I0648040

The
Charlemagne
Murders

The Murder of Six World War II Generals
Leads to the Greatest Manhunt in History

Carl Douglass

Neurosurgeon Turned Author Writes with Gripping Realism

PO Box 221974 Anchorage, Alaska 99522-1974
books@publicationconsultants.com—www.publicationconsultants.com

ISBN 978-1-59433-628-7
ISBN 978-1-59433-629-4 eBook
Library of Congress Catalog Card Number: 2016939629

Manufactured in the United States of America.

DEDICATION

To the warriors, the defenders, the restorers, and the historians

TABLE OF CONTENTS

PROLOGUE

The Inscription over the Vestibule of Hell
Through me you pass into the city of woe:
Through me you pass into eternal pain:
Through me among the people lost for aye.

Justice the founder of my fabric mov'd:
To rear me was the task of power divine,
Supremest wisdom, and primeval love.

Before me things create were none, save things
Eternal, and eternal I endure.
"Lasciate ogne speranza, voi ch'intrate"
"Abandon all hope, ye who enter here."
-Dante Alighieri, *Divina Commedia di Dante: Inferno*
[The Divine Comedy - Dante's Inferno], Canto III: 1–21, 1317

Butugychag Tin Mine, Soviet Gulag Camp for German POWs, Kolyma River, Siberia, USSR, April 1953

Across the gravel empty space between the camp security gate and their barracks, two thin graying men shuffled painfully, eyes down, pushed and shoved by brutal camp guards. They were crawling with lice on their bodies which had not been bathed in a year, and their clothing was covered with cassiterite—tin ore dust—which had accumulated since the previous year's washing. The two specters—barely living ghosts with skin stretched across their bones—wore all the clothes they owned on their backs—ill-fitting maximum security special treatment uniforms consisting of thin woolen pants and camp jackets with dull gray and maroon horizontal stripes and the same decrepit combat boots they were wearing when they were captured eight years previously. A close inspection of their faces would reveal they were twenty years older than their chronological age. They had been reduced to what was known in the *Sevvostlag* system of hard labor and minimal or no food as helpless *dokhodyaga* [goners].

They were POWs and known to the Soviets as *zeks*—slave laborers—who had lost their identity within the system, and no one in their native France was aware they were alive or had any idea where they had been for more than a decade. The two men and seventeen other survivors were all that remained of the eighty-one members of their 33rd Waffen-Grenadier SS Division when they were originally captured. The *Schutzstaffel* officers' prison—since being captured in Berlin by victorious Soviet troops during the last days of the Third Reich—was the Butugychag Tin Mine, a Soviet gulag camp known as the "Valley of Death"—the most notorious of the infamous Soviet internment camps. The majority of gulag camps were positioned in extremely remote areas of northeastern Siberia beyond the Arctic Circle. The Butugychag camp was part of the *Sevvostlag—severo-vostochnye lagerya—or SVITL* [The North-East Camps located along the Kolyma River]. A nearby area along the Indigirka River came to be known as the Gulag inside the Gulag. In one village in that region, a record low temperature of -96 °F was recorded. Under the supervision of Lavrenty Beria who headed both NKVD and the Soviet Atom bomb program until his demise in 1953, thousands of *zeks* like Antoine and Michaele were used to mine uranium ore and prepare test facilities at Novaya Zemlya, Vaygach Island, and Semipalatinsk.

Somehow—by what had to be a nearly superhuman instinct for survival—the nineteen POWs and a handful of non-POW internees—mainly political dissidents, academics, and intellectuals—approached the gate alive. A year into their incarceration, their predicted longevity statistically approached an infinitesimally small chance that they would have lived to see this day. The conditions of their internment were inhuman by any civilized standards. Most of the men had lost over a third of their body weight owing to the imposition of forced hard labor and minimal or no food by the Dalstroy Agency which administered the area for the Soviet Union. The hapless prisoners were housed in seriously overcrowded, stinking, poorly-heated barracks.

The overcrowding problem was alleviated by the high death rate—more than 500,000 prisoners perished there. As the fat and flesh melted from their bodies; so, did all human emotions—love, friendship, concern for one's fellow man, compassion, hope for praise, credit, or fame, honesty, envy, or even hate. Prisoners lived in a camp surrounded by a barbed wire fence, unfeeling thugs of armed guards overlooking in watchtowers. Upon occasion, the watchtower guards had shooting events to kill prisoners arbitrarily at random to see who could put the most accurately placed bullet into a designated bodily kill zone. The prisoners themselves descended into the level of primeval animals—brutal and violent—who cared only for their own survival. Fellow prisoners turned informers for a crust of bread. Cannibalism was commonplace.

Prisoners in the gulag received their *paika* [food ration] according to the amount of work they performed that day. This was an incentive scheme the Soviets learned from the Nazis in their slave labor camps, including both coercive and motivational elements applied universally in all camps. It consisted in standardized formal "nourishment scales"—the size of the inmates' rations depended on the percentage of the work quota delivered. A full ration barely provided enough food for survival. If a prisoner did not fulfill his daily work quota, he received even less food. If a prisoner consistently failed to fulfill his work quotas, he would slowly starve to death. The gulag was created as a system where people were worked to death with the certainty that there would always be more *zeks* coming into the "corrective labor camps." Disease—especially tuberculosis—claimed half the prisoners who entered the camp. Guards read out the names of those to be shot every evening.

The elements were as harsh as the other prison conditions: there were two seasons—nine months of winter and three months of fall with temperatures ranging on average from -40° to -5° F during the winter months with spells of temperatures falling to incredible lows of -60° to as low as -90° once or twice a winter. Many of the *dokhodyaga* gave up the ghost on those days. Gulag guards in the *Sevvostlag* were not concerned with finding escaped prisoners: they would die anyhow from the cold and severe winters. Prisoners who did escape without getting shot were usually found dead miles away from the camp.

The man known as 1945-WC 2200186 survived because he found a way to grow carrots and onions. The other man, also known only by his prison number—1945-WC 2208592—grew cabbages and was a ruthless thief, willing to steal another prisoner's food and let him starve to death or freeze. He killed more than one man to get food or the man's mittens that would let him live one more day.

Although the two men were walking towards the gate, it did not seem to be much different from the routine of any other day. After ten to twelve hours of inhumanly hard work in the mine, they received a bowl of potato soup and a slice of frozen black bread if they were lucky. Antoine and Michaele survived the Siberian death camp partly because they were able to find the occasional raw, frozen, or even putrid dead owls and small rodents, or because they killed or stole to live.

There was some variation in the routine. Owing to the condition of the internees, it was often difficult to find people who were even able to gather firewood or to bury the dead. Sometimes when the numbers of the dead became so high that the stench bothered the guards, the guards suspended work in the tin mines and assigned inmates with a record of obedience to operate bulldozers to bury the partially frozen corpses. Sometimes they created huge mass graves and pushed stiffened bodies—thousands of bodies, thousands of skeletal corpses—with their twisted fingers, putrefying toes, frozen stumps, dry skin marked with blood and sores, and those starved staring eyes. Other times they were taken into the forest to labor at sawing, chopping trees, and digging rocks.

Rebellious prisoners were punished by being isolated in tiny cells of frozen concrete. For them, suicide was more common than the murders going on outside their putative coffins. In the slave camps of Kolyma, the vast majority of inmates—women, men, and children—never survived more than two years.

In the eight years they had been interned in the NKVD special camp, the two surviving men had never been allowed to approach closer than thirty yards from the gate or any fence line. Now they were slowly being herded to the entrance gate of the Valley of Death. It was evident that a new thing was happening, and new things were rarely good in the *Sevvostlag*. Unknown to the nineteen surviving officers and men of the 33rd Waffen-Grenadier SS Division and the few non-military detainees—about half of political prisoners in the gulag camps were imprisoned without trial—the Dastroy Agency was starting a period of mass amnesties and the release of most political prisoners, and even the scant few remaining war criminals. Some nonessential producing camps were scheduled to close between 1953 and 1956.

Former SS officers, now known only as Antoine [1945-WC 2200186] and Michaele [1945-WC 2208592] were pushed roughly into an American-made Studebaker 6X6 troop truck without any explanation as to why or about their destination. The truck was modified to hold twenty men. Antoine and Michaele were two of forty-one men crammed into the inadequate space. It was still cold—but in northern Siberia, it was always cold in what passed for spring. The men were used to it; it had become a part of life; and they were glad to be alive, though they often groused to each other in their native French that they would just as soon live in hell. The truck jounced and swerved over slick slushy ruts in the wholly unpaved Stalinist "Road of Bones" for 1240 miles with occasional latrine stops and for a scanty serving of gray turnip or potato soup and black bread fortified with sawdust that had been their usual fare for the past seven years in the gulag. For one lunch of the weeklong journey, they were given the luxury of a slice of American Spam—said to be only one of two things that the USSR liked about America, the other being the Studebaker trucks.

The two men and thirty-nine others–sitting in relative misery in a conveyance that could have been hauling pigs or sheep–were from an assortment of countries and backgrounds. They sat on hard benches along the sides of the truck bed and were chained to the floor by one ankle. At night they slept on the still frozen ground chained to each other. When one turned over, they all had to turn. None of this was anything particularly different from the comforts of the camp. Taiga Yukaghirs in old NKVD uniforms drove the truck and served as the never gentle guards.

Finally—after a seven-day trip—the truck pulled up to a stop in front of the dilapidated municipal police station in the middle of Magadan, the very isolated main city of the Chukchi Peninsula and largest port of northeastern Russia. Their ankle locks were released; the men were given their discharge papers—dated, bewilderingly, October 1, 1945— and the men were herded off the truck clutching the papers which were their only worldly possessions other than the clothing on their backs. The truck then wheeled about and headed back in the direction from which it had come, leaving the bemused men alone in the street.

The men had been in Magadan before as part of their painful journey to slavery in the Valley of Death. After being captured, they traveled by train to Siberia. That trip proved to be a harbinger of their future. The trains were unbearably cramped and stifling. Only death of prisoners afforded a little more leg room. On the trains, the heat was terrible. There was serious lack of fresh air, and the dreadful overcrowded conditions exhausted the semi-starved men. Many of the elderly prisoners, weak and emaciated, died along the way; and their corpses were left abandoned alongside the railroad tracks.

The worst was yet to come. The survivors of the grueling Trans-Siberian Railway train ride—the longest in the USSR—were disembarked at the Nakhodka transit camp. There, they encountered the bitter unrelenting cold. After three days, they were moved to Khabarovosk, which was part of the gulag archipelago. They then were forced onto decrepit ships and transported across the Sea of Okhotsk to Magadan's natural harbor. Conditions aboard the ships were even harsher than they had endured on the train. The Soviet prison ships were sewage-ridden hellholes. Of the original three train loads of POWs, thousands died during the crossing. Antoine and Michaeles' ship was caught for several weeks in early gathering ice. When it reached the Magadan port it carried only crew, guards, and two thousand prisoners—5,200 POWs were left dead on the ice. The two men spent a month in Magadan working as slave labor on the fishing fleet. The seaport was only fully navigable from May to December, and the Dastroy Agency lashed and kicked the men onto the fishing trawlers to get as much free labor out of them as possible. The dwindling numbers of hardy remaining prisoners were hauled by cattle trucks to their new home in the Butugychag tin mine camp beyond the Arctic Circle.

Now, in 1953, the novelty of being free to walk about in Magadan and away from the slave-labor camp soon gave way to more primal concerns. Antoine Duvalier and Michaele Dupont were the only Frenchmen on the truck—and for all they knew—were the only members of their regiment still alive. They moved away from the other former prisoners, a natural grouping in which countrymen tended to find some similitude of camaraderie with their own. Hungarians, Serbs, Germans, and Baltics went their separate ways two-by-two. They were soon all lost among a populace of exceedingly poor and deprived Northern Russians who were just eking out a living in an unforgiving land. Most of those people had arrived during the recent war as displaced persons and were only a little better off than the newly released prisoners of the gulag. No one took an interest in anyone else. No one had the strength or resources to give help to another human being. Antoine and Michaele were out of prison, but only slightly better off than when they were in the camp. Their first priority was to find food.

Recipe

Rat Stew—for 1 or 2 Diners

Ingredients (as available):
4 lg rats. May substitute 2 gophers, 3 frozen owl carcasses, 10 squirrels, or 1 stolen chicken. May use leather belts or straps.
Any vegetables in as large amounts as findable and as season and/or availability permits, may add grass, green leaves, or fruit or vegetable peelings from refuse bins. Avoid wild mushrooms since they may be poisonous.
Spices: anything available with salt as a premium

Preparation
Skin animals, cut off beaks and claws and discard.
Place meat items in the largest pot available, add 1–2 gal. of the cleanest water obtainable.
Bring to a hard boil until meat is putty soft (crucial to avoid food poisoning)
Add vegetables for last 30–60 min. of boiling.

Serving
Place in regulation tin pots or pans and consume while still very hot. Recipient will remove bones and inedible portions. Do not save as leftovers (also crucial for safety)

BOOK ONE

WHAT

CHAPTER ONE

Arkhangelskoye Military Convalescent Home, Moscow, USSR, October 9, 1961

Lieutenant of *militsiya* Trushin Vasilyovich Stepanovich drew the black bean and now sat in his cramped and untidy office in the *MYC* [Moscow Criminal Investigations Department] building on Petrovka 38 Street to wait for the boredom of a quiet weekend to pass.

The Moscow Criminal Investigation Department [Russian-*MYC*]—established in 1722—is the Main Department of Internal Affairs of the city of Moscow. It was usually called simply the Moscow Police, and was the largest municipal police force in Russia with primary responsibilities in law enforcement and investigation within Moscow City. The Muscovite Police [more accurately, *Militsya*] is one of the oldest police departments established in Russia. Since the days of the tsars, its headquarters have been in the famous Petrovka 38 Street in the Tverskoy District, central Moscow.

First Secretary of the Communist Party of the Soviet Union Nikita Sergeyevich Khrushchev's grip on the USSR was only slightly less draconian than that of his predecessor Iosif Vissarionovich Stalin—the Man of Steel—despite Khrushchev's program of de-Stalinization. As the unopposed leader of Russia and its satellites during the Cold War, the First Secretary was concerned with the great struggle with the corrupt capitalist West. He maintained brutal control of the security forces, including the *Militsya*, which served the Soviet Union as its police force. Petty crime and murder rates plummeted during Stalin's and Khrushchev's reigns, and made Lt. Stepanovich's life as a homicide detective a relatively easy one.

Stepanovich coughed a little from his latest Belomorkanal and took another sip of his cup of ersatz coffee in the drab office. The minor vices passed for cigarettes and coffee, respectively, in Soviet Russia. Lt. Stepanovich wondered at the popularity of the two because he detested both of them. He shrugged and continued to puff and sip. The pseudo cigarette came in the form of a papirosa—a hollow card board tube with no filter, a sort of disposable cigarette holder. Stepananovich compressed the tube into two separate surfaces. He so seldom had a real cigarette—a Western brand—that he no longer considered the way Russians were reduced to do their smoking to be odd. The coffee—so-called coffee—was a nearly unpalatable blend of roasted acorns, chicory root, beechnut, potato peelings, and wheat bran. The militia lieutenant thought he detected a hint of actual coffee in this latest rendition. It made him smile—the glorious Soviet industrial engine at work.

Trushin was twenty-seven years old, one of the youngest lieutenants of police in the entire Soviet Union. He was tall—five feet, ten inches—for a man born during the lean, starving times, when Stalin's iron fist determined who should grow what; and who should get enough to eat. He had been seventeen years old when he volunteered for service in the Red Army in 1940. His first posting was to Pomerania, to assist in driving out the entrenched Wehrmacht, Waffen-SS, and the French Charlemagne Division. There, in the bitter cold, he had become a man, seen death, known defeat, and finally revenge. He had been in a troop truck when the Charlemagne Division stragglers, blundering into an open field, were duly slaughtered. That was enough horror for him, but his unit had been sent on to Berlin to secure the German capital. He was one of the very few Red Army soldiers who survived without a wound. His heroism led to him receiving the Order of the Red Star and the Order of the Patriotic War, 1st Class, something that pleased him greatly, but about which he never told anyone except his wife, Katrinka.

His face was lined with memories of the terrible struggles and sacrifices he had witnessed and experienced. He was a slender, handsome, man in a hard way, with heavy dark hair and slightly olive complexion. He wore a Stalinist mustache; otherwise, he kept his scalp hair very short and militarily neat. His uniform was always newly cleaned and crisp, thanks to Katrinka. An old knee wound occasionally made him limp, but he decided he would do everything possible to avoid appearing like a needy old soldier. He was a hard worker, which gave his arms and legs deeply carved muscular definition. He avoided smiling because his teeth were crooked and overlapping, and there were gaps where he had lost three teeth to decay.

He finished two days' worth of *Pravda*, sighed, and reluctantly began to pick up folders from his inbox to get the reports read and signed off. It was a routine that bored him almost to the frantic state. The Soviet Union was a giant records machine, and Stepanovich hated being a cog in it. But it was his job, and it brought in a meager salary that kept his own and Katrinka's bodies and souls intact for another week.

The telephone jangled.

"*Dah*," he said, "Stepanovich here."

"We have a murder at the Military Convalescent Home," *Efreitor* Lebedinsky stated crisply.

"Somebody killed some old vet?" Stepanovich asked, unable to keep the incredulity out of his voice.

"That's right, Lieutenant. And it's likely to have political consequences."

There was nothing Stepanovich liked to hear less than "political consequences."

"Maybe you should come promptly, Lieutenant, if I may suggest."

"I'll be there. Secure the scene and nobody goes in or out of the home."

"Yes, sir. Already done."

"Political" meant hurry up, and it meant trouble. Anything political in Stepanovich's experience meant it could never be done right, never proceeded by police rules and procedures, and if blame were attached to the investigation, he would get it. If credit were to be attached to the investigation, some bureaucrat up the line would garner that.

Lt. Stepanovich got up, checked the press of his uniform and the shine of his boots, and walked down the hall to the enlisted mess room. Four privates leaped to attention as their lieutenant entered the room.

"Sit back down," Stepanovich ordered.

"Lada, come with me. We have a case out at the Arkhangelskoye estate. It will take all day—probably the whole weekend.

Lada Kornikova stood at attention. A senior private and the only woman in the on-call unit that day, she was also the brightest of all of the privates and one already being considered for promotion to sergeant. The lieutenant had to make an effort not to be obvious in his appreciation of her Nordic beauty. She came from Viking stock—the original Rus—and looked every bit the blond athlete or western movie star dressed in the humble soldier's uniform. She filled that uniform out well enough that men had to remember to shift their gaze to avoid embarrassment. Lada would have been alluring in a gunny sack.

Lada was special in other ways. She served as a street cop alongside Trushin, a decidedly unusual assignment in the paternalistic society of Russian law enforcement. Although women constituted a significant proportion of *militsiya* staff, they were usually not permitted to fill positions that carry risks—such as patrolman, guard, SWAT—but were allowed to carry firearms for self-defense. Instead, they were widely represented among investigators. Lada had the respect of her tough fellow *MYC* [Moscow Criminal Investigations Department] for both her prowess in situations with risk, and for her investigative skills.

"Yesipov, you drive," Trushin ordered.

Neither street patrols nor detectives were allowed to drive police vehicles themselves; so, a specialist driver—either a serviceman or a civil employee—was assigned to each car and was also in charge of its maintenance. Private Georgy Yesipov stood beside Lada in a demonstration of his readiness. Georgy was illiterate and coarse, but was loyal to Stepanovich to an almost embarrassing level because the lieutenant had fetched him from a brothel which had been declared counterrevolutionary by the NKVD one evening. He would have been branded a minor enemy of the state and considered suspect ever afterward had it not been for Stepanovich's timely and improper intervention. Georgy was a huge stolid Slav, slow and steady, and incredibly strong. Stepanovich always wanted him to accompany him on high profile or dangerous assignments because he knew Georgy would always have his back. This assignment could easily require such protection, if past experience with "political" was any indicator.

Lieutenant Stepanovich called in his backup, *Efreitor* [Lieutenant] Zakhar Rumyantsev, to take over the office duties for the rest of the weekend while Stepanovich looked into the odious "political" case. Zakhar's voice sounded hung over, but he said he would be at the police station in less than an hour. Unlike in some other countries' police agencies, *militsioners* were not assigned permanent partners; instead, they worked alone or within larger groups; so, Trushin was obligated–as always–to work with his entire investigation unit; and he was also required to provide a unit in the office in his absence. Fortunately for Trushin, Rumyantsev was resourceful.

It was raining out—heavy, soaking, cold rain—the *Rasputitsa*—the twice annual season when the usually poor Soviet Union roads become muddy, rutted, and very nearly impassable. The other such season which made traveling so onerous was spring, with the melting snows from the Russian winter. Yesipov pushed the ponderous Lada Militia car expertly through the heavy muck of the road. Kornikovna sat in the front passenger seat—which had almost no cushion left—and Stepanovich sat in the backseat with the crime-scene equipment and the weapons.

It was difficult to see through the fog, low-hanging mist, and continuing downpour, to the turnoff road into the Arkhangelskoye Estate twelve miles west of the militsya *MYC* in Tverskoy District, central Moscow. Yesipov found a place to park next to *Efreitor* Lebedinsky's metro police vehicle, and the three *militsya* officers hurried to get in out of the rain. The architectural center of the Arkhangelskoye Estate is the Yusupov Palace, a beautiful edifice on a sunny day. But today, they were unable to see even its outlines. They walked into the entryway to the long façade of the Stalin-era Military Convalescent Home. The home is located close to the Moscow Automobile Ring Road [MKAD]. It was built in the 1940s for the Red Army elite and is closed to visitors. Its terraces overlooking the river are accessible, and its staircases are the best way to reach the riverbank, a sodden mass at the moment.

Underofficer *uchastkovyi militsioner* Lebedinsky was standing at rigid attention as Lt. Stepanovich and his junior officers strode into the Palladian-style building. One unique feature of *militsiya* policing approach is the system of territorial patronage over citizens. The cities—as well as the rural settlements—are divided into *uchastoks* [English: "quarters"] with a special *uchastkovyi militsioner* [quarter policeman"] assigned to each. The main duty of *uchastkovyi* is to maintain close relations with the residents of his quarter and gather information among them. In particular, *uchastkovyi* should personally know each and every ex-convict, substance abuser, young hooligan, etc. in a given *uchastok*, and visit them regularly for preemptive influence. The *uchastkovyi* are the first line of defense against criminals and the principal conduit of intelligence for the police apparati. Lebedinsky excelled at both.

Nearly three dozen hospital personnel were lined up in three neat rows facing Lebedinsky, all with solemn faces and drooping shoulders. Each man and woman was carefully studying his or her shoes.

"Greetings, Comrade Lebedinsky," said Lt. Stepanovich. "It is good to know that you are on the job. Would you please tell us all you know about what is going on here in the vets' home?"

Stepanovich meant it when he said he was glad that Lebedinsky was on the job. He was a thorough and efficient police officer and *uchastokovyi* for the section of Moscow surrounding the Arkhangelskoye Estate, Yusupov Palace, and the Military Convalescent Home. Lebedinsky's sobriety, attention to detail and to duty, and his loyalty to the *militsiya* was comforting to *Operativniy Rabotnik* [Detective] Trushin Vasilyvich Stepanovich. Nearly one in every three policemen in the USSR was a psychopath or an alcoholic, the result of the attraction that police and military service had for such people. There was no psychological screening of applicants, and the sense among many in the service was that—as militiamen—they were beyond the reach of the law. This was especially true of the higher ranks and those with connections to the communist party elite.

Ivan Lebidinsky was very tall and rail thin. His uniform was perfect with knife-edge creases, starched shirt, and well polished brass buttons. His shoes had a perfect shine all the time, a characteristic that sometimes made Trushin wonder if the fairies came in the night and polished them while the policeman slept. Lebedinsky had earned his rank of *Efreitor*—the highest non-com rank in the militaristic police— the hard way, by dint of inexhaustible hard work and sucking up to his superiors. His face was now—as always—freshly shaved and ruddy from exertion. Trushin had never known him to have an unshaven face for even a day, nor to have a hair out of place on his scalp. Despite his long-distance runner physique, Ivan was very strong; and he was quick. He had saved several civilians and occasionally a police officer by lightning-fast movements when he and the others had come under fire. He was a good man to have on your side, even if he was boring and entirely devoid of a sense of humor.

Ivan pointed at the downtrodden-looking men and women of the convalescent home staff and said, "Comrade Stepanovich, thank you for coming so soon. We have assembled the entire staff—even the gardeners—so far as we can tell."

"Good work, Comrade Ivan Viktorovich. And I presume the crime scene is pristine?"

"Yes, sir, Comrade Trushin Vasilyvich. Two of my men have it under guard."

"All right, please take Private Kornikova and me there. Georgy, take one of Underofficer Lebedinsky's men with you and begin questioning the staff. Keep them separate from each other and unable to communicate with anyone until they are interviewed by you."

Georgy saluted and began herding the thoroughly cowed staff towards a row of office and storage rooms.

Ivan led Trushin and Lada into the convalescent center proper and down an immaculate hallway to a bank of patient rooms flanking both sides of the polished linoleum floor. He gave the two Moscow officers a serious look and opened the door to the room being guarded by two metropolitan *uchastkovyi* police underofficers. Although Trushin Vasilyich was in the Great War from beginning to end, the sight that he saw as he entered the room gave even him a moment of pause. Lada had a little sharp intake of breath, betraying her shock.

The well-appointed small room contained a single bed, two bedside tables, a writing desk, a closet, and two places to sit, the larger of which was a comfortable overstuffed chair with a matching ottoman. Sprawled out on the chair was a frail old man who was naked, adding an obscene element to the specter. His head was slumped on his chest which was impaled with a handsome cavalry saber that penetrated all the way through the back of the chair. There was a small trickle of blood on his chest and only a little more on the floor in back. The blade was evenly smeared with blood.

"Is that his own sword?" Lt. Stepanovich asked.

"Yes, sir."

"Is this who I think it is?"

Lebedinsky nodded. "Lieutenant General of Cavalry Grigory Yegorivich Lagounov, Cavalier of the Order of the Red Banner, for his service in the Great War and for his service afterward in the management of the far northeastern prisoner of war system."

"I presume he is the highest ranking officer in the home?"

"By several grades."

"Do you think this savage murder had anything to do with his military service?"

"I have no idea, although it seems more than happenstance or weapon of convenience that the general was killed by his own saber."

"If that is true, it is possible that the murderer was just a tool of someone of more political importance pulling the murderer's strings."

"That has occurred to me as well. I hope it is not true; but often, in our business, what we hope for does not happen."

"Like a quick, easy, and quiet solution to the problem, eh, Ivan?"

"Yes, Trushin, like that."

Lada employed her well-used personal *Hasselbladski*—Kiev 88 model—camera to document the scene. The complicated and bulky camera was a knockoff of the fine German Hassleblad 1600. The communist aspects of the Kiev company assemblage were heavy and rather difficult to use—interchangeable backs and Ukrainian made lenses which were shamelessly based on old WWII Zeiss designs. The advantages of the *Hasselbladski* were the viewfinders that were directly interchangeable with the original high quality Hasselblads, and the fact that the lenses had a satisfyingly wide range of optical choices.

Stepanovich and Lebedinsky started at opposite corners of the room and looked with intense scrutiny at every part of the small room for even the smallest and most obscure clue. They met at the halfway point and double-checked each other's work. The killer had been scrupulous in clearing away any traces of blood on the floor that might have contributed a shoeprint, and there was no evidence of an effort to wash off blood in the bathroom or anywhere else.

Stepanovich and his *MYC* [Moscow Criminal Investigations Department] were enamored of fingerprint evidence and—without admitting the source—copied the forensic fingerprint identification procedures established in 1905 as the Bureau of Criminal Identification of the US Department of Justice. By 1946, the FBI had processed over one hundred million fingerprint cards. The USSR had joined the IAI [International Association of Identification] in 1932 and endeavored to make fingerprint identification a staple part of Soviet police and intelligence service work. Lt. Stepanovich was proud of his personal facility with fingerprint science but deferred to the superior memory of Private Lada Kornikova for day-to-day work.

He and Lebedinsky began a systematic dusting of the entire room and found several dozen different sets of fingerprints. Evidently, the killer had not been aware of fingerprint evidence, or did not feel he (or she) had to be concerned. Stepanovich took great pains to dust every part of the sword to identify prints and was able to identify prints indicative of the last person to hold the sword's handle. He had Lada make very careful and close-up photographs of the prints. Then, he extracted the sword from Lt. Gen Lagounov's chest; and Lada photographed the entire weapon with a series of photographs. Stepanovich concentrated on the blood smears on the blade and found no prints, and confirmed that negative finding with fingerprint dusting powder. Because of the importance of the fingerprint evidence, Lt. Stepanovich dispatched Private Kornikova back to the *MYC* headquarters to get the tedious search for the owner of the fingerprints underway.

"Comrade Ivan Viktorovich, would you please arrange for the deceased's body to be taken to the police morgue and to have the autopsy done as a first priority? The body is to be kept cold and preserved as best as is possible in case certain important political officials wish to ascertain for themselves the validity of our work. Once your subordinates have that project underway, please join Lada and me back in the main section of the home to get through the interviews of the staff."

"Immediately, Comrade Lieutenant Trushin Vasilyovich."

Lebedinsky made a smart about-face and left the murder scene bedroom. He was flattered that the lieutenant would treat him with courtesy, even saying "please" more than once. He made a mental note that Lt. Stepanovich was going places in the services; and he, Lebedinsky, was going to attach himself to the rising star's coattails.

Russian Recipes

Cold Russian Borscht—for Six

Ingredients
-2 lbs small new beets. Boil then peel and cut into quarters, 11 cps water, ±½ cp red wine, ¼ cp + 1 tbsp sugar, ¼ cp fresh lemon juice, 2 tbsps cider vinegar, salt and freshly ground pepper, 1 med. Yukon Gold potato, peeled and cut into ½ in. cubes, 1lb Kirby cucumbers—peeled, seeded and cut into ½ in. cubes, 1 cp finely diced radishes, 4 thinly sliced scallions, 3 lg peeled and coarsely chopped hard-cooked eggs, ¼ cp coarsely chopped dill, ¼ cp coarsely chopped flat-leaf parsley, sour cream or crème fraîche, for serving.

Preparation

-In a large pot, cover quartered beets with water and bring to a boil. Simmer over moderately low heat until beets are tender when pierced with a fork, about 30 minutes. Using a slotted spoon, transfer beets to a plate and peel.

-Coarsely shred beets in a food processor or with grater. Return them to the pot and add sugar, lemon juice and cider vinegar; season with salt and pepper. Refrigerate soup until chilled, for at least 4 hours or preferably overnight.

-Meanwhile, bring a small saucepan of salted water to a boil. Add potato cubes and cook until tender~7 mins. Drain and cool under cold water. Pat dry and transfer to a med. bowl. Add cucumbers, radishes, scallions, eggs, dill, and parsley.

-Ladle the chilled borscht into bowls. Garnish with the vegetable and chopped egg mixture, top with a generous dollop of sour cream and serve.

Note: Borscht can be refrigerated for up to 3 days and safely used. Garnishes should be prepared shortly before serving. Borsht served with a dollop of very cold, rich, tart sour cream and salad type garnishes: cubed boiled potatoes, diced radishes, chopped hard-boiled eggs, and coarsely chopped dillweed.

Russian Black Bread—1 Loaf

Ingredients

-2 cps coarsely ground dark rye flour, 1½ cps finely ground white flour, ½ tsp coarse brown sugar, 1 tsp salt, 1 cp 100% all-bran cereal, 1 tbsp crushed caraway seeds or sunflower seeds and ¼ tbsp fennel seed, 1 tsp instant coffee powder, 1 tsp onion powder, 1 (¼ oz) pkg active dry yeast, 1¼ cps water or strong dark ale, 1 tbsp vinegar, 2 tbsp dark strong molasses, ½ oz unsweetened chocolate, $\frac{1}{4}$ cp salted butter, ½ tsp cornstarch, ¼ tsp cold water or beer

Preparation

-Combine flours, then, in a large bowl, thoroughly mix 1¼ cps flour mixture, sugar, salt, cereal, caraway seed, coffee powder, onion powder, fennel seed, and undissolved yeast.

-In a sauce pan combine 1¼ cps water or beer, vinegar, molasses, chocolate, and butter.

-Heat liquid mixture over low heat until liquids are very warm (120°–130°F). Mix in butter and chocolate without melting.

-Gradually add heated liquid mixture to dry ingredients and beat (with electric mixer if available) for 2 mins, at med. speed, scraping bowl occasionally. Add ¼ cp flour mixture. Beat at high speed for 2 minutes, scraping bowl occasionally. Stir in enough additional flour mixture to make a soft dough. Turn dough on to a lightly floured board. Cover dough and let rest for 15 mins.

-Knead dough until smooth and elastic (about 10–15 minutes). Dough may be sticky. Place dough in a greased bowl, turning dough to grease the top. Cover bowl and place in a warm, draft-free place to rise until doubled in bulk~1 hour.

-Punch dough down; turn out onto a lightly floured board. Divide dough in half. Shape each half into a ball, about 5 ins. in diameter. Place each ball into the center of a greased 8-in. round cake pan. Cover; let rise in a warm, draft-free place until doubled in bulk~1 hr.). Bake at 350°F for 40–45 mins., or until done (check with toothpick).

-Meanwhile, combine cornstarch and cold water. Cook over medium heat, stirring constantly, until mixture starts to boil; continue cooking mixture for 1 min., stirring constantly.

-As soon as bread is baked, brush cornstarch mixture over top of loaves. Return bread to oven and bake 2–3 mins. longer, or until glaze is set. Remove loaves from pan and cool on wire racks.

Serve hot.

CHAPTER TWO

Lt. Stepanovich and Private Kornikova returned to the main row of offices and storage rooms where Private Georgy Yesipov and Militsioner Private Yuri Inozemtsev, Lebedinsky's next-in-command, were well into their interviews with the convalescent center staff. Stepanovich took Yesipov and Inozemtsev aside for a progress report.

"Where are we in the effort to question everyone on the staff, Georgy Artyomovich and Yuri Alexandreovich?"

"About a quarter of the way along, Trushin Vasilyovich," Georgy replied.

Lt. Stepanovich pondered a moment. "Why is that, Yuri Alexandreovich?"

"Because most of the people are young, female, and frightened of us. It is like pulling teeth to get them to calm down and answer questions, and then they don't know anything."

"We need to become more efficient. We need answers before this day is out. I propose a different approach."

He scanned the list of staff members and made several quick marks on the sheets.

"I have divided the list into four groups, one for each of us. Now, the list is pared down to only those people who work in the area of Gen. Lagounov's room. That is a manageable number. I will start with the security staff. If any one of you finds a lead, let me know immediately; so, we can pursue it and not spin our wheels chatting with uninformed and anxious worker-bees."

Stepanovich drew a blank in his interviews with the security personnel—two elderly military veterans who were looking forward to their pensions and a bright and overly energetic young man who told Stepanovich at least six times how much he admired the officers of the *MYC*—especially Lt. Stepanovich—and how much he wanted to join the force. The elderly vets had lived long enough under Soviet rule to know not to give anything but yes and no answers, and the younger man's excessive verbiage was useless.

Lada Kornikova was the first interviewer to get anything of use. She left her interview room as soon as it was evident that she at least had someone who was in regular contact with the murder victim.

"Trushin Vasilyovich, I have something. The sister who tends to the general almost every day reports the visit of a stranger to the unit."

Lt. Stepanovich dismissed the man he was interviewing, and he and Lada went directly back to her room.

"Sister Ludmila Mikhailovna, this is our senior officer, the man I told you about. Please tell him what you told me," Lada said to the submissive country girl.

She stammered for a moment, then gathered her courage and told Lt. Stepanovich, "The general has been in the center for a long time—since before I was given the privilege of working for the glorious Soviet Union in my humble capacity. During the time I cared for him, he never had a visitor, never wrote a letter, never made a telephone call. Then early this morning, a man dressed in gardener's clothing came onto the unit and asked the head nurse, Sister Maria Nikolayovna Ilyushkin, about where the general's room was. She talked to him for a few minutes then ordered me to lead the man to the general's room. I stayed with the two men for a few minutes, long enough to tell that the general was not happy to see the man. The man stood up strong and tall like a military officer; so, I thought he was one of the general's officers from the Great War. The man ordered me to leave, and I did."

"That was fine, Sister. Remain calm and tell me anything you heard the man say to Sister Maria Nikolayovna or to Gen. Lagounov."

Ludmila wrinkled up her brow in thought.

"The man seemed unhappy with Sister Ilyushkin. She said something to him that I could not understand—maybe in German—and the man spoke back to her in what I think could be French. She was shaking her head, and she looked like she might be frightened. The man looked angry. He said '*Gott verdammt, wo is er?*' I understood that. It means

... a swear word then a question, 'Where is he?' Sister Ilyushkin just shrugged and pointed down towards Gen. Lagounov's room."

"What did you see and hear next, Ludmila?"

Ludmila Mikhailovna was comfortable now. She did not like the domineering and abusive head nurse. She had done nothing wrong, and the policeman was just trying to find out what happened to the old general. She was a simple farm girl, which one could discern at the first glance at her soft, corpulent, bovine figure and round, guileless face. She inspired trust for what she had to say by her more than evident innocence.

"I walked with the gardener man down to Gen. Lagounov's room. He opened the door and walked in like he was family, or he owned the place."

"Did you challenge him?"

"No, sir. I do not have authority to challenge."

"*Of course not*," Stepanovich thought to himself; but as he was getting information from the homely young woman, he did not want to upset her and interfere with the flow.

"Did he say anything?"

"Who?"

"Either of the men."

"The gardener man did. He told me to leave. Not very nice about it either. As I was walking out of the room, the gardener said, 'Kind of surprised to see me, no, General?'"

"Were those his exact words?"

"Yes, sir."

Trushin made a note in his murder book.

"Then what happened?" he asked.

"The gardener man closed the door."

"What did you do?"

"I was busy; so, I left."

"Did you hear or see anything else that concerned the general?"

"No, sir."

"No noise or voices or anything?"

"No, sir."

"Have you seen the man before? Maybe on the grounds or in one of the maintenance sheds, Ludmila?"

"No, sir. I don't think the man was a gardener or that he worked here."

"I'm sure you would remember him if he was a longtime employee, but what makes you think he wasn't a gardener?"

"He looked like a soldier—an officer. Short haircut, tall, large strong hands. And he had a scar on his left face like the German officers sometimes have. His face was hard and mean. I didn't like to be near him."

"Did you ever meet a German officer, Ludmila Mikhailovna?"

Stepanovich looked at her face. Her eyes were down. She had paled. He thought she was about to cry.

"Don't be afraid, my sweet girl, you are safe with me. Did something happen in the war, something that you don't like to remember?"

Now she did cry—a soft, quiet cry that came from somewhere down deep in a tortured soul.

"Yes, sir. I don't like to talk about it."

"Please tell me, Ludmila. It will be our secret. I promise that no harm will come to you if you tell me the truth. I think it may be important for my investigation."

Ludmila squared her shoulders and said in a voice a little above a whisper, "I am from Stalingrad. I was sixteen when the Germans came. My family and I lived on a farm outside of the city. The Germans marched into the area and came to our house. They took all of our food and murdered my father and mother. An officer—a man who looked something like the gardener man who came to our convalescent home today—grabbed my arms. He had a cruel face ... he hurt me."

Ludmila wept out loud now, the horrors of that day and that battle etched into the lines of her face.

"I don't like to say ... I am a good girl...."

"You don't have to say any more. I know you are a good girl. You have been a real help. Please don't say anything to anyone else about what you saw this morning, all right?"

"Yes, sir," she managed to say.

"Ludmila, could you do another thing for me?"

"If I can."

"My assistant, Lada, is a police sketch artist. Would you sit down with her and see if you can remember the man's face? It would be a great benefit to the Rodina."

The young woman had no doubt suffered terribly for the Motherland already. She was a true Russian dedicated to the Soviet Union which had saved her city. She was willing to do anything this Soviet officer required of her.

"I would consider it to be my duty, sir."

"Good girl, Ludmila. Please sit here until Lada can come to help you with a picture. Oh, by the way, do you happen to know were Sister Ilyushkin is now?"

"No, sir. No one has seen her since this morning when General Lagounov's body was found."

Trushin headed straight of the interview room where Lada was currently interrogating the charwoman who had found Gen. Lagounov's body.

"Lada, let Georgy take over here. I need you to make a sketch. I think your drawing is likely to be of the murderer. Once Ludmila is satisfied that the picture you draw is of the man she saw, bring it to me. We will get it out to the militia all over the city. The NKVD can make sure it is copied and spread around the entire union."

"I think this woman ... her name is Oksana ... Oksana Leonidovna Tkachenko ... also saw the man. He might have just finished killing the general."

Stepanovich told Oksana to stay in her seat while he went to find Georgy, but he ran into Private Inozemtsev first.

"Good, Yuri Alexandreovich, I have an important job for you. Do whatever it takes to find the head nurse on Gen. Lagounov's unit. We must get hold of her. I think she may be the linchpin to this whole plot. If you cannot find her in an hour, come back here to get a picture of our presumed killer. We will have to get that spread around the whole of the Rodina. Move as fast as you can."

Inozemtsev snapped to attention and saluted Lt. Stepanovich, did a sharp about-face, and hurried out of the room.

Oksana had a surprisingly good memory and a keen eye for details of the stranger's face when it came her turn for Lada to sketch her image of the presumed murderer. Lt. Stepanovich's interrogation of the old lady yielded only that when she attempted to enter Gen. Lagounov's room for the morning cleaning, the man whose face she described to Lada came to the door and rudely closed it in her face. She never saw him again.

It was starting to be dusk out before the militsioners completed their work, pulled back onto the MKAD [Moscow Automobile Ring Road], and drove back to Petrovka 38 Street and the *MYC* building. The first order of business was to get photocopies made of Lada's drawings—the two women had described and signed off on remarkably similar images. Lt. Stepanovich and Lada knew that in Western police headquarters, it was a simple thing to make large numbers of faithful photocopies on the office Xerox machine. It was an altogether different story in the Soviet Union as the 1960s began. All copy machines were held under tight control by the KGB for political reasons—that is, to counteract the dissident activity of *samizdat.*

Counterrevolutionaries all around the Soviet bloc nations reproduced censored publications from government sources and also produced their own crude typed products. The copies were passed from reader to reader by hand, and that grassroots practice designed to evade officially imposed censorship was fraught with nightmarish danger. To be caught with such a document meant that the culprit would receive very harsh punishments meted out in KGB prisons like the Lubyanka. No one emerged from the Lubyanka unchanged.

Copy machines in the Soviet Union were knockoffs of the American-made Xerox technology and never quite worked satisfactorily; but for most of the less technological needs for copies, the Soviet technology served. Photocopy machines were a nightmare for the KGB, and many members of its vast army spent their time policing the use of those machines secreted into the country. The 1960s, like the 1950s, was a culture of secrecy, often carried to absurd degrees. The lack of a photocopy machine was a frustrating nightmare for the nation's police services; and the exhausted lieutenant of militsya, Trushin Vasilovich Stepanovich, ground his teeth as he set about trying to obtain a machine for the KGB.

This was not the first time Lt. Stepanovich had had to go around proper channels to get a machine. As he usually did, Trushin put a call in to his old Great War commanding officer, Boris Vadimovich Ilyushin, now colonel general—*komandarm* commander first rank—of the Red Army. It was a measure of the respect accorded Stepanovich that he could get through to the colonel general at all, and an indication of the commanding influence the old man still had that he was able to get through to none other than Alexander Shelepin, the cruel, crafty, and ultimately secretive current head of the KGB [*Komitet gosudarstvennoy bezopasnosti*—Committee for State Security].

Half an hour later, Shelepin rousted the sleepy and moderately drunk Rudolph Vladimirovich Fedorchuck II and made things happen. At this point of the early 1960s, the ruling Soviet elite included the KGB's Fifth Directorate, responsible for ideology and countersubversion, and the Agitprop Department, the party's main watchdog over "ideological" matters, had full control over the introduction of newly invented photocopying machines—technically speaking, newly stolen from the American company Xerox—and Fedorchuck was its secretive and harsh watchdog of the watchdogs.

Half an hour after that—at midnight—Fedorchuck had twelve new photocopy machines delivered to Petrovka 38 Street. Ever the optimist, Stepanovich had two dozen service staff brought in from around Moscow to launch the largest manhunt in the history of the city to date.

CHAPTER THREE

Alaskan Bear Lodge, Excursion Inlet, Alaska, August 7, 1962

General Glen Gabler, USA ret., his three sons, and his long-suffering aide-de-camp, Major Rick Saunders, also USA ret., caught a MAC flight through the VR-3 naval air squadron based at Joint Base McGuire-Dix-Lakehurst, New Jersey. Their first stop after a grueling nine-hour flight was at the Maintenance Squadron VR-8 in the Naval Air Station Moffett Field, California. After a day's layover, the five men flew in a C-130 to Bellingham, Washington. The USAAF closed the military airfield in 1946, and its two diagonal runways fell into decrepitude. The property reverted to the port and city of Bellingham. Special permission to land on the airport's single maintained runway was granted because of Gen. Gabler's high rank and prominence. The last leg of their flight was to Juneau, Alaska, on a de Havilland Canada DHC-3 Otter, a single-engine, high-wing, propeller-driven, STOL [short take-off and landing] aircraft.

Juneau is the capital city of Alaska. The city was named after gold prospector Joe Juneau. It was once known as *Rockwell* and then *Harrisburg* after Juneau's coprospector, Richard Harris. The Tlingit name of the town is *Dzántik'i Héeni* ["Base of the Flounder's River"]. The Taku River just south of Juneau was named after the cold *t'aakh* wind, which occasionally blows down from the mountains.

They had a six-hour wait before their ferry sailed; so, the general obtained two jeeps, and the men took a side trip to see the Mendenhall Glacier.

Rick complained that they did not see any calving from the glacier.

Gen. Gabler informed him, "The Mendenhall is not a tidewater glacier, my boy"—referring to the fifty-eight-year-old man—"It doesn't break off into the ocean."

It annoyed Rick that he had forgotten that little factoid and allowed Gen. Gabler to have yet one more small one-upmanship victory since he had been stationed at Haines with the general and was in Alaska as long as he was. He had to shake his head in acknowledgment of Gen. Gabler's encyclopedic memory for arcane facts—factoids—and trivia. A much smaller man than the general, Saunders strongly resented a reference to himself as a "boy." He was from the South, and being called a "boy"—even in jest—grated despite the decades that had passed when he was first assigned to the large man who became a noted general.

From Juneau, they sailed on the *MV Malaspina* ferry via the Alaska Marine Highway to Haines. The cobalt blue water was relatively smooth that day, and the five men and their fellow passengers had the chance to see "big brownies"—the huge coastal grizzly bears for which Alaska is famous—bald eagles, and a small pod of Beluga whales. The captain made a point of stopping to give the passengers a good look and opportunity to take photos and of sailing perilously close to the shoreline searching for the bears. The Alaska Marine Highway System operated along the south-central coast of the state, the eastern Aleutian Islands, and the Inside Passage of Alaska and British Columbia, Canada. The ferries served communities in Southeast Alaska that have no road access, transporting passengers, freight, and vehicles. The service route included 3,500 miles that went from Bellingham, Washington on the far south, to Unalaska/Dutch Harbor in the Aleutians on the far west.

This was the peak summer season for deep-sea fishing. The *MV Malaspina* and the important retired general and his entourage moved up the Lynn Canal from Juneau—a penetrating natural waterway into the interior that connects Skagway and Haines, Alaska, to Juneau and the rest of the Inside Passage. The canal is more than 2,000 feet deep, the deepest fjord in North America and one of the deepest and longest in the world. It is the main hub of the water highway. Gen. Gabler wanted to take a short nostalgic stroll around Haines, one of his old stomping grounds during the war. Haines—located in the Alaska Panhandle—has a long US military history. Fort William H. Seward was constructed south of the town in 1904. In 1922, it was renamed

Chilkoot Barracks. It was the only United States Army post in Alaska before World War II.

During the war, and the time when Gabler and Saunders were stationed there, it was used as a major supply point for some US Army activities in Alaska and a POW camp for a time. The fort was deactivated in 1946, and Gen. Gabler and Major Saunders were assigned to France and West Germany to oversee repatriation of US POWs and to investigate Germans held as POWs to identify those suspected of being Nazi war criminals. Both men were late middle-aged but still vigorous and loved rafting in the Chilkat River, hiking and hunting in the Takshanuk Mountains, and deep-sea fishing in the icy-cold dark waters of the Inside Passage with its 1,000 islands, 15,000 miles of shoreline, and thousands of coves and bays. Haines is one of only three cities in Southeast Alaska that are accessible by road to another city.

Late that afternoon, the fishermen boarded a renovated de Havilland DH.98 Mosquito bomber floatplane provided by the Alaskan Bear Lodge and flew smoothly to the Excursion Inlet Seaplane Base located forty miles west of Juneau. The water base surface—1,000 by 1,000 feet—had room for only one seaplane. Excursion Inlet—population eight—was 60 square miles in size with 0.2 square miles of that being water. The area was originally an Alaska Native village. During World War II—when Gen. Gabler served in Alaska—it was used as a prisoner-of-war camp and a strategic base for the Aleutian Campaign. Excursion Inlet also had a fishing cannery that opened in 1891 and was rebuilt in 1918. It was still functioning to process pink and chum salmon, salmon roe, salmon caviar, halibut, and sablefish, when Gabler returned to Alaska for the first time since his service there. The cannery was one of the largest in the world, and the Alaskan Bear Lodge and its competitors provided one of the largest sports fisheries in the world.

"Hey, General," the party was greeted by the bluff mountain of a man who owned and ran the lodge. "Welcome, welcome! We've got booze for your parched throats, a nice hot shower for your beat-up bones from that miserable plane ride, and dinner's almost done. C'mon up. The boys'll bring up your gear."

"We're glad to finally get here after that hazardous trip," Gen. Gabler said, laughing. "Let's go up and see if this rascal's description of his place is anything more than puffery."

There were striking similarities and equally striking differences between the two men and between the two sets of sons. The fathers were both big men—tall, heavily muscled, and showing their age in their ponches. Both men had lined leathery faces from long days in the sun, and both men were beginning to show their age in their faces and small but definite bags under their eyes and turkey-wattled necks. The fathers' differences were also notable: Glen Gabler had white, short cropped hair in a military brush cut; and his hard face was etched in frown lines from his years of hounding men who did not want to work or to go into battle to face bullets and bayonets; and there were scars which attested to his willingness to lead his men into those battles. His silver-steel blue eyes were as unforgiving as ice and carried a hint of sadness, a remembering which he could never shake.

Neille Bastrup had red hair—not sandy or pale reddish yellow or strawberry blond—and it was red enough almost to glow like an ember in the dark. As if to call attention to himself in any crowd, Neille's hair was kinky-curly and stood out from his scalp like a clown hat. Unlike Glen, Neille's face radiated kindness and bonhomie. His lined face showed smile lines and crinkles around his eyes which told of laughter, invitation, and goodwill—and, perhaps, a measure of rascality. It was evident that he had eaten well up there in the Alaskan outback, but his was still a formidable physique.

The sons of both fathers were all tall, athletic, and muscular, like runners, and unlike their fathers who were built more like powerlifters than racers. Glen's three sons—Glen, Jr., Trace, and Jackson—favored their mother who was a handsome and willowy brunette. Neille's four sons—Kevin, Able, Michael, and Donovan—all had red hair, freckles, and mischievous facial expressions—young men who might short-sheet your bed but who would be there to save you from the furies of the Arctic Ocean. It was as if they were born by reverse partheno-genesis and had no female genetic contribution. Their mother was a statuesque honey blond who looked ten years younger than her husband and drew looks from the sparse population of men in Excursion Inlet—visitors and locals—that many of them lived to regret. Neille had a well-deserved reputation as a jealous man.

Two hours later, besotted with drink and satiated with two-inch thick slabs of baked halibut and baked potatoes covered with hot secret-recipe chili, the Gabler party collapsed into their comfortable beds to get restored enough to start the following day of fishing at the crack of dawn.

Glen, his sons, and Maj. Saunders knew that the Bastrups had been up late readying the boats and had gotten up early to prepare a fortifying breakfast of scrambled eggs, slabs of bacon, racks of Russian rye toast, fruit bowls, and steaming coffee. They respected the lodge owner and staff, and showed that they did by pitching in to carry the day's gear and food to the two fishing boats swaying gently against the docks. The *Arctic Sun* and the *Winter's Haven* were old but well-kept motor and sail boats that could sleep ten men each with all of their gear. The fishing boats, safety gear, and fishing equipment were all seaworthy and in good working condition. Gen. Gabler took all of that in and appreciated the nearly military quality of the preparations, supplies, and conveyances.

The predawn light was just becoming noticeable when Neille announced, "Okay, look alive! We'll head for Hoonah to pick up some extra food stuff and bait for today, then we'll head off for Elfin Cove and try our luck in Cross Sound and the Icy Strait."

It was still early morning when the *Arctic Sun* and *Winter's Haven* put in at the rather rickety dock. Nielle watched as two dock workers hitched the mooring lines. Personnel changes were infrequent at the small Tlingit family operation, and he had never seen a non-Tlingit employee working there. That was—he presumed—because of a mutual distrust and general dislike between whites and the Alaska natives. He made a mental note to ask the Tlingit patriarch, Charlie Sobelev, when he got the chance. Something else nagged at the back of his mind: the two men were older than usual. Dock work was heavy physical labor—young man's work—and there was something about the two that suggested Russian. Nothing concrete, but if it was true, it would be a distinct departure from the status quo because generally the Tlingits disliked Russians owing to the fact that they routinely mistreated the Tlingit women.

He, Kevin, Able, and Michael walked to the gee-dunk to get some snacks and soda pop. Donovan stayed back to mind the boats. Neille had told him to keep a close watch on the two possible Russians; but as soon as they moored the boats, they disappeared. The fishermen were all happy to stay aboard and fall back to sleep as the soft cradle rolling waves lulled and gently rocked them. In a few minutes Neille and the boys returned and stowed the luxury supplies. Donovan untied the mooring lines, and they headed off towards Elfin Cove.

Elfin Cove is located in a small flask-shaped harbor on the north end of Chichagof Island. There were no roads—just a one mile boardwalk, a sleepy village consisting of a handful of buildings—a post office, liquor store, and a general store. Neille dropped in to the liquor store, shared a few jokes, then told the owner his plans for the day and promised to check in again at day's end—a standard safety precaution.

Just to wow the Gablers and Maj. Saunders, they took a small detour to have a look at the Glacier National Monument. In 1794—when it was first described by Captain George Vancouver—there was virtually no bay or inlet. Instead a massive glacier filled the area. It was more than 4,000 feet thick in places, up to 20 miles wide, and extended more than 100 miles to the St. Elias mountain range. In 1879, the famous naturalist John Muir reported that the ice had retreated more than thirty miles, and by then there was an actual bay. By 1916, naturalists reported that the Grand Pacific Glacier—the main glacier which carved the bay—had melted back sixty miles to the head of what became known as Tarr Inlet. Since 1951, the Arctic warmed roughly twice as much as the global average; and the area of arctic ice shrank by one-fifth as the 1960s dawned; and the Gabler and Bastrup party were amazed—more accurately, shocked—by the obvious growth of newly exposed land and the retreating moraine line.

Back outside the protected harbor of Elfin Cove and Glacier Bay, the two small fishing boats passed into Cross Sound and the Icy Strait. It was a bright sunny day with clear views of the rugged coastline of Chichagof Island and its coastal beaches, deep fjords, and plethora of tidewater glaciers. Looking back, they could see the snow-capped mountains and glacial fields of the national monument and the Fair Weather Mountains. The setting was perfect, and Neille unabashedly prophesized that they would take their limits that day.

The Bastrup boys put out the trolling lines over half a mile then dropped anchors—two for each boat. Each fisherman had a belt with a cup for the handle of his fishing rod and settled down holding the fishing gear for a happily anxious wait for the first cry of "hook-up." Most of the guests were sliding back into a pleasant slumber in the cool Alaskan sun. The *Arctic Sun* and *Winter's Haven* were the only boats visible, and Neille liked it that way. At nine-thirty, a Tlingit craft from

Hoonah passed by—a bit too close for Neille's comfort. He thought he had been out in the sun too long because he was sure on his first glance that he saw the two Russian-looking men. On second glance, he could not see them, and decided that his mind was playing tricks. He vowed to avoid hitting the sauce so hard the night before a big fishing trip.

The Gabler party members were all so drowsy that they relinquished their fishing rods to the Bastrup brothers who patiently waited for the first hit.

"Hook-up!" yelled Kevin, startling everyone and throwing both boats into a controlled frenzy of activity.

Kevin knew he had either hooked into a huge sunken log or he had a mammoth fish on his line. He handed the rod to Gen. Gabler and warned him about how to bring the lunker in without losing it.

"Pull up on the pole, General, then as you let the end, go down reel some line in. Don't jerk it, and don't be in a hurry. This is going to take considerable time!"

Gen. Gabler began to work.

Neille called out to the rest of the men, "Slowly reel your lines in. Let's check the bait and lures. If you get a hit, let it set for a couple of times then give a medium jerk to lodge the hook. No real fast moves!"

Trace Gabler shouted, "Hook-up!" and Donovan Bastrup moved alongside him to be sure he had a secure hit.

Another hit came on the line that Donovan Bastrup was holding, and he handed the line off to Jackson Gabler. Able Bastrup got the next hit and gave his pole to Glen, Jr. Now it was pandemonium.

Rick Saunders whooped from the deck of the *Winter's Haven*, "Got one! Feels like a whale!"

His face was red from excitement and strain. Every man on the two boats had a fish on his line except for Neille on the *Arctic Sun* and Michael on the *Winter's Haven* who had their hands full controlling the boats and lending a hand to the fishermen to keep them from entangling their lines or sawing off each others' lines as they battled their fish.

Gen. Gabler was sweating and beet red from the exertion. Neille was beginning to worry about whether the general's heart could handle the strain. Trace pulled a bright orange fish alongside the Arctic Sun, and Neille gaffed it.

"Hey, man," Neille shouted, "you've got your year's limit on Yelloweye rockfish! That beauty weighs a good thirty-five pounds, maybe forty. Great job?"

He clubbed the fish's head and threw it into the cold locker, then he rebaited Trace's hooks and helped him drop the line to the proper depth.

Kevin brought in a Coho salmon that weighed twelve pounds, and Jackson Gabler landed a Chinook (King) salmon that weighed in at twenty-two pounds. Ten minutes later Jackson Gabler pulled a pink (humpy) salmon in that weighed five pounds.

"That's great eating! My favorite, Jackson," Michael told him. "We'll have that for supper!"

In rapid succession Glen Jr. landed an eighty-pound lingcod, and Jackson pulled in another one that weighed a healthy sixty-two pounds.

"Ugly boogers, aren't they!" Neille said, admiring the two ancient fish that were so ugly that they were beautiful. "They're my absolute favorites. We'll have the best fish supper you guys have ever eaten tonight! Great work!"

Two hours later, Neille stopped to take stock of the haul to be sure the two boats had not brought in more than the limit. There were four kings weighing between twelve pounds and thirty-seven pounds, six Cohos weighing in at a hefty range of eight to fourteen pounds, four halibuts weighing from sixty-two to one hundred eighty pounds, three Lingcods ranging from a low of fourteen to a high of seventy-one pounds, eight rockfish of assorted colors and weights, twenty-one Chum (dog) salmon with their reputation as hard-hitting and fun sport fish—which on that successful day ran from eight to eighteen pounds, with one exception a twenty-four pounder, and the limit of twenty sea bass which almost finished filling the cold locker. The nearly exhausted general was still working on whatever he had on his line, and now all eyes were on him.

"Let's give it a rest," Neille announced. "Save some for tomorrow."

"You okay, Dad?" Glen, Jr. asked the general, working to conceal the concern in his voice.

"I think so," his sweating and extremely tired appearing father answered.

"How about I spell you off for a bit?" Glen Jr. offered.

The general was reluctant, but decided that wisdom was the better part of valor; and he had plenty of ammunition for bragging rights from whatever was on that line.

As soon as he transferred his pole to his eldest son, the fish took a dive for the bottom.

"Great fish," Neille said. "Hang in there. Maybe we've got a record on the line."

The "record" consumed three more hours of work and the efforts of every member of the Gabler party. A very tired Rick Saunders brought the even tireder fish up to a point near enough to the surface to be able to see it."

"That's got to be the biggest halibut we've ever seen, don't you think, Dad?" Jackson asked Neille excitedly.

"Maybe so. Hey, Rick, how about letting the general have the honor of the final work before we put the gaffs in that lunker?"

Rick was only too glad to relinquish his role. He had been doing similar services for the general for more than twenty-five years; so, this was nothing new. Gen. Gabler staggered a little as he switched seats and sagged into the action seat. Rick stood by and gave a little assistance as the huge fish was brought up to the hull of the *Arctic Sun*. Kevin and Able each wielded a gaff and pinioned the great fish to the side. Neille, Michael, and Donovan were able to drop a net from the swing beam and the five men maneuvered the fish into it. The winch engine did the rest of the work. The halibut weighed in at a colossal 454 pounds—not a record, but a whole lot of great eating to come.

On the way back to Excursion Inlet and the Alaskan Bear Lodge, Neille discussed a plan to take a day off from fishing and have a nice restful hunting trip along the coastline. He predicted that they would see at least two big moose and a couple of nice coastal brown bears. The would-be hunters could only mumble their assent as they sagged into the discomfort of their deck chairs and fell asleep.

Back at the lodge, everyone helped to unload the gear and the day's catch before they went inside to shower and change clothes. Neille glimpsed out into the inlet before going to his room and thought he saw the same Tinglt boat he had seen out on the Icy Strait during the midmorning. He shook his head. It could be anybody doing anything to or from Hoonah; so, he put it out of his mind.

The maids and cooks—two Tinglt girls and an Athabaskan Indian girl from the Yukon territory—made a dangerously large dinner including ptarmigan, moose, bear stew, fresh baked halibut, and grilled Coho salmon. The girls had made a trip to Hoonah for fresh vegetables, including little new red potatoes that they pan fried in butter with a heavy dusting of spices to a hard crispiness, and had baked a large chocolate layer cake for dessert. There was water, milk, three kinds of beer, a pleasant Chardonnay, and an assortment of mind-numbing cocktails to drink. Neille decided to leave off the booze and to fortify himself with milk; so, he would not have a repeat of his hallucination of the Russian dock workers coming back. He was not entirely ready to dismiss the memory, no matter how faulty it might be, however.

Glen asked a lot of questions about the extent of the retreating of the great glacier in Glacier Bay.

"Shame," said Neille. "I guess it was about the time that Vancouver sailed into the area that the Little Ice Age was starting to come to an end."

"Right. And it looks like the process is still going on. Glad we could be here to see it in time. My times in Alaska have been an altogether too short but great part of my life. After the terrific fishing trip today, I could die a happy man."

Alaskan Recipes

Bear Stew—Serves Six

Ingredients
-Fresh bear meat-2 lbs, cut into 1 in. cubes.
Vegetables: 1 lg yellow onion, 2 cloves coarsely chopped fresh garlic, carrots, potatoes, celery, ±brussel sprouts, brown mushrooms cut into ½ inch cubes, fresh frozen or canned corn and fresh or frozen baby peas, 1 12 oz can strong dark beer, 2 tsps (may increase to taste) beef buillion.
Spices: 1 tbsp Worchestershire Sauce, sea salt, and coarsely ground pepper to taste

Preparation
-Lightly flour bear cubes, brown in extra virgin olive oil with salt and pepper and set aside.
-Sauté onions and garlic until golden brown and set aside
-Heat beer to near boiling, add bear meat, buillion, Worchestershire, onions, and garlic
-Add remainder of vegetables except for corn and peas when meat is almost done. Add corn and peas just before serving.

-Simmer until vegetables are cooked but still firm.
-Alternatively, may cook in crock pot or bake in an oven. May make dumplings for the pot.

Poached Halibut—Serves Six

Ingredients
-Halibut: 4 lbs thick sliced halibut cut into 6 equal pieces, milk-sufficient to cover fish, ⅓ cube butter.
-Spices: Salmon/trout mix or sea salt, ground powdered garlic, lemon pepper, ±cumin, dry parsley to taste.

Preparation
-Place spices and butter into milk and heat to near boiling. Lightly dust more spices on halibut itself and add to hot milk
-Cook in oven for 30 min. at 350° or until halibut is thoroughly cooked (by sampling), but do not overcook.

CHAPTER FOUR

Alaskan Bear Lodge, August 8, 1962

Nasnana—the Athabaskan girl—got up before everybody else and hurried around to get the breakfast preparations underway. She checked by the men's rooms to see if any of them were awake and needed some coffee. Most of the doors were closed, but the famous general's door was ajar. She knocked timidly—too timidly she decided, because there was no response—so, she knocked again and in so doing pushed the bedroom door half open. Then she screamed.

The first responder to the frightened scream was Asaaluk, the Tlingit girl from Hoonah. She joined in the ear and heart-piercing screams. Thirty seconds later everyone in the Alaskan Bear Lodge was a mute witness to the horror of the image of General Glen Gabler, USA ret., hanging from the ceiling beams of his room, his face contorted in agony, bloated, and purple.

Donovan—the youngest and least tactful Bastrup boy—exclaimed before he thought, "Why would the general kill himself?"

His father responded by backhanding the boy across his cheek.

Neille turned to the Gabler sons and Maj. Saunders and said, "Please ignore him. He has not learned to turn on his brain before he puts his mouth in gear."

"Obviously, everyone here has just had the same question, Mr. Bastrup," Glen Jr. said sadly. "What do you think about this unthinkable situation?"

"It's not suicide. Look at his wrists."

Everyone lifted his or her eyes and looked at Gen. Gabler's wrists and hands, glad not to have to look at the man's grotesquely distorted face.

Maj. Saunders spoke first. "Ligature injuries. Look at how swollen and cut they are."

Able Bastrup added, "And he has a huge bruise on the side of his head."

"Murder," Neille said. "Everybody clear out of here. Nobody touches anything. Michael, you stand guard. Whatever happens no looky-loos get in here. I'll call Juneau."

Neille called the Juneau headquarters of the Alaska state troopers. A sleepy dispatch operator answered.

"Alaska state troopers, how may I direct your call?"

"This is Neille Bastrup up at the Alaskan Bear Lodge."

"Where is that located, sir?"

"Excursion Inlet."

"What is the nature of your problem, Mr. Bastrup?"

"There's been a murder at the lodge. We need troopers and a crime scene unit. We have secured the scene."

"Oh, dear me!" the flustered voice of the young woman in Juneau said.

There was a pause.

"Are you still there, ma'am?"

"Yes, sir. Sorry I got kind of flustered. I've only been on the job for a week."

Swell, Neille thought.

"Can you get a trooper to talk to me?" he asked.

And hurry it up, he thought to himself.

"Sorry, Mr. Bastrup. But we've got a problem here. The troopers are all out of the office. The bank got robbed, and a couple of people were killed. Everybody's either at the bank or out looking for the robbers. I'll do my best to get hold of someone, but I can't leave the phone. I'll call some people who live by the bank and get them to give the message to the troopers and the town policemen. It'll take a while."

"Seriously!?" Neille said, trying unsuccessfully to hide his exasperation. "While we sit around twiddling our thumbs, the killer or killers are getting farther and farther away. There must be some way to get the law up here!"

"We have a reciprocal agreement with the RCMP. You could give them a call. They have a small post in Atlin, B.C. That's really not that far from you. I could give them a call and ask for help. Would that be okay?"

"Anything would be better than our present situation. Get the Mountie to give me a call at this number."

He gave the girl the number for the lodge and repeated it slowly. He had her repeat the number.

"I'll get right on it, sir. And I'll do my best to get a trooper to call you as soon as possible but don't expect a miracle."

"I won't expect anything like a miracle. A little help would be better'n nothing."

He put the phone back on its cradle, steepled his fingers on his forehead, and tried to think. Neille was a man used to getting things done and had a logical mind that functioned at its best in an emergency.

The rest of the occupants of the lodge were gathered in the main floor sitting area waiting for Neille's report, except for Donovan who had not left his post as guard at the murder scene door. He took the stairs two at a time to see the fishermen and his employees.

"All right, here's the deal: the troopers are dealing with a bank robbery and double homicide in Juneau; and the little new girl on duty as the dispatcher has her hands full. It'll be a while before we can get any trooper up here. If we don't do something, the killer or killers will be long gone before any cop gets here. The dispatcher is putting a call through to the RCMP for help. The troopers and the Mounties have a working arrangement. Maybe we can get at least temporary help.

"I'll stay by the phone. Able, take the Lund boat over to Hoonah and go talk to Henry or Anotklosh Peratrovich. Get them to send out their boats to see if they can see any suspicious strangers. I doubt this is the work of any locals ... at least I certainly hope not. Tell Henry to pay some serious attention to the two new dockworkers—maybe Russian. Put both 25 hp Evinrudes on and get over there as fast as you can move.

"Nasnana and Asaaluk, rustle up some breakfast for everybody. It's gonna be a long hungry day.

"I know you are shocked; and it's been a terrible blow to you Gabler boys; but if you're up to it, why don't you get with Kevin and Michael and have a quiet look around the area back of the lodge. See if you can see anybody back there that shouldn't be there. Don't do a thing except look. Whoever did this is dangerous ... to state the obvious. We should have the law here before too long.

"Rick, how 'bout you check out the boats and the plane and see if anything's been stolen ... maybe used for a getaway. Report back here in no more than an hour. I don't want to have to send out any search parties. Okay, everybody, look lively!"

Major Saunders returned in less than five minutes.

"Neille, we have a real problem: the plane's gone!"

"That means the murderers are in the wind. Who knows when they killed the general and how far they've gotten to? The plane's tanks were full to the brim."

The phone rang.

"Neille Bastrup here."

"This is Constable Daniel Olsen with the RCMP at the Atlin station. The Juneau trooper office tells me you have a problem and could use some help."

"Thanks for getting back to me so fast, Daniel. We do, indeed, have a problem."

Neille told the Mountie everything he had learned.

"Sounds bad. There's just me, but I'll fly over there as fast as possible. I presume you have a floatplane dock, eh?"

"And it's empty and waiting," Neille said ruefully.

"I've got a good map, Neille. Mind if I call you Neille?"

"You can call me Mary Jane, if you want, Daniel. I'll be that grateful for your help."

"Anyway, I don't think I'll have any trouble finding you; but maybe you could put a colorful flag or two on your roof and send up a flare when you hear me overhead."

"Will do, and thanks again."

As soon as he hung up the phone, he ordered Kevin to tack every flag they had in the lodge on the top of the roof and to get the flare guns out of the fishing boats. Then they all sat down to the communal table and wolfed down breakfast.

Neille and Donovan were the only ones left in the lodge. Even the two girls wanted to be in on the adventure of hunting for the killers. Neille was all but certain that the killers were long gone and the search would be both fruitless and safe unless someone fell down and broke a leg or something. That would fit the day, he thought.

It was less than an hour before the drone of a plane's engine sounded over the lodge. Neille and Donovan ran outside and each fired a flare. Five minutes later, a floatplane touched down in the inlet and coasted comfortably into the Excursion Inlet Seaplane Base. Neille walked out to greet the Mountie and helped him moor his plane to the dock.

"Thanks for coming, Constable. We have left the crime scene alone just as we found it. I sent out our people to get some help from the Tlingits over on Chichagof Island and some are out looking around in the bush behind the lodge. All of that is probably looking for the horse after leaving the barn door open, though; because, whoever did this probably flew off in our own plane."

He gave the constable all the information he had.

"Did you call it in to Juneau?"

"Yes, and I called your headquarters in Vancouver."

"That's good. So, let's take a look at the scene."

Constable Olsen picked up his crime scene kit and camera. He gave the lodge a quick once over look then concentrated on Gen. Gabler's bedroom. There, he took several dozen photographs, dusted for fingerprints and, finding dozens, he painstakingly lifted them and taped them to evidence cards. There was no blood anywhere except on the general's head; so, Olsen concluded that there was nothing more to be done in the room except to remove the body. He had a body bag with him, along with his crime scene kit. Olsen worked quickly and efficiently. His entire persona radiated calm and efficiency. He had a well-worn uniform which had obviously seen long service. Everything about the man indicated cleanliness and a Spartan life in the out-of-doors. He had short-cropped dark brown hair, a neatly trimmed mustache, and high cheek bones. His face and hands—all the skin visible—were deeply tanned. His hands were rough and calloused, but deft and careful. He was medium everything—height, weight, dress, and manners—a prototypical nice, mild-mannered Canadian.

Neille and Daniel climbed on ladders and respectfully cut the rope from the noose and lifted the body down to the floor. Daniel checked the body temperature in the general's rectum and then put a needle into the right upper quadrant of his abdomen and checked the liver temperature. Then the two men put the body into the body bag. Gen. Gabler's body was moderately stiff.

"The rigor mortis is incomplete," Constable Olsen said. "That suggests that the murder took place between three and twelve hours ago, probably closer to five or six hours. His liver temp confirms that—30 degrees centigrade. Although there are a lot of variables, the living body temperature of 37.5° C loses about 1.5° C per hour until the temperature of the body is that of the environment around it—the ambient temperature."

"What's that in American, Daniel?"

Daniel did a quick calculation.

"Eighty-six degrees Fahrenheit."

Neille did a quick check on the time on his watch—eight-thirty.

"So, the time of the murder was about three, three-thirty this morning?"

"Let's consider a range—something like three a.m. to five a.m., give or take."

"The girls start to stir around five; so, I'd guess it was closer to three than to five," Neille said.

"Sounds reasonable. He's cooling down fairly rapidly, Neille. Decomp will begin to set in soon. Do you have a big ice locker and plenty of ice where we can store the body until the troopers arrive and can take over?"

"You betcha. That I've got."

The searchers returned, reported seeing nothing out of the ordinary; and Neille enlisted the help of Kevin and Michael to carry the general's body down to the ice shed. The Gabler boys were huddled around the telephone conveying the terrible news to family, friends, and business associates down below.

The Tlingit headmen, Henry and Anotklosh Peratrovich, moved into immediate action in the Huna Tlingit village on Chichagof Island. The villagers spread out and gathered up the men and women working on the docks, in the Hoonah Packing Company facility, and every fisherman not already at sea as soon as Able Bastrup located the leaders. Women and children left their breakfasts and homes and began searching all over the island. Every available boat put out of Port Frederick and into the Icy Strait to begin the sea search. The village was empty when the Alaska state troopers arrived from Juneau at eleven-forty-five.

CHAPTER FIVE

Regional Major Crimes Unit [MCU], Alaska Bureau of Investigation Post, Juneau, Alaska, August 9, 1962

The RCMP investigation along with the searches conducted by locals in the Icy Strait area led to the conclusion that the murderer or murderers of Gen. Gabler had fled the state. Constable Olsen reported his findings to Lt. Oscar Perez from the MCU and flew back to British Columbia. All of the fishermen, owners, staff, and guides from the Alaskan Bear Lodge and Henry and Anotklosh Peratrovich from Hoonah, were transported to the Juneau MCU [Major Crimes Unit] post by late afternoon the day after the murder for further questioning.

"Hello, I am Major Higgins—Darrin Higgins. I am the MCU chief officer here in Juneau. Thank you for coming," the state law enforcement officer said as soon as the group was gathered in the post conference room.

As if we had any other choice, Maj. Saunders thought, but kept his negative remarks to himself.

Higgins was an all-business, squat muscular man with an almost thuggish look about him despite his fat-free physique and his careful attention to the appearance of his uniform. He shaved twice a day, but that was not enough to keep him from having five o'clock shadow at noon. His hair was a dark brown and totally unruly thatch which he kept bulldog short style to avoid the frustration of combing. His bushy eyebrows were consistently longer than the hair on his scalp. He did not smile often but when he did, his observer or listener was unable to remove his attention from the prominent gap between his front two incisors.

"I don't think it will be necessary to keep our two Hoonah headmen very long. We'll get you some supper and on back to the island as soon as we get done here. I just wanted to get the information directly from you guys and to ask a favor. First off, tell me what you found. I know that you already talked to Lt. Perez, but please do me the courtesy of telling me again."

"Some of the people found a rude campsite near the entrance to Glacier Bay at Bartlett Cove. There were remnants of salmon bones, tails, and heads, huckleberries, salmonberries, and thimbleberries, along with some trash. Some of that trash included fairly recent copies of the *Petropavalovsk-Kamchatsky Journal.* Two boys out fishing found an abandoned boat—one of ours from Hoonah—on the Point Adolphus feeding area for humpback whales. Some trash they found around the boat had brochures from the Alaskan Bear Lodge and the plane's document packet."

"That sound like your stuff, Mr. Bastrup?"

"Absolutely."

"So it appears that the murderer or murderers were able sailors and pilots, that they stole a boat from the dock at Hoonah, that they sailed to Excursion Inlet, killed General Gabler during the night; and one took the boat and sailed it to Point Adolphus while the other flew the floatplane down there; and finally, they flew out of Alaska," Maj. Higgins summed everything that was known about the case—precious little, at that, and even less about who the killers were or where they went.

"Our plane shouldn't be that hard to find," Neille said.

"What kind is it?" Higgins asked.

"A renovated vintage de Havilland DH.98 Mosquito bomber floatplane. The tail number is number N7952Z."

An aircraft registration is a unique alphanumeric string of numbers and alphabet letters. Because planes usually display their registration numbers on the aft fuselage just forward of the tail, or more often on the tail itself on older planes, the registration is usually referred to as the "tail number."

"I'll get out a BOLO and an APB and get hold of the Russkies, the Canucks, and INTERPOL in case the killers flew to Siberia or BC, or to parts unknown," Higgins said and motioned to his second in command who left the room to get the international dangerous fugitive search underway.

"Let INTERPOL know that we will give them the information on names of fugitives as soon as we can get the; so, they can get out a Blue Notice."

They all sat for a moment while Higgins had dispatch get through to the Petropavlovsk-Kamchatsky Metropolitan Police Department. The speaker phone option was turned on.

"Kamchatka Krai Police," the foreign operator answered in Russian.

"English, please. This is the American police—Alaska state troopers—calling."

There was a few moments pause and some clicking noises.

"I am an English speaker," came the gruff commanding voice of a man. "What is the nature of your problem?"

Higgins took over from the dispatcher. "I am the head of the criminal investigation service in Juneau, Alaska. There has been a murder of a senior American general here in our area, and we have some reason to believe that one or maybe two Russian nationals may have been involved. At least, they are persons of interest. We need any information you can give us about any recent suspicious incidents on the peninsula."

"What are the names of this 'persons of interest'? My department would have nothing to go on to conduct an investigation without such minimal information."

"We don't know. The murder happened yesterday; and the only people in our remote area not accounted for were one or two men who have been described as Russian-looking, whatever that may mean. But we do have evidence that they stole a plane, and our best conclusion at this early part of our investigation is that they may have flown in your direction. Do you have any information on such a plane?"

"Describe the plane."

"It is a recently renovated vintage de Havilland DH.98 Mosquito bomber floatplane. The tail number is number N7952Z."

"I will look into it. But be aware that such incursions by Americans are not rare, and this sounds every bit like a CIA operation. I will call you. Do not call me again. If we find the plane, we will examine it most carefully to see if it is fitted out for espionage. If it is, we have an international incident on our hands. I will not allow any danger to come to the Rodina on my watch. Good day, Major Higgins, or whatever your name may really be."

The line went dead.

Higgins paused for a moment, then turned to the two Hoonah headmen.

"That's the kind of cooperation I expected. I have a favor to ask of you. You have contacts on Kamchatka and do business back and forth between Hoonah and Petropavlovsk-Kamchatsky. The Alaska state police and the Gabler family need to know as much as possible about the events surrounding the death of Gen. Gabler. It will take forever for us to get any worthwhile information from the Soviets, if we get any at all. This Cold War business makes ordinary interchange all but impossible. Would you be willing to travel over to the peninsula and nose around, see if there is any report of an unauthorized plane having landed there, and if you can find out anything about the pilot or passengers? For one thing, were they Russians? We're making an almost wild supposition. If not Russians, any information that would lead us to who they are would be of great help."

The Peratrovich brothers glanced at each other and gave a slight mutual nod.

"Yes," Anotklosh said, answering for both Tlingits.

"Done," Maj. Higgins said and stepped away from his chair to shake hands with Henry and Anotklosh.

The handshake was sufficient as a bond, and the two Tlingits left the conference room for their dinner and a flight back to Hoonah.

"Now, as distasteful as it is and as difficult a time as this is, we need to establish the whereabouts of each the Gabler party members during the presumed time of the general's death. The question I will put to each of you—and I will do it separately—is this: where were you between two-thirty or maybe as late as three to about five-thirty a.m. night before last?

"Lt. Perez will escort you to separate rooms before he and I will question you. Thank you all in advance for your cooperation."

The two MCU officers questioned Maj. Rick Saunders first.

"So, Major, do you have an alibi for the time in question?"

Saunders looked the two Alaska law enforcement officers directly in their eyes without sign of evasiveness, guilty conscience, or nervousness. He had lived most of his adult life under the shadow—and, indeed, under the thumb—of Glen Gabler. As a result, he had developed a thick skin and an ability to avoid flinching or looking away when challenged. He was only five foot four inches tall and 145 pounds soaking wet, but he had genuine courage—proved in battle—and had not feared another man—even the general—for more than twenty years. He was a thin man with a monk's tonsure male pattern baldness, a sallow complexion, wore thick horn rim glasses, and had crooked teeth that had never been properly aligned. He was the quintessential Casper Milquetoast in appearance but not in character.

"I was in my bed asleep," he answered without hesitation.

"Anyone able to corroborate that, Major?"

"All of the young Gablers and I played cards—bridge and pinochle—until a little after one, maybe one-twenty, then we made our way to the bathrooms. We got together with the general at about two-fifteen for a final celebration drink and retired into our separate bedrooms. The next thing we knew of each other was when the young staff girls screamed after finding the general hanging from the rafters."

"Do you know who the beneficiary is or who are the beneficiaries of Gen. Gabler's will, Maj. Saunders?"

"I do know that. Each of the sons receives an equal portion of fifty percent of the estate. I receive ten percent. The final forty percent goes to the Army's disabled veteran's programs."

Maj. Higgins and Lt. Perez got almost identical answers from all of the Gabler sons. The stories sounded unrehearsed and not word-for-word as if scripted, but the gist was the same.

Maj. Higgins reassembled the Gabler party and asked one more small set of questions: "Did any of you hear or see anything suspicious throughout the rest of the night? Any sounds of a struggle, any possibility of blows being struck? Anyone walking in the hallways?"

The answers were uniformly "No," and the two MCU officers believed them.

"All right, gentlemen. You are free to go. We'll get you back to the Alaskan Bear Lodge, and they can see to your needs. Sorry to have inconvenienced you, and we are genuinely sorry for your loss. Leave your names, addresses, and telephone numbers; so, we can contact you if need be and to give you updates. Thanks again for your cooperation, and we wish you all the best from here on out."

The questioning of Neille Bastrup and his staff was less genteel and more like a serious cross-examination which went on for several hours. Everyone involved was exhausted, offended, distressed, and—in the end—frustrated, at not knowing anything more about the murder of Gen. Gabler than they had nearly forty-eight hours before when his body was first discovered. The Bastrup contingent was flown home to the lodge and—like the Gablers and Maj. Saunders—slept the sleep of the dead until late morning the next day. Glen Jr. made arrangements for the transfer of the remains of his father back to the lower forty-eight, then their gear was collected and travel arrangements completed.

"Don't worry about the fish. I'll get it all cut up, packaged, and frozen. We'll get it to you by the first flight out on Friday, and you should have it late the same day. If there's anything else I can possibly do for you, don't hesitate to let me know," Neille said, and he meant it.

CHAPTER SIX

Lomas de los Carolinos, Córdoba, Argentina, August 9, 1962

Carlos Aguillara-Dominguez left his business office on Alberto Soriano Street early on a cold August afternoon to keep an assignation with his mistress, Anna Maria Lobos, as he did every Friday. He wore an anticipatory smile, his best suit, and a new pair of shoes imported from Italy; and he carried an extravagant bouquet of flowers, as he did every Friday as he walked the six blocks to Anna Maria's apartment on Avenida San Pedro y Paulo. In all ways, Carlos was a creature of habit. He looked a decade younger than his sixty-four years thanks to a fine limited nip and tuck maintenance job of plastic surgery done the year before in Buenos Aires and to regular discreet hair dying which kept his full coiffure an even jet black. His facial appearance had changed dramatically from what it had been fifteen years ago when he had his first facial reconstruction. His generally handsome mature face was slightly marred by the presence of a transverse dueling scar on his left cheek. He had once been mildly bothered by the presence of the scar for several reasons; but Anna Maria told him it was sexy; so, he got over the negative sense of his appearance. He was slim, patrician, and fit, even martial, in appearance. Carlos never went out in public dressed in anything but the tailored ensemble that befitted his status as a wealthy and successful import-export company president and the employer of one-hundred-seventy-five loyal workers.

Carlos's only health issue for the past seventeen years had been a mild hand tremor which was coming under control with the help of an eminent psychologist in the capital city, Robert Mueller. Dr. Mueller and Carlos were members of the same Germanophile organizations and charities and moved in a close-knit and exclusive circle of helpful friends. On Fridays—Carlos smiled to himself—he lost the tremor altogether knowing that shortly any and all of his stress-related concerns would evaporate for a few hours.

When he arrived at the bottom of the stairs that led up to the apartment building where he owned the apartment now occupied by his latest paramour, Carlos was annoyed to encounter a homeless man–an intolerable disgrace in this very affluent, neat, scrupulously clean section of Córdoba.

The sight of the disheveled man disturbed Carlos's ebullient mood and brought out in him an authoritarian side he usually made an effort to suppress in public.

"*Hier raus, Faulpelz!*" [German: "Get out of here, lazy bum!"] he ordered imperiously. "*Finden Sie ein Loch woanders verstecken!*" ["Find a hole to hide in somewhere else!"]

The man ignored him. Carlos shook his head at his own mistake. Of course, this *untermenschen* would not know the *Zunge des Vaterlandes* [Tongue of the Fatherland]. Certainly no self-respecting German would appear in such a state in this place in this modern age.

"*Leave a la vez, o le enviaré a la policía!*" [Spanish: "Leave at once, or I will send for the police!"] he corrected himself by changing to Spanish.

Obediently the eyesore slowly pushed himself up to a standing position. There was something about the man that caught Carlos's attention. It came to him in a flash of recognition: it was the unabashed stare of the man's steely blue eyes.

The man flashed a gleaming razor-sharp machete and unerringly swung it with both hands at Carlos's neck above the line of his immaculate white shirt collar and floral print necktie. Before he could react, Carlos Aguillara-Dominguez's head separated from his body and rolled grotesquely onto the clean side walk. The homeless man stepped back and avoided the gouts of blood rhythmically spurting from the momentarily still standing corpse. He walked away briskly down Avenida San Pedro y Paulo. The murder was witnessed, but all the witnesses could recall when questioned by the police was the horror of the decapitation and all that blood on the previously pristine sidewalk. It was as if the homeless man was invisible, as might be expected in Lomas de los

Carolinos where few homeless ever ventured into the neighborhood, and even fewer merited any notice.

Córdoba is located in the geographical center of Argentina, in the foothills of the Sierras Chicas on the Suquía River, 435 miles northwest of Buenos Aires. It is the second-largest city in Argentina after Buenos Aires. It was founded July 6, 1573 by conquistador Jerónimo Luis de Cabrera, who named it after Córdoba, Spain, his city of origin. It was one of the first Spanish colonial capitals of the region that is now Argentina.

The wealthier suburbs west of the city are located at slightly higher altitudes, which allows cool breezes to blow in the summer bringing drier, comfortable nights during hotter periods, and more regular frost in the winter. The General Cerro de Las Rosas area is located a little less than four miles from downtown Córdoba. Lomas de los Carolinos on the old Camino a La Calera is one of the oldest sections of Córdoba. Lomas is a very affluent neighborhood famous for its schools, shops, and educational institutions. The main thoroughfare through the rich neighborhood is Rafael Núñez Avenue, which stretches for a few miles. It features posh restaurants, expensive European boutiques, banks, and other institutions and trendy shops. Most of the affluent inhabitants such as Anna Maria Lobos—kept by Carlos Aguillara-Dominguez— have moved to gated communities because of growing security reasons.

Sargentopoliciaprovbsas Policía de la Provincia de Córdoba, PPC [Corporal, Police of the Province of Córdoba] Manuel de Jesus received the first of several frantic calls from dispatch regarding a gruesome murder in Lomas de los Carolinos, one of the most panicked having come from *Oficial de Policía* [Police Officer] Gerhardt Möller, the most German of the men on the force. Well aware of the rarified atmosphere of the richest and oldest neighborhood in the city, he immediately called his friend from the academy, *Teniente* [Detective] Jose Emanuel de Corsos, to go with him and to take charge of the investigation.

Manuel was a small Indian/Latino man with dark brown skin and irises and a head of thick, coarse, black hair. He had the inscrutable face of the people whose world was taken from them by Spaniards four hundred years ago. Nimble and quick, he constantly wore a pair of aviator's dark glasses. He was neat and entirely proper in his uniform.

Detective de Corsos was thick and bulky. He appeared to be slow— both in movement and in intellect—but he was neither. His movements were quick and precise, and he could—if required—move with alarming speed in dealing with an uncooperative man in the course of an investigation. He had a reputation of being effective—and that was known to be "unorthodox" (code for brutal) when necessary to obtain crucial information. His face was fleshy and suggested gluttony, which was at least partly true; but it also suggested slovenliness, which was not true. His civilian linen suit was always pressed, a monumental feat in the hot, wet climate of Córdoba. He never went out without a freshly starched white shirt and a high quality silk tie. He had a preference for gaucho boots.

The two men bounded down the stairs of the headquarters building and ran to their blue Argentine Ford Falcon. De Jesus drove, lights and sirens scattering the crowded streets as they went. Upon arrival at the scene on Avenida San Pedro y Paulo, the two provincial policemen saw a ramrod stiff police officer standing guard over the grim scene. They approached him and noticed first the massive amount of blood that had spattered the sidewalk and the street, then a man's head detached and lying a full three yards away from his blood-drenched body, then a patch of vomit a few feet away, and finally, the gray-green color of the officer's skin. His knees were locked, and he stared vacantly straight ahead.

De Corsos barked an order, "*Oficial* Möller, bend your knees; or you will faint!"

A swift softening look of relief seemed to come over the man's ashen face—which, instead of showing the hoped-for flushing indicative of return of consciousness, turned deathly white. He fainted and fell face forward like a felled tree into the thickening pool of blood, making no effort to shield his face.

Fury showed on de Corsos's face, and he fought his desire to scream at the hapless police officer or at the gathering crowd or even at his partner on the scene, Corporal de Jesus. He counted to five, regained composure, and gave de Jesus a series of orders.

"Manuel, disperse the crowd. Make them stand no closer than fifty meters away. Use the car radio and get us a squad of officers here to get control of the scene. When that is done, get Henckel on the line for me."

"Henckel" was Adolf Henckel, the *Inspector de Policia*—third ranking field officer in the Córdoba Provincial Police Service. He was respected and feared but considered to be both the smartest and the toughest police man in the province. It was rumored that he had a military background, and not exactly the Argentine military.

He was forty-two years old but looked more like thirty. His hair was deep brown without a trace of graying or balding. Unlike the other police officers, he had relatively long hair which covered the tops of his ears. He had thick eyebrows, deepset brown eyes, and a face cratered with old small-pox scars. His chin was cleft with a deep dimple. He was tall and muscular and had large sinewy hands. He wore a jet-black suit and matching tie with a starched white shirt. His black wingtip shoes were nearly new and were polished that morning.

De Corsos unceremoniously took hold of the still unconscious policeman by his ankles and dragged him away from the corpse, leaving an almost comical blood smear attesting to the folly attending the scene. He took care not to add his own footprints to the already grossly contaminated murder site.

Henckel came right to the point: "Why are you calling me, Detective? Is there something you cannot handle by yourself?"

De Corsos gave a very quick Dick-and-Jane description of the scene, then added, "From the appearance of the victim, I would say that we have an *hidalgo* [son of someone of importance] here."

"Have a name?" Henckel asked.

"Not yet. I don't recognize the face. Looks European."

"European" was police code for German, and often implied *German*, "one of those *Germans*."

"I'll get there as soon as I can, and I'll bring a photographer. We need to know who this is *muy pronto*. It's beginning to sound like one of those cases that never happened. Treat it that way for now. Get rid of the onlookers."

"Yes, sir," de Corsos said; but the line was already dead.

De Jesus was very efficient. The reflexively obedient citizens of Lomas de los Carolinos were standing quietly looking on from more than fifty meters away.

"What now, *Jefe*?" he asked.

"Henckel is on his way. None of these people are to be here when he arrives. And neither is that boob, Möller. Let's get to work. Get us two big men to carry him off. Loosen his tie and shirt collar. Throw some water on his face. Put him over there, behind the bushes on the side of the apartment building. I'll get the crowd out of here, then go in and order everyone in the apartments to stay where they are. We have very little to go on, but we can make a first supposition that the man was here to conduct business or that he lives in the building."

"He was very dressed up, José. There is an expensive bouquet of flowers by him. Maybe he had an assignation in the building."

"Likely. Let's make it an early priority to find her."

"Or him," de Jesus suggested dryly.

"He's 'European,' that's not particularly unlikely. You know how they are," de Corsos said softly enough; so, no one but he and de Jesus could hear.

De Jesus selected two burly laboring types and headed back to the corpse with them. De Corsos stretched his arms out to the crowd of onlookers and signaled them to gather in front of him.

"Go home. Now. The excitement is over. Do not speak of this. So far as you are concerned, it never happened. It is better for you that way, *comprende?*"

They understood, all right. This was a people who would not soon forget the most recent—1952–1955—administration of Presidente Juan Peron, the *Batallón de Inteligencia* 601, and "*los desaparecidos*" [the "disappeared ones"]. Three minutes later the streets near the murder scene were empty. That included two mediocrely dressed European men who had been standing in the middle of the crowd.

Inspector Henckel came with two carloads of police officers, secretaries, and crime scene technologists. Henckel acknowledged de Corsos with a cursory nod then began setting his team to work. Two men set up a command tent in the street. Another man put up police tape around a large area outside where the body, head, and blood of Carlos Aguillara-Dominguez lay festering in the cold August sun. A distinguished portly Germanic appearing gentleman stepped out of a gray van marked *Equipo Argentino de Médico Forense* and was followed by three other members of the medical forensic team. They photographed the scene very thoroughly, then one of the technicians—dressed in white coveralls and rubber boots—stepped carefully up to the corpse and riffled through his pockets. He extracted a wallet and found a national identification card and driver license. There were black and white photographs of a dowdy woman and a handsome well-dressed European man with their four grown children and a full color photograph of a strikingly beautiful statuesque blond woman wearing a décolleté evening gown which displayed a more than ample cleavage to turn the head of a priest. Glued to the bottom of that photo was a name and address: Anna Maria Lobos, 76 Alberto Soriano Str., Apt. 12.

He retraced his steps and handed the wallet—opened to the photograph of the beautiful woman—to Dr. Schmidt, who smiled.

"The man must have suffered from dementia if he had to keep the name and address of this one in his wallet in order to remember her."

The technologist laughed. "No man I know could forget such a one," he said.

Konrad Schmidt von Dresden walked briskly over and picked up the severed head with a gloved hand. He held the man's wallet in his left hand and compared the photograph of the man in the family photo with the face of the disembodied head.

"Our victim is Carlos Aguillara-Dominguez, Inspector Henckel," he announced then tossed the wallet to the police inspector.

While Dr. Schmidt did a cursory and preliminary examination of the body, Henckel sent a team to canvass the neighborhood and finally spoke to de Corsos, "Detective, have your corporal get the preliminaries done; and then the three of us will go into the apartment and talk to the woman in this photograph and the other people in the building."

De Corsos nodded his understanding to his superior officer, then turned to Corporal de Jesus, "Manuel, get Möller—if he is able to stand up by now—and go to every apartment and order the people to remain in their rooms. Start questioning them about anything they saw today that was out of the ordinary, anything they know about this Aguillara-Dominguez, and the woman … Anna Maria Lobos, in apartment 12."

Henckel spoke to his chief lieutenant, "Send some men to the address of the man's wife and see what we can learn. I want to know if she knew about the mistress, if Aguillara-Dominguez had an insurance policy on his life, and if he had any enemies. We'll try a gentle approach to begin with."

The detective signaled to a couple of uniformed police officers, and they left promptly to carry out the inspector's orders.

"All right, then, de Corsos, it's time to go see Anna Maria. It's hard work, but someone has to do it. That's why they pay us the large salaries," Henckel said.

De Corsos laughed with the inspector, and they walked into the apartment and up to the twelfth floor.

De Corsos knocked. Two minutes later they heard a high and melodious woman's voice say, "*Ist, dass Sie, lieber ein?*" [Is that you, dear one?]

"Police. Open the door, please," de Corsos ordered.

There was a slight shuffling behind the door, then the door opened. Anna Maria had hastily put on a sheer nightgown which left little to the imagination. The platinum (suicide) blond folded her arms across her chest to lessen the impact she knew she had on men. She was smoking an original French Gitanes Brunes, the French cigarette with the strong bite popular in Argentina and Chile.

"Come in," she said, switching to accented Spanish.

"Are you Anna Maria Lobos?" de Corsos asked unnecessarily.

"Yes, sir. What is this about? Where are my manners—please have a seat."

"A police investigation, Miss Lobos. Do you know a man named Carlos Aguillara-Dominguez?"

She hesitated a moment, apparently considering whether or not to lie.

"Yes, sir. Why do you ask? Has something happened to Carlos?"

"We will ask the questions for now, Miss Lobos," Henckel answered, taking over.

"Did you see him today?"

"No, sir, but I was expecting him," she said and had the humility to blush.

Henckel and de Corsos suppressed a smile.

"What is your relationship with Herr Aguillara-Dominguez, please?"

She blushed in earnest now, which would have been enough of an answer even if she made no reply.

"We are very good friends, Officer."

"Were you his mistress, Anna Maria? Is it all right if I call you by your first name?"

"That's fine … and yes, I guess that is what you would call it."

"How long have you known him?"

"Three years."

She was looking downcast now. She was not stupid; she had caught the reference to her lover in the past tense.

"Does he pay for this nice apartment?"

"Yes."

"Do you have work?"

"Yes, sir. I am a model for *Casa Vogue*."

"The Italian woman's fashion magazine?"

"Yes. It is popular here in Argentina as well."

"Did Herr Aguillara-Dominguez have an insurance policy naming you as beneficiary?"

"I don't think so. He's dead, isn't he?"

Her lip quivered, and she began to cry.

De Corsos found a box of tissues and gave it to her. It took her a few minutes to regain her composure.

"I'm afraid so, young lady. That's why we're here. We are sorry to have to tell you this," Henckel said. "But as difficult as it is, we have to get information that can help in our investigation. You understand."

"Yes. Anything. Please tell me what happened."

"He was attacked. He was killed. I'm sorry," Henckel said quietly.

"*Oh, mein Gott!*" Anna-Maria said, lapsing back into her native German. She looked stricken, but maintained her composure.

"Who could do such a thing? He was such a sweet man? Was it a robbery?"

"That's a lot of questions, Anna Maria. First, we are investigating, and for the time being we do not know who could have killed him. To answer your question—no, it was not a robbery. He appeared to have been targeted."

"I think he might have had some enemies ... from the war. It is a big secret, but I guess it is time for the authorities to know. He came here from Germany and was being hunted for questioning about war crimes. He told me this."

"That is most interesting, Anna Maria. Did he have enemies connected with his business? Do you know if he had links to criminals like the Sicilian Cosa Nostra or the 'ndràngheta from Italy? The 'Honored Society' is known to ship cocaine from Córdoba through Spain to Milan and Turin."

"Please do not let anyone know that I tell you something. They will kill me, if you do. They are very bad men."

"If you tell us the truth, we will protect you," Henckel told her, echoing the same lie that police have told potential witnesses all over the world and for time immemorial.

CHAPTER SEVEN

Central de Policia de Cordóba, Av. Colón 1254, Cordóba Capital [Police Headquarters, Provincial Capital, Cordóba], the same day

Anna Maria proved to have a minor treasure trove of information, which had been gained through pillow talk. Inspector Henckel listened to her for nearly an hour, then decided to move her incognito to the central police headquarters in the city for her own protection and to ensure that her information could be preserved for eventual prosecution of the case. During and even after the revolving door regimes of Juan Peron, evidence of wrongdoing and even people possessing such knowledge that touched the regime—even tangentially—seemed to have a vexing habit of disappearing. Henckel was determined that he was not going to let that happen in this case. That is why Anna Maria entered the law enforcement edifice under an assumed name.

Once settled in and fed properly, Henckel and de Corsos continued to grill Anna Maria. De Jesus and Henckel's men remained at the crime scene area in Lomas de los Carolinos to try and find witnesses.

"Can you give us some names of people in the Cosa Nostra or the ʿndràngheta, Anna Maria?" Henckel asked her.

In the relative safety and comfort of the fortresslike police head-quarters—and after a few glasses of Barbera from the grape fields of Mendoza province, the inferior domestic red wine which was a crude mixture of an assortment of wines and wine grapes made with little pride or product control—Anna Maria began to relax. Henckel would not drink the stuff; it was no wonder that Argentina was a net importer of wines in these early 1960s so far as he was concerned.

Anna Maria asked for a pen and paper and began writing as fast as she could. Occasionally she would stop for a moment and think, then resume until she had filled ten pages with names, addresses, telephone numbers, and company names. When she looked up—indicating that she was finished—Henckel asked her a question.

"Who did Carlos have trouble with?"

Anna Maria responded by putting a check mark by about fifteen names.

"And which of those do you think employs killers to get their way?"

Anna Maria said, "I'm not sure. But maybe these."

She underlined five of the names.

De Corsos waited until there was a pause in the interrogatory before inserting a question of his own.

"Tell us what you can about his life before he came here. Any known Nazi connection?" How about the ODESSA?"

"He didn't talk much about that, you understand; but I caught a few things over the past couple of years. He once told me that he was a chemist for a while, and he worked for IG Farben in a secret plant that made weapons."

"Chemical weapons?"

"Yes."

"Remember any names of the chemicals? Think hard, Anna Maria. It's important."

"Once, he talked about a man he was afraid of, maybe someone he came to Argentina from Germany with. I think the man might have been in charge of making a very bad gas, in fact, two kinds of gas."

"Can you remember the names of the gasses? Even if you could give us a name that sounds like the chemical?"

"Oh, just a second—I remember the man's name. It was August Neubert—something like that. I don't know for sure, but he might have come here. He and Carlos were helped by the ODESSA in 1946. They were in the French section of West Germany, I think. It's also possible that they parted ways before they came here, but one thing I do remember is that this August Neubert was perfectly willing to kill anyone who might be able to identify him or who knew where he ended up. Carlos was truly afraid of him. He had plastic surgery to hide what he looked like and changed his name of course. Once when he was very drunk and was speaking German, I called him Carlos—and he got angry and told me never to call him that again. He was Hörst Dietsel, and it was a name he was proud of. When he sobered up, he told me to forget that name because it would be the death of him if anyone ever found out."

"Is that anyone you are familiar with, de Corsos?" Inspector Henckel asked.

Detective de Corsos shook his head. Henckel shrugged.

"Can you remember the names of the gasses, Anna Maria? You have done very well so far. Give it a hard try."

He gave her time to think.

"I am almost sure that Carlos told me that the weapons were called tabun and sarin gas. One of those was called GB or GD, I think. A very tiny spray in the air could kill a man in minutes. A tiny tiny drop in a glass of wine would kill a man in half an hour—maybe less—depending on the man's size."

She had a small involuntary shudder.

"Never heard of them," Henckel said, "You?" he asked, looking at de Corsos.

"Above my pay grade, apparently."

"Look into it, Detective. Maybe knowing about that or about this man Neubert got him killed. Or maybe the Israelis found out about him. I'll get you the clearance."

Córdoba, Argentina Recipes

<u>Córdoba Dove Empanadas—6–8 Servings</u>

Ingredients
-Dove meat—2.5 lbs deboned and skinned dove breasts
-Vegetables—2 large peeled carrots, 1 large red pepper, 1 medium
yellow onion, ¼ tsp ground ginger
-Spices—Black and red pepper, sea salt (or garlic salt), and paprika to taste
-Premade round pastry discs or use filo dough.

Preparation
-Cut vegetables and meat into small cubes.
-Sauté vegetables with extra virgin olive oil.
-Remove and set aside vegetables then sauté meat until tender.
-Mix all ingredients and season mix to taste
-Fill the premade pastry rounds and bake for 15 minutes at 350° or until golden brown.

Argentine *Chimichurri* olive oil and spice rub for steak

Ingredients
-Spices and herbs—¼ cp oregano (fresh is best, but dried (4 tsps) is a decent substitute), 4 garlic cloves, 2 cps firmly packed fresh Italian parsley leaves, ½ tsp red pepper flakes, ½ tsp kosher or sea salt, ½ tsp freshly and finely ground black pepper, ½ tsp red pepper, ¼ cp red wine vinegar, 1 cp extra virgin olive oil

Preparation
Note: It is best to make the chimichurri a day in advance and refrigerate to bring out flavors.
-Peel and smash garlic cloves
-Place parsley, garlic, oregano, vinegar, red pepper flakes, salt, and pepper (all to taste) in the bowl of a bladed food processor. Process until finely chopped, stopping and scraping down the sides of the bowl with a rubber spatula as needed, about 1 minute total.
-Keep motor running, and add oil in a steady stream. Scrape down the sides of the bowl and pulse a few times to combine. Transfer sauce to an airtight container and refrigerate at least 2 hours—better up to a full day. Before serving, stir and season as needed. The chimichurri will keep in the refrigerator for up to 1 week.
Serve on the side for 1–2 inch thick, 1 lb Argentine steak (which should be cooked "*jugoso*"—medium rare) and apply the chimichurri to taste.

CHAPTER EIGHT

Jardin du Luxembourg Park, Rue d' Assas Entrance, Fauborg Saint Germain-des-Prés, 6ᵗʰ arrondissement [6ème], Paris, Assumption Day, August 15, 1962

The morning heat was indicative that it was going to be a typical August day in Paris—hot, muggy, and soporific. The city was not in its usual vibrant state, a change that took place every August. Most Parisians had abandoned the capital for the overpacked beaches of the Cote d'Azur or the Atlantic Coast, and the invasion by global tourists was its usual annoyance to the citizens who were obligated to remain for work or due to some sort of infirmity. The tourists exuded noisy enthusiasm, and the people of Paris unlucky enough to have to endure August in the City of Lights and Love exhibited an increase in their usual gloomy dispositions and famous sullenness.

A cloudburst the previous day had transiently dissipated the heavy air and oppressive heat to make the beginning of Assumption Day an almost pleasant one for a retired general. He knew the heat and humidity would retake control by noon; but for the moment, his regular early morning walk was delightful. The veteran of two wars—World Wars I and II—was still in good condition and would have been able to wear his tailored uniform complete with medals if required, a fact that appealed to his rather considerable vanity. His thick crop of hair was silver, but had not a hint of balding; and he had improved the growing topographical wrinkles of his hard face with a little adroit plastic surgery.

His wife had made him a particularly pleasant *petit déjeuner*—a light meal of fresh baguettes, whole wheat cereal, Greek yogurt, a fresh peach, and café au lait. Enough that he felt invigorated for his meeting with his mistress, but not too much; so, his prowess would be affected. It was proving to be a fine day.

Gen. Étienne Malboeuf was an ardent Catholic, born into the faith and sustained by it during his long years in the colonies and in the European wars. He was on his way to the center of the extensive Jardin du Luxembourg Park for an Assumption Day religious program. The elderly soldier walked briskly across the wide boulevard and into the park, making sure that he was not late. Malboeuf lived a life of military grade rigidity, punctuality, adherence to schedule, and scrupulous compliance with the etiquette of his class. France was a very class-conscious society, and he made no concessions to the growing fashion of breaking down the civilized barriers of the class-stratified society or the ascension of women. He did not have to deign to acknowledge manual workers or other peasants. It was his due owed him for his long service to his country and by the God-given privilege and responsibility of the upper-crust stratum into which he was born.

Malboeuf particularly loved the romantic Fontaine de Médicis—built for Marie de Médicis—a shady and peaceful spot overlooking a pond filled with fish and the statue of the beautiful Marianne, the symbol of the republic as a motherland. She stands for the rallying cry of "liberty, equality, fraternity," and seeing her never failed to ignite a small adrenaline rush. He knew she was modeled after the movie actress, Brigitte Anne-Marie Bardot. He had never seen one of the young woman's films, but she was for him—and millions of other French men and women—the personification of France as the motherland. Gen. Malboeuf thought the iconic figure in the statue looked more like his mistress, Antoinette, who was at the moment sleeping quietly in the *pied-a-terre* he maintained for her on Rue Vavin. His wife—who was his childhood sweetheart and lifelong heart's friend—was at home on Rue d'Assas baking bread for the family dinner that evening. He allowed a faint smile to curl his thin lips. Life was good, as it should be in a civilized country.

In the opinion of Gen. Malboeuf, France was the most civilized of all nations, and the 6th *arrondissement* was the best neighborhood in the city. There are twenty different *arrondissements* which spiral out numerically from the center of Paris, starting with the Louvre as 1e. The city is further divided almost exactly in half—north and south—by the Seine into the *rive gauche* [left bank] and the *rive droite* [right bank]. As a general rule, those *arrondissements* closest to the geographic center of the city are the wealthiest, and the suburbs to the west and south of Paris tend to be more affluent than those to the north and east. The 6th [6ème] is on the left bank—the heart of the *rive gauche*, Malboeuf would insist—on the vibrant bank of the river. The 6th and the 7th A.s rank close to each other in average wealth, and that is considerably higher than the average in France. In fact–but nothing the general would admit–the 7th A. was the richest in the city.

The 6th was beginning to change from its earlier character as the meeting place for bohemian artists and intellectuals into a more upscale neighborhood of trendy new boutiques, high-priced modern art galleries, exciting, even daring, new restaurants, and quiet *pied-a-terres*; nearly twenty percent of apartments are secondary residences—enough to raise an amused eyebrow among French sophisticates. The Latin Quarter is part of the 6th. Being one of the old school Frenchmen, the general still preferred the older and more famous cafes such as Brasserie Lipp, Cafe Flore, and Les Deux Magots. Nouveau rich and sophisticated buyers and younger residents had begun to supplant the previously seen famous artists and writers such as George Sand, Pablo Picasso, Ernest Hemingway, Oscar Wilde, Gertrude Stein, and Ezra Pound. Charm was replacing the solid old buildings and narrow and interesting streets, leaving a mix of the new and the historic architecture. The Musée de Cluny remained as the best museum dedicated to the arts of the Middle Ages—again, in Gen. Malboeuf's educated opinion. Its Gothic architecture had resisted all the modern changes, a fact that pleased the old general greatly.

Gen. Malboeuf paused for a moment for a brief rest. He extracted a Gitanes Brunes from its classic black, blue, and white colored box with the fetchingly obscure picture of a gypsy, all part of the vibrant French culture he had loved for so long. He had always been a small man, but once had been erect and imperious. Now—to his chagrin—he was small, bony, and bent with arthritis. He wore skin creases that gave evidence to the pain the crippling joint disease caused him. His once desert-bronzed face now had an unpleasant sallow complexion which intensified the loss of the soft tissues and gave him an appearance of a man who was all of his seventy-four years and more, and a man whose sojourn among the upper echelon Frenchmen he admired so greatly was nearing its end. He hated the fact that his once full head of hair which the women around him prized now consisted of little more than a few wispy white feathers. He had to wear a beret or one of his army uniform caps whenever he went out in public. He had the Frankish nose—once part of the hauteur he knew his face conveyed in those halcyon years—but that was about all that was left of his once forceful and authoritative demeanor. As he held the brown cigarette to his lips, his gnarled fingers shook, an observation that pained him.

He entered the park and gave a brief but heartfelt salute to the row of *tricoleurs* lining the avenue. The Jardin du Luxembourg is a favorite garden oasis and rendezvous spot for Parisians, and the general always enjoyed his walks through the park with his mistress. The beautiful and peaceful gardens were designed in the formal French style featuring broad avenues lined with precisely planted trees and trimmed hedges, immaculate lawns, statues, and fountains, including the ever-popular octagonal pool full of toy sailboats. He gave a smile at the children of well-to-do families playing with their boats. Overlooking the Luxembourg gardens was the grand Palais du Luxembourg, built in the seventeenth century to remind its first owner Marie de Médicis, widow of Henri IV, of her native Florence, Italy.

Bowing to the fact that his glory days were behind him, he turned to walk to the center of the park where—for a brief moment—he would be selected out for praise for his service and reminded of what he once was. He glanced around, admiring the garden and thinking that Paris architecture was stable—quite homogenous—in its beige tones and beautiful even though many of the buildings could do with a good sandblast cleaning. He made a mental note that there was something a bit unusual in the garden. Whereas ordinarily, visibly armed police were a noticeable presence throughout the city—particularly in urban areas and where crowds gather such as he was seeing in the Jardin du Luxembourg Park on auspicious occasions such as this Assumption Day—he could not recall seeing even one today. They regularly exercised their right to stop any person and demand to see documents of identity. It was a bit odd that he was not seeing the gendarmerie. It was not worth more than a bored shrug.

Witnesses differed considerably about what happened next. They all agreed that Gen. Malboeuf was shot to death—shot in the back. The number of shots varied from one to six; the location of the entry wounds varied from the back of his head to as low as his waistband; and the description of the murderer—or murderers—could have incriminated half the men in Paris. Some reported a black man, probably one of those lowlife immigrants from Morocco. Others described a man in a gray morning suit wearing a large fedora. The man seemed to have been a provincial to some, a Parisian to others; to some, tall, to others, short, and to one witness, a cripple with a pronounced limp. More than half of the many witnesses described a lone killer; but two persons told investigating officers that there had been two killers, each firing a handgun. One older woman was sure she saw three killers. There was even a report that the killer had been a tall blond woman.

No one made the slightest effort to apprehend the culprit. There were an assortment of excuses, but no really valid reasons other than that they did not want to get involved, or that they were no physical match for the assailant, or that they were not close enough to be of any use.

Grégoire Laurent De Vincent had a wife—Claire—and eleven children. He came from a family of twelve children, and all of his siblings had demonstrated a nearly equal degree of fecundity. The huge extended family lived in what amounted to a compound, no nuclear family further away than a city block. It was not that Grégoire did not like or love his large noisy family—which invaded his privacy at will and with regularity—but being a contemplative man by nature, he longed for moments of peace and quiet. His profession demanded that he be able to think undisturbed when he was involved in a case, and he was highly respected for his ability to sift the wheat from the chaff of a case and find the kernel of truth that led to solving even very complicated and emotionally charged cases. He had chosen exactly the right profession for himself for several reasons: he was indomitable and indefatigable in his pursuit of the truth, and he loved the chance to get away from the hordes of relatives from time to time.

Life was good for France and for Grégoire. France had emerged from World War II in the 1960s, and the work of rebuilding the country physically and the nation's national identity through the French Fifth Republic was well underway under President Charles de Gaulle, elected in 1958. Under the leadership of the famous general, France was making progress to regain its status as a great power. Senior civil servants like Grégoire and his family had been able to move into better housing and neighborhoods in the early 1960s as the middle class numbers and its economy began to expand.

Grégoire was an *enquêteur* [plainclothes detective] in the *Sûreté Nationale,* Préfecture of Police of Paris—an agency of the national government of France. He had been assigned to the homicide division for the past twenty-two years and enjoyed his job immensely—especially the part where he got to see murderers he had arrested sweat in court. Grégoire was relieved when the call came from Place Louis Lépine, at 1 rue de Lutèce—police headquarters—that he was to report to the Jardin du Luxembourg in Saint Germain-des-Prés to head up a sensitive murder investigation. He took pains not to show his enthusiasm for the assignment and its promise of taking him away from the cacophony and chaos of the family gathering to celebrate Assumption Day.

"Alas, *ma légitime,*" he said to his long-suffering wife, suppressing a smile of relief, "but I am called to work—a serious murder."

"They are all serious, *mon amour*; and they all seem to occur during big family gatherings," she responded with her usual affectionate resignation.

He smiled sheepishly and went to change into his suit and tie.

Inspector De Vincent arrived first at the Rue d'Assas/ Rue Vavin entrance to the Jardin du Luxembourg Park and stood for five minutes impatiently twiddling his thumbs as he waited for his favorite investigative partner to show up.

A dyspneic old Peugeot driven by Gendarmerie Research Unit Lieutenant Sylvain Piétri coughed its way to a stop at the intersection; and the frail, tiny, academic-appearing officer stepped out and gave a small wave to De Vincent. The two men could not have been more different in appearance and manner. Piétri was wiry, energetic to the point of seeming frantic, and never appeared in public out of his gendarme uniform. He was deferential to De Vincent who technically outranked him even though they worked for different services. He had a dark complexion, close-set eyes, and aquiline nose that hinted at a Moorish genealogy. He spoke with a stammer that continually caused him embarrassment, which is why he seldom talked to anyone except

Inspector De Vincent, and why he jealously guarded his out-of-the-public-scrutiny research job.

De Vincent was a ponderous man—obese, rotund, jolly—unable to find a suit that fit or shoes that could hold a shine—but underneath that untidy exterior, he was a quiet and slow-moving thinker. Piétri supplied the raw information, and De Vincent made sense of it. The inspector's tie had stains from meals enjoyed months ago. He had a pudgy, ruddy face, the joviality of which belied the great intelligence behind it. Many a criminal and his or her attorney were shocked at what happened to them when they underestimated the slovenly and none-too-bright appearing Sûreté officer who surprised them by delivering a rapier-sharp synopsis of the case against the criminal in his clipped, cultured, and precise, Parisian Sorbonne accent.

"I hope you have more information about this case than I do, *mon ami*," said De Vincent by way of greeting.

"Only a little—some research I picked up in a hurry at headquarters before I raced to meet you at the scene."

De Vincent raised one eyebrow and looked askance at his longtime, and almost always, late friend. They both knew that the chronic tardiness stemmed from the inadequacy of Piétri's decrepit but beloved little car. They shared a brief comradely laugh.

De Vincent led the way towards the presumed crime scene, if the teeming crowd of onlookers was any indicator.

"Tell me," he said as they picked their way through the milling hordes of the curious, "what do we know at this point?"

Victim is … or once was, famous. Name is Étienne Malboeuf. Does that have a ring in your memory, Grégoire?"

The inspector thought a moment. "Army?"

"Retired. He was a *Général de division* who led French troops into the final battle in Berlin along with the Americans. He and his unit received the Croix de guerre with palm during the battle that put an end to Hitler and almost all of his defenders."

"He got a great deal of fame and reward from De Gaulle, I recall."

"True, but there were some Frenchmen who considered him to have been overly ruthless during that engagement."

"Ah, yes," De Vincent said, finally making the connection. "As I recall, he was fighting Hitler's elite 33rd Waffen-Grenadier Division of the SS, not so?"

"Indeed ... the all-French unit."

"A strange bunch, and I can see how they or their families might hold a grudge. Good work, Sylvain. It will be worth looking into."

The two men were now inside the perimeter being manned by the gendarmerie. The retired general's body lay face down on the grass a few meters from where the Assumption Day speakers' table was sitting. Several people—including several old men—were openly crying. A few waved small red, white, and blue French flags.

A uniformed Sûreté lieutenant intern greeted them and commenced to tell the two detectives what was known about the crime.

"I am sorry to report," the one-striper said, "we have little to go on. The victim entered the park to take part in the Assumption Day festivities. There was a gathering crowd; so, no one noticed the murderer or murderers slip up behind him and fire three shots into our victim's back, killing him instantly. I say three shots because that is the number of entrance wounds I can see without disturbing the body. Witnesses—if you can call them that—seem not to have seen nor heard the shooters or the shots."

"So, this is the usual gathering of deaf and blind people, eh, Lieutenant?" De Vincent said with a tinge of anger in his voice.

"Yes, sir. That would appear to be the case. Or—more accurately—it is a gathering of Parisians—hear no evil, see no evil, speak no evil."

De Vincent and Piétri nodded their understanding with resignation. It was ever so when Parisian police talked to people crowded around a crime scene. Like New Yorkers, they did not want to get involved.

"Have you herded the closest witnesses into a guarded area, Lieutenant?"

"Of course, *Monsieur Inspecteur*," the lieutenant said and clicked his heels.

He did not smile at his almost mock militaristic response, but the two more serious officers did.

"Of course you did ... and *merci*. Anything else to contribute?"

"I did get to speak to a few older people who knew him. He was a bit stiff, but not really unfriendly. Kept to himself. He was ... how should I say it ... something of a racist and not even courteous to women—a man of the old school, definitely the old school."

"Any friends?"

"None that I could find."

"Enemies?"

"No one would say; but I gather he was not popular; but probably no one around the neighborhood disliked him enough to put three bullets in his back."

"Relatives?"

"A wife ... lives at 47 Rue d'Assas. Neither I nor my staff have had a chance to meet with her yet."

"Meaning you left the unpleasant task of informing the widow of what happened to her husband to me."

"Not intentionally, *Monsieur*; but we have only been on the scene for about half an hour."

He shrugged—a Parisian junior officer shrug.

De Vincent understood. It was why he was paid so much more than the junior lieutenant.

"All right then. Sylvain, please evaluate the scene and the body. Accompany the general to the morgue and learn everything you can about the man, the bullets, anything in his pockets. I suppose for completeness sake we should rule in or rule out a robbery. Lieutenant-intern, please do the preliminary fact-finding on all witnesses, and that includes anyone anywhere near this crime. No one gets to leave until you have your information; and Lieutenant Piétri and I have had a chance to determine who stays, who leaves, and who gets a ride to 1 rue de Lutèce. Understood?"

"Perfectly."

The three men went their separate ways. The 6th arrondissement is ideal for walking. Inspector De Vincent liked the hint of the past as his feet worked their way over cobblestone streets. It was an active day, and business was thriving. In the years following World War II, philosophers, movie makers, artists, writers, and musicians met in the Saint Germain-des-Prés cafés, establishing the neighborhood as a center of intellectual thought. The 6th was full of good local bakeries and patisseries, fruit and vegetable shops, butchers, cheese shops, and small supermarkets, all of which were full of customers. Nonetheless, it only took Inspector De Vincent ten minutes to walk to the front stoop of 47 Rue d'Assas.

CHAPTER NINE

47 Rue d'Assas, Fauborg Saint Germain-des-Prés, 6th arrondissement [6ème], Paris, Assumption Day, late morning

"*Oui*?" came the raspy voice of an elderly woman from inside the apartment. Just finishing her *petit déjeuner,* she did not care to be disturbed.

"*C'est le gendamerie, Madame,*" Inspector de Vincent responded.

Three locks were deactivated, and the heavy metal door opened.

"How can I be of service to the police?" Madam Malboeuf asked with a measure of apprehension without inviting the two policemen inside.

"May I step inside, Madame?" de Vincent requested. "I have important questions we need to put to you."

She looked doubtful, but, after a pause, opened the door and showed the police officer into her parlor.

"Yes?"

"I am sorry to disturb you, Madame, but are you the wife of General Malboeuf?"

A dark shadow of fear momentarily crossed her sallow and wrinkled face. She tugged at the front of her worn and none-too-clean dressing robe.

"I am indeed Monica Roussin-Malboeuf. How may I be of service, gentlemen?"

She presumed now that they were from the de Gaulle government, and she had dreaded this day for years.

"I am afraid I have some unfortunate news for you, Madame Malboeuf."

"Please tell me," she said, her voice now barely a whisper.

"It is my sad duty to inform you that your husband, General Malboeuf, has passed on."

"How is it that he died?"

She said it with resignation and a sigh.

Inspector de Vincent shook his head sadly, "I am afraid that he was murdered—shot."

She reflexively crossed herself and fought to restrain insistent tears.

"May I be excused to make myself more presentable, gentlemen?" she asked.

It was obvious that she needed a moment. She was gone fifteen minutes and reappeared in a highly presentable ensemble and with fresh facial makeup.

Inspector de Vincent resumed his questions, "As difficult as this time is, Madame, I am obliged to ask you some questions to aid our investigation."

"But of course. Please feel free. Anything I can do to help I will do."

"Did the general have enemies?" de Vincent asked, knowing that becoming a general in anyone's army produced many enemies.

"He did. There were people from the war … wars, of course. He was active in the postwar efforts to track down Nazis and Nazi sympathizers; so, the ODESSA probably harbors keen resentment against my husband. Then there was the unfortunate Algerian war … perhaps you are familiar."

De Vincent was indeed thoroughly familiar and was glad that Madame Malboeuf brought up the subject first. *Général de division* Étienne Malboeuf was stationed in Algeria in the mid-1950s and early 1960s when forces for independence from France—largely the FLN [National Liberation Front]—launched the Algerian War of Independence which pitted the nation of France against the fighters associated with the several independence movements. The vicious struggle lasted from 1954 to 1962 and finally resulted in Algeria gaining its independence. Gen. Malboeuf and his fellow senior officers pledged themselves to defending the honor of France—as they perceived it—to the bitter end. The war—like many civil and revolutionary conflicts—descended into barbarity consisting of a complex conflict involved in guerrilla warfare, maquis [guerrilla resistance fighters] fighting, terrorism and counter-terrorism operations characterized by inhuman measures including the use of torture by all sides. Gen. Malboeuf and many of his colonial compatriots entered into the civil war between loyalist Algerians supporting a French Colonial Algeria and insurrectionist Algerian Muslim fighters. The conflict shook the foundations of the French Fourth Republic (1946–58) and led to its eventual collapse and a legacy of enmity.

President De Gaulle told the people of France and the French army in Algeria that he believed the war in Algeria was militarily winnable, but it could not be defended politically on the international stage. Finally, he announced that France would no longer contest the colony's eventual independence. Gen. Malboeuf very publically voiced his anger and his sense that Frenchmen and the army were deeply offended. The French settlers and the French city-dwellers—joined by the dissident members of the army—were so enraged that they staged two armed uprisings. Reluctantly de Gaulle sent regular army units and fanatical foreign Legionnaires to the colony to suppress the settlers and troops. During the second uprising, in April 1961—with Gen. Malboeuf as one of the principal leaders—a threat of invasion of France itself was raised in what came to be known as the Generals' Putsch. Rebel paratroops landed on French soil. Retaliation was swift, excessively brutal, and decisive. A noisy and chaotic demonstration in Paris—which came to be known as the Paris massacre of 1961—led De Gaulle's government and police to machine-gun dissidents and herd them into the River Seine to drown. The Algerian rebels and angry colonial soldiers made several attempts on de Gaulle's life.

The massacre and the assassination attempts were kept secret for decades. De Gaulle won decisively and was then faced with the thorny issue of what to do with the French generals in Algeria who had defied him in armed conflict. De Gaulle was a thoroughly unforgiving man, but also a pragmatist. His overwhelming victory could easily have been capped by executions or other draconian punishments visited upon his officers. He knew, however, that reprisals would expose to the world and to his own people the fragmentation of the French armed forces and would explode the myth of French honor and cohesiveness. Against the advice of many of his senior officers who had remained loyal, President de Gaulle decided to show leniency ... with a price. Every Algerian officer of the rebellion who preferred life over execution had to choose to resign his commission, to retire into silent obscurity, to foreswear any political activities for the rest of his life, and to accept a subsistence-level pension.

De Vincent nodded his understanding to Madame Roussin-Malboeuf.

She continued, "My husband—the proud Étienne Malboeuf—had to eat humble pie and to live like one of the *racaille* [riff-raff] in a city apartment. He had to gnash his teeth whenever that pompous ass, de Gaulle, made some new gaffe in his public pronouncements. It ate away at his innards; but his life depended on his silence; and so he kept quiet—even with me."

"I understand that Gaullists retaliated against some of the old-guard army men and searched them out. Many were taken away and disappeared over the next few years; a few had unfortunate and unexplained accidents; and a few were frankly murdered with the murders never solved," de Vincent added in his slow soft voice.

As Madame Roussin-Malboeuf had been talking, he had been unobtrusively reading his extensive file on her husband provided by Lieutenant Piétri.

Madame Roussin-Malboeuf nodded her agreement, and added, "And their estates were confiscated. My Etienne and his fellow officers lived in terror. We moved many times, changed our names, and tried to become invisible. We were visited at random times by big men from the Deuxième Bureau. Did you know that they have a whole section devoted just to the 'appenings in the colonial wars, especially Algeria? Until today, I thought that de Gaulle might have forgotten or forgiven my Étienne, and life had returned to some semblance of normal."

At the end of the Second World War in 1945, the Deuxième Bureau became the modern French counterespionage service—the SDECE [*Service de documentation extérieure et de contre-espionnage*. English—Foreign Documentation and Counter-Espionage Service]; but for the Algerians and old French cops it would always be the Deuxième, and would always be regarded with suspicion and distaste seasoned with a generous dollop of fear.

"Any names come to mind?" asked de Vincent.

"I will compose a list," Madame Roussin-Malboeuf said with a hard set to her features.

The general's wife was bent from arthritis and spinal osteoporosis, and her face showed every insult and deprivation to which she had been subjected. But in her gray-blue eyes was still the fire of determination and the need for revenge. She was wrinkled, and her skin was sallow. Surprisingly to the detectives, as a result of her fifteen minutes of regaining her composure, Madame Roussin-Malboeuf was well-dressed, at least by the strict rules of the 1950s French style when Paris burgers ruled the fashion world. Her archaic ensemble included a mink coat with hairless patches and considerable jewelry. Had he bothered to ask, the detective would have received the answer, "Because it is the style, *Monsieur*." True enough, but off by more than a decade.

Enquêteur De Vincent was sure the elderly woman locked in her time warp would produce a list that would include serious de Gaulle officials, and its release to the public would create an international sensation that could topple the de Gaulle presidency and might well result in his and Lieutenant Sylvain Piétri's deaths.

He simply nodded noncommittally to the widow and took a new tack in his questioning.

"You have children, I understand," he said, recalling Piétri's hasty research back at Paris Police Headquarters at Place Louis Lépine, 1 rue de Lutèce, before he drove his pathetic automobile to the Jardin du Luxembourg Park and his quick study of the file he carried.

"Yes, *Monsieur*, my husband and I were blessed by the Virgin to have two sons, René and Damien."

"What is their relationship with you and their father, Madame?"

She paused before answering.

"Somewhat strained I'm sorry to say, *Monsieur Enquêteur*."

"And their relationship to you?"

"Better. Much better, I am pleased to say."

"What was the problem between your sons and their father?"

"I am not entirely sure, but it had to do with money and business, a subject that none of the men in the family share with their women. Relations with the Roussin side of the family have not been good these past six or seven years. I think that was part of the money and business problem. You will have to take that up with René and Damien."

"Would you please write down their addresses and telephone numbers, Madame Roussin-Malboeuf?"

She nodded and began to write.

"I am sorry to have to bring this up, Madame, but I am afraid that it may have something to do with the tragic events of today," de Vincent said in his slow and deliberate way.

She gave him a quizzical look.

"My associates and I searched the general's belongings and found a photograph, a name, and address of a young woman. It was prominently displayed. Can you shed light on that finding? A daughter, perhaps?"

She snorted.

"You mean his *putain* [whore]—the *catin* [strumpet] Antoinette de Baudry—the famous model!"

She spat out the words with acidic venom.

"What can you tell me about her, other than the obvious, Madame?"

"She was passed from rich man to rich man. First, an Italian count— maybe a Mafioso—then the son of some wealthy de Gaulle appointee, then just before my husband, she did the dirtiness with a chief criminal of the *Unione Corse* [Corsican crime syndicate]."

"Do you have a name for any of those men?"

"Only the last one. He was called Benedettu Paganucci. But, knowing that lot, it could be a fake name. For that matter, I can't be the least bit sure that the *catin*'s name is what she says it is."

"It gives us a start," de Vincent said and paused a moment to take notes.

"Anything else?" he asked, then flipped a few pages in his notes. "Ah, yes, the will—it slipped my mind.

"Madame Roussin-Malboeuf, the gendamerie are familiar somewhat with the general's career and that he came from a well-to-do family. Can you tell me about the extent of his estate?"

"First of all, the general did not share with me his business dealings, including the value of his estate. I do know two things: first, he took from me my inheritance from my Roussin relatives, which was valued in the millions of francs; second, de Gaulle allowed him to keep his money and property in recognition of his long service to France and as a way of demonstrating that he forgave him. So, I am certain that he died a very wealthy man.

"I know he had a will, revised only recently when he set up the *catin* in her own *pied-à-terre* not far from here. I cannot tell you what evil she seduced him to commit against his wife and his children, but I would not be surprised at anything."

De Vincent glanced away from the newly created widow and shrugged.

"I will leave you to mourn now, Madame. It is possible that I or others from the police may return with more questions. Please do not leave the area."

"Of course. I have no means to leave at the moment."

CHAPTER TEN

26 Rue Vavin, Fauborg Saint Germain-des-Prés, 6th arrondissement [6ème], Paris, Assumption Day, 1962, early afternoon

Lieutenant Piétri arrived back at the park with a new folder of papers containing his research, and he and *Enquêteur* de Vincent drove to Mademoiselle Baudry's apartment in Piétri's wheezing old Peugeot. As they drove, de Vincent quizzed his partner about what he had learned concerning his findings regarding Mlle Baudry's several former lovers.

They knocked, and the door opened wide to reveal a statuesque blond fashionably dressed in evening wear although it was not yet two in the afternoon. Her full-skirted evening gown made of vermillion silk had a disturbingly low décolletage and close-fitting waist that further accentuated her hour-glass figure. Antoinette Baudry's face was equally beautiful, and her skin—of which a considerable amount showed—was flawlessly white. She was tall, and her height was enhanced by her matching stiletto heels. The impact was momentarily distracting enough to make De Vincent stammer slightly as he introduced himself.

"We ... we are sorry to disturb you, Madame ... Mademoiselle. This is Lieutenant Piétri of the Gendarmerie, and I am Detective De Vincent of the Paris police. May we have a word with you?"

"Please come in, gentlemen. I am about to be joined by my gentleman friend for an important Assumption Day gathering; so, I will not have long to talk. May I ask what this is about?" she asked as she showed the men into her sitting room.

De Vincent carried the conversation at this point, "Are you Mademoiselle Antoinette Baudry?"

"Yes. Why do you ask?"

She was not entirely a stranger to visits by law enforcement officers, and now she was on her guard.

"Is your gentleman friend General Étienne Malboeuf, Mademoiselle?"

"Yes, he is," she replied, entirely focused on the *Enquêteur's* face.

"I am afraid that we are the bearers of bad news, Mlle Baudry. It seems that the general has been the victim of a crime … he has been murdered in the park."

Antoinette gasped and threw her hand to her mouth. Her eyes demonstrated her consternation and bewilderment. She did not cry. It appeared she could not yet process the information entirely.

"We are most sorry for your loss and wish that we did not have to intrude on your privacy at a time like this, but the circumstances are under investigation. Time is of the essence, and we must gather information that can lead us to the murderer or murderers. We are in need of your help, *Memwzel.*"

Antoinette worked to regain her composure.

"May I sit down, please?" she asked in the voice of a confused young girl, no longer the fashionable sophisticate.

She absent-mindedly brushed back her honey-blond hair to expose her ears. The hair quickly resumed its original ear-covering position.

"But, of course, *Memwzel.* We will take seats as well. We know this is a shock for you."

"Please call me Antoinette. I would be more comfortable with that."

"Certainly. We hope our conversation can be quite informal."

"Now … how can I help you, Officers?" Antoinette said, having regained her voice and most of her composure.

Quiet tears were slowly running down her well made-up cheeks.

"Please tell us what you can of the general, his family, his friends … and his enemies, Antoinette. If you don't mind, my partner will take notes as we talk."

She nodded. "My Etienne, is … was … a retired *Général de division* in the army, a hero of three wars. Perhaps you are aware that he was … shall we say … on the wrong side in the General's Putsch and opposed our beloved president. He was forgiven his mistake. He has been silent on the subjects of politics, that war, and in fact, anything to do with Algeria since I have known him."

"How long was that, Antoinette?"

"About three years."

"Go on."

"Let me think. What can I tell you that might help in your investigation? I do recall one unfortunate encounter with a member of the de Gaulle government … a man named Louis Charles de la Reynie. I remember because he was quite threatening and insisted that both of us never forget him or his name because he would be watching our every move. I believed him, but my Etienne told me not to worry. He could not fool me. He was worried, and always looked over his shoulder when we went out."

"Any other government officials, Antoinette?"

"Two that I can remember for the moment. They did not seem to be so threatening, but Etienne told me to be careful what I said around them. One is a man you probably know: Jean-Baptiste Berryer."

Both de Vincent and Piétri blanched at the name. Berryer was the sitting lieutenant general of police, the commander of all police forces in France. They knew that Antoinette would do well to be careful of that man who had the ear of de Gaulle and a reputation as a most political and unforgiving man.

Antoinette nodded in acknowledgment of the impact Berryer's name had on the two police officers. She gave Piétri a moment to make his note.

"The other man was named Louis Thiroux d'Albert, an ugly man with a deep scar on his left cheek. He had a limp. We met him at a reception for old World War I veterans, a dinner that took place in Lyon. He warned Etienne not to attend any more army gatherings. He was being watched, and the president might consider such attendance to be a violation of his promise not to associate with officers in public or private. It was the last army function we attended."

Louis Thiroux d'Albert was a shadowy figure. De Vincent assumed he was the head of de Gaulle's intelligence service, or at least a senior officer and a man more to be feared than Berryer or anyone else in government except de Gaulle himself. De Gaulle created the BCRA [*Bureau central de renseignements et d'action*] in 1942 under the auspices of the Free French government-in-exile in London. The third iteration of the BCRA became the SDECE [*Service de documentation extérieure et de contre-espionnage,* the Foreign Documentation and Counter-Espionage Service] in 1945. D'Albert was known to be—but seldom mentioned to be in public—the most senior officer in the SDECE, and one of the most feared individuals in French history.

Piétri gave de Vincent a quick look that said, "CAUTION," a message that was unnecessary to the senior detective.

"Anyone else from the government?"

"Not that I recall."

"Any other potential enemies, Antoinette? Even maybe associates of yours? Anyone who might like to see Etienne dead?"

"Not really, except for his sons."

"Let's leave them for the moment. How about your … friends, or former friends?"

"I presume you have reference to my lovers and … protectors … before Gen. Malboeuf came into my life. Probably you already know about Benedettu Paganucci and Dominic Rizzuto or Tony Lagomarsino. We are all still friends. Actually, I think Benedettu still sort of loves me. He asked me to move back to France for my own protection. It was during a time when the Italian government had one of their crusades against the Mafia. We keep in touch. Benedettu is not a jealous man, and Dominic and Tony work for him. Sometimes when I can have a vacation, I go to Sicily and pal around with the three of them … on the quiet, if you know what I mean."

De Vincent nodded.

"Now, how about Gen. Malboeuf's sons?"

"René and Damien. He had an older son named after himself who was killed in the war. We never talked about him. It was a very sensitive subject and made Etienne emotional. René and Damien were estranged from their father over some business enterprises that went sour. They knew that he made a new will a couple of years ago and presumed that they were cut out of their inheritances; so, they were very angry."

"Angry enough to kill him?"

"Maybe, but they were wrong about the will—at least partly wrong."

"How so?"

"It was a big secret while Etienne was still alive, but I am sure it will come out in your investigation and in the papers, I suppose. René and Damien's and Etienne's wife Monica's portions of the estate were cut in half, but that was still several million francs. Monica came to my apartment twice and threatened to have me killed. Etienne told her to mind her own business. He never told his sons, because they refused to talk to him."

"What is to become of the other half of the estate?" Piétri asked, looking up from his note-taking.

"One half of it comes to me, and the other half goes to the army veteran's pension fund."

"I take it that Gen. Malboeuf kept very few secrets from you, Antoinette," Piétri said.

"That is one of the reasons Etienne kept me. We are ... or were ... friends. We were lovers at the beginning; but you know, he was getting a bit too old for much of that. He knew about Benedetto and said that he didn't mind so long as I did not leave him. He needed someone to confide in that he could trust."

"Have René and Damien made threats against you?"

"Yes, veiled ones, but I took them seriously."

"We have heard rumors during our investigation that the general might have had some business dealings with criminal elements over the years. Can you tell us anything about that?" asked Piétri.

"I don't know much about that except from hints I picked up from Etienne. Sometimes he had me go on vacations and deliver messages in sealed envelopes to Benedetto. I think Etienne had some dealings with the *Unione Corse* [Corsican crime syndicate]. A couple of times he mentioned another Italian, Enrique Lambiase, who he also referred to as 'Big Ears' and a man he called 'the Greaser.' I think his real name is something like Giovanni Vigliotti. They are from the Mafia, I'm pretty sure; but I really don't know anything about Etienne's business with them."

"Anything else, Antoinette?"

"I can't think of anything else right now. Maybe I might later. Can I give you a call?"

"That would be good. Now, two last questions before we leave—this may be a hard one, but we have to ask it anyway, Antoinette. You stand to become a very rich young woman now that the general has been killed. Where were you this morning?"

"I have been waiting for that question. I was right here, but I was not alone. I was with my girlfriend, Carol Watson. She is from America. She and I used to do some modeling together."

"Do you have her address and telephone number?"

"While we were talking, I wrote it down—here."

She handed Lieutenant Piétri a small piece of paper to include in his notes.

"And finally, Antoinette, did you arrange for someone to murder your lover, Gen. Malboeuf?"

"I did not. I loved him. He was very good to me."

She said it with convincing sincerity.

"Thank you for your time and for your candor, Antoinette. You have been more than helpful. We must ask you not to leave the area. We will be back to see you again in all likelihood."

"I am at your service."

The policemen left and, once back in the Peugeot, Piétri summed up their situation, "This is going to be a tough investigation, Grégoire. What we have here is too much information. We have enemies from three wars, from his family, and maybe from the *Unione Corse*, the Mafia, and the government of France, including—let us not forget— the SDECE and our own departments. Do we have the *burettes* [French slang for balls] for this?"

"We'll have to wait and see," Detective de Vincent responded in all soberness.

"Ready for *le déjeuner*, Grégoire?"

The corpulent inspector gave a small laugh.

"What do you think?" Grégoire replied to the unnecessary question. "What's your fancy?"

French Recipes

Sea Salted Caramel Halves—Serves 4–6

Ingredients
-For batter dry ingredients—1 cp all-purpose flour, ¼ tsp salt, 1 cp granulated sugar
-For batter liquid ingredients—2 eggs, ½ cp milk, ½ cp water, 2 tbsps melted butter
-For salted butter caramel—½ cp salted butter, ½ cp heavy cream, ½ cp water, 2 pinchs of sea salt

Preparation
Crepes—Mix all ingredients in a blender until the mixture is smooth. Allow the batter to rest in the refrigerator for at least 20 min. before making into crepes.

-Melt a little butter in a crepe pan or large skillet over low-medium heat.

-Add 3 tbsps batter to the pan and swirl until the bottom of the pan is covered with a thin, even batter. Cook the crepe for 1 minute, or until the crepe is slightly moist on top and golden underneath. Do not overcook. Loosen the edges of the crepe, slide the spatula under it, and then gently flip it upside down into the pan. Cook for 1 minute and transfer the cooked crepe to a plate ± into warming oven to keep warm.

Sea Salted Caramel—In a saucepan set over medium-low heat, melt butter in heavy cream. Immediately remove from the heat and set aside.

-Place the sugar in a separate saucepan set over medium heat. Sprinkle the water over the sugar and allow it to dissolve over the heat without stirring. As the sugar begins to caramelize, occasionally shake and swirl the pan to evenly distribute the color.

-When the caramel is a rich golden color, remove the pan from the heat and carefully add the hot cream and melted butter to the caramel. Take care to stand back during this process; the hot caramel will bubble up the sides of the pan.

-Return the caramel to the lowest heat setting, whisking constantly. Cook and stir the salted butter caramel for 2 minutes over the low heat.

-Remove from the heat and season the sauce with the sea salt; stir until it is dissolved completely.

Assemble crepes:

-Spoon 2 tsps caramel sauce down the center of a warm crepe and roll into a cylinder. Alternately, spoon 2 tsps of the caramel sauce onto the center of a warm crepe and then fold into quarters.

-Garnish with vanilla Chantilly cream and sautéed apples. Drizzle the crepes with additional caramel sauce, as desired.

Honeyed Fruit Salad: Serves 4–6, and Accompanies Crepes

Ingredients
-Dry—½ teaspoon lemon zest, 1 tbsp granulated sugar, 1 pint hulled strawberries, 2 ripe cored pears, 2 pitted peaches, ¾ cup pitted sweet cherries, 1 kiwifruit.
-Liquid—½ cup dry white wine, 4 tbsps honey, 2 tbsps lemon juice.

Preparation:
-Process liquid ingredients, lemon zest, and sugar in a blender until smooth. Chill 20 mins. before serving.
-Halve or quarter strawberries, cut pears and peaches into ¾ inch pieces, and cut cherries in ½. Cut the kiwifruit in ½ then cut each ½ crosswise into ¼ inch slices. Toss the prepared fruit with the desired amount of dressing and serve immediately or chill.

CHAPTER ELEVEN

Ludwigshafen am Rhein, Bundesland State of Rheinland-Pfalz, Germany, August 22, 1962

Prior to World War I, Ludwigshafen was a thriving industrial city in southwestern Germany located in a picturesque pastoral setting along the Rhine River across from Mannheim. Ludwigshafen, Mannheim, and Heidelberg made up the Rhine Neckar Region. The area was prosperous owing to the efficient and industrious German people, the homogeneity of the population, and—more importantly—to the presence of chemical and oil plants in Ludwigshafen and Oppau owned by IG Farben [German full name: *Interssengemeinschaft* Farben. English: Association of Common Interests]. The large complex of companies and plants was the property of a consortium known by the cumbersome title of *Badische Anilin and Soda Fabrik* or BASF, a powerful union of German companies Bayer, Hoechst, and others. BASF produced pharmaceuticals, fuels, fertilizers, potash and salt, inks, cosmetics, and textile dyes among many other products, and provided a stable prosperous economy which encouraged education, innovation, and cooperation.

The adventurism of Kaiser Wilhelm I and the very conservative and jingoistic Junkers produced World War I and the nearly catastrophic destruction of the cities of the region and of the plants and the economy. During the war, the industrial plants played a key role in Germany's war machine producing munitions, poison gas, Zeppelin factories, and expertise for the military. The area became a prime target of Allied attacks, including the first aerial bombardments. Following the war, Germany was hamstrung with reparations assessments, and the return of the economy to its prewar status was slow. The economic recovery encountered a major setback in the form of a huge industrial explosion that killed five hundred citizens and injured another couple of thousand. A great many of the newly rebuilt buildings were destroyed, and the area had to begin again. Foreign workers began moving in by necessity to provide the labor for reconstruction and to man the plants, adding an entering wedge of diversity and confusion.

Fortunately for Ludwigshafen and Oppau, BASF produced such robust profits that reconstruction of a much changed group of cities proceeded fairly rapidly. The result was a greatly changed city, now built on the efficient and unattractive styles of postwar European housing developed for efficiency and not for attractiveness. Unfortunately for Lugwigshafen and its sister cities, another dictator brought in another round of adventurism and disaster.

In what was dubbed the Oil Campaign of World War II, Allied B-17 and B-24 bombers wreaked havoc on the IG Farben plants so that output dropped to zero, and the economy dropped to a subsistence level. Allied historical records indicated that the area was inundated with explosives for two years with an incredible 13,000 bombers engaging more than 120 separate raids, dropping over 50,000 bombs—including high explosives and nearly two and a half million magnesium incendiary bombs—which wrecked the cities and the plants and brought production to a permanent halt. In a single raid in 1945, Allied bombers laid down 1,000 high explosives and almost 10,000 incendiary bombs that killed scores, started hundreds of fires, destroyed over 350 homes, and put 1,800 people out on the streets with no means of support or protection. The cities were ruined, and the economy appeared to be destroyed beyond recovery.

In the aftermath of World War II, foreign workers began to stream in along with displaced Germans, including not a few war criminals with new identities provided for them by the ODESSA. Old generational associations were disrupted, friends went permanently missing, and the newcomers assimilated easily during the chaos. When BASF rebuilt its factories, the newcomers became an integral part of the community and the economy with hardly any questioning of the past histories of the new generation of citizens.

During the 1960s, Ludwigshafen was part of the French occupation zone, a prominent city of the newly founded Bundesland (state) of

Rheinland-Pfalz and the Federal Republic of Germany. Reconstruction of the devastated city and revival of the economy was supported by the Allies, predominantly by American financial aid. By 1948, American citizens pitched in. The "Pasadena Shares Committee" sent packages of blankets, clothing, food, and medicines to help the residents; serious friendships formed. In 1956, Ludwigshafen am Rhein and Pasadena, California, became sister cities.

Much of the city was completely ruined; but because BASF soon made enormous profits again, the city administration became wealthy enough to rebuild Ludwigshafen according to the architectural taste of the current era—the 1950s and 1960s. Projects included the *Hochstraßen* [highways on stilts], the new main station—which was the most modern station in all of Europe—several tower blocks, and a complete new suburb—the satellite quarter Pfingstweide north of Edigheim.

Largely forgotten was that the partner company of the American Rockefeller industries, *Interessengemeinschaft* [Association of Common Interests] Farben—IG Farben, for short— participated in the destruction, plunder, and murder of countless thousands of cities and millions of people throughout Europe. The company formed by the association was a powerful cartel of BASF, Bayer, Hoechst, and other German chemical and pharmaceutical companies. It was the single largest donor to the election campaign of Adolph Hitler. The year before Hitler seized power, IG Farben donated 400,000 marks to Hitler and his Nazi party. Accordingly, after Hitler's seizure of power, IG Farben was the single largest profiteer of the German conquest of the world, and one of the most criminal organizations fostering the Second World War.

One hundred percent of all explosives and synthetic gasoline used in the war came from the IG Farben conglomerate factories. As the German Wehrmacht moved from country to country conquering and subjugating the population, IG Farben followed close on its heels, systematically taking over the industries of those countries. IG Farben participated in the plunder of Austria, Czechoslovakia, Poland, Norway, Holland, Belgium, France, and all other countries conquered by the Nazis. Following the war with all of its chaos and the massive incentives to facilitate the rebuilding of Germany as a bastion against the growth of Stalin's Soviet Union, IG Farben prospered; and there was hardly a ripple on the surface of the company's profit history.

One of the newcomers to the reawakening city complex of Lugwigshafen was a relatively young man by the name of Heinrich Rudolf Gajewski, a German IG Farben war criminal who had helped in the manufacture of sarin and tabun gas used in the execution chambers. His principal occupation during the war was the procurement of slave labor, which proved to be a full-time effort because of the unconscionably high mortality rates among the workers due to starvation, overwork, and neglected disease. His talents were also utilized in the postwar triage of returning German POWs, and he gained enormous power of life and death over the returnees. If they could not pay, they languished in the camps and often starved before final repatriation. He returned to Ludwigshafen with the help of ODESSA and assumed a new life under the innocuous name of Gunther Emil Sondregger. Because of his expertise, he was assigned to the human resources division of the BASF system. Because of his being included on the Allies' most wanted war criminal list, his position in the company was a relatively minor one and one unlikely to attract attention to himself or to the company for harboring him.

Gajewski/Sondregger settled down in the obscure Ludwigshafen suburb of Hemshof in the older original North district of *Nördliche Innenstadt* located between the main station and main cemetery. Hemshof and the North District were known for their high proportion of foreign inhabitants, making them culturally diverse. He never married, never had children, joined no church or political organization, or even the union at his work. He had a few acquaintances, but no friends or confidants—especially no confidants. He avoided veterans' groups and did not attend memorial services. He was approached by the *Deutsche Reichspartei*—the postwar far-right political party—but politely rebuffed them saying he wanted to be left alone. So far as he knew, he was not on any foreign or domestic war criminal list such as Operation Paperclip, nor had he come to the attention of the *Verfassungsschutz* [Federal German Intelligence Organization]. He considered himself lucky not to have fallen into the hands of the occupiers in the French zone because he was well aware of the many thousands of Germans who were beaten, robbed, raped, and murdered. It would be a mastery of understatement to say that Gunther Emil Sondregger kept to himself. In fact, if one were to make an effort, Sondregger would be found not to have existed prior to 1952 when he joined the influx of workers and foreigners who poured into the city.

Sondregger situated himself in a corner of the large business office and avoided communicating with his fellow workers unless it became absolutely necessary. His manner was stiff and correct, polite, but neither cordial nor forthcoming. From his SS days he had adopted the habit of sitting squarely upright in a sturdy right angle high back chair. This was in part habit, and in part the uncomfortable chair assisted him to maintain his attention on his mind-numbing work and on any other workers or visitors who might pay attention to him. He was assiduously careful about that. Even with the end of military occupation in 1955, Sondregger did not let down his guard. He even dressed to be so ordinary and innocuous as to approach invisibility. He wore a gray suit— he had five of them—a white shirt, and one of three quietly patterned gray and black neckties. His shoes were post-occupation production black lace-ups, and he kept them neat and clean and occasionally polished, but nothing extravagant. He combed his hair straight back; it was neither very short nor very long. He carefully avoided having any facial hair. His eyeglasses were cheap; there were tens of thousands of those discount frames throughout Germany. He made sure he did not call attention to himself by gaining or losing weight. He had weighed 182 pounds since he turned thirty.

On August 16, 1962, Sondregger was seated at his desk checking the accounting sheets of hours worked against pay received during the past month by two thousand workers. The work was deadly dull; but he never forgot the importance of maintaining a low profile; and he was glad to have a job in a difficult economy. The truth was he was very happy to be alive and not rotting in a postwar prison or worse. He was unaware of a person behind him dressed in ordinary factory workers' garb. He was unaware that the individual was wearing a cummerbund with two heavy 100 Franc coins sewn into folds in the center of the cloth. Before he could react, the assassin behind his chair back-whipped the cummerbund over Sondregger's head and expertly situated the lump of coins in the exact center of his neck. Powerful hands and arms applied killing pressure for five minutes, fracturing Sondregger's hyoid bone and cutting off all blood and oxygen supply to his brain. His death was swift, silent, and unseen.

Owing to his reclusive nature, no one paid attention to the accountant slumped over his small desk until quitting time, and only then because he appeared to refuse to leave the building in response to repeated demands. One of the human resources division secretaries happened to say good evening to the obscure accountant; and when he failed to respond in any manner, she looked more closely. She suspected something was very wrong; so, following protocol, she informed the workroom foreman before he could exit the building for the night.

The workroom foreman called security, who recognized that the accountant was dead, and in fact that his neck was encircled by a heavy strangulating cloth. The security officer rushed to close off all exits; but it was an act of futility because most of the workers had already left the building; and no one who worked anywhere near Gunther Sondregger remained in the room.

"Call the *Landespolizei* [Bundeslandt State Police]," the senior security officer ordered. "Call the Kripo office directly."

"*Kriminalpolitzei*, Detective Branch," the dispatcher answered crisply. "How may I direct your call?"

"Get me *Kriminalkommissar* [Detective Lieutenant] Horst Schäfer, please. This is an emergency."

"Whom shall I say is calling, sir?"

"Joachim Becker at Farben Administration. I am the security officer."

"I will ring his office. Hold the line for a moment, please, sir."

After a two-minute pause, Schäfer responded, "What can I do for you, Joachim?"

"Solve a murder, catch a murderer—your specialty, Cousin."

"At Farbens?"

"Yes—a garroting in the administration building. The body has not been disturbed."

"I'll get Eberhard and the crime scene team and be right there. I presume you have collected everyone in the building for me?"

"Too late. Most of them already gone. It's ten minutes after the whistle."

"Too bad. That's just more work, but that's why I get the huge salary."

It was a standing joke between the two first cousins, because the plant security position paid far better than the police position.

Fifteen minutes later with lights and sirens on, the police contingent pulled up to the main headquarters building of the BASF complex. Schäfer ordered an officer to take each of the three doors to the building, and he and Senior Constable Zimmermann led the forensics team into the office building through the main entrance where they met Joachim.

"Tell me what you know, Joachim."

"There's not much to know. One of our accountants and minor administrators by the name of Gunther Emil Sondregger was strangled to death ... garroted by an unknown assailant earlier in the day."

Schäfer raised a questioning eyebrow.

Joachim was a small wiry man who had been in awe of his much larger cousin during their youths; and even now at thirty-one, he was still a bit intimidated. He shook his dark curly hair—a lifelong habit which came out when he was nervous.

"Nobody's fault, Horst. The man was a recluse—never talked to anybody, never made a suggestion, or reported an error. He sat in his ridiculous stiff old chair and worked leaning over his desk. It wasn't until quitting time that anyone noticed that he was not moving. The supervisor determined that he was dead and called me."

"So, Joachim, how long do you think he has been dead?"

"I can only make an educated guess. He is stiff as a new broom; so, he has been dead no less than three hours and no more than twelve hours."

"This is not too helpful, Cousin. When did he come in to work?"

"He was like a machine. He clocked in every day at exactly eight in the morning, and he clocked out at exactly five o'clock in the evening, having spent nine hours in his chair."

"So, he was killed between eleven and five."

"Approximately."

Det. Schäfer raised his questioning eyebrow again.

"There's more to it than just the passage of time; but I'm just a humble security officer, not a medical examiner or a lofty detective. We probably should ask Herr *Arzt* [Doctor] Miller."

"Where is the lazy old Nazi anyway?"

"Traffic. Police band said that there was a communist bombing on *Universität Strasse*. He probably got caught in the police blockade."

Schäfer gave a small shrug, indicating he was mollified for the present.

"Tell me about the witnesses, please."

"Sorry, Horst. We don't have a single person who indicates that he or she saw or heard anything. Not a one."

Horst sighed and did a little stretch exercise. He was an impressive man—well over six feet tall and weighed more than 220 pounds. He was lean and had sharply defined muscles and large powerful hands. He was an old-school German right down to a dueling scar on his left cheek like so many former officers of the Wehrmacht and the SS. Unlike his wiry, dark, curly-haired, olive-skinned cousin, Horst was an Aryan through and through. He could easily have been taken for a Norwegian with his blond, almost white, short-cropped hair, narrow and lined face, and piercing blue eyes. He wore a gray business suit, fashionable dark gray shirt, deep purple tie, and black penny loafers—an affectation he had picked up from the Americans. He wore the academy ring on his left hand, and his broad band gold wedding ring on the right like most German men. His nails were manicured.

After relieving his tension and frustration with his minor exercise routine, he turned back to Joachim and to Eberhard—his partner— who had been standing quietly listening to the other two men talk.

"Joachim, please get your men out and bring every worker who was on the victim's work floor back in for questioning. Eberhard, dig into the company records and then in the police and military records to see if you can get a handle on who our victim is and then we three can begin to figure out who had a reason to kill the man."

"We do have the instrument of death. I thought you would like to examine it."

"Good, I'll do that first. After that I am going to follow up on a line of inquiry I have been thinking about as you have told us what you know, Joachim. Let's take a look at that garrote."

The heavy cloth cummerbund was thick and sturdy, well worn and rather nondescript gray in color.

"Looks something like a Turk or Arab might wear. We'll have to do a little looking into the foreign labor pool," Horst told Joachim.

Joachim nodded. "Let's open it and see what the lump is."

Horst opened his pocket knife and sliced the tough cloth open to reveal two worn 100 franc coins.

"Cousin, while you're at it, check and see if there are any Indians on the payroll. This looks something like an old Thuggee assassin's weapon."

"I'll get on it."

"Call Eberhard about what you learn. I need to see some people about this. I was going to work with you to question the employees, but I am feeling pushed to follow up my idea. I will be surprised if anything comes from the interrogations, but we need to make sure that we follow every reasonable avenue. Thanks for the help. See you at the family reunion next Friday night."

CHAPTER TWELVE

Bundeskriminalamt **[BKA-Federal Criminal Police Office], Office of *Der Polizeipräsident in Wiesbaden* [The Police Chief of Wiesbaden], Thaerstrsse 11, Wiesbaden, Germany, August 23, 1962**

Getting an appointment with Chief Friedrich Schneider Graf von der Lippe was a considerable strain and an even more considerable risk for Detective Schäfer. Chief Schneider outranked Schäfer by a stratospheric dimension. He was old aristocracy with all of the perquisites that title granted him even though–of course–the new German constitution forbade any such entitlement or any right to pass the title on to his heirs—just the name referring to a count of one of the oldest and most distinguished old German noble families. That alone would have prevented such a lowly personage as a mere detective from having any meeting with the chief of the entire German federal criminal police force. Chief Schneider's extended family came from entrenched Junkers who still had a staggering amount of personal wealth.

The man's very appearance shouted wealth, influence, power, patrician background, and entitlement. He was tall, slim, and handsome with a topographical Nordic face and snow-white hair. He was dressed in a light grey afternoon suit made exclusively for him by his tailors— Bespoke Tailoring—which Chief von der Lippe kept current by a personal suit consultation at the Berlin Capital Club am Gendarmenmarkt. His tie was an intricate silk paisley from Hong Kong, and his shoes handmade in the Northampton Shop in Spitsbergen. He eschewed belts, preferring leather braces from South America. All of that spoke of him being untouchable, unapproachable, and impervious to criticism.

Detective Schäfer had none of those entitlements, and his long years of service had not allowed him to rise in rank beyond a steady workman's status for all of his successes.

What Schäfer did have—and now took a risk in revealing—was an incredibly precise, accurate, and complete memory. What he knew was who served and where in the old prewar and World War II eras of the *Kriminalpolizei* [Criminal Police], and–for the first time in his career–he allowed a hint to be conveyed that he did know such remarkable things.

From its inception, the *Kriminalpolitzei* was popularly known as the Kripo. The best comparison was that it was the German equivalent of the British CID. Over the nineteenth century, the Kripo expanded until all major cities in Germany had a branch or—in larger cities—sometimes more than one. While the Kripo had units tasked to investigate political crimes from the beginning, Kripo detectives in general prided themselves on being essentially apolitical, regardless of their outside political backgrounds and interests. When Horst Schäfer joined the force, he made a vow that he would continue that policy even as the Nazis insidiously began to take over the police forces throughout the country.

The Kripo—thus constituted—was considered to be a problem within the ranks for the Nazis who were hell-bent on full control of all authoritarian entities. There were Nazis in positions of power who wanted a purge of all German police forces, and to replace them with the SA [*Sturmabteilung*] which was widely considered to be nothing more than a gaggle of thugs by the rank and file regular police, and they resisted. Nazis with real police backgrounds blocked the Nazis with a series of subtle maneuvers. This resulted in a de facto separation of the *Kriminalpolitzei* and a mutual enmity between the two factions until war's end.

Most ordinary Germans did not know that the *Kriminalpolizei* divided into two quite separate divisions when the Nazis took over. The political branch—for lack of a better term—became the Gestapo and gained life and death power over the German populace and later the citizens of occupied countries. The distinction was not clear to ordinary citizens; but there was a criminal investigation branch that continued throughout the prewar era, during the war, and well into the devastating aftermath, to be exactly what the name conveyed—police who investigated and brought to justice criminals for such crimes as burglary, forgery, assault, rape, and murder. *Kriminalkommissar* Horst Schäfer had always been an honest cop in the criminal investigation division. He never rose in rank because he never joined the National Socialist political party. Nor did he ever consider himself to be part of the combined political and apolitical branches—the SiPo [*Sicherheitspolizei*-Security Police]. For his own long-term protection, he began keeping careful records of cases in which Nazi police committed crimes and atrocities under the cloak of authority. By the time he came to Wiesbaden to meet with his police chief, his notes and documents filled several volumes.

One of Chief Schneider's assistants ushered Detective Lieutenant Schäfer into the most ornate and opulent office he had ever seen. It was expected to awe and intimidate people who did not belong in the upper echelons of Germany. Chief Schneider had learned a thing or two about being intimidating during the war, and his appearance that day—like all days—was meant to intimidate. His was a hard face, one used to frightening his subordinates and other inferiors. His eyes were an almost luminescent silver gray, rather peculiar and therefore riveting. He used them and his jutting square jaw to full advantage. He started a staring down contest with the lowly detective, and Schäfer finally blinked first. Schäfer was awed but not intimidated, and he considered the stare-down to be a cheap trick beneath his continued participation.

He had not come all this way from Ludwigshafen am Rhein to surrender to that. Rather—either out of bravery or foolhardiness—he had come to Wiesbaden to do a little intimidating on his own.

Schneider dismissed his subordinate and then turned a steely gaze on the lowly detective.

"So, what is so urgent and what is so important that you thought to ingratiate yourself with me by making reference to our past service together, Schäfer?"

Schäfer was pleased that the man did not waste time on pleasantries.

"I have a murder to solve at the BASF administration building in Ludwigshafen. The victim is a man who has no past, at least none that my forensic team or the human resources department of BASF can find. He either sprung out of the ground at the end of the war, a prime example that there were never any Nazis in the country, or … someone created an elaborate legend for his existence. The man was a cipher, an invisible, colorless, inoffensive functionary with no social or business life, and not a single friend or enemy that we can discover."

"What has that to do with me, young man?" Schneider asked brusquely.

"I need your help. To get right to the kernel of the matter, we both know that kind of history is a creation of the ODESSA. My theory of the case is that my victim was likely considered to have some knowledge about someone in the party who very strongly wishes to have that knowledge disappear forever. I have no contacts or influence in the upper reaches of the federal police, in the senior levels of the Bundestag German Parliament, in the Bundesrat [Representative body of the Länder-Germany's regional states], at the Chancellery, in the *Bundesgerichtshof* [Federal Court of Justice of Germany], or in the Federal Constitutional Court (*Bundesverfassungsgericht* [Federal Constitutional Court]. I could go on, but you get my drift. I want to talk to the people who know things—the ODESSA, or some of those police and government people I suggested. I do not want my investigation to be impeded or compromised. I do not want to be ignored or evaded."

"Or what, you silly upstart? Just why should I–of all people–be of help to you, a nothing detective?"

"Detective Lieutenant."

"Not impressive. So, answer my question."

"Are you sure you would like me to do that?"

"I order you to do so."

"May 7, 1942, arrest of fifty-three Latvian civilians. I have photographs of their executions. Your face features prominently. December 18, 1944, there is a photograph of a man in a Kripo uniform shooting German soldiers in the back of their heads … an execution of German soldiers."

"Deserters."

"Likely so, but the photo has been suppressed until now. Don't bother to intimidate or threaten me. The evidence is in the hands of an American journalist—an expatriate German … a Jew with the *New York Times* newspaper, along with a ream of written testimony which more than incidentally lists your name and exploits. If I so much as fall down some stairs, get the stomach flu, or—God forbid—I should meet with a fatal accident or be charged with a major crime, the information will appear in that newspaper with banner headlines. Americans do not like Nazis—especially the Gestapo—and I am almost certain that you would not like to be their story of the month. Chief Schneider, I will have the information I seek.

"And if I refuse your blackmail?"

"Watch for a front-page article in the near future."

"I could crush you like a bug. You know that," the chief said and began another staring contest.

This time Chief von der Lippe lost.

"And if I should be able to discover some of the people who might be of help in leading you where you want to go?" he asked.

"Nothing."

"No money, no rank increase?"

"Just information. And no one needs to know that you were the source."

"You are a hard man, Schäfer. I am surprised that you did not rise higher in the *Kriminalpolizei*. I will see what I can do for you."

Schäfer stood for a few moments while the chief looked down at his papers. The detective took his cue and left, satisfied that he had done a good day's work.

§§§§§

Landespolizei [Bundeslandt State Police] *Kriminalpolitzei*, Detective Branch, Wittelsbachstrasse. 3, Ludwigshafen am Rhein, August 25, 1962

Joachim Becker, IG Farben Administration security officer, delivered the first report to the investigation group regarding the murder of Gunther Emil Sondregger.

"In the past thirty-six hours, the entire security staff at the BASF factory complex has interviewed every man and woman who works in any capacity in the administration facility. We extended our canvass to include friends, relatives, and anyone those who interviewed considered to be a possible risk to the factory or to any employee. We drew a complete blank when it came to the name of Herr Sondregger. BASF employee records contain only his employment application and work records which began on May 19, 1952. There are no company records with any information about the man before that date.

"I went over his application for work very carefully. What was interesting about that form was what it did not contain—or rather, what could not be deciphered. His handwriting was terrible. I could not read a single item related to his previous place or places or employment, his place of birth, or where he lived before moving to Ludwigshafen.

"In short, the man is a ghost who appeared whole cloth on the day he applied for work at BASF. Furthermore, he had no association with anyone or any group inside or outside of work. He turned down promotions four times, apparently so he could keep his same desk and could have work that would not draw any attention to himself. He was highly successful at that for ten years."

Senior Constable [*Oberwachtmeister*] Eberhard Zimmermann, Schäfer's working partner was next. He was assisted by a very senior secretary in the *Kriminalpolitzei* forensic sciences division. Her name was Hilda Weiss-Krüger, and she was well known throughout the *Landespolizei* system as an assiduously careful and thorough analyst and investigator. Lieutenant Schäfer had requested that she be placed on temporary leave from her regular assignment and moved to the special investigation unit.

Eberhard was a cop's cop. He did not give a fig for all the grandiosity of the senior officers. Instead, he admired efficiency, cleverness, and thoroughness in getting the job of identifying, finding, and arresting criminals through the collection of evidence that would defeat any defense attorney's arguments. For that he would have followed Horst Schäfer into the mouth of hell. He was the oldest man in the entire Kripo division of Germany. He had more experience that the rest of the detectives put together. He had not risen in the ranks because he did not want to, and he seemed to go out of his way to avoid making friends with the inspectors and above who could give him a step up. He was professorial in appearance, a senior citizen with salt and pepper hair and full beard. He wore old-fashioned horn-rim spectacles which usually hung from his neck on a leather lanyard. He had a pocket full of pens, pencils, and notebooks. His suit was old, never pressed, but never looked actually dirty. He was small and prissy, easily offended, and never forgot anything.

Zimmermann carried the weight of the Kripo reporting initially, "We—and by that I mean mainly Hilda—dug into every avenue for moving strangers into the BASF system, especially in the late 1940s and early fifties during the period where the French and Americans ran the internment camps and displaced persons interviews. We ran into a number of intentional roadblocks and appeared to be stymied. We followed your directions at those points, Lieutenant, and put in a call to Police Chief Schneider's office in Wiesbaden to clear the way. It was magic. Once the chief knew who was asking, one of his subordinates wired an approval. Rather than have the bother of us calling all the time, Chief Schneider sent us a formal letter directing anyone we asked for records to comply promptly or answer to him. It was like Moses parting the Red Sea.

"After the first day, we had more records than we knew what to do with. Once again, Hilda used her skills and wiles...," Hilda snorted and gave Zimmerman a theatrical frown, "to winnow out the obvious junk and to get us down to about twenty names that seemed appropriate for further investigation. Six of them were taken to the United States in Operation Paperclip; eight ended up in nuclear science projects in England; two were rounded up by the French military police and served sentences that kept them in prison until last year and now work at menial farm or factory jobs—all under their genuine names. That left us with four persons whose histories could be our Herr Sondregger. We have put in long hours trying to find them. With the help of good Chief Schneider, we were able to contact ODESSA people who reluctantly assured us that they knew about three of the men who had been exfiltrated by ODESSA to Argentina. The names of two of them—if it matters to you—are Dieter Schwartz, who became Carlos Aguillara-Dominguez, and Rudolf Heinz-Köhler von Krupp, who became Federico Gonzales."

"What happened to the record in Argentina?" Schäfer asked.

"Quite formal and accurate as near as we can tell. Dieter Schwartz, aka Carlos Aguillara-Dominguez was murdered—decapitated—by person or persons unknown in a subdivision of the city of Córdoba, Argentina, called Lomas de los Carolinos, in early August this year. Von Krupp—yes, those Krupps—drowned off the Mar del Plata coast in January 1961. We have good local police records and some documentation from ODESSA. Neither of these men was our victim or seemed to have any association with him."

"I take it you're saving the best for last."

"You are right as always, Herr Lieutenant," Zimmerman said with a small grin.

"So, who is our victim?"

"His real name was Heinrich Rudolf Gajewski, a German IG Farben war criminal who had helped in the manufacture of sarin and tabun gas used in the execution chambers. He was a genuine war criminal. The war crimes commission records indicated that he was the executive in charge of procuring slave labor for the BASF factories, including those at Auschwitz. Apparently it was hard work and a full-time occupation because of the high mortality rates among the workers—most of whom were Jews, homosexuals, or gypsies. They were worked to death, starved, and grievously neglected. At times Gajewski and the other beasts had to step over the bodies of those who died the previous day to deliver the new workers. Other concentration camp victims had to clear out the bodies to make way for the next crop of unfortunates. Any number of survivors could bear Gajewski enough of a grudge to want to murder him, but it would have been all but impossible for them to learn with any certainty who any of those monsters were without having access to the Allies' records.

"It may be more productive to know that in the last days of the war in in the early postwar period, he was assigned triage detail of returning German POWs, and he gained enormous power of life and death over the returnees. If they could not pay, they languished in the camps and often starved before final repatriation. The names of those people may be obtainable, and many of them should still be alive."

"So, this is our lackluster minor functionary at BASF administration, Gunther Emil Sondregger."

"That's what we think."

"We have solved only the very first part of this puzzle, Lieutenant," Hilda said, making her presence known for the first time. "Our next project has to be to find out why this apparently unimportant little man was killed. God knows he deserved to be murdered; but that is not for us to decide, or even to ponder."

"That's true, Hilda; and we have to keep that in mind all of the time. One way of looking at this murder and the slimy person the victim was is to presume that whoever killed him is very likely to be an even worse person."

"Or part of a conspiracy," she pointed out.

"And there's that," Schäfer agreed. "So, Hilda, where do we go from here?"

"Sweat and shoe leather. Good old *bulle* [German slang for cop] work, and getting the *Goldfasan* [German slang for Golden pheasant, a reference to high-ranking Nazis, and sometimes for high-ranking military or police officers]."

Hilda was as tough as all the other Kripos put together. She was manly in appearance and definitely not one you would want to meet in a dark alley despite her gender. Her dishwater blond hair was cut short and brushed into a tangle of bristles. She seldom smiled, and did so almost exclusively when her research produced a definitive result. She had a plain face–which was deceiving because behind that face and those eyes was a brilliant analyst–a brain that was regularly capable of exercising great insight, clarity of perception, real wisdom, and often genius-level serendipity. All of that was belied by her choice of uniform—drab, wrinkled, and baggy enough to be her older larger sister's.

"All right. Eberhard and Hilda, you do the sweat and shoe leather work; and I will beard the lion in his den," Horst said.

CHAPTER THIRTEEN

Thirty minutes later

"Please inform Chief Schneider Graf von der Lippe that *Kriminalkommissar* Horst Schäfer is calling and it is both important and urgent that I speak to him immediately."

"He won't be happy, Lieutenant. I hope for your sake that your communication is both important and urgent. He does not suffer fools."

"I'll take the risk. Get him on the line … *bitte*!" Schäfer said, emphasizing the 'please.'

"What now, Lieutenant? You are beginning to try my patience."

"And a good morning to you, sir. I am hoping to solve an important case with your help, which should add to your already sterling record of bringing to justice criminals no matter what their rank or position."

"You are troweling on the crap too thick now, Schäfer. I repeat: what do you want now?"

"Nothing much. I just want to talk to the main führer of the ODESSA." Schäfer delivered the outlandish request totally deadpan.

Schneider sputtered momentarily, then began to laugh uproariously.

"Have you gone completely *verrückt* [crazy]? You wouldn't last a minute if you were to knock on the führer's door. For that matter, what makes you think I know anything about the ODESSA?"

"I am sure that the chief of criminal police for the entire German nation has heard of ODESSA and regards it his business to monitor the information coming in from the intelligence department. I only wish to share a part of that. I need a name and a useful introduction, or you will certainly be right: I won't get in the door; I might get killed; and nothing will be gained in my investigation of a murder."

"Will I be quit of you if I do give you what you ask?"

"Probably, unless the lead points to another area of your expertise."

"Schäfer, I have half a mind to promote you to the Wiesbaden office where I can keep my eye on you."

Schäfer laughed.

"I have successfully avoided that fate for my entire career. It probably wouldn't work out all that well."

"After considerable and deep thought, I'm sure you're right; so, I withdraw the offer."

They both laughed.

"I'll get back to you this afternoon. Stay close to a phone."

He hung up.

§§§§§

Schloss Krupp, southeast corner of Lietzenburger and Pfalzburger Strassen, Charlottenburg Section of City West, Berlin, Germany, six hours later

The Krupp limousine picked *Kriminalkommissar* Schäfer up at *Flughafen* Schönefeld [Berlin Schönefeld Airport] and drove him in a style to which he was not accustomed to *Schloss* Krupp, in the very affluent Charlottenburg section of City West, Berlin. Never in his wildest imaginations did blue collar *bulle* Horst Schäfer see himself being driven by a liveried chauffeur in a stretch car to a castle. Chief Schneider came through in grand fashion, and Schäfer knew that he would owe the chief a marker for the rest of his career. He only hoped that it would prove to be worth it.

Charlottenburg used to be the heart of West Berlin and stretched between the Ku'Damm—jointly shared with Wilmersdorf—and the Charlottenburg Palace in the north. The southern part of the district was one of the wealthiest areas of Berlin with several *schlosses*, posh villas, and apartments. Although rebuilding was continuing in the less affluent parts of the capital city, Charlottenburg already had mature broad streets and sidewalks, parks, and spacious residential buildings, especially around the southern Kurfürstendamm area where the Krupp castle stood.

He was stopped in front of the huge front door ornamented with the brass logo of the Krupp dynasty—three intersecting rings emblematic of the *Radreifen* [no-weld railway wheels] patented by Alfred Krupp in 1851. He was thoroughly patted down by two security guards and was glad he had paid heed to Chief Schneider's admonition not to wear a firearm. Then a man in a tuxedo, whom Schäfer presumed was the butler—but who did not speak—led him what seemed to be nearly half a mile to his destination. The butler directed Schäfer to a stiff-backed chair in a long hall lined on both sides with medieval armored knights and very professionally mounted animals from around the world. The floor was polished walnut that reflected the lights that lined the hall. The walls and ceiling were covered with highly polished, recently dusted, carved oak with scenes of famous battle victories of the Teutonic Knights. The lieutenant from unimportant little Ludwigshafen tapped his fingers impatiently as he waited for a full hour before the master of the house entered the hall from a side door.

Anton Friedrich Krupp von Bohlen und Halbach was a reed-thin straight-back patriarch with a full head of precisely trimmed long hair and sculpted beard of snow white. His face was lined with the cares of the world which he bore with the equanimity that only the immensely wealthy can afford. He was dressed in traditional green wool field hunting attire including the dress style field hat, all perfectly tailored for him. His patrician figure was accentuated by his perfectly polished knee-high leather boots and small clinking spurs. Other hunters were obligated to wear red when out in the field, but the Krupps were exempt for such foolishness on their own extensive property, and probably everywhere else, Schäfer surmised.

Krupp did not offer his hand or any pleasantries, and he stood as ramrod stiff as a first sergeant reporting to his colonel in the Prussian army.

"You are the police officer from … where is it?"

"Ludwigshafen."

"Ah, yes, the IG Farben town. Chief Schneider briefed me about your visit and your request. I agreed reluctantly and with conditions. They are as follows: nothing I tell will ever be traced back to me; my name will never be used in print or in conversation, even in official police records; no suggestion will ever be made to anyone that I have even the slightest acquaintance with the criminal organization known as ODESSA. Do you agree to my conditions?"

"Yes."

"Good. You will find me to be a most unforgiving man if I learn that you have violated our agreement."

"Herr Krupp, I am investigating the murder of a former Nazi SS lieutenant colonel by the name of Heinrich Rudolf Gajewski—his original name—also known as Gunther Emil Sondregger, a pseudonym he adopted in the postwar period having erased his past records; or so he believed. He was a complete recluse in his work at BASF and a virtual unknown in the society of the city and his workplace. The only avenue of investigation we have to follow to seek out someone who meant the man harm is that he was known to the ODESSA which arranged for his disappearance on German and Allied records and his reappearance as a new person in Ludwigshafen. We speculate that perhaps the man had knowledge that could incriminate a former Nazi or perhaps some of the SS men involved with ODESSA. We need your help and direction to allow us to meet with men who may know the answers to our questions."

"Well and succinctly put. I have prepared a list of individuals who may have such knowledge. They will speak with you only when you give them a set of code words—Alpha Wolf. When your investigation is completed, you will forget those words and never utter them again. Understood?"

"Perfectly."

Krupp handed Schäfer a crisp heavy bond manila envelope then turned on his heels and exited the way he had come in. Immediately after the master of the house closed the door, the butler reappeared as if part of an illusionist's conjuring trick. Schäfer was all but frog-marched out of the castle and placed in the limousine for his return to the airport.

On the plane he read his department's intelligence report on the ODESSA as preparation for a thorough study of the men whose names appeared on Krupp's papers. The report on the history regarding the people involved came from the work of a Jewish survivor of the concentration camps—Simon Wiesenthal. The information regarding the financial intricacies of the efforts to protect the war criminals came from the *Kripo* intelligence division. The reluctant old SiPo members, Nazi hunters from the allies, and police analysts working on the German and Austrian denazification project provided the final pieces of information Lieutenant Schäfer and his team needed to get on with their work.

ODESSA is the acronym for the German *Organization Der Ehemaligen SS-Angehörigen*, [Organization of Former SS Members]. It was founded in 1944 at the behest of Reichsleiter Martin Bormann, Hitler's private secretary, with the express purpose of helping Nazi members to flee Europe and to escape justice. The pioneering meeting took place in the Maison Rouge Hotel in Strasbourg on the tenth of August of that late year of the Second World War. Besides a very carefully chosen few SS officers, the men attending the meeting included coal tycoon Emil Kirdorf, owner of a major coal conglomerate; Georg von Schnitzler of IG Farben chemical works; Gustav Krupp von Bohlen und Halbach, the great steel and railroad magnate; Friedrich "Fritz" Thyssen, German industrialist who dared to oppose Hitler and spent time in several concentration camps; and banker Kurt von Schroeder. Their common bond was partly their allegiance to Hitler and the Nazi party, but wholly to profit.

The war profiteers and the objective SS officers—including Bormann—in the meeting recognized the impending defeat of Germany and the serious repercussions that any SS member would eventually face. These pragmatic idealogues, opportunists, thieves, and murderers recognized that they had sufficient power to exercise either of two options: first—continue the rapidly deteriorating German position in the war and hope to be able last out long enough for their plethora of secret weapons such as rockets and deadly chemical warfare agents to become fully operational, which could resuscitate Germany's chances of victory. This was the vain hope to which Hitler clung; or, second, they could begin the process of moving their still huge hordes of money, technology, and dedicated personnel to ensure the continued survival of the Nazi Party and the SS in an elaborate scheme to begin again to build the mythical Fourth Reich.

The men present at the meeting made a brilliant decision: they chose both courses of action. The meeting was not the first time these courses were considered. The movement began to take shape as a potential safety net early in the war. The German leadership nurtured Italian, German-Argentine, German-Brazilian, and other South American dictatorships in a cozy and mutually profitable set of labyrinthine interconnections. In addition, they secretly fostered other extremely valuable cooperative arrangements. As the war wore on towards its inevitable negative conclusion, the SS and German financiers and industrialists developed firm agreements with such diverse groups as the Vatican, multiple high-ranking Roman Catholics in a score of countries, Italian fascists, senior governmental officials in Argentina, Italy, Switzerland, Sweden and—not inconsequently for the SS—the Allied intelligence services. Two other organizations worked in secret to help the SS members left in Germany—*Die Spinne* [The Spider] and an organization established by Gudrun Burwitz—the daughter of Heinrich Himmler—called *Stille Hilfe* [Silent Help].

Those three and several other organizations aided fugitive Nazis, established and maintained secret escape routes and transportation—known as ratlines—subverted Italian, Swiss, Vatican, Middle Eastern, and South American governments, and murdered people who interfered or who were targeted for revenge. Ratlines were a system of escape routes for Nazis and other fascists fleeing Europe at the end of World War II. These convoluted and expensive escape routes usually led toward semipermanent havens in South America, particularly Argentina, Paraguay, Brazil, Uruguay, Chile, and Bolivia. But others led to the United States, Great Britain, Canada, Southeast Asia, and the Middle East. There were two primary routes: the first went from Germany to Spain, then on to Argentina; the second from Germany to Rome to Genoa, then to South America; the two routes developed independently but eventually came together to collaborate.

During the chaos at the end of hostilities, the underground network called *"Die Spinne"* supplied false papers and passports, safe houses, and contacts that could smuggle war criminals across the unpatrolled or actively involved Swiss borders. Once into Switzerland, the Nazis moved on quickly to Italy, using what came to be called the "Monastery Route." Roman Catholic priests—especially Franciscans—helped the ODESSA move fugitives from one monastery to the next until they reached Rome—all with the blessing of Pope Pius XII. One Franciscan monastery–Via Sicilia in Rome–became a routine transit station for Nazis, an arrangement made possible by Archbishop Romani [not his real name]. By their own admission, the motive for most of the priests was a notion of Christian charity. Once in Italy, the fugitives were out of danger, and many then dispersed around the globe.

By 1946, there were hundreds—perhaps several thousands—of Nazi war criminals in Spain; and thousands of outwardly former Nazis and fascists. Vatican cooperation in turning over asylum-seekers in those Catholic countries was negligible. Pope Pius XII was active in the efforts to put former Nazis and other fascist war criminals on board ships sailing to the New World. He was instrumental in getting ex-Nazis out of the terrible conditions in Allied POW camps in zonal Germany, and there was a trickle-down hierarchal support system to keep the Vatican or Roman ratlines effective. Similarly, the Vatican emigration ratline operation in the ratlines of Spain was fostered by the Vatican.

Archbishop Carlo Romani of Graz was an outspoken rector of the *Pontificio Istituto Teutonico Santa Maria dell'Anima* in Rome, a seminary for Austrian and German priests. He was often refered to as the "Spiritual Director of the German People resident in Italy." After the end of the war, he became active in ministering to German-speaking prisoners of war and internees then held in camps throughout Italy and assisting them in ways the Vatican at first denied. However, in 1944 the Vatican Secretariat of State received permission from the pope to appoint a representative to attend to the needs of the German-speaking civil internees in Italy—an assignment enthusiastically filled by the archbishop.

Romani used this position vigorously to aid the escape of wanted Nazi war criminals, including some of the most notorious of the Nazi concentration camp officers. He made no attempt to conceal that activity on his part, never expressed regret or shame. One of the means he employed to conceal the identity of these wanted men was to ensure that they had no identity papers; so, they could be enrolled in camp registers under innocuously false non-Germanic names.

The financial cost of maintaining the ratlines was enormous, and the Vatican assisted Nazi organizations in establishing an efficient system. A growing source of precious metal came from Nazi concentration camps and death camps, where all property was taken from the victims, and included personal effects such as wedding rings, pocket watches, cigarette cases, jewellery, and gold teeth. The Swiss National Bank— the largest gold distribution centre in continental Europe before the war—was the logical venue through which Nazi Germany could dispose of its gold. During the war, the SNB received $440m in gold from Nazi sources, of which $316m is estimated to have been looted.

By 1945, the Vatican had confiscated 350 million Swiss francs in Nazi gold for what it termed "safekeeping." Of that massive treasure, 150 million Swiss francs were impounded by British authorities at the Austro-Swiss border, thus confirming the Vatican and Swiss culpability. The balance of the *Raubgeld* ["stolen gold"] was held in one of several of the Vatican's numbered Swiss bank accounts. Postwar intelligence reports found that more than 200 million Swiss francs—mostly in the form of gold coins—were eventually transferred to Vatican City or to the Institute for Works of Religion (aka the Vatican Bank), with the assistance of Roman Catholic clergy and the Franciscan Order. In the late 1950s, leading ex-Nazis later publicly thanked the Vatican for its vital assistance.

The financial arrangements for assistance to the escaping Nazis were rigid and formal. In return for providing safe haven and new identities, the involved organizations and nations were provided massive loans from the plunder of the conquered and occupied nations and from the Jews of Germany and the lands of occupation. There was at least an implicit "pay-it-forward" pact with those who were saved that they would reimburse and help to finance future ODESSA projects when they could, and the occasion required them to do so.

It was a win-win arrangement for both the lenders and the borrowers. The SS recognized that Germany's ill-gotten assets would fall into the hands of the rapidly approaching enemies if they were not transferred and hidden to be retrieved and used in the future. Out of the 1944 meeting in Salzburg, a pact with the devil was made. The party lent huge sums of money to industrialists all over the country and to sympathizing financiers in the former occupied countries.

This enabled them to set up separate and secret postwar organizations abroad, which provided an additional layer of hidden assets to facilitate the saving of the SS members and allowed for the enrichment of the industrialists and the subverted friends and political officers in the targeted countries. As collateral, the industrialists paid back to their Nazi benefactors an ongoing portion of their earnings from abroad. Together the corrupted industrialists and the Nazi hierarchy built well-funded and protected resources abroad, so that a strong German Reich would reemerge after the defeat and would be manned by zealots even more jingoistic that those of the vanquished Third Reich.

As the war drew towards its close, Nazi treasure began to be distributed to 750 corporations around the world, all of which were sympathetic or at least cooperative with the Third Reich. In 1944, George W. Merck was a senior advisor for President Franklin D. Roosevelt in his capacity as the American biological weapons industry director. His input related to strategies for employment of that kind of weaponry. He retained his position as president of Merck and Company, Incorporated, and in the spring of that same year, the company received a very large cash contribution from Martin Bormann. That infusion of cash allowed Merck to secure a virtual monopoly over the world's chemical and pharmaceutical industries. Publically, the money was contributed to provide for Germany's economic recovery. Quietly, the massive monetary contribution was targeted towards the assurance of the rise of the hoped-for the *Neuordnung* [New Order]—the Fourth Reich.

The Rockefeller partner company, IG Farben, received huge sums of money from the Nazi war chest to actualize Hitler's proclaimed vision of a Third Reich and world empire, and subsequently towards the putative Fourth Reich. The project and the money originated from Martin Bormann as head of the Nazi Ministry of Economics. This was outlined with clarity in a document that was accompanied by a letter of transmittal from the Führer to the Bormann-led Ministry of Economics

The head of Perónist government's Information Bureau coordinated the work of intelligence and immigration officials in Argentina and throughout South America directly from from his office in the Casa Rosada, Argentina's White House. Incoming SS officers, one named Hörst Dietsel, but better known by his new name, Carlos Aguillara-Dominguez, was recently murdered, Lieutenant Schäfer learned. Such officers were willing conduits and facilitators for the flow of gold and Nazi fugitives. The Argentine connection was powerful, diverse, and ruthless.

In addition to the Argentines, there was a multinational and polyglot cabal of Vichy French, Belgian Rexists, Croatian Ustashi, and Roman Catholic cardinals from several countries, acting with the blessing of the Vatican. According to interviews with some of the people apprehended over the years, they were all motivated by the vision of an international brotherhood of Catholic anti-Communists, and not by greed or vindictiveness. Schäfer read that information with more than a grain of salt and with a healthy dose of world-weary police skepticism.

Carefully husbanding the treasure they sent to Argentina, the SS organizations purchased huge tracts of land in South America and elsewhere. Large, apparently legitimate corporations were established which conducted research begun in Germany to create the master race by careful pseudoscientific eugenic protocols and by developing profitable industries. *Sperrgebiete* [secure areas] grew up in the welcoming atmosphere and created whole towns, airfields, highways with all the amenities of civilized German life—free of Jews, Negroes, Gypsies, retarded people, or homosexuals. Fascist countries, including Spain under Franco, and Italy under Mussolini–as well as those in South America–became secure and safe havens.

The establishment of the state of Israel after World War II led several Middle Eastern Arab nations to welcome Nazis who shared their hatred of the Jews. The ulterior motive of the Islamic world was that the unreformed Nazis would use their expertise in rocket science to enable the final annihilation of the Jews who—at the time—were gaining the upperhand in the ongoing Arab-Israeli conflicts. The Allies—including the United States—were eager to the point of near frenzy to exploit the knowledge and work of Nazi war criminals.

America created a pattern of postwar SS relationships with South American governments and formed false corporations to keep Nazi scientists out of the clutches of the communist governments which were also on a frantic crusade to gather in the bomb makers, rocketiers, and weaponized poison makers to their side.

For all of that massive expenditure and complexity of maneuvering, some war criminals—including Heinrich Rudolf Gajewski, aka Gunther Emil Sondregger—failed to find a way out, and—during the chaos—ODESSA found ways for them to remain in Germany and take on new identities and to manage to get themselves successfully and unobtrusively reentered into postwar German society.

"*The question for us Kripos is how did they do that?*" Schäfer asked himself. "*And who cared? That question has to relate to who killed the man.*"

Recipe

Großmutter's Dumpfnoodles—Serves 8

Ingredients
-Dry—4 cps all-purpose white flour, 2 pkgs dry yeast, 1 tsp salt, 1 tsp garlic powder,
1 large Russet potato, 2 lbs ground sausage (your choice as to spiciness).
-Liquid—1 cp lard, 2 cps potato water, 4–5 tbsps extra virgin olive oil
-Sauerkraut: just buy packaged product—will cut time significantly.

Preparation
-1. Mix yeast and potato water (boil the potato until it is soft enough to fall apart) using sufficient amount for proper dough consistency.
-2. Add salt and lard, mix very well.
-3. Add flour. Knead until it sticks to your skin.
-4. Place in warm area of the kitchen or in very low setting of oven, let dough rise to double its size.
-5. Punch dough down, let it rise once more, and punch it down a second time.
-6. Let dough rise a third (and final) time to double the original size.
-7. While dough is rising, fry sausage on medium heat. Add sauerkraut, may pour off excess moisture. Add garlic powder to mix of meat and sauerkraut.
8. After the dough is done, make 2–3 inch balls and roll them out into medium-flat circles.
9. Fill fairly full with sauerkraut and meat mixture; and squeeze the edges of the dough together to make pouches.
10. After the pouches are made, let dough rise again for 30 min.
11. If dough is sticky, use wax paper during preparation.
12. Heat medium high 2 tbsps oil for each high sided, nonsticking frying pan. Test heat by splashing a little water in the pan. It should skitter and make sounds of frying. Then add ¾ cp water.
13. Place fully risen pouches in pan—as many as will fit.
14. Once in the pans, place lid on and fry until there is no water left, About 30 min. Smell the fried dough to be sure cooking is complete.
15. DO NOT take off the lid until it smells fried and no water sloshes.

CHAPTER FOURTEEN

Landespolizei [Bundeslandt State Police]
Kriminalpolitzei, Detective Branch, Wittelsbachstrasse.
3, Ludwigshafen am Rhein, late evening,
August 28, 1962

Oberwachtmeister [Senior Constable] Eberhard Zimmerman, Schäfer's working partner, and Hilda Weiss-Krüger, the most experienced and well-respected analyst/secretary in the *Kriminalpolitzei* forensic sciences division, had a breakthrough after a grueling twelve-hour day. Both officers were sure they would go blind from the eyestrain after pouring over the prodigious amount of documentation Chief Schneider had delivered by courier from headquarters in Wiesbaden.

Unable to contain themselves, they interrupted Lieutenant Schäfer's late evening lunch—leftovers of a sandwich he started at lunch the previous day. He was weary but happy, because he, too, had made a breakthrough which would send him on what he hoped would be a productive search.

"Horst!" Zimmerman called out to his boss in a burst of enthusiasm. "We hit a great lead!"

"All right, Eberhard, you and Hilda go first; then I will tell you my little success."

"We have a list of four names that Leopold Boehm in the FIU [Financial Intelligence Unit] here in Ludwigshafen gave us; they are his paid confidential informants. Their specialty is informing on former Nazis, especially the SS; and *Kriminalkommissar* Boehm says these people—one of whom is a woman—know a great deal about the inner workings of modern-day ODESSA. They are all risk takers, and informing on the SS and ODESSA is very much a risk; so, they expect to be paid handsomely."

"I know Leopold. We talked about our decision back when we were first approached whether we would go SiPo or stay Kripo. We both knew that our careers would never amount to much, but we have both been able to sleep nights. He knows as much as anyone in Germany about organized crime since it is so money-driven," said Schäfer."

Hilda added, "Leopold was willing to arrange a meeting with all four of them—separately, of course; so, Eberhard and I scheduled meetings all over Ludwigshafen for tomorrow morning."

She grinned in triumph and with the knowledge that she and Eberhard had scored a serious point in the ongoing one-upmanship battle with their usually successful lieutenant.

"So, what have you got, boss?" Eberhard asked.

"I only have one name, but it came from Chief Schneider himself. He called me this afternoon. This is a man that the headquarters office knows all about and has considerable leverage over. In exchange for information about anything going on in the organized crime world here and abroad or about the ODESSA, the entire *Kriminalpolitzei* turns a blind eye to his very lucrative enterprises that include human trafficking, gambling, illicit drug trafficking, prostitution, and a host of white collar crimes. The chief thinks it is a good trade and said he would make the arrangements for us to interview him if we promise not to use anything he tells us against him, and he never gets connected to any arrest that might take place as a result of the information he shares."

"Who do we go after first, Horst?"

"Let's flip a coin."

Eberhard laughed out loud. He had been through this several hundred times—long enough and often enough that it had become a tradition and a standing joke.

Horst smiled back, extracted a coin, flipped it, and gave it a quick glance as it sat out of range of Hilda and Eberhard.

"Heads," he said. "I win. We go and see my hot prospect first."

Eberhard laughed heartily, but Hilda looked like she had been violated.

"Hey," she demanded, "I didn't get to see that! What I did see was a magician's trick. That's not fair."

Horst pushed the dorsum of his hand towards Hilda and smiled, "See—heads."

She gave him a stern look which she could not maintain and started to laugh with her two male partners.

"How come I think I have just been had?" she said.

Both men shrugged and gave her an affectionate smile.

§§§§§

Suite 2212, Haus Cumberland Office Building on the Kurfürstendamm Avenue between Bleibtreu and Schlüterstrasse, Charlottenburg, Berlin, August 29, 1962, three o'clock in the afternoon.

Horst, Eberhard, and Hilda were fully aware of the activities of the Rebscher crime syndicate of which the man they were to meet—business executive Herr Kohler—was a leading executive. West Germany did not have a fully professional international criminal organization in comparison with the Allies. However, the Rebscher German crime syndicate profited significantly from their loose connection with the Sicilian and Russian Mafias, the Camorra, the Triads, and the Yakuza. They were tolerated by those better-established organizations because they provided a conduit into the newly growing German economy and assisted in helping the other syndicates gain a toehold in a new market.

On their own, the Rebschers became rich as partners of the ODESSA, with all of the Third Reich's hidden treasure at the ODESSA's disposal when needed. Those monies allowed the legal front company, the WestBerlinImportExport GmbH Corporation to prosper by pursuing a legitimate export business involved in the moving of commodities such as motor vehicles, machinery, chemicals, electronic products, electrical equipment, pharmaceuticals, metals, transport equipment, foodstuffs, textiles, rubber, and plastic products. The ODESSA and its remaining secretive SS officer directors reaped a very acceptable harvest from the twenty percent portion of the company's profits which reverted back to them. Neither the ODESSA nor the corporation were likely to be forthcoming about their own involvement, but Chief Schneider assured his Kripo squad from Ludwigshafen that a trip to Berlin would be useful.

The three Kripo officers were shown to comfortable hand-crafted leather swivel chairs in the sumptuous conference room of WestBerlinImportExport GmbH Corporation. *Stellvertretender Direktor* [Deputy Director] Heinrich Kohler entered the room within minutes. He was a tall, handsome, Aryan gentleman—every bit the personification of the ideal German mensch envisioned by the leaders of the Third Reich. Kohler was all blond, blue-eyed, authoritarian, and unquestionably in charge of the proceedings about to take place. He was dressed in the latest Parisian fashion—custom-tailored, conservative, charcoal gray, form-fitting, three-button silk and wool blend suit, crisply starched white shirt, and hand-knotted bow tie. His black shoes gleamed with a shine applied that morning. Horst thought he was nearly a clone of Chief Schneider Graf von der Lippe.

"Welcome. You are here because Chief Schneider asked us to see you. A few ground rules: you may not inquire as to our business except as it directly applies to the search for individuals associated with one Heinrich Rudolf Gajewski, former SS officer whom I understand is deceased. You may only be given information regarding his associates and particularly his actual or putative enemies. A few documents pertaining to the man have been prepared and copied from certain files to which we have access. You may not have access to any other documents, and understand at the outset that no subpoena will be honored that demands more, as per the directive of the chief of the Federal Police of West Germany.

"Any questions?"

"No. Thank you, Herr Deputy Director. What can you tell us about Herr Gajewski?"

"The man was an employee of IG Farben/BASF since 1934. His education was in chemical engineering with a specialization in production of industrial gasses. He became involved in the top-secret manufacture of sarin and tabun gasses which—as you may know—was used in the execution of undesirables. Gajewski was found to have an important skill in personnel management. His principal occupation during the recent war was the procurement of slave labor which proved to be a full-time effort so that his other work in the actual production of industrial gasses became only tangential. Few of the workers who possibly knew him or of him remain available in Germany, as you might imagine. I have here a list of fourteen. The names and addresses are accurate and current.

"His talents were also utilized in the postwar triage of returning German POWs, and it is said that he gained considerable power of life and death over the returnees. In that position, he was susceptible to bribery. If the Germans returned from POW camps in America, France, England, and Russia could not pay the bribes, they were ignored and languished in the camps and succumbed to various causes before final repatriation. Some of those POWs were SS members who were captured by the Russians and had harsh treatment. We have a list of 142 such Germans possibly living in West Germany and another 255 who may be living in the East at present.

There are—as near as we can determine—fourteen men now living in France. They were an interesting subset of SS officers. They were all from the 33rd Waffen-Grenadier Division of the SS. The remarkable thing about that particular group is that they were all originally French citizens. Even more remarkable is that they were among the few SS troops who fought to the bitter end during the Battle of Berlin against the Red Army. Our listing of those men is only patchy and not nearly as reliable as our listing for German citizens. Every one of them fell into the category of those triaged to remain in the postwar German internment camps. It is to be presumed that they knew of Gajewski and did not regard him with any favor.

"Finally, there were several Russian POWS who encountered this Gajewski as the triage officer. He was especially harsh in his treatment of them. Although he personally murdered or ordered others to murder many of those Russians, most of them are not of interest to your investigation. However, three of the murdered men had strong connections with elements of the Russian mafia—which, in turn, had then and has now a connection with the Soviet government. There are several men who still remember Gajewski with a venomous hatred and might well have wished him great harm. We have a list of those people's names; but, unfortunately, we do not have addresses or any access to them. You are on your own if you decide to investigate Soviets.

"A remote possibility is that he had to have come into contact and shared secrets with American, British, French, and Russian military officials who no doubt caused unfair and real suffering on the part of some of the German POWs. We have included a complete list of all of the Allied officers and enlisted men who were involved—it numbers well over a thousand names. We have no direct knowledge of connections with Gajewski or who shared diabolical secrets with him and might fear that he could implicate them. However—for what it is worth—you have their names and their whereabouts. Good luck sifting through that large list.

"He returned to Ludwigshafen with the help of ODESSA. In order to obtain his place with the ODESSA operatives, Gajewski murdered two POWS and was able to expropriate their family holdings, a not inconsiderable sum of money. We have spoken with the two families— the Beckenbauers and the Fenstermachers—both from Hamburg. That bit of self-preservation cost both families their fortunes and reduced them to a life as minor tradesmen just able to eke out a humble living. They hate Gajewski with a passion but are of the opinion that he finally died during the chaos of that period.

"Gajewski received the necessary documentation to assume a new life under the innocuous name of Gunther Emil Sondregger. There were two other candidates among the ex-SS officers who were murdered by Gajewski to remove them from competition for the few places the ODESSA could provide in Ludwigshafen. They have a total of six friends from their days of service during the war, and they have not forgotten what Gajewski did to those two men. Although we do not have evidence that they know his new identity, it is not outside the realm of possibility. We include in our list the names and current addresses of those men. As you would no doubt assume, their identities have been radically altered; and they are most secretive. We have quietly contacted them, and they are willing to help in any way they can with the obvious condition that their identities remain secret. Two of them expressed real distress upon learning that Gajewski had been murdered—not because of any sorrow for the man, but because they had wanted to be the agents of a long and painful death for the man. The six names and addresses are available to you; it is unlikely that they have enough information to be useful or to have been the murderers; but you never know.

"Because of his expertise and his ruthlessness, he was assigned to the human resources division of the BASF system. Because of his being included on the Allies' most wanted war criminal list, he elected to be given a position in the company that was a relatively minor one and one unlikely to attract attention to himself or to the company for harboring him. We have no information on any possible enemies the man may have collected since moving to Ludwigshafen. Have you any further questions?"

The three Kripo officers glanced at each other and shook their heads in the negative.

"None. Thank you, Herr Kohler. You have been very helpful. The lists will give us considerable work, and we would like to get started as soon as possible. Would it be all right if we contact you by telephone from time to time for clarification of details that might come up?"

"It would be my pleasure. I have taken the liberty of writing down my private number. Please be discreet."

The Kripos nodded their agreement.

CHAPTER FIFTEEN

Headquarters, Metropolitan Police Service/New Scotland Yard, Criminal Investigation Department [CID], Victoria Embankment, August 21, 1962

The day was hot and soporific. The large ceiling fans in the London Army and Navy Club were inadequate to the task. The City of London had largely been evacuated, with everyone who could get away heading to the countryside. There were only two members in the exclusive club's bar that morning, and they were preparing to leave to escape the oppressive mugginess. Major Algernon Donelly nodded briefly at the oldest member of the club—Lieutenant-General Sir Cyril Goeffrey Robert Hill-Brownwell, RA, Ret.—who came to the club every day in his declining years. The major considered the general to be a hero and exemplar, and was, therefore, always carefully respectful whenever he encountered the old gentleman.

The general was slow in getting to his feet and had rather poor equilibrium, but Major Donelly knew better than to embarrass the fine old man by offering to help. He strode to the front door deliberately; so, he could watch the general and see if he might need help. He was about to open the door when an unthinkable event occurred. A man—quite evidently one of the help and dressed in the gray tunic and trousers of the club staff—darted out from behind the bar where he had been polishing ale glasses and rushed towards the general. Almost more quickly than Major Donelly could see—let alone act—the kitchen worker flashed a length of shining metal and pushed his hand against the posterior neck of the general, waited a moment, then allowed him to slump forward as if he had fallen asleep reading the *Times*.

Major Donelly hurled himself at the attacker and succeeded in enveloping his abdomen with a rear bear hug. The man in gray twisted violently and jabbed the major in his temple with the hard sharp bone of his right elbow. The movement and blow caught the major unawares and rendered him unconscious. When Major Donelly awakened—groggy and disoriented—he found himself alone on the floor beside the stuffed armchair in which Gen. Hill-Brownwell was sitting in unmoving repose. He was alone with the famous general and mildly frightened. At first—as his mind only slowly tried to develop a clear focus on the real world—he felt he had fallen asleep and had had a disturbing violent dream.

His mind cleared, and he worked his way to a standing position—made sure of his equilibrium—then assayed his surroundings. The most striking thing in the room was the handle of a monogramed club ice pick sticking directly in the middle of the back of Lt. Gen. Hill-Brownwell's neck. Less than half an inch of the bright steel of the pick was visible. The major avoided any disturbance of the room or the general, knowing that the old gentleman was dead. He did not require a doctor's opinion. His years of combat had offered him sufficient examples of death to allow him a comfortable level of expertise on the subject.

Major Donelly recovered his senses quickly, another benefit of having engaged more than once in hand-to-hand combat. He was short, powerfully built, and agile. He had a considerable amount of male pattern baldness which he partially disguised by keeping his hair clipped to less than an eighth of an inch long. His face was flat, a characteristic accentuated by his having suffered several nasal fractures which led to him having effectively lost the bridge of his nose. That defect was made up by his very prominent Adam's apple. His teeth were crooked and he was missing several; so, he kept his lips closed by entrenched habit. That made him appear to be perpetually somewhat angry or grumpy. His facial skin was clear of any blemishes, deeply tanned, and—by dint of scrupulous grooming—free of any facial hair, even sideburns. He was dressed in a casual afternoon olive-drab corduroy sports jacket, light tan military shirt, and heavy tweed trousers despite the oppressive heat. He wore riding boots, an affectation borne of his long suppressed desire to have been in the cavalry. He was sweating.

Evidently, no one else had witnessed the heinous act; so, it was up to the major to act and to act appropriately. He strode purposefully to the cord hanging from the ceiling near the doorway which connected the kitchen and the waiters' lounge to the gentlemen members' area. He gave two sharp pulls; and, in less than two minutes, a sleepy waiter in his starched club livery moved into the room.

"Brewster, there has been a crime here, my man," Major Donelly stated authoritatively. "Summon the Old Bills [slang for policemen] immediately."

He pointed at the obvious murder weapon sticking obscenely out of the back of the fine old veteran's neck.

Brewster had never seen a civilian murder victim before, and he required a gulp before he could react. He paused long enough for the major to move to get his attention.

"Get yourself together and ring up Whitehall 1212. I will mind the crime scene until the Bills get here."

Brewster was connected immediately to the dispatch operator at the CID.

"What is the nature of your problem, sir, and how may I direct your call?"

"This is Brewster, the majordomo at the Army and Navy Club. Put me through to the homicide division. We have had a murder here—a murder most foul!"

"Oh, dear, my good fellow, I will get the Special Branch right away! Please hold on the line."

She reached the office of Detective Chief Inspector Lincoln Crandall-White.

"DCI White here."

"Chief Inspector, do you have the duty this afternoon?"

"I do. Can I presume that you are about to disturb my plans for a comforting and restorative nap?"

"I'm afraid so, sir. I'm sorry to have to report that there has been a murder at the Army and Navy Club. The majordomo is on the line at this moment."

"This smells like a case that will interest the grand level of the MET divisional superintendent at the least. Lucky me."

"As they say in the States, 'Have a nice day, CID Crandall-White.' Now, I will turn the majordomo over to you."

"Majordomo Brewster is it?" Crandall-White asked. "May I ask your first name?"

"Clifford, sir."

"This is CID Crandall-White at this end. Are you in the club?"

"I am. I can see directly into the gentlemen's bar—the scene of the crime as it were."

"Is anyone else there, Brewster?"

"Only the major who found the body."

"Major...?"

"Oh, yes, Major Algernon Donelly, active duty RA."

"Has anyone disturbed the remains or anything in the room since the deceased was found?"

"No, sir. The major witnessed the murder itself not more than three or four minutes ago. He is minding the room. Nothing has been disturbed, let me assure you."

"We'll be there in two shakes of a dead lamb's tail. Keep up the good work."

The three CID coppers—DCI Crandall-White, DI Angela Snowden, and DI Anthony Bourden-Clift, arrived fifteen minutes later at 36-39 Pall Mall in St. James Square and parked their vehicle in front of the square box-shaped metal and glass seven-story building, not bothering to use the secure underground car park on the site. The two younger officers were mildly awed by the features of the West End—Mayfair and Covent Gardens, and the many attractions that neither of them could afford. Originally the building was built on number 18 St James's Square, at the north corner with King Street, with its exterior inspired by the Palazzo Corner in Venice. The latest iteration of the venerable old club was the more prosaic and modern building reconstructed in the 1950s after the war.

The three detectives moved quickly through the front entrance on the west side of St. James's Square and into the wood-paneled and heavily carpeted bar area. Major Donelly and Brewster stood stiffly to the side of the doorway into the bar to allow the police detectives to pass.

"Majordomo Brewster and Major Donelly, I presume," DCI Crandall-White said as he shook both men's hands warmly.

Each of them enjoyed the recognition, which set a friendly tone for the beginning of the interviews.

"No one else here this afternoon, I take it?"

"No, sir, just the two of us."

"Well, then. We'll get started. I would like Mr. Brewster to step into the office with me. DI Snowden and DI Bourden-Clift, please take Major Donelly to another room for interviews."

The office was set off from the members' area. It had the feel of a man's office—wood, leather, cigar smoke smell, and clutter. Brewster sat at his desk, and DCI Crandall-White took a seat in a comfortable old leather overstuffed armchair facing the majordomo. The DCI took a moment to observe the man he was about to interrogate—tall, lean, military bearing, and short-cropped haircut. He had an impressively well-sculpted curly dark brown mustache and beard cut in a neat combination of sideburns, muttonchop mustache, and Van-Dyke style beard which left his neck clean shaven. Scalp and facial hair were the same length. Brewster had a lean, lined, and tanned face bespeaking years outside. That and the well-tailored olive-drab, gold button, epaulets at the shoulders, and spit-polished black boots of his uniform spoke loudly of a military background—probably some long ago cavalry experience.

His military experience and the necessities of his duties as the majordomo of a very exclusive and expensive men's club had developed in Brewster a similar penchant for sizing up a man whom he faced. The DCI was a large, powerful man whose inexpensive civilian suit did not quite disguise the muscularity of his frame or his military bearing. The DCI had a simple mustache, more in the current British style than Brewster's own. Crandall-White had a full strong face—not handsome, but one that commanded attention. His eyes were keen–nearly cobalt blue–and steady. He was early middle-aged, but his lean athletic figure belied that. He was dressed in a blue serge suit, one of several he owned. His tie matched his suit. His shoes needed a polishing; and his white shirt and his suit needed pressing; but Brewster was quite sure that Crandall-White did not care a whit for such vain interests. He was all business.

DCI Crandall-White waited a full minute before speaking, then he went directly to the heart of the matter as Brewster expected that he would, "Who were Gen. Sir Hill-Brownwell's enemies, Brewster?"

"I have been waiting for that question, Chief Inspector. I did not know the man personally to any degree, but I have had the opportunity to observe him and his interactions with the other members for more than a decade. He was a regular here. He served on the western front in the first war, and I recall one member who confronted him some years back for his behind-the-lines service. The gist of the heated conversation was that the lieutenant general was quick to order men to charge out of their trenches to what he must have known were near-suicidal and futile attacks, and the men serving under him despised him. Sir Hill-Brownwell's response was a counter accusation—essentially that the man confronting him might well be one of the cowards who had conspired to assassinate him as the commander. The staff had to come between the two. Sir Hill-Brownwell's position in the club was of such an elevated nature that his accuser was forced to resign."

"Name?"

"I can't bring it to mind at the moment, but I will do some research and get back to you on that, if that would be acceptable, sir."

"I would appreciate it. Any other confrontations or enemies?"

"Not directly. However–like any senior officer–there were petty jealousies and perceived slights by his junior officers. I have sat in pubs and listened to bits and pieces of conversations among the enlisted who served under him—enough to know that he was a highly unpopular officer in both wars. Again, the gist was that he enjoyed his comforts in the safety of his command post while keeping well out of harm's way, if you get my drift.

"He was deemed to be an extremely harsh disciplinarian, even an unfair one by many officers and enlisted alike.

"His areas of service might well have generated enemies as well. I don't know if you are aware, but Sir Hill-Brownwell served as head of the military police department in the British sector of Berlin at the close of the last war. Many officers—I understand—bore him ill-will for the ruination of their reputations and careers owing to his penchant for rushing to judgment and for his dictatorial style which did not allow for what the men considered an adequate defense which might take in extenuating circumstances or even opposing testimony. Several complaints were filed against him during that period."

"You seem to be quite well-versed in the general's career, Brewster. I have to ask: were you one of those men who was treated shabbily by the general during or after the war?"

For the first time there was a moment of emotion that showed in his face, but it passed like a distant rain cloud.

There was a very brief but telling pause before Brewster responded.

"Well, since you bring it up, I did have a black mark placed on my record as a result of decisions made by the general during that period. You may check the records yourself, Inspector, but basically this is what happened: Sir Hill-Brownwell had a specially selected team of investigators and enforcers whose task was to monitor and to control the German POWs returning to the British sector after their release from military prisons. The general hated the Nazis passionately, and went well out of his way to find ways to make the transition back into civilian life for the Germans as difficult as possible. The records are sealed, and few people in the general public are aware of just how brutal and unjust the occupying forces were throughout Germany up to the end of the occupation. I served under the general in a more-or-less mundane roll as a military policeman. I saw a great deal of brutality—even murder— of former POWs, and I made the personal mistake of reporting such improper actions up the chain of command.

"In my own defense, there is developing documentation that something on the order of a million Germans were killed—most murdered—by Allied occupiers, and that was a fact that the officers in charge were determined to keep secret until well after their own deaths sometime in the far distant future. My report came to the attention of Lieutenant-General Sir Cyril Goeffrey Robert Hill-Brownwell."

His voice cracked slightly with what was obviously long pent-up emotion.

"I was never brought up on charges nor had a chance to defend myself in the commanding officer's summary hearing. I was not informed of such a hearing and certainly had no opportunity of having the services of a judge advocate general's attorney. No, indeed. I simply was given a formal written reprimand, demoted one rank, and transferred back to the ranks serving at Sandhurst—well away from the occupied territories. Within a year, I was informed that I was to be discharged from the service. A young officer informed me that it would be most imprudent to protest because that would result in me receiving a bad conduct discharge. I tucked my tail between my legs and found work in the private sector, namely in the Army and Navy Club. It was real test of my mettle to keep quiet day after day when I was obliged to serve and to be obsequious and deferential to the man I so despised."

"Were you the man who stabbed Sir Hill-Brownwell and fought off Major Donelly, Brewster?"

"I was not, much as I would have enjoyed doing so."

DCI Crandall-White allowed an awkward silence to descend on the interrogation. Both men locked eyes, and neither blinked.

"Did you and Major Donelly join forces to murder the man?"

"No. The murder took place just as the major described."

"How do you know that, Brewster? Were you an actual witness?"

Brewster paused briefly.

"Well, technically, no, I did not actually witness the killing. I did not see the man Major Donelly described. I assumed that the major is a man of honor and upright British character and had no reason to lie."

"That remains to be seen, I suppose. What do you know about the major? Do you have any knowledge of ill-will between him and the general?"

"I have only seen entirely proper and courteous interchanges between the two men, Chief Inspector. In my recollection, such encounters were few and far between since the major was an infrequent guest on the premises. I would say that the men passed only most limited and casual greetings—polite but neither cordial nor inhospitable."

"Um hmmh. Please tell me your impression of the major. Is he a man prone to anger? Has he expressed grudges, especially such ill feelings toward the general?"

"Major Donelly tends to keep to himself. Not very talkative to anyone. I have never heard him express any kind of ill-will towards any individual. He, too, was involved in the occupation forces at the end of the war. As I understand it, he was an officer in charge of the interim camps where returning German POWs were processed after returning from the Soviet prison camps. The only thing I ever recall him saying about that is that those men were deserving of the harsh lives they had endured under the Soviet gulag system, and they would not be men ever to be allowed to occupy significant positions in the new Germany being created by the Allies. Donelly was a captain at that time, as I recall."

"It's time for a spot of lunch," the DCI said, and the three coppers left for Charlie Brown's Railway Tavern on West India Dock Road.

Charlie Brown's lived up to its designation as a public house, a true pub. The place was a world apart from cafés, bars, *bierkellers*, and even brewpubs. It had a sort of museum—a collection of curiousities patrons had brought in from all around the world. Its windows were made of smoked glass to obscure the clientele from looky-loos on the street. It was a decidedly decadent working class joint with bare board floors covered with sawdust to absorb the spitting and regular spillages—so, it was one of the 'spit and sawdust' pubs the gentry would never admit to patronizing. However, the place was always full of gents and coppers despite the hard uncomfortable seating accomodations. They got a laugh out of the place. Charlie Brown's was a gastro-pub, one of the best in the city for all of its seediness and apparent lack of sanitation.

The three detective inspectors ordered family-style plates of corned beef and sausage with mustard and pretzels, goat cheese and roasted tomato with sourdough bread and olive oil, and crispy pig's ears served with lime, kosher salt, and chili. They splurged by ordering bakewell tart with heavy clotted cream for dessert, and took a few turns at trap shooting before settling down for their meal and beer.

English Recipes

Bakewell Tart—Serves Three or Four

Ingredients
-For shortcrust pastry—6 oz white flour, 2½ oz chilled butter, 2–3 tbsp cold water.
-For the filling—1 tbsp raspberry jam, 4½ oz butter, 4½ oz caster sugar, 4½ oz ground almonds, 1 beaten egg, ½ tsp almond extract, 1¾ oz flaked almonds.
-For the icing—2¾ oz icing sugar, 2½ tsp cold water

Preparation
-Pastry—put flour into a bowl and rib in butter with fingertips until the mixture is the texture of fine bread crumbs. Add water, mixing to form a soft dough. Roll out the dough on a lightly floured work surface and use to line an 8 in flan tin. Chill in the fridge for 30 mins.
-Preheat the oven to 400° F.
-Line the pastry case with aluminum foil and fill with baking beans. Bake blind-15 mins., then remove the beans and foil and cook for a further five mins. to dry out the base.

-Filling—spread the base of the flan generously with raspberry jam.

-Melt the butter in a pan, take off the heat, and then stir in the sugar. Add ground almonds, egg, and almond extract. Pour into the flan tin and sprinkle over the flaked almonds.

-Bake about 35 mins. If the almonds brown too quickly, cover the tart loosely with foil to prevent burning.

-Icing—Sift icing sugar into a separate bowl. Stir in cold water and transfer to a piping bag when ready. Remove tart from the oven, pipe the icing over the top in a zigzag design.

-Devonshire cream— Pour 2 pts heavy, lightly pasturized cream into a heavy-bottomed oven-safe pot. For extra richness, may add ¼ cube whipped butter. Fill to 1–3 ins. Cover pot and place in oven at 180° F for at least 8 hrs. It is done when a thick yellowish skin forms above the cream. That skin is the clotted cream. Cool pot at room temperature then in fridge for another 8 hrs. Apply liberally to the pastry at time of serving.

CHAPTER SIXTEEN

The Army and Navy Club in London [popularly known as The Rag], 36-39 Pall Mall, St. James Square, Sixth Floor Conference Room

In the conference room five floors up at the same time as DCI Crandall-White was questioning Majordomo Brewster, Major Donelly was stiff and ill-at-ease. That was not surprising given his recent experience. It was evident that he was none too keen on having to submit to questioning by the police. When the police officers first arrived on the scene, he had naively felt that his word as a Royal Army officer would suffice, and that would be the end of it. DI Bourden-Clift stood behind his partner Angela Snowden, projecting a calm but calculated menace. That image had its desired effect—that of unnerving Maj. Donelly. He calmed down as DI Snowden asked the first question.

Snowden was such a striking figure of a woman, that most men—even those of rank—were a bit in awe of her. She had coal-black shiny hair which–at the moment–was done up in a tight bun, and snowy white unblemished skin. She did not wear any makeup, yet her lips were full and rosy; and her cheeks had that hint of color that women everywhere try to emulate with their makeup. She was tall and buxom, even in her sensible black shoes. She wore a fine woolen lady's suit and a light-blue silk blouse. Although her bosom strained the material, DI Snowden had been meticulous to be certain that no hint of what lay beneath the shimmering blue material was allowed to see the light of day. She gave Major Donelly a brief friendly smile and then started with hard, direct questions without any attempt at ice-breaking social chit-chat.

"Are you aware of any animosity on the part of Majordomo Brewster towards Lieutenant-General Sir Cyril Goeffrey Robert Hill-Brownwell?"

"I am to some extent—nothing I could actually document, however, Inspector."

"This is just preliminary fact-finding, Major. Let us be the judges of what may be important or not."

"I have noticed that Brewster seems to avoid—seems to have avoided—the general during the times I have frequented the club. That was unusual since being affable and helpful are part and parcel of the majordomo's duties. I once commented on that to the general just by way of making polite conversation, and he was quite brusque with me. 'Not your concern, young man,' he said, or words to that effect. I am naturally inquisitive; so, I did two things: first I queried Brewster; and second, I got into the regimental files a bit. That was not particularly difficult.

"I hope I am not telling tales out of school...."

"That would mean that you may not have the right to give the information you are prepared to give, or even that you are not entirely certain whether or not your information is correct. It also could mean that you would be breaking some sort of gentlemanly code of conduct that would make your communication mere gossip and that you might indiscreetly reveal private matters, secrets, or confidences. Let me remind you that this is a police investigation, and none of that is applicable here. We need your information, and withholding such information could be considered obstruction of justice," DI Bourden-Clift stated with unsmiling authority, taking over the questioning—a smooth transition between the two partners to keep the person being interrogated off-guard and ill at ease.

"Of course, of course. I understand completely. One evening after regular hours, I invited Brewster to join me in the gentlemen's bar. We tossed back a few and were somewhat in our cups. I asked the man if there was some issue between him and the general. It was the first time I saw Brewster let down his guard. He told me that he had served as a sergeant major under Sir Hill-Brownwell in the British sector after the cessation of hostilities. He related a tale of having had a discrediting mark placed in his service file by the general. It is a matter of record that Sir Hill-Brownwell headed up the British occupation military police regiment. Brewster told me that the general had a specially selected team of investigators and enforcers whose task was to monitor and control the German POWs returning to the British sector after their release from military prisons. It was Brewster's conviction that the general hated all Nazis, and that he went overboard to make the transition back into civilian life for the Germans as difficult as possible. He even indicated that there were atrocities. That is more than just Brewster's opinion. I am a witness myself, and I can state without equivocation that all of the Allied occupation forces inflicted vengeful acts of retribution against former military and government personnel, their families, and on random civilians. There was torture, job and educational discrimination, and even murder—maybe upwards of a million—maybe more—deaths. Brewster complained that the official records are sealed, and few people in the general public are aware of just how brutal and unjust the occupying forces were throughout Germany up to the end of the occupation. I am afraid that I am of the same opinion. During my service I saw things, heard things, and read things, which would be a great disappointment to the British people.

"Brewster told me that in his capacity as a sergeant major he served under the general in a more-or-less mundane role as a military policeman. He rattled off a litany of brutality, even witnessing murder of former POWs. His very words were, 'I made the personal mistake of reporting such improper actions up the chain of command.' Apparently that report made its way up the chain of command to the desk of Sir Hill-Brownwell."

Donelly paused and looked over at the two detective inspectors to gain permission to continue. They nodded their heads.

"Brewster told me that he was never publically brought up on charges, but he never had an opportunity to present his side of the story ... not even when charges were brought up against him in the commanding officer's summary hearing conducted by the man he was accusing. Brewster said he was not even informed of such a hearing and was never assigned the services of a judge advocate general's attorney to defend him. He was peremptorily given a formal written reprimand, demoted one rank to first sergeant, and transferred back to the ranks serving at Sandhurst—well away from the occupied territories. Although his ambition was to retire on a pension after a thirty-year

unblemished career, he was discharged from the service with the nota-
tion that the discharge was a routine matter of reduction of forces for
peacetime. Brewster went on to tell me that a young officer told him
in no uncertain terms that it would not at all be in his best interests
to protest. When he started to argue, he was told point blank that he
would receive a bad conduct discharge if he did so—and that would
haunt him for the rest of the days.

"He shut his mouth and left with his pension. It took him a year or
two, but he finally found work in the private sector, specifically here in
the Army and Navy Club in London. Brewster was not an emotional
man; that evening with his tongue loosened by the demon rum, he
said it was a severe burden for him to keep his lips zipped day after day
when he had to meet, serve, and be obsequious and deferential to the
man detested and whom he believed to be a war criminal."

"I see. And how about yourself, Major, do you bear the general ill
will? Do you share Brewster's opinions?" asked DI Snowden.

"I agree with Brewster's analysis of postwar occupation issues in the
British sector. I personally only served in the returning POW camps.
I have to say that it was difficult to me as a former enemy combatant
against those bestial Nazis to have to treat them with any degree of
civility. If it had been up to me, I would have executed the lot and let
God sort out the guilty from the innocent. I don't believe that would
have been all that difficult. Less than a handful would have fallen into
the innocent category. There were even Frenchmen who served in Nazi
SS regiments who returned to my camp. Did you know that?"

When there was no answer, Donelly continued his narrative. "My
fellow officers from the UK, the US, and the other allies felt the same
about them. We did not give them any privileges; but by the same
token, we were fair and decent in our treatment of them. No murders
or tortures by my POW camp officers. I am afraid it was different in
the civilian population. It seems likely that Brewster was correct in his
complaints. He seems a decent sort; so, I am inclined to believe his
personal rendition of his and the general's interactions."

Major Donelly took a few needed breaths and regained his composure completely before DI Bourden-Clift resumed the questioning
started by DI Snowden, now taking a different and harder tack.

Bourden-Clift was the polar opposite of his partner, the attractive
DC Snowden. He was a black man, one of the few black detectives in

the entire police force. He was as black at his end of the continuum as Snowden was white on her end. He was decidedly unattractive with a flat nose and flaring nostrils; his irises were so dark that it seemed that he did not have pupils. His lips were large and two-toned, and offputting where Snowden's small cupid's bow lips drew people to listen to her. The two partners played off each other seamlessly, and usually to the detriment of a guilty perpetrator they were tag-teaming.

"Major, you were alone in the bar with the general. Is that your statement?"

"Yes, until the murderer came in from the bar pantry and launched his attack."

"Are you sure the murderer was a man?"

"Yes. I did see his face. His bodily movements were that of a man."

"How far away were you standing when the murderer attacked Gen. Hill-Brownwell?"

"Perhaps ten or twelve meters. I was about to exit the building when I caught a glimpse of the man rushing in to inflict what I at first believed was a blow—a sort of judo chop—to the back of the elderly man's neck, a despicable cowardly act."

"Indeed. But you learned differently later."

"I did. First, though, I rushed to try and save the general. I tried to tackle the villain; but he was apparently adept in the military hand-to-hand arts; and he got the better of me I am ashamed to report."

"I take it that you have a well-developed skill set in the martial arts yourself, is that not the case, Major?"

"I take a modicum of pride in my training and skills. I have won tournaments and have had direct experience in unarmed hand-to-hand combat during my career. I have to admit that the murderer was better than me. It was obvious that I had engaged a trained soldier or perhaps a skilled assassin. Whatever the case, he knocked me cold. I guess I should feel lucky to be alive."

"What did you discover when you came to?"

"It took a while, but finally I studied the scene. It was quite evident that the general was dead. I had been wrong about what the assailant was doing. It was certainly no judo chop. I saw the handle of one of the bar's ice picks driven into the junction between his skull and his neck—a favorite killing site. I myself was trained to try to stab or bayonet an opponent through what the anatomists call the foramen magnum. That results in an instant death due to a cut or transection of the brain stem. This murderer knew with precision what he was doing."

"It would seem that you yourself are quite knowledgeable on the subject, Major. What you are telling us that the general had been pithed—apparently quite expertly. I have to ask: did you murder Gen. Hill-Brownwell?"

Major Donelly looked shocked.

He raised his voice, "I most certainly did no such thing! I am neither a murderer nor a liar, and I take great offence at your inference."

"No need for a display of anger, Major. These are just questions that have to be asked. DI Snowden and I are just doing our jobs, however distasteful they may be. I'm sure you understand," DI Bourden-Clift soothed.

Major Donelly worked to ratchet down his emotions several notches and nodded his understanding. He could not entirely erase the look of resentment from his facial expression.

"Major, the Army and Navy Club is a gentleman's club for commissioned officers of all ranks in Her Majesty's Regular Army, Royal Navy, and Royal Marines. Is that correct?"

"Yes."

"Although it must seem beyond any reasonable possibility, is there any member or person on the staff at the club who could have committed this terrible crime?"

"Not for the life of me can I think of a living soul who is a member or on the staff here. But then, I did not really know many of the members or staff that well."

"How about Brewster? Did he have motive enough, means, and opportunity, do you think?"

"Circumstantially, I suppose. However, my encounters with the man face-to-face would not lead me to consider him to be a suspect. I looked into the face of the killer. It was not Brewster. Furthermore, as I think about it, if he did want to kill the general—even by use of a proxy—why wait until today, years after the incidents which angered him took place? Surely there was a more opportune time or place during that decade or so."

"It would seem," DI Snowden agreed.

"Oh, and it occurred to me that the man I put my arms around to tackle was taller. Besides—and most obvious to me—I saw his face. He was older than Brewster, had short white hair, and several facial scars which looked altogether like dueling saber scars. Strong and swift as he was, I think I saw a bit of a limp as he was running towards the general."

"That is helpful, Major. Do you have any further questions for the major, Tony?"

DI Anthony Bourden-Clift shook his head.

"Then, that should be it for now, Major Donelly. Thank you for your assistance and cooperation. Please don't leave the city. We may have further questions as our investigation continues."

After Donelly left the room, Bourden-Clift, asked, "So what's your take, Angela?"

"He seems genuine, but the circumstantial evidence points to him as the first person of interest and to Brewster as the second."

"Or the pair of them as the third," Bourden-Clift added, and Snowden nodded her agreement.

"Both of them are experienced military veterans, fit, and, at least—in the major's case—young and athletic," Bourden-Clift went on. "I can't get it into my head that either of them would murder for the reasons we have heard. They are practical men, and revenge would seem like an inadequate motive this far out."

After they joined DCI Crandall-White on the first floor, the three detectives went over what they had learned.

The DCI added the final note, "We have our work cut out for us, and we ought not to jump to any hasty conclusions. We need to know everything there is to know about our three persons of interest first, then about the membership and staff of the club; and finally, we will have to get into the old military records and the files on the POW camps. Maybe we just don't know about some revenge-seeking German who finally snapped and came after our general. One of those former POWs could be our man. We will have to wear out some shoe leather and do some regular 'Old Bill' flatfoot work. This is not going to be a simple or quick investigation. Since we are dealing with a senior army officer, we will likely encounter some flack and considerable lack of cooperation both from the army and from her majesty's government."

"I'll work on the British records," said Angela, the star analyst of the team.

"I'll put in a few calls, and try and see if there are other murders like this one. If this is a revenge murder, it is possible that the perpetrators hold a grudge against other men and even foreign nationals," Tony offered.

"I'll shepherd the evidence and run interference with the chiefs of the 'Old Bills,' the government tops, and push the brass at Northwood. I will probably run into a lot of static, but there is more to this crime than meets the eye. It was certainly no robbery. Sir Hill-Brownell had a Rolex watch, a diamond pinky ring, and a billfold full of pound notes, all untouched."

"Before this is over, Boss, and you have talked to the man—and we have offended the veterans and the foreign nations, we will probably conclude that we have really stepped in it," Angela said.

"That's why we get all the rhino and the nicker [centuries-old British slang for ready cash or big money]," DCI Crandall-White said.

The team of three left the Army and Navy Club and drove back to the CID on Victoria Embankment.

BOOK TWO

WHY

CHAPTER SEVENTEEN

Magadan, Siberia, April 1953

The two men were too exhausted to be able to enjoy a psychological, spiritual, or philosophical sense of being free men after eight years of enslavement in the harshest of all the world's prisons. They were gaunt, sallow complexioned, and shrunken. After little more than an hour of cautiously savoring the novelty of being free from the homicidal confines of the Butugychag Tin Mine—the Soviet Siberian gulag on the Kolyma River camp for German POWs who were designated for "special treatment"—the novelty gave way to more primal concerns. Paramount of these concerns was the need for food. The two men were starving, just as they had been for the past eight years. And it was cold; they needed better clothing and some sort of shelter.

For all they knew, they had the dubious distinction of being the only members of their regiment still alive. They moved away from the other former prisoners, a natural grouping in which countrymen tended to find some similitude of camaraderie with their own. Hungarians, Serbs, Germans, and Baltics went their separate ways two-by-two. The two men—who looked like emaciated raggedy hoboes—were soon all lost among a milling populace of exceedingly poor and deprived Northern Russians who were just eking out a living in an unforgiving land. Most of those people had arrived during the recent war as displaced persons and were only a little better off than the newly released prisoners of the gulag. No one took an interest in anyone else. No one had the strength or resources to give help to another human being. Although it was somewhat better than the gulag, it was still a Hobbesian world.

Antoine and Michaele were used to hard work; the basic philosophy in the camp had been work or die. So, they set to work. They stole a grubbing hoe with a heavy iron head and an old shovel and dug themselves a rude pit in the side of an embankment which allowed at least some respite from the biting wind. They waited until darkness fell before daring to venture out to steal food. Both men were sure that the semi-starving wretches in the city and on the hardscrabble farms would guard their caches of food to the death. It was bitter cold and a starless dark night; both of those climatic conditions worked in their favor. They were accustomed to working in near darkness and to being cold. They knew from bitter experience that they had to keep moving, or they would die. They also knew that without food another day, they would weaken and become unable to forage or to defend themselves.

A light ahead alerted them to the possibility that they were seeing a farmhouse, and they began to hope for the possibility of food. They kept to the brushy areas along the road, and the going was slow. Antoine hand-signaled for Michaele to move to the rear of the rude hut while he moved slowly and quietly towards the front on the opposite side. He heard a woman singing a *vesnyanky* [song invoking the spring season] in an old scratchy voice. There was accompaniment by a *Yat-kha* [long zither similar to Korean *gayageum*]. Antoine had a brief moment of nostalgia. He had heard the local people living outside the Gulag prison occasionally singing folk music and playing on their very different string instruments. He shook his head to clear his thoughts. He and Michaele had work to do, not the sort of work that could allow any softness like nostalgia to intrude.

He peered in the window. It appeared that there were only two people in the room—old ones dressed in dirty ragged peasant tunics, not so different from his own. A woodstove was ablaze, and on it was an iron pot filled with a thick bubbling stew. The reaction in his salivary glands and stomach was so intense that it was painful. The reaction drove out every other thought than food. He moved to the back and signaled Michaele. His gesture pointed towards the interior of the hut. He returned to the front; and—when he was set–he gave two sharp shrill whistles.

Antoine smashed through the door; and Michaele pushed his way into the living quarters, passing through a pen containing pigs, sheep, and goats. The old lady fainted, and the old man put his zither vertically in front of himself in a reflex defensive move. He did not utter a sound. When Antoine swung his shovel at the old man's head, the victim did not flinch or throw his forearms or hands up in defense. The sound of the shovel blade striking the peasant's head was like a watermelon being struck. Michaele smashed the old lady's head with the heavy iron blade of the grubbing hoe. From the time of entry into the hut until the couple was dead, less than three minutes had elapsed. The two former Gulag prisoners dragged the bodies out of the hut and up to the top of the low hill behind it. They shoveled out a shallow pit in the snow and chopped down a pile of birch tree branches to cover the bodies. The deaths of Karp and Marita Petrenko were not discovered for three years, two years after Antoine and Michaele were herded aboard busses and taken via the Kolyma Highway [known to the local populace as the "Road of Bones"] and loaded onto uncomfortable buses and troop trucks to Tommot where they were herded onto the Amur-Yakutia Mainline train for a fourteen-day starving trip all the way to Moscow.

The Petrenkos were among the limited number of survivors of mass deportees from all around Russia at the outset of the successful Bolshevik revolution. Their crime was that they were Kulaks—supposedly rich farmers, almost as antithetical to the communists as if they had been part of the bourgeoisie. Their records were lost, and anyone who knew of them back in Stalingrad where they were born would presume that they had long since perished in the barren frigidity of the far north.

The two starving men ate the entire cauldron of rich vegetable and mutton soup. It was savory and delicious and full of fresh vegetables. They engaged in a frenzy of devouring their first decent food in almost a decade. Antoine and Michaele ate too much and too fast for stomachs unused to being filled up, especially with cream and mutton fat-based broth. The two ex-POWs cursed and laughed as the rich meal exited both ends of their alimentary tracks in a night-long orgy of vomiting and diarrhea. Once they were cleaned out and able to be up and about again, they commenced a program of eating the year's supply of food they discovered in the kitchen, the pantry, and the pens of their victims. Having vowed to exercise more prudence, they waited a day then slaughtered one of the goats and made another stew. It was as good as the mutton stew, and this time they were able to eat smaller portions and to savor the rich meat—something lacking in their diets for the past eight years.

At first Antoine and Michaele alternated guard duty in an around-the-clock vigil to defend themselves and their invaluable treasure of food and warm clothing. After a few months—and no one came to bother them—the two men relaxed and became Siberian farmers, tilling the fields, planting, and harvesting. They were none too good at farm work, however; and over the next several months, their efforts were not nearly as productive as the Petrenkos' had been. When the harsh fall began to change to bitter winter, Antoine and Michaele finally had to admit that the idyllic peaceful and safe pastoral life they had envisioned for themselves was not going to persist. By late October, they were out of food. Both men had regained body weight, fat, and muscle, and could go for perhaps a month before they would begin to deteriorate seriously.

Having advanced their life's condition to the point that they were genuinely healthy, neither man had any intention of returning to the condition they were in when they lived in the tin mine gulag. They decided to become hunters. The former prisoners knew they had to exercise great caution to avoid detection or capture—or even drawing attention toward themselves. They worked only at night and walked many miles away from their small home on the outskirts of Magadan. During the first week, they were able to steal two decent horses and enough provisions to last them a week. The horses gave them a wider latitude for their predations; and by mid-December, they had accumulated a food storage sufficient to keep them going for the next two months. They decided not to go out again until it was absolutely necessary, even if it meant having to kill and eat their horses.

The ground was still hard frozen down to the permafrost, and the nearly constant early March wind blew away patches of the accumulated snow, leaving stretches of bare ice. The cold was dreadful—falling as low as -45 to -65 degrees Fahrenheit most days. The early spring winds drove the effective temperature to fifteen degrees colder than that every night and until noon most mornings. Antoine and Michaele suffered from the cold, but considered it an advantage because no one but a mad man would venture out. Taking a breath at that level of cold would result in actual freezing of a man's lungs.

They had not factored into their life's equation the concept that others besides lunatics would venture out. There were also desperate men out there whose approaching starvation would drive them to attempt to take the two farmers' food, even at the risk of being killed in the effort.

§§§§§

In the very early morning hours of a bitterly cold night, Michaele awakened with a start. Antoine was snoring like a tank engine. Michaele gently placed his hand over his companion's open mouth to silence him. Antoine became instantly awake. Michaele put his right index finger to his lips in the universal request for silence.

"What, *mon frère?*" Antoine whispered.

The two men listened so intently that they hardly breathed.

There it was again. The horses were restless and apparently rearing and kicking.

"Wolves?" Antoine asked.

Siberian Peasant Recipes

Pot Roast of Horse—Feeds 4

Ingredients
-2¾ boneless hindquarter roast, cut to fit pot. 2 tbsps oil-melted horse fat will do well; salt and pepper to taste.
-1 tbsp Worcestershire sauce, 1 tsp beef boullion, 1 tsp crushed dried basil, $\frac{3}{4}$ lb new potatoes and or 2 med. sweet potatoes, 1 lb carrots or 6 medium parsnips, peeled, cut into 2 in. pieces, 2 onions, cut into wedges, 2 celery ribs cut into 1 in. pieces
-$\frac{1}{4}$ cup flour

Preparation
-Trim fat from meat. Brown meat on all sides in hot oil in a 4– to 6–qt Dutch oven or pot. Drain fat.
-Mix 3/4 cup water, Worcestershire sauce, bouillon, basil and salt and pepper to taste; pour over roast and bring to boil. Reduce heat to simmer, covered, 1 hr.
-Quarter all new potatoes or peel and quarter sweet potatoes. Add potatoes, carrots, onions, and celery to pot. Return to boil. Reduce heat. Then simmer covered, until tender~45–60 mins. Add water as needed. Check for tenderness. May have to boil tough horse meat longer. Do not overcook vegetables.
-Transfer meat and vegetables to platter. Reserve juices.
-Prepare gravy: skim off fat, add juices and enough water to make 1½ cps. Return to oven.

In a small bowl, stir ½ cp water into flour. Stir into pan juices. Cook, stirring, on med heat until thickened, then 1 min. more. Season to taste. Serve with pot roast.

-After browning meat and adding liquid mixture to pan, bake, covered, for 1 hr at 325° F.

-Add prepared potatoes and vegetables to meat. Bake, covered, until tender, another 45–60 mins. Add gravy.

CHAPTER EIGHTEEN

Magadan, Siberia, March 1954

Michaele slipped silently out of the bed they shared and crawled on his hands and knees towards the rude window facing out to where the horses' corral was located. What he saw caused him to crawl like a man possessed.

"Not wolves," he said, "at least not the four-legged kind."

"*Voleurs* [thieves]?" Antoine hissed.

Michaele nodded, and he and Antoine moved into efficient and determined action which was second nature to them after their long careers as soldiers. They had set aside an assortment of weapons, including two Kalashnikov rifles they had managed to procure during one of their own nightly raids as *voleurs*.

Each man took a window to reconnoiter the magnitude of the threat and the direction from which it would came. They knew that thieves that brazen would not hesitate to kill them, even if only to buy a period of silence. The Patrenkos had purchased Antoine and Michaele two years of relative safety at the cost of their lives.

It was clear that all activity was taking place in the rear of the hut; and, for the moment, at least, all attention was centered on their horses. There were four men—men larger than the old Kulaks still eking out a living on the permafrost, and considerably larger that the indigenous Yakutsks—all dressed in heavy padded clothing and all carrying Kalashnikovs and swords. This was going to be fight, one that would require more brains than brawn if the two former gulag prisoners were going to survive.

"Out the front. You go left, and I'll go right," Antoine said. "We'll get behind them. They won't expect us coming from there."

Each of them was armed with a Kalashnikov, a hatchet, and a machete. The cold was numbing to their bodies and to their minds, but it was a mutual enemy for both sets of combatants.

They outflanked their unsuspecting predators. On a signal from Antoine, he and Michaele screamed the battle cry of their division, "*Gott mit uns* [God with us]!" and hurled themselves at the unsuspecting thieves.

One of the thieves was able to think very quickly under the stress of the surprise attack.

"*Dieu avec uks!*" he shouted.

The effect was stunning. All six men stopped in their tracks for a crucial moment upon hearing the same battle cry uttered in French with the clarity of a native-born speaker. Six automatic rifles continued to point at the chests of putative opponents. No one spoke; they hardly breathed during that pregnant moment. The most important thing was that no one squeezed his trigger.

"*Wer Sie sind* [who are you]?" Antoine asked, breaking the stalemate.

"*Charlemagne,*" one of the men replied in an unmistakable Parisian accent.

"*Driunddrissigsten* [thirty-third]?" Michaele asked calmly.

"*Oui, trente-troisième,* I am *Waffen SS-Obersturmbannführer* [lieutenant colonel] Serge Alain Rounsavall," the apparent leader of the four estwhile thieves announced.

The other three men introduced themselves:

"*Waffen SS-Sturmbannführer* [Senior Battalion Leader] Hugues Beauchamp."

"*Waffen SS-Sturmbannführer* [Major] Jean Luc Latendresse."

"*Waffen SS-Hauptsturmführer* [Head Company Unit Storm Leader] Jérôme Christophe Mailhot, at your service."

Antoine and Michaele glanced at each other and gave a crisp nod of reassurance.

"*Gruppenführer und Generalleutnant der Waffen-SS* Antoine Duvalier."

"*Waffen SS-Oberführer* Michaele Dupont."

In an almost instantaneous semirobotic simultaneous motion, five right hands saluted General Duvalier with the *Hitlergruss*. Then the six men broke into laughter, grins, and embraces. For each of them, it was the first genuine moment of pleasure they had enjoyed since they were captured and imprisoned in the inhuman gulag.

"I was afraid that I was the only one left from the division," Latendresse said.

"Until the two of us met and finally, we were able to identify Mailhot and Beauchamp," said Rounsavall.

"We were of the belief that only the two of us had survived from the entire division," said Dupont.

In fact, the division numbered only sixty men by May 1945, and less than a third of that number by the time the last German POW was released by the Soviets in 1956.

"You four are four more than we thought existed," Antoine said. "We should start up another regiment."

The four newcomers were as healthy, well-fed, and fit as Antoine and Michaele. Serge was the acknowledged leader, largely because of his markedly superior physical strength. He had a heavyweight lifter's rotund body packed with muscle. He had a peasant's bland face which belied the fact that he was a professional killer and a survivor against all odds. He had stringy brown hair down to his shoulder blades and a full face beard that made him look like Rasputin. He was dressed in heavy furs—pants included—taken from another pair of old Kulaks. His eyes were squinty and small; in fact his vision was none too good owing to his lifelong myopia [severe nearsightedness] and the nonavailability of suitable eyeglasses. Once the men retired to the warmth of Antoine and Michaele's cozy cottage, Serge stripped down to his bare chest, which made all the men laugh because his chest and back was so hirsute that he looked like he had simply changed sets of furs.

Hugues was lanky and somewhat awkard. He had large hands and even larger feet. No shoes had been available for him in the internment camp, and he had had to make do with rags and rabbit skins. Now, he wore crude—but adequately fitted—hand-sewn horse hide mocassins lined with rabbit fur. His face was lined with the stresses he had suffered since 1945 when he was captured after the Battle of Berlin, but he had somehow retained his youthful look. His face and his hair did not match. He had turned gray after the end of the twelve-day Battle of Berlin due to having little or no sleep, or food, or relief from the constant bombardment and the accompanying soul-searing stress. He stood six feet six inches tall and changed from the skeleton he was during the camp years into a tall, fit, and rugged appearance. He had a wispy beard and head of hair, unlike Serge; but like Serge, he had never bothered to cut it. He was wearing a Russian peasant tunic and trousers made out of heavy gray wool. His trousers were held up by a four-inch wide black belt that he and his comrades had found in a cabin of an old Cossack whom they had murdered. One holdover from his prison days was a cadaverous gray skin pallor which gave him an almost zombie look. No one could win in a blinking contest with the still surviving Charlemagne soldier.

Jean Luc Latendresse was born a peasant and had resigned himself to grubbing out a meager living from the ground of Alsace-Lorraine. The occupation by the Germans had changed all that. When he was sixteen, his ardent Catholic and even more ardent anti-communist parents had gotten him admitted to the University of Lorraine in Metz to study in the theology department with the hope that he would become a priest one day. He learned Catholicism and the duties of the priesthood, of course; but he learned it from a faculty of rabidly anti-communist, French nationalistic, priests who were dedicated to the destruction of the Antichrists, as they termed the Reds. As soon as he was big enough to pass for eighteen, he traveled with two dozen other young men from his village and volunteered to join the Wehrmacht. In less than a year he was an officer in the SS.

Jean Luc had the great advantage facilitating advancement in the SS of being an indisputable Aryan. Not only was his appearance Nordic—strong-jawed, tall, and straight—but the recruiters were given full access to his family's eight-generation genealogy—not a hint of any variant in the purity of the Aryan legacy. His face was open and ruddy, rather innocent-looking for all that he had done for the SS. He had no scars; his nose was Frankish and large; but for the first time in his life, that was a plus. At the moment he was dressed in three layers of peasant clothes stolen from farmers' houses while they were out in their fields. He was still looking for a pair of boots that fit.

Jérôme Christophe was the only olive-skinned man among the four newcomers to Antoine and Michaele's growing military force. He had Italian blood from two generations previous to him; and, apparently, the genetic marker was a strong one. He had the dark curly hair, fine straight nose, and delicate facial features of his Sicilian ancestors. He had a charm and roguish look that appealed to girls in every village he and his French volunteers had pillaged during their days with the Charlemagne Division. He was not a big man, but he was an agile and almost acrobatic one. He could climb, run, fight, and endure hardships with the best of men. His clothing had been purloined from a peasant woman's line of washing, and he was wearing her linen blouse covered by two of her sweaters. He was quick enough with a butterfly switch-blade knife to discourage anyone from making disparaging remarks about his appearance or choice of clothing.

The four newcomers had met at the tin mine and had become close allies after they were unceremoniously dumped into the unfortunate society of Magadan, Siberia. They took to calling themselves the four musketeers. Serge became Porthos; Jean Luc became Athos; Jérôme Christophe became Aramis by default; and Jean Luc was the consensus choice to be d'Artagnan. Once they got to know Antoine, they occasionally called him by the name of M. de Tréville, captain of the Musketeers. That name did not stick, since Antoine was not much for games and pretenses.

CHAPTER NINETEEN

Magadan, Yakutia, Siberia, late April 1954

The "regiment" proved to be mutually beneficial for all of its six members. They worked together to improve their living quarters, their small vegetable gardens, and when they carried out foraging raids. They saw themselves as being invincible and having the effective power of a small SS independent fighting unit living off the land.

"*Wir sind Gebirgsjäger* [We are light infantry alpine-mountain troops]," Antoine told his men, harking back to the 6th Waffen SS Mountain Division *Nord*, an elite unit all of the former POWs admired, holding the unit in almost mythical respect.

That division held the distinction of being the only Waffen SS unit to fight in the Arctic Circle. Their successes and sacrifices in Finland and northern Russia between June and November 1941 were trumpeted by Hitler and became perhaps overrated as Aryan giants to be emulated by all SS troops.

"*Ja, es ist wahr, Mein General,*" Michaele echoed. "*Wir sind die letzten Totenkopfverbände. Es ist unsere pflicht als speerspitze für die neue Vierte Reich!*" [Yes, my general, we are the last SS Deaths Head Unit. It is our duty to be the spearhead for the new Fourth Reich].

His enthusiasm was shared by the other members of this increasingly arrogant band of brothers; now they were elite soldiers with a purpose that transcended their current meager status. It mattered little to any of them that the original *Gebirgsjägers* were drawn from the most brutal and thuggish concentration camp guard troops. The new *Gebirgsjägers* were also realists about their own situation and recognized that they would fight as a cohesive unit, or they would be imprisoned or killed. There could be no flinching at what had to be done. Every man knew that it was imperative that they leave no witnesses.

Each of them had experienced the terrors of becoming the subject of arrest for crimes against the Soviet Union. They were determined never to fall into the clutches of the only government more brutal and less compassionate than their own SS regiment. Murder of nearly defenseless men, women, and children became a necessary modus operandi as they began to accumulate more resources, including food, weapons, and warm clothing. The six men were fascinated by the fact that many of the former Kulaks had considerable treasures in gold, jewelry, and rubles which they had been able to hoard when they were transported to the northeastern Siberian region of Yakutia—which included Magadan—and had undoubtedly increased by dint of their extremely hard work and frugality.

The six former POWs enjoyed their good life to the maximum. They had good food, even a few luxuries like chocolate. They had all the vodka they wanted, good quality boots, fur caps, parkas, and sturdy woolen clothing. Things went so well that Antoine relaxed his iron grip on his men and began to allow daytime raids and to permit the men to neglect their gardens. One problem that was likely to come to endanger them was the woeful lack of even the most rudimentary intelligence about the area beyond their small isolated rural part of Yakutia. Michaele pointed that fact out a number of times before Antoine allowed two of the men—Hugues Beauchamp and Jean Luc Latendresse—to check out the situation in Magadan.

Hugues and Jean Luc meandered carefully through the muddy streets of Magadan frequently looking over their shoulders or into reflective store windows to see if they were being observed or followed. At noon, they entered a small café and took seats near the rear exit. Both men sat on the same side of the table facing the front door and the main front windows. Hugues ordered reindeer steak, and Jean Luc had a salad and borscht with beef strips. They had a Celta-Pils ale and a large glass of red wine that was not very good. The black rye bread was delicious and still hot from the oven. They smothered their pieces with heavy cream butter and consumed half a loaf each. The salad and the ale were the first they had enjoyed since 1945.

"Don't be obvious," Hugues said, "but there are KGB troops in the street. They're getting out of a troop truck. That can't be a good thing."

Jean Luc nodded his head.

"Let's watch and shovel the food in, leave some rubles, and get out by the back door. Seeing them before they saw us is the kind of intelligence we came for. Antoine will have to decide what our plan will be."

"Think they're after us?"

"I doubt it. We aren't worth the trip from Moscow or Vladivostok or wherever they came from. This must have something to do with the city—maybe some dissidents or suspected counterrevolutionaries. There's a small army out there, and I see one officer we both know."

"Which one?"

"There by the Zil. That's Lieutenant General of Cavalry Grigory Yegorivich Lagounov—the head commissar—or I'll eat my hat," Hugues said.

"Is he back to run the SVITL [Russian: *Sevvostlag: severo-vostochnye lagerya*. English: Directorate of North-Eastern Camps]?" Jean Luc asked quietly, feeling like someone had just walked on his grave.

"Who knows? I thought the Sovs had shut them all down and had repatriated all of the *Kriegsverurteilte* [German-POWs]," Hugues whispered, his voice also subdued by the presence of the infamous director of the camp system who was reputed to have participated in the shooting contests from the guard towers using random prisoners as targets.

"The man pushed my head into a *kanalizatsiya vedro* [sewage bucket] and almost drowned me because I ran too slow carrying logs to the stockpile."

"He killed men for less than that," Hugues said with a gravely growl, his eyes blazing with hatred.

"He killed men for nothing. Let's get out of here before he sees us."

Hugues and Jean Luc set out at a steady lope for the "*Gebirgsjäger*" camp, leaving all of their purchases behind to freeze in the snow.

They were too late. A Red Army unit surrounded the encampment and had rounded up all of the former POWs, placing them in shackles when the two men got close enough to understand what was going on. Jean Luc shrugged and whispered that they had to get away from there before they were recaptured and joined their fellow Frenchmen/former SS elite comrades in what was obviously a round up to force them back to the gulag. They had been living in a dream, and now it was a nightmare. They bent low and moved as silently as they could through the snow and into the increasingly dense forest.

It was a futile try. The Red Army sergeants had anticipated that stragglers would try and slip away into the cover of the trees and deadfall. They were waiting and took Hugues and Jean Luc by complete surprise. There was no use putting up a fight; they knew they would be dead before they could raise their weapons; so, they meekly put their Kalashnikovs down and set their faces towards a distant day when they might possibly be free. For the time being, it was enough to be alive. That had been the unspoken motto of all of the surviving POWs while they languished, froze, and starved in the tin mine. At least they were starting out in better condition than they had been in when they first entered the brutal gulag in 1945.

The six totally dispirited prisoners marched through the snow and darkness all the way back to Magadan, arriving there just before midnight. In the Yakutsk, winter lasts from early October into May with temperatures sinking to as low as negative fifty-five degrees. Even in summer, temperatures in the range of thirty degrees Fahrenheit were so frequent as to be the rule. The men were shackled to each other and to steel spikes driven into the frozen ground at intervals. The Soviet soldiers never spoke to them. They shivered and stomped the ground to prevent frost bite and succumbing to hypothermia. Sleep was out of the question. They were famished and exhausted by the time the sun came up in the morning.

They were kicked awake by Soviet enlisted men and forced to their feet—a slow and awkward process owing to their stiffness.

A lieutenant marched stiffly and stood in front of the former POWs.

"*Vnimaniye sobaki* [attention dogs]! I am Lieutenant Sobrieski. It is my honor to present Lieutenant General Lagounov."

The general stepped in front of his lieutenant flanked by two powerful-looking military policemen. He was slender with a hawk's face and skeletally slender long fingers. He wore a new and perfectly pressed uniform. His eyes were close set and cruel. He had a carefully practiced efficiency of movement. He did not tolerate the least hint of insubordination as he perceived it. His aide-de-camp, Dimitri Sobrieski, was a short man who justified his manhood by the level of his cruelty. He exercised steely discipline never to smile and never to allow a prisoner to look him in the eyes. He was obsequiously deferential to Gen.

Lagounov and anyone else who outranked him or could give him an advantage in the rank-conscious KGB. He was as clean shaven and neat as his superior officer, and a trifle less Slavic and more handsome in appearance, although he would never have hinted at that fact. He had wideset eyes—his only facial flaw, a perfect Roman nose, thick lips, and unlike almost any other Russian, his teeth were straight, free of cavities and all present. He kept his uniform and boots as near perfectly cared for as the privates he dominated could manage in the mud and filth of the Siberian streets.

Gen. Lagounov spoke up again, "This is a happy day for you miserable *sobaki*," he said, "You are to be repatriated back to Germany today. You will have the opportunity to report on the fair and decent treatment you have received while POWs. You will find that the Soviet Union does not take kindly to complainers and those who would criticize or try to undermine the great peoples' government. We will travel by truck to the railhead, and then you will have the luxury—the undeserved luxury, I might add—of transportation by train the rest of the way west."

The general said it with not a hint of irony or smile.

Every man standing in the cold waiting for transportation west remembered in vivid detail the painful journey to slavery in the "Valley of Death." After being captured, they had traveled from Berlin by cattle train to Siberia. That trip prepared them for the horrors to come. The trains were unbearably cramped and stifling. Only death of prisoners afforded a little more leg room. On the trains in the west, the heat was terrible. There was serious lack of fresh air, and the dreadful overcrowded conditions exhausted the semi-starved men. Many of the elderly prisoners—weak and emaciated—died along the way, and their corpses were left abandoned alongside the railroad tracks. The worst was yet to come. The survivors of the grueling Trans-Siberian Railway train ride—the longest in the USSR—were disembarked at the Nakhodka transit camp. There, they encountered the bitter unrelenting cold. After three days, they were moved to Khabarovosk, which was part of the gulag archipelago. They then were forced onto decrepit ships and transported across the Sea of Okhotsk to Magadan's natural harbor. Conditions aboard the ships were even harsher than what they had endured on the train. The Soviet prison ships were sewage-ridden hellholes. Of the original three train loads of POWs, thousands died during the crossing.

The general had aged considerably since any of the still surviving German POWs had seen him. He remained ramrod stiff, but his frame was no longer lithe and wiry—just thin and stringy. His face still had the chiseled-in-granite frown of authority, but now his skin was sagging and grayish—the hallmarks of a sick man or at least an old one. Even when he spoke, his lips were nothing more than a line in the lower part of his face. Presumably, those lips had never lost control and smiled. Lagounov had never been an even remotely handsome man. Now his very bushy eyebrows and tufts of hair on his ears had become salt-and-pepper gray which—added to his sharp aquiline nose—gave him a cruel hawklike face. His eyes were still the same harsh blue-gray—the color of gun metal—and gave one the impression that he could see deep into that last box hidden in a tortured man's brain where his final secrets were kept.

He was dressed in the KGB version of the Zhukov-style officer parade uniform complete with battle medals—not just the ribbons. In keeping with the cold, the uniform was gray napped wool and closely fitted to his lean body, unlike the poorly fitted clothing of his junior officers and enlisted men. He had a spotlessly clean field officer's cap with a cornflower blue band and gold piping. The cap's band mounted a two-piece M55 parade cockade and emblem. He wore thick leather gloves of fine custom construction. Despite the muddy conditions, his knee-high cavalry boots gleamed with a just finished spit-shine.

The emblems, medals, and insignias conveyed the desired effect— awesome power. Gen. Lagounov's body and face were diminished into a death's head appearance, which only added to the fear his gaze struck in a prisoner who had to face the mass murderer.

None of the *Kriegsverurteilte* expected breakfast, and they were not disappointed. Gen. Lagounov gave an order to his lieutenant with a mere nod of his head, and the repatriates were shoved aboard the cramped troop trucks and sat in maximum discomfort on uncushioned steel benches. The trucks lurched forward.

CHAPTER TWENTY

"People speak sometimes about the 'bestial' cruelty of man, but that is terribly unjust and offensive to beasts; no animal could ever be so cruel as a man, so artfully, so artistically cruel."
-Fyodor Dostoyevsky

Oymyakon, Yakutia, Siberia, June 1954

The four trucks made it as far as the towns of Oymyakon and Susuman by the end of the first two weeks of their journey across the Yakutia region—ten times the size of Germany. They traveled on what the Soviet Union called the Kolyma Highway—but known to the prisoners and former inhabitants of the region as the "Road of Bones," because so many died during construction of the track through the mountains which did not merit the designation as a highway. The track followed the circuitous Kolyma River through the mountain range of the same name. That region of Yakutia was so remote that much of it was not even explored until as late as 1926. It is the coldest area in the northern hemisphere. In the 1950s, the Soviet Union's Council of Ministers did not deem the area to be of sufficient economic value to provide any services.

The trucks were still all intact as they passed the ghost town of Kadykchan, known as the "City of Broken Dreams" to the seven thousand people who used to live there. Two abandoned coal mines stood in decay just outside the city. Without time to prepare for deportation from their home city, all the inhabitants received 80 to 120 thousand rubles to purchase another apartment somewhere else—and were left to their own devices as to how to get to that other place. The power supply to Kadykchan was cut; the heating plant was dismantled; and the private homes were burned; so that the owners could never return. The only people they saw were reindeer breeders who lived in prehistoric conditions in a settlement called Ust-Nera, about 600 miles from their start on the Kolyma Highway.

The region through which the truck passed is located in the far northeastern area of Russia. It is commonly and mistakenly called Siberia, but is technically part of the Russian Far East. It is bounded by the East Siberian Sea and the Arctic Ocean in the north and the Sea of Okhotsk to the south. Part of the area is within the Arctic Circle and has a subarctic climate with extremely cold winters which some years last up to six months of the year. Permafrost and tundra cover a large part of the region, making it bleak and uninviting even to the eye. Even in June as the trucks made their way slowly west, it was very cold. That particular portion of Yakutia remained cold year-round. This was a portion of Siberia where the great permafrost belt remained in perpetuity. Permafrost extended three feet deep into the ground. At frequent intervals, the struggling trucks could not make it across a stream, up a grade, or over a particularly rough and rock-strewn stretch of road. The men were ordered out of the back of the trucks and half of them were harnessed to the front of the truck like draft horses and obliged to pull their conveyances while the other half pushed from behind. It was very slow going, and every night they slept on the frozen rocks. Rations were skimpy.

The steep, winding route ran through narrow ravines and alongside jagged cliff faces. When the way opened up, there were endless snowy expanses, frozen lakes, and rivers. The first death occurred on the fourteenth day—more precisely during the fifteenth night. One of the enfeebled former SS officers/former gulag survivors gave up the ghost and froze to death while shackled between two other men in fairly similar condition. The guards had to heat a kettle of boiling water to get the dead man's corpse loose from where it was stuck to the frozen ground. Two other *Kriegsverurteiltes* were ordered to dispose of the body. They dragged it fifty yards from the strewn rocks that passed for a road. There were no trees to fell or rocks that could be pried up to cover the body; so, they simply hollowed out a trench in the snow and covered the man over with snow and packed it down. It would have been easier to bend the dead man over double and to have made a smaller depression in the snow; but rigor mortis was in full rigidity; and they had to place him in the hole like a bundle of sticks. The two gravediggers expropriated the man's ragged clothes and added them to their own layers. The column pressed on.

Every other night, another man died in his sleep and was similarly left as a frozen reminder of what the former POWs endured on the "Road of Bones." None of the makeshift graves had any kind of a marker, and no record was kept. They simply became additional statistics in the horrors of World War II. When the four trucks arrived for the second to the last night's stay before getting to the rail head, one of the trucks threw a rod, thus ending its service. Failure of a connecting rod in those days in the western world was not particularly frequent. However, in the Soviet Union, throwing a rod was one of the most common causes of catastrophic engine failure in trucks. In the case of this small convoy, almost every known cause of failure of a connecting rod was operative. There was failure and improper excessive tightening of the rod bolts, overrevving of the engine beyond its ordinary capacity going up the frequent steep inclines, lubrication failure due to faulty maintenance, and freezing. A further problem of maintenance came from the common Soviet practice of cannibalizing parts to keep at least a fraction of a fleet going. Unschooled mechanics had assumed that the big end caps were interchangeable between connecting rods when rebuilding an engine. No care was taken to ensure that the caps of the different connecting rods were not mixed up. The result was that the truck's engine suddenly froze up and stopped, pitching the occupants hard against the metal seats and dashboard. The engine glowed red and burst into flames.

Unfortunately, the truck had to be declared kaput and abandoned. Fortunately, no one suffered severe injury—just broken noses, two broken legs, and one broken arm. Also fortunately—in a perverse way—the number of dead men had reduced the overcrowding on the four trucks. That made it possible for the three remaining trucks to be able to handle the remainder. They had completed about 250 miles of the overland journey and had only about twenty-five to thirty miles left before they arrived at Tommot, the capital of the Sakha Republic and the eastern railroad terminus of the Amur-Yakutia Mainline.

The next morning, they slogged onward for about fourteen miles until they became bogged down in the jelly slick mud of early spring breakup. The three remaining trucks could only advance about two miles that day, and overnight the wheels froze in the six-inch ruts they had created. No heavy machinery was available; so, those trucks also were abandoned after a heroic struggle by the occupants, including the guards. The leading officer ordered a forced march to Tommot. Being a pragmatist, he knew the emaciated and exhausted men would not make it all the way. He divided up the remaining food, and the guards and their prisoners ate one last meal—the best of the entire journey for the *Kriegsverurteiltes*.

The first hill of the forced march proved to be too much for former *Waffen SS-Sturmbannführer* [Major] Jean Luc Latendresse. He was walking alongside Antoine when he suddenly clasped his chest and screamed in pain. Before Antoine could catch him, Jean Luc collapsed dead at his feet.

"Heart attack," Serge Rounsavall observed matter-of-factly.

His *Kriegsverurteilte* comrades in the makeshift *Gebirgsjäger* unit buried him in a hastily dug snow pit and moved on. Someone in the Soviet Union estimated that at least thirteen million mammoths were encased in Siberia's permafrost belt along with the human unfortunates who pass that way. Major Jean Luc Latendresse joined the great beasts for eternity. Now, there were five remaining members of the 33rd Waffen-Grenadier Division of the Nazi SS—the renowned Charlemagne Division.

Soviet Emergency Rations

-Biscuits (tinned or sealed cardboard/paper wrapper) 17.5 oz
-Concentrated food—Course I (2.6 oz of instant soup or enriched biscuits)
-Concentrated food—Course II (7.0 oz of more of the same)

Where available after late 1942:
-Lend-Lease Tins or even some prepackaged ration items, such as British biscuits or dripping spread)—not available in Siberia during the 1950s.
-Smoked sausages 3.5 oz (by 1954, substituted by lard, fish conserves, ± bacon)
-Sugar 1.2 oz, tea 0.07 oz, salt 0.35 oz

Twice during the long journey from Yakutsk to Tommot, the guards and POWS received surprise meals obtained from locals—mostly leftover from troop encampments, including:

-raw vegetables, small red potatoes, some fresh and delicious, even raw; some rotten, chunks of red or green cabbage, and a smear of lard in a mess tin.
-"portable meat"—chunks of almost rock-hard blood sausage wrapped in oiled brown paper or thin smoked bacon.
-stale Russian black rye bread, unsliced, bags of hard-boiled eggs, some smelling faintly of H2S
-A small paper bag of macaroni or uncooked grits, and once, a small bag of apples, hard pears, prunes, and sunflower seeds (wrapped in a handkerchief).
-Tinned or dried varieties of fish—sprats, mackerel, or herring fish.
-very coarse loose-leaf tea. Some loose-leaf tobacco: the only way the men could tell the smoking tobacco from the tea is by boiling it. Cigarettes were unheard of.
-Salt: a small amount of salt and an ounce of plain sugar of a piece or hard lump candy twisted into some brown paper
-dry ingredients for nettle soup.
-a few sheets of latrine paper—Russian newsprint and leaflets.

POW Camp Recipes

Stinging Nettle Soup—Serves Four

Ingredients
-1 lb stinging nettles, 2 tbsps salt, 1 tbsp extra virgin olive oil, 1 diced white onion
-¼ cp basmati rice, 4 cps chicken broth, salt and pepper to taste

Preparation
-Bring a large pot of water to a boil with 2 tsps salt. Drop in the stinging nettles and cook 1–2 min. until soft to remove most of the sting. Drain in a colander, rinse with cold water. Trim off tough stems, then chop coarsely.
-Heat olive oil in a saucepan over medium-low heat and stir in the onion. Cook until the onion has softened and turned translucent~5 mins. Stir in rice, chicken broth, and chopped nettles. Bring to a boil, then reduce heat to medium-low, cover, and simmer until the rice is tender~15 mins. Puree the soup, and season to taste with salt and pepper.

CHAPTER TWENTY-ONE

Tommot, Aldansky District, Yakutia, Siberia, July 1954

Tommot was a dismal dot on the map of Siberia, but for the guards and *Kriegsverurteiltes* it held four distinctly positive attributes. First, it was about twenty degrees warmer—the name of the town was derived from a word used by the indigenous Yakuts to mean "not freezing." Temperature-wise, that was a decided plus. Secondly, there were houses and even a couple of taverns with smoke issuing from their chimneys with the promise of warm food. Granted those structures were somewhere between log buildings and mud huts; but, to the *Kriegsverurteiltes,* they might have been palaces. Thirdly, Tommot was situated on the banks of the Aldan River, which would allow the sick and filthy travelers access to clean water—something not taken for granted by men who had been without such amenities for a long time. Fourthly, the town constituted the terminus of the passenger trains of the Amur Yakutsk Mainline railroad and the chance to get to the west. For the *Kriegsverurteiltes,* it meant travel on real seats, meals prepared by the train crew, no more stinging nettle soup, and no more forced marches or having to pull trucks up stony inclines or out of snowbanks and mud pits.

Not everything was positive. The ranking sergeant and two privates commandeered a 1940 Studebaker President automobile maintained by the town's mayor for delivery of any VIPs who might come from Moscow to the "Aldan International Airport" a few miles away from Tommot. By anyone's standards, the airport was hardly international; in fact, it barely qualified as an airport. There was one pockmarked

runway and one hangar. The runway accommodated only small pro-
peller planes that did not require a long runway. Lt. Gen. Lagounov,
head commissar of the *Sevvostlag,* and his aide, Lt. Dimitri Sobrieski,
alighted from the comfort of their seats in the warm cabin of the An-2
"Annushka" biplane the general was able to commandeer in Magadan.

The master sergeant pulled the Studebaker up to the lowered steps of
the plane and hurried out to open the rear passenger door for the general. His two privates rushed to collect the luggage, and one of them
hurried back to the car to open the rear seat for the lieutenant. The
four enlisted men somehow squeezed themselves into the front and sat
uncomfortably on the inadequate bench seat. Half an hour later they
pulled up in front of the assembled POWs, and the occupants of the
car extricated themselves from their cramped seating arrangements.

"*Achtung!*" barked Lt. Sobrieski. He repeated the command in
Russian, "*Vnimaniye!*"

The POWs who were still able to stand came to rigid attention.

Two men were bent over and another, Jérôme Christophe Mailhot—
one of Antoine's *Gebirgsjägers*—was being held up by Antoine. Gen.
Lagounov strode down the line. When he came to the first man standing
with his hands on his knees trying to get fully upright, he kicked the
man's knee so that he fell face down on the rough and frozen ground.

Gen. Lagounov looked down at the fallen man with utter disdain
and muttered, "*Dokhodyaga*" [goner].

He struck the second ailing man in the back with his sharp elbow,
and the man crumpled to the ground, too exhausted to make a protest.

Then he stood in front of Antoine and Jérôme Christophe Mailhot.

"*Slabovol'nyy chelovek* [weakling]!" he hissed and kicked at Jérôme,
who was unable to protect himself.

Antoine made a swift pivotal move and pulled Jérôme out of harm's
way. The old general's balance was put off by the unexpected move,
and he tottered and almost fell. Two privates ran up alongside their
general and glared at Antoine, who now became the focus of attention
of everyone present. Both privates pointed at Antoine menacingly with
their Kalashnikovs.

Gen. Lagounov calmly removed a short stout quirt from his uniform
belt. He did it slowly and deliberately locking eyes with Antoine. Antoine
held the general's gaze long enough that the senior officer blinked first.
Lagounov then whipped the quirt backhand across Antoine's face with

all of the force he could muster. The cruel little weapon opened a cut across the right side of Antoine's face. Antoine steeled himself not to flinch or cry out. His face became a calm mask of hatred.

The general looked at Antoine's face for a moment, then smiled his patented cruel lipless smile.

"This will not be forgotten, fool," he said.

Antoine snarled inwardly, "*You can bet your life on it, cafard* [cockroach]!"

His fellow *Gebirgsjägers* fully expected Antoine to be shot on the spot; but Gen. Lagounov shook his head "No," and the moment passed.

The surviving *Kriegsverurteiltes* were herded onto the decrepit passenger cars of the Amur-Yakutia Mainline bound for Moscow Kazanskiy Central train station over 3,000 miles to the west.

CHAPTER TWENTY-TWO

Moschendorf Transit and Release Camp, Occupied Germany on the Bavaria, August 1954

The Amur-Yakutia Mainline moved at the rate of glacial erosion across the vast and frozen expanses of Siberia. Antoine and his men at least had seats and some freedom to move about in the passenger cars to stretch their legs. The guards frankly did not care if any of their prisoners escaped; there was no place to go; and the only alternative to the train was death in the snow from freezing or starvation. They crossed the Baikal-Amur Mainline after a week of tedious travel, traversed the Gilyuy River twice, and chugged their way over the Aldan Highlands and the Stanovoy Mountain pass. The distances were vast. It took the train six days to plow through the snow-covered tracks the 684 miles from Tayshet—where they obtained water for the steam engines—to Severobaikalsk on Lake Baikal.

There were two stops before reaching Lake Baikal to take on fuel and food. At Neryungri—about seventeen miles from the cutoff to the Baikal-Amur Mainline, they were allowed off the train to stretch their legs. For three days rations were doubled, and the quality of the food improved. Up to that point, the meal and meat rations were infested with insects and their eggs and larvae because the corrupt Soviet commissars and food depot managers sold off all of the good quality rations on the black market and left the rotting food for the prisoners. All of the men were in improved condition when they reached Severobaikalsk on the northern bank of the great lake. At Goudzhegit, the prisoners were ordered off the train cars and onto the beach. There they were ordered to strip naked and throw their putrid ragged clothing into a pile which was then set afire. Red army trucks from Severobaikalsk hauled in a truckload of used Soviet uniforms, including boots, and laid them out on tarpaulins according to size.

The master sergeant now in charge of the transportation detail herded the shivering men into the hot springs and then into a natural 40–50 degree natural spring to refresh. None of the men had been truly clean for months, and the experience was reviving. The army brought huge cauldrons of rich thick stew made of reindeer meet and canned vegetables. There was even beer. The army issued blankets for sleeping on the rest of the railroad journey to Moscow. The POWs felt like they had died and gone to heaven—a destination none of them expected ever to reach. For the rest of the railway journey, the men enjoyed the relative comfort of blankets, full bellies, and decently fitting clothing—albeit well-worn hand-me-downs.

When the train arrived in Moscow's Kazanskiy Central train station after a 3,000-mile journey to the west, the prisoners were not allowed out of the passenger cars even to stretch their legs. News of their impending arrival brought out thousands of Muscovites who clogged the streets and entrances to the train station. Many of them carried hoes, shovels, rakes, pruning hooks, and a wide assortment of other improvised clubs. They were bent on wreaking their pent-up fury in an orgy of revenge on the German soldiers who had raped their country. Peasants and ex-soldiers made their way from as far away as Stalingrad to have their day of vengeance.

Between midsummer 1942 and midwinter 1943, the daunting German Wehrmacht pitted its might against the hapless city in the Siege of Stalingrad. The conflict was the single bloodiest battle in the history of warfare and probably the turning point in World War II. In the aftermath, the body count included over 1.1 million total casualties, which left tens of millions of Russians with a bloodlust against Germans. On their part, the Germans and their allies in the battle lost 400,000 Germans, 200,000 Romanians, 130,000 Italians, and 120,000 Hungarians killed, wounded, or captured. The bodies of the dead Axis soldiers were left to rot outside the walls of Stalingrad. When a German Red Cross group was allowed to visit the city after the war, they complained to the city's officials and to the Soviet government that it violated all rules of war and civilized conduct to leave the corpses and skeletons in plain view.

The response from the victims of the German atrocities was: "The skeletons stay. This is what defeat looks like."

KGB and Red Army divisions were mustered around the train station to protect it, the trains, and the hated returning POWs. Tensions were so electric and the dangers of a riot with thousands of civilian casualties so high that the government forced the train to move on to occupied Germany. The final destination of the transcontinental journey was the Moschendorf Transit and Release Camp, a miserable and inadequate holding pen for thousands of German POWs and translocated German civilians destined for Allied forced labor camps in the west.

The Moschendorf facility was constructed as a concentration camp located in the northeastern part of Bavaria near the Saale River close to the eastern border of Germany. For convenience of receiving the hordes of displaced persons, slave laborers, and POWs, the camp was located immediately along the railway yard between Regensburg and Moschendorf. Early on it served as a transit camp for displaced persons—including civilian prisoners, persons expelled by either or both the Nazis and the Allies, and returnees, and had accommodations for five thousand people. Soon, however, the numbers swelled out of all proportions and ability of the camp to provide food, water, shelter, and even rudimentary medical assistance. A novel solution was agreed upon by the Allied commanders.

Antoine and his four French companions who had fought for the SS—the *"Gebirgsjägers"*—arrived hungry and weary but in reasonably good condition considering what they had been through. The camp was overcrowded, none too clean, and the ration portions were between 1200 and 1500 calories a day. It was better than many of the places where they had "lived" since 1945, and the best thing was that there were barracks which could protect them from the omnipresent miseries of the elements. The five men presumed that they would soon be released, and that things could only get better. They were wrong on both counts.

They, like the vast majority of the rest of the internees in the Moschendorf so-called "Transit and Release Camp," had no idea about the decisions arrived at by the Allies regarding disposition and treatment of Germans and other displaced peoples in the postwar period.

During the Allied commanders' Tehran conference in 1943, Soviet premier Joseph Stalin laid the groundwork for the disposition of peoples. He demanded four million Germans be turned over to the Soviet Union as forced labor. In 1944, the Morgenthau plan included forced labor for not only the Soviet Union, but also for the rest of the Allied powers. Slavery was accepted and included in the final protocol of the Yalta conference signed in January 1945. The signatories included UK Prime Minister Winston Churchill and US President Franklin D. Roosevelt. The result was the prolonged internment of and exploited labor from many thousands of former POWs and displaced civilians—some for many years. The ultimate fate of 1,300,000 German POW's in Allied custody remains unknown; they are officially listed as missing. The German Red Cross—in charge of dealing with tracing the captives—estimated German POW casualties from the east and west, and in war and peacetime, to range from 600,000 to 1,000,000.

The August 16th evening meal was the best the men had in the Allied camps up to then, or would ever have during their incarceration. Most of the food was obtained from the German civilian populace and was more often than not forcibly taken from the people who had barely enough nutrition to do their work, including from small family stores like the Tante Emma Laden chain. Rationing in Germany was introduced in 1939 immediately upon the outbreak of hostilities. The meat ration at the war's beginning, for example, was 500g per week per person. After the German invasion of the Soviet Union in June 1941, however, this changed to 400g per week. The meat ration dropped by up to eighty percent during the five months of fighting in Russia. After May 1942, civilian rations in Germany were dropped to 8000 grams of bread— about a half loaf a day—1200 grams of meat—less than .1 lb. per day— 600 grams of general foods, and 130 grams of sugar. By war's end, any adult was lucky to be a third of that ration, and then only if the commodity was available on the day the German did his or her shopping.

Margarine replaced butter; the margarine was colored with a purple dye to salve the complaints of the farmers about losing their dairy business. Rationing or not, meat became scarce; so; the Germans raised rabbits. By the early 1950s, there were hardly any rabbits left. Flour for bread was stretched using ground horse chestnuts, pea meal, potato meal, and barley. The populace learned to make do with powdered eggs. Wild plants—edible tubers, mushrooms, plants, and seed—were foraged from the countryside to replace fresh vegetables. Other items were not rationed, but simply became unavailable as they had to be imported from overseas: coffee in particular, which throughout was replaced by substitutes made from roasted grains. The Reich Food Estate collapsed altogether late in the war.

The *Gebirgsjägers'* grand meal consisted of intentionally overcooked rice mashed into patties and cooked in mutton fat to become small patties of ersatz meat. Rice patties mixed with onions and oil reserved from tinned fish became ersatz fish—which did not prove to be the *Gebirgsjägers'* favorite—and mock goose. Cooked nettles and goat's rue or *pestilenzkraut* [plague herb] also known as French lilac, the mucilaginous leaf juice of which tastes bitter and astringent. The bad smell emitted by bruised leaves of the herb is responsible for its most widely known common name. Before the war the plant was used as cattle feed. The nettles and goat's rue were served mixed as a substitute for spinach.

Any illusions the *Gebirgsjägers* harbored after that fine repast were shattered on August 17. On that day, hundreds of men and women were lined up under Allied military guard and placed on trains, planes, buses, and troop trucks for translocation to other camps with no mention of even eventual freedom.

German Civilian (for POWs) Recipe

MockGoose—Serves 2–4 Average Adults

Ingredients
-1 cp dried split lentils, 2 slices wholemeal bread breadcrumbs, 1 onion, 1 chopped sage, a little butter, some chicken stock (or if that is not available, can make vegetable stock, salt, pepper, garlic, and lemon to taste.

Preparation
-Place 1 cp rinsed dried lentils and 3 cps hot water into a saucepan and cook for 15 mins., drain and squeeze some lemon juice and sprinkle salt and mix together.
-Chop onion and place in a pan with a little butter and saute lightly, add a little chicken or vegetable stock (~ 1½ oz) and continue to cook and reduce a little. Mix in breadcrumbs, salt, pepper, chopped sage, and mix thoroughly.
-Spread half of lentils in a shallow dish and press down.
-Spread the breadcrumbs/sage mixture over the lentils and again press down a little.
-Cover with the remaining lentils.
-Cook at about 200 C for ~30 min. until the top is lightly browned.
Tastes very faintly like goose. Children do not usually enjoy the dish.

CHAPTER TWENTY-THREE

Schlosskirche [Palace Church], Ellingen, Bavaria, August 22, 1954

Antoine and Michaele waited by the camp fence during the darkest hours of August 20—from midnight to two a.m.

Michaele fidgeted, then after more than two hours of silent waiting, he finally whispered, "Do you really think he'll come, Antoine? We don't know the man that well."

Antoine whispered very quietly, "*Obersturmführer* [SS-Senior Storm Leader] Jacob Friedrich Bunnemann has three very important reasons to come and to give us every assistance. First—my friend—he has been supplying us black market luxuries through this very fence for as long as we have been here with the blessing of the ODESSA. Second, he has been promised a very great deal of money for the help he will provide—five percent of the *Schlosskirche* treasure. Third, he knows that we know he was with us during the last days of the Battle of the Führer Bunker. He escaped because we helped him and got captured as our reward for that bit of foolish charity. We can reverse his good fortune in the blink of an eye. All we need to do is to supply what we know to the Soviets who keep peeking through the concertina wire. His life would be hell on earth, and he is not about to take that risk just because he is a trifle fainthearted right now. He'll come."

Michaele shrugged his answer, and they waited another fifteen minutes.

"Hsst," came a short soft signal.

"Hsst, hsst," Antoine replied.

No one further away than ten feet could have heard the two sounds or differentiated them from the ambient diverse sounds of the night.

"Antoine?"

"*Oui.*"

"It is I, Jacob. I have a truck on the gravel road just across the canal. I'm afraid Michaele will get a bit wet."

"He won't melt, my friend. He's ready. You know who we are. We always keep our promises, Jacob. Do right by us, and you will be rich beyond your wildest dreams. Betray us, and...." He let the rest of the sentence hang.

"I would never betray you. We are brothers."

"Indeed," said Antoine. "Farewell, Michaele. We will next meet in our homeland. We will be rich as Croesus, and our sufferings will be over. I trust you with my life, my brother."

"And I, you."

Jacob whispered harshly, "We only have a few minutes. We have to hurry. Come on, Michaele."

Antoine and Michaele embraced and saluted each other with the *Hitlergruss*, then Michaele disappeared through a hole cut in the wire of the camp fence.

The water in the canal moved almost imperceptibly and was fetid and cold. Michaele and Jacob pushed through the greasy water and struggled up the embankment, slipping and sliding on the heavy wet grasses. They lay face down on the edge to catch their breath.

Jacob was overweight by fifty pounds, soft and pudgy after ten years of life as German "civilian who had never been in the war", was "never a Nazi, and, most certainly, never in the SS [The *Schutzstaffel* (German), Protection Squadron (English)]." Had a passerby asked any German in 1953 if he or she had been a Nazi or if he or she knew anyone who had been a Nazi ever, the answer would not only have been "No," but the tone of the answer would have suggested that it was a ridiculous question since no one except those actually tried, convicted, sentenced, and served their sentence—i.e. the great leaders of the Party—was ever a Nazi. What a silly and offensive question! Jacob had a pockmarked, puffy, and red face owing to a prodigious capacity for fine German and Austrian dark lager. He walked with a moderate limp from a shrapnel wound received during the Battle of the Bunker in reality, but which had morphed into an industrial accident in the chaos after the war.

Jacob was short, thick—in both body and mind—and easily fatigued. However, he had real value because he knew former Nazis, movers and shakers of the ODESSA, and the back roads from the Moschendorf Transit and Release Camp on the border of Austria and Hungary to their destination in Ellington, Bavaria. He adjusted his hat. His one nod to vanity was that he wore a small-brimmed construction worker's cap all of the time—even in bed—because he was as bald as a bowling ball.

He took a deep breath and whispered to Michaele, "We have about two hours of complete darkness left; so, we have to hurry. You are lucky you have me as a guide; you would never make it to the rendezvous point without someone who knows every inch of this area."

"*And who expects to be amply rewarded when this was all over,*" Michaele said silently to himself.

For purposes of secrecy and security, the two men hiked along obscure paths in wooded areas to Steiermark, hampered by Jacob's inability to keep up the pace and his need to take a breather. The second time they took what Michaele considered to be an unnecessary rest, and Jacob lit up a Spud cigarette which he—like many Bavarians—obtained at discount prices from American GIs, Michaele grabbed him by the lapels and slammed him up against a tree.

"No more smoking, you wheezing blimp! Someone may see us, and you can't breathe well enough for us to make it to where we have to go tonight in time if you keep fighting for breath."

Jacob whined, "But, you don't understand, Michaele, I have to smoke. I *need* to smoke—calms my nerves."

"You can have nerves when we get there. Now, get going. Worry about me. Do you understand that? I am your worst worry; so, don't upset me."

CHAPTER TWENTY-FOUR

"Evil begins when you begin to treat people as things."
                                    -Terry Pratchett, *I Shall Wear Midnight*

Bad Kreuznach—Lager Galgenberg und Bretzenheim PWTE—Bad Kreuznach District, Rhineland-Palatinate, Germany, August 18, 1954

At five o'clock in the morning, American enlisted men rousted four barracks full of POWs and displaced persons without warning and ordered them to stand at attention in the cold morning. The commandant of the camp, Lieutenant General Glen Gabler and his aide-de-camp, Major Richard "Rick" Saunders, marched along the line of anxious men and stopped crisply and made a sharp left face.

Seven hundred sleepy-eyed men listened with intensity as Saunders spoke.

"By orders of Commander-in-Chief of SHAEF, General of the Army Dwight D. Eisenhower, you men are to be transferred to a new camp in France where you will be processed for discharge. Take twenty minutes to gather what you can carry in one duffel bag and present yourselves at the west entrance of the camp. It is my pleasure to introduce Lieutenant General Glen Gabler who will accompany you to your new station and will assume command of the base. General Gabler."

The general was an imposing man physically as well as militarily—showing to full advantage his impressive chest full of campaign ribbons, a silver star, and two purple hearts. He was tall, heavily muscled, but beginning to show his age by a ponch which overlapped his Army issue belt. He had a lined leathery face from long days in the sun with wrinkles around his eyes and mouth from long days spent staring into a bright sunlit horizon. Gen. Gabler had salt-and-pepper, grey-white, short cropped hair in a military brush cut; and his hard face was etched in frown lines from his years of hounding men who did not want to work or to go into battle to face bullets and bayonets; and there were scars which attested to his willingness to lead his men into those battles. His silver-steel blue eyes were as unforgiving as ice and carried a hint of sadness—a remembering of things he had seen which he could never shake.

"Men," he announced, "your next assignment will be Bad Kreuznach—Lager Galgenberg und Bretzenheim PWTE—Bad Kreuznach District of the Rhineland-Palatinate. That site is designated as a work camp where internees work to pay back for the harm they have done and thereafter to be released back to their homes. You have the opportunity to be among the first groups of internees here at Moschendorf Transit and Release Camp to be moved to this newer and better camp. The army of occupation has constructed nineteen facilities known as the *Rheinwiesenlager* camps. They are a group of camps built in the Allied-occupied part of Germany. They are designed to hold captured German soldiers from the close of the Second World War until the internees are repatriated. You will learn—if you are not already aware—that I am a fair man, but a stern disciplinarian."

The *Rheinwiesenlager* [English: Rhine meadow] camps, were a group of concentration camps built in the allied-occupied part of Germany by the US Army to hold captured German soldiers including POWs repatriated from the United States. The camps were officially named Prisoner of War Temporary Enclosures [PWTE] for an important ulterior motive. They held between one and almost two million surrendered *Wehrmacht* personnel from April until September 1945. Prisoners held in the camps were designated Disarmed Enemy Forces, not POWs. The decision had been taken in March 1943 by SHAEF Commander-in-chief Dwight D. Eisenhower because of the logistical problems arising from appearing to adhere to the Geneva Convention of 1929. By not classing the hundreds of thousands of captured troops as POWs and substituting the disingenuous appellation "Disarmed Enemy Forces", the problems associated with accommodating so many prisoners of war according to international treaties governing their treatment was negated, not that many people in the Allied countries cared a whit.

Well after the war, studies indicated that one of the camps with the highest mortality was Bad Kreuznach [Lager Galgenberg und Bretzenheim)], which was occupied by US troops in March 1945 and thus stood under American military authority. The studies revealed that:

- The army lost track of some of the locations where POWs were held.
- The number of prisoners greatly exceeded expectations.
- Organization of the camps was left to prisoners, which too often led to fatal results.
- Food and water supplies were insufficient. The 1200 to 1500 calories ration that the Disarmed Enemy Forces were receiving after August 1945 was inadequate to sustain normal weight in a grown man. The lack of food led in many cases to extensive malnutrition.

Much later legal historians determined that the Allies violated international law regarding the feeding of enemy civilians, and directly and indirectly caused unnecessary suffering and death of large numbers of civilians and prisoners in occupied Germany, often as a spirit of postwar vengeance. For example, the directors of the camp purposefully created circumstances that contributed to the deaths of Bad Kreuznach prisoners. There were strict orders to US military personnel and their wives to destroy or otherwise render inedible their own leftover surplus so as to ensure it could not be eaten by German civilians.

Most estimates of German deaths in these camps range from between 3,000 to 10,000, but some have claimed that up to 1,000,000 prisoners died. Many died from starvation, dehydration, and exposure to the weather elements because no structures were built inside the prison compounds.

Major Saunders developed a quick, unguarded smile and rolled his eyes, a response not lost on Antoine. Antoine was the unquestioned leader of his small band of former French SS soldiers. He was standing beside Serge Rounsavall, Hugues Beauchamp, and Jérôme Christophe Mailhot, the last of his "*Gebirgsjägers*" still in the camp. He missed Michaele.

"What is the meaning of PWTE?" whispered Serge out of the side of his mouth.

Antoine shrugged. Given the American major's minimal but telling momentary change in facial expression, Antoine was pretty sure it did not mean anything good for the prisoners.

Gen. Gabler continued, "As such, you can count on two things from me: every man will be treated the same as every other man. I keep my promises; and if you do your work satisfactorily, the day will come when you will be set free to resume your prewar life. I am sure you remember your SS motto for the camps holding the Jews: *Arbeit Macht Frei*. The same statement applies in your new camp. Do what you are told, as soon as you are told, and everything you are told—and you will be recorded as a model prisoner. The work will be strenuous enough to keep you out of trouble. Should you fail in any of those requirements, disciplinary action will be swift and memorable. Is there anything about what I have said that you do not understand? Speak up now or keep your mouths shut. You do not want to appear before me at the camp. Mark my words. On the other side of that coin is that if you do work, you will go free. You can trust me on that.

"There will be no transfers permitted should you think life is hard at one camp. They are all the same, and I command them all."

None of the prisoners dared to speak.

Ten minutes later, the prisoners were all in assigned seats on one of the four olive drab US Army buses with one foot chained to a circle screw bolt fixed to the steel floor. They received no food or drink during the long bus ride. Antoine viewed that fact as a harbinger of things to come.

"*Call me a pessimist*," he thought.

Antoine could not have been more accurate in his opinion if he had been in charge of the three hundred American soldiers guarding the new camp instead of having a measly three men— his *Gebirgsjägers*—under his "command."

That very day, he and the rest of the prisoners privileged to be transferred to Bad Kreuznach learned exactly what PWTE meant: they were in hell. Even if they had known about the heinous maltreatment of the POWs, most victims of the Nazi regime would only have shrugged and said, "They deserve everything they get." In retaliation for acts of resistance, French occupation forces expelled more than 25,000 civilians from their homes. Some of these civilians were subsequently forced to clear minefields in Alsace.

Contrary to Section IV of the Hague Convention of 1907—*The Laws and Customs of War on Land*—the *SHAEF counterinsurgency manual* included provisions for forced labor and hostage-taking. German prisoners were forced to clear minefields in France and the Low Countries. Allied critics of the practice who visited the camps reported to disinterested readers, listeners, and authorities back home that everywhere in the Allied POW camps there was callous self-interest and a desire for retribution determining the fate of German prisoners. Sick or otherwise unfit prisoners were forcibly used for labor, and in France and the Low countries this also included work such as highly dangerous mine-clearing. As early as September 1945, French authorities estimated that two thousand prisoners were being maimed and killed each month in accidents—largely explosions. The prisoners were the canaries in the mines, and the dogs in the minefields.

Over 740,000 German prisoners transferred in 1945 by the US for forced labor in France came from the Rheinwiesenlager camps. Those forced laborers were already very weak, many weighing slightly over 110 pounds.

The first thing that Antoine and the *Gebirgsjägers* noticed was that—aside from guard houses, barracks for the US Army military police, and an administration building—there were no buildings. Hugues pointed out to his fellow former SS officers that a bare dirt field in the center of the camp had rows of shallow depressions in the dirt. Running alongside the rows of ground depressions were latrine trenches. No internees were anywhere to be seen at the time the *Gebirgsjägers* and the other new prisoners were being treated to their first vision of camp life.

"No mess tent or mess hall," he said unnecessarily.

"Plenty of guards and dogs, though. They must have some sort of facilities. Dogs are valuable, and they have to have plenty to eat to keep them in top form," Jérôme added.

There was no gallows humor intended in that observation. It was just an objective statement of the obvious. None of the arriving prisoners were at all prone to making jokes.

"At least we aren't likely to be as cold as we were in the Butugychag Tin Mine," Serge said in a vain attempt to find at least one feeble bright lining to the black clouds that surrounded them.

Gen. Gabler finished his introductory remarks, "Now, your work will commence under the capable supervision of Sergeant Major Owen Briggs. He will be your foreman, supervisor, police captain, judge, jury, and perhaps executioner if need be. You will address him as Senior Master Sergeant Briggs and all American military personnel by their full titles. You will not address me at all."

With that cheerful introduction to camp life, the general and the major retired from the dismal landscape and walked into the officers' club for a lunch of baby back pork ribs, mashed potatoes and gravy, steamed broccoli with melted cheese, Folger's coffee, and chocolate cake. The prisoners were not given food that day.

When Gen. Gabler said "now" as the time for work to commence, he meant it quite literally. The taciturn and seldom verbal senior master sergeant signaled to his lower-ranked enlisted men who marched forward and separated the two hundred prisoners into twenty-five groups. That activity took ten minutes and required the overworked Americans to club the prisoners who moved with insufficient alacrity. The guards were experts. They inflicted pain but no disabling injuries for the most part. As the club blows struck, even sick and weary men began to hurry.

Antoine Duvalier had a fifteen-minute tutorial on the dismantling of Nazi land mines. Fortunately for him, he was familiar with the devices and how to render them harmless because he had been in charge of burying more than a hundred thousand of them during his career in the SS. The instruction was given by a haggard, ragged, and filthy internee—one all too reminiscent of the POWs at the tin mine. Antoine was certain he was not going to prosper in his new environment. His real concern was whether or not he would survive. Other prisoners were less fortunate than him. They were assigned to the ignoble task of marching as human shields through known minefields at bayonet point to discover and destroy land mines without anyone having proper equipment or knowledge of the whereabouts of the mines.

The death rate was beyond anyone's worst predictions. The Allied officers and NCOs cared very little. There was an inexhaustible supply of mine-destroying fodder coming in; and, after all, they were hardly humans. Moreover, they deserved whatever they got.

After eight hours of work—the work having to cease because it was too dark to see any longer—the staff sergeant in charge of his detail ordered the men to finish disarming the land mine they were working on then to line up for return to the main "living" area. One of the prisoners—an old man with thick glasses and trembling hands—did not move quickly enough. His NCO kicked him several times in the ribs and lateral thighs, making him even more unsteady. The NCO walked back fifteen yards—the mandatory distance to be maintained by American servicemen from the "dogs" in the mine-disarming work. It was a good thing for him that he did, because the man's trembling hands jerked a wire he should have cut, and the bomb exploded, blowing him to pieces.

The NCO groaned, knowing that this would make him late for supper.

Antoine had the misfortune to be standing near the NCO at the time.

"You. Get three men and go clean up that mess. The trash bags are over there by the dump. Fill a couple of trash bags—that's all you'll need—seal them very well, then carry the bags to the dump. Hurry it up!" the American ordered.

Antoine had seen worse; so, he got right to it. Perhaps his willingness to hurry would be noted; and even if not, at least they would all get back to chow a bit earlier. One of his chosen helpers had not been in combat; so, it was too much for him and he fainted. That brought upon him scorn from the American guards and a series of heavy blows with a club. Antoine was blamed for his choice and took six blows himself as an educational strategy. He swallowed what little pride he had left and his feeling of Vesuvial anger and rushed to do the other man's share of the work. They arrived too late to the communal pot and found no food. One of the older men gave Antoine and his coworker/human bomb detector a few dirt cookies to fill their stomachs before they went to sleep. Antoine and his handpicked fellow workers each found an unoccupied ground pit and went to sleep famished. It had been an inauspicious first day in his new home.

Allied POW Camp Recipes

<u>**Dirt Cookies—Serves 12–15**</u>

Ingredients
-2–3 quarts of fine clay dirt, water sufficient to make a smooth, fluid, but not watery consistency; salt, sugar, butter, cream, bacon drippings to taste (as available).

Preparation
-Break up and grind dirt until it is powdery fine. Sift out pebbles, hard pieces of dirt, and extraneous matter.
-Gradually add water (or milk, coffee, tea, beer, or cream as available) to the dirt until a fine smooth batter is created. Avoid excess water since cookies will crumble as they heat.
-Place smooth mud mixture on a flat surface, cut 3 in. cookie shapes and dry in the sun until firm.
-Then carefully slip a pancake turner (or broad bladed knife) under each cookie and transfer to the area of longest and most intense sun through the day and leave until the cookies are almost as hard and brittle as clay pottery.
-Break off bite-size pieces, chew carefully so as not to break teeth or to swallow pieces large enough to catch in the throat.
-It is also a good idea to suck the cookie pieces to soften them—that takes time and allieviates stress as the nutrition-free delicacies work their magic of filling the stomach and damping down the pangs of hunger.

<u>**Toasted Rat—3 Rats Constitute 1 Serving**</u>

Ingredients
-10–12 large rats, salt, pepper, curry, garlic, cooking oil—as available.

Preparation
-To catch rats, gather several handfuls of dry grass; light it afire to create smoke. Place smoking grass into opening of a rat hole; wait several mins. then retrieve dead rats.
-Skewer rats with hard wood or metal skewers as available.
-Hold rat to open fire until all hair is gone and rat is the consistency of potato chips.
-Break off pieces and eat like crackers (skin, bones, muscles, guts, extremities, and tails)
-Add spices as available to improve taste. This manner of preparation of rat is considered to be an acquired taste.

Note: a variation when equipment and materials are available is to deep-fry rats in oil until they are as brittle as wafers; break off pieces, as above, and enjoy. For stew, it is best to skin the rats first as the hair remains annoying.

CHAPTER TWENTY-FIVE

Bad Kreuznach—Lager Galgenberg und Bretzenheim PWTE—Bad Kreuznach District, Rhineland-Palatinate, Germany, August 22, 1954

Local farmers Berthold Küppers, Rolf Kohns, and Franz Joseph Dheil entered the main gate of the camp and were escorted to the administration building by four US Army military policemen. The road leading to the building passed through the area between the rows of army barracks, officer's quarters, BAQs, and storage facilities on one side and the perimeter fence on the other. The intention of placement of the road there was to present an effective sight barrier against the local Germans seeing what went on in the interior of the camp. The farmers' purpose in coming to the camp was to protest the high demand the Americans had for their produce and the low price the farmers were being paid. More importantly, they were well aware that the Americans were withholding fresh food from the inmates and selling it on the black market. They were practical men, not humanitarians. What the Americans did with their prisoners was of only minor interest, but they would no longer be able to keep farming if the American officers did not get control of the black market operations so that market forces could bring food prices up to a fair level outside the compound.

The three farmers were led into a spacious and well-appointed Quonset hut and seated on comfortable chairs at a solid walnut conference table. Gen. Glen Gabler presided at the weekly meeting with local providers along with his aide, Major Saunders. A full complement of assistant officers took up the rest of the chairs: the G1 [chief of staff], G2 [intelligence], G3 [operations and plans], G4 [logistics], G5 [civil affairs], G8 [resource management], military police, and Sergeant Major Briggs. The assemblage was daunting to the farmers, but they were determined to be heard and to try and convince the Americans to get control of the black market operations associated with the camp.

"Welcome to our weekly conference with local officials, gentlemen," Gen. Gabler said. "We have read your petition and wish to have you present the information you have on your complaints."

Berthold Küppers had been elected spokesman for the farmers of Bad Kreuznach and Bretzenheim.

"General, Officers, we are but humble farmers; and we have come to seek your help. We live in a fertile farming area and can grow all of the fruits and vegetables you need for your camp and also for our local citizens. With the help of your transportation services, we have been able to deliver our produce to you in the amounts you order and on time. It is an efficient operation. Our problem is that prices for our produce continue to go down as the black marketeers siphon off the fruits and vegetables and sell them at very reduced prices—below what it costs us to plant, grow, and deliver our goods. We will not be able to farm if our costs and a reasonable profit for our labors are not met."

"So, I take it that you are applying for an increase in payment for your goods. Is that correct, Herr … Küppers?"

"Partially so, General. The American occupying forces have taken over all police control, and nothing is being done to curb the greed and success of those who obtain our produce without our knowledge or consent and undercut us by selling them throughout the area at ridiculously reduced prices."

"You are speaking of German criminals, are you not, Herr Küppers?"

"Yes, but…."

"We on the base fail to see how this involves us. You are not quite correct about control of police forces. German civilian police have been selected to deal with nonmilitary German matters. Black marketeering is one of those matters. We sympathize, but see no way we can interfere with what is a civilian matter."

"The source of the illegally sold produce is the Bad Kreuznach—Lager Galgenberg und Bretzenheim PWTE. That is the long and short of the matter. The German police do not have the money, authority, manpower, or weapons to deal with the problem; and neither they nor the merchants and farmers of the area have any say in what happens to the produce once it comes into the PWTE. We implore you to put a stop to the profiteering taking place at the camp."

As soon as he said it, Küppers knew he had been intemperate in his language and had gone too far.

"That sounds very much like an accusation, Herr Küppers. You, perhaps, are not mindful of the great generosity of the Americans and other Allies towards the enemies—the defeated enemies—of our countries. This camp is an example of that generosity. We rehabilitate criminals so that they can eventually be reassimilated into German society without creating the Nazi menace you, like us, suffered from. We are mindful of the extra costs coming from a growing German economy. I will have my G5 and G8 officers look into the possibility of increasing payments for your products if it seems to them that such action is warranted. I suggest that you take up any supposed criminal matters with your local German authorities and police. That is all, gentlemen. You are dismissed."

The three Germans were not successful in hiding from their facial expressions their contempt for the Americans and especially the general, but they said nothing and departed promptly under guard.

Gen. Gabler turned to his G2.

"Mike, do a background check on those three men. I suspect we'll find a Nazi or two in the woodshed. Perhaps an object lesson will need to be learned by complainers, and with rehabilitation here in the camp for a few months, we will have a more compliant and grateful population—one that understands its place and—more importantly—learns what defeat means and why they should never allow another militaristic society to raise its ugly visage again in this despicable country."

The conference room cleared.

Major Saunders caught up with Sergeant Major Briggs before he headed back to the work area.

"Sergeant Major, a word please."

"Certainly, Major, sir. How may I be of assistance?"

"I need the figures for the last two months. The minefields around the area are fast being cleared, and we are hearing scuttlebutt that we will have to start closing down the camp gradually in the next three or four months. We need to get everyone paid, and our extra operation closed down before then. The general is especially interested in how well the Swiss accounts are doing."

"I will have the information in your office this afternoon, sir. If I may speak candidly, sir?"

"Of course, Sergeant Major."

"We may have a problem brewing. There are too many men for us to handle or feed. The Red Cross has become increasingly demanding that they be allowed access to the prisoners. The ODESSA is operating actively in the area, and we know that several of the more senior SS officers interned here are going missing. This is probably related to the trucking in and out of the camp. We will have to address each of those problems."

"Thank you, Briggs. The general and I are aware of those problems and will have to take measures to control them, but we have to tread lightly or we will jeopardize our enterprise. The ODESSA and certain criminal syndicates are—like it or not—involved in our operation unofficially—of course—but nonetheless actively. It is possible that they know too much and may eventually be an embarrassment to all of us who may have … profited from this windfall of funding."

"I will see to it at my end, sir."

"Good man. Keep me posted."

The POWs, Disarmed Enemy Forces, and Displaced Persons interned in the PWTE lived in squalor in shallow pits in the ground without real shelter. They did not wash, and wore the same clothing every day until they were nearly naked before they were handed a new set. They received an average of 1200 to 1500 calories ration which was inadequate, and the food they got was substandard to be euphemistic. Antoine and his *Gebirgsjägers* were very aware that they were weakening a little more each day. They saw men who had died of starvation and privation carried away every day. The lack of food made men weak, slow-witted, and a danger to themselves and the rest of the camp inmates. Some of that inhuman treatment was not entirely the fault of the army.

The number of prisoners so greatly exceeded expectations that the army itself had begun to lose track of some of the locations where POWs were held. Organization of the camps was left to prisoners, and starving and brutalized men are notoriously poor humanitarians. In many camps—Bad Kreuznach, Lager Galgenberg, and Bretzenheim PWTE included—society descended to a primeval Darwinian/Hobbesian level of existence, not unlike the conditions in the Russian gulags.

The period soon after August 1945 had been, overall, the worst period; and supplies improved later. However, the black market profits drove previously honorable and honest men to seize the moment to become rich by depriving the despised internees. They convinced themselves that the POWs and "Disarmed Persons" deserved everything they got, and ordinary American soldiers turned a deaf ear and a blind eye to the plight of the prisoners as they themselves grew rich. Swiss banks did a landslide business.

Reports to Washington that the Allies were violating international law regarding the feeding of enemy civilians and both directly and indirectly causing unnecessary suffering and death of large numbers of civilians and prisoners in occupied Germany were received by Allied capitals with indifference. This attitude was guided largely by a spirit of postwar vengeance, and no effective interest occurred to correct the circumstances that contributed to that suffering and those deaths. On the contrary, Washington sent out strict orders to US military personnel and their wives to destroy or otherwise render inedible their own leftover surplus so as to ensure it could not be eaten by German civilians or former combatants.

"We will die this year if we don't get out of here," Hugues Beauchamp told his fellow remaining members of the 33rd Waffen SS Division.

It was a statement of the obvious, but all of them recognized the need to do something and soon, there was no need for them to send delegates to the camps.

They all looked to Antoine.

"I have made contact with one of the guards. He is the head of the transport detail that moves food and other supplies in and out of here. He told me about the camp's deal with the black market to profit by giving us the dregs and selling the fresh healthy food on the outside. He has some contact with the ODESSA which gets part of the food to help former SS people and their families. They informed the American that this camp is going to be disbanded soon, and that we will be transferred somewhere. I pressed him for more information which he would only give me for a price. I have a contact through the fence with an ODESSA operative who provided the money. This is what I learned:

we are known to the ODESSA. That means they believe we have a treasure cache and that they can support their SS people. Therefore, it is in their best interests to help us escape. Because of the impending—but presently secret—move, security has been heightened to the point that they cannot help us now. They will find out where we are sent and get us out of that place."

"If we live that long," groused Serge.

"I grant you the honor of having made the argument of the day. Hang on and let's find food. That will be our first priority," Antoine said.

"And don't get careless and trip one of the mines," Jérôme added.

The following morning, Antoine made contact with his guard and with the ODESSA contact.

"My three men and I have to get out of here in the next three or four days or we will be dead from starvation and overwork, and you will not get the promised payday."

It was dark and raining, and none of the men had any inclination for light conversation.

"No can do," the American corporal said, "too much scrutiny on the fences and gates. I will be headed with you to the new camp, but even I don't know where it is. Once I know, I can let our ODESSA friend here—who shall go unnamed—where you and I are. With that intel, we can get the show on the road for you to disappear."

Antoine had picked up considerable English during his stay in Bad Kreuznach, and that included army slang, but he was missing some of what the corporal was saying.

"Does 'no can do' mean it can't be done? And does 'get the show on the road' mean something like starting a diversion?"

The corporal laughed, "'No can do' is pretty obvious, but 'getting the show on the road' is an old traveling carnival expression which means that we can do what is necessary to make things happen—things we want to have happen, okay?"

Antoine nodded his understanding.

"My friend on the outside—the one with the treasure—has to have someone to contact," the American corporal asserted, "Our silent friend here from the ODESSA has got to give me an address or telephone number; so, my friend can contact him. I assure you that I am not a spy for anybody, and I am not a threat," he said.

The ODESSA operative nodded to the corporal.

"It's okay. Here is the number. Have your guy call between 1900 and 1910 hours every night starting one week from now. He will need to be able to provide a meeting place for the ODESSA people and him, and—absolutely—he will have to prove that he has the moola."

Antoine gave him a quizzical look.

"The money," the corporal said.

CHAPTER TWENTY-SIX

"There were many words that you could not stand to hear and finally only the names of places had dignity. Abstract words such as 'glory,' 'honor,' 'courage,' or 'hallow' were obscene."
-Ernest Hemingway, American novelist and WW1 veteran, in *A Farewell to Arms*, 1929

POW Camp 63 Brienne le Chateâu, France [*Kriegsgefangenenpost* 62: POW Post Office], August 29, 1954

Preparations for the move began a week later. Rations were cut to 800 calories. In two days, no one was capable of working, but that was of little concern because the vast majority of the German land mines had been removed, blown up, or otherwise rendered harmless. The *Gebirgsjägers* largely lay in their ground hollows in misery because of a spate of summer rains. After another screening of the POWs, the Americans began releasing old men and boys of the *Volkssturm* [Lit. "people's storm"—which was a German national militia formed in the last months of World War II from conscripted males between the ages of thirteen to sixty years] who were considered to be harmless and even possibly of potential benefit to a new, controlled German economy.

All prisoners were assembled in the open area. A team of army doctors, nurses, and corpsmen made all of the men remove their shirts. Most of them were little more than skeletons.

"Five push-ups," the sergeant major ordered.

Less than half were able to do even one. All of the *Gebirgsjägers* were able to eke out five and to struggle back to their feet. About two hundred of the 2,500 survivors were able—barely able—but many of the others just lay down in the mud ready to be shot. They did not even have the strength to protest. The head doctor walked along with a corpsman taking notes. He pointed his finger at the men who had performed the task. He nodded to Sergeant Major Briggs and Major Saunders, then the medical unit returned to the clinic building.

Sergeant Major Briggs barked, "Follow me. No talking in line."

The two hundred fittest men—a decidedly relative distinction–fell into a queue and followed the senior enlisted man to the front of the building where seven buses were waiting. He ordered them to get aboard and passed out ham and cheese sandwiches and bottles of beer. He even gave each man a package of the Americans' favorite cigarettes called Camels. Antoine noticed that there were two healthy-appearing men being loaded onto the bus he was on. They were both overweight and were wearing good sturdy working clothes.

"What are your names, gentlemen?" he asked, curious about their late appearance in the Allied concentration camp system, and more than a bit suspicious.

"Berthold Küppers and Rolf Kohns," the larger of the two men answered grumpily, "what's yours?"

"Antoine. Antoine Duvalier."

It was one of the few times Antoine had given his real name out loud in ten years.

"What brings you here? You obviously aren't POWs. Are you communists or gypsies?"

He laughed when he said it.

"*Nein*! We are accused of being unrepentant Nazis. We are guilty of suggesting that the general was allowing the black market to steal food from the prisoners to make an obscene profit.

"Are you guilty?"

Antoine asked it with a smile.

"*Ja. Ja wohl!*"

"Are you Nazis?"

"*Ja.*"

"*Wehrmacht?*"

"*Nein*," Berthold said with defiance in his face and in his tone. "*Schutzstaffel!*" he said emphatically, looking Antoine directly in the eye."

"*Wie lautet Dein Eid?*" [What is your oath?] Antoine asked, posing the central first question of the SS Hitler oath as a test.

"*Ich schwöre Dir, Adolf Hitler, als Führer und Kanzler des Deutschen Reiches Treue und Tapferkeit. Wir geloben Dir und den von Dir bestimmten Vorgesetzten Gehorsam bis in den Tod. So wahr mir Gott helfe!*" [I vow to you, Adolf Hitler, as Führer and chancellor of the German Reich loyalty and bravery. I vow to you and to the leaders that you set for me, absolute allegiance until death. So help me God!]

"*Also glaubst Du an einen Gott?*" [So you believe in a God?] Antoine continued.

"*Ja, ich glaube an einen Herrgott.*" [Yes, I believe in a Lord God.].

"*Was hältst Du von einem Menschen, der nicht an einen Gott glaubt?*" [What do you think about a man who does not believe in a God?]

"*Ich halte ihn für überheblich, grossenwahnsinnig und dumm; er ist nicht für uns geeignet.*" [I think he is arrogant, megalomaniacal, and stupid; he is not one of us.]

Antoine was joined by Hugues Beauchamp, Jérôme Christophe Mailhot, and Serge Alain Rounsavall.

Serge spoke for the *Gebirgsjägers*, "You are one of us. Stay close. We work to protect each other.

Berthold nodded, answering for himself and for Rolf Kohns.

A well-armed unit of guards walked onto the bus and stood in the aisles with menace on their faces. Sergeant Major Briggs spoke briefly to the first bus driver then stepped off and returned to the field where the weaker men were still lying on the ground. Major Saunders walked across the field to the small set of barracks that housed the known senior members of the SS and presumed war criminals. The regular POWs and Disarmed Enemy Forces personnel had a fairly large area where they could move about fairly freely so long as they remained ten feet from any fence. The senior SS officers had an exercise area measuring about twenty by twenty feet. They were only allowed out at night; so, they were seldom seen. Major Saunders's detachment ordered the officers out of their barracks and began to talk to them about the changes taking place in the camp. Suddenly without warning, four of the American enlisted men opened fire on the SS officers, who crumpled like wheat being cut for harvest. Behind them a graves registry unit moved in and loaded the corpses into a truck and took them to the center of the open area and dumped them in a pile. The senior NCO ordered the truck to the dump, and his men loaded the long-standing pile of body bags into the back of the truck and dumped them on the other bodies.

Two men doused the pile with ten gallons of gasoline, then another casually tossed and lit cigarette lighter onto the pile, causing an almost explosive inferno. The graves registry unit and the assassination unit left the open area and returned to their barracks. It was all done with Germanic efficiency. Then Gen. Gabler joined Major Saunders and Sergeant Major Briggs in front of the men lying huddled on the ground. Many of them were crying softly, expecting the worst.

"You men are worthless for work, and our orders do not permit us to execute you; so, today you are free. We will open the gates and put you on the street. Do not venture close to the camp again or you will be shot," the general said; and he, too, returned to his quarters.

The major and the sergeant major gathered the troops and did whatever was necessary to push, walk, or drag the remaining men and to place them on the four streets running alongside the perimeter fences. Perhaps they thought that the populace would provide food, water, clothing, and shelter. Perhaps not. None of those subhuman monsters deserved even a passing thought, each American thought to himself.

Cooperation was not complete. About fifteen men somehow found strength or were crazed by fear, hunger, and thirst; and they made a sad—almost slow motion—dash for the fence, apparently not aware that the gates were open. The sentries opened fire, and all fifteen were dead before they reached the fence. Grave's Registry was summoned back and added the new bodies to the still crematory-hot fire. The remaining men still able to stand in the queue for the bus each got a swift blow from an American's club to punctuate the lesson they had just witnessed, as if any further emphasis was needed.

The buses entered the city streets driving very rapidly. It was immediately apparent why: the streets were lined with furious and sullen townspeople who had only a few days before collecting the dead, dying, and severely ill PTWE concentration camp victims from the streets around Bad Kreuznach. The American guards on the buses were afraid the angry crowd was going to block the streets and attack the buses. That would precipitate an armed response with mass killings of German civilians which would lead to an international incident, which in turn would lead to exposure of the deplorable conditions of the camp and treatment of the prisoners, and would result in America being identified as being no better than the Nazis with their concentration camps and horrific POW camps or the Soviet gulags. The bus drivers were ordered to push full speed ahead and not to stop for anything. The people scattered, and a riot was averted.

They drove at breakneck speed to the Bad Kreuznach railroad station. The American guards alighted from the buses, and ten of them ran to the station master's building and ordered him to ready the train for immediate departure despite the disruption of the schedule all down the line. The rest of the guards force-marched the weary and weak prisoners out of the buses and onto the trains. While the American soldiers were brow-beating the civilian train personnel to get them to hurry away from the station against all regulations, the train master sent two employees to local food stores to empty their supplies of meat, cheese, bread, and beer. In the chaos that swirled around the departure frenzy, the food was rushed aboard and distributed by the Germans to their fellow Germans.

Much to the displeasure of the Americans, most of the food had been consumed by the time order was restored. Some of the prisoners had gobbled the rich food so quickly that they were vomiting in the aisles. Recognizing that it was too late to prevent their prisoners from getting their fill, the Americans decided to forget about it and ordered the train to move out, wishing the prisoners good riddance. The prisoners had learned a thing or two about Americana and almost to a man, stuck their hands out the windows and gave their cruel American keepers the finger.

Six hours later, the train pulled into the station in Brienne le Chateâu, a commune in the Aube department in the Champagne-Ardenne region of north-central France. Its population was 1500 people. The town was located a mile from the right bank of the Aube River and about ten miles from the POW internment camp located on the American AAF base.

The prisoners were herded off the trains and into buses with the same urgency that had attended their boarding them in Bad Kreuznach and for much the same reason. Violently angry French people—men, women, and children—had somehow gotten wind that the German

POWs and Disarmed Persons were going to arrive in the town's railroad station that afternoon. The towns in the Champagne-Ardenne area had been ravaged by the Nazis well within the memories of all of the citizens except for small children. Even they had been thoroughly schooled in hatred for the Huns.

During the Nazi occupation, the military base had been an SS headquarters. From 1940–1945, men from every country under German control were trained there to become conscienceless SS officers. A subcamp of the Dachau concentration camp was located in the town. It provided labor for the *SS-Junkerschule* and the *Zentralbauleitung* [Central Administration Building]. As the need for more and more slave laborers for Nazi projects progressed, the base itself became a major holding area. Most of the inmates died during their stay, but that was of no great interest to the SS men and women who ran the camp because the sources of new slaves were many, and the slaves were both cheap and plentiful.

During the war, the base was also a large medical center. There were persistent rumors that heinous medical experiments were carried out there. A legacy of hatred towards the Germans was created, and no one in the region believed that even the slightest sliver of mercy should be shown by the victors to the vanquished. When the Americans and Free-French began to close in on the airfield, the SS purposely flooded the bottom floor of the headquarters to destroy all of their records. A pond was formed due to water seeping out of the building, and that pond was still standing when the POWs were moved into the concentration camp that now belonged to the Americans.

In November of 1953, the 10th Special Forces Group Airborne arrived at the former AAF base/then SS base. The former *SS-Junkerschule* became the base of the US Army's First Battalion headquarters. The French living in the region cared little about what occurred on the base or in the concentration camp. They were happy when the emaciated camp internees were marched out in ever widening concentric circles to clear the Nazi minefields. It made life safer in the fields, on the streets, and in the forests for the French citizens, and they were not dismayed when they heard a bomb go off—one less Hun. Or when they saw the plumes of black smoke come from the southwest corner of the camp—many less Huns.

The arrival of the train was another opportunity for the citizens to vent their pent-up and unquenchable rage. As the men were quickly marched off out of the passenger cars of the trains and into the waiting US Army troop trucks, the townspeople rushed forward to club the POWs with hammers and clubs made from tree branches, picks, shovels, and rocks. Considerable blood was shed in the process, but no one was killed or critically injured–much to the chagrin of the French people. Of the *Gebirgsjägers*, only Antoine had a wound that left another scar on his forehead.

At the gates of the camp, the buses were met by a contingent of International Red Cross volunteers who—against the wishes of the new commandant of the camp—passed out water, croissants, crusty bread, cheese, fresh fruit, and coffee. The prisoners—knowing this was better fare than they were likely to see for sometime—gobbled down the offerings like pigs at a trough. The Red Cross volunteers were disgusted and dismayed by the spectacle, but made an effort to remain stony-faced. Among themselves, they muttered that it was no more than might have been expected from these vermin. When the prisoners tried to tell the volunteers thank you, they were met with expressionless faces and silence.

At the entrance into the American/British POW camp, they were met by the commandant—currently a British general taking his rotation—and four large and menacing other ranks: a corporal, two lance corporals, and a Fusilier. The commandant's introduction to the camp was terse and harsh.

"You were sent here to die. You are responsible for the deaths of countless Americans, British, and French soldiers and civilians. Do not expect treatment any better than what you gave to the Jews in your murder camps. Do not make trouble. If you do, you will be shot and then burned on a trash dump. No one will ever know you were here. That is all."

They were not fed again for two days. During that time, they were required to dig out shallow pits in the dirt by hand for their sleeping arrangements. They were deloused, and their bodies were shaved of all hair except about the groin. They were prodded into the pond by the former SS-*Junkerschule*—now administration building for the 10th Special Forces Group Airborne—given bars of crude rough soap and brushes. Those who were unable or unwilling to use the brushes on their newly shaved and nicked skin were assisted by camp prisoners already interned there who were promised a hot meal if they were especially vigorous with the stiff-bristled brushes. After drying with rough towels, they were issued prison clothes—bright red and white striped shirt, trousers, soft brimless cap, and shoes with uppers made of canvas and soles made of used and discarded rubber tires.

The *Gebirgsjägers* had experienced brutality, indifference, neglect, injustice, and all had witnessed wanton murders by psychopaths; but in the British commandant, they saw and experienced an even worse monster. He was a sadist of the worst kind. The Geneva Convention meant nothing. He actually took pleasure when inflicting pain or if a German suffered. Of all of the beasts they had suffered under, the officers of the 33rd Waffen-Grenadier Divison of the SS hated this man the most.

Antoine made the cardinal mistake of protesting when the general whipped a Wehrmacht officer until he was unconscious and covered with blood. For that, he was driven to the ground with an electric cattle prod; until he, too, was unconscious.

When he regained consciousness and found himself lying in the mud, confused, and feeling pain in every muscle and joint in his body, Antoine swore an oath, "*This man will pay and will pay dearly. I will stay alive no matter what it takes to destroy him.*"

CHAPTER TWENTY-SEVEN

POW Camp 63 Brienne le Chateâu, France [Kriegsgefangenenpost 62: POW Post Office], September 1, 1954

This was an important day for the camp. The operation of the prisoner facilities and labor force was being turned over to the newly reorganized French army. This was the prisoners' opportunity to meet the new commandant–the first French officer to take over an American or British base. It was much heralded in town—Brienne le Chateâu—and in the region—Bar-sur-Aube, Troyes, Chaumont, and Saint Dizier newspapers and magazines. There was even a mention in *France Soir* in Paris the next day. It was a matter of monumental indifference to the prisoners. That day was regarded as no different from the day before; none of those days were another day in paradise, or even the upgrade to the equivalent of a Parisian slum.

At ten in the morning all prisoners were brought back from their now far-flung fields of labor disarming mines and as slave labor for local farmers. The Americans started the practice, and it was continued by the British during their turn at running the camp. The unspoken policy was akin to the black market in Germany, but it had a distinct stamp of French flair—please the officers and guides of the camp with profits over and above their military salaries, please the townspeople and farmers who benefited from having free labor, and the concerns of the prisoner/slaves be damned. From September 1945 on, it was estimated by the French authorities that two thousand prisoners were being maimed and killed each month in accidents.

Outgoing British camp commandant Lieutenant General Sir Cyril Goeffrey Robert Hill-Brownwell, RA, stood before the assembled prisoners and announced, "Per orders from SHAEF headquarters, the American and British occupation of the prisoner of war system comes to an end today. Henceforward, the French army will assume its rightful role as the master of its own destiny in matters military in France. We have the honor to be the first American or British base to turn over command to the French, and it is particularly fitting that the new commandant is to be *Lieutenant Général de division* Étienne Malboeuf, hero of the Battle of Berlin. I give you, with pride and pleasure, General Malboeuf."

Antoine and his *Gebirgsjägers* remained at attention with only their facial expressions telling of their intense hatred for the man. Each of the former French officers of the 33rd Waffen-Grenadier SS Division remembered with a fiery exactness the man who had served as the second in command to *Maréchal de France* [Marshal of France] Philippe François Marie Leclerc de Hauteclocque, and who had ordered the summary execution of what the French believed were the last twelve men who served the Nazis with great courage and pitiless excess since the unit was established in 1942.

The men had been defeated, captured, and rendered defenseless in the last few days of the war. The scene was a clearing in a woodland near the Bavarian village of Karlstein. They were brought before General Malboeuf of Leclerk's Second Armored Division, a man who walked with the strutting pride of a martinet in front of the wholly conquered men. His face assumed the disdainful and condescending expression of a haughty great avenger—the god of the day. After a stinging condemnation of each man as a traitor to his country and to civilized humanity, he turned his back to them, and, with a mere flicking of his swagger stick, ordered the firing squad to machine gun the prisoners. He was not aware that another fourteen French members of the 33rd Division witnessed the executions. It would not have mattered a whit to him anyway, and no one was ever to hear about or from those men. They were subsequently captured by the Red Army and eventually transported to Siberian gulags.

The hauteur and rigid pomposity of the French general was unchanged on this day as he stood in front of the helpless prisoners from his demeanor on that dreadful day in 1945 when the atrocity was committed. His uniform was perfectly tailored—a new one in the cavalry style, personally designed by the general himself. His képi of a *ereal de division*—with its red top, wide brim, high cap, and wide black band bearing a striking gold oakleaf cluster—his knee-high riding boots, polished to a degree that they reflected the sun, his epaulets with three stars, and his spotless freshly pressed coat, blouse, and trousers bespoke a man of supreme authority, inflexible rigidity, and an insufferable dandy. His vanity was stroked by his wearing the medals he had won—not just the campaign ribbons. He was less a handsome man than he was regal with a thick crop of well-coifed silver-white hair without the slightest hint of balding. He carried a hardwood swagger stick containing a concealed blade under his left armpit, and affectation he had copied from American General George S. Patton.

Gen. Malbeouf spoke in a high-pitched, almost falsetto voice, "Stand at attention, defeated German swine! You are in this corrections camp to make restitution for your crimes during the recent war which you started, and which you lost. When you have paid the uttermost farthing, you will be returned to your country of origin to join those unhappy souls living in poverty and misery brought on by your military misadventures. You will work, and you will obey. Your new masters will tolerate no one who is a slacker and no one who will not obey instantly.

"You will not look a guard or an officer in the eye. You will never speak unless spoken to. When you walk, you will look down at the ground. When you approach a gate or a door, you will wait until a guard appears and gives you permission. You will not register complaints. You will not ask for more food, better clothing, or improved housing. You do not deserve even what you have or will yet be given. Remember when you used to say, '*Es ist nicht ein Mann; es ist ein Jude?*' ['It is not a man; it is a Jew.'] You are now the Jews. You once brutalized and tortured the French people. Now you will feel the sting of their hatred and righteous wrath. You are dismissed. Get back to work."

Antoine watched the general strut past the front row of prisoners. One man made the mistake of looking up at the officer and received a hard swipe of Malbeouf's swagger stick, an object lesson for the first day. Antoine and his *Gebirgsjägers* were kicked, shoved, and driven with cattle prods to their work sites and began another day of unearthing mines and disarming them. Gen. Malbeouf was driven by his staff car to his house in the Hôtel de ville Square in Brienne-le-Château for a celebratory picnic with the mayors of the region's towns, the sheriffs, the French army officers in the Aube department in north-central France, and the American and British army officers who were preparing for their return to the United States and the UK. Malbeouf did not approve of women being invited to such important gatherings.

Malbeouf expressed his personal gratitude to Lieutenant General Sir Cyril Goeffrey Robert Hill-Brownwell, RA for the generosity of the United States which provided the slave labor for the now French camps—740,000 of them (with the promise of 560,000 more) over the course of the upcoming year. The British were credited with handling the administration of the huge prisoner transfer. The annual death rates for the prisoners held in American-run camps—as brutal and neglectful as they were—was about one percent. The French succeeded in raising that number to 2.6 percent. On one occasion during the period of internment, nearly 1000 SS officers were poisoned to death by bread laced with arsenic.

Malbeouf and his guests enjoyed a sumptuous *déjeuner* of *pâté de Foie Gras, Salade Nicoise,* savory buckwheat galette filled with ham and cheese, and for dessert, *pain au chocolat* and *Croque Madame.* They quaffed Brut Réserve champagne from the house of Billecart-Salmon flown in from Paris for the occasion. The one meal of the day for the POWs and Disarmed Persons was a further lesson and warning for them: grass and weeds picked by their own hands and placed in a tin can containing a thin soup canned specially for the French prisoners. It was more than evident that Gen. Malbeouf and his Frenchmen and Lt. Gen. Hill-Brownwell and his Brits intended for them to die in this place and be forgotten. It was one of the few times the French and the British agreed on anything, and it was cause for another round of champagne.

Over the next several weeks, the men became emaciated and suffered raging dysentery. Many were too weak to dig latrine trenches and few could make it to such a trench if one were present. They were packed into crowded conditions so severe that many could not get to food when it was made available by dumping it on the ground. The slit trenches which were still open were so crowded that many men simply lay down and fell asleep in their own excrement, too exhausted to move or to care. Those men died. None of the French guards made a move to help them, and there was no medical assistance of any kind.

The irony of the camp was that many of the men were nothing more than sharecropper farmers and unskilled workingmen. They were simple and ignorant, and even if they had been soldiers, they were more victims of the Nazis than they were perpetrators. Work results fell to a minimum despite the vicious beatings delivered upon slackers. The world of the French slave labor POW camp became a Hobbesian nightmare peopled by zombies, many of them having lost their minds. Some of those used their last vestiges of strength to make an insane and suicidal dash for the river to get something to drink and were strafed with machine gun fire.

Antoine and his men were an exception to the starvation. The ODESSA and their former providers—American corporal Jimmie Clemmons and his black marketeers—who brought in food for the *Gebirgsjägers* in return for the promise of a larger share of the Nazi gold they were assured would be available to them once Jérôme Christophe Mailhot was able to escape with the help of the ODESSA. They were recognized as being able to work and joined approximately four thousand other men who were able to be productive to one degree or another. They were trucked to labor on farms, the minefields having been largely sanitized.

The trucks left the camp at six in the morning on the dot and returned at eight in the evening with equal precision. Any German prisoners who were so exhausted that they staggered, fell down, or lagged behind were clubbed to death—not being considered to be worth a bullet to the head. The bodies were dragged to the side of the road by the other prisoners and left there to be picked up by a burial brigade when they could get to them. Not a few of the men intentionally fell to their knees and awaited the inevitable, preferring a quick death to the slow starvation back at POW Camp 63, which was known to the prisoners as the "killing fields."

French Officers Mess Recipes

Croque Madame—Serves 4

Ingredients
Dry—3 tbsps all-purpose flour, ¼ tsp salt, ⅛ tsp black pepper, ⅛ tsp freshly grated nutmeg, 3½ oz (1⅓ cps) coarsely grated Gruyère cheese, 8 slices firm white sandwich bread, ½ lb thinly sliced high quality cooked ham, 4 lg eggs.
Liquid—5 tbsps unsalted butter, 2 cps whole milk, 4 tsps Dijon mustard

Preparation
Sauce:
Melt 3 tbsps butter in a 1–1½-qt heavy saucepan over moderately low heat, then whisk in flour and cook roux, whisking, 3 mins. Whisk in milk and bring to a boil, whisking constantly. Reduce heat and simmer, whisking occasionally, 5 min. Whisk in salt, pepper, nutmeg, and ⅓ cup cheese until cheese is melted. Remove from heat and cover surface directly with a sheet of wax paper.

Sandwiches:
-Spread 1½ tbsps sauce evenly over each of 4 slices of bread, then sprinkle evenly with remaining cheese~¼ cp per slice. Spread mustard evenly on remaining 4 bread slices and top with ham, dividing it evenly, then invert onto cheese-topped bread to form sandwiches.
-Lightly oil a 15- by 10-inch shallow baking pan.
-Melt 1 tbsp butter in a 12-in. nonstick skillet over moderately low heat, then cook sandwiches, turning over once until golden, 3–4 min. total. Remove from heat and transfer sandwiches to baking pan, then wipe out skillet with paper towels.
-Preheat broiler. Top each sandwich with ⅓ cp sauce, spreading evenly. Broil sandwiches 4–5 inches from heat until sauce is bubbling and golden in spots, 2–3 mins. Turn off broiler and transfer pan to lower third of oven to keep sandwiches warm.
-Heat remaining tbsp butter in nonstick skillet over moderate heat until foam subsides, then crack eggs into skillet and season to taste with salt and pepper. Fry eggs, covered, until whites are just set and yolks are still runny~3 mins. Top each sandwich with a fried egg and serve immediately.

Note: The egg yolks in this recipe will not be fully cooked, which may be of concern if salmonella is a problem in your area. You can use pasteurized eggs (in the shell) or cook eggs until yolks are set, but while safer, the runny eggs are better.

Terrine *pâté de Foie Gras*—Serves 10

Ingredients
-1½ lb. fresh duck *foie gras*, ⅓ cup good-quality sauternes, sea salt and freshly ground black pepper, 1 finely chopped black truffle.

Preparation
Prepare *foie gras*:
First, allow chilled foie gras to warm up so that it's tender and manageable because cold liver is brittle, and its veins harder to locate and remove intact. Pull any bits of translucent membrane from the surface and separate the two lobes using a knife to sever any connecting veins. Inspect the folds for patches of bitter green bile that could mar the terrine and extract them with a knife.

Second, clean and devein. For a smooth terrine, you must remove the thick, branched main vein that runs through the center of each lobe. Dig into the middle of each lobe with a paring knife, catch the vein under its tip, and pull it out.

Third, soak deveined *foie gras* pieces overnight in ice water to draw out any excess blood.

Fourth, the next day, break the liver into pieces and marinate it for 2 hrs in sauternes.

Fifth, cook the *foie gras* in a *bain-marie*. Considerable fat will be rendered. This fat is precious, both for flavoring and preserving the terrine. Save excess fat and refrigerate. To store terrine, pour melted fat over *foie gras* to seal it.

-Place *foie gras* in a medium bowl, break into even pieces, and add sauternes. Season with salt and pepper and allow to marinate 2 hours.

-Preheat oven to 400° F. Remove *foie gras* from marinade; press into a 2 ½-cup terrine, leaving a bit of space at top. Place terrine on 3 folded-over paper towels in the bottom of a deep skillet, and fill skillet with hot water to reach halfway up sides of terrine. Cook until internal temperature of foie gras reaches 115° F on a meat thermometer~30 mins. Pour off fat and reserve. Cool terrine.

-Cut a piece of cardboard to fit inside top of terrine and wrap it in plastic wrap. Gently press cardboard onto *foie gras*; weight with a small can for 1 hr. Remove can and cardboard, return reserved fat to terrine, cover, and refrigerate 1–2 days.

-To unmold, dip terrine in a bowl of warm water for 30 secs, run a knife along edges, and invert onto a plate. (Reserve fat in terrine.) Serve thinly sliced, garnished with truffle, if desired. If covered in reserved fat leftovers, the *foie gras* will keep if refrigerated for 1 wk.

CHAPTER TWENTY-EIGHT

Schlosskirche [Palace Church], Ellingen, Bavaria, August 19, 1954

Three of the six trucks of the ODESSA convoy parked in separate groves of trees in parks near the *Schlosskirche* while it was still dark, but only after a three-pass reconnoitering operation per Michaele's orders. Michaele and Jacob Bunnemann turned off the headlights of their truck and inched through the opaque darkness of the starless night past the front of the *Schlosskirche* and drove to the abandoned parking lot in the back. The church had been condemned as unsafe by the Nazis and later by the Americans and was declared off-limits to all personnel. In 1943, Antoine Duvalier and Michaele Dupont had been instrumental in that declaration and for providing security to keep citizens and military members away. The Allies inherited the partially demolished old building and let it go to ruin, never questioning the veracity or necessity of the prohibition.

Michaele strained his eyes and reaffirmed that the fine old church was still looking seedy and had not been repaired from its war damage. The barriers he and Antoine had placed there in the early forties were still in place and had not been disturbed. The German signs were still posted around the building, "*Zutritt verboten!*" [Entry forbidden—Keep out!] He tried not to get his hopes up too high, but this was the Holy Grail. It had to be; he and his men had suffered too much for it not to be. In a matter of days, he and his ODESSA companions would either be fabulously wealthy; or they would be in prison or dead.

To the uninformed—including Jacob and his ODESSA assistants—there were no safe or even possible entrances. Rubble-jammed doorways and the windows were boarded shut. The rear wall of the church near the entrance had crumbled, with the ceiling of the first floor collapsed over it so that tons of bomb-destroyed construction materials put up an impassable barrier. Michaele led Jacob to an old well on the northwest side of the churchyard, and the two of them pried off a wood plank cover hidden beneath undergrowth and trash. Michaele shined his flashlight briefly down into the well and was pleased to find it empty and to have the ladders he and Antoine had placed there in 1943 still in place.

"Let's have a quick look, Jacob. I'll go first and you shine the light, then you come down; and I'll shine the light for you. Make it quick."

The ladders were sturdy, and descent was easy. Both men stood in utter darkness at the bottom for a few moments. Then Michaele flashed his light around in a circle and revealed a tunnel intersecting at right angles to the vertical shaft of the well.

"This way," he said.

The air was dank and dusty, but the going was easy because down there they could use their flashlights without fear of detection from above. About fifty yards from the vertical shaft, they came to a heavy set of wooden doors which were bolted and secured with two large locks holding a heavy iron bar in place across the two doors.

"Uh-oh," Jacob said with discouragement in his voice.

"Watch," Michaele said.

He walked to one side of the tunnel where a wooden box covered with dust sat. They pried open the lid. The box was full of dusty spikes, bolts, nuts, and assorted other metal pieces. Anyone looking into the box would have presumed that nothing there would be of help in opening the door. Certainly there was no key. Jacob looked into the box soberly.

"Help me move it," Michaele ordered.

The two men struggled to move the heavy box a couple of feet away. The floor of the tunnel was extremely dusty, and only drag marks from the moving of the box showed any alteration in the dust cover. Jacob was becoming more dubious by the minute. Michaele was becoming increasingly enthusiastic.

Michaele ran his hand around in the dust where the box had been sitting. He found a minor depression in the floor and wiped the dust away from around it. Jacob's flashlight revealed a circular cut in the floor and a metal plate the same color as the dust and the nearby concrete floor. He pushed his finger into the depression and pulled up a metal ring about the size of a Deutschemark coin. He pulled on it. For a few minutes nothing happened, and Michaele strained harder.

Finally, the round metal plate pulled out of its depression in the floor to reveal a shallow pocket. Jacob's flashlight caught the glint of two large brass keys. Michaele took them out and walked to the locks on the door. Despite the years that had passed since the last time the locks had been opened, they gave easily. He lifted the heavy iron bar that had been holding the double doors fixed in place and pulled the doors open. Both men shined their lights into the cavernous basement storage room of the *Schlosskirche*, and then were transfixed by what they saw.

CHAPTER TWENTY-NINE

Schlosskirche [Palace Church], Ellingen, Bavaria, August 19 to September 14, 1954

Jacob was a man of forty-five years of age who had led a prosaic life, which—aside from his period of service during World War II—was spent scratching out a living as a farmer. In all of his life he had never seen more than a thousand Deutschmarks together all at once. But now, sitting before him was a stupendous and brilliant gleaming treasure. There were a dozen pallets loaded twenty rows high with gold ingots, huge ornate paintings of religious figures in heavy gold frames, boxes full of jewelry and gold and silver artefacts—candelabras, statuary, and platters—and open trunks full of diamonds and other precious stones. This was the riches a Kaiser would covet and men would kill for.

Michaele's mind began to review his plan for moving the massive fortune out of the church basement without attracting the wrong kind of attention. He already had a good working estimate of the combined value of what he and Jacob were gazing at.

Jacob snapped out of his reverie. "How in the world do we get all of this out of here and to where we can store it without getting caught?"

"Antoine and I have a plan. We built a means to get it out way back in '43 when we hid it here. We need to get back out of here and explain to the rest of the men what we need to do. Let's move quickly before it gets light outside."

For two days the men rested up in a house Jacob had rented several months earlier for use in this endeavor, although he had had no idea at the time why he had been ordered by Antoine to rent the place. They spent their time understanding Michaele's elaborate plan and working out how to carry it out. It was audacious–just audacious enough that it might work–they all decided. The extent of the treasure—as described by the awestruck Jacob—would cloud anyone's mind enough to ignore the obvious risks. Michaele assured them that it was going to work.

To get the plan ready to proceed, two men drove the trucks to a commercial vehicle painting company and had them altered to look like city maintenance trucks. They purchased lumbar and heavy tools and arranged to rent a backhoe and a heavy WWII tractor with a large snow removal blade. Two men returned to ODESSA headquarters and had regulation-appearing Ellingen City maintenance workmen's uniforms and caps and two Ellingen municipal police uniforms made. They purchased a large mess tent for use as an enclosure. Michaele and Jacob had large signs printed which read: "*Achtung: Abbruch und Wiederaufbau im in Fortschritt. Behalten Heraus!*" [Attention: Demolition and Reconstruction in Progress. Keep Out!] and heavy rope with signs that read: "*Extreme Gefahr. Das Gebäude Baustelle Nähern Sie sich Nicht!*" [Extreme Danger. Do Not Approach the Building Construction Site.] attached to the rope at intervals. The ODESSA volunteers were very efficient; and the organization had a large contingent of willing workers; so, the preparations were completed in twelve days.

On the last day in August, the work crew gathered en masse at the *Schlosskirche* and set out to cordon off the church grounds. The four large trucks and the heavy equipment pulled into the area behind the church immediately adjacent to where the subterranean tunnel was located. Two dozen workmen appeared and began to demolish the rear of the church building, making sure to leave structural supports in place. The large tractor with its heavy steel blade began to remove the mass of debris blocking the rear entry to the church building proper. When that was done, the large tent was placed near the entrance and the backhoe was put into use to dig a deep wide hole all the way down to the bottom of the church's old rock foundation. The hole was wide enough to accommodate the trucks. A team of construction workers built a truck ramp with a solid concrete foundation reinforced with steel struts—enough to bear a massive weight.

Two weeks later when the job was finished, the ODESSA crew boss was assured by Jacob that the men would all be paid in due time—and not a very long due time. As the real project for which Michaele, Jacob, and their men had come to Ellingen to accomplish began, only the original truck drivers and their coworkers remained for the work. A total of ten men would be the only ones to know the incredible secret. The ODESSA men knew better than to ask unnecessary questions.

Jacob warned the mayor and police chief in advance that they would be employing explosives on the first of September. Michaele was an explosives expert, and he set the charges to make a precise opening in the foundation wall so that the contents of the basement could be removed with ease, but not so large that the explosion required to create the opening would raise eyebrows. The plan was unfolding so openly that no eyebrows had been raised yet. It was a Bavarian city where the officials and the populace were used to avoiding questions or intrusions.

The explosions created a jagged hole which the men trimmed to avoid damage to the contents as they were moved to the trucks. Heavy mine trolleys were chained to the trucks and pulled out of the hole at the rear of the church in a test which was completely satisfactory. The next day, the workers were permitted to enter the chamber where the Nazi treasure had rested for the past thirteen years. After the first intense reaction to that magnificent hoard of valuables passed, the men began to ask how Michaele had managed to accumulate the treasure and get it to the church without attracting attention.

Knowing that he was among former SS men who did not blanch at the details of what Hitler's elite corps had done since the 1930s, Michaele felt that he owed them a real answer.

"The expropriation of the enemies' riches which could later easily have been used to attack the Third Reich began in the late 1930s when the *untermenshen, Juden*, and other undesirables were dealt with. Their funds and treasures were moved into safekeeping in the Reich. In 1940, the ERR [*Einsatzstab Reichsleiter Rosenberg für die Besetzten Gebiete* (the Reichsleiter Rosenberg Institute for the Occupied Territories)] was formed to bring German efficiency and effectiveness into dealing with the large volume of captured resources. The first operating unit, the western branch for France, Belgium, and the Netherlands—called the *Dienststelle Westen* [Western Agency]—was located in Paris after the surrender and establishment of the armistice between Germany and France on June the twenty-second.

"Antoine Duvalier and I helped form a division of French soldiers to help our German counterparts stave off the Bolsheviks and the undesirables who planned to destroy civilization. Some of us were assigned to head up the French division of the *Dienststelle* with orders to collect the materials and to secure them. Early on, *Schloss* Neuschwanstein was chosen as headquarters of the *Einsatzstab Reichsleiter Rosenberg*, and our division had the honor to keep the secrets, transport the gold, currency, and degenerate art to the *Schloss* for safekeeping. It soon became apparent that the *Schloss* was neither large enough, secure enough, nor secret enough, to be the appropriate location for what we had collected.

"Antoine suggested to *Reichsleiter* Rosenberg that it was necessary to disperse the treasure in order to keep it secure, with the aim of transferring it all back to the *Vaterland* once we had vanquished the so-called Allies who perpetrated that wicked war on the innocent German nation. It was our destiny. I have to say now that it is our destiny *and* our responsibility to use the treasure to fund the new Fourth Reich which will come. God wills it!

"In addition to gold, silver and currency, cultural items of great significance were confiscated—some quite bulky, including paintings, ceramics, books, and religious treasures. That necessitated considerable planning and work. Sonderkommando Kuensberg created 1,050 repositories in Germany and Austria by the end of the Great War, and Antoine and I were his executives."

Realizing that he had allowed his emotions to cloud his thinking, Michaele returned to the direct information that he wished the men to know and to understand, "*Sonderkommando* [Concentration camp inmate enforcer] Führer Kuensberg ordered us to move the divided treasure troves to their hiding places, including the one here in the *Schlosskirche* Ellingen. In addition, Antoine and I had direct responsibility to maintain the safekeeping of the Nazi *Raubgold* [lit. "Stolen Gold"]. We supervised the transfer of gold and other assets such as fine art to Swiss and overseas banks in return for them providing the currency that funded our glorious war effort. It is ironic that some of those banks are located in the United States, and some are even owned by the *Jüdisch untermenschen*. The Americans, British, French, and lesser 'Allies' do not know the half of the extent of the secret account numbers. Only Antoine and I know them all and can obtain the money in a heartbeat as soon as we can break free of their illegal imprisonment of our soldiers. Even without factoring in the interest earned by those funds, Antoine and I can put our hands on over half a billion dollars in gold and other precious metals, jewels, and currency already in safe-keeping in Switzersand to be put to use by the ODESSA."

"Where did the money come from during the war, Michaele?" asked Jacob.

"The bulk of what we know about—that Antoine and I and the Charlemagne Division had responsibility for—came from France, Belgium, and the Netherlands. Others undoubtedly had responsibility for other areas of funding and protection of the treasury they procured."

"We read of the Allies finding many caches of treasure hidden by our people. Is that true?"

"Unfortunately, it is true. There have been some traitors among us who alerted the enemy to where the treasures were hidden in order to serve themselves and their escapes. Never forget the names of Hörst Dietsel and Heinrich Rudolf Gajewski to name but two. Those two men were able to make good their escapes to no one knows where by telling the Allies about *Schloss* Neuschwanstein, *Musée Jeu de Paume* in Paris, Nazi headquarters in Munich, and the mines in Merkers, Altaussee, and Siegen. Their day will come, you can be certain of that."

"Surely there are more such places still hidden, *Oberführer*. This place cannot be the only one."

"Indeed, you are right. In time, as the Fourth Reich comes into its own, we will be free to return to them and to use the *Raubgeld* funds for their proper purposes."

Raubgeld constitutes the gold transferred by Nazi Germany to over-seas banks before, during, and after World War II. The regime executed a policy of looting the assets of its victims early on to finance the war, collecting the looted assets in central depositories. The occasional transfer of gold in return for currency took place in collusion with many individual collaborative institutions including the Vatican, Swiss, and American banks. The precise identities of those institutions–as well as the exact extent of the transactions–remain unclear to the present day. During World War II, Nazi Germany continued the practice on a grand scale. Germany expropriated some $550 m in gold from foreign governments, including Belgium and the Netherlands. Over and above those thefts from national governments, there was a massive fortune—

including gold, jewelry, and precious artifacts—taken from private citizens or companies.

As Germany's outlook diminished drastically after 1943 and especially after 1944 and through to the war's end, many thousands of Nazis and wartime collaborators from France, Croatia, Belgium, and other parts of Europe looked frantically for a new home—preferably one as far away from the Nuremberg Trials as possible and as hospitable as could be made available. Argentina welcomed onto its bosom thousands of them; the country and its government publically agreed with the vicious anti-Semitism of the Nazis; and the Perónist regime actively courted them, especially the wealthy ones. Argentina was full of Nazi spies, and Argentine officers and diplomats held important positions in Axis Europe. Argentina sent agents to Europe to provide easy passage—including provision of authentic travel documents and in many cases covering expenses temporarily—usually on a loan basis.

Many influential Argentines—including wealthy businessmen and members of the government—were openly supportive of the Axis cause, none more so than Perón himself, who had served as an adjunct officer in Benito Mussolini's Italian army in the late 1930s. Even criminals–including those accused of the most heinous crimes–such as Ante Pavelic—whose Croatian regime murdered hundreds of thousands of Serbs, Jews, and Gypsies—Dr. Josef Mengele—whose sadistic medical experiments were the stuff of nightmares—and Adolf Eichmann—Hitler's architect of the Holocaust—were welcomed with open arms into the Argentine society and economy.

Eva Peron alone had an estimated $800 million dollars in bank deposits in 1945, 4,600 carats of diamonds and other precious stones, 90 kilograms of platinum, and 2,500 kilograms of gold. The total value of all assets stolen by Nazi Germany remains uncertain, but it is clear that only a fraction of the stolen treasures has ever been returned to the rightful owners. For example, best estimates indicate that almost 100 tons of Nazi gold produced in Portugal—not a small fraction from gold teeth extracted from murder victims—were laundered through Swiss banks, with only four tons being returned at the end of the war.

Even after Germany was defeated, there were many powerful men in Europe who had favored the Nazi cause and continued to do so. Spain was still ruled by the fascist Francisco Franco and had been a *de facto* member of the Axis alliance; many Nazis would find safe–if temporary–haven there. Switzerland had remained ostensibly neutral during the war; but many important leaders had been outspoken in their support of Germany; these men retained their positions after the war and were in a position to help the ODESSA. Swiss bankers–out of greed, sympathy, or both–helped the former Nazis to move and to launder funds. Many more of those outspoken Nazi/Fascist supporters were allowed to go to Argentina instead, because the Allies were reluctant to hand them over to their new communist rivals, where the outcome of their war trials would inevitably result in their executions. The Catholic Church also lobbied heavily in favor of these individuals not being repatriated. The Allies did not want to try these men themselves— only twenty-three men were tried at the Nuremberg Trials—nor did they want to send them to the communist nations that were requesting them; so, they turned a blind eye to the ratlines carrying them by the boatload to Argentina, Chile, Paraguay, Brazil, and Uruguay.

To be cynical, it was clear that there was a financial incentive for Argentina to accept those criminals. Wealthy Germans and Argentine businessmen of German descent were willing to pay the way for escaping Nazis. Nazi leaders plundered untold millions from the Jews they murdered, and a significant amount of that money accompanied them to Argentina. The ex-Nazis were given landing permits and visas, and many of them were even given jobs in Perón's government.

Pragmatic Nazi officers and collaborators saw the writing on the wall as early as 1943 and began setting aside gold, money, valuables, paintings, statuary, coin collections, etc., usually in Switzerland for later transfer to the coffers of accepting countries and benefactors. Ante Pavelic and his criminal cronies had multiple chests full of gold, jewelry, and art they had stolen from their Jewish and Serbian victims: this eased their passage to Argentina considerably. They even paid off British officers to let them through Allied lines. The cynicism of Argentina was revealed when—in the last month of the war—she declared war on Germany to end up on the victors' side. The main reason for doing so—in reality— was to be able to plant Argentine agents in Europe who were in a very advantageous position to continue the Argentine assistance for ODESSA. Antoine, Michaele, and their *Gebirgsjägers* fully intended to emulate those predecessors.

The effort of transferring the Nazi loot to the trucks required both a prodigious amount of physical work and a great deal of careful calculation. Michaele had considerable experience in dealing with the problems of moving bulky treasures around Europe and finding hiding places for them. This was not much different from his war assignments. He and Antoine had several important administrative experiences during their SS careers. They handled problems in the "solution" camps that many of even the hardest of the other SS men shied away from. They moved the gold, art treasures, and money, and killed anyone whom they suspected was about to betray the great secret of the Third Reich. They managed the almost impossible problems of supervising the obtaining, transporting, and managing the local slave labor forced to move 600,000 horses for use by the SS and the Wehrmacht during the invasion of Russia. *Oberführer* Dupont could handle this one treasure trove with relative ease.

He relegated all final decisions to himself. Time was short, and space in the trucks was finite. This required a process of rapid triage on Michaele's part. His first painful decision was to leave behind all of the beautiful frames from the paintings and only to take the most valuable canvasses. He was angry with himself that his knowledge of the value of art was so inadequate, but one does the best one can. The next choice was to sift quickly through the trunksful of jewelry and to limit the transport to only one large trunk. He was better educated in jewelry and was sure that he had made good choices. The boxes full of gold wedding rings, exterminated concentration camp internees' gold teeth, and the bales of currency were all loaded onto the trucks with dispatch because they were relatively light and manageable.

The gold ingots had to go into the trucks, but they were extraordinarily heavy. Two fork lifts were employed to lift down the heavy pallets and move them into position for loading onto the ramp. It took all of the men in a tug-of-war with just one pallet to drag it into position on the exit ramp they had created where the truck could then pull it out of the ground. With several dozen pallets, the work proceeded with glacial celerity. In the back of the cache, under bales of fine silks, the men discovered ten more pallets piled high with silver ingots. An additional half a day of effort was required to get those pallets out and onto the trucks. The trucks were beginning to groan under the weight.

Finally, the best silks, furs, and fine linens were added. The carpenters made oaken boxes to store the tons of gold and silver artefacts, much of which was in the form of useless religious artefacts such as Passover candlesticks, whose only value—so far as Michaele was concerned—was what they could bring when melted down into ingots. Of course, there was no time for that at the moment; so, they were dumped haphazardly into the boxes. Michaele could not help but think that it was rather like the way the former owner's bodies had been piled in trenches or burned with no record of who was who or what belonged to them.

One of the ODESSA assistants came to Michaele on the twelfth day of backbreaking and psychologically stressful work.

The assistant reported, "Herr *Oberführer*, we cannot add anything else to the trucks. The only way to transfer more is to get more trucks. To do that, we will have to steal from the farmers. My superiors are afraid that will attract attention to us before the trucks can get out and onto the road to Switzerland."

"I agree," Michaele said without a moment's hesitation.

He had been worrying about that possibility for several days now.

"We will move the trucks out tonight. You and your men dismantle the 'construction project,' and when the area is clean, plant the explosives. Be absolutely certain that no busybody can find a way in to have a look at the treasure we have to leave behind. Perhaps, we will be able to come back again and remove what is rightfully ours."

The irony was lost on him.

"We move out as soon as it is dark," he told the ODESSA truck drivers and security men.

He and Jacob poured over Jacob's maps to plot the best routes from Bavaria to the Swiss border which would avoid major throughways.

CHAPTER THIRTY

Konstanz Cathedral in Konstanz, Baden-Wurttemberg, Lake Constance Border Region, September 25, 1954

Michaele, Jacob, and the ODESSA volunteers did not hear any explosion as they drove through the night with the final goal of making it to the Swiss bank that was the repository for the Nazi *Raubgold* already accumulated. The presumption was that the men left in Ellingen would destroy the entryway and any access to the basement of the old Romanesque and Gothic *Schlosskirche* [Palace Church]. They were extremely tense as they wound their way through the city streets, expecting at any time to encounter police which would provoke a firefight. They headed west on Veterinärstrasse, then left onto Professor-Huber-Platz, then right onto Ludwigstrasse, then left on Leopoldstrasse.

To confuse anyone who might be following them, they turned on Odeonsplatz, then onto Brienner Strasse, then Maximiliansplatz der Opfer des Nationalsozialismus, then Lenbachplatz; then—in a dizzying set of left and right turns—they drove onto Elisenstraße, Marsstraße, Arnulfstraße, and finally Landshuter Allee at the edge of the city. They pulled into a vacant lot by an abandoned building and waited until it was sure that all six trucks had been able to keep with the erratic pattern. The ramp to Salzburg was in view.

They waited an hour before deciding that they had not been followed before driving as fast as possible to Saarbrücken. Predawn light made Michaele nervous; so, he ordered Jacob to find a place to spend the rest of the night and the next day where they would not create any reason to be noticed. That was not difficult. There were still many bombed out buildings where once business thrived before the Nazis came, then the Americans came after them with a vengeance.

In the morning, Jacob left the convoy to make contact with the priest in the Church of the Twelve Apostles. He was the ODESSA's conduit to the Vatican and from the Vatican to the bank in Switzerland where they could deliver the treasure. At the time, the Vatican was acting as a crucial way station to provide forged documents for Nazi fugitives. Pope Pius XII considered the entire communist movement to be atheistic and antithetical to the beliefs, aims, and purposes of the Church to the point of being the Antichrist. As a result, he was sympathetic to the violent anticommunism of the fascists and especially the Nazis whom he felt were serving the ends of the Church. Publically, he kept his distance from Hitler and his senior cronies; but privately he condoned, and, in fact, supported the Nazis before, during, and after the war. During the war, Pope Pius displayed an implacable public stance of indifference to the German Holocaust and to all of the other atrocities committed against the defenseless Jews. He turned away thousands of pleas from the Jews, telling them that his hands were tied, because the Vatican had to remain neutral like Switzerland. He was instrumental in setting up the network to move Nazi treasure from Germany and Nazi-occupied countries and aided the ODESSA in its efforts to move SS personnel to Switzerland, Italy, and Argentina.

The US State Department described the Vatican's participation as "the largest single organization involved in the illegal movement of emigrants." That was rank hypocrisy given the immense effort by the Americans to save Nazi scientists and to incorporate them into the warp and woof of American scientific and engineering life via Operation Paperclip. The facilitator of the Vatican's activities was a rich and enthusiastic Swiss Nazi collaborator named François Caussidière.

The Vatican was very efficient the day Jacob contacted the priest at the Church of the Twelve Apostles. Through the mediation of the Vatican's *Pontificio Istituto Teutonico Santa Maria dell'Anima* in Rome—a seminary for Austrian and German priests and the Roman conduit for the Swiss/Argentine Ratline—Jacob was able to speak directly to Caussidière.

"Caussidière here," the Swiss collaborator answered.

"ODESSA code 'SpecialSwissEmigration No. 1945,'" Jacob answered.

"What is needed?"

"Documents for twenty-four to allow safe transit into Switzerland, avoidance of search of my six trucks, and a warm welcome at the UBS in Geneva."

"Your documents will be prepared by the Vatican Emigration Service and the *Commissione Pontificia d'Assistenza* [Vatican Refugee Organization] and will be ready in six days. Stop at the Konstanz Cathedral in Konstanz, Baden-Wurttemberg, Lake Constance region. Pope Pius XII raised it to a papal Basilica Minor. You cannot miss it. Lake Constance is the only area in Europe where no borders exist, because there is no legally binding agreement as to where the borders lie between Switzerland, Germany, and Austria. You will have no difficulty."

"And, once we are in Switzerland?"

"Immediately across the border, you will be met by trusted men who answer to me. They will see to your safe passage."

"I cannot thank you enough, Herr Caussidière."

"It is my humble duty. *Heil* Hitler!"

"*Seig Heil* [Hail, my Leader]!" Jacob answered and ended the call.

Dusk was approaching by the time Jacob returned to the convoy. He knew the men would not have been able to get out for food and water and had to be famished. He stopped at a restaurant and bought twenty full meals. He was received with enthusiasm.

Jacob conveyed all he had learned to Michaele, then asked, "What next, *Oberführer*?"

"We head to Brienne le Chateâu to get Antoine and the others out of that hellhole."

"It is possible that we will run into trouble and will endanger the mission, *Oberführer*."

"Saving Antoine and the '*Gebirgsjägers*' is every bit a part of the mission, *Obersturmführer* [SS-Senior Storm Leader] Bunnemann. Never under any circumstances ever think differently."

"*Ja wohl!*" Jacob replied vigorously.

"Have the men check the weapons and ammunition, *Obersturmführer*. We will be ready for whatever comes. We are SS."

Jacob nodded without demurrer and gathered the other men. When it was fully dark, they moved out and drove to the preplanned rendezvous for restocking and planning their crossing into Switzerland. They stopped in a copse of trees to the north of the Konstanz Cathedral in Konstanz, Baden-Wurttemberg. The cathedral was run by priests who were part of the Vatican Refugee Organization and who were waiting for them.

Michaele insisted that they trust no one at this point. He ordered the men to hide their trucks, and he went alone to the rear door of the cathedral. He reasoned that—if he were taken—the mission still had a chance to succeed. He rapped softly on the door in a pattern which had been agreed upon during Jacob's telephone conversation with François Caussidière—the Latin Gregorian chant, *Adoro Te Devote*. The rhythm of the chant was simple, easy to remember, and so familiar that any priest throughout the world was familiar with it. Michaele and Jacob had practiced the beat repeatedly to avoid confusion.

It was obvious that he was expected. A man's voice came from behind the heavy oak door.

"What is wanted?"

"I come with the Holy Father's blessing," Michaele said, repeating the prearranged identification code.

"State your purpose."

"We are émigrés with intent to travel into Switzerland to obtain religious freedom and to fight godless Bolshevism."

"You may enter, Brother."

With that invitation, the great door swung open; and five bearded young men in Franciscan Friars Minor Capuchin brown cloaks and hoods stood facing Michaele with automatic rifles pointing at his chest.

"Pardon our caution, Brother. With the Americans and the communists, one can never be cautious enough. Are you alone?"

"I am alone at the door, but my men are close. Is it safe?"

The priest nodded his head.

The priests escorted Michaele into the main area of the cathedral—a simple cruciform plan with a nave of four square bays, a square crossing, a transept that projected by half a bay one each side, and an apse. There were no aisles. The building combined both Romanesque and Gothic styles which had not been altered nor improved in two centuries. There were rows of frescoes along the walls which had deteriorated from damp and decay. The floors were covered with what had once been very handsome inlaid tiles, but which had become chipped and some areas replaced with mismatching pieces. The Order had not had the funds to maintain the cathedral as it should have been, let alone to make improvements. The promise of reward from Nazi treasure was no small incentive to the Franciscans. Michaele was led to a small chapel located at right angles to one arm of the cruciform extensions. It was much better kept and had well-maintained tall Gothic windows designed and periodically cleaned and releaded by German craftsmen from the same families who made the originals. The pews were made of deep dark hardwood and polished to a waxy gleam. They were built at hard right angles to maintain the proper level of discomfort.

"Behind the altar is where we do the document preparation. Our work is masked by genuine work being done to restore medieval manuscripts. We have fourteen copies of the *New Testament* under way. You and your men will have to come in; so, we can make photographs for the identification cards and papers; and so we can produce papers with reasonably plausible birthdates and physical descriptions. We have only a few hours before it becomes too light to be safe; so, please fetch your companions; and we'll get underway," Brother Luke requested.

Michaele was led back outside and hurried to where the ODESSA men were secluded. All eight men trotted back to the cathedral which was only a silhouette in the dim light, its Romanesque bell tower and sharp turret looking like a menacing specter suggestive of the guard tower of a large POW camp. Six hours later, Michaele was satisfied with the quality of the brothers' work, especially the details of aging and wear that indicated frequent use. There were now eight new Swiss citizens ready to cross the border.

Brother Luke nodded to four of the brothers who left the chapel and were gone for ten minutes. When they returned, they were pulling a cart laden with FN machine guns and crates of ammunition.

"Is this sufficient?" Brother Luke asked Michaele.

"Better than we could have hoped," Michaele answered.

The friars and ODESSA men took the weaponry to the trucks and loaded them into secure but accessible locations.

"Go then in peace, my son," Brother Luke said. "Remember us in your prayers."

Michaele had to laugh inwardly at the possibility that a prayer of his would have efficacy, but he kept his expression strictly neutral.

"We will do better than that," he said.

He whispered to Jacob, who went out to the lead truck and returned with four gold ingots loaded on the cart.

Brother Luke said with heartfelt enthusiasm, "We are grateful to you, my Brothers and to our God that He has made us part of this holy work. We were privileged to visit and to provide comfort to many of the victims in the heinous American and French prisons and concentration camps such as Bad Kreuznach—Lager Galgenberg und Bretzenheim PWTE and Brienne le Chateâu. It was with God's grace that we have been able to give aid and to help some of them escape with false identity papers. Bless you, my sons. May God and the holy saints protect you as you continue your pilgrimage."

With that blessing, the hardened Nazis left their cover in the trees and headed for Brienne le Chateâu and POW camp 63.

UBS [Union Bank of Switzerland], Rue des Noirettes, 35 Centre des Acacias 1227 Carouge, Genève, Switzerland, September 28, 1954

Michaele and Jacob decided to take only one vehicle to POW Camp 63 in order to avoid creating interest in their activities. They moved the trucks into Heinrich Schläger's large dairy barn and covered them with tarpaulins. All eight men loaded into a modified troop truck which now passed for on of Heinrich's dairy delivery vehicles. With three men in the front seat, there was room for the five ODESSA men who had assisted with the retrieval of the *Schlosskirche* treasure and the efforts to keep the secret thus far, and for eleven more men in seats and perhaps six more standing in the truck's rear compartment. It would be crowded—especially with the weapons and ammunition—but it would be quite possible, and they might need a fairly large fighting force if things went badly.

The weather conditions were favorable—light rain, heavy clouds, and fog. There were very few cars or trucks in Brienne le Chateâu and even fewer pedestrians at that time of night. Jacob parked the truck half a mile from the eastern fence of the POW camp and cautioned the ODESSA men to be silent. He and Michaele retraced their path from the truck to the camp used the night Michaele was extracted. The mud was thick and cloying and made the going difficult, but the sound of the rain and the sound insulation of the mud made the two men as quiet as rabbits. They were no more visible than the bushes along the stream bank.

Per their prearrangement with US Army Corporal Jimmie Clemmons, they each carried an ingot of pure gold. They had arranged for him to appear at the exit point in the fence every night between two and three a.m. The arrangement was built on the two prime movers of trust: the expectation of reward, and the guarantee of retribution. Clemmons knew the ODESSA operatives could destroy him in two ways: assassination or exposure to his superiors, which would be as sure an assassination as if he had been shot in the head.

It was two-fifteen, and the corporal was as good as his word.

"Treasure," Michaele whispered from the darkness on the outside of the fence.

"The men are ready," Corporal Clemmons responded with the established reply.

Michaele and Jacob stood up from where they had been lying on the bank of the stream and walked up to the fence. A bush artfully camouflaged the area in the chain-link fence that had been cut to let Michaele out when he had left to go to the *Schlosskirche*. The two men made sure the man talking to them was indeed Corporal Clemmons.

Then Michaele said, "Surprised to see me, Corporal?"

"I have to admit that I am. Surprise me again."

He helped the two men edge their way through the opening in the fence.

"Where are our people?"

"A whistle away."

Michaele and Jacob put their gold ingots at the corrupt corporal's feet. He gave a whistle that sounded almost exactly like the extravagant song of the Bavarian wood lark. In a few moments, eight specters slowly moved up to where the three men were standing by the fence. Four of them were the original "*Gebirgsjägers*": Antoine Duvalier, Serge Alain Rounsavall, Hugues Beauchamp, and Jérôme Christophe Mailhot. Berthold Küppers–the farmer–had earned his place by his suffering alongside the *Gebirgsjägers* and because the ODESSA vouched for him. There were three men who were unknown to Michaele.

"Who are these three?" Michaele asked Antoine suspiciously.

"SS. Not from the 33rd, but loyal men. I vouch for them. Meet Clause Fischer, Willibald Movius, and Gerhard Jungermann—all officers who fought to the end."

Michaele remained dubious and uneasy, but he shook their hands.

"Jacob, go back to the truck and bring one more ingot for Corporal Clemmons. We will cross the fence as soon as you get back," Michaele ordered.

Jacob was through the fence in half a minute and disappeared into the blackness of the soggy night. He was back in twenty minutes out of breath and stinking from the fetid canal. He handed an ingot through the fence to Clemmons, who accepted it and nodded. He turned his back on the fence and stood guard as the eight men made their escape. He had more than kept his word. He had seen to it that all of the men had received good food while Michaele was gone, and they appeared considerably healthier than previously. None of the men looked back. Clemmons pushed the edges of the cut chain-link fence together and pulled a few branches of the bush into place to hide the opening. It took him four anxious trips to get his ingots back to his secret stash. Only then he allowed himself a stiff jolt of Jim Beam and a quiet laugh. He knew that the camp was going to be shut down in a month, and he already had a signed and dated discharge from the Army. He was officially a short-timer and soon to be a very rich civilian. His plan was to lay chilly for the next month and keep safe.

The eight filthy sopping-wet escapees joined their comrades in the back of the truck and kept silent except for a short exchange of whispers which passed for introductions and greetings. Jacob drove back to the Schläger dairy farm and rousted the drivers into action. It was four in the morning when they pulled out of Brienne le Chateâu and set their sights on Geneva. Their first goal was to get out of France, return to Bavaria, and to cross the border into Switzerland from the contested Lake Konstanz area—hopefully without ever having to stop at a border crossing between Germany and Switzerland. To do so, they kept to the back roads and traveled only under cover of darkness which extended the time of their transit by one hundred percent and their level of anxiety by nearly the same degree. They stopped only once, which was as the daylight hours appoached.

The men and their trucks were hidden on a farm run by two brothers with ODESSA ties. At the farm in the outskirts of Konstanz, Baden-Wurttemberg—near where they had obtained their forged documents two days previously—they were all able to clean up, put on fresh clothing—standard south German farm wear—and to eat two hearty rural German meals. At dark, they left with full bellies and high hopes that their ordeals were almost over.

Master Sergeant Nathan Lee Howard, USA sat in his jeep smoking a Camel and relaxing into a long night of watching the web of back ways into and out of Switzerland used by smugglers and Nazis wanting to avoid the official border crossing station outside of Konstanz. His unit consisted of fourteen men–including himself–and all of them considered the assignment a barely necessary nuisance during the waning months of the Allied occupation of Germany. It was boring, and that was a good thing. He had spent nearly ten years off and on in the American occupation forces of Germany and Austria with sporadic periods of violence from escaped POWs, ODESSA militia, and smugglers. Things were quiet now; and all he had to do was last out one more month; and he would go home to Iowa and full retirement. He considered himself lucky not to have been called up during the Korean conflict and to have been posted to that godforsaken backwater. Retirement could not come a day too soon.

There were three vehicles in the unit—his jeep, an FV 106 Saladin light armored car, and a 1952 Alvis FV603 Saracen, a heavily armored car (sixteen inches of RHA—Rolled Homogenous Armor). The Saladin and the Saracen were both holdovers from the Brits, and a comfort to his men because they were reliable and formidable. The men were distributed with four in the Jeep, four in the Saladin, and eight in the Saracen. They were separated two miles apart on three potential alternate roads used by the illegals.

Despite the lack of recent action in the area and the absence of violent encounters, the unit was almost comically over-armed with two AAT-52 [Arme Automatique Transformable Modele 1952] general purpose machine guns, eight Enfield wartime .303 Bren Guns, eight Remington M870 combat shotguns, M-1 Garand service rifles—one for each man with six spares, Smith & Wesson SW Model 29 [.44 Magnum] handguns—one for each man with six spares, and six crates of M-26 and M-61 fragmentation hand grenades. Every spare square foot was packed with ammunition for the weapons. The men called their arsenal being "loaded for bear." Master Sergeant Howard thought they had enough to start World War Three.

The six ODESSA converted army trucks laden and slowed down by the heavy burden of treasure they carried lumbered along the rutted and rocky gravel road four miles away from what they calculated would be the Swiss border. François Caussidière —their Swiss contact and fixer—had arranged for a map of the area and general instructions for the farmer to give the ODESSA men and promised a unit of Swiss Defense Forces to be at the crossing—which did not have a formal customs post—in case of a challenge by Americans, Germans, or French occupation forces on the lookout for escaping Nazis. That was helpful; but the closer they got to the putative border line, the more heightened their expectation of danger was.

Antoine—ever the pessimist and always overcautious—ordered a halt at a crossroads three miles from the border. Caussidière's map showed the roads all leading to the same point; so, Antoine decided to send the trucks on three separate approaches. If one truck was intercepted, the others would get through.

Michaele touched Antoine's arm and whispered, "I think we need to send out scouts—one for each route."

"I agree. Let's send two men down each road for two miles and then return and report. If the Americans are closer than two miles from the border, we can make an all-out run for it. Tell them to stay in the tree lines and be as quiet as bunnies."

The six men moved silently into the fringes of trees along the roads and were out of sight within minutes. Antoine and Michaele remained behind with the rest of the men to guard the precious cargoes in the four trucks. The wait was agonizing. Every minute they expected to hear the rattle of gunfire which would signal a potentially lethal end to their quest.

The first four men returned in half an hour to report that they had seen nothing. Everything was clear. After another nail-biting thirty minutes, the last pair returned out of breath.

"An armored vehicle and about eight or nine Amis parked in the middle of our road. When we watched for a few minutes, another one showed up. The two teams talked for a couple of minutes, then split up. We don't know where the larger of the two armored cars went exactly, except it was to the north," reported Clause Fischer.

Antoine took less than half a minute to decide.

"First three trucks go south; and Michaele, Clause, and I will go up the middle. Try not to get into a shooting match until the very last minute if you can."

"You want us to move slow or fast, *Gruppenführer?*" asked Willibald Movius, who was to drive the lead truck of the group of three.

"Good question, Sergeant. Let's move out slowly at first and keep the noise and dust down to a minimum, then go as fast these crates will go if an attack comes."

"Ja wohl, Mein Führer."

Willibald was a dyed in the wool Nazi who considered the loss of the Third Reich to be ony a temporary setback. He had his sights set on the upcoming Fourth Reich, and considered Antoine and the *Gebirgsjägers* to be the last best hope for realizing that ambition. He knew that this small group of dedicated Nazis would be the nucleus of the new Germany and for worldwide domination—Hitler's prophetic dreams would be accomplished by these pioneers. He was none too bright, which made him an excellent choice for a follower. That he was entirely amoral was another plus.

He had the look of a Bavarian farmer—inexpressionate facies, vapid eyes covered by Coke bottle bottom-thick spectacles, nondescript nose and lips, and a small round symmetrical head. He was overweight and had a prominent neck wattle to go along with his belly which protruded over his belt line. His arms and fingers were short and pudgy. He had bow legs from childhood rickets. He tended to wear the same set of clothes—a peasant tunic over baggy pants and ankle-high surplus Wehrmacht boots—almost every day. Antoine presumed that he had several interchangeable outfits. The idea that he wore the same single set of clothes all the time was more than his Prussian sensibilities was prepared to accept.

Clause Fischer was shorter and squatter than Willibald. Although he was actually brighter than his old friend, he had little to say; so, he was usually considered to be even less intelligent than Willibald. He had much the same bodily habitus in general, one that did not inspire confidence in the idea that he was strong, or quick, or soldierly. That would be to underestimate the man. Claude could move with alacrity and with surprising endurance when it was required of him, and he had remarkable strength when he put his mind to a task. He was as much of a killer as any of his SS comrades and had a record of killing which made him a good friend and a bad enemy. His face was duller, fuller, and more vacuous in appearance than Willibald's; and he was every bit as much of a follower. His only claim to being better than Willibald was that his clothes were of a better quality, variety, and fit. He usually wore olive drab Bavarian hunting clothing which was durable and as attractive as clothes could be on a man with a physique as unremarkable as his.

Gerhard Jungermann was a tall fit man who wore either farmer's clothes, or—like many former German soldiers—wore his old uniform without any rank designation or insigniae. He was efficient and relatively intelligent, which made him an asset to the *Gebirgsjägers.* Despite his height of six feet four inches, he had the build of a muscular shorter man. He had the telltale pockmarks of childhood small pox, and his right leg was somewhat smaller than his left as a sequelae of his having had polio as an adolescent. His face was deeply lined with natural furrows in his cheeks, a deeply dimpled, nearly cleft chin, and forehead lines earned from hatless years in the sun. His only nod to fashion was that he had a series of colorful tee-shirts he had purchased from a displaced Indian merchant who had had to flee from Berlin to Ellingen, Bavaria, as the Soviets closed in on the city at the end of the war. Gerhard wore a different, rather gaudy, shirt under his open uniform shirt every day.

Jacob Bunnemann was the least likely of the men to be considered a fighter. He had been a baker for the SS and still retained his rotund baker's figure. His apparent obesity was real, and did not hide large muscles. His benefit to his fellow conspirators was that he was bright and resourceful. He was very good at maths, subjects in which he had excelled in school. He had been held in a favored status in his SS unit because he could always come up with a decent meal for them, even when they were on the move. He had established a small bakery business on the side, but like his friends had subsisted on what his meager farm could produce. His shirt strained to cover his bulk; his pants had to be held up by suspenders; and his shoes were slip-ons because he could not reach down far enough to lace up boots. He did not cut a dashing figure, and he did not care.

The engines of the vintage trucks were noisy even at a slow rate of speed. It could not be helped. They traveled at one mile an hour, slow enough that two men were able to go ahead of the convoy as scouts. The three trucks made it to the point that they could see some moonlight glinting off the vehicles and weapons of the Swiss soldiers across the border. They stopped off the road in a sparse grove of evergreens and waited.

Antoine remained in his truck; and Michaele took point, walking about fifty yards ahead.

Suddenly, Michaele whirled about and ran as fast as he could back the truck, waving his arms frantically. Antoine stopped and turned off the engine.

It took a few minutes for Michaele to get full control of his breathing; then, he blurted out, "An armored car, maybe six men milling around it!"

"Arms?"

"I didn't see any rifles or machine guns. As best as I could tell, they were taking a leak and just had their side arms. What do you want to do?"

"Grab an FN and two bandoliers of ammunition each. The sound of the truck will send them back to their vehicle for weapons that will almost surely outgun us. We'll use the only advantage we have—the element of surprise."

Antoine and Michaele set off at a trot, keeping to the cover of the trees along the roadside so that the moonlight would not allow them to be seen by the enemy. They were able to make it to within fifteen yards before they were almost certain to be detected.

"Crawl," ordered Antoine. "Take out as many as possible by stealth, then we have to kill all of them even though we make a racket that will be heard for ten miles. Go."

Michaele cut the throat of an Army PFC who was enjoying a leak and a smoke—breaking one of the cardinal rules of combat by allowing the glowing end of the cigarette to give away his position, and the smoke to interfere with his own vision and concentration.

Antoine encircled another American's neck with his wiry but still powerful left arm, jerked the man off his feet, and shoved a combat knife into his right costovertebral angle, slicing his renal artery in half and penetrating all the way across his kidney. The sudden pain of the knife thrust is well-known by commandoes to have a paralytic effect which prevents an outcry. Even if the man had lived long enough to shout, Antoine's arm was so tight around his neck that his vocal cords were compressed; and no sound could leave his throat. Both former SS men were able to kill one more man each, which dispatched one half of the force outside the armored car. They regrouped to whisper.

"The rest are too far away for us to get to them without them raising an alarm," Antoine whispered. "Let's split up and get them in a cross-fire. Wait for my first burst."

A burst of three shots from Antoine's FN killed two American non-coms instantly. Michaele killed the remaining two before they could react. Antoine ran as hard as he could to the armed car and pulled open the door. A startled and terrified private stood in the doorway with a grenade in his hand, apparently the first piece of weaponry he could put his hands on. Antoine shot him three times in the chest; and he fell down in the entryway, dropping his grenade. Two more Americans pushed their Garands out the door, but they were too late. Antoine flipped off the grenade clip and tossed it into the interior of the car. One of the Americans fell to his knees trying to get hold of the grenade before it exploded, but he was too late. All he accomplished was to toss the grenade further back into the interior of the armed car as it exploded. Except for the open door, the car was like a heavy metal drum built to keep the force of the explosion inside. In less of a second, everyone inside was dead and scarcely recognizable as human beings.

No words needed to be spoken. Both Antoine and Michaele turned about and began running for their lives back to their truck. Although the truck was heavy and relatively slow, they had the clear advantages of speed and momentum over any pursuers. The pursuers had the added disadvantage of not knowing exactly where the fighting was taking place. By the time they arrived at the scene of the massacre and got their bearings, they were so far behind the ODESSA truck that all they saw was its taillights as it crossed the border into Switzerland. They also saw a strong force of Swiss Frontier Guards surrounding the truck and lining up at the border. The cardinal rule of the Allies was to respect Swiss neutrality at all costs. They turned back.

To their shock, three large German troop transport trucks bore down on them at breakneck speed, coming from two directions. The Americans leaped out of their Jeep and their Alvis FV603 Saracen and formed a skirmish line behind the lightly armored personnel carrier. Clause Fischer and Willibald Movius bore down on the Jeep and smashed it into the only protection available to the master sergeant and his three PFCs. They did not have a chance. The other two trucks pulled up front to side of the Saracen; and the men rolled out firing their FNs, which forced the Americans to keep their heads down. The close proximity of the ODESSA trucks—and the fact that the Americans were not able to set up machine gun posts—evened the odds considerably.

Fischer and Jungermann were killed by an American grenade, and Jacob Bunnemann died when an American staff sergeant courageously ran around the back end of the Saracen and poured half a dozen rounds from his Bren gun. That sergeant and three other Americans were killed and three were wounded. There was still sporadic but ineffective shooting underway when—to everyone's profound surprise—a contingent of twenty men in Swiss Frontier Guard uniforms swept across the border and pulled up behind the ODESSA trucks.

The highest ranking American soldier still alive, Corporal Dennis Smith, from Tuscaloosa, Alabama, held up a white flag.

"Come out!" the lead Swiss guardsman said. "Leave your weapons and come out with your hands above your heads."

There were six men able to stand; two of them had minor wounds.

"We have four men in urgent need of medical attention," Corporal Smith said as soon as he and his men were assembled in front of the ODESSA operatives, former POWs, and the men in the Swiss uniforms.

The leader of the Swiss looked hard into Antoine's eyes, then into Michaele's. The two high-ranking former SS officers—former POWs—did not even have to look at each other. They set their FNs to full automatic then raised them quickly and cut the Americans to pieces by firing first from left to right about navel high then by firing right to left at the level of their nipples. It was over in forty-five seconds.

Antoine gave a head jerk in the direction of Serge and Hugues. They walked around to the back side of the Saracen. Six shots rang out, and the two former 33rd Waffen-Grenadier SS officers, former Soviet, then US, then French POWs returned and took their places in the line of their comrades-in-arms.

The leader of the Swiss contingent stepped up to Antoine and said, "*Gruppenführer und Generalleutnant der Waffen-SS* Antoine Duvalier, I presume," and gave a smart *Hitlergruss* which was promptly and precisely returned.

The Swiss officer repeated his greeting, "*Oberführer SS* Michaele Dupont, I presume," and gave a second crisp *Hitlergruss* to Michaele who responded correctly.

"I am François Caussidière, Swiss national. I believe you have heard of me?"

"We most certainly have, and we owe you our lives. The Fourth Reich will rise out of the ashes; and you will be one of its remembered heroes, Herr Caussidière. It would be difficult to repay you for what you have done and for what you are yet to do today."

"Ah, *Mein Bruder* [my brother], that is simple. I get ten percent of what you are bringing in. There are a great many people who have participated and need to be compensated."

"Fair enough."

"Then, it is time for us to disappear and to leave it to the Allies to figure out what happened here and how it gets reported."

François Caussidière was dressed in a cream-colored linen suit, light beige silk shirt, an elegant Chinese red silk tie, and tan lace-up oxfords with a perfect spit-shine despite the lateness of the hour and the inappropriateness of the attire for a potential battle. But then, Caussidière was not a man who got his hands dirty—either literally or figuratively. He had other men to handle such things. The contingent of phony Swiss guards was one such example. He was of a fairly uncertain age— probably middle-aged—with only a few gray hairs beginning to show over his temples. His hair was ridiculously well coifed and recently cut for such an outing, but his hair grooming was an ingrained trait he had adopted so that he could always emenate a persona of importance and wealth. He was handsome in a somewhat dissolute way; he was a connoisseur of fine wine and tested more than his share. He had a fine crisp little mustache and a triangular beard the size of one Swiss franc coin located just beneath the margin of his lower lip. He put out an energetic–even theatrical–level of affability and bonhomie. Its lack of genuineness was not lost on Antoine who studied men by watching their eyes. François's eyes were cold, calculating, and cruel— the equivalent of probing x-rays—devoid of warmth. His smile never made it to his eyes.

All six ODESSA trucks were drivable, and the former POWs and their newly acquired Swiss friends crossed the putative border into Switzerland with lights on and at full speed. When they were thirty miles inside the border, Caussidière signaled a halt in a large truck farm parking lot. The "Swiss" got out of their vehicles, stripped to their skivvies, and put on civilian clothes. The uniforms were placed in a fifty-gallon barrel holding one gallon of gasoline and set ablaze. The convoy pulled into Geneva at ten in the morning. Caussidière took all of the SS officers to a Turkish bath where they were scrubbed clean, shaved, and received gentlemanly haircuts. They were then taken to a fine men's clothing store Caussidière owned and outfitted them with fine suits, underclothing, stockings, shoes, shirts, ties, cufflinks, tie tacks, and leather belts. No one who knew any of the men two days ago would have recognized the newly transformed Swiss gentlemen.

Their next stop was significantly grander. They arrived by limousine at Rue des Noirettes, 35 Centre des Acacias 1227 Carouge, Genève— the UBS [Union Bank of Switzerland]—where they were met by liveried valets who escorted them into the top floor offices of the principal investment and savings director. Eight men had been left behind at the offices of Ganoush Enterprises International to guard the treasure trucks as a precaution.

CHAPTER THIRTY-TWO

UBS [Union Bank of Switzerland], Rue des Noirettes, 35 Centre des Acacias 1227 Carouge, Genève, Switzerland, September 28, 1954

Not unexpectedly, François Caussidière made the introductions all around. Every man in the meeting was impressed with the man's prodigious memory. Antoine was in the process of changing his mind about the man facet by facet as each new aspect presented itself. No longer did any of the *Gebirgsjägers* think of Caussidière as just an opportunist, or just a wanna-be SS officer, or just a fixer, or just the best connected man in the postwar world. He was all of those, and undoubtedly more.

"It is with pleasure that we welcome you to Switzerland and to the UBS," Liert Beili Amstutz said with a broad smile on his face.

Antoine had to laugh inside because he knew that the man would not have met his glance had he come into the bank looking to deposit a hundred francs to his account, let alone had they met when he and the other *Gebirgsjägers* were in the gulag, or in Bad Kreuznach—Lager Galgenberg und Bretzenheim PWTE, or in POW camp 63.

He was also amused—and again did not show it—at the fussy little man's appearance. He was perfect, but in miniature. Amstutz was barely over five feet tall and had tiny hands and feet. His gleaming black wingtip shoes had to have been custom-made. He had a Rolex watch that would have fit a ten-year-old and a discreet but beautiful diamond pinky ring. His suit—presumably custom-tailored—was black as coal and free of any design. It was practically an antiadvertisement for pinstripes or colored flecks in the material. He was wearing a deep maroon tie—bow tie, of course—who would have expected anything any different? He had on a freshly starched French cuff white dress shirt without so much as a spec of dust or a loose crumb from his morning coffee cake. He had a handsome—more accurately, pretty—face, and a fine-boned small one. His eyes were silver-gray and intelligent. He did not miss a thing. His nose was slender and his ears were small and attached close to his head. He had curly black hair which had obviously been cut that morning. Not a hair was out of place. He had a pencil mustache which could have been painted on by an artist and a perfect small triangle of a beard below his thin lower lip.

The effect on Antoine and his men was exactly what Liert Amstutz wanted it to be. They were immediately convinced that the man was the very definition of rectitude and safety. Their money and treasure would be safe with this man.

"Now, gentlemen, I have been given to understand that you are bringing a significant-sized set of commodities which are of rather impressive value."

"Yes, they do," Caussidière answered for the SS men, which annoyed Antoine and Michaele.

"Have you a round figure estimate of the value of the commodities you wish to entrust to the care and keeping of the bank?"

Caussidière opened his mouth to answer, but Michaele gave him a look that said, "Don't."

"We can do better than that, Herr Amstutz. I have here an itemized list of what is in our possession. Granted, the figures are only estimates; but you will note that the value is considerable. Of course, the bank will have to have professional evaluators give you and us a more precise value."

When he saw the figure on the well-preserved ledger sheet Michaele had prepared during his travels of the ODESSA trucks, Amstutz allowed a tiny crack to appear in his serious mask of a face. It was what passed for a smile in the austerely careful banker.

"We will be happy to provide security for your goods, gentlemen. Our director of security will discuss where the valuables are being kept for safekeeping, and how to transfer them to the UBS vaults. Our appraisers will evaluate the valuables; and after that analysis is complete, we can meet again to determine the disposition of the total assets according to your wishes. For the moment, the bank's main question is whether or not you wish to include this set of assets in your already active account; or if you will prefer a separate account."

Antoine answered, "Include everything in the same account with the same requirements for access, codes and passwords, and withdrawals, please, Herr Amstutz."

"Very well. Would a meeting in a week suit your convenience?"

"Yes. However, we think it will take somewhat longer to tally the assets. We are prepared to wait in Geneva for the results."

"Of course. How shall we contact you?"

"Through Herr Caussidière. However, one of our men will be present with the assets at all times, twenty-four hours a day, and at whatever location the assets are kept."

"Perfectly understandable, General. In addition—per bank policy—our security staff will also be constantly present. Let me assure you that they are most capable, heavily armed, and absolutely serious about their work."

"Thank you, Herr Amstutz. We look forward to our next meeting."

Bank security staff escorted Antoine, Michaele, and François Caussidière out of the bank to waiting limousines.

"Where to?" asked Caussidière.

"The valuables," Michaele answered with authority.

The men who had remained with the trucks asked a flurry of questions, most of which were premature, and for which the answers were usually, "We have to wait for the final tally. That is likely to take some time."

Michaele set to work to organize a schedule of security responsibilities for the *Gebirgsjägers* for the next month, planning ahead for a longer-than-expected effort to obtain accurate appraisals in an atmosphere of almost paranoid security. Antoine gave some hard and unpopular orders: no drinking, clubbing, women, phone calls except for the business at hand, and no loose lips. Caussidière arranged for the men to stay in the elegant Hotel des Bergues, the city's first hotel, founded in 1834 at 33 Quai des Bergues on Lake Geneva. The men laughed out loud when they heard the price of a night's stay and compared the hotel accommodations to their lodgings for the past ten or so years.

Antoine asked Caussidière if he was keeping track of expenses.

"But of course *Mein Freund*, I am first a Nazi and second a businessman. The accounting will be complete in due time."

Antoine thought to himself, *I can just bet.*

The *Gebirgsjägers* were famished; so, François hurried them to the Domaine de Châteauvieux in the the magnificent Satigny vineyards of the Château de Peney, fifteen minutes west of central Geneva. The ambiance was inspiring: original sixteenth century beams and paneling, cobbled walls, a period fireplace, solid wood furniture, and walls covered with expensive artwork and statuary. The place inspired a much needed atmosphere of calm and tranquility, and everyone expected it to be the perfect setting to enjoy a gourmet *dîner*. The maître d showed them to the Chef's Table.

Caussidière addressed the maître d, "For starters bring us the seared force-fed duck liver *Foie Gras*, green tomato and strawberry chutney, caramel with spices, and mixed plate of shellfish and chanterelles." He paused for a moment to peruse the menu before continuing. "For the entrée, let us have a family-style arrangement with the baby leek, chinese cabbage in Mount Lebanon saffron threads sauce, Zucchini flowers filled with red-clawed crayfish mousseline in almond and tarragon sauce, Ile-d'Yeu fillet of sole cooked with mushrooms crust, razor shell clams stuffed with frégola and shellfish in pink champagne, poultry jus flavoured with oxalis. It's a celebration; so, we can be wasteful. Include the gilt head bream and the razor shell clam stuffed with frégola."

The meat course was Limousin rack of lamb and hay cooked in a sealed casserole, Zucchini flower filled with nicoise vegetables, lemon puree, jus perlé with olive oil spit roasted chicken from bresse stir-fried broad beans and artichokes, jus enhanced with savory. Dessert was left to the choice of the maître d.' It was a gastronomic extravaganza: hot and creamy pure Venezuelan chocolate biscuit, with Tahaa vanilla ice cream, and "Arlette" caramelized puff pastry with red berries, lemon thyme jus and torrified pistachio ice cream.

The appetites of every man after years and years of want were fully surfeited, and the resulting abdominal pain was soothed with appropriate wines with each course: for l'entrée,—the fish and chicken required Neuchâtelois; and the lamb required Rosé Champagne. The dessert was topped off with sweet Domaine Le Grand Clos, empreinte Passerillé, and the fine Cuban cigars were served with the Michelin-starred restaurant's best Merlet C2 Cassis and crackers daubed with soft bris.

It was sheer gluttony and a beginning and partial payback for the past decade of deprivation.

§§§§§

Despite Antoine's lingering doubts about Caussidière, the man came through for the *Gebirgsjägers* again during the week they waited for the bank to complete its exacting work.

He took Antoine and Michaele aside as soon as they were settled into their suites at the hotel and said, "I mentioned earlier that your identity documents issued by the *Commissione Pontificia d'Assistenza* [Vatican Refugee Organization] are not sufficient in and of themselves. They were, rather, the first stop in a paper trail to pass muster for permanent and genuine passports, travel overseas, birth certificates, union membership, and the like. However, I have taken standard measures to take care of that minor glitch in the system. I have invited Archbishop Carlo Romani, *C.S.Sp.* of the Vatican's liaison office with the ICRC [International Committee of the Red Cross] to meet us at the hotel today to explain the ICRC and the Vatican's role in the final process.

"As he makes his way to us, let me tell you that I and the ODESSA have often sought Archbishop Romani out; and his role in assisting escapes is very well known on the Nazi grapevine. He is hardly the only Catholic priest who helps our cause. We sometimes use Father Jason Gallent-Dupres who is very effective in funneling our people through his Vatican-approved Hungarian Refugee Charity. He has experts in the preparation of what appear to be authentic ICRC documents."

Archbishop Romani got up from an adjacent table and walked briskly across the room to the table where Antoine, Michaele, and Antoine were sitting. As he approached, Caussidière explained the importance of the man.

"He is what is known as a Spiritan here in Continental Europe. The English and Americans call them Holy Ghost Fathers. Their order is the *Congregatio Sancti Spiritus sub tutela Immaculati Cordis Beatissimae Virginis Mariae* or Congregation of the Holy Spirit under the Protection of the Immaculate Heart of Mary. His name or title includes the initials C.S.Sp. after his name. What that means for you is that his word is believed without question and his influence is boundless among Catholics, including governmental officials. He is our friend … one of our best friends."

He was a tall, elderly stick thin man with piercing dark eyes, aquiline nose, full lips, and high cheek bones. His slightly olive-tinted skin coloration made it difficult to guess his ethnic origins. He was dressed simply—a black cassock with amaranth trim and purple fascia, along with a pectoral cross and episcopal ring—making no attempt to disguise his prominent position in the Roman Catholic ecclesiastical hierarchy. The general effect gave him the appearance of the Keeper of the Crypt.

"May I?" the high-ranking Vatican prelate asked politely.

"Of course, Your Grace," Caussidière said deferentially.

"I understand that you men are in need of the intercession of the Vatican in an important matter. Am I correct?"

"You are," Caussidière responded quickly.

"I thank God that He and the Holy See have granted me permission to visit and comfort many victims in their prisons and concentration camps and to help them escape with false identity papers. The so-called 'Allies'' war against Germany was not a crusade for the right as they would have the world believe, but the rivalry of rich Western economies for whose victory they fought. Make no mistake, this was business; and it depended on crass advertisement. They used catchphrases like democracy, race, religious liberty, and Christianity as a bait for the ignorant masses. Because of what I have seen myself, I have felt duty-bound since 1945 to devote my whole rather extensive charitable work to aid former National Socialists and Fascists, especially the so-called 'war criminals.' We help with logistical support and money. We have agents who find and maintain escape routes, and more importantly we can provide false papers including identity documents issued by the Vatican Refugee Organisation (*Commissione Pontificia d'Assistenza*) which are unassailable.

"These Vatican papers are technically not full passports, and not in themselves enough to gain passage overseas. They are–instead–the first and most important stop in the paper trail required by the so-called 'Allies.' We can–for example–provide a displaced person passport from the ICRC, which in turn could be used to apply for visas. In theory, the ICRC performs background checks on passport applicants; but in real-world practice the word of a priest or particularly a bishop such as me is good enough and is accepted at face value. I can also use my position as an archbishop to request papers from the ICRC made out according to my exact specifications.

"How may I be of service to you unfortunate displaced persons?" he asked without a hint of guile on his priestly face.

"These gentlemen are newly arrived in Switzerland and have been able to come here through the kind ministrations of the Vatican already. They have papers from Konstanz."

"Ah, I understand," the prelate said. "You are displaced persons in need of formal documentation, including visas and passports. Because you are displaced persons who have suffered greatly, your own papers have been taken from you. This would make you men without a country, which is a cruel unkindness that the Holy Church feels is uncivilized and unchristian. It is something I can remedy. Without being boastful, it is true that I have a certain degree of influence. Despite the current spate of illegal, stolen, and forged ICRC papers, my signature will remove any darkness of doubt about the authenticity of your documentations. Would you like me to do that for you?"

Antoine and Michaele answered in unison, "We would be most obliged, Your Grace."

Antoine added, "How could we repay you for this great service?"

"No such payment is necessary or needed. My fellow clerics and I consider it our duty to help pilgrims such as yourselves who have suffered from the ungodly communists. Perhaps it would not be asking too much for you to continue to further the struggle against the atheists."

"Certainly not. We have every desire to serve the Church in that end. Thank you, Your Grace."

Archbishop Romani C.S.Sp. asked no further questions and wrote a letter to his personal contact in the International Red Cross—a man who owed his position to the archbishop—who then issued the genuine visas, passports, and necessary foundational identification documents. Two days later, they were in the hands of the *Gebirgsjägers*.

Eight days later, a call came through from UBS, Geneva, to Caussidière Enterprises International. The caller insisted upon talking only to Antoine or Michaele and would not leave a message. He was willing to wait while one of the two men was found.

It took ten minutes to locate Michaele.

"Yes," he said into the receiver.

"Liert Beili Amstutz from UBS. Our experts have finished the appraisal and the accounting. With your approval, we are ready to move the assets into the bank's vault. Would two o'clock fit your schedule?"

"I will make it fit. Thank you for calling, Herr Amstutz."

Antoine was still in the hotel sitting down to *Frühstück* [breakfast] with Willibald Movius, Rolf Kohns, Jérôme Christophe Mailhot, Hugues Beauchamp, Serge Alain Rounsavall, and Heinz Rudolph Grüber who had succeeded to the head of the ODESSA unit that had traveled to Brienne le Chateâu, POW camp 63, to extract the *Gebirgsjägers*. His superior officer had died in the battle at Konstanz, Baden-Wurttemberg. They were finishing a heavy German meal of porridge, cold meats, sausages, pickles, cheeses, a variety of breads smeared with sweet butter, jam, marmalade, and honey, soft-boiled eggs, and a bowl of fresh-cut fruit in orange juice. Michaele strode into the breakfast and whispered to Antoine.

Antoine said, "We'll all go. We are now partners."

Michaele looked briefly askance at Antoine who stood up, faced him, and mouthed, "Only real members of the 33rd will still be standing in the end."

He led the men back to the Caussidière compound to take their turns watching the treasure trucks. Everyone was as anxious as children until one-thirty finally arrived. The stroke of the half hour was heralded by the arrival of a heavily armed Swiss army unit and six armored vehicles from the bank that joined the *Gebirgsjägers* and ODESSA partisans. Needless to say the two-mile trip was uneventful. Swiss people are conditioned not to pay attention to the business of other people; and no one seemed to notice the convoy of army, bank, and civilian security forces driving into the basement of the bank.

Herr Liert Beili Amstutz met the Germans and Caussidière in the basement and had them escorted to his office.

He was not a man for idle chatting. A servant poured a glass of water for each man, then Amstutz spoke.

"There are only two planned items on the agenda for this gathering. First, I will hand out copies of the appraisal and accounting sheets; then, we will determine the disposition of the assets. I presume that only generals Duvalier and Dupont have the password code."

Antoine nodded.

"And, further, that is your preference for the future?"

Both Antoine and Michaele nodded in response to that question.

"Do you wish all men gathered here to see the appraisal and accounting, generals?"

"We have no secrets from these, our brethren," said Antoine.

"Good. We will proceed."

He handed out a copy to each man. None of them could keep a placid expression. They began to smile, to laugh, and to salute each other.

What the men saw was an accounting sheet with the UBS letterhead which gave subtotals and totals of value in US dollars (USD), Great Britain pound sterling (GBP), Swiss francs (CHF), and Deutschemarks (DEM) at the day's exchange rates. The accounting was for cash only with the amounts for tangible items to follow. The cash tally read:

1100 hours, September 28, 1953 exchange rates: USD 1.0, GBP .36, CHF 4.37, DEM 4.2	
SUBTOTALS (current deposit)	TOTALS (including assets from 1943)
USD $582,000,000	& $1,700,000,000
GBP £295,598,970	& £612,000,000
CHF SFr 2,543,340,000	& SFr 7,429,000,000
DEM DM 2,444,400,000	& DM 7,140,000,000

None of the men had ever seen any one man's name or small group of men's names linked to such staggering numbers. They had never known a man or a family with seven *billion* marks, and now they were to share equally in this colossal windfall. It almost made their time of suffering in the camps worth it. But not quite. Each man—in his own heart of hearts—intended to see that the Allies and the traitors pay every farthing the *Gebirgsjägers* were owed before satisfaction would be achieved, even if it required battle.

Herr Amstutz summed it up for the Germans: "This is a magnificent treasury to start the Fourth Reich, but that great accomplishment will wait for another day and will likely require Shakespeare's pound of flesh—as he said in *The Merchant of Venice* and a great deal of blood."

He adroitly left out the fact that the character who uttered that bit of quotation that would likely stand the test of time for as long as civilization persisted ... was Shylock, the Jew. There was not a Christian or a Hebrew among the Germans; but they all agreed with the JudeoChristian Bible where it required eye for eye, and tooth for tooth.

Amstutz took Antoine aside and asked what he wanted done with the physical assets other than the great masses of cash money.

"I will work with Herr Caussidière to convert those physical assets into bank account values. We will need to take a year or two to melt down the loose gold."

He was referring to the wedding rings and other jewelry and the gold teeth contributed by the Jews at the *Konzentrationslagers* [concentration camps] such as Auschwitz, Buchenwald, Treblinka, Dachau, Mauthausen, Bergen-Belsen, and the scores of lesser known camps—and to the plan to sell off the resulting gold ingots and to make wise investments outside the low-yield prospects of banks. It was about numbers and wise investments. None of the men had even a passing nag from his conscience about the human cost.

Swiss French Recipes

Ile-d'Yeu Fillet of Sole Cooked with Mushrooms Crust—for 16
Ingredients
•For the sole—7.2 kg sole (900g/ piece), 40 g black truffles, pinch of French sea salt "Fleur de sel," 160 g slightly salted butter, 160 g truffle perfume crust.
•For the truffle crouton (400g)—g butter, 160 g bread crumbs, 64 g minced truffle, 40 g puree of truffles (see below), 2 g garlic.
•For the truffle puree (600 g)—720 g truffle, 2.0 cl truffle oil.
•For the truffle-scented spinach (880 g)—180 g spinach, 120 g truffles diced small, 200 g heavy cream, 40 g butter, 40 g truffle oil, 180 g shallots, chopped, salt and pepper to taste.
•For the champagne sauce (5.2 l)—440 g butter, 800 g mushroom of Paris, sliced, 20 g coarse-ground black pepper, 400 g shallots, sliced, 200 g celery, 40 g lovage, sliced, 300 dl champagne, 800 g lobster claws, 8 dl champagne, 200g lobster claws, 8 dl shellfish jus, 20 dl heavy cream, 160 g lemon.
•For the clarified consommé (2.4 l)—200 g green part of leek, 600 g sole trimmings, 4 matured tomato, about 240 g, 320 g egg white, French sea salt "*Fleur de sel*" to taste.
•For the consommé of sole (1.0 l)—Sole bones, 160 g butter, 200 g shallots, 200 g onions, 400 g mushrooms, 4 pieces tip of thyme, 2.0 pieces laurel leaf, 240 cl water, 160 cl champagne, 1.0 cac chili, parsley stems, French sea salt "*Fleur de sel*" to taste.
•For the crawfish (6.0 kg)—20 kg large 'red-legged' crawfish, 2.0 kg concentrated fumet of crawfish (see below), 20 l court bouillon (nage écrevisse, see below), 4 g ascorbic acid.
•For the nage ecrevisse (20 l.)—20 cl white vinegar, 400 g coarse grained salt, 20 g white pepper in grain, 20 g coriander in grain, 45 g dry fennel, 300 g lemon, 32 g garlic
•For the fumet of crawfish (2.8 kg)—16 pieces big 'red-legged' crawfish, 320 pieces crawfish heads, 24 cl olive oil, 240 g butter, 320 g butter of fennel, 80 g

garlic, 480 g very matured tomato, 200 g tomato paste, 40 cl dry white wine, 40 cl cognac, 200 cl fumet of lobster (see below) 120 cl water, 4 pcs scent bouquet (tails of parsley, thyme, 2 laurel leaves), 20 g dry fennel, 2 bunches basil, 8 g black pepper.

•For the lobster fumet (2.8 kg)—24 heads lobster without shell, 400 g fresh fennel, 400 g white onions, 48 g garlic, 2.0 kg tomato, 210 g tomato concentrate, 16 cl fine champagne, 40 cl extra virgin olive oil, 320 g butter, 4 bunches fresh basil, black pepper grains, wild fennel.

•To finish (per serving)—4 pc sole, 200 g truffle-scented spinach, 120 g champagne sauce, 200 g consommé of sole, 80 g mushroom of Paris, 20 g truffles, 180 g crawfish.

Preparation:
•For the lobster fumet:
-Cut the entire lobster bisque and the lobster heads into large round slices. Cook in a cast-iron casserole with some olive oil. Add butter and caramelize. Add onions, fresh fennel, and garlic with skin. Sweat without browning, then add the tomato paste and fresh tomatoes and let stew to remove the acidity.
-Deglaze with some brandy, reduce the liquid. Moisten with concentrated fumet, add the dry fennel, and cook for 40 minutes over low heat. While cooking, skim off the impurities without removing the grease. Add the crushed pepper grains and the basil bouquet and leave simmering for 20 min. on the corner of the heat source.
-Drain the stock of carcasses, and then crush them in a fat-masher and filter.
•For the crawfish fumet:
-Cut the crayfish into small regular cubes, heat the olive oil in a cast-iron casserole, and sauté quickly with the crayfish heads. Add the garlic cloves and the precut aromatic garnish. Sweat for 3 minutes, then add the tomato paste and caramelize everything in butter.
-Deglaze with the cognac and the white wine. Let the alcohol evaporate and add the fumet of lobster and some water so that the crayfish is completely covered. Add the bouquet of aromatic herbs and the dry fennel and cook for 30 minutes. At the end of the cooking, add a half-bunch of basil and the grains of black pepper and leave to infuse for 15 minutes.
-Pass all ingredients through a fat-masher to extract the maximum flavor and filter through a sieve.
•To make the concentrated fumet, cook to reduce to 520 ml.
•For the court bouillon of crawfish (*Nage écrevisse*):
-Cook all ingredients together with 20 l of water.
•For the crawfish:
-Bring 16 l of court bouillon to boil. Kill and clean the crayfish. Boil in the court bouillon, normally around 2 minutes to reach boiling point. Shell immediately. Keep the crayfish tails in 1 l of cold bouillon with 4 g of ascorbic acid. Reserve in a vacuum bag, on ice. When needed, roll the crayfish in the concentrated fumet of crayfish.

•For the sole consommé:
-Drain the fish bones over a sieve. Wash, drain, and sieve the mushroom trimmings. Peel, wash, and chop the onions and the shallots in a regular size. Make an aromatic bouquet with parsley stems, the thyme, and the laurel-leaves. Melt the butter in a casserole, add the aromatic bouquet, and sweat without coloring.
-Add the fish bones and cook gently for 5 mins. without coloring.
-Moisten with cold water and the champagne; add the bouquet, the sliced mushrooms, and some salt. Bring to boil, then simmer gently for 20 mins. and skim as often as possible. As soon as the cooking time is over, remove the pan from the heat, add pepper, and let the consommé settle for 10 mins.
•For the clarified consommé:
-Wash the green part of leek and pat dry. Remove the stem of the tomato, wash, cut the tomato into quarters, and remove the seeds. Mince the sole trimmings, leek, and tomato finely. Add the egg white, lightly season with sea salt, and mix vigorously.
-Transfer the sole consommé to a pan high enough to skim off the scum. Stir constantly until it boils. Gently simmer for 10 mins. on the edge of the stove so that a cap is formed for clarifying the stock. Adjust the seasoning; filter the stock through muslin placed over a stainless steel container. Cool immediately.
•For the champagne sauce:
-Quickly fry the lobster claws in butter without browning. Add the shallots and celery, sweat on the corner of the stove. Deglaze with half of the champagne. Reduce half of the *jus*. Add the sliced mushrooms, the shellfish juice, and the cream and concentrated fumet. Cook for 30 mins. over low heat.
-Add the lovage and the pepper. Leave to infuse for 20 mins.
-Filter, store in freezing compartment. To use, heat the preparation to 80°C, season. Add the rest of the champagne and 160 g of emulsified butter.
•For the truffle scented spinach:
-Blanch the spinach in salted water (80 g salt/L).
-Cool, drain, squeeze, and finely chop the spinach. Sweat the shallots in butter and oil. Add the diced truffles, pour in the cream, cook for 5 mins., and add the chopped spinach. Correct the seasoning and set aside.
•For the truffle puree:
-Sweat the truffle in a little olive oil. Moisten with mineral water and cook, covered, over low heat for 20 mins. After cooking, mix the truffles with the cooking juices in a thermo blender to obtain smooth puree.
•For the truffle croutons:
-Melt the butter in a frying pan, add breadcrumbs, and stir constantly with a whisk until golden. Remove from heat and cool over ice. Before it is completely cooled, add the chopped truffle, the truffle puree, the chopped garlic, and a tour of the milled pepper.
-Spread the crust between two sheets of baking paper. Make sure that it is regular and as thin as possible. Let harden. Cut out a rectangle 12 cm x 3 cm and store in the freezer.

•For the sole:

-Clean and gut the sole. Remove the white and grey skins. Fillet and remove delicately the outside membrane with a thin-bladed knife. Flatten the fillets by placing them between 2 plastic sheets that have been previously moistened to prevent the meat from sticking to the plastic sheets. Spread the thicker fillet (from the side opposite the stomach) on a board. Butter the fillet lightly, season with a little French salt and lay down slices of truffle. Season again with some French sea salt and put the other fillet on top of the truffles. Roll the fillets by enveloping them tightly in plastic wrap for vacuum cooking (pressure at 3.2/ welding 7).

-Immerse the vacuum bag of fillets in a bath at 85°C for 5 mins., and then leave the fillets in the vacuum bags to rest for 2 mins. Remove the fillets from the bag. Put the truffle crouton on top and brown lightly under the broiler. Bevel the sole.

•To finish:

-Put the truffle-scented spinach in the centre of a Reynaud rectangular plate. Put the sole on top of the spinach. Spray the plate with the emulsified champagne sauce.

-Put 3 frozen crayfish in a separate bowl. Decorate with a thin julienne of truffle and sticks of mushroom. Serve the broth in a transparent sauce boat. Decorate the plate with chervil and truffle juliennes.

CHAPTER THIRTY-THREE

Corporate Offices of European International Conglomerate, No. 13 Upper Belgrave Street, London, February 2, 1959

The five-story metal and glass office building stood out like a proverbial sore thumb in its neighborhood and had been the subject of such vitriol when it was first proposed to the Council of the City of London in 1955 that it failed as a business venture almost before construction was complete. The failure of the building left a vacant eyesore so incongruous with the wealthy center of the world's foremost financial center that the residents and citizens of The City had serious cause to reflect on their choice. Because of the massive expense of the construction, no buyers came forward even with the asking price having been cut by three quarters. The City felt there would be no recourse but to raze the building and incur a massive expense which would strain the municipal coffers to the limit.

Upper Belgrave Street extended from the southeast corner of Belgrave Square to the northeast corner of Eaton Square in the very center of the City of London—the most prestigious and expensive area of The City. The street was a wide one-way residential street lined with very imposing white stuccoed buildings, most of which were originally exclusive large single family residences—and remained among the most expensive properties in the world. It was adjacent and comparable to Eaton Square. After World War II, some of the largest houses ceased to be used as residences or townhouses for the country gentry and aristocracy; but the new uses were generally restricted to certain categories, including embassies, charity headquarters, and professional institutions. By 1955, many of the houses were being divided into expensive flats, an indicator of the trying times in England's economy. Number 13 had been the home of the Duke and Duchess of Wellington, then the summer residence of his nephew who proved to be a wastrel and allowed the building to deteriorate. His son was a humiliation to the family and allowed the once elegant mansion to burn almost to the ground during a particularly wild party in 1948.

The building was razed, and the property remained vacant until 1955 when a consortium of wealthy foreigners proposed to the City Council that they be allowed to build the first commercial building on the neglected property. It was the lesser of evils; so, a waiver of exception was given by the council and permission was granted for construction of the new building, despite general misgivings. The mistake made by the council was to fail to require an escrow account to return the building site to its pristine empty condition in the event of bankruptcy. By November of 1958, the homeowners and other concerned citizens of the exclusive area began to demand that something be done. The council passed a plan for razing the new building at the expense of the taxpayers—£9,000,000. The original project had cost £71,000,000, and the great losses were considered to be a serious political issue for the upcoming elections.

Then, in December, the chairman of the council, Sir Sedwick Grayson, received a communication from a prominent Swiss financier by the name of François Caussidière who represented clients backed by UBS of Geneva. The chairman of the bank's investment department—Liert Beili Amstutz—and Caussidière made an offer of £5,000,000 and a guarantee that the building would be restored to full value. The guarantee was in the form of an escrow account valued at £9,000,000 should the venture fail. The council chairman was convinced that the purchase of the property and building was a godsend, and he convinced the council and the neighbors that this was the best solution they would ever see.

The sale was completed in record time, and renovation began almost immediately. By the fifth of January 1958, the building was formally dedicated for business with the Lord Mayor and every member of the city council in attendance. The senior partners of the new ownership group, Laird Eagen and Randolph Bellwether, were also in attendance but chose to occupy an inconspicuous role. Herr Caussidière was the public spokesman for the consortium. The owners occupied the upper two floors as their offices for the Corporate Offices of European International Conglomerate. No one questioned particularly strongly exactly what the business of the conglomerate was.

On February 2, 1959, Messrs. Eagen and Bellwether met in their private offices with representatives of a Russian interest group and several others regarding expansion of their business activities. The two senior Russians—Leonid Zaslavskevich Breslava and Nicolai Andreavich Putansky— and their *Byki* [Lit. bulls– bodyguards] had had to clear several hurdles to be able to come to the meeting. The Politburo itself had needed to grant a temporary exit visa for the men to fly to England, a rare exception to the guarded policy of the Soviet Union in the era of the Cold War. They had some difficulty finding the correct recipients of a generous gift they felt obliged to offer to receptive officials. Finally, they had to make elaborate arrangements to travel incognito with carefully crafted false documents because they were considered persona non grata in the United Kingdom owing to their alleged connections with Russian organized crime.

Breslava was the *Pakhan*—the Boss or *Krestnii Otets* [Godfather] of the *vory v zakone* [thieves-in-law] *Solntsevskaya Bratva* [brothers or brotherhood; bratva is a brigade], and Putansky was Breslava's Brigadier [or *Avtoritet* (Authority), similar to Caporegime in Italian-American Mafia crime families and Sicilian Mafia clans, the intermediary through whom Breslava controlled his four close personal criminal cells, each having six *Boyeviks* and *Shestyorkas* [the organization's errand boys who form the lowest rank in the *russkaya mafiya*]. Breslava had a close business relationship with the premier of the Soviet Union and his cronies in the *nomenklatura* [the power elite of the country, corrupt officials all] who ran the Soviet Union along with criminal bosses. Breslava considered the *nomenklatura*—for good reasons—to be partners in his criminal enterprises.

The *Pakhan* could have passed for Communist Party General Secretary Leonid Brezhnev—dark brown hair with a low set forehead, very bushy eye brows, thuggish face, bad teeth, cheap suit and all. Breslava would be the first to deny vehemently the resemblance in private and the last to deny it in public; it would be impolitic to do so.

The other Russian in the room was Ivan Dragonovich Brudzinski, the Sovietnik [support person, advisor, and close trusted friend of Breslava], comparable to the Consigliere of Cosa Nostra. He never spoke except to whisper into Breslava's ear occasionally. Ivan was the invisible gray man who was seldom seen, almost never heard; and whose influence and power was never questioned. He and the *Pakhan* laughed about the intellectuals comparing them to the seventeenth century *Éminence Rouge* [the red-robed Cardinal de Richelieu] and his advisor behind the scenes, the *Éminence Grise* [the gray-robed Capuchin Friar François Leclerc du Tremblay, the right-hand man of Cardinal Richelieu].

The organization of the *russkaya mafiya* was very complicated, and Breslava was limited in which of the men in his system he could bring. He settled on his brigadier, but had to keep the brigadier's 'Two Spies' in a separate set of rooms and not bring them to the meetings. It was their job to watch over the action of the brigadiers to ensure loyalty and that none of the four became too powerful. He elected to bring his *Sovietnik* (support group man) and to leave his *Obshchak* (security group man) at home, a choice that made him uneasy. Breslava left his *Krysha*—literally "roofs," or "covers"—always extremely violent enforcers and sometimes cunning individuals. The *Krysha* were employed by Breslava to protect his business from other criminal organizations. It was a significant measure of his trust for Antoine and Michaele—in the phony identities Breslava knew—that he left some of his men he would never travel anywhere in Russia without. He left his Torpedo [contract killer] in Moscow, but he brought his two *Byki* with him. He never left his house without at least two of them.

From France was Pierre Saint-Denis who was the godfather of the Paris *Milieu*. Pierre was a dandy; he walked with a minsing step; he dressed in flamboyant colors; and his long honey-blond hair and delicate features were very suggestive. No one living had ever questioned Pierre's masculinity, however. For the time being—following a masterful coup—Pierre was also the boss of the most well-known local criminal underworld in Belgium—the *Milieu Liègeois*, which was headquarted in Liege. The *Milieu Liègeois* is a loose-knit web of organized criminals from the impoverished suburbs and towns surrounding the city of Liege. They planned and executed brutal armed robberies on security vans. Pierre Saint-Denis commanded respect in that corner of the European underworld because of his well-earned reputation as a violent and hair-trigger killer. He developed the modus operandi of using military-grade weapons such as AK-47s and grenades to obtain the contents of armed cars. Saint-Denis's other criminal activities in Belgium and France included the more mundane crimes of extortion of businesses, illegal investments in real estate, drug, and weapons trafficking. Another major activity that had in the past led to particularly sensational trials was the perpetrating of contract murders. After his third such trial ended in yet another acquittal, he was usually called by the flattering moniker of "Slick Pierre."

While there was no British comparable to the Cosa Nostra or *Solntsevskaya Bratva*, Gregory "Freight Train" Withers was the nearest thing to a godfather the Brits had at the time, having defeated the Sabini family of the old Clerkenwell area of London—the previous dominant crime family. Withers and his East Enders were in the process of establishing their dominance, which was a bloody ongoing process. Withers was the polar opposite to Pierre Saint-Denis in appearance and mannerisms. He was a thug—or as the cockneys who were his main men called him, "a spiders and bugs." His hair was cut short with no attempt to be in style or groomed or even clean. It was graying, but might well have been more of a brown color after one of his rare showers. He had a pugilistic face with bent nose and cauliflower ears. He had had his two front teeth knocked out in a fight and never bothered to have any cosmetic dentistry done to repair them. He loved to grin at men he was about to pulverize. His suit was too large in the shoulders and too small at the waist. He wore a gray shirt that was once likely white and a gravy-stained tie. His shoes were never polished, but they fit his huge feet comfortably. He wore a ring on every finger of both hands. No one with good sense ever criticized his attire, his bodily aroma, or his choice of jewelry. The public, the newspapers, and the coppers refrained from referring to him as a "spider and bugs."

"We're glad you could make it today. As Mr. Bellwether and I told you when we requested that you meet here, we would like to establish a profitable and safe syndicate. I don't need to tell you that there have been too many wars within and between organizations. We will fare better if we agree to some common ground rules. We're here to decide those rules, whether or not we can control our own spheres of influence, and whether we can trust each other."

Antoine and Michaele had never divulged their pseudonyms to anyone outside of the very tight circle of confidants in Switzerland.

"War is wasteful and makes it so we can't enjoy the profits we earn. Probably the best example is the Bitch Wars in Russia. *Vor* Breslava can certainly relate to this. For those of you who are not familiar with Russian history, let me give you a very brief overview: after Hitler's invasion of the Soviet Union during World War II, Stalin was desperate for more men to fight for his nation. He offered prisoners in the gulags freedom if they joined the army. A great many men in the gulags considered themselves to be Russian patriots despite all that Stalin had done to them, and they agreed to help out in the war. This was based on the questionable idea that they could trust Stalin. This is where our proposal for an agreement comes in.

"The agreement and joining the army betrayed one of the main oaths sworn by the Thieves' World that there could be no agreement or cooperation with the government. Trust in Stalin proved to have been a mistake. When the German war was over, Stalin sent every known prisoner back to the gulag. The Thieves-in-Law who had fought in the Stalin's war referred to those who had not as traitors—*sukas* [bitches]. The fighters heavily outweighed the *sukas*; so, the bitches landed at the bottom of the hierarchy of the Thieves-in-Law. The *sukas* became outcasts and separated from the majority and formed their own scattered groups and power bases by collaborating with prison officials in the gulags which got them the luxury of comfortable beds and decent clothing and food.

"As might have been expected, the bitterness between the groups boiled over into a series of what the Thieves called 'Bitch Wars' that lasted from 1945 to 1953, with many useless killings every day. The prison officials laughed at the Thieves-in-Law and actively encouraged the violence and killing because it was a convenient and easy way to empty the gulags and cut down on the cost of running the system. For the first six or seven years, the gulag officials—more corrupt and murderous than the Thieves-in-Law—profited handsomely. They failed to report the deaths and continued to receive rations and funding for the prisoners still on the rosters. They turned around and sold the food on the black market while the prisoners starved or ate worm-ridden meat and weevil-infested wheat."

"And we agree with Laird and Randolph that we don't need that crap anymore. Bad for business. I say we oughta hear the two of them out," Breslava interjected.

"So what's your plan, Laird?" asked Pierre Saint-Denis of the Paris *Milieu*.

"I'll get right to it," Antoine answered. "First of all, Randolph and I will withdraw our people from the prostitution, bookmaking, horse racing, protection business, gambling, extortion, drug trafficking, and smash-and-grab raids—all of the local rackets—and turn all of our territories to the rest of you provided you agree today."

"Youse goin' soft and legit?" asked "Freight Train" Withers.

"I think you don't need me to answer about the 'soft' part, but the 'legit' of your question is fair. We plan to grow our legitimate businesses—especially our banking interests—in order to protect ourselves from law enforcement while we handle your money affairs. Think of us like a *Solntsevskaya Bratva Kassir* or *Kaznachey* [the bookmaker who collects all money from various *brigadiers* and bribes the government and other legal entities] who tends to the *Obshchak* [money intended for use in the interests of the group as a whole]."

Breslav was impressed with Antoine's intimate knowledge of the inner workings of the *russkaya mafiya*.

"And you get a cut of our 'money affairs'?" he asked pointedly.

"In a nutshell. We take five percent of all goods and money you bring to us as the price for money laundering. In the end you get a much better rate and a safer situation than you have now. We work with some Swiss banking interests as well as some in Belgium, South Africa, Hong Kong, and Canada."

"How about America?"

"Too volatile. Too many of the Mafiosos are in jail or are dead."

The rest of the men nodded their heads in agreement with that observation.

Michaele took a turn, "We will keep a somewhat more active hand in certain other areas. We plan to do some real estate, unions, transportation industry, and construction industry investing that will require some of our ... let's say well-established methods. We have excellent contacts in almost fifty countries for gunrunning. What we would like to do there is to assist in the transactions between your organizations, the manufacturers, and the buyers. That will be for our usual five percent cut."

"Sounds pretty tame," observed Pierre Saint-Denis. "You just going to sit around in your office like legal advisors, Laird?"

"Not quite. There are two other areas where we will take an active but behind-the-scenes role. We have comparable links to local and national governments, senior police officials, judges, prosecutors, and prison officials, to those of the *Solntsevskaya Bratva.*"

Breslava's interest perked up. He did not like the sound of this.

"Don't get yourself all heated up," Antoine told him. "Nothing changes in the Russian sphere except that you get to make use of our contacts and vice versa when situations demand. The rest of us will have full use of our present contacts and those we develop in the future. As evidence of good faith, we will take only five percent—our usual fee—based on the amount of the transaction involved. When it becomes necessary for us to intervene in a court case, we will request a flat fee—one that will be reasonable."

"Sounds like fairy dust to me," said Withers. "We all have our soldiers. We all have a lot of blood on our hands and don't care if we get a little more. Don't seem to me that that's gonna change. Seems to me that your fairy dust ideas will fail because there's no control from one outfit to another."

Antoine gave Withers a direct and disconcerting look.

"That brings us to our last proposal, Gregory, and everybody else. You know that we are effective and efficient. We have an excellent intelligence service. Since we will not have territory to protect or business interests to steal, we can keep ourselves free of alliances on one side or another. What we propose is that our organization become the universal enforcers between organizations. You can all keep order in your own territories and among your own people for the most part. When there is a growing friction between groups, we step in to take care of it. You come to us and present your cases. We become the impartial judge and jury and decide what will be done to prevent a war. We will be for the whole group what the *Boevik* [warriors] and the *Kryshas* [violent enforcers who protect businesses of the winning side from the losers] are for the Russians."

"You'll do the contract killings, Laird?"

"Exclusively. Our participation will be extremely secretive and discreet. No one will ever be able to pin anything on you. Think of it like the role of the ancient Spartans of Greece. When two city-states found themselves so unable to agree that war became imminent, they would 'send for the Spartan,' a man of high respect in Sparta—the most potent military machine in the world. He would come to the area and listen to both sides, then deliberate. He would then deliver a decision which would be obeyed by both sides or the dissenting side would face the Spartans in a war that could only be considered suicidal. If the Spartan sent to do the deliberation was injured or killed, the offenders would face Sparta and extermination.

"We ask that power and responsibility, and for that, just compensation and silence. Our people are warriors, make no mistake about that. Cross us and you will pay a sevenfold price. Once we are crossed, there will be no place for you to hide. However, if you abide by the agreements, you will have peace—and you will have it at a reasonable price."

"It'll take us some time to consider this revolutionary proposal, Laird," Breslava said.

"It doesn't have to take too long. It depends on your power, strength, and will. I ask each of you the key question: can you control the people and organizations in your sphere of interest? You go first, Leonid Zaslavskevich, if you please."

Thus challenged, Breslava responded, "We guarantee the cooperation of the *Dolgoprudnenskayas* [Russia's second largest criminal gang] and every organized outfit throughout the Rodina and in all of the Soviet satellites. How's that?"

"Great. How about you, Pierre?"

Saint-Denis was very much in favor of Antoine's proposals, especially since it would increase his wealth, his security, and his power.

"The *Milieu* guarantees the full participation and cooperation of every local *Milieu* working, and that includes every major city in France—Marseille, Grenoble, Paris, and Lyon. We can persuade, and—if necessary—control, the Corsicans, the Maghrebis, the French Blacks and the *Gitans* [ethnic Manush and Yeniche], the *Tractions Avant*, the French Connection, the Guerinis, Venturis, and the *Brise de Mer* Gang which are small but can be difficult. They will act in their own best interests and will not pick a fight with the *Milieu*. In all honesty it will take time to reign in the North Corsican traveler gangs we call '*Gitans*' or '*Voyageurs*' because they are so nomadic and violently independent. The *Hornecs* are sensible men and can be influenced by the promise of easier and more money and better protection. They can bring the other travelers around in … let's say, six months, at the outside."

Antoine turned to Gregory "Freight Train" Withers, "So, Mr. Withers,what can you bring to the table?"

"We're in a bit of a state of flux at the moment," he said, squirming a little, "and not all that big of an outfit. I can guarantee the East End and what's left of the Sabinis and probably the other Mafiosos whose connections to Cosa Nostra aren't too strong, which is most of them. We are almost in full control of the boxing scene and the Jewish bookmakers. No one has ever been able to control everything in Great Britain, and we have no influence over the West side club rackets. We'll need real help there. Agree to help us without horning in on our business when we get control, and we are your guys. The new interest in drugs and upscale escort services and houses is an area we can get control of from the get-go with a little help."

"You have our help—just ask," said Michaele. "I think we may have a viable interest in the heroin and cocaine trade that we might be able to assist you in developing. For a modest price, of course."

Of course, "Freight Train" said to himself.

CHAPTER THIRTY-FOUR

Corporate Offices of European International Conglomerate, No. 13 Upper Belgrave Street, London, September 8, 1960

The final intelligence reports came into the office by courier. Obtaining the information had required two years of work by employees of the intelligence department of the European International Conglomerate, the *Solntsevskaya Bratva*, and the *Dolgoprudnenskaya*, a Washington, DC, branch of the Cosa Nostra, a confidential informant in the Argentine *Secretaría de Inteligencia*, a woman who worked for the French Ministery of the Interior who had an encyclopedic knowledge of the intelligence services of the National Police and a cocaine habit that allowed her to be the victim of blackmail, and a source inside a loose British criminal network. All of the individuals were paid a king's ransom to betray their masters, and all of them knew full well that they would die if they were found out. The cost of obtaining the information would have been staggering to any ordinary office, but was considered just the cost of doing business by the two men who considered it to be invaluable—something for which they had been waiting fifteen years. The information was in the form of dossiers on men from the Soviet Union, the United States, Argentina, France, and Great Britain.

The opulent office in which the two men were sitting had gold lettering on the pane glass of the door reading: "Private Library of CEO Laird Eagen and President Randolph Bellwether." The names were only two of the many pseudonyms employed by the men over years. As huge and rich as the corporation was, the two were virtual unknowns in the UK; and that is the way they liked it.

"Once we get this done, will you be thinking about retiring and disappearing? We're not getting any younger," Michaele asked his long-term partner.

Antoine just shrugged.

The two men met with their trusted confidants, the *Gebirgsjägers,* and the four men who survived the Allied occupation camps with them after the war and their misery in the gulag.

"We have enough money now to do pretty much whatever we want. More than two hundred million dollars pour into our legitimate business channels every month, and another three hundred comes in from our other activities—which includes and necessitates our money-laundering service," Antoine said. "Michaele and I think it is time for us to phase in more legitmate business enterprises and to phase out our secret activities. We look to the time—maybe ten years from now—when we have no involvement in criminal activities or with criminals. That would mean that we could retire with wealth and without risks from the law or the other side of the law. We want to know what you think about it."

"I see it differently, Antoine. The power that our wealth gives us is the real insurance. We own coppers, prosecutors, judges, and prison guards. That is expensive and getting more expensive all the time. I want those layers of protection; so, I don't have to trust anyone. I don't know anything about legitimate business; so, I would be like a lamb going to the slaughter," said Serge.

He knew he could say his piece without getting Antoine angry, and he certainly did not want that. He had been present when Antoine felt like he was betrayed. No one survived Antoine's impression of betrayal.

"Anyone else?" asked Antoine.

The men were quiet for a few moments, then Willibald spoke up, "Antoine, you and Michaele and I have gone through a lot. I wish you would stay on in our business. I don't see myself sitting in a soft chair in my smoking jacket and slippers sipping peppermint snapps for the rest of my life. If you're serious about it, maybe we could separate with a substantial nest egg for those of us who want to go it alone."

"I guess I should ask: who is going to stay with Michaele and me?"

Hugues Beauchamp and Jérôme Christophe Mailhot nodded their heads, and the three other men—Willem Dortman, Fritzi Gerhardt, and Adolf Wagner who joined up with the *Gebirgsjägers* after the escape from POW Camp 63 in Brienne le Chateâu, France, followed suit. Willem always went where Adolf went, and Fritzi was Michaele's bodyguard. The choice was not difficult for any of them.

"Michaele and I respect your decisions. I ask one thing of you and Willibald," Antoine said, his attention on Serge Rounsavall who had been captured by the Russians on the same day in 1945 as Antoine, Michaele, Hugues, and Jérôme.

"Name it, Antoine."

"We have unfinished business with the Russians, Americans, French, Argentines, and the Brits. It will take our whole team. I think you and Willibald want to see a little justice come out of our miserable lives before we decide to fade away. I don't demand it—or require it of you—but I ask as an old friend: will you help us with a few erasures?"

"Of course. I have waited what seems like a lifetime to be able to even our scores."

"We'll never be even, Serge; but we can get some satisfaction. We are simple men, and we don't ask for much. It'll take a lot of planning."

"And some nerve."

"We're good at both," Michaele said. "We should get started today."

CHAPTER THIRTY-FIVE

Arkady Hotel, Central Moscow, USSR, October 8, 1961

The preparations, planning, bribing, and efforts to convince Leonid Zaslavskevich Breslav—the *Pakhan* of the *vory v zakone* [thieves-in-law] *Solntsevskaya Bratva*—consumed most of the ensuing year, and nearly five million dollars. Leonid Zaslavskevich argued that the project that Antoine and Michaele were planning could compromise the goodwill with Khrushchev that had taken so long to foster; and besides, the mission would require a great many men and considerable supplies. It was likely that some of the *russkaya mafiyas* would get injured, killed, or compromised, which would jeopardise his organization. Antoine saw Breslav's protests as disingenuous bargaining and was certain that the *Pakhan* would lend his support in the end.

Antoine and Michaele took rooms in the Stockholm Grand Hotel under assumed names. They kept to themselves and did not venture out of the hotel. They ate a late dinner in the hotel's exclusive restaurant—a small gastronomic event. The beginning of the courses involved little brown paper surprise bags holding krisp bread. Antoine had a selection of Soup of Morels from Turkey with poached egg and green asparagus. Michaele had French onion soup, as good as was served at the Hotel de Crillon in Paris. Both had thick, brown crusty bread spread with thick salted butter. The next course was crisp round croquettes of nettles from Kälinge farm served with a half lemon and dusted with sea salt.

For his second course, Antoine selected fresh white asparagus from Rhineland-pfalz and rilette of crab, egg, and parsley. Michaele ordered breaded fillet of lemon sole from Kattegatt. The fish was presented as two rectangles of golden sole with a generous line of black caviar on the mid-center surface lying on a bed of piped celeriac cream. Both men ate too much bread, but they were still unable to pass up the desserts displayed for them on a silver platter. Since it was the start of the Swedish rhubarb season, they indulged themselves too generously in the fried raw rhubarb from Holland, lemon sponge cake, quenelle of vanilla ice cream, and browned sugar.

Sweden did not produce anything exciting in the way of wine because it was too cold to ripen grapes properly. Sweden's favorite—and national drink, and the only thing the two men liked about Russia—was vodka made from rye, wheat, corn, and potatoes. They topped the vodka off with generous goblets of Zumbali Chenin Blanc from South Africa. The formerly destitute concentration camp internees who had spent more than a decade in the worst that three nations had to offer laughed at how marvelous the food was and at the fact that they had consumed almost enough to make themselves sick. How far they had come.

It was sobering to get up early the next morning, to change identities into the appearance of common Swedish workers, and to wonder together if they were about to wreck their now almost idyllic existence. With directions from the concierge, they took the train to the harbor then went by ferry to the Tallinn, Estonia Soviet Socialistic Republic. The process of getting into the Soviet satellite buffer state was as unpleasant as the Soviets could make it—long, complicated, slow, and ponderous, with every one of the six separate border representatives they encountered being surlier and ruder than the next. The outside world's policy of nonrecognition of the Soviet state of Estonia gave rise to the principle of legal continuity, which held that *de jure*, Estonia remained an independent state under illegal occupation throughout the period after the war. The officials of the regime–high and low–resented what they considered the disrespect of the westerners and their condescension. However, the two "*Gebirgsjägers*" spoke the universal language—money—which significantly greased the skids for their entrance.

"I remember now why I hated them so much. It was the world's greatest mistake that the Soviets won the war. The Fourth Reich can't come too soon," Michaele said.

"True enough, but don't say anything like that again until we are safely back in England, Michaele. No mistakes," said Antoine soberly.

Michaele nodded and frowned. He had not needed to be told.

The two men arrived in the capital of the Estonian SSR on October 7, the USSR Constitution Day celebration. On the streets there was lackluster enthusiasm—no outright protests, but occasional mutterings. The Tallinn citizens were unhappy about two things. The Soviets had chosen to continue their destruction of Estonian graveyards and war memorials even during what was supposed to be an important day of celebration, with the powers in Moscow granting a day off work for all workers. The graveyards were still in the process of being dismantled, and the materials hauled away with no attention paid to the dismay that project caused the citizens of the city and the country. The Tallinn Military Cemetery was almost denuded of its original gravestones which were placed there between 1918 and 1944. Since then, that graveyard was being used by the Red Army.

The Baltic German cemeteries were now nothing but empty fields. The Kopli and Mõigu cemeteries from the seventeen hundreds and the oldest one in the city—the Kalamaja cemetery—which was established in the sixteenth century, were becoming unrecognizable. The monuments erected by the Republic of Estonia were being knocked down; and to add insult to injury, the stones were being used to construct drab utilitarian soviet block buildings. The Red Army had a designated Destruction Battalion with bright red right shoulder patches that made them stand out as perhaps the most despised unit of the most despised armed force in the country save only the KGB.

Two years after the end of World War II, Estonian private business disappeared, and along with it any vestiges of prosperity. The once vibrant city with its colorful Hanseatic League buildings was now a dull soviet gray with many of the war-torn buildings still windowless hulks. Even a brief step outside rekindled the hatred Antoine and Michaele had for the entire soviet regime. The citizens—now nearly fifty percent ethnic Russians—walked about like inmates of a huge prison compound, heads and eyes down, not speaking to one another. The majority of the intelligentsia, military officers, university professors, and respected businessmen were sent to Russian prison camps and never heard from again. The remaining people were as docile and colorless as their cities. The missing professors at the universities were replaced by politically reliable stooges, many of whom did not even have an education in the subjects they taught. The Balkans were a shadow of their former selves and a sad comparison for Antoine and Michaele who had now lived for years in the splendor of Paris, London, and Bonn.

The famous Song Festival of Estonia was in full swing such as it could be in those stodgy and penurious Soviet years, but it was only a forme fruste of its original vibrant self. That accounted for the hangdog expressions worn by the populace festively dressed in their colorful national costumes. Before the Germans and before the replacement tyranny of the Soviet Union, the Song Festivals were a national institution held in July once every five years with massive choruses from all over the country, indeed from all over the Balkans. Some of those choruses had as many as 18,000 singers. It was a time of meeting kin and old friends, of starting romances, of drinking and rollicking let down of inhibitions, and of producing the best choral music and dance that a nation of enthusiastic performers could bring to the capital. The foreign authorities—the hated Soviets—determined to use the Song Festivals in their own interests. The Soviet regime tied the Song Festivals to the "red holidays," and forced the people to produce them several times a year. Soviet Constitution Day in October was one of them. Foreign and propagandist songs had to be sung in order to preserve the chance to sing Estonian songs at all. During this three-day period–as in the past several years–the people cautiously turned the festivals into minor mass demonstrations, spontaneously singing a few national songs and hymns, both of which were strictly forbidden. Even a few intrepid Estonian rock musicians played briefly and furtively.

On the morning of October 8, Antoine and Michaele hired a lorry to take them unobtrusively to the bus station where they caught the cross-border bus to the former St. Petersburg–called Leningrad ever since the Bolshevik revolution. They had only thought the transit from Sweden into Estonia was cumbersome and tedious. They got a university-level education in what bureaucratic obfuscation and inefficiency was like when they joined a silent queue to walk across the border into Russia.

Every individual border official wore a KGB uniform with its blue insignias. Every man and woman in the border guard had a permanent frown tattooed onto his or her lower face. Every syllable was a growl, and every facial expression was one of distrust and suspicion. The visitors' documents were scrutinized with a thoroughness of a diamond cutter, including with magnifying lenses. There were six stations to go through, and each one of them required the applicants for entry into the communist paradise to answer the same litany of mind-numbing questions. They were patted down none too gently and prodded on to the next station. Their bags were emptied six times and had to be repacked. For Antoine and Michaele, it was a very unpleasant reminder of the mind-set of the gulag where they spent their first years after the fall of Berlin.

Finally they emerged on the other side of the gauntlet and began to search for transportation to the train station. Their Russian was good, and they took every advantage they had to pass for Russians. That advantage evaporated at the Leningrad to Moscow train station, where everyone who passed through passenger check-in went through a vetting as vigorous as they had encountered at the border. Their papers identified them as foreigners which entitled them to pay double the train fare that the citizens paid. They were hungry, thirsty, tired, and out of sorts like every other prospective passenger when they finally made it to the waiting area on the dock alongside the tracks. The only thing that lightened the mini-ordeal was the fact that the train station was a work of art—art deco with heroic paintings and statuary—and as clean and shining as an operating room.

Given the difficulty of finally getting to the point that they could board the comfortable train car their tickets entitled them to, they were highly surprised and relieved to find themselves ensconced in plush comfortable seats—in Soviet gray, but newly recovered—and to be served a decent meal which was included in the fare. They had been warned to buy platform food to supplement the filling but not necessarily interesting onboard food from rows of smiling babushkas who sold everything from freshly picked raspberries to home-smoked fish. There was fragrant bread, boiled eggs, and still-hot boiled potatoes flavored with butter, salt, and pepper, and dill. They put pancakes filled with goat's cheese into their carry bags and had a quick small bowl of strawberries and sour cream.

The train kitchen crew provided borscht, caviar, a tepid cabbage soup with meatballs, and coarse brown bread. There was the expected freely provided national drink, vodka. Most Russians did not consider the water fit to drink. As an after-dinner drink, they were each given a small glass of *champanskaya* [champagne], not the equivalent of the French variety, but not bad for Russia.

Precisely on time, the Russian locomotive class U-U-127, Lenin's 4-6-0 oil-burning compound locomotive, chugged out of the station for an overnight journey to Moscow. The sounds of the locomotive's old engine and clickety-clack of the steel wheels on the joints of the tracks was like a lullaby to the two tired men, and they slept soundly the entire way into the Moscow train station. The station was massively crowded and hectic; so, no one paid attention to the two foreigners who looked every bit like the rest of the Russians around them. No one checked their papers.

Antoine and Michaele had been warned by the British foreign office to avoid Gypsy cabs, but friends had assured them that crime was rare. They elected to take one of the nondescript Fiat 124s which circled the train station, since in Moscow any car can legally be used as a taxi. There is a long tradition of Gypsy cabs, and they comprised most of the city's meager fleet. They stepped up to the curb and raised their hands. A dented and rusting Fiat pulled up, and the driver leaned towards the open window. The driver and the two passengers—all speaking street Russian—negotiated a price, and a handshake bargain was stuck. The driver did not talk the entire way to the Arbat Hotel in central Moscow. The hotel was midrange in price and would not be likely to attract attention to the two men. It was completed in 1960 and still had a sense of newness about it. The accomodations and in-house restaurant were decent.

Per arrangement with the *Pakhan* Leonid Zaslavskevich Breslava, one of his *Kryshas* [extremely violent *russkaya mafiya* enforcers, employed to protect the organization's business from other criminal organizations] named Artur Vsevolodovich Denisov, knocked on Antoine and Michaele's room door—a series of four quick knocks followed by a single loud knock, followed by four more. Michaele responded with two sets of three knocks then opened the door. Denisov was a huge man—six-foot seven and weighed nearly three hundred pounds. He was heavyset with muscles—not fat—and his almost neckless body looked uncomfortable in his wide-lapelled black suit that looked more like a character from 1930s Chicago mobster film than a modern 1960s businessman—the looked he hoped to convey. He had a gray shirt, black tie with an eagle tie tack, and matching cufflinks. His broad black shoes could have used a shine.

Artur Vsevolodovich's brown hair was combed back and pomaded into a neatness that was almost waxen. The neatness did nothing to soften his face, which would have been chosen as the year's best thug face for the movies if such a contest existed. He had several facial scars, and half of his right ear was missing. The left earlobe held a medium-sized gold ring, which gave that side of his face a piratical quality.

"*Dobryy vecher, on poslal menya, chtoby pomoch* [Good evening, he sent me to help]," the Mafioso said, presuming that "he" needed no further characterization.

CHAPTER THIRTY-SIX

Arkhangelskoye Military Convalescent Home, USSR, October 9, 1961

"*Spasibo za to* [Thank you for coming], Artur Vsevolodovich," responded Antoine in the same language, gesturing a welcome to the formidable man.

"You have to be at the place by seven in the morning when they have the change of shifts. I will be parked at the loading dock of the Arkady at O six hundred. The traffic will get too heavy after that," Artur said without taking a moment for greetings or a chat.

"Do you have weapons for us?"

"They will be in the car tomorrow. Too dangerous to have such things in your possession these days if you don't have to. The *ments* [cops] and the KGB goons are always on the lookout."

Antoine nodded his understanding. Michaele brought a small tray holding three medium glass tumblers half-filled with vodka. The three took their glasses and chorused the traditional salute.

"*Bóo-deem zda-ró-vye*, [To our health]!"

The following morning, Antoine and Michaele took no chances. They stood shivering in the autumn cold and darkness at five-thirty, making sure they were as obscure as possible by standing in the shadows of a stack of packing boxes.

"There's Artur Vsevolodovich," said Michaele as a shiny new ZIL-135LM slowly pulled alongside the dock.

He and Antoine slipped quietly into the backseat, and the Mafioso sped out into the growing traffic. They slowed down after going a short distance on the MKAD [Moscow Automobile Ring Road], while Artur squinted to find the road he wanted. He turned off twelve miles west of the militsya *MYC* in Tverskoy District, central Moscow, and into the Zrkhangelskoye Estate. The architectural center of the Arkhangelskoye Estate was the Yusupov Palace, a beautiful edifice on a sunny day. But today they were unable even to see its outlines due to fog and drizzling rain.

"Here's your guns. Keep them out of sight," Artur said, and the two newcomers quickly slid the weapons under their trench coats.

They were dressed in hospital groundsmen uniforms supplied by the *vory v zakone* [thieves-in-law] *Solntsevskaya Bratva* [brothers or brotherhood]. Artur parked off the gravel parking area beneath a copse of white birch trees to wait for them.

His parting warning was, "Don't be long. Once the body is discovered, the *ments* will be here in a matter of minutes."

Antoine and Michaele walked into the entryway to the long façade of the Stalin-era Military Convalescent Home which was built in the 1940s for the Red Army elite and was closed to visitors. Its terraces overlooking the river were accessible, and its staircases were the best way to reach the riverbank, a sodden mass at the moment; but the two men navigated the terrace to the main patient area unnoticed as a fortunate result of the limited visibility. They stepped into the Palladian-style building, and Michaele found a sofa in an out-of-the-way corner and settled into it, fingering his gun. His job was to protect Antoine's back this time. His turn would come.

Antoine made sure there was a minimum of people in the hallway where the thieves-in-law had told him he would be able to locate his quarry. He encountered a young woman dressed in the uniform of a senior nursing officer.

"Are you Sister Maria Nikolayovna Ilyushkin?" he asked using the name *Pakhan* Breslava had given him.

"Do you work here … outside?" she responded brusquely.

"Never mind that. Answer my question."

The man had the air of a military officer despite his humble uniform. Maybe he was KGB.

"I am Sister Maria, the head nurse. What do you want?"

"The *Pakhan* sent me."

Maria blanched. Her sister had borrowed money from the *russkaya mafiya* during a time of desperation and had never been able to pay off the exhorbitant interest let alone the principal of the debt. The choice she faced was prostitution or involve the entire family in a lifetime of favors for the criminal syndicate. There was no escaping, and this was hardly the first favor required of her to protect her sister.

"I will help anyway I can," she said with dread in her voice.

"Where is General Lagounov? Be quick about it."

"It is against the rules. I am not supposed to divulge where our important veterans live, sir, please."

Acting on a hunch about the man, she asked in German, "*Sind sie Deutsch, mein Herr. Warum Sie die Allgemeine möchten, bitte?* [Are you German, sir? Why do you want the general, please?]"

Antoine let his stress and anger at the nurse's obstructionism get the better of him.

He snarled, "*Gott verdammt, wo is er?*"

This was worse than she had imagined. It was bad enough for a friend of the *russkaya mafiya* who was owed a favor to be challenging her, but this was a German. This meant that the favor must be evil indeed. She had lived in Stalingrad during the war—during the siege—and she was well aware that Germans were the spawn of the devil. She felt faint.

Antoine calmed down, seeing that his bullying was counterproductive. It had been a terrible mistake to have seemed to be a German to the woman and to have responded when she spoke the language of the Fatherland. He tried another tack to soften his presence and to get her to cooperate without calling more attention to him.

He spoke quietly in his native language, "*Je suis désolé de vous avoir inquiété, Sœur. Je suis un grand admirateur du général et souhaite qu'à lui présenter mes hommages. Aidez-moi, se il vous plait.* [I am sorry to have worried you, Sister. I am a great admirer of the general and wish only to pay him my respects. Please help me.]"

Sister Maria decided he must be one of those poor souls who was interned by the Germans and had lost his gentlemanly skills. Gen. Lagounov must have liberated him. It was a fiction she needed.

She called to the nurse-apprentice who was standing nearby and listening too intently, "Ludmila Mikhailovna! Take this man to General Lagounov at once!"

The timid country girl sprang to an upright posture and strode quickly up to the man and Sister Maria.

"Yes, Sister. Follow me, please," she asked.

The general's hospital room was fifty yards down the long hall. The door was open, and the general was sitting slouched on his easy chair listening to the music of Tchaikovsky's *Swan Lake*—his favorite—on his vintage gramophone. Antoine stayed behind the young nurse to obsure his presence until the last possible moment.

"What do you want now, you witch?" the old man demanded imperiously, his usual demeanor.

He looked at Antoine without recognition at first, then something from somewhere deep inside him seemed to jell.

Antoine smiled grimly. The pleasure of the moment was almost too much to contain. He turned to the rather homely young nurse.

"Get out," he said, "now!" in a voice that came from inside a crypt.

Ludmila Mikhailovna turned quickly and walked towards the door, shivering.

She heard the unpleasant man say, "Kind of surprised to see me, no, General?" as she walked out the door.

Antoine took his time. The first thing he did was to close the door to the old man's room. Then he picked up the general's prize cavalry saber and admired it, stroking it lovingly.

BOOK THREE

THE HUNT

CHAPTER THIRTY-SEVEN

MYC [Moscow Criminal Investigations Department]
Building, Petrovka 38 Street, Moscow USSR,
October 9, 1961

The on-scene investigation at the Arkhangelskoye Military Convalescent Home was finished—all leads exhausted—at eight-thirty in the evening, and lieutenant of *militsiya Operativniy Rabotnik* [Detective] Trushin Vasilyvich Stepanovich ordered his crew to gather at the main office for a final presentation of the progress of the day in the investigation of the murder of Lieutenant General of Cavalry Grigory Yegorivich Lagounov, Cavalier of the Order of the Red Banner, which occurred in his room at the home. While he waited for the rest of the police officers to gather, he gave his wife Katrinka a belated call to their fifth-story central Moscow apartment. In the 1960s, that was about all any Moscow cop could afford.

"Hello," she said in the peeved voice he had come to recognize and expect at the end of a long day of doing his duty.

Her lack of enthusiasm was warranted–he knew–because she was just waiting for him to tell her that he would not be home in time to put the children to bed ... if he made it home at all.

"Sorry, I couldn't call. I was at the scene all day. This is proving to be not only difficult, but also political. I'll make it up to you, Kat."

"No need to be sorry. I'm not upset; but I worry that you work too hard; and I feel sad that you can't be here to watch the children grow up every day the way I do. More than that, I worry that you may not be safe."

"I'm fine, Kat. It's just boots on the ground *ment* [cop] work, nothing exciting or dangerous. I have a great team; and for the moment, we are just beginning to sift through the evidence. I'll be pretty much tied up tomorrow as well, but let's splurge and take the children to the lake on Sunday for a big picnic. Maybe your mother and father would like to come along."

Nothing made Katrinka feel better than having Trushin be nice to her parents. It was a great way to dispel ill will. Katrinka knew it was a ploy, but it was a well-intended one—and it worked.

"See you tomorrow, my Trushin Vasilyovich. Get something good to eat, and don't let Lada Kornikova get you off into a little room someplace there at Petrovka 38."

She laughed, and he joined her. It was a standard joke between the couple whose marriage was rock-solid. Lada and Katrinka were the best of friends, and she often tended the Stepanovich children when Kat and Trushin had a rare evening out together. The brief conversation with his wife led him into a few moments of nostalgic woolgathering. They had first made love on the grass by the edge of Lake Glubokoye, the deepest lake in the Ruzsky District of the Moscow oblast. She was beautiful: Scandinavian blond, striking flawless white skin, laughing eyes, small feet and hands, and a kissable mouth. Two children later and a typical Muscovite life for the past ten years notwithstanding, Katrinka was still beautiful and still the object of his dreams and fantasies.

Trushin sighed and forced himself back into the present as the rest of the team made their way into the small and cluttered conference room. Lada set about to make a pot of ersatz coffee; the men lit up their noxious Belomorkanals; and Trushin set up a blackboard and easel.

"All right," the lieutenant said, "Let's hear what you've come up with."

Senior Private Lada Kornikova spoke first, "I'll tack up my crime scene photos on the board," she said, referring to the north wall of the office that was covered with corkboard.

She moved aside her *Hasselbladski*—Kiev 88 model—camera and efficiently placed the photos in an array that showed the room as if one were looking at every wall, the floor, and the ceiling laid out before him. The men all blushed at their quick reaction to the statuesque Nordic beauty as she moved her curvaceous body in quick, graceful moves which allowed momentary stray thoughts. None of them would ever have touched her. They were all protective of the charming bright girl; Lada was their little sister; and perhaps the best detective among them after Lt. Stepanovich; but she was like a fine painting, with her beauty only suggestively hidden under her dumpy uniform. The gruesome scene of the murder was shown in unforgiving clarity of light and color from her excellent photographs, including the impacted sword, the small amounts of blood on the floor, and the considerable amounts in the bathroom.

"We typed the blood, and the blood type was the same as the general's—B positive—with no other contributor. We questioned every member of the staff; and Georgy, Ivan, and Yuri Alexandreovich are all agreed that no one knows anything or saw anything except for the head nurse, Sister Maria Nikolayovna Ilyushkin, and the floor nurse, Ludmila Mikhailovna Kovalevsky. Yuri questioned the Kovalesky woman. He can tell you what came of that."

"She was very excitable and very feminine; by that I mean emotional … no disrespect to you, Lada. However, she held to her story that she overheard the man speaking to Head Nurse Ilyushkin in both German and French. He also spoke Russian to her. Ludmila overheard the man saying something to the general to the effect that 'You don't seem surprised to see me,' or maybe 'You seem surprised to see me,' which suggested that the two men knew each other."

Lt. Stepanovich listened intently and took notes but did not have anything to say at that point.

"I talked to the head nurse, Sister Maria Nikolayovna Ilyuskin," Ivan Viktorovich Lebedinsky said. "I am convinced she knows more than what she is telling, and she might be telling outright lies in some of the particulars she related. She denied speaking French or German to the man. All she would say is that she told the unknown male that he did not have a proper pass to go to the general's room. He should not even be in the convalescent home at all."

"So, what excuse was given for his presence?" Lt. Stepanovich asked.

"Maria said that he had a pass from General Lagounov's longtime aide-de-camp, Colonel Dimitri Sobrieski; so, she got Ludmila to take the man to Gen. Lagounov's room—and that was the last she saw of the mystery visitor."

"Did anyone talk to Sobrieski?" Lt. Stepanovich asked.

"Not yet," Ivan said. "He lives in Pushkin outside of Leningrad. Maybe you remember it better as Detskoye Selo. The name was changed after the October Revolution."

Trushin nodded.

"We have sent for him. Our dear friends in the KGB have authorized it. Seems they are more than a little interested in our case."

"How nice for us," Trushin said almost under his breath.

"He should be here by tomorrow afternoon if our soviet engineering marvel of a fast train doesn't have an unfortunate malfunction owing to sabotage by the counterrevolutionary cabal that is still here, there, and everywhere, trying to undermine our glorious triumph."

All of the police officers present in the cramped office turned their heads aside to avoid their sudden smiles from showing too completely for safety.

"I'd like to handle that interview personally," Lt. Stepanovich said. "What else?"

"Ivan and I dusted for fingerprints, Trushin Vasilyovich," Yuri said. "The room was full of them. It will take a long time to sort them out, and I am afraid that we will have to ask help from the American FBI to get anywhere."

"Our new KGB friends won't like that," Trushin said.

"No, sir, they won't. You get to approach them. That's why you get all the extra rubles and all the glory, Lieutenant," said Ivan Viktorovich.

Trushin just grumped.

The following morning, Lt. Stepanovich sent underofficer Lebedinsky and five of the brighter young *MYC* to dig into Gen. Lagounov's official records. Stepanovich made the call to the number two in the Moscow KGB office and was surprised that he agreed to allow–and even to help in–Trushin's investigation. Apparently the KGB did not like to have its senior officers murdered and was more than happy to help the *MYC* find the killer. It would cost Trushin and his *MYC* something: once they had the perpetrator in custody with sufficient evidence to convict him and anyone who aided him, the KGB would take custody and deal with any questioning, trial, conviction, and sentencing, and would do so out of the public eye. The Soviet Union was a giant records machine, and Stepanovich hated getting bogged down in it. He thought to himself that he would owe Lebedinsky a steak dinner when this was over.

Trushin and Lada interviewed two former officers who served under General Lagounov, intending to learn as much as possible about the dead man's relationships during his career and whether or not he had cultivated any serious enemies. The first man was Col. Gavriil Davidovich Nabatov.

"Col. Nabatov, let me assure you that you are not under suspicion and you are in no trouble. This is a routine part of an important case the *MYC* and the KGB are conducting, and you need only answer questions honestly. Once we are satisfied with that, you will be free to go. Do you have any questions, sir?" Lada asked courteously, playing her part of the soft *ment*.

"I will have nothing to say unless I am questioned by someone of equal rank to me or who outranks me. You certainly are not that person. And, furthermore, I will not be answering any questions before I know fully what is going on and why I am being questioned."

"I certainly mean you no disrespect, Colonel. However, this is a serious *MYC* matter, and we have our policies and procedures. The first of which is that I ask the questions, and you answer them. You give the information requested, and I record that information and evaluate it. The second matter of policy is that you have the right to be questioned by the KGB and likely by ranking officers. If you exercise that right, we will have you delivered to the Lubyanka this very morning. What is your choice?"

"My choice is to call your bluff, young lady. Perhaps you should get back to the kitchen or to tending the kiddies where you belong. I am leaving now. I shall report your insolence to my superiors and yours. I suspect you will be singing a different tune by the end of this morning."

He stood up stiffly and started for the door of the interview room. He looked back to see Lada's reaction, unaware that he was being observed through a two-way mirror. Lada raised her index finger in a laconic gesture. Col. Nabatov opened the door; and two burly KGB noncoms stepped up beside him, grasped his arms and twisted them around his back, and placed him none too gently in handcuffs.

"Sit," the larger and uglier of the two sergeants said, and Nabatov was shoved down hard into an uncomfortable straight-back metal chair.

The noncom dialed a number from memory.

He listened then said, "Sergeant Dragnarovich."

There was a reply which no one but the sergeant heard.

There was a five minute pause during which no one spoke.

Then Sergeant Dragnarovich placed the receiver of the telephone against Col. Nabatov's ear and said, "KGB Col. Rudolph Vladimirovich Fedorchuck II."

Col. Nabatov did not speak; but he evidently listened, because his face paled; and he started to sweat. He knew all about the man speaking to him, although he had not met him in person. Fedorchuck was head of the KGB's Fifth Directorate, responsible for ideology, countersubversion, and the Agitprop Department. He was one of the most powerful men in the Soviet Union, and probably the most universally feared.

"I understand, Colonel, and I will comply completely. Then I will report back to you as ordered." There was a short pause. "Yes, sir. I will see to it that every resource at my disposal will be put into the manhunt." Another brief pause. "Yes, sir, Comrade Colonel, every man under my command will cooperate with the police investigation. You have my guarantee."

Nabatov stared daggers at Lada; but when he returned to his seat in the interview room, he was deferential.

"Now, where we, Colonel…?" she asked.

"I was about to tell you what I know about the unfortunate General Lagounov. Ahem … where shall I start….? Lieutenant General of Cavalry Grigory Yegorivich Lagounov served the revolution in a Workers and Peasants' Red Army cavalry unit headed by Gen. Budenny before 1922 when he was just a boy. His first service was during the insurrection of General Alexey Maximovich Kaledin's Volunteer Army in the River Don region. He rose rapidly in the ranks owing to his … how shall we say…? particularly effective methods. Lagounov was credited with having come up with the motto of the Cheka troops: "Exhortation, Organization, and Reprisals" which was widely considered to express the necessary discipline and motivation to ensure that the Red Army would achieve tactical and strategic success. His first real command was over the Cheka Special Punitive Brigades which conducted summary field courts-martial and executions of deserters and slackers. That stiffened the backbones of any would-be slackers."

"And perhaps caused him to have some enemies, Colonel?" Lada asked as if it were merely an aside.

"Not perhaps, Comrade Kornikova. Lagounov was widely known as one of the Great Leader's men-of-steel. Slackers, deserters, and fifth columnists learned early on to hate him, but to fear him more than that. He was an innovative and determined leader whose record in the Great War was cited by Comrade Iosif Vissarionovich Stalin then and afterwards in the period leading up to the Great Patriotic War.

"You are obviously too young to remember the Great War, Comrade Kornikova; so, allow me to share a bit of pertinent history. During that time, the war became a deadlock of trench warfare and futile—near suicidal—mass attacks. Then Captain Lagounov developed the concept of having selected shock troops attack weak points along the Austrian lines. General Brusilov agreed and put the captain in charge. Lagounov selected the best of the best soldiers and cavalrymen and had them detached from the main army lines. He sent them to infiltrate enemy positions. Then, he would call for short ferocious artillery fire on the weak point so that that point was attacked from both the front and the rear. Often that resulted in a narrow, but important breakthrough. The senior officers opposed him and his tactics because it violated the army's fixed plans. His men were considered to be no better than mere spies by some of the generals. The shock troops grumbled some about the high rate of casualties they suffered and blamed that on Captain Lagounov. When he learned of their discontent, the captain had them shot in front of the surviving troops as an object lesson. Despite the complaints from above and below, Comrade Iosif Vissarionovich continued to support him; and Lagounov was considered to be untouchable. He was awarded the honor of becoming the youngest officer ever to be named a Cavalier of the Order of the Red Banner for his instrumentality in breaking the cohesiveness of the enemy's lines."

"We will need names of men who might have borne Lagounov a lasting grudge and who could still be capable of carrying out an assassination. I want you to prepare such a list for us in as much detail as is possible to be found, Colonel," Lt. Stepanovich interjected for the first time.

"It will be done," Col. Nabatov declared.

"Please submit your list to my subordinate, *Militsiya* Underofficer Ivan Viktorovich Lebedinsky. I expect the list within seventy-two hours."

"Comrade Lieutenant—with respect—that is an impossible request to fulfil in that period of time. I can assign a team of a dozen—maybe more—of my best technicians and analysts; but just finding such records will take a great deal of time and considerable persuasion. Am I permitted to use Gen. Fedorchuck's name as the senior authority?"

"You have that authority, Colonel, and to show that I am a reasonable man, you are allowed seven full days to complete your task," said Lebedinsky.

Lada Kornikova resumed her questioning of the colonel, "Please continue your narrative, Colonel."

"Ten years after the Great War, Lagounov was elevated to the rank of *kombrig* [equivalent of brigadier] in the Cheka. Exactly when he was formally transferred to the chekists is uncertain, but not long after the end of the Great War."

"And in that organization, I presume he created enemies in addition to those he acquired during the war," Lada said.

"Every chekist did, and many of them were murdered by peasants, successful deserters, and regular army officers who were appalled by the excesses of the secret police. It would be impossible even to number the multitudes of people who hated Lagounov, let alone compose a list of them."

"Get us the names of some of the most prominent, Colonel," Trushin ordered.

Nabakov shrugged but nodded his head.

"Again, some history is pertinent. It is really not very useful to separate Lagounov's involvement with the Cheka, the NKVD, the MVD, the NKGB, the MGB, or finally with the KGB we have today. There were a series of reorganizations; and by and large, it was only the most cruel, unfeeling, and violent of the people—including some women—who survived and advanced in rank. The chekists or any of their later titles had a lot of jobs: they requisitioned food for the Red Army troops, tortured political opponents, put down rebellions, quelled riots, conducted summary executions of deserters; and I am quite sure that Lagounov's last assignment related to policing labor camps. I think he was in charge of releasing the longest-held prisoners—some as late as the mid-fifties."

"Making enemies by the hundreds all along the way."

"More like by the thousands—or tens of thousands if you include the families of the victims. They were arrogant in the extreme and took no effort to hide what they were doing. They strutted around in long shiny flowing leather coats and hightop black boots. The chekists had an affectation. They all had amber worry beads that they took pleasure in fingering as they conducted torture and massacres. It was sort of a mark of distinction—an in-group kind of identifier. They laughed at their torture victims and the families, all but daring them to try and resist or to plan revenge. Lagounov used to be particularly open about it. He is was ... probably the only man who went to the camps who actually enjoyed the experience."

"A sadist."

"Of the first order. No better than Hitler."

"Is there really anybody left that we might find records about who might hold a murderous grudge, or even some kind of group that could be sponsoring revenge? Come to think of it, Lada, we need to check around to see if there have been any other suggestive murders," Trushin said.

"I'll check the databases from outside the Rodina—even outside the satellites—after we get done here," Lada said thoughtfully.

"He headed up the so-called 'Special Punitive Department or Extraordinary Commission' with mass arrests, imprisonments, and executions of presumed enemies of the people—the class enemies like the libertarians, socialists, clergy, bourgeoisie, and anarchists, even people strongly on the left of the communist political spectrum."

"With hundreds of thousands of potential suspects for us to sift through," Lada said.

"I'm afraid you're too conservative, Comrade Kornikova. Just the deserters alone numbered more than three million men, and more than two-thirds of them were arrested. Add to that the numbers of surviving family members and your counts go up to numbers that could populate a medium-sized country."

"We have to pare down the numbers somehow, Colonel," said Trushin. "Do you think you could get us into the records of the worst cases, so we would have someplace to start?"

"Actually that is a good idea, because there are records of the Military and Revolutionary tribunals both inside and outside war zones and of the gulags. Strangely enough the commisars were fanatics about keeping records. The secret police shot deserters, shot hostages to force deserters to give themselves up, and tortured people by the hundreds of thousands. I read a report that said that the worst torturers ended up with psychopathic disorders and had to be hospitalized in lunatic asylums. They became alcoholics and drug addicts. The psychiatrists writing the reports tended to trivialize the problem, concluding that it was just an occupational hazard.

"I can get records of the worst kinds of atrocities—which General Lagounov undoubtedly supervised—and maybe you can find a very few survivors but more family members and friends. I have seen records of people being skinned alive, beheadings, beheadings by fixing a man's body in place then twisting his head on his neck until the head was separated from the body, scalped, impaled on Poles; so, they did not die immediately but suffered agonies, hanged, stoned, boiled, jammed into barrels with spikes studded on the inside and rolled about, tied to posts along the street in winter and covered with water so that they became ice statues, and being tied down while starving rats ate them alive. The government in the last two years has declared such things illegal, and police are allowed access to the records."

"Colonel, that sounds like a good place to start. Thank you for your service," Trushin said, and everyone was aware of a significant thawing in the atmosphere.

"I apologize for my attitude at the beginning. I actually want to help, but please do not let my name be known. I will not last a day if you do."

"You have my word."

Russian Supper Recipes

Basic Russian Vareniki or Pelmeni Dough (Russian Pierogi)

Ingredients
•For dough:
-1 large egg, 2 tbsp sour cream, ¾ cp water, 1 cp water, 1 cp whole milk,5 cps all-purpose flour, plus about 1 cup more for dusting.
•For the filling: potato and onion, blueberry, cherry, and ground pork and turkey
•For toppings
•For potato-filled vareniki:
Zazharka: Saute bacon and onion in butter and drizzle over your finished vareniki/pierogies.
For meat-filled pelmeni:
Melted butter. Also good dipped in vinegar or ketchup.
•For fruit filling:
Dust finished product with some sugar to keep from sticking and dip in sour cream.

Preparation
•Basic Pierogi dough:
-Whisk together egg and sour cream until well combined. Whisk in milk and water. Using a spatula, mix in flour 1 cp at a time.
-Place the dough onto a floured surface. Using a food scraper, knead the dough by turning and folding it with the food scraper. Dust the dough with flour as you need it until it is soft and doesn't stick to your hands—around 1 cp more flour. Knead for 6–8 mins. Don't add too much flour or the dough will become hard to work with.
-Place the dough under a bowl and let it sit at room temperature for about 1 hour. Cut the dough into 4–6 pieces. Work with one piece at a time and keep the rest covered with plastic wrap.
-Form the chunk of dough into a log and cut off small pieces one at a time. Pieces should be a little larger than a gumball. Dust rolling pin and cutting board with flour and roll out a piece of dough until it is ⅛ in thick and 3 in. in diameter.
-Fill these circles with the desired filling (potatoes, cherries, blueberries, or meat). Fold the dough over the filling to form a crescent and seal the edges tightly with your fingers. If making pelmeni (meat filling), pinch the two edges together to form a "diaper" shape. Place the finished pierogis on a cutting board dusted with flour until ready to boil.
—Bring a large pot of salted water to boil. As you finish the first batch of pierogies, place them in boiling water. After they float to the top, cook about 2–3 mins. more, then remove them with a slotted spoon to a bowl. Drizzle the pierogies with melted butter.
-Repeat steps with the rest of the dough.

Russian Beef Stroganoff—Serves 4

Ingredients
-1 lb round steaks or 1 lb skirt steak, $1\frac{1}{2}$ tbsps cornstarch or all-purpose flour, $1\frac{1}{2}$ tsps olive oil, 1 large onion, thinly sliced, 8 oz sliced mushrooms, $\frac{3}{4}$ cp beef broth, $\frac{3}{4}$ tsp salt, $\frac{3}{8}$ tsp black pepper, $\frac{3}{8}$ cup sour cream, 3 tbsps parsley, 8 oz egg noodles.

Preparation
-Cut steak diagonally across the grain into thin slices. Combine steak and cornstarch or flour in a small bowl and toss well.
-Heat oil in a large nonstick skillet over medium-high heat. Add steak and saute 5 mins. Add onion and saute 1 min. Add mushrooms, cover and cook 2 mins. Add broth, salt, pepper.
-Reduce heat and simmer uncovered for 5 min. Remove from heat; stir in sour cream and parsley.
-Serve over egg noodles.

Russian Tea Cakes—Serves 48

Ingredients
-1 cp softened butter, $\frac{1}{2}$ cp powdered sugar, 1 tsp vanilla, 2 $\frac{1}{4}$ cps all-purpose flour, $\frac{1}{4}$ tsp salt, $\frac{3}{4}$ cup finely chopped nuts, ½ cp powdered sugar.

Preparation
-Heat oven to 400° F.
-Beat butter, powdered sugar, and vanilla in large bowl and mix well. Stir in flour, salt, then nuts.
-Shape dough into 1 in. balls. Place about 2 ins. apart on ungreased cookie sheet.
-Bake 8 to 9 min. or until set but not brown. Immediately remove from cookie sheet; roll in powdered sugar.
-Cool completely on wire rack. Roll in powdered sugar again.

CHAPTER THIRTY-EIGHT

MYC [Moscow Criminal Investigations Department] Building, Petrovka 38 Street, Moscow USSR, October 9, 1961—afternoon

The An-24 "coke" twin Progress engine turboprop military transport aircraft carrying KGB Colonel General Dimitri Sobrieski landed at Moscow's top secret Sheremetyevo Airport an hour late—1300 hours. *MYC* Lts. Stepanovich and Zakhar Rostislavovich Rumyantsev—Stepanovich's backup officer during the Lagounov investigation—had been waiting since 1100 hours. Used to the inefficiencies of the soviet state, they did not even bother to grumble. Rumyantsev was bluff and red-faced, the stigmata of his alcoholism that he tried to hide. He had unruly mousey medium brown hair that stuck out from his police cap like clacks of old straw. His abdomen was protuberant from alcoholic ascites, and his complexion was pasty. Trushin knew his old friend did not have long to live but kept him on to protect his pension for his wife. The rest of the *MYC* unit involved in the Lagounov murder investigation were toiling away back at the office, beginning the gargantuan task of sorting through the boxes of files provided by Col. Nabatov.

Sobrieski had been the aide-de-camp to Gen. Lagounov with the rank of lieutenant when they had both been in the NKVD [literally, the People's Commisariat of Internal Affairs]. Lagounov had been the general in command of the Directorate of North-Eastern Camps—the *Sevvostlag* or SVITL [*severo-vostochnye lagerya*]—which constituted the majority of gulag camps in extremely remote areas of northeastern Siberia along the Kolyma river. The two men had risen in the ranks and survived the purges and changes leading to what became the KGB [*Komitet gosudarstvennoy bezopasnosti*-Committee for State Security]. Sobrieski rose to his rank of colonel general after Lagounov retired, and he assumed command of all KGB forces in Siberia.

The flight from Novosibirsk Tolmachevo Airport situated in the town of Ob, ten miles from the center of the capital, Novosibirsk, to Moscow is 1,740 miles. It took nine hours for the trip and required refueling stops and interminable machinery and bureaucratic delays every four and a half hours. The aircraft was capable of flying a maximum 540 mph and a cruising speed of 267 mph, and should have taken no more than five hours total even with refueling stops. Sobrieski was out of sorts when he deplaned and met the Moscow Criminal Investigations officers.

"Get me to a decent chair and some decent food and drink," Sobrieski said abruptly as soon as Lt. Stepanovich stood before him. "My back is killing me."

"Sorry, General. We'll see to your comfort in short order. I want you to know that we appreciate you coming to help in our investigation and that you will be doing a great service for the Rodina."

"And I am happy to do it. The murder of such an important KGB general cannot go unpunished. If I have anything to add, I am enthusiastic to do so. Forgive an old man for griping about his aches and pains."

Then he actually smiled, showing his soviet gold and silver fillings and tooth caps. He extended his hand and shook Stepanovich's hand enthusiastically. Trushin thought he had just fallen across some invisible line into another world for a moment.

Trushin conducted the interview with Gen. Sobrieski himself because he did not have full faith in Sobrieski's assertions that he wanted the whole truth to come out. Trushin was certain that no officer who served in the Red Army or KGB units assigned to the gulag system was going to be entirely forthcoming about his own or a friend's actions during that postwar vengeful era.

"General, let me first assure you that this is not an investigation of what went on in the *Sevvostlag* except to identify those who might have a grudge against Gen. Lagounov—who survived the camps, who are likely still alive, and finally, who might have resources at hand now to carry off such a murder. It is our suspicion that the *russkaya mafiya* may have assisted. If that is true, it could not have been an easy or inexpensive cooperation."

Sobrieski sipped on his Stolichnaya vodka and snacked from the platter prepared for him on wild Caspian caviar—fresh, shiny, and each egg separate from the others as good caviar should be. He savored the relaxation and especially the small beads of sturgeon roe rolling across his tongue, dissolving into little fishy-salty bursts. The opulent platter held almost all of the soviet favorites in small dishes: pickled cucumbers, tomatoes, and mushrooms; *salo* [raw fatty bacon] with Russian bread and garlic, fermented cabbage, Russian meat jelly, boiled small new potatoes, salami with cheese; marinated herring and fresh black bread; lamb *shashlik*; *ukha* [fish soup]; borsch topped with *smetana* [sour cream]; and *olivje* salad [dense cold salad made of boiled potatoes, mayonnaise, wurst, and green peas]. He had enough from the platter of snacks to lessen his hunger pangs and of the vodka to loosen his inhibitions and his tongue.

"You have done well by me, Comrade. I am glad to have the *olivje* salad. It will serve as a table pillow when I can no longer hold my head up," he joked.

"Good, Comrade General. Now perhaps we can get to some important questions."

Lt. Stepanovich had never met the general before. He had met very few generals before. The man was rail thin with wispy salt and pepper hair cut short. His eyes were narrow and too close together; and along with his sharp nose, Sobrieski had a rather ratlike face. His teeth were bad; he had been a soviet citizen all his life with most of his adult years spent in war and in Siberia; so, it was not surprising that even a man in his high position would show the stigmata of poor dentistry that plagued soviet citizens throughout the immense country. His uniform was perfect: new, pressed to knifelike crispness, starched; and his boots were polished to a mirror finish.

"My first question—and I ask your forgiveness for my directness—is: do you know of any person or number of persons who fit my description of who we are hunting for?"

"Angry survivor, still alive, and possessing adequate resources to be successfully involved with the *russkaya mafiya*? My answer is maybe, and perhaps it is fortunate that there can only be a few such people who knew my general in Siberia who fit that description. I would have to say that most of the men who fit all of those criteria are officers and former officers of the army or the KGB. Once you have finished with your questions, I will give you a written list of those men.

"As to the inmates, I have to say that not many are still alive; most of them are still in Siberia living as soviet citizens, but there are a few classes of prisoners which could bear some scrutiny. You no doubt know that *GU lag* is the acronym for *Chief Administration of Corrective Labor Camps and Colonies*, of which Lieutenant General of Cavalry Grigory Yegorivich Lagounov was the commanding officer. The gulags themselves were seldom called by the official term, 'corrective labor camp.' Tens of thousands or more people died en route to the area or in the series of gold mining, road building, lumbering, and construction camps of Kolyma just as they did in Uzbekistan. Very few inmates—men, women, or children—survived longer than two years. In the death and labor camps of Kolyma USSR records I can provide for you show that more than three million prisoners died between 1935 and 1955—about the time Stalin died. Polish, German, Rumanian, and Finnish war prisoners who worked in the gold fields were the third generation of Soviet slaves. For many, suicide was more common than murder. We have accurate documentation of at least 11,000 people who were shot in Kolyma camps by the state security organ, the NKVD. All causes of death were closer to 500,000, maybe as many as a million persons.

"As you may be aware, there were nearly three million German prisoners of war who were captured by the Soviet Union during the Great Patriotic War, most of them during the great advances of the Red Army in the last year of the war. German soldiers were kept as forced labor for many years after the war. The last German POWs—those who were sentenced for war crimes—were released in 1956. According to Soviet records 381,067 German Wehrmacht POWs died in NKVD camps—356,700 German nationals and 24,367 from other nations. German estimates put the actual death toll of German POW in the USSR at about 1.0 million. They maintain that among those reported as missing in action were men who actually died as POWs.

"After Nazi Germany's defeat by our glorious army under the man of steel, Great Leader Stalin, 'subordinate' camps to the gulag were set up in the Soviet Occupation Zone of postwar Germany. These 'special camps' were former Stalags, prisons, or Nazi concentration camps such as Sachsenhausen—special camp number 7—and Buchenwald—

special camp number 2. According to German government estimates, 65,000 people died in those Soviet-run camps or in transportation to them. According to German researchers, Sachsenhausen—where 12,500 Soviet-era victims have been uncovered—should be seen as an integral part of the gulag system.

"The large majority of prisoners at most times faced meagre food rations, inadequate clothing, overcrowding, poorly insulated housing, poor hygiene, and inadequate health care. Most prisoners were compelled to perform harsh physical labor. Cannibalism was commonplace. While Stalin pleaded with the British to rush more aid and take further action, the NKVD labor camp guards were doubled in number from 500,000 to one million heavily armed men...."

Sobrieski paused to take a breath before summing up: "Such camps can only be described as extermination centers."

It was the first time he had quoted those mind-numbing statistics to men outside the closed ranks of KGB officers of the first rank, and he was prepared to defend his own involvement as being only obeying Lagounov's orders if he were challenged. He preferred to let any detailed personal defensive comments remain unsaid if possible.

"You must realize that these things are not spoken of outside the ranks of men who were actually there, not even to their wives or best friends. Since the closure of the camps, this has been considered to be greatest ... and worst ... secret of our times ... of our Soviet Union, gentlemen of the Moscow Criminal Investigations Department; and they can never see the night of day.

"Our officers and men did their duty, however distasteful, and followed their orders to the letter. Remember, *prikaz yest' prikaz*; *befehl ist befehl* [Russian and German: orders are orders]. Every one of those Germans—those atrocious sadists and war criminals, all of those homosexuals, all of those deviants and retarded persons, all of those criminals who supported Hitler and the German people, all of those Christian clerics who would not bow to the greater law, and all of the lower forms—the Jews—deserved to die. They had to die for the greater good of the great Soviet state and to bring about the final triumph of the dialectical materialism over the bourgeoisie and thereby to enable the new, just, and powerful Soviet world to rise out of the filth and corruption of the capitalistic world. Stalin said it best—as he always did—'Ours is a just cause; victory will be ours!'"

It was a long rant which made Gen. Sobrieski tired over and above the soporific effect of the copious amount of alcohol he had consumed. Stepanovich was afraid he would fall fast asleep before the team could get him down to specifics.

"General, we have been at this for quite a while. Let's get some air and a little exercise. We'll all go out to the playing fields and take a run."

They did six fast laps until all of them were sweating and breathing hard. Gen. Sobrieski seemed to be much better for the exercise. His eyes cleared, and his face took on a renewed look of determination that had been lacking as soon as he started imbibing in the vodka. Back inside the interview room, Trushin ordered all vodka to be removed and substituted with ice water.

"General, we are but a few officers of the law working with limited resources. We are told that Comrade Stalin said, 'The death of one man is a tragedy; the death of millions is a statistic.' We will have to leave alone the statistics and pare down the numbers to find the most likely suspects we possibly can. From you, now, we need to have names of no more that fifty men who wanted Lagounov dead and could have committed the murder this week. Concentrate on that list, if you would, sir."

"Ah, yes, of course. I do get to speechifying when I have too much vodka. My mind is now clear. There were only three officers who hated Lagounov enough to want him dead. The man he replaced was intentionally undermined by Lagounov, humiliated, reduced in rank to a colonel, and sent back to Moscow in disgrace. He lost his commission as an officer altogether after Khrushchev reviewed his record. I personally heard him vow to kill Lt. Gen.Lagounov on more than one occasion. His name is Abram Kirillovich Yerkulayev. He took down his two aides when he fell from power. Their names are Konstintin Leonidovich Zubkov and Matvei Nikitavich Akhremenko—and they likewise hated the late general with passion. I have written down their names and how they can be located."

"The general was fond of corporal punishment and humiliating his officers in front of the men was he not, Comrade General?"

"He was. Many thought he was too quick with the lash. However, there were so many who were given that kind of punishment that the scars on their backs became a sort of badge of courage, a kind of indelible mark of honor. I myself bear such scars, and do so with pride. I most certainly harbor no ill will worthy of killing my superior officer because of my scars."

Trushin unobtrusively wrote down Sobrieski's name in his murder book notes.

"I anticipated your question; so, I have two names for you to consider. I warn you to be careful: these men now occupy offices on the sixth floor of the Lubyanka. Do you still want me to give you the names?"

"Yes."

"The first is Vitali Mikhailovich Bakatinshov, second in command to Ivan Aleksandrovich Serov when he was the chairman from 1954 until 1958; and the other is Vladimir Yefimovich Semichastny who was once second in command to Gen. Lagounov in Siberia. I presume you know who he is at present, Lieutenant?"

"Of course I do, General. There is not a breathing person in all of the Soviet Union who does not know the name and face of the current chairman of the KGB. Look me in the eye, General, tell me that this is not a trap for me and my officers."

"I assure you on my honor as an officer and a gentleman that this is no plot against you and certainly not a joke. I know firsthand that they both hated Lagounov. I presume they have no confidence in you that you can solve the murder. If either of them did it, you will get a great deal of help, most of it misinformation. On the other hand, if they did not do it, they will turn over heaven and earth to find the killer. That someone could kill one of the ranking KGB officers and get away with it, would be anathema to them personally and to the secret police. Can't have any chink in that armor, you understand. I think you will be successful in getting to talk to them, and I am quite sure that you will be safe in doing so as long as you are respectful. Whether you get any helpful information is quite another thing."

CHAPTER THIRTY-NINE

MYC [Moscow Criminal Investigations Department]
**Building, Petrovka 38 Street, Moscow USSR, October 9,
1961, late afternoon**

"Tell me about Lagounov's chekist years and anyone you might suspect from that era, please," Lt. Stepanovich asked, making a strong effort not to show any reaction to having just been told that he might have to interrogate two high-ranking KGB officers who held life and death control over him.

"A time better left in the past. Ordinarily I would order you not to follow this course of questioning; but I am as good as my word. I will tell you what you need to know—and nothing more—to aid in your efforts to hunt down the murderer of the superb officer, General Lagounov.

"Perhaps we should begin with a little history, then I will give you two or three names. The Cheka was created in 1917 as the first state security agency—the military and security arm of the Bolshevik communist party—and it has remained very much the same organization until the present day other than changes in names, personalities, and a few organization changes.

"The first two men I want to suggest to you as possible suspects came into Lagounov's life late in 1918 near the end of the Great War. The commissars were putting pressure on the Red Army and Cheka officers to root out the *Kulaks* [successful farmers who often employed farm workers and owned more property than one family needed]. Oleg Petrovich Latsis was the son of an especially prominent and educated

Kulak family in the Stalingrad area. Lagounov ordered me to name him as a traitor, a deserter, and his family as money-grabbing capitalist farmers who were grinding in the face of the poor. Lagounov made a public example of the sixteen-year-old boy who was–in fact–serving altogether faithfully in the Cheka. He was whipped nearly to death and sent off to the gulags. His family was forcefully removed from their lands and put on a train for Vladivostok, where they remained and somehow survived until a year ago when they showed up in Moscow, a fact known only to me. I admit to having provided them help over the years, and saved their lives. I ask you not to divulge that fact."

"I won't. Did Oleg survive, and did he return?"

"He did. Oleg was a sturdy boy, and he became a hard man—not one to be trifled with. He remained loyal to me, but from time to time when he had too much vodka he would hint at his desire to get revenge against Lagounov. I can get you to him, but I do not want him to see my hand in that."

"You mentioned others from that time, General."

"There are many others like Oleg, and I will give you a list of the few that I know who survived and whose whereabouts are known to me. There is another man who is probably more dangerous than all of those put together. You are aware that the chekists were assigned to destroy religion branch, trunk, and root. We targeted clergy to make examples of them and to strike the fear of God into their followers;so,they would get the message and abandon their superstitious beliefs and practices. Many priests were killed, tortured, and exiled. Most of them finally died in the gulags, where they were singled out for 'special treatment' much like the political opponents of the conservative Marxist-Leninists and the German officer corps POWs. I know of only one of them who lived in torment under Gen. Lagounov, survived it all, and has made it back to the west. He lives in Leningrad and operates an underground church and also a secret organization dedicated to the overthrow of the ruling communist leaders—particularly Chairman Khrushchev— whom he blames for the current persecution of the church and its clergy. So far–to my knowledge__they have not assassinated anyone, but eventually they will."

"I will need that one's name for sure, General. He could be our cul-prit. He certainly would seem to have motive."

"Presbyter Athanasius Mogila named for the *hieromartyr* Athanasius of Brest-Litovsk. He lives on Obukovskoy Oburon Street in Leningrad near the Alexander Nevsky Monastery. My men can take you there."

"Thank you."

"And I can send you the short list of surviving clergy from Siberia. Few of them have enough fire left in them to fight any longer or to be part of an assassination plot. Some of those few are true Christians who would never participate or condone murder, even of one they deemed to be deserving of the death penalty, not even the Antichrist."

"What about more recently—the Great Patriotic War?"

"A few deserters who were persecuted by the KGB … in the persons of Gen. Lagounov and myself. We killed most of them, and not a few of their families. However, there were three escapees who were due to be repatriated and then sent to the gulags but were able to get back to Germany—to Hamburg, to be exact. I have KGB records on them, on their families, and on their associates. They live under assumed names, but they have been indiscreet in expressing their opinions about the USSR, Chairman Khrushchev, the KGB, and specifically about Gen. Lagounov whom they seem to hold responsible for the murderous repatriatiation program ordered by Stalin himself. Lagounov was neither the creator nor the main officer in charge of the program, but you could never convince those three of that."

"Names?"

"Oh, yes. My mind seems to be wandering a little. Their German names are Karl Rudolf Kirschstein, Jakob Josef Potthoff, and Rolf Herman Schwindt. They all live in Hamburg in the Altona-Nord quarter of the Altona Borough. We can find them easily."

"Even with your excellent work to narrow down the field, General, we have a huge list of names to investigate, and who knows if they had anything to do with the murder of Gen. Lagounov. What about the inmates—the seemingly indestructible survivors?"

"Perhaps it may not be so difficult, Lieutenant. I do have a list of men that are—in my mind—the most likely to be involved. They are the last men to be released from one particular gulag in Siberia—the Butugychag Tin Mine—a camp known as the "Valley of Death." It was a place that Gen. Lagounov took a special interest in. He seems to have been especially harsh there because that particular gulag had the senior SS officers who were officially designated for 'special treatment' by the politburo. I will spare you the details, but here is the list of names of some of the most violent survivors.

"*Gruppenführer und Generalleutnant der Waffen-SS* Antoine Duvalier, *Oberführer der Waffen-SS* Michaele Dupont, *Waffen SS-Obersturmbannführer* Serge Alain Rounsavall, *Waffen SS-Sturmbannführer* Hugues Beauchamp, *Waffen SS-Hauptsturmführer* Jérôme Christophe Mailhot, *Waffen SS-Sturmbannführer* Jean Luc Latendresse, and *Waffen SS Obersturmführer* Jacob Friedrich Bunnemann."

"Except for Bunnemann, all of the names sound French," Stepanovich observed.

"Yes, indeed. They are French, from an all-French—Vichy French— SS unit which served Hitler in all sorts of capacities throughout the war and stayed until they were captured after the fall of Berlin. They were part of the 33rd Waffen Grenadier Division of the SS."

"French?! I never heard of such a division. One more mystery of the Great Patriotic War."

CHAPTER FORTY

US Army Alaska Defense Command/Alaska Department, 83rd MP Det CID [Criminal Investigation Division], Office of the Special Agent in Charge, Building 47645, Fort Richardson, Anchorage, Alaska, August 20, 1962

Staff Sergeant Randy Turnblom received a heads-up call from Major Darrin Higgins Chief officer MCU [Regional Major Crimes Unit, Alaska State Police] in Juneau at 1540 hours.

"Staff Sergeant Turnblom, CID. How may I assist?"

"This is Major Higgins, Alaska State MCU. I am calling to report a murder investigation underway in our office. It involves a former army general who was stationed in Alaska during the war. I think I should speak directly to SAC Nicholsen."

"I'll fetch Special Agent Nicholsen. Please hold."

Sgt. Turnblom walked into Nicholsen's office without knocking.

Tucker Nicholsen was sipping a cup of steaming black coffee trying to get his nerves in shape to start another boring day of routine police work which would require only his official presence. His men were great; and he felt superfluous, which made him crotchety. Nicholsen was a fitness fiend, and the only thing that kept him sane besides his morning cup was running ten miles every morning and hunting whenever he could. He had been the SAC at Fort Richardson for six years—five and a half years too long. His wife got cabin fever and did not last the full first winter;so, she flew back down below to Arkansas to stay with her parents. He only sees her three times a year, and the anticipation of those poignant reunions was about all that he looked forward to throughout the years.

He was an overly fit forty-two-year-old cop at heart and army military policeman by training and experience, and almost by rote. He wore an old-style white wall super-square flattop haircut that suited his square-jawed face and was proud that his hair was still thick and black. SAC Nicholsen was the base boxing champion and had an unrepairable crooked nose from three too many broken noses. He was dressed in civilian clothes—a blue denim shirt, Levis, and hiking boots.

"What?" he asked irritably. "This better be important."

"I have Major Higgins from Alaska State Troopers holding on the line, sir," Sgt. Turnblom said.

He was used to the SAC's evil moods in the morning and knew that it was nothing personal.

"Okay," Nicholsen said grumpily, "put him through."

"What can I do for you this fine afternoon, Darrin;or is this is just a social call?"

"Hardly, I have a murder on my hands;and it could become a problem for you, Tucker."

"How so?"

"A big-time general. You probably remember him. Glen Gabler—full four stars."

"Murdered!? Today?"

"No, coupla days ago. We are just getting our investigation underway."

This was the chance Nicholsen had been waiting for the past six years. He was not about to pass it up, hunting buddy or not.

"Whoa!" he said. "This sounds every bit like an Army case. The brass will be all over me if I don't handle this case."

"Whoa yourself, Tucker. We caught the case in our jurisdiction. The man is retired; so, officially he is a civilian; and we have already started checking out potential leads."

"Still our case, Darrin. Sorry to go federal on you, but it's either me or the fibbies that will take it over. Take your pick."

Like every local cop who had an ounce of pride left, he hated the FBI for its arrogance, glory-hogging, and disdain for local law enforcement. He knew Tucker was right. The choice was obvious, but he was not about to fold that easily.

"Look, Tucker, you may be right. I'll never get a sliver of information back from the Fat Boys. How 'bout you and me work it together? We share the credit and both of our careers get a little jump. Whatta you say?"

"Let me think on it."

"Time's a wastin'.' We need to pool resources and get on this. We can't afford to blow this one, you know that. If it looks like we dragged our feet or allowed precious time to get by us because of a squabble, it could hit the fan for both of us."

"Who'll be in charge?"

"Nominally you, but in the trenches our guys and your guys will pool resources and work on it as equal partners. And, Tucker, this is a trust kind of a deal."

"I'm thinking about agreeing with you, Darrin; but I'm also thinking about a bear hunt on Kodiak where sometimes it's a bit tough to get a license."

"You are corrupt, SAC; and you drive a hard bargain. And I'm not promisin' anything, but some of the troopers have a hunt comin' up in October. I don't see why I couldn't do a little persuadin' and open up another coupla slots. If I have a reminder 'long about the first week in September, and if I feel good about things...."

"Who's corrupt? It's a deal. I'll bring along Sgt. Turnblom. His first name's Randy. So, how about we get to work? Tell me what you've got."

Major Higgins became all business.

"General Glen Gabler, USA, retired, came up here to fish with his family—three sons—and his former aide-de-camp on the seventh. They settled in at the Alaskan Bear Lodge then went fishing the next day and a half. Had good luck. Everything seemed copacetic—nothing out of the ordinary or suspicious—until the night of the eighth. Three or three-thirty to be as precise as possible. That morning—still the eighth—his dead body was found hanging from the rafters by a couple of the local girls who work at the lodge. The aide-de-camp took charge of securing the scene and got the owner's sons to round up everybody who was in the lodge that night to be sure nobody took off. The owner—a local character named Neille Bastrup—called our dispatch in Juneau, but every trooper in the office was out on a big bank robbery. Bastrup is a resourceful guy and not one to be put off;so, he put in a call to the RCMP station across the water in Atlin, BC. The troopers and the

Mounties have a real good working relationship, and the Mountie in charge at the time—a guy named Daniel Olsen—responded.

"Constable Olsen flew over in a floatplane and took charge of the preliminaries of the investigation and did a good job so far as I can tell. He put on gloves, checked to see if anything had been taken, dusted for prints, and examined the body which he described as about halfway into rigor—about as much as he could do under the circumstances. He told a couple of Bastrup's boys to cut the body down and leave the rope in place. He said that it was too warm in the lodge to keep the body without decomp getting the best of it. So, the boys carried him out to the game cooler. The rest of the people went out and searched all around the lodge but didn't find anyone or anything suspicious with one big exception: the lodge's floatplane was missing, obviously stolen by the perp or perps and used for a getaway.

"The locals and the troopers did a wide area manhunt including the only really inhabited island up there. It's called Chicagatov Island. There's nothing there but a Tlingit town—more like a hamlet—and a salmon processing plant called the Hoonah Packing Company facility. The dockworkers in Hoonah remembered two unfriendly newcomers to the docks and a few people thought they might have been speaking Russian. That's not confirmed. The two headmen of the island did find some definite evidence about the killer or killers. They described a rude campsite near the entrance to Glacier Bay, at Bartlett Cove. There were remnants of salmon bones, tails, and heads, huckleberries, salmon-berries, and thimbleberries along with some trash. Some of that trash included fairly recent copies of the *Petropavalovsk-Kamchatsky Journal*—Russian. Two boys out fishing found an abandoned boat—belonged to the Tlingits from Hoonah—on the Point Adolphus feeding area for humpback whales. Some trash they found around the boat had brochures from the Alaskan Bear Lodge and the plane's document packet."

"What about the plane, Major?"

"It's a recently renovated vintage de Havilland DH.98 Mosquito bomber floatplane. The tail number is number N7952Z. Nobody's seen hide nor hair of it."

SAC Nicholsen made a note.

"If that's all the crime scene and timeline information, please give me some details. First, some names."

"Are you ready to write?"

"Ready."

"Okay, here goes. Stop me if I go too fast. There's Neille Bastrup and his sons—Kevin, Able, Michael, and Donovan. They run the Alaskan Bear Lodge on Excursion Inlet. There are two native girls working there by the name of Asaaluk. She's a local Tlingit girl. The other one is Nasnana, an Athabaskan girl from the Yukon. Gen. Gabler's sons are Glen Jr., Trace, and Jackson. The general's former aide-de-camp's name is Major Richard 'Rick' Saunders. He's retired Army and now has several businesses in Texas. The two Hoonah headmen are Henry and Anotklosh Peratrovich. The Mountie is Constable Daniel Olsen."

"I presume you took notes."

"I did. I'll send 'em down to you in the next post."

"Oh, you mentioned Kamchatka. Were you able to make contact with any of the nice Russkies, maybe a *ment* or two?"

"Nice ones, no. But I did get through to the Petropavlovsk-Kamchatsky Metropolitan Police Department and spoke to an English speaker. That was a complete bust. The guy thought it was a CIA plot and wouldn't talk to me about any plane unless or until they locate one and give it a thorough going over to be certain it's not a spy plane. Can't be too careful."

"These are cold and careful times, Darrin."

"Aren't they ever?"

The Kamchatka Peninsula, Commander Islands, and Karaginsky Island constitute the Kamchatka Krai of the Russian Federation. The Kamchatka Peninsula is a 780-mile long outcropping of the mainland of Siberia in the Russian Far East. It lies between the Pacific Ocean to the east and the Sea of Okhotsk to the west. The 270-year-old Cossack settlement of Petropavlovsk-Kamchatsky metropolitan area is one of the oldest Russian cities in the Far East. More than half of the population of the peninsula live in that one city, including almost all of the eight thousand indigenous Koryaks. Across Avacha Bay from the city is the Rybachiy Nuclear Submarine Base—Russia's largest—established during the Soviet regime. The entirety of Kamchatka was a Soviet military zone closed to all foreigners and any Russians who did not actually live there, which accounted for the expected paranoid interaction between Maj. Higgins and his Soviet counterpart.

"Got any ideas about where to go from here?"

"I do, actually. First, I think it will be futile to requestion anybody local. I don't think they have any useful information. There's no evidence, and my gut tells me that they didn't have anything to do with this murder. I think we have to dig deeper into Gen. Gabler's past, especially the military part. He's bound to have made some enemies along the line, and that Saunders guy was with him almost every step of the way. We didn't have enough time with him."

"Where is he now?"

"Dallas, I think."

"Maybe the two of us should take a little trip down below and call on the major in Dallas."

"Dutch treat," I presume.

"It'll have to be. The feds and the army won't be willing to fund a junket until we have something substantial to go on."

"Alaska won't be all that willing to part with money either; so, I think we have our work cut out for us from the get-go."

CHAPTER FORTY-ONE

Fort Sam Houston, Camp Bullis Army Base Military Police Office, Bexar County, Texas, Northwest of San Antonio, August 20, 1962

As soon as he said good-bye to Major Higgins at the Alaska State Trooper MCU, SAC Tucker Nicholsen had his staff sergeant find a number for retired major Rick Saunders in Dallas. He was not satisfied that the state troopers had mined Saunders for all of the pertinent information he had, whether he was purposely withholding anything or not.

"Hello," a man answered brusquely.

"Is this Richard Saunders? I am Staff Sergeant Randy Turnblom calling from the 83rd Military Police CID."

"What's this about?"

"I am calling for Special Agent in Charge Tucker Nicholsen. He would like to speak to you, sir."

"Alaska, you say?"

"Yes, sir."

"I already answered every imaginable question put to me by the state troopers regarding the death of Gen. Gabler. I am very busy at the present time and will not be able to talk to anyone else on the matter. Try me again in a couple of weeks."

SS Turnblom gave SAC Nicholsen a negative look and shook his head.

Tucker took the phone from Randy.

"This is the special agent in charge, Criminal Investigation Division, US Army Alaska Defense Command, Major. I have important police business to discuss with you, and I need to do it now."

"I'm retired and am not subject to your authority. Good day, Mr. Nichols."

He started to hang up, but Tucker caught him before he could.

"It's SAC Nicholsen, and yes you are subject to my law enforcement authority even though you are retired. Check the Army regs, Major. We can do this the easy way and have a chat on the phone now, or we can do it the hard way."

"You can't threaten me, whatever your name is. The only way for you to get me under your thumb is if I was on active duty. I'm not," Saunders said and hung up.

"Hmmh," Tucker said.

He was mad, and Randy could tell. The SAC never raised his voice, swore at people, or made threats. You could tell he was mad because he became very quiet, very calm, and had a look in his eyes that could laser-cut marble.

"We'll see about that," he said after a few moments to get back into full control and to decide if he needed to do what he was thinking.

He did.

"Randy, I need the Provost Marshal General in DC. Not his aide, the general himself."

As the Army expanded following World War II; so, too did the crime rate. Criminal investigations failed to keep abreast of the expanding crime rate. Commanders did not have the personnel or the funds to conduct adequate investigations. In December 1943, the Provost Marshal General was charged with providing staff supervision over all criminal investigations. The Criminal Investigation Division of the Provost Marshal General's Office was established in January 1944. The Provost Marshal General rendered staff supervision over criminal investigation activities, coordinated investigations between commands, dictated plans and policies, and set standards for investigators. Originally in the interest of efficiency, the Army CID was centralized at the theater Army level. Practicality determined that control of criminal investigation personnel be decentralized to area commands during the 1950s and then down to the installation level during the early 1960s. In the case of Alaska, it was in the headquarters of the Alaska command. While the Provost Marshal General still had overall supervision of criminal investigation activities, the operations were conducted at the local level. The Provost Marshal General still had overall supervision of criminal investigation activities, but the operations were conducted at the local level.

There were exceptions to be made when a serious investigation crossed jurisdictional lines, and this was one of those times. The motto of the Army CID, and one which Tucker believed in completely was: "Do what has to be done." The importance of the Provost Marshal General who Tucker insisted on speaking to was underscored by the fact that the general answered only to the Chief of Staff of the Army and the Secretary of the Army, and he could get done what had to be done.

Randy raised an eyebrow, but it was obviously not a time to have a discussion. He had the office of the general on the line in two minutes;and after a short description of the local problem, Lt. Gen. Drake Foster came on the line.

"Give me the short version," Gen. Foster said.

"We have a murder up here, sir. We have good reason to believe that it was not a local matter; and it is possible that a retired army major knows more than he is willing to tell; or maybe he is even involved somehow."

"Is the victim anybody I should know about, SAC Nicholsen?"

"Yes, sir. General Glen Gabler, USA retired."

"I heard about it."

"Who's the reluctant SOB?"

"Name's Richard or Rick Saunders, Major USA, ret. He was a longtime aide to the general. He refuses to answer any questions over the phone and says that I have no jurisdiction over him because he is retired."

"Wishful thinking on his part. I guess you know that, SAC Nicholsen. Mind if I call you Tucker?"

"I'd prefer it, sir. And yes, I know he's off base. More importantly, I think he's hiding something, and it is probably important."

"Well, Tucker, we could fight it through the JAG office, but that would take months. Our work in the CID can't muddle around while the bureaucrats worry their pointy heads about niceties. If the man were to be ordered back to active duty, all of that would become moot. Right?"

"As rain. And, sir, I truly believe we can't let any more time be wasted while he takes measures to hide his involvement or prepares a scenario to protect someone who did kill Gen. Gabler."

"I answer only to the Army Chief of Staff and the secretary of the Navy. I am owed some favors, and it just so happens that I have a golf date with the two of them in an hour. This is a timely call, and

I am itching to get the CID back into the game in a righteous way. I'll give you a ring about fourteen-thirty your time. That should be enough time to get the brass who can make it happen, want to make it happen. I am guessing that should be around eighteen-thirty or maybe nineteen-hundred DC time."

The call came at fourteen-hundred, ideal for Tucker. It meant that the wheels of the DOD could whir at maximum speed, and Major Saunders would be receiving a visitor that very evening.

Rick and Patricia Saunders were sitting watching the tube holding long neck bottles of East Side beer. It was Sunday night; Elvis the Pelvis was on the *Ed Sullivan Show*; and Rick laughed uproariously as the clown belted out Jail House Rock. Patty was offended. If she had her way, she would be down there with the thirteen-year-olds when Elvis left the theater the back way and ran into the horde of screaming and fainting girls.

They were both annoyed when a firm knock came on the door.

"Who could that be at this hour, Rick?" Patty asked.

He grumbled but got up to see.

Standing at the door was a stiffly proper lieutenant jg. He stood at attention and saluted—a salute as crisp and well-checked-out as his uniform. His face was flat and expressionless.

He said, "Major Richard Avery Saunders?"

"Retired, son. A long time ago."

"I have the duty to inform you that you have been called back to active duty. I have a set of orders from BuPers. You are to accompany me and Sergeant McCord here tonight. We will see you to your destination."

"What???!" Saunders asked incredulously;—this could not be happening.

He took a quick look at the orders; and, to his dismay, they appeared to be perfectly genuine.

"Lieutenant, who are you? What is this about? Look at me. It's been almost ten years since I wore the uniform. I can't even fit into it."

He knew he was dithering, but it was about all he was able to stammer out. He finally got enough control of himself to stop spouting nonsense.

"Listen, Son. I am completely in the dark. Did world war three start and I wasn't watching the news?"

"Not that I know of, sir. I do not know why you have been called up. But, like me, we will both just follow orders. My name is Martin Grant Fowler, lieutenant jg, USA/AD."

"It'll take me a few to get my things together. Wait here."

"No, sir. My orders are to escort you forthwith. Everything you need will be provided at your destination. You are permitted to inform your wife that you have been recalled to duty, and you are required to leave without delay."

"Where are we going? At least tell me that."

"Sorry, sir. I have not been informed. I assume that we will both know when we get there. I have sealed orders in our unit out front."

The unit was a jeep.

Rick was about to launch into a tirade but thought better of it when he looked into the unfeeling face of the sergeant major accompanying the lieutenant. This was a nightmare. Was he asleep, drunk, or hallucinating?

Major Saunders, Lieutenant Fowler, and Sergeant Major Harvey Birtsnell drove to Love Field military hangars and boarded an old OV-1A Mohawk fixed-wing CAS [Close Air Support] for the short flight to Fort Sam Houston. One and a half hours later they touched down in Bexar County just outside San Antonio on a small landing strip on the northeast corner of Fort Sam Houston. They were met by a troop bus and driven to Camp Bullis Army Base, a 28,000-acre former training camp, then POW camp, which presently served as a testing ground for tires fuels, tanks, and medical training—an unlikely combination. It took Major Saunders a few minutes to adjust to what he was seeing. During the post-World War II period, Camp Bullis Army Base was outfitted to accommodate two hundred prisoners; but it became a tent city for many more. Rick then realized that he had been stationed here for a few months in the mid-fifties aiding Gen. Gabler in the transfer of German POWs who were being unwillingly sent back to French-occupied Germany to be interned in an Allied slave labor camp at the request of the French authorities. The orders had come from SCHAEF, Gen. Eisenhower, and with the blessing of President Truman.

The bus driver drove the three men to one of the older buildings on the camp property, a blocky cinder brick construction edifice devoid of any esthetic features which might offset its somber appearance. There was a sign over the lintel of the main entrance: MILITARY POLICE, CAMP BULLIS.

They were led to a section of the building where a group of Spartan rooms sat adjacent to a series of four holding cages. The rooms had a cot, a toilet, a washbasin, and a set of wall pegs for hanging clothing. There were no decorations of any kind. Small windows looked out into a packed sand exercise yard surrounded by a high concertina wire fence. The yard was illuminated by unforgiving klieg lights which resulted in the impression that it was a patch of the earth bathed in eternal scorching desert sunshine. At each corner of the yard were manned guard towers. It was a most forbidding place.

Saunders was led into his assigned room, handed a set of scrub suit pants and shirt, and skivvies, all marked "Brooke Army Medical Center," a kit containing a toothbrush, toothpaste, hairbrush, comb, two rolls of recycled brown toilet paper, a bar of rough lye soap, a hospital issue washcloth, and a towel. He was allowed to keep his shoes, but the laces were removed. The bus driver took all of the clothing Saunders was wearing when he arrived and had the major sign a detailed sheet listing the articles. When that bit of bureaucratic housekeeping was completed, the driver walked out of the door and locked it from the outside. As keyed up as he was, Saunders was able to sleep off and on for a couple of hours before it was lights on. He never saw his escorts from Dallas again.

Army CID SAC Nicholsen and Alaska state trooper Major Higgins arrived at the Fort Sam Houston airstrip by a Bell UH-1 Iroquois [unofficially *Huey*] helicopter from Dallas Love Field about the time that Major Saunders was settling in for a lonely, disconcerting, and hungry night in a box of a room about the size of three bathtubs wide. It was starting to rain as the two lawmen were escorted to the base BOQ for the night. They were in time to get a good prime rib and baked potato dinner.

Major Higgins asked, "Hey, Tucker, do you want to get the interrogation started tonight?"

"Nope. I'd like him to sweat a little and feel the pinch of hunger first—throw him off his game."

"And, besides, we can have another coffee, a piece of pie, and a cognac," laughed Darrin.

CHAPTER FORTY-TWO

Fort Sam Houston, Camp Bullis Army Base Military Police Office, Bexar County, Texas, Northwest of San Antonio, August 24, 1962, midmorning

Breakfast was good: bacon, over easy eggs, wheat toast, corned beef hash, milk, and a jelly Danish. Both law officers enjoyed Uncle Sam's largesse, and felt fortified for the day of interrogation lying ahead of them. Rick Saunders—on the other hand—did not particularly enjoy his watery scrambled eggs–with no salt, pepper, or Tabasco sauce–fried corn meal mush, graveyard stew, and the quintessential favorite of US military people since the Revolutionary War which can only be served on a shingle. His already foul mood worsened when two burly Bexar County Sheriffs Office Jail guards rousted him from his cell with the creamed chipped beef only half-eaten and escorted him rudely to a small conference room on the south end of the police building. He was handcuffed to a heavy steel ring welded to the tabletop and to another on the floor.

It was 0900. Tucker entered the well-secured conference room accompanied by four jail guards who stationed themselves in the four corners of the room. Their stances and facial expressions conveyed a silent but completely apparent attitude of vigil, indefatiguability, and intense purpose. None of them blinked if he received a side glance from Saunders. It was unnerving.

SAC Nicholsen entered the room as the first of the two law officers who would tag-team the questioning that day.

"Hello, Major Saunders. I am the senior agent in charge of the Alaska CID. We spoke on the phone yesterday morning."

"What is the meaning of this? Have I committed some sort of crime? Why handcuffs? I guess you made your point about being able to question me whether I agreed or not."

"I ask, you answer. That's how this works. As for the situation, you will remember that I offered you the option of a courteous phone call which you refused. Rudely, I might add. You are here and will tell me everything I need to know because what I need to know is important. We Army people do not take kindly to our generals being murdered, and it is my mission to find out why and by whom."

Appropriately whipped and chastened, Rick waited morosely for the first question.

"Did you kill Gen. Gabler?"

It was a shock and was meant to be.

"I most certainly did not."

"Who did?"

"I have no idea."

"How do you profit from the general's death?"

"I don't … well, I think there is some small amount set aside by his will for me."

"How small?"

"I don't know the details. He was a stingy and ungracious old curmudgeon; so, it is altogether possible that he left me nothing for twenty-five years of service to him."

He saw the look on the SAC's face and instantly regretted having opened himself up to questions about his personal relationship with Gen. Gabler.

"Hmmh," Tucker hummed, "it would seem that there was something short of brotherly love between the two of you, Rick. All right if I call you Rick?"

"No. You got me back on active duty. You can refer to me as Major Saunders or sir, whichever suits you."

Once again he regretted his rude pomposity. He knew he should be cultivating whatever goodwill he could with this hard-nosed cop. He resolved to school his tongue in the future.

"Of course, sir. You and the general had a long and varied career together. I want you to tell me in detail about how he treated you, how he treated other people; and I especially want to know specifics about his aptitude for disciplinary action and his methods. I want to know about whose feathers he ruffled in the Army, who he disliked, and who disliked him. Then, I want you to give me a very detailed account of your postwar service in Europe. As you might have surmised, I already know quite a bit; so, lying by commission or omission will be futile. Do you want me to repeat my outline of the interrogation?"

"No, I have it. He was Lt. Col. Gabler when we first met as World War Two was beginning to look like the US would be involved. He was in charge of training boots for the Seventh Infantry Division at Fort Ord in California, and I was his exec. I was a lieutenant jg back then. We were a good team, I guess. It was obvious that he was on the joint chiefs' short list for promotion; and his star would rise; and I would not get anywhere on my own; so, I stuck with him. We shipped out for North Africa to fight the Nazis with the first units to land there. Our first battles—Operation Torch—were with the Vichy French army assigned by Hitler to prevent an Allied amphibious landing at Casablanca or the establishment of a beachhead. From there, we led men into almost every major campaign in the European theater. Both of us were wounded, and both of us were decorated during the rapid advance towards Germany after D Day. We were caught in what came to be called the Void, because the tanks and other armor so far outdistanced the infantry. After the liberation of Germany, we ended up in Alaska—on Chichagof Island—for a few months where a rudimentary POW camp was set up to hold the Germans captured in the battles on the Aleutians.

"Gabler made a name for himself as a POW camp commander; so, we were sent to Texas—right here at Fort Sam Houston to oversee the POWs who were being prepared for shipment to France. The Frenchies wanted forced laborers and were strongly of the opinion that they should get such unwilling workers as reparations from the jerries. They also felt that the jerries deserved every punishment that could be meted out to them. Ike and his SHAEF commanders and the brass all the way to the top agreed to send something like a million of our Germans back. In fact, we sent something like 750 to 760,000 of them back. Gen. Gabler with me as his assistant were in charge of that transfer which was a monumental task.

"Our last assignment before we both retired was to be the commanders at a huge POW complex called the Rheinwiesenlager camps. Our main posting was the final destination of the transcontinental journey for the repatriated Germans, especially those from America. It was the Moschendorf Transit and Release Camp, a miserable and inadequate holding pen for thousands of German POWs and translocated German civilians destined for Allied forced labor camps in the West. I hate to admit that, but I am sure you already know about it."

Tucker nodded.

"When the *Kriegsverurteiltes* [repatriated war returnees] moved on, Gen. Gabler and I moved with them because of our accumulated expertise. Our next assignment was to an even worse place—called Bad Kreuznach—the Lager Galgenberg und Bretzenheim PWTE—Bad Kreuznach District, Rhineland-Palatinate, Germany."

"What does PWTE stand for?" interrupted Tucker.

"Officially Prisoner of War Temporary Enclosures."

"Go on."

"We stayed there until the end. That's where we mustered out."

"What happened to the POWs?"

"Shipped on to be slaves in France; most of them to a particular cesspool called POW Camp 63 Brienne le Chateâu, France."

"Were you or the general ever there?"

"No."

"So, you don't know what became of the men you guarded at Bad Kreuznach?"

"No. And to be clear about it, I don't care. Those monsters got what they deserved. Not many of them made it all the way through. Good riddance, I say."

"You have done a good job giving the short version of your careers, Major. Now it's time to answer the rest of my questions—the who, the why, and the generation of personal enemies. We'll take a short break. You've earned a little exercise. Get out to the yard for an hour, then we'll meet back here for some lunch."

It was no kindness and no privilege to be ordered to the exercise yard that day. San Antonio was having one of its infrequent weird storms—furious winds, torrential lashing rain, and frightening drum rolls of thunder and a sky rent with bursts of lightning coming in electrical sheets. Major Saunders took the moments of misery to think about his own responsibility for what happened in the Allied POW camps. There was a nagging repetition of Coleridge's poem, "The Rime of the Ancient Mariner," which had the line, "He hath penance done, and penance more will do."

Grill Sergeants Brig Food Recipes

Shit on a Shingle—Serves 12

Ingredients
-6 tbsps sweet cream salted butter sticks (total 4–16 oz), 6 tbsps all-purpose flour, 3¾ cps warm milk, 3 (8 oz) jars dried chipped beef, 3 pinches cayenne pepper.

Preparation
-In a medium saucepan over low heat, melt butter. Whisk in flour all at once to form a roux. Whisk in milk a little at a time, increase heat to medium-high, and cook, stirring until thickened. Bring to a boil, stir in beef and cayenne, heat through, and serve hot over toast (shingle).

Fried Corn Meal Mush—Serves 16

Ingredients
-2½ cps cornmeal, 5 cps water, 1 tsp salt

Preparation
-Mix together cornmeal, water, and salt in a medium saucepan. Cook over med. heat, stirring frequently until mixture thickens–5–7 mins.
-For frying, pour mixture into a loaf pan and chill completely. Remove from pan, cut into slices, and fry in a small amount of lard over medium-high heat until browned on both sides. Serve with sauce of your choice if available. Butter, salt, and pepper can substitute. Best if eaten quickly.

Graveyard Stew—Serves 12

Ingredients
-12 slices Wonder Bread, 3 cps whole milk, 12 patties of butter, lard, or margarine

Preparation
-Butter bread, heat milk to just below boiling. Soak bread in hot milk, then eat.

CHAPTER FORTY-THREE

Fort Sam Houston, Camp Bullis Army Base Military Police Office, Bexar County, Texas, Northwest of San Antonio, August 24, 1962, afternoon

Rick came into the conference room soaking wet and shivering. He was angry and had had enough of being treated like a criminal. He had made up his mind not to answer any more questions, and the over-zealous MP could just lump it. He knew he could not be kept there incognito forever. There were laws.

He grabbed a napkin from the lunch table and wiped his face.

Before he looked around the room at anyone, he made his emphatic declaration, "I want a lawyer. You have kidnapped me. I am not a material witness, and I am most certainly and absolutely not a criminal. I know my rights under the UCMJ. Get a JAG officer here before you ask even one more question."

Rick had not noticed that there were now two men sitting at the conference table finishing their sandwiches, French fries, and beer. It was not until the man spoke that he realized that he was facing the same Alaska trooper—the main Alaska investigator—who had questioned him in Anchorage the day after Gen. Gabler was killed.

"Sit down and be quiet. You don't have to say another word if you don't want to. But you do have to hear what I have to say. It is in your best interests," said Major Darrin Higgins, chief officer of the MCU, Alaska State Police, in Juneau.

Rick did not feel well. The presence of the state law enforcement officer caused a sudden loss of his prepared bravado. He slumped into a chair. He was no longer hungry.

"I have news for you," Major Higgins said in his quiet and unhurried fashion, which had lulled many a criminal into a false sense that they were dealing with a simple and backward country bumpkin Sheriff Taylor from Mayberry, North Carolina–a television character. "This file is a very thorough record of your financial holdings and transactions for the past ten years. We started working on the discovery investigation in Gen. Gabler's case the day we learned about it. You and his sons have been subjects of interest since that day. I won't bore you with the complete set of documents, but let's you and me take a gander at the underlined items together."

Rick wanted to scream. How in the world had this happened? It was only a few days ago that everything was rosy. He was getting ready for a fishing trip of a lifetime. Then, as if the general's murder was not enough, he was about to see his very private and very personal economic history be made public—or at least police—property.

"What happened to my rights as an American citizen? You have no right to have my private information. I insist on having a lawyer … I insist on being released from this jail immediately."

He was desperate to avoid having the police be able to use his financial history against him.

Major Higgins looked at Rick calmly and for a full two minutes before speaking.

"Just shut up. There aren't going to be any lawyers for a while. You're under the rules of the UCMJ, and we have a very valid subpoena to search everything you have or ever had. Once we go through all this boring number stuff, I am going to make you a one-time offer. I have every expectation that you will be anxious to cooperate at that time."

Tucker Nicholsen sat and observed as Major Higgins undid Major Saunders. It was masterful. An experienced team of forensic accountants had scrutinized every line item in Saunders's portfolio and transaction sheets. There was a small briar patch of little glued-on markers sticking out from the pages of the records.

Occasionally, Major Higgins would ask, "What is this about?"

Rick answered like a man on powerful drugs, knowing that life as he had known it was over; and there was nothing to gain by stalling or lying.

Beginning a year ago, there were twelve equal credits to the Saunders account for a total of one and a half million dollars. Rick paled and had a couple of moments of humming and hawing each time one of those numbers was identified.

For the first five months worth of credits into the accounts, Major Higgins asked the same question, "Where did this money come from? Where did it go? And, what was the intended purpose of the money?"

Rick was balky when challenged the first two times, but after that gave up and spilled the truth like it was coming from a fire hose.

"All right, all right ... it's a payment for consulting work ... for services rendered."

"What consulting? What services? Do you think I just fell of the turnip truck, Rick? I have something to give, and you're not going to get it unless you give me the truth."

"I want immunity if I give you the full information. No immunity means no info."

"Get real. There's not going to be any immunity. The question is going to be whether or not you get the chair or life in prison. You understand?"

It was over.

Rick dropped the bombshell he had been keeping secret for so long.

"I was promised a million and a half dollars over one year and another two million the next year to keep a certain organization apprised of Gen. Gabler's whereabouts, especially when he planned a relatively long stay in one place. That's all I had to do. We needed that money. Our debts had piled up, and we did not have any way out from under that load. I didn't see the harm. Besides, the old tightwad treated me like a second-class citizen servant ... after everything I did for him."

"We can argue the morals and the legalities later. No more coy evasions. Give us names and where we can find those people."

Rick sighed. "European International Conglomerate. At least I think that's the main company. I went through something like six different holding companies, LLCs, trusts, and corporations until I came to the end of the line at this EIC Corporation. Never could get a good handle on the principals of the company, though. I checked carefully because it seemed too good to be true. I worried about what I was getting myself into. The guy on the phone had a mixed European accent; so, I wasn't inclined to trust him right off the bat. I had my doubts about getting the money and about the guy's promise that he meant the general no harm. I insisted on that, and he seemed honest enough. The money came in like clockwork every month as promised."

"Is that all you agreed to do, Rick? Your life depends on your answer, and I'm not being melodramatic."

"That's all I agreed to...."

"I sense a 'but' somewhere in there."

"Yeah, well, it was like any military mission or group activity I was ever part of; there are always Murphy's Law kinds of things—the standard SNAFU."

"So, tell me, Rick, what got SNAFUed?"

"Nobody but the boss and me were supposed to be in the lodge that night. But, apparently, the lodge owner—Bastrup—had some difficulty with some incoming guests: they were coming in earlier than planned. We needed to postpone our dinner out in town until the next evening. That kept everybody together in the lodge. I met the two guys in the forest behind the lodge; they wanted to meet with the general as planned and told them the meeting was off. There were too many people in the place. It would be impossible for the meeting to be secret. 'Maybe some other time,' I told them. They were not nice men ... I mean, definitely not nice men."

"How so? And Rick, you seem to be of reasonably average intelligence. It seems disingenuous that you hadn't had an inkling that they meant Gen. Gabler harm before that meeting."

"I swear I didn't think about it. Probably naïve of me, in retrospect."

"To say the least, but keep going."

"Well ... where was I? Oh, yeah—then they made a demand of me, something I had never and would never have agreed to. I had to help them get the general alone and then had to do some heavy lifting with them. I balked and tried to beg off, but no soap. The older guy said, 'You got our money. You finish the mission.' He made a throat-slitting motion with his right finger across his throat. I got the message, all right. I thought I was going to be a goner just like the general that night. And, yes, I wasn't naïve anymore."

"So, you helped in the murder that night?"

"Actually, not in the murder. I mean I helped; but the two guys hid in his room until we came back to his room after a big dinner. He had a lot to drink and was very drowsy; so, I told him he needed to get some rest because we had a big day of fishing the next day. They let him get sound asleep. They were very patient. It wasn't until something like two or three in the morning when the younger one slipped into bed with the general, put his arm around his neck, and made a two-hand quick snap of his relaxed neck. Gen. Gabler never felt a thing.

"All I had to do was to help hoist him up far enough off the floor to make it look like a suicide. It's not like I actually killed him. How could I know what those guys had in their minds?"

"Ever hear of felony murder, Rick?"

"I think so, but I never paid much attention to the term. I just always figured that all murder is a felony."

"No, Rick, it's a technical legal term; and you need to get serious about it. In most states the felony murder rule is that when a person is killed during the commission or attempted commission of a felony—such things as burglary, arson, rape, robbery, kidnapping, and—of course—murder itself, even if by accident, all participants in the crime may be charged with first degree murder. That would include the driver of the get-away car or the individual who lures the victim or if the get-away car runs over a pedestrian while fleeing. In short, Rick, that's you."

"Even if I had no intent to kill him or if I was more or less forced?"

"That would be very hard to prove. Your presence and help during the commission of the murder would be considered primae faciae evidence of your involvement. In short, even if you had been there for a kidnapping or to steal from Gen. Gabler and he fell down the stairs trying to avoid you, that would be felony murder."

"Then I've had it is about what you're saying."

"Rick, felony murder—like a lot of things in the law—is complicated. I have considerable wiggle room in what goes down here. Maybe you help us, and we help you."

"What can I possibly do? I'll do anything … anything. My life just can't end this way."

"I have a plan that could involve you and might just help us get the real killers. First off, it involves learning anything and everything there is to know about the men who killed Gen. Gabler. We'll want you to give us a very careful description and have one of our police artists work with you to get a useful sketch we can put out on an APB. We'll be getting hold of INTERPOL and run this manhunt worldwide."

"I just thought of something. I don't know if these guys were just hired assassins or if they were the ones who masterminded the whole crime. Whichever, they seemed to be smart and to have planned the crime down to the last detail. I'll be glad to help with a sketch. I'm pretty good with faces and memory—part of my training and military experience. And, and I just thought of something," he stammered: "the two men had a hard look—no smiles, no jokes, all business. They had accents I couldn't quite trace—seemed like a kind of combination of French and German, but something else ... I think Russian or some other Slavic kind of accent in there. And, you know—somewhere way in the back of my mind—I have a kind of fleeting thought—maybe a memory—that I might have met or seen them before. I'll rack my brain.

"Throw me a crumb. If I help, what will you do for me?"

"Before I get to that, I want to tell you about our plan. It might involve some risk for you. You have to have had some way to communicate with the killers. Find a way to do it. Then you can let them know that you really like the easy money, and maybe there's somebody else you can finger for them. Find out what kind of person or what particular person they're after. I want some names. You are the only lead we have to get to that point. Make it happen for us and we can finagle for you."

"What can you do? This felony murder thing sounds like an open and shut case with no bargaining."

"No. That's not quite true. There are a couple of ways SAC Nicholsen and I can go. You are here in Texas, and we could run the murder through the Texas courts. They have the standard felony murder policy and you would get fried. Or we could stick with Alaska. Alaska is a funny place; its felony laws do not make felony crimes with a death into first degree murder like most places—like Texas—do. Alaska Statutes § 11.41.100(a) has a set of rules where Alaska delegates some felony murders to second degree murder. That is up to the law enforcement people, the prosecutors, and the judges. It's complicated. Or, the best way you could get prosecuted is under the UCMJ. The Manual for Courts-Martial only allows for the death penalty if the accused was the actual killer."

SAC Nicholsen interrupted briefly, "In case you've forgotten, that's Part II, MCM 1984, RCM 1004(c) (8)—Voluntary Manslaughter [Article 119(1), UCMJ]." No death penalty, maybe a possibility of parole."

"Like I said, I'll do anything."

SAC Nicholsen said, "That's a good attitude, and we will likely test you to the limits. For your information, the army CID motto is: 'Do what has to be done.' That is exactly what we intend to do. You up to it?"

"Absolutely. You scratch my back and I'll scratch yours in a fair deal, okay?"

"All right, here's the plan...," the senior Alaska state trooper said.

CHAPTER FORTY-FOUR

Central de Policia de Cordóba, Av. Colón 1254, Cordóba Capital [Police Headquarters, Provincial Capital, Cordóba], August 10, 1962

Adolf Henckel *Inspector de Policia* [Inspector of Police—third-ranking field officer in the department] *de la Provincia de Policía de Córdoba, PPC,* and José Emanuel de Corsos, *Teniente Policía de la Provincia de Policía de Córdoba, PPC* [Detective, Police of the Province of Córdoba], were excited about the information pouring out from Anna Maria Lobos. She was the extremely attractive mistress of the murder victim, Carlos Aguillara-Dominguez; and it was beginning to appear as if what she had learned through pillow talk was likely to break the politically charged case in record time. She was on a roll, and they let her talk as freely as she wanted.

She handed them a list of five names culled down from fifteen after Henckel asked her to list those acquaintances of the murder victim, Carlos Aguillara-Dominguez, aka Hörst Dietsel, who would commit murder to get what they wanted or to preserve secrets.

"These," she said. "Remember, you promised to protect me."

"And we will."

None of the names were familiar to the police inspector or the lieutenant of detectives. The first three names were Italian; and without having to speak to each other, Henckel and de Corsos mutually agreed that these had to be Sicilian or Unione Corse Mafiosos—Dominic Rizzuto, Tony Lagomarsino, and Benedettu Paganucci. The next two were obvious German names. The policemen surmised that they were likely ODESSA or maybe organized crime figures working out of either West Germany, or perhaps from inside Cordóba—Fritzi Hoeltzel and Hänsel Stahlecker.

"Thank you, Anna Maria. We will focus our investigation on these men. However, we cannot ignore other aspects of your 'friend's' life. As you told us, Señor Aguillara-Dominguez at least once indicated that he had another name–perhaps his original one—and it was German. Hörst Dietsel, you said. Can you tell us anything more about that? Did he have meetings with important Germanic people or officials that you know about?"

"You're asking about the ODESSA, is that not right?"

"Yes. That relates to how he came to live in Argentina. While we were talking earlier today, our office did some research. It is apparent that Señor Aguillara-Dominguez did not exist here in Argentina before 1945. Now, none of us are children or are naïve. The influx of Germans–at least the wealthy ones—around that time were Nazis. Officially, our government does not inquire about how such Germans got here or about their politics; and they do not allow outsiders to inquire. We—as the police–are not interested in your 'friend's' former life or what help Nazi organizations gave him except as it may relate to his murder. Please think for a moment about anything that might relate to the Nazis."

"I know very little. He rarely mentioned anything about Germany, the war, or the Nazis. I don't recall him ever saying that he had been a Nazi or a Nazi sympathizer. However, I know he was deathly afraid of someone in the ODESSA. He told me that much. I do remember one man's name. Did I tell you about him? It was August Neubert—I'm pretty sure about that. I don't know for certain, but he might have come here to the apartment. I think this Herr Neubert and Carlos were helped by the ODESSA in 1946. They were in the French section of West Germany, I think. It's also possible that they parted ways before they came here, but one thing I do remember is that this August Neubert was perfectly willing to kill anyone who might be able to identify him or who knew where he ended up. Carlos was truly afraid of him. He had plastic surgery to hide what he looked like and changed his name of course from Hörst to Carlos. Apparently he was able to escape from Germany with the help of ODESSA agents; but he must have betrayed someone who was waiting to come. Whoever that was, he got left in a concentration camp; and Hörst had nightmares about that man. I call him Hörst now because we are talking about Germany.

"This will maybe sound crazy, but Hörst once said that the man—or maybe more than one man—might have been French. A French Nazi in the German army. Hörst might have been drunk and confused, or maybe he was just trying to confuse me; so, I could never give clear information if the police or the Mossad ever questioned me. Sorry, that's as much as I know about his German past."

"You spoke of the Mossad. Are you aware of any contact or surveillance that Israeli organization might have had with your 'friend,' Anna Marie?"

"Not really. Carlos or Hörst or whatever his real name was had a great fear ... how do you say in Spanish or German ... unreasonable fear of the Mossad coming after him."

"Paranoia," de Corsos offered.

"That's it. Sometimes we would walk in crazy circles or hide in an alley or in a crowded store because he thought he saw someone watching him. He was sure the Jews were after him, and the watchers had the Jewish look. He often talked very quietly about the Jews and the Israelis and about how much he hated them. When the Mossad kidnapped ... the famous Nazi—I forget his name—in 1960, Carlos wanted to move to some other part of the country or even to Paraguay. He even talked to a priest in Buenos Aires about getting help to flee. When the Israelis hanged the Nazi, Carlos went so far as to travel to Asunción to find a place, but he eventually calmed down and came back. But he always was more careful after that."

"You mean SS-*Obersturmbannführer* Adolf Eichmann, do you not, Anna Marie?" Inspector Henckel suggested.

"That's the one. I think Hörst or my Carlos might have once worked with him or for him. He told me that when the Mossad kidnapped him, it was too close to home. He said they never gave up. They were like a pack of wolves on a carcass. Eventually they would get him, Dr. Mengele, the medical scientist who experimented on children, Ustasha Dinko Šakić, the former commandant of the Auschwitz of the Balkans [Jasenovac concentration camp], Richard Walther Darré who served as part of the Führer's cabinet, and especially one of Hörst's personal friends ... Erich Boehme who owns a delicatessen in Manriquez-

Huelsmann. He's the vice president of the German-Argentinian Cultural Association there.

"Many former Nazis live there. Maybe that would be a place for you to go to question people who might know about the ODESSA or might even know Hörst's friends. Boehme looks just like his old SS photos. He was thinner then, but his heavily tanned arms are remarkable for having deeply cut lean muscles. He still has the face, extremities, and powerful body of a frequent outdoorsman. Anywhere else in South America Boehme would have seemed out of place—perhaps even an overzealous German tourist—but not in the transplanted German town of Bariloche."

"Thank you, Anna Marie. You have been very helpful."

"You must not ever tell anyone that I said anything about the mafia people or the ODESSA at all. I will become … how you say … paranoid also, if you do. I am sure somebody like that killed my Carlos or Hörst; and it would be very easy for them to find me and to kill me, too."

"Your secrets are safe with us," Henckel assured her.

De Corsos was not quite so sure, but he kept his doubts to himself.

After they left Señorita Lobos, Henckel and de Corsos discussed what their next steps should be.

De Corsos favored going to Bariloche first, and Henckel wanted to start with the Mafiosos. They compromised with de Corsos convincing Inspector Henckel that his team could get the necessary information on the IG Farben poison gasses—GB or GD—probably tabun and sarin gas. And they could find the whereabouts of the Mafiosos which would be no small task. That way the two of them—Henckel and de Corsos—could go to Bariloche where it might be easier to find information, while the rest of the team made headway into the difficult task of finding and arranging to meet the Mafiosos. That would require very senior police commanders to be part of the arrangements, and that would be time-consuming. Henckel agreed, and Detective de Corsos called Manuel de Jesus, *Sargentopolicíaprovbsas Policía de la Provincia de Córdoba, PPC*, and Gerhardt Möller, *Oficial de Policía* [Police Officer] *Policía de la Provincia de Córdoba, PPC,* and gave them instructions

"You have confidence enough in your men that they can work without supervision?"

"Absolutely."

"I envy and applaud you, *Teniente*" Henckel said, "I can't say that I am that effective of a leader of the people directly under me. Perhaps I should be mindful of you and protect my job," he smiled as he said it.

§§§§§

Police Station 28, San Carlos de Bariloche, Rio Negro Province, Argentina, early evening

Bariloche is an anachoristic Bavarian city situated at the bottom of the world in South America. It sits in the foothills of the Andes that form the border with Chile. The small city is surrounded by snow-covered peaks on the southern shores of Nahuel Huapi Lake. The residents of the region call it the "Little Switzerland of South America." It is altogether reminiscent of the Bavarian Alps; so, that appellation is warranted. The police station was a three-story gray-brown tuff stone, slate, and fitzroya cypress conifer log structure like the city center's other official buildings. The log portion of the front of the station bore scorch mark damage not yet repaired from a recent protest over a police killing of a young thief. The thief's father and two friends launched a protest. Protests were strongly frowned upon in the town and especially by the historically Teutonic police. It was a typical dry, windy summer evening in the Rio Negro.

Henckel and de Corsos had called ahead to avoid appearing to be abrupt, officious, or to be imposing their superior law enforcement authority on the local officials. They made courtesy visits to the army's *12 Regimiento de Infantería de Montaña* [12th Mountain Infantry Regiment] and its *Escuela Militar de Montaña* [Argentine Army Mountain Warfare School], and to the German-Argentinian Cultural Association Offices. Col. Jorge DeCanzo and his adjutant, and Lt. Col. Gerd von Santiago—the commanding officers of the two important institutions respectively—greeted the police officers in full dress uniforms and graciously offered any help Henckel and de Corsos might need.

Erich Boehme at the cultural association was less inviting and was strictly and formally polite. He was the man they had come to see, and both officers took their measure of the man without being overly obvious about it. They had photographs from his days in the SS, and he had not changed appreciably with the passage of time. His thin unsmiling face and his ramrod stiffness looked very much as they did in the formal photographic portraits taken when he was a senior SS officer during the forties. For the rest of the world, that man had disappeared from the face of the earth at the end of the war. He was thinner, but still looked the way Anna-Marie Lobos had described. He, however, did not look like an overzealous German tourist. He looked every bit the unrepentant Nazi.

He had on brown Hansel lederhosen, a rough olive drab short-sleeved shirt, and matching knee-length stockings. His shoes were hard-soled mountain brogans which were a holdover from his strenuous rock hiking in the 1940s during his off-duty periods. Although he was an accomplished, even renowned boulderer, he never gave in to the newer thin and light shoes. He did not feel safe in them.

"Greetings, *Hauptsturmführer*. We appreciate you taking time out of your busy schedule to speak with us on such short notice," *Inspector de Policia* Henckel said.

"Former *Hauptsturmführer*, gentlemen. And very former SS, I might add. Not many know of my association with the Reich. I trust that you have been discreet."

"Indeed so," de Corsos said.

He loathed the former Nazis with their history of atrocities and their hubris in his country, but he made a serious effort to keep that to himself.

Henckel said, "Herr Boehme, we must meet with the police chief and then we would very much appreciate it if you would join us at Number 28—say half an hour from now?"

Boehme grunted an almost surly affirmative reply, and the two officers left for the police station.

Bariloche Police Chief Pedro Carriz-Mueller had set aside a small conference room on the second floor of the station. Chief Carriz-Mueller was one of the few mestizos or castizos in the city. The mixed race population in Bariloche itself was closer to two or three percent, with the rest being mostly Bavarian Europeans. The mestizo population of Argentina as a whole was about six percent. In Latin America, *castizo* is used to describe individuals born of the union of a European and a Native American resulting in a mixture of seventy-five percent European and twenty-five percent Native American. Although he was known to be a castizo, phenotypically, the chief looked more Southern German than he did Latin or mixed race. He was of medium height, medium weight—and not in excellent physical condition. He had brown eyes—a giveaway of his ancestry—light olive skin, dirty blond hair combed up and back in a pompadour, and a finely chiseled face. He wore a recently cleaned and neatly pressed blue police uniform with four stars on each shoulder. His large chief's badge was prominently displayed above the left chest pocket on his uniform jacket.

"I am afraid that it will be necessary for me to be in attendance during your questioning of Herr Boehme. There is concern about the suggestion that he might have to get into areas that the local citizens consider … delicate. I'm sure you understand."

"We do, Chief Carriz-Mueller. But we have a murder on our hands—one of our countrymen—and a man with a significant military history. We are here to learn what–if anything–the murder of Carlos Aguillara-Dominguez–aka Hörst Dietsel–has to do with his past or his present associations. We are determined to find his killer. As you know he is now the sixth former SS officer to be murdered in our country in the last year and a half. The president himself is determined to see to it that this spate of killings comes to an end. I am sure you are of a similar mind, Chief, are you not?"

"Of course. Some of our better known citizens are beginning to feel threatened. Their reports to my officers seem to suggest an Israeli behind every tree. We intend to work with you, but every former German officer or enlisted man is understandably leery about what will happen to the information they give."

"We are interested in identifying, arresting, and bringing to justice the killer or killers of Dietsel and any other of our citizens of Germanic ethnicity. We are not—and I repeat with emphasis, we are not–interested in pursuing the manhunts being conducted by the Jewish organizations, the hypocritical Americans, and the reformed Europeans. Please assure the people we question here that we have no interest in them unless they are somehow connected with the murder or murders."

Chief Carriz-Mueller said, "*Hauptsturmführer* Boehme is waiting in the entry hall. Shall I have him sent in?"

"Please do. I think this should prove most interesting," said Inspector Henckel.

"It is approaching noon, gentlemen. I will have our secretary bring lunch," the chief said.

Lunch Recipes for San Carlos de Bariloche

Curanto ("Hot Stone" in Mapuche Indian)

Ingredients
-Sufficient amounts of pieces of beef, lamb, pork, chicken, *chorizos* [pork sausages], potatoes, sweet potatoes, apples, and hollowed-out pumpkins stuffed with cheese, cream, and peas.

Preparation
-Dig a pit about two feet deep in the ground. Start a roaring fire with available oak, mesquite, or applewood—but not aromatic woods like eucalyptus—then place river stones on top of the fire. Once the stones are heated, remove them from the fire and place in the pit. Arrange a bed of leaves on top of the stones. The selection of meats and vegetables are then stacked on top of the leaves. The food may be seasoned with a variety of spices to taste.
-Then cover with leaves and damp sheets to keep the heat from escaping. Finally, cover the damp sheets with soil which results in the cooking process becoming something like a pressure cooker.
-After a couple of hours, smoke and steam start billowing out of the ground. The end result is a unique and delicious meal which has a hint of smoke and a slight earthy flavor.

Cordero Patagónico al Asador con Salsa Chimichurri Roja

Ingredients
For the lamb: skin, clean, and splay (butterfly) open one full fat lamb.
For the red chimichurri sauce: ½ tsp black pepper, 1 tsp kosher salt, 1 tsp crushed red chili flakes, 1½ tsp smoked paprika, 1 tbsp dried oregano, 2 tbsp fresh lemon juice, ¼ bundle fresh cilantro, 1 bundle fresh parsley, 1 red bell pepper, seeds and pitch removed, 2 trimmed green onions, 6 cloves, 1 peeled garlic, ⅓ cp red wine vinegar

Preparation
For the lamb: Make a *leña* (fire of wood oak, mesquite, or applewood) and burn down to a *brasa* [red-hot coals]. Place whole lamb splayed out on a spit, oriented vertically over the wood fire, and slowly rotate over the central fire for at least 3 hours. It is the duty of the *cocinero* [cook] to marinate the meat periodically with a mix of salt, water, and local herbs, all the while testing the choice pieces for the perfect tenderness.

For the chimichurr: In a food processor, combine the pepper, salt, chili flakes, paprika, oregano, lemon juice, cilantro, parsley, bell pepper, green onions, garlic, and vinegar.

-Blend on low while simultaneously drizzling in the oil, emulsifying until it forms a wet saucelike paste. To serve, drizzle the red chimichurri on grilled meats or vegetables and enjoy. Should serve with a Malbec—a strong and slightly spicy red wine.

Grilled Whole Cow

Ingredients -1400 lbs of beef, split in half, salt and pepper

Preparation: Skin the cow, split it down the middle, and splay the salt-and-pepper-rubbed meat slabs on a sturdy metal, crosslike contraption that has one or two sharp, speared edges on the bottom. Jam the entire setup into the ground and angle toward a slow-burning wood fire, marinating frequently (butter, wine, beer, various jams) and rotating often.

Serve: When done—as determined by the *cocinero*—cut off slabs of meat, chitlins, and internal organs (such as liver, kidneys, pancreas, heart) and serve with or without bone-in.

Zapallo en Almíbar, Candied Squash

Ingredients
-3 cps firm squash [butternut, kabocha, acorn, or hubbard], 3 cps light rum, 1 tsp natural vanilla, 4 cps water, 4 cps sugar

Directions
-Peel and deseed the squash. Cut into medium-large cubes, about 1½ in. in size. In a medium bowl, combine the squash and rum and set soak for 24 hours, stirring occasionally to make sure all the cubes are covered.
-Drain squash, discard rum. In a medium nonreactive stock pot, heat water and sugar over medium-high heat. Stir frequntly, and when the sugar is completely dissolved, add in squash and vanilla. Heat to a boil, then reduce heat but maintain the mixture at a simmer until the squash becomes translucent—about an hour.
-Remove the mixture from the heat and let cool completely. Place the squash in a jar and cover with the syrup and a lid. May refrigerate for up to 2 wks. Serve with a tray of meats, cheeses, and olives as a snack, as part of a predinner appetizer, or as a dessert course with fruit, nuts, and cheeses.

CHAPTER FORTY-FIVE

Police Station 28, San Carlos de Bariloche, Rio Negro Province, Argentina, 1900 hours, August 26, 1962

Former SS *Hauptsturmführer* Erich Boehme strutted into the conference room as if he were there to assume the helm as the new commander of the installation. Hencke, de Corsos, and police chief Carriz-Mueller, stood up in respect to greet the old unrepentant Nazi. It galled the two visiting police officers no end to have to accord the old butcher such tokens of respect. They considered his hubris to be an affront. If they had their way, he would be in prison or awaiting the hangman. The reality of the situation was–however–that they needed the information he could give them. They had to convince him in their first few sentences that it was in his best interest to help in the murder investigation of Hörst Dietsel, aka Carlos Aguillara-Dominguez. They were well aware that it would be a difficult sell to convince the crafty old SS man to divulge anything after so many years in hiding. To add sting to the police officers' agitated psyches, they had to break bread with the man and to serve him from the fine lunch they had ordered to be catered for the local Bariloche policemen.

"Thank you for dropping by," Chief Carriz-Mueller said, to start the interview.

"I understand that you three seek justice for the murder of one of my countrymen, a former German officer who acquitted himself with honor during the time of the Third Reich. If that is truly the case, then I will do my best to help. If ... however ... if this is some sort of ruse to inveigle me into a plot to assist the despicable *Untermenschen* [sub-

343

human] *Judenschwein* [Jewpigs] to pull off another Adolf Eichmann kidnapping—only two years ago, mind you—then I will see right through you in an instant; and I will be gone. The Jewsows have murdered over a thousand of us to date, and there will be no more if I have anything to do with it. Do we have an understanding?"

"As we said earlier in the day, *Hauptsturmführer*, our only aim is to find and punish the murderer of Hörst Dietsel," Henckel said.

"I will give you the benefit of the doubt."

"Thank you. Now kindly answer a few questions for us. Did you know Dietsel personally?"

"As a passing acquaintance. We met and passed the time of day at a few Argentinian-German celebrations. We were not intimates."

"Are ... or were you aware of Dietsel's wartime activities?"

"I was. He acquitted himself well in his work for the cause."

"Do you know anyone or any group that might know of the real identity of Carlos Aguillara-Dominguez? Anyone still living that knew him during his service to the Third Reich? Or anyone who associated with him in his escape from the Jews and Americans and his coming to the *Provincias Unidas del Río de la Plata* [United Provinces of the Silver River]?"

That loving reference to the original name of their country put Boehme more at ease.

"I will answer your questions. First, let us concentrate on those who might bear him ill will. There were many SS officers who were assisted by the ODESSA. Of course, that help came at a price since it was a costly venture to bring together everything and everyone who was needed. I recall a certain IG Farben chemist who was somehow able to usurp the position in the queue waiting for placements in Germany. As I recall, he was named Heinrich Rudolf Gajewski. There was great resentment against him, and more than once I heard Herr Dietsel swear a vendetta against the man. I also know that the leaders of the ODESSA quietly took Dietsel aside and warned him to keep his mouth shut because he had made Gajewski into an enemy, and Gajewski had powerful friends who would not hesitate to erase him—Dietsel—if anything happened to Gajewski. There were several others whose opportunity to go to Argentina was lost because of Gajewski's and Dietsel's connivings. Strangely enough, they were senior SS officers who were French part of the Führer's special guard at the last. They were superb officers and loyalists, but they considered themselves to have been betrayed by several men who made it to Argentina, including Dietsel. I may get the names a bit wrong here, but I am sure of the ranks. All of them were Hitler's Gauls—part of the 33rd Waffen Grenidier Division of the SS. I have to say that they probably hold me at least partly responsible for what happened to them: they were captured by the vile Russians and sent off to the gulags. Probably died there."

"Are you sure of that?"

"No, but from what I have been told, less than a handful survived. It is also possible that the few wretched survivors may still be rotting up there in the frozen north."

"Do you recall any of their names, Herr Boehme?"

"A few come to mind—just the higher ranks. I recall *Gruppenführer und Generalleutnant der Waffen-SS* Antoine Duvalier, *Oberführer der Waffen-SS* Michaele Dupont, *Waffen SS-Obersturmbannführer* Serge Alain Rounsavall, *Waffen SS-Sturmbannführer* Jérôme Beauchamp, *Waffen SS-Hauptsturmführer* Jérôme Christophe Mailhot, *Obersturmführer SS* Jacob Friedrich Bunnemann, and *Waffen SS-Sturmbannführer* Jean Luc Latendresse. There were certainly a few more, but I regret to report that I am unable to recall any more names. Old age, I guess. These men I knew well and found them to be loyal men of respect."

Lieutenant de Corsos abruptly shifted the questions to another area, partly to keep Boehme off his stride.

"Thank you for your help with those names. We know you to be a successful man of the world and have some knowledge of people of importance in all walks of life, *Hauptsturmführer*. Perhaps you could help us with an area where we are largely excluded."

"It is true that I have a wide circle of family, friends, and associates. How can I assist you?"

"We are aware that important clergy from the Church, associates of Cosa Nostra, *russkaya mafiya*"—de Corsos deliberately used the Russian term to convey to Boehme that the police were working with precise knowledge—"some quasi-legitimate businessmen, and other organized criminal elements have been instrumental in aiding the ODESSA or helping individual patriots get to safety. Our sources suggest these organizations may be involved. Could you put some thought into that area and come up with some names, sir?"

Boehme paused before answering, wondering whether or not this line of questioning could lead to him, his friends, or organizations he supported.

"I want careful assurances on this, Officers."

"We repeat that we will treat everything you tell us with the same rigor as the confessional."

"All right; first, the clergy: all of the priests connected with the Christ the Savior Cathedral in Buenos Aires—Bishop Manuel Ortega-Rodriguez from the archdiocese of Rio Negro and Abbot Francoise Hercule and the brothers at the Mount of the Trinity Abbey in Monasterio Benedictino Santa María. Second, Corsican syndicate: almost any Mafioso or gang might be involved, but I am sure of three members—Benedettu Paganucci, Dominic Rizzuto, and Tony Lagomarsino. There have been some ODESSA dealings with Russian Mafiosos from a city called Yelizovo [a town in Kamchatka Krai, Russia]."

De Corsos nodded his understanding and made a strong mental note to pursue the Yelizovo lead further.

"Thank you, Herr *Hauptsturmführer*. Would it be possible for you to introduce us to any of the people you have named? That would be a very useful assist in our investigation and a favor that we would not forget."

"Although I have considerable influence and am held in a high level of respect in several communities in Argentina, Germany, and abroad, I do not have authority to order anyone to talk to you; and they are not at all likely to communicate willingly with police, intelligence officers, or anyone asking questions that even hint of an interest in the ODESSA. If I were to do so, I would become one of the *desaparecidos* [disappeared ones]—a permanent situation, if you understand my meaning."

"We do," said Henckel, "and we certainly do not have any wish to bring harm to you. If you think of anything else that might assist our investigation, please give us a call. We will treat any and all such communications with the utmost level of security."

Boehme nodded and stood up to leave.

"I am an enemy of anyone who seeks to find or to harm *meine Brüder* [my brethren]. I will quietly listen and encourage conversation. Should I learn anything, I will contact you. It is possible that I will learn something that will demand immediate attention, and my comrades-in-arms will be obliged to attend to that. I may have to contact you after the fact. You understand."

"Yes, sir. But we would prefer to have the police handle such things. For one thing, our involvement would put you at arms length and remove you from danger of reprisal. Bear that in mind, *Mein Herr.*"

After Boehme left, Henckel and de Corsos discussed what they had learned thus far: there were more persons of interest than they could interview in a lifetime—if the subjects would even prove to be willing to talk to police officials. Everyone who had suggested a line of questioning or had proffered some names had an agenda of his or her own. Every direction of inquiry would lead to great and powerful organizations and individuals, none of whom would be likely to believe that the police had a limited scope of interest—that they were merely trying to catch a single murderer and not trying to stir up the Argentine–German–Jewish–Peronista hornets' nests. No matter which direction they headed, they were going to run up against political, military, financial, and church self-interests that would likely provoke homicidal intentions. With the exception of the Jews and Israelis, the links among Argentina, the US, Germany, Austria, Switzerland, the Vatican, France, Spain, the Mafia, nationalists, and would-be dictators lived in the shadows; and anyone seeking to cast light into the dark corners would become a target. Any such quest would be suicidal.

"We have a few leads we can pursue without overtly suggesting an involvement by the ODESSA, the Nazis, the American Paperclip operation, the church, the Allied atrocities or the knowing involvement of law enforcement so long as we keep our investigation aimed at individuals and not at organizations," de Corsos said, more hopefully than with any certainty.

"I think we can work from behind the scenes and use a surrogate that will keep us out of the direct light," Henckel said. "I am pretty sure that we are not dealing with a single person with an overwhelming urge for revenge. My bet is that there are other killings and more than one killer."

"How do we find out about that? Are you suggesting that this may involve other cities, other police forces, even other countries?"

"Could well be. I am on fairly good terms with INTERPOL. When they did some Nazi hunting in Argentina a couple of years back, I helped one of their agents track down a notorious concentration camp guard. We had an agreement to keep the Mossad out and to make it a French affair since the froggies seemed to be the least threatening to Argentine interests at the time. I think INTERPOL will be willing to explore the question of whether or not this has international implications and to help us narrow the field down to a handful of real suspects."

He took a brief look at his notes.

"We have some names to start with which should be fairly safe to investigate. We have heard about the Corsican syndicate: almost any Mafioso or gang might be involved, but I am sure of three members of the Corsican syndicate—Benedettu Paganucci, Dominic Rizzuto, and Tony Lagomarsino. The pope wants to put some distance between the church and the Nazis they helped; so, they might be willing to sacrifice a scapegoat or two—like the priests of Christ the Savior Cathedral in Buenos Aires, Bishop Manuel Ortega-Rodriguez from the archdiocese of Rio Negro, and Abbot Francoise Hercule and the brothers at the Mount of the Trinity Abbey in Monasterio Benedictino Santa María.

"Boehme gave us the names of some French Nazi officers, and I would bet my hat that the ODESSA would not go to war over a few French SS criminals. We have Antoine Duvalier, Michaele Dupont, Serge Alain Rounsavall, Hugues Beauchamp, Jérôme Christophe Mailhot, Jacob Friedrich Bunnemann, and Jean Luc Latendresse from the 33rd Waffen-Grenadier SS Division to start with. We should be able to find out about them from the Allied POW records, maybe even from the Russians. We have a place to start. I'll call Eugène Dentremont at the Lyon INTERPOL office to get us started. You give our German friends a call about the old Nazi Heinrich Rudolf Gajewski and about the West German criminals Anna Marie Lobos told us about—Fritzi Hoeltzel, Hänsel Stahlecker, and August Neubert. Maybe that will give us a back door look at the ODESSA and their connections with our Argentine Nazis without having our names be known, José."

Le *Bureau Central National (BCN) d'*INTERPOL *pour la France* [The International Criminal Police Organization, or INTERPOL], Office of Senior Detective Chief Superintendent Eugène Léon Dentremont, 200 Quai Charles de Gaulle, 69006 Lyon, France, August 28, 1962

The telephone line flashed yellow, indicating a call from a foreign nation. Office hours had officially begun only five minutes ago.

"General Secretariat, INTERPOL, Criminal Information System. How may I direct your call?"

"Please ring the office of the Senior Detective Chief Superintendent," the voice asked in French with a German accent.

"Yes, sir."

There was a two-minute wait.

"Office of the Detective Chief Superintendent, Criminal Information System."

"I need to speak to Eugène Léon Dentremont, the *senior* chief super-intendent, not just one of the detective chief superintendents. This is Adolf Henckel. I am the *Inspector de Policia de la Provincia de Policía de Córdoba,* Argentina. It is imperative that I speak to the senior detective ... *ahora!* Give him my name, young lady."

"Would you repeat your name please, sir?"

Henckel did and also spelled it out slowly.

"One moment."

Henckel could hear loud voices coming over the line but could not make out what was being said. Thirty seconds passed.

"Is this Adolf Henckel of the famous organized crime unit of Córdoba?"

"Yes. I am in hopes that you remember the humble assistance our CID unit gave your INTERPOL investigative unit two or three years ago."

"I do, Adolf, my friend. You are too modest. Your unit was crucial in INTERPOL's case against the Corsicans. I owe you. What can I do to repay you?"

"I ask as a friend and a fellow law enforcement officer, Eugène, and not as someone seeking to even a score between us. Whatever you decide in the matter I put before you, my department stands ready to assist INTERPOL whenever needed."

INTERPOL had to tread lightly before deciding to pursue an international case. To keep INTERPOL as politically neutral as possible, its charter forbids it from undertaking interventions or activities of a political, military, religious, or racial nature or involving itself in disputes over such matters. As a result, its work focuses primarily on public safety and battling terrorism, crimes against humanity, environmental crime, genocide, war crimes, organized crime, piracy, illicit traffic in works of art, illicit drug production, drug trafficking, weapons smuggling, human trafficking, money laundering, child pornography, white-collar crime, computer crime, intellectual property crime, and corruption. An apparently straightforward murder case in Argentina would not seem to fit the mandate. However, Chief Inspector Dentremont was not always inclined to accept limitations, especially when he encountered a case that interested him.

"I know that, old friend. Now what can I or my ICIS resources do for you?"

"There has been a murder in Lomas de los Carolinos, one of the nicer neighborhoods in Córdoba. It was particularly gruesome."

"I recall the place. Lovely. And very German. Does my memory serve me correctly?"

"Yes, and that is tied into the problem for which I am calling you, Eugène. May I explain?"

"Please."

"A man named Carlos Aguillara-Dominguez here in Argentina is of German extraction—born Hörst Dietsel—he was murdered on a public street in the neighborhood on Friday, August 9th. An apparently homeless man sitting in the gutter suddenly stood up and attacked

Señor Aguillara-Dominguez. The victim was decapitated. There were no witnesses."

"Of course not. There never seem to be any."

"There is a great fear about in the neighborhood because–in fact–the deceased is a prominent German, apparently one of those who emigrated from Europe at the end of the war."

"And that is always a problem for you and your fellow officers."

"Yes. We find ourselves tangled up with the country's military, former Nazis, the government, Corsican mobsters, possibly with Sicilian and Russian Mafiosos, possibly the Church, and perhaps even the Mossad."

"That is a toxic stew my friend. What can INTERPOL do to help?"

"I will give you a list of possible suspects—mind you, we have no evidence against any of them—and perhaps you can tell us more about them. We would like to know first off if they are even alive, if they are involved in crime, if such crime has anything to do with our victim, and who we can talk to to get us on the way to a solution. I do not need to caution you about the delicacy of this case. We are handling it with kid gloves."

"You can certainly count on our discretion, Adolf. What did you say the man's German birth name was? I must have missed it."

"*Mon dieu!*" said Adolf. "My mind must be slipping. He was known as Hörst Dietsel before he showed up in Argentina. Please look into the man and his German connections. That will probably lead you to the ODESSA. Please be sure to leave out any mention of me or my department. I would likely become another police statistic—line of duty death—if my part becomes known."

"I will put my secretary on the line, and she can take down the names of your potential suspects as you give them. It will likely take me a few days before I can get anything solid for you; so, be patient, please."

"I don't expect miracles, Eugène. Do what is necessary. I will try to practice or maybe just learn patience. It is not one of my strong suits."

The secretary came on the line, and Adolf read off the list of criminals, former Nazis, and French SS troops.

"An unusual mix, Adolf, but not untirely unheard of, except for the Frenchmen in the uniform of the SS. That is a new one even for me. I'll call you at the police station in San Carlos de Bariloche, Rio Negro Province, by tomorrow afternoon at the latest," Dentremont, who was listening in, said.

"Thank you. I will owe you, old friend."

As soon as Adolf put down the telephone receiver, the number two criminal investigation officer for INTERPOL began his methodical work under the chief superintendent's direction. He checked the dailies to see if there were any recent similar crimes in the countries served by INTERPOL and was not entirely surprised to locate an unexplained murder in Moscow on October 1961, another on August 8, 1962 in Alaska, and nearly a dozen somewhat similar murders around Europe—especially France—and in Russia. The Moscow and Alaska murders involved senior allied generals, which set off alarm bells.

Dentremont set his office into overdrive to find out if there were any connections between the two generals. The only similarity found was that the two senior officers had commanded allied POW camps for German internees. He let Adolf Henckel know his findings and told him that they should be patient and look for a pattern. Moscow was not quite as forthcoming as the European and American sources.

By August 15—Assumption Day—confirmation of his suspicions was brought to him. The morning report told of the murder of a famous or infamous French general depending on one's politics. The killer or killers were as much a mystery as in the first two murders, but there was a similarity that could not be mere coincidence. The general had been the commandant of a French-run POW camp for German detainees. He excitedly called Adolf Henckel and told him about the new death.

"That has to be the link, Eugène. Great work. I will help in anyway I can, but none of those seems to be linked directly to my murder. I don't have any evidence that my victim was a military man."

"Perhaps not, but there may be a broader aspect to this which involves the war, the connections between the generals, the prison camps, and who knows what else? We will keep working. I suggest you do the same and find out any connections between allied POW camps and any men who made it to Argentina separately. I am not a betting man; but if I were, I would put money on there being more such men involved and who have made it to the relative safety of your country."

"I'll keep working on it," Henckel said.

Inspector Henckel could not have made a better choice in the selection of a working partner outside the confines of the Germanophilia of Argentina and the risks of choosing a partner from the questionable ranks of German law enforcement: both had more than just a taint of Nazi nepotism. The other thing Henckel liked about Dentremont was his apparent—but deceptive—ordinariness and self-effacing demeanor. The man was intellectually brilliant but often shrank into the background during discussions which all too often brought out the hubris of his fellow peace officers both in and out of INTERPOL. He was average height, average weight, had average graying brownish hair, and wore frumpy clothes off the rack. He had a jowly face with rather thick, wet lips. He was able to appear every day with the same one-day old beard stubble. His eyebrows were thick like his sideburns, and his thinning hair always seemed to be about two weeks beyond the reasonable need for a haircut.

If one took the effort to scrutinize his unexciting face carefully enough, the observer would be impressed with his keen, intelligent, curious eyes. He was easily overlooked and underestimated by criminals and his competitors in law enforcement ranks. That he held the senior detective chief superintendent's position in INTERPOL was not due to any record of average accomplishments. Dentremont had an almost uncanny knack to detect liars, to undo fakers, to think ahead of criminal "masterminds," and to arrive at the correct conclusion well ahead of his subordinates. He had been eligible for retirement for the past five years, but no one even hinted that it was his time to leave permanently for the Villefranche-sur-Mer beaches near Nice in the South of France which he so loved in the years when he could spend his month off on vacation away from Paris and Lyon.

On August 18th, Senior Detective Chief Superintendent Dentremont found another murder of a general, this time a British officer who was killed by being pithed by a skilled assassin in his private club. The clincher for Dentremont was learning that the Brit had been the commandant of a POW camp like the other generals. He put into motion a global search for anyone who knew anything about Allied prisoner of war camps. What he learned astonished him, but it did not explain the murder in Argentina or several others around the world that involved possible wartime grudges but without involving senior officers or POW camps directly. Still, Dentremont had a nagging suspicion that he was on to something with these murders and suspected a connection but one that he could not yet prove.

Dentremont was known to be frustratingly thorough even when his staff thought they were dealing with an open-and-shut case. For all of his work on the Allied POW connection, the chief superintendent refused to limit his case; he doggedly worked to track down any links to former Nazis, organized crime, petty grudges, business or criminal enterprise conflicts, or even love triangles.

Chief Inspector Dentremont assigned officers to a team tasked to solve all of the murders, which he now deemed with almost religious intensity to be interrelated. His German deputy stationed in Wiesbaden, Alina Hertzog, was assigned to gather every piece of information available from both official and unofficial sources about the German/Nazi/ODESSA connections to every one of the murder victims. He chose Alina because she was highly experienced and adroit in dealing with the still Nazi-infiltrated law enforcement agencies in Germany, Austria, Italy, and South America and,–as far as he could tell–she was untainted by the close proximity to the Nazis or neo-Nazis. He ordered the Italian, Giuliano Pasqualone, to work with Inspector Henckel in Paraguay and Argentina to get a clear vision of what motives might be driving the Nazis and neo-Nazis to remove one of their own. His own number one deputy, Roger Lahillonne, was assigned the thankless task of winning cooperation and gaining information from the Soviets and to learn all there was to know about the Allied POW camp systems. Axel Baird—the agent in charge in New York City—was chosen because he had been directly involved in the American CIA Paperclip Operation which resulted in thousands of Nazi scientists being secretly transferred from Europe to the United States.

The chief superintendent considered himself blessed that he had been able to seduce Axel away from the CIA to be his SAC in New York. Axel had a well-earned reputation for control under stress, courage in the face of personal danger of any kind, a dogged determinism in pursuing evidence, and a demonstrated capacity to fight or even kill as the situation required. He knew that Axel seldom had to resort to fighting when in a confrontational situation. He was so big—six feet six inches tall, and a weight of two hundred fifty pounds—that only a fool would directly challenge him. More importantly was that certain look he got when threatened—an intensity that threatened serious harm to come to the man foolish to issue the threat; an intensity that said, "You made the mistake of bringing a knife to the gun fight."

Axel was a smart dresser; he always worked in a clean, neat, new or almost-new suit. He wore silk shirts and silk neckties, usually colorful ones. Where work was considered, there were no casual Fridays. He was handsome in a hard sort of way, and his auburn hair was regularly refreshed in Kenneth's on 19 East 54th Street, which was a place of fun, almost a club. The salon, which filled four stories just off Fifth Avenue, was wildly colorful and had a plethora of patterns meant to evoke the circus. Kenneth [Kenneth Battelle—who created the soft coiffures worn by stars like Lauren Bacall, Audrey Hepburn, and Marilyn] did Axel's hair. Presidents' wives wore his style, including Jackie Kennedy. Marilyn was wearing a do by Kenneth the night she sang *Happy Birthday, Mr. President*, to JFK. The salon served finger sandwiches and tea and was reputed to be a favorite meeting place for New York's gay community.

Women constantly, but briefly, attempted to win Axel's interest; but he never succumbed. There were men who said that Axel was married to his work and had no time. There were a very few people who speculated that he could perhaps be gay, a man so handsome that he was almost pretty. None of those people had ever done so to his face. They were all convinced without the need for conformation that Axel might have a violent streak.

Dentremont elected to take on the most difficult and delicate section of the investigation: to look into the inner workings of the European organized crime syndicates to find out which of them might be funding the work of the gangs and the ODESSA and Spider organizations. He was determined to learn who had the most burning grudges against the murder victims and also had the resources sufficient to pull off the murders spanning such a great distance and such a diverse subset of society. First, though, like any real Frenchman, Eugène needed to decide on what to have for lunch and where.

Mid-Day French Recipes

Quick French Onion Soup

Ingredients
-6 cps low salt beef broth, 3 lg sweet onions, one chopped, two thinly sliced lengthwise, ¾ to 1 oz dried porcini mushrooms, 1 tbsp unsalted butter, 1 tbsp olive oil, 1 tsp finely chopped fresh thyme, ¼ tsp paprika, ¼ cp medium sherry, e.g. amontillado, kosher salt to taste, 4 ¾-inch-thick slices French baguette, lightly toasted, 6 oz Gruyère cheese, coarsely grated (about 2 cps).

Preparation

-In a 4-quart saucepan, bring the broth, chopped onion, and porcini to a boil. Reduce to a simmer and cook for 15 mins. Strain through a fine-mesh sieve lined with damp paper towel into a large bowl. Clean the saucepan and return the broth to the pan.

-Meanwhile, heat the butter and oil in a 12 in. skillet over medium-high heat until the butter browns, about 2 mins. Add sliced onions, thyme, and paprika. Cover and cook until the onion is soft and golden, stirring occasionally, about 10 mins. Add sherry and stir to scrape up any browned bits on the bottom of the skillet. Add the contents of the skillet to the broth. Add 1 and ½ tsp salt and bring to a boil. Cook for 2 mins. then turn off heat.

-Position a rack 6 in. from the broiler and heat the broiler on high. Place four broiler-safe 12-oz soup crocks or deep bowls on a rimmed baking sheet. Divide the soup among the bowls and top each with a slice of baguette. Evenly distribute the cheese over each. Broil until the cheese is melted and bubbling (1–2 mins). Serve very hot.

The recipe is quick by saving time caramelizing the onions for this classic soup. Because sweet onions are already sweet, starting with them means they need less time to make them so. The secret to this soup's deep flavor comes from infusing the broth with dried porcini.

Spring Niçoise Salad

Ingredients

-6 baby beets, greens removed and washed, 2½ tbsps red-wine vinegar (more as needed to taste), 1 lemon, halved, plus 1 tbsp freshly squeezed lemon juice, 8 trimmed baby artichokes, 1 cp + 4 tbsps extra-virgin olive oil, ¼ cup dry white wine, 2 sprigs fresh thyme, red pepper flakes and kosher salt to taste, ¾ lb new red potatoes, 1 clove garlic, pounded to a smooth paste—add a pinch of salt, 1 tbsp Dijon mustard, 1 lg egg yolk, 1 lb ahi or yellowfin tuna, cut into even slices about 1 in. thick, freshly ground black pepper to taste, 2 lightly hard-boiled eggs, peeled, 1 handful wild arugula, or ½ handful arugula and ½ handful young dandelion (~1 oz. total), washed and dried.

Preparation

-Heat oven to 350° F. Put the beets in a single layer in a baking dish. Add water to come about ½ in. up the side of the dish. Cover with foil and roast until the beets can be pierced with a sharp knife~45 mins. When cool, peel and cut them into ½ in. wedges and toss with 1 tbsp of the vinegar and salt to taste; let sit for 10–15 mins.

-Fill a large bowl with cold water. Squeeze the juice of the lemon halves into it. Trim off the top quarter of the artichokes and snap off the tough outer leaves. Using a small, sharp knife, peel the stem and the base of the artichokes, then cut them in half and scoop out the choke with a spoon. As you finish trimming each artichoke, drop it into the bowl of water and lemon juice to prevent browning. Just before cooking, drain the artichokes well.

-Warm a medium skillet over medium heat. Add ¼ cp olive oil, the artichokes, wine, ½ cp water, the thyme, and a pinch of red pepper flakes. Season with salt and simmer, uncovered. Stir occasionally until the artichokes are tender when pierced at the base with a small, sharp knife~10–15 mins, depending on the size of the artichokes. If the liquid evaporates before the artichokes are tender, add a splash more water. Let cool at room temperature and then taste for salt.

-Put the potatoes in a shallow baking dish or pan just large enough to hold them in a single layer. Drizzle with 1 tbsp oil; season with a generous amount of salt, and toss well. Add a splash of water~just enough to create a little steam as the potatoes cook. Cover tightly with aluminum foil and bake until the potatoes can be easily pierced with a small, sharp knife, 30–40 mins., depending on the size of the potatoes. Remove from the oven, vent the foil, and let cool at room temperature.

-To make the vinaigrette, combine the garlic, mustard, 1½ tbsp vinegar, and 1 tbsp lemon juice in a small bowl. Let sit for 5–10 min. Whisk in egg yolk, then slowly whisk in ¾ cp oil. Thin the vinaigrette with a few drops of cool water as necessary to be thin enough to drizzle easily. Adjust with more salt or vinegar if necessary and set aside.

-Shortly before serving, halve or quarter the potatoes and season with~1½ tbsp vinaigrette and set aside.

-Season the tuna on both sides with salt and freshly ground black pepper. Warm a large skillet, preferably cast iron, over high heat until very hot. Add 3 tbsps oil and place the tuna in the skillet. Cook, without moving, until seared and nicely browned~2–3 min., depending on the thickness of the tuna. Turn and cook on the opposite side for another 2–3 min. The tuna should be pink in the center. Transfer to a plate and set aside.

-Drain any liquid from the artichokes and discard the thyme. Cut the eggs into quarters and season with salt and freshly ground black pepper. Scatter about half of the arugula around a large platter or individual plates. Tuck the potatoes, artichokes, beets, and eggs in and around the greens. Using your hands, break the tuna into rough rustic pieces, or slice it with a knife and nestle it in and around the other ingredients. Drizzle~¼ cp vinaigrette over the platter, or~1 tbsp over individual portions. Serve immediately, passing the remaining vinaigrette at the table.

CHAPTER FORTY-SEVEN

*Le Bureau Central National (BCN) d'*INTERPOL *pour la France* [The International Criminal Police Organization, or INTERPOL], Office of Senior Detective Chief Superintendent Eugène Léon Dentremont, 200 Quai Charles de Gaulle, 69006 Lyon, France, August 30, 1962, late afternoon

After a thorough study of the cases he had learned about—and an especially careful evaluation of the German case—the first call Chief Superintendent Dentremont made was to Friedrich Schneider Graf von der Lippe, police chief of Wiesbaden, to smooth the way for Alina Hertzog to learn what she could about the current status of the ODESSA and to get any records available that would shed light on the relationship of ODESSA functionaries and the German murder victim.

Before he could make direct contact with the chief, Dentremont had to talk to three secretaries and five subordinates, and had to spend nearly thirty minutes twiddling his thumbs while his inquiry made its way up the chain of command. Finally, von der Lippe came on the line.

"Senior Chief Superintendent Dentremont, it is an honor to have the opportunity to speak with you. I hope you have not been kept waiting long. I trust that Florina and the children are doing well."

"My family is fine, thank you, Chief. How are Gretchen and Addler? I presume they are the only children who have not yet flown from the nest?"

"They are overactive but excelling in school; so, I suppose that is about as much as a father can reasonably hope for."

"Did Agata come through her surgery all right?"

He knew that the chief's wife had been undergoing treatment for ovarian cancer, a fact known to only a very few insiders in the German law enforcement community.

"She did very well. They found no spread of the tumor, and we are all hopeful that she will make a full recovery and, in fact, will be cured."

"I am gratified to hear that, Friedrich."

"It goes without saying that I very much prefer to keep the information about Agata and the rest of the family private for the sake of security."

"Of course. I have to go to the same lengths to protect my family. It is one of the curses of our profession, I am afraid."

"So, Eugène, how can I be of service to INTERPOL today?"

"We have very recently been made aware of a series of murders around Europe, South America, and the US that may be related. We have launched an investigation—thorough but quiet—to find links–if any exist–among the murders in order to cast light on possible suspects. I received a call this morning from an Argentine—Inspector of Police Adolf Henckel—about the murder of a prominent citizen of Córdoba who was living under an assumed name in an upscale neighborhood."

"Let me guess. The victim was a former Nazi?"

"Yes. His name in Argentina was Carlos Aguillara-Dominguez, but we—actually Inspector Henckel—have been able to trace the victim's birth name. He was Hörst Dietsel, formally a ranking officer in the SS."

"The assassinations of such men can't be terribly common in your country but is not all that uncommon in South America, Eugène. I would presume that the Mossad had a hand in the killing—they usually do."

"We are looking into that possibility, of course, Friedrich;but suggestive connections to other murders lead us to look more intensely into the ODESSA and Spider organizations; and we need your help in that area."

"I presume you are well aware of how close-knit and closed-mouth the ODESSA people are, my friend."

"Of course. But we are not investigating the ODESSA for its crimes—past or current—rather we are looking for leads related to our murder and possibly the series of murders that have come to our attention."

"I will help, but you must assure me that there will be nothing that will lead from you to the ODESSA and back to me. They are almost as powerful as the government, far more powerful than the police, and more lethal than either you or I can imagine."

"You have my assurances, of course, Friedrich."

"I have already had some inquiries and requests for intervention from our own German law enforcement authorities, and I am quite sure the matter is under investigation—an almost subliminal investigation. I was called by *Kriminalkommissar* [Detective Lieutenant] Horst Schäfer who is looking into a murder that took place in the IG Farben factory in Ludwigshafen.

"I have the records here. Let me see ... ah, yes. The victim was known as Gunther Emil Sondregger at his work and had been since the end of the war. Schäfer learned that the man's birth name was Heinrich Rudolf Gajewski, and that he was highly respected in the chemical aspects of the Nazi war machine working under top SS officials and the IG Farben conglomerate. I called in a number of important favors and arranged for *Kriminalkommissar* Schäfer to meet with the second-ranking ODESSA officer in Germany–Heinrich Kohler–who is a well-established executive of the WestBerlinImportExport Corporation. In fact, Kohler is the *Stellvertretender Direktor* [Deputy Director] there. Since then *Kriminalkommissar* Schäfer has been working with *Kriminalkommissar* Leopold Boehm, head of the FIU [Financial Intelligence Unit] of the *Bundespolitzei* and their very capable staffs. I believe it would be of considerable value to work with those teams in the *Bundespolitzei* and to avoid the rest of law enforcement in Deutschland, if you catch my drift."

"I very much value your candor, Friedrich; and I will tread lightly. My deputy in Germany is a fine officer by the name of Alina Hertzog. I will have her get in touch with Detective Schäfer and see if our combined resources can shed light on the murders."

"I would wish you luck—if I believed in luck, Eugène; so, I will hope for your success ... and for your safety. If there is anything else I can do as the investigation proceeds, let me know."

"Thank you, Friedrich, I will do that. And I will keep you posted as to our success."

"*Good luck on any of that,*" Chief von der Lippe muttered to himself after the telephone connection was severed.

Senior Detective Chief Superintendent Dentremont put down the phone and immediately dialed the *Landespolizei* [Bundeslandt State Police], Kripo division.

"*Landespolizei*, how may I direct your call?"

"*Kriminalpolitzei*, Detective Branch, please."

"Who may I say is calling, sir."

"Senior Detective Chief Superintendent Eugène Léon Dentremont, INTERPOL."

"Yes, sir, right away," the receptionist said.

It was always gratifying to hear or to see the response on his listener when he gave his full name and title. On a personal level Friedrich loathed the grandiosity of his or any other officer's title, but it often hastened the work along; so, he used his credentials to his maximum advantage more frequently than he cared to admit to himself.

"To whom would you like to speak, Senior Detective Chief Superintendent?"

"Detective Lieutenant Horst Schäfer, please."

Schäfer came on the line in less than two minutes.

"Yes sir, Senior Detective Chief Superintendent. This is Horst Schäfer. How may I be of service?"

"I believe we can serve each other in a common cause. First, however, could we dispense withthe cumbersome titles? I prefer to work with people using first names. Mine is Eugène. May I call you Horst?"

"Of course, Si … a … Eugène."

"I will be brief, Horst. This morning I received a call from a detective in Argentina related to a murder of an Argentinian citizen named Carlos Carlos Aguillara-Dominguez, aka Hörst Dietsel, formerly a German citizen and Nazi SS officer. I was informed by Chief von der Lippe in Wiesbaden that you were familiar with another similar case—that of Gunther Emil Sondregger aka Heinrich Rudolf Gajewski and were already well underway in an investigation that interests us at INTERPOL. We are most interested in Dietsel's and Gajewski's connection to the ODESSA, and Chief von der Lippe thought you were well ahead of me in that regard. Would you be willing to collaborate, Horst?"

"With enthusiasm, Eugène. However, I have to tell you that security will have to be extremely tight. I have had several warnings, some not so pleasant. We are treading on sensitive toes in this case."

"I understand fully. My deputy in Germany–Agent Alina Hertzog– is waiting for your call in our office in Berlin. I would appreciate it very much if you would contact her today, if that is possible. We have considerable resources we can offer to you and hope you are willing to share. INTERPOL is not interested in taking credit or usurping authority. We want these criminals brought to justice. If the ODESSA or a few Mafiosos along the way happen to fall into our net—well, all to the good."

"I am excited to collaborate, Eugène. I will call Alina as soon as we hang up."

"Then, don't let me cause you delay, Horst. Good bye."

Before Eugène could make his next call—to Adolf Henckel—his phone rang with a call from Moscow, which was a rarity in Eugène's long experience.

"Hello," he said, "this is Senior Detective Chief Superintendent Dentremont."

"Thank you for taking my call, Chief Superintendent. I am Lieutenant of *militsiya* Trushin Vasilyovich Stepanovich, the Moscow police officer in charge of the investigation into the murder of Lieutenant General of Cavalry Grigory Yegorivich Lagounov."

Eugène's interest was piqued immediately. Investigations had a way of taking on a life of their own; and if this call was related to the other murders, then "the thick was beginning to plotten," as he like to joke with his subordinates. They spoke English together, the common language between them.

"Please fill me on the details, and I will see if or how we can help, Lieutenant. Also, would it be all right if we used first names. It is easier to remember and to say Trushin and Eugène than to go through all of the titles."

"Thank you, sir. Russian names are difficult on the ears of people outside the Soviet Union; so, 'Trushin' may save us time as we work together."

Eugène liked the authoritative presumptiveness of the young man and was hopeful to have any new information be a valuable addition to the growing investigation.

"Ordinarily I would not consider this case to be within the purview of INTERPOL, Eugène; and, of course, the Soviet Union does not recognize INTERPOL—we have 'socialist legalism' as you know. There are officers above my position who would have my job in a minute if they knew that I was talking to you. The reason I want to collaborate about the murder of Gen. Lagounov is that my administrative assistant found newspaper articles from several countries which detailed murder cases very similar to ours. Maybe it is just a hunch, but I am becoming more and more convinced that we are seeing an international criminal conspiracy or linked crimes in multiple countries."

"I am inclined to agree with you, Trushin. Can you bring me up to date on what you have discovered so far in your case?"

"Certainly, and I assume you can make your findings available to me as well."

"Easier said than done, my friend, since the Soviet Union has not yet elected to join the rest of the world in sharing criminal record information. How can we go about this sharing?"

"My administrative assistant—*Militsiya* Private Lada Kornikova—is very capable of utilizing the new communications machines, and I think we can transmit written material by telex, telegraph, and Morse code apparatuses. She is also very much able to handle secrets properly. Do you have someone she can work with, Eugène?"

"I certainly do, Trushin. We are fully aware of the delicacy of communications between our two services; so, we will make every effort to keep transmissions strictly between us."

Eugène listened to the cacophony of telex, telegraph, and Morse code machines being operated by more than forty technicians in the large room outside his private office, and made his decision.

"I will have my senior technician, Forensic Specialist Marianne de la Reynie, contact your *Militisyi* Private Kornikova to begin the exchange of information. Would that be satisfactory for you?"

"Yes. However ... and this is a sensitive problem between our two services ... can we be certain that there will be no undue influence from the Nazi sympathizers remaining in your organization, Eugène?"

"Another officer would possibly be offended by your question, Trushin; but I am all too aware of the dark history of INTERPOL during the war. It is true that INTERPOL submitted to Nazi authorities in World War II and later refused to pursue war criminals. It is also true that INTERPOL has preferred to camouflage behind the rule that it must avoid all involvement in politics. There are some who still have that bias. I give you my word that I am in the business of pursuing criminals of all stripes and will not flinch in the least if we encounter Nazi criminals during our investigations. Do you feel that you can trust me, Trushin? Our association will hinge on our mutual trust."

"I do. But the test of our trust will come as we move along. You and I must have an open and candid communication at all times to deal with such questions. If you can agree to that, I will take the very considerable risks attached to my inclusion of your service into my investigation. I will hold nothing back. It is more than my life is worth to be betrayed to my superiors."

"I will protect you with every resource at my disposal, Trushin. My team is hand-picked with one requirement being that they–like me–are truly nonpolitical. Another requirement is that they must be highly professional and competent. Finally, they must be entirely loyal. For the past nearly twenty years, I have found my team to have an excellent record in all of those aspects."

"Good enough for me, Eugène. Let me start with a summary of our findings."

CHAPTER FORTY-EIGHT

Le Bureau Central National (BCN) d'INTERPOL pour la France [The International Criminal Police Organization, or INTERPOL], Office of Senior Detective Chief Superintendent Eugène Léon Dentremont, 200 Quai Charles de Gaulle, 69006 Lyon, France, August 30, 1962, later that same day

Lieutenant of *Militsiya* Trushin Vasilyovich Stepanovich had gone to considerable effort to prepare for this conversation with the senior detective chief superintendent of INTERPOL. He was fully aware of how much was at stake—mutual trust and security and conveying to the INTERPOL officer that he and his *MYC* [Moscow Criminal Investigations Department] were worthy of being considered to be a professional police department and not one that served as a puppet of the Soviet regime. He would be a dead man if it became known that he was entering into a partnership with a bourgeois capitalist organization with a dubious background with the Nazis. He determined to enter into the partnership fully and to accept the risks of his decision.

"We have begun inquiries in several directions, Eugène. Lada and Marianne can deal with the rather large quantities of background documentation separately."

"That sounds good, Trushin. We have extensive contacts around the world outside the Soviet Union, and already they are beginning to look into different areas of interest involved in the possibly connected murders internationally."

"So, Eugène, this is what we have learned.—I will spare you the details for the moment unless you ask questions: On October 9, 1961, Arkhangelskoye Military Convalescent Home, USSR, retired Lieutenant General of Cavalry Grigory Yegorivich Lagounov was murdered by a sword thrust during daylight hours. The murder itself was not witnessed, but several members of the Arkhangelskoye facility did see a stranger enter the general's room and close the door. Within minutes, Lagounov was found dead.

"Our investigation revealed that Lagounov had accumulated a very significant number of serious enemies during his career, which is not altogether unusual for a senior leader of the Soviet Union. We have narrowed the general categories to these: Lagounov served the revolution in a Workers' and Peasants' Red Army cavalry unit headed by Gen. Budenny before 1922 when he was just a boy. His first service was during the insurrection of General Alexey Maximovich Kaledin's Volunteer Army in the River Don region. There is not a White Russian living who does not know his name and who would not volunteer to kill the general if the opportunity were to arise.

"Another significant area where enemies developed was in the ranks of officers and enlisted personnel during his military activities. These included civilian and military victims of the 'Special Punitive Department or Extraordinary Commission' which he commanded before, during, and after the Great Patriotic War. Any student of real Soviet history since the revolution knows the motto of the Cheka troops—'Exhortation, Organization, and Reprisals'—was authored by Lagounov. He was the supervisor of innumerable atrocities while he was the head of the Cheka Special Punitive Brigades; there are serious men still living among Red Army officers who opposed his so-called 'shock troops' tactics during both the Great War and the Great Patriotic War because they violated the army's traditional fixed plans. His Cheka and shock troop men were considered to be no better than mere spies by some of the generals—a few still living. There were complaints about the high rate of casualties they suffered and blamed that on Captain Lagounov. When he learned of their discontent, the captain had the senior officers shot in front of the surviving troops as an object lesson. Hundreds or perhaps thousands of soldiers and their families were humiliated, tortured, and often murdered when Lagounov accused the soldiers of cowardice, slacking, and desertion.

"Literally millions of enemies were created during his tenure as the head NKVD German POW camps during the Red Army advance into Germany and as head of a special treatment gulag in Siberia. The West German government estimates the actual death toll of German POWs in the USSR at about 1.0 million. The last German POWs—those who were sentenced for war crimes—were released in 1956, and it is presumed that many of those who survived are still living in Eastern or Western Europe and are nursing intense grudges. There is one special subset of gulag victims to consider and that is the last group of Germans and Russians who were repatriated. They were arrested during the war–some before 1945–and kept as slaves in Siberia. They were assigned to special punitive conditions and were tortured and murdered by the scores. Some few are known to have survived. There were even a few Frenchmen who were part of Hitler's elite guard during the Battle of Berlin. Both the French and the Russians insist that all of them are dead, but there are some records that indicate that a very few may have lived long enough to be interned in the slave labor POW camps run by the Americans and French. There is no record of them after that."

"You are right about me having never heard of a French unit serving Hitler until today. The longer I live the more I learn about that terrible conflict. I am in hopes that you and Lada have been able to narrow the field better than millions of persons of interest, Trushin."

"We have tried, Eugène. The list is still lengthy; so, maybe it would be better to leave that to Lada and Marianne."

"My mind is already in a whirling haze, my friend. I think you are right about getting a committee to work on what you have unearthed. Congratulations. I look forward to our cooperative endeavor."

After they disconnected, Senior Superintendent Dentremont squeezed his temples and wondered what he had gotten himself into. He collected himself and put in his delayed call to Inspector Henckel in Córdoba.

"Hello, Adolf. This is Eugène. I have learned a few things and would like to convey those to you while they are still fresh on my mind."

"Thank you. I will take notes."

Dentremont filled Henckel in on the reported assassinations of French *Général de division*, Ret., Étienne Malboeuf in Paris, US Army General Glen Gabler, Ret., in Alaska, British Lieutenant General Sir Cyril Goeffrey Robert Hill-Brownwell, RA, Ret., in London, and

Lieutenant General of Cavalry Grigory Yegorivich Lagounov, Ret., in Moscow. He outlined his suggestions for the special investigations unit working out of INTERPOL headquarters in Lyon.

"I am not sure if you are familiar with our agent in Italy, Giuliano Pasqualone. He is a very fine cop and has several geniuses working in his analysis unit. Would you be willing to work with him to advance the investigation into both Paraguay and Argentina to get a clear vision of what motives might be driving Nazis and neo-Nazis to remove one of their own, or what other motives might be behind a connection of Nazis to your victim, Carlos Aguillara-Dominguez, aka Hörst Dietsel?"

"Of course, Eugène. Have him call me, and together we can get our two sets of geniuses into action. He will get to know my hand-picked unit: José Emanuel de Corsos, *Teniente Policía de la Provincia de Policía de Córdoba, PPC* [Detective, Police of the Province of Córdoba], Manuel de Jesus, *Sargentopolicíaprovbsas Policía de la Provincia de Córdoba, PPC* [Corporal, Police of the Province of Córdoba], and José Emanuel de Corsos, *Teniente Policía de la Provincia de Policía de Córdoba, PPC* [Detective, Police of the Province of Córdoba], Dr. Konrad Schmidt von Dresden, Córdoba Provincial Police Medical Examiner, and Gerhardt Möller, *Oficial de Policía* [Police Officer] *Policía de la Provincia de Córdoba, PPC.*"

"I can see that this is going to be a very complex case, Adolf. I think it best to have my office serve as the administration and communications center and to pool our findings. Does that meet with your approval, Inspector Henckel?"

"Yes, sir, Senior Superintendent."

The use of official titles made the agreement between gentlemen and friends formal.

Eugène's next call was to Axel Baird, the INTERPOL agent in charge in New York City.

"Hello, Axel. This is Eugène. I hope I'm not calling at an inconvenient time."

It was six-thirty in the evening Paris time and midday—twelve-thirty p.m. in Manhattan. Superintendent Baird was having a Spartan business lunch with his agents in the office conference room. Baird did not believe in fancy lunch or dinner meetings.

"Not at all, Eugène. We are just having our regular lunch meeting."

"That reminds me that I'm hungry; so, I'll make this brief. I have learned of the murder of a rather well-known retired American general—Glen Gabler. I am sure you are fully aware of it, but I doubt that the Amis have asked for INTERPOL assistance yet."

"True. So, how does this become an INTERPOL problem?" Alex asked.

"For most of the day today, I have been communicating with law enforcement officers in Moscow, Paris, Weisbaden, Córdoba; and I will call London as soon as we hang up. In brief, we have reason to suspect that the murder of Gen. Gabler may be linked to murders in all of those diverse cities. I will fill you in by telex; be warned, the transmission will be extensive. I would like you to get hold of the appropriate American police authorities to get them to cooperate with the investigation. We are willing to share everything we get and hope they will do the same.

"I am—indeed—familiar with the killing, Eugène. It took place in Alaska. It won't be difficult to make contact and to get cooperation with the Alaska State Troopers who are—no doubt—handling the investigation there. However, we will not be able to avoid the FBI; and who knows how they will react? They might want to take over the whole investigation. They will certainly want to make any arrests and to take full credit for any successes, you realize," Alex said with a shrug of resignation.

"And INTERPOL can take full credit for all failures, *Est-ce pas à peu près correct* [isn't that about correct]?" Eugène asked with a small Gallic laugh.

Axel's French was very good, and he replied in kind, "*Vous ne connaissez pas la moitié de celui-ci* [you don't know the half of it]."

"Our INTERPOL agents should have a conference call in a couple of days. Expect to hear from me, from Giuliano Pasqualone, Alina Hertzog, Marianne de la Reynie, and Roger Lahillonne soon. In the meantime, please get the Amis on board as much as possible and hand-pick a special unit of geniuses and people as discreet as monks to handle your end of things. As you may well imagine, we are entering into tiger country when we get Washington, Moscow, and the ever touchy French, to try to cooperate."

"I wouldn't trade you jobs for all the tea in China, Boss," Axel said.

The two men exchanged pleasantries about politics and family news then hung up to get on with the formidable tasks of the manhunt looming ahead.

Axel put in a call to the Regional Major Crimes Unit [MCU], Alaska Bureau of Investigation Post, Juneau, Alaska, as his first official act in the international investigation and manhunt for the killers of General Glen Gabler. He had been on two fishing expeditions to the frigid US territory and had met the chief of the state troopers and also Major Darrin Higgins, head of the Alaska MCU, on one of those trips. He asked for Higgins.

"Hello, Axel. Looking for another fishing trip?"

"I'm afraid not, Darrin. I have an INTERPOL investigation that should include you."

"Uh-oh, that sounds bad."

"The American part is undoubtedly well in hand by you already, Darrin. We have an interest in the murder of Gen. Glen Gabler."

"We're on it."

"Of course. May I ask if the FBI is also?"

"Not yet, but they'll be involved soon, I'm sure. The DOD is in it. I am partnered up with an Army CID detective by the name of Tucker Nicholsen. He's the SAC of the 83rd MP Det CID at Fort Richardson."

"I'm glad not to have to deal with the FBI right off the bat, I'll tell you that, Darrin. Let me tell you why we think INTERPOL should be involved."

He took a few minutes to tell the state trooper about the international implications of Gabler's murder—as much as he had gleaned from Eugène Dentremont.

"Sounds like a global conspiracy. That makes it a lot more interesting. I have no objections with cooperating with you, Axel. I can't speak for the fibbies."

"I have to call them as soon as we get off the line. Senior Superintendent Eugène Dentremont from the General Secretariat in Lyon, France, is heading up our end of things. With your okay, I'll have him telex the information to you and to SAC Tucker. Would you mind giving him a head's up?"

"I'll be glad to. I think he'll be happy to have the extra help. He's a good guy to work with and a very smart cop. I'll send you what we have found out so far."

"Thanks."

"I'll go you one further, Axel. I'll smooth the way to the FBI by getting together with a contact of mine in DC."

"I'll take any help I can get."

Darrin contacted Tucker Nicholsen at the base and told him about the call he had just received from INTERPOL about the projected manhunt. Tucker agreed to contact the Army and the DOD. Darrin's next call was largely a courtesy call, but hopefully one that would help prevent trouble with the ubersensitive FBI in the future.

"Department of Justice, main switchboard, how may I direct your call?"

"This is Major Darrin Higgins, chief officer of the major crimes unit, Alaska State Police in Juneau. Please connect me to Spencer Reynolds, assistant attorney general for the criminal division."

"Thank you, sir. I will connect you with the criminal division office." The pause was brief.

"Department of Justice, criminal division, office of the assistant attorney general."

"Thank you for taking my call. I have an international criminal issue which requires that I speak to the AAG himself."

"I'll see if he is available, Major Higgins."

Less than thirty seconds later, AAG Reynolds answered. "What can I do for you, Major?" the authoritative bassoprofundo voice asked; and the stage was set for the start of the greatest manhunt in the world's history.

INTERPOL Office Party Recipes

Cheese Fondue and *Fonduebourguignonne*—Serves 4
Traditional Swiss Cheese Fondue

Ingredients
-2 French sticks, cut into cubes, 1 garlic clove, 0.3 l dry white wine, 3 tsp corn flour or cornstarch, 400 g Vacherin Fribourgeois, 400 g Gruyere cheese, dash of kirsch, pepper to taste.

Preparation
-Peel and crush the garlic, rub it round the *caquelon* [a special ceramic pot with a small burner underneath it to keep the fondue at constant temperature]. Dissolve the cornstarch in the kirsch. Pour the wine into the caquelon, add the grated cheese, and melt together carefully on a very low heat on the kitchen cooker, stirring continuously with a wooden spatula. Add the kirsch (cherry brandy) and the pepper.
-Transfer to the serving stand, whose burner should be kept at a steady temperature.

-To eat the fondue: you need special fondue equipment, consisting of a heavy pan (*caquelon*) and a special stand containing a burner with an adjustable flame. Spear the cubes of bread on forks (preferably specially designed long fondue forks), and dip them in the cheese, stirring all the time to prevent the mixture from sticking on the bottom of the pan. Be extra careful not to let your bread drop off your fork.

Fonduebourguignonne

Ingredients
4 cps vegetable oil or mix of vegetable and olive oils, 8 oz beef tenderloin cut into small cubes or strips, 8 oz chicken breast, boneless and skinless, cut into small cubes or strips, 1 tbsp extra virgin olive oil, salt and pepper to taste, ¾ cp ground pork, ½ tsp minced garlic, 1 tsp minced shallots, 1 egg yolk, 1 tsp mustard, 4 small red-skinned potatoes quartered and cooked until tender, ½ cp each of 3 sauces~Aioli, barbecue sauce, Bearnaise and/or horseradish cream)

Preparation
- Heat oil in a fondue pot or 2-quart saucepan at 375ºF until very hot.
-While oil is heating, cut beef and chicken, toss with olive oil, and season with salt and pepper. Combine pork with garlic, shallots, egg yolk and mustard, and form into tiny meat balls. Decoratively arrange meats, meatballs, and potatoes on a large platter, or on 4 individual plates. Arrange sauces in individual dipping bowls or plates.
-Place fondue pot of oil in center of table over a small candle or sterno, and adjust flame so that it bubbles but does not sputter when meat is added. Spear meat, meatball, or potato on long metal or wooden forks or skewers, place in pot and cook 20–30 seconds until crispy. Remove meat from fork before eating; fork will be burning hot.

Traditional Swiss Raclette—Serves 4

Ingredients
-8 small/medium potatoes, skin on, 1½ lb Raclette Cheese, *Buendnerfleisch* (cut in paper-thin slices),1 jar pickled gherkin cucumbers (cornichons), 1 jar pickled onions, freshly ground pepper, and paprika to taste

Preparation
-You must have a raclette grill or raclette melter.
-Wash potatoes and boil in a pot filled with salted water~20 min. Test with a knife to see if the potatoes are done. Keep warm until ready to use in an insulated potato basket.
-In the meantime remove the rind of the cheese and cut into 1/16 in. thick slices using an adjustable wire slicer.

-Arrange gherkins, onions, and *Buendnerfleisch* on a platter and set aside until required.

-Turn raclette on to begin to heat up (allow for at least 5 mins. before using).

-To serve: For Raclette grills: Each guest takes a slice of cheese, places it in their pan, and slides it under the raclette grill to melt. It takes approximately 2 mins. to melt to a creamy consistency and 3 mins. for a crispier top. Remove the pan from under the grill once it's reached its preferred consistency and hold the pan onto its side to scrape the cheese out, using your wooden spatula. Place a potato on your plate and cut it into a few pieces and eat it and the *Buendnerfleisch* with cheese. Gherkins and onions are added taste ticklers.

-To serve: For Raclette melters: Each guest prepares potatoes and side dishes on their plates. When the cheese starts melting on the wheel, scrape the cheese onto the plate. Season to taste with freshly ground pepper and paprika.

Swiss Chocolate Roll Cake

Ingredients
3 eggs, ½ cup caster sugar, ¼ cup plain flour, 2 tbsps cocoa, 1 cp heavy cream, 1 tbsp icing sugar (plus extra to dust), ½ tsp vanilla essence

Preparation
-Preheat oven to moderately hot~395º F. Lightly grease a Swiss roll tin (12 x 10 in.) and line the base with baking paper, extending the edges over the two long sides.

-Beat the eggs and ⅓ cp of the caster sugar with electric beaters until thick and creamy. Using a metal spoon, gently fold in the combined sifted flour and cocoa. Spread the mixture into the tin and smooth the surface.

-Bake for 10–12 mins, or until the cake is just set.

-Meanwhile, place a clean tea towel on a work surface, cover with baking paper and sprinkle with the remaining caster sugar. When the cake is cooked, turn it out immediately onto the sugar. Roll the cake up from the short side to roll the paper inside the cake. Stand the rolled cake on a wire rack for 5 mins., then carefully unroll and allow the cake to cool to room temperature.

-Beat the cream, icing sugar, and vanilla essence until stiff peaks form. Spread the cream over the cake, leaving a ½ in. border all the way around. Reroll the cake (without the paper). Place the cake seam-side down onto serving tray.

-Refrigerate until serving—dust with extra icing sugar before serving. Cut into slices to serve. A little vanilla or dark chocolate ice cream wouldn't be bad with this famous dish either.

CHAPTER FORTY-NINE

United States Department of Justice, Office of the Assistant Attorney General, Criminal Division, 950 Pennsylvania Avenue, NW, Washington, DC, August 30, 1962, 12:35 p.m.

"We have a situation here in Alaska that has now become an international criminal issue," Major Higgins said.

He told AAG Reynolds about the call from INTERPOL.

Reynolds told him, "The FBI director and I have had several conversations about the murder of Gen. Gabler. We have been getting regular updates through the DOD from the SAC of the MP Det CID at Fort Richardson, and have been debating whether or not to offer the services of the FBI."

"Technically, SAC Nicholsen is the lead investigator in Gabler's murder, and I think he is doing an excellent job. He and I are more or less acting as partners and have done a fair amount of investigation on our own. The involvement of the Senior Detective Chief Superintendent of INTERPOL has altered the landscape, to say the least. As of this morning, Nicholsen and I have conceded the lead in the wider case to INTERPOL because we are convinced that they have the best and the most up-to-the-minute global information. Frankly, Mr. AAG, all of us are more than a bit leery about getting the FBI involved because of their history of riding roughshod over other law enforcement agencies, and this is a case that cries out for delicacy and sensitivity," Higgins said.

"Political correctness?"

"You could phrase it that way; but to be accurate, it is more about getting the job done before anymore senior officers fall victim; and everyone involved in the investigations in four or five countries wants to avoid publicity or domination. If the FBI is to be involved, then they will have to curb their enthusiasm for making appearances in the news and from tromping on the toes of people who won't put up with it."

Reynolds laughed. "I don't have any quibble with your descriptions or with your concerns, Major Higgins. There are three things working in your favor here. First, we have a new director of the bureau; second, I am his boss; and third—and the trump card—I am in agreement with you about how this case should be handled.

"What does your gut tell you about whether or not this is a huge conspiracy as opposed to a group of murders with some similarities but no genuine or provable connection, Major?"

"It's too soon to be sure of that, Sir;but the red flags are there: major WW2 players murdered by individuals or organizations with serious resources and manpower and similar modus operandi. I have been at the law enforcement business for my entire adult life, and have investigated murders for the majority of that time. My gut says this is bigger than just the killing—maybe assassination—of an important American general. If my gut is right, I don't think we've heard the last of this."

"I'm inclined to agree with you, Major, much as it pains me to say so. If you won't consider me to be presumptuous, maybe it would be best for me to get together with Director Gaines. I think it might smooth the way and protect the sensitivities of the French, the Argentines, the Germans, the British, and the Soviets, of all people."

"I would appreciate your help, and I think I can answer for my boss on this global investigation. I don't know if you know Senior Superintendent Dentremont. He is a cop's cop and a brilliant investigator and administrator. He never seeks personal publicity and would probably be all right with the FBI taking credit when all is said and done. Back to my gut: it tells me that any credit should be parcelled out to the cops in each of the involved countries. That would go a long ways toward present and future relations."

"I will bear that in the front of my mind throughout my discussions with Warren Gaines, who is not a bad sort, by the way. Let's keep in touch."

"Yes, sir. Might I suggest that we use the INTERPOL main head-quarters in Lyon as the central information center? That way, we are less likely to have personality and nationality clashes which would hinder the work."

"Major Higgins, you sound like a seasoned politician/law enforce-ment officer who is headed for bigger and better things," AAG Reynolds said with a quiet low chuckle.

"Perish forbid, sir. I am just a simple trooper turned large. Being head of the criminal division in Alaska is exactly where I want to be. I have no ambitions to turn up in Washington and being eaten alive."

Several communications and events occurred within the next few min-utes. AAG Spencer Reynolds had a long talk with DFBI Warren Brent Gaines who reluctantly agreed to be involved with the INTERPOL investigation but only after a few unkind descriptors of "that Nazi sym-pathizing bunch of froggies" and a surly pouting vocalization made to his superior in the DOJ about not being the least bit happy about "playing second fiddle in any investigation." And a muttered sotto voce that "we'll see how that goes."

New York City INTERPOL Superintendent Axel Baird did–indeed–find the way smoothed to have useful conversation with the DFBI. Axel agreed to drive up to Washington, DC, that afternoon to set the man-hunt in motion with the United States fully involved. Axel reported to his superior, Senior Chief Superintendent Dentremont, who received the news with pleasure but was inclined to keep his feelings about the US FBI close to his vest.

Eugène arranged with his secretary to hold a conference call to France with himself, Marianne de la Reynie, and Pierre Papon on his staff, Superintendent Guy Mutz of the Paris INTERPOL office in the western suburb of St. Cloud in Paris, and *Enquêteur* [Detective Inspector] Grégoire Laurent De Vincent and his assistant, Gendarmerie Lieutenant Sylvain Piétri, Research Unit Officer in Paris.

"Thank you for taking our call, Detective Inspector and Superintendent. Before we start, would it be all right if we used first names? The titles and last names are so cumbersome."

Everyone agreed.

"My secretary informed you of the purpose of our call. In brief, we have reason to believe that the murder you are investigating—that of retired *Général de division* Étienne Malboeuf may be part of a much larger conspiracy and a series of murders of similarly prominent individuals. If we are correct, it seems self-evident that cooperation with each other would be mutually beneficial."

"We here in Paris are inclined to agree," De Vincent said in his usual laconic fashion.

"Please do us the favor of bringing all of us up to date on that unfortunate crime."

Grégoire gave as thorough a presentation as he could while still as brief as necessary.

"On fifteen August 1962, General Malboeuf was shot to death in broad daylight with a crowd of people watching in the Jardin du Luxembourg Park in Paris. He died of a single gunshot wound to his back. We believe there was only one killer, but witness evidence varies considerably. Some witnesses claim more than one, and there is no consensus on a description of the murderer or murderers. There are people who described the killer as a black or Moroccan man, some an older limping man, some even a blond woman. He was seen as tall, short, old, young, male, or female. The most common description was of an older man in a gray morning suit wearing a large fedora.

"My staff has done a considerable amount of effort to delve into Gen. Malboeuf's life to determine if he had enemies or others with reason to kill him. He had a mistress who was well known to his wife of many decades; so, there is the potential for a motive involving jealousy. He had children who stand to inherit his considerable fortune. He was a career army general who accumulated virulent enemies along the way. Those included soldiers who considered his disciplinary measures to be overly harsh and the remnants of a German SS army division manned entirely by expatriate Frenchmen. There are rumors of atrocities connected with the surrender of members of that division, and it is not outside the realm of possibility that family members of that division have carried grudges for all of these years since the war's end. Following the war, he was active in the efforts to track down Nazis and Nazi sympathizers; so, the ODESSA probably harbors keen resentment against our murder victim.

"Those areas of inquiry have not been leading us anywhere as yet, but we are beginning to focus our attention on his postwar activities in Algeria—in the unfortunate Algerian war. I presume you are well familiar with that debacle."

His listeners made brief replies to assure him that they—like everyone in France—were all too familiar.

"I will spare you the details except to say that the general was stationed in Algeria in the mid-1950s and early 1960s when forces for independence from France—largely the FLN [National Liberation Front]—launched the Algerian War of Independence. That uprising pitted the nation of France against the fighters associated with the several independence movements. The vicious struggle lasted from 1954 to 1962 and finally resulted in Algeria gaining its independence. Gen. Malboeuf and his fellow senior officers pledged themselves to defending the honor of France—as they perceived it—to the bitter end. The war—like many civil and revolutionary conflicts—descended into barbarity and produced thousands of lasting examples of personal and group-defined enmities. Gen. Malboeuf and many of his colonial compatriots entered into the civil war between loyalist Algerians supporting a French Colonial Algeria and insurrectionist Algerian Muslim fighters. The conflict shook the foundations of the French Fourth Republic (1946–58) and led to its eventual collapse and a legacy of enmity.

"President De Gaulle finally decided that the war in Algeria could not be defended politically on the international stage. Finally, he announced that France would no longer contest the colony's eventual independence. Gen. Malboeuf very publically voiced his anger and his sense that Frenchmen and the army were deeply offended. The French settlers and the French city-dwellers—joined by the dissident members of the army—were so enraged that they staged two armed uprisings. Reluctantly de Gaulle sent regular army units and fanatical foreign Legionnaires—which included remnants of the German POWs who had no homes to which they could return—to the colony to suppress the settlers and troops. During the second uprising, in April, 1961—with Gen. Malboeuf as one of the principal leaders—a threat of invasion of France itself was raised in what came to be known as the Generals' Putsch, as you well know. Rebel paratroops landed on French soil. Retaliation was swift, excessively brutal, and decisive. In the Paris massacre of 1961—De Gaulle's government and police machine gunned dissidents and herded them into the River Seine to drown. The Algerian rebels and angry colonial soldiers made several attempts on de Gaulle's life.

"The massacre and the assassination attempts were kept secret for some time. De Gaulle won decisively and was then faced with the thorny issue of what to do with the French generals in Algeria who had defied him in armed conflict. De Gaulle was a thoroughly unforgiving man, but also a pragmatist. His overwhelming victory could easily have been capped by executions or other draconian punishments visited upon his officers. He knew—however—that reprisals would expose to the world and to his own people the fragmentation of the French armed forces and would explode the myth of French honor and cohesiveness.

Against the advice of many of his senior officers who had remained loyal, President de Gaulle decided to show leniency ... with a price. Every Algerian officer of the rebellion who preferred life over execution chose to resign his commission, to retire into silent obscurity, to foreswear any political activities for the rest of his life, and to accept a subsistence-level pension. Gen. Malboeuf was one of those.

"His life depended on his silence, and so he kept quiet and chose obscurity over the chance of almost certain death for ever speaking out. Gaullists retaliated against many of the old-guard army men and searched them out. Many were taken away and disappeared over the next few years; a few had unfortunate and unexplained accidents; and a few were frankly murdered with the murders never solved. Our working hypothesis is that Malboeuf was likely one of the casualties. We have something more than just policemen's hunches. Malboeuf's mistress reported a visit by one of de Gaulle's administration figures—a man named Louis Charles de la Reynie. Ring a bell?"

"We are all familiar with de la Reynie. A rough character, reputed to do some of the president's dirty work," Eugène remarked.

"Another man mentioned by the mistress may prove to be a problem for us all. I have to be certain that what is said here is kept in strictest confidence."

"You have my word."

"The man is one you certainly know: Jean-Baptiste Berryer."

Berryer was the sitting lieutenant general of police, the commander of all police forces in France.

"My associate and I warned the mistress that she would do well to be careful of that man who has the ear of de Gaulle and a reputation as a most political and unforgiving man. We should all know to tread lightly."

Unseen by De Vincent, all of the listeners on the conference lines nodded their heads in agreement.

"One other man was mentioned by the mistress: Louis Thiroux d'Albert, whom she described as an ugly man with a deep scar on his left cheek and walks with a limp. At a reception for old veterans in Lyon, this d'Albert warned Gen. Malboeuf not to attend any more army gatherings. He told the general and his mistress that they were being watched, and the president might consider any further such attendance to be a violation of his promise not to associate with officers in public or private. It was the last army function the general ever attended."

Louis Thiroux d'Albert was indeed a shadowy figure, and a man well known to INTERPOL. He was the head of de Gaulle's intelligence service—the BCRA, or as it later became known—the SDECE [*Service de documentation extérieure et de contre-espionnage*, the Foreign Documentation and Counter-Espionage Service]—and a man more to be feared than Berryer or anyone else in government except de Gaulle himself. D'Albert was known to be—but seldom mentioned—the most senior officer in the SDECE, and one of the most feared individuals in French history.

Eugène asked only one other question, "Our brief research suggests that the esteemed general might have had dealings with organized crime, many members of whom sympathized with the Algerian generals against the Gaullists. Anything to add on that, Grégoire?"

"The general's wife suggested—and his mistress confirmed—that there was interaction between the general and perhaps his two sons and a Corsican syndicate criminal named Benedettu Paganucci. Seems that the mistress had previously had an affair with Paganucci. She insisted that the parting was amicable, which would seem to be the case since the general is known to have had business dealings with the Corsicans after he took up with the former mistress of the gangster. We haven't ruled a gang killing out, but we don't have any useful evidence."

Haute Cuisine or Grande Cuisine Recipes

Note: *Haute cuisine* is characterized by meticulous preparation and elaborate, artful, and careful presentation of food by skilled chefs or teams of chefs— usually at a commensurately high price level—and accompanied by expensive wines. Georges Auguste Escoffier is credited with the change from regular French to *haute* [high] dining in 1900, which became known as *cuisine classique*.

Julia Potatoes—Serves 6-8

Ingredients
-2¼ lb peeled potatoes, 5 tbsp goose or duck fat, 6 cloves of chopped garlic, pinch of sea salt, pinch of ground peppercorns, parsley for garnish.

Preparation
-Slice potatoes as thinly as possible, no more than ¼ in. thick.
-Melt 2 tbsp of goose or duck fat in a large saucepan, adding potatoes and a pinch of salt once hot. -Allow to simmer for 30 mins., turning occasionally with a spatula.
-Add in an additional 1 tbsp of goose or duck fat, along with chopped garlic, and cover for 2–3 mins. or until browned.
-Serve potatoes sprinkled lightly with salt, ground pepper, and parsley.

Ratatouille

Ingredients
¼ cp extra-virgin olive oil, 1 large onion chopped into chunks, 3 minced garlic cloves, 1 small red bell pepper, 1 small yellow bell pepper, and 1 small green bell pepper, all cut into 1 in. squares, 1½ pounds fresh tomatoes coarsely chopped (leave in skins and seeds), 1 small can tomato paste, ½ tsp dried thyme, ½ tsp dried rosemary, 1 tsp dried basil, 1 dried bay leaf, 1 tsp salt, ½ tsp pepper, 1 med. unpeeled eggplant, cut into chunks, 2 average-sized unpeeled zucchini, cut into chunks.

Preparation
-Heat oil in a large pot with a heavy bottom over med. heat. Add onions and sauté until translucent, then add garlic and cook for an additional min. Once onions are a light golden color, add peppers and cook for five mins.
-Mix in tomatoes, tomato paste, thyme, rosemary, basil, bay leaves, salt, and pepper. Then add eggplant and zucchini and cook for~5 mins.
-Reduce heat to low, cover and simmer until vegetables are tender~30 mins. Remove bay leaf.

Sole Meunière

Ingredients
-½ cp all-purpose flour, Kosher salt and freshly ground black pepper, 4 fresh sole fillets 3–4 oz each, 6 tbsps unsalted butter, 1 tsp grated lemon zest, 6 tbsps—3 lemons—freshly squeezed lemon juice, 1 tbsp minced fresh parsley.

Preparation
-Preheat the oven to 200º F. Have 2 heat-proof dinner plates ready
-Combine flour, 2 tsps salt, and 1 tsp pepper in a large shallow plate. Pat the sole fillets dry with paper towels and sprinkle one side with salt.
-Heat 3 tbsps butter in a large (12-inch) saute pan over medium heat until it starts to brown. Dredge 2 sole fillets in the seasoned flour on both sides and place them in the hot butter. Lower the heat to medium-low and cook for 2 mins. Turn carefully with a metal spatula and cook for 2 mins. on the other side.
-While the second side cooks, add ½ tsp lemon zest and 3 tbsps lemon juice to the pan. Carefully put the fish fillets on the ovenproof plates and pour the sauce over them. Keep the cooked fillets warm in the oven while you repeat the process with the remaining 2 fillets. When they're done, add the cooked fillets to the plates in the oven. Sprinkle with the parsley, salt, and pepper and serve immediately.

Classic French Soufflé

Ingredients
-Melted butter, to grease, dried (packaged) breadcrumbs, to dust, 50 g (~⅓ cp butter), 40 g (¼ cp) plain flour, 1 cp milk, 1½ cps coarsely grated vintage cheddar cheese, 4 eggs, separated.

Preparation
-Preheat oven to 375° F. Place a baking tray in oven. Grease a 6-cp capacity ovenproof dish with butter. Dust with breadcrumbs.
-Heat butter in a saucepan over medium heat until foaming. Cook flour, stirring for 2 mins. or until it bubbles and comes away from the side. Remove from heat. Gradually whisk in half the milk until mixture is smooth. Gradually whisk in remaining milk until smooth and combined. Whisk over medium heat for 3–4 mins. or until sauce boils and thickens. Add cheddar and stir until cheddar melts and mixture is smooth.
-Remove saucepan from heat. Quickly whisk in egg yolks until well combined. Transfer the mixture to a large bowl. Use an electric beater to beat egg whites in a clean, dry bowl until firm peaks form. Be careful not to overbeat the egg whites. Add ⅓ of egg white to cheddar mixture. Use a large metal spoon to fold. Repeat, in two more batches, with the remaining egg white.
-Spoon into prepared dish. Run your finger around the inside rim of the dish. Place on preheated baking tray. Bake for 25–30 mins. or until golden.

French Parisian Bistro Steak Tartare

Ingredients
-3 med. oil-packed, rinsed and minced anchovy fillets (adjust salt if added), 2 tsps brined and rinced capers, 3 tsps Dijon mustard, 2 lg egg yolks, 10 oz prime beef tenderloin cut into small dices, cover and refrigerate, 2 tbsps red onion and

2 tbsps Italian parsley leaves all finely chopped, 4 tsps olive oil, 3 dashes Tabasco sauce, 4 dashes Worcestershire sauce, ¾ tsp crushed chile flakes.

Preparation

-Keep beef covered and refrigerated until you are ready to use it. Combine anchovies, capers, and mustard in a nonreactive bowl. Using a fork or the back of a spoon, mash ingredients until evenly combined; mix in egg yolks.

-Use a rubber spatula to fold remaining ingredients into mustard mixture until thoroughly combined. Season well with salt and freshly ground black pepper. Serve immediately with toast points or French fries.

CHAPTER FIFTY

Headquarters, Metropolitan Police Service/New Scotland Yard, Criminal Investigation Department [CID], Victoria Embankment, August 31, 1962

Eugene's next call in the series was made the following day to New Scotland Yard, where he asked to speak to Detective Chief Inspector Lincoln Crandall-White, the New Scotland Yard senior homicide detective who had the lead in another recent case—the murder of Lieutenant-General Sir Cyril Goeffrey Robert Hill-Brownwell, RA, Ret.

"This is Crandall-White," the detective answered crisply—his usual professional telephone pattern.

"Thank you for taking my call, Detective Chief Inspector. I am Eugène Dentremont, Senior Detective Chief Superintendent of INTERPOL. I am calling in regards to your investigation of General Hill-Brownwell. I believe I can be of some help."

"How would that be, Senior Detective Chief Superintendent?"

"Before we get down to details, would it be possible to do this on a first name basis, Inspector? The titles are awkward and tedious, in my opinion."

"Efficiency is always best. My name is Lincoln, but people who know me call me, Linc."

"I am Eugène."

"What do you have for us, Eugène?"

"I will be very brief on the phone, Linc, but I can telex a ream of material on a series of murders that may well be related to yours. Would that be all right?"

"Of course. And I presume you intend the information to be kept in confidence?"

"Indeed, as both of us do in police matters; but especially in this case. I have recently learned of murders in Argentina, France, Germany, the USSR, and the United States that are very similar to yours. It is entirely possible that there are more to be found as we go along. While there are almost infinite possibilities that could be part of the cases and almost that many persons of interest, we at INTERPOL have formed a loosely arranged committee of fellow police officers to winnow down the field and to make all of our investigations more manageable. This is what we have learned thus far that seems to have pertinence to all of the cases."

Inspector Dentremont gave Detective Chief Inspector Crandall-White a succinct description of each of the murders and of the history of the victims—all of whom seemed to have made a great many enemies during their careers. He stressed the tentativeness of the information dredged up during the investigations in the several countries, but gave Linc the benefit of his long law enforcement experience's hunch.

"I think the main thread is something that happened during or especially shortly after the war. There may be ties to organized crime; but, more likely, these killings are assassinations related to war time or to POW experiences. We are not neglecting the mountain of evidence that is accumulating about multiple avenues of investigation, but our group is moving in the direction of the military careers holding the secrets that are most germaine to all of our inquiries."

"And you would like us Brits to join you with INTERPOL as the lead, is that about it?"

"Only as a central clearing house. We will serve and not be in the news, if you get my meaning. We have no desire or need to take credit or to interfere. I think a brief chat with some of your mates in the law enforcement community around the world will confirm how I work."

"I am aware, Eugène. Your reputation precedes you, and we will be happy to join you. What can I do now?"

"Please bring me up to date on your case thus far, and then telex the larger amount of details to my office in Lyon. When you finish your communication, I will give you the name of my people who are receiving and collating the information and will ask that you get them in touch with one individual on your team who can link up with us. We want to keep this as tidy as possible."

"All right Eugène, on the twenty-first of August, last, a call came in to the CID at the Metropolitan Police Service/New Scotland Yard reporting a witnessed murder in an exclusive men's establishment—the London Army and Navy Club. As the name implies, it caters almost exclusively to military men—both past and current. As the detective chief inspector, I was assigned the case. DI Angela Snowden, DI Anthony Bourden-Clift, and I proceeded directly to the London club. There we found an elderly male victim, identified as Lieutenant-General Sir Cyril Goeffrey Robert Hill-Brownwell, RA, Ret. We interviewed an eyewitness, Major Algernon Donelly, and learned that the general was assassinated with an ice pick to his brain by a man the major presumed was one of the help because he was dressed in the uniform of the club attendant staff. Major Donelly attempted to capture the assailant, but was knocked unconscious in the struggle. The killer was not seen by anyone else and was not apprehended.

"We interviewed the only other person in the establishment—the majordomo—a man named Clifford Brewster. He informed us that he did not really know the general personally. However, in his capacity as a senior servant at the club for more than ten years, he did pick up a nugget or two from the other members, and the majordomo himself had a history of having suffered a serious setback to his career by the actions of the general. He clearly had reason to resent the man. Overall, Gen. Hill-Brownwell was not popular, not well thought of. Brewster learned that the general served on the western front in the first war, and one member confronted him in Brewster's presence some years back for his behind-the-lines service. The gist of the heated conversation was that the lieutenant general was quick to order men to charge out of their trenches to what he must have known were near-suicidal and futile attacks, and the men serving under him despised the man. Sir Hill-Brownwell's response was a counter accusation—essentially that the man confronting him might well be one of the cowards who had conspired to assassinate him as the commander. The staff had to come between the two. Sir Hill-Brownwell's position in the club was of such an elevated nature that his accuser was forced to resign.

"Our investigation turned up the name of the accuser—an elderly former colonel by the name of Matthew Templeton. Unfortunately, Templeton died nearly five years ago. Along that same line, the majordomo reported overhearing conversations among the enlisted men who frequented the same pubs as him. He gleaned enough to know that Sir Hill-Brownwell was a highly unpopular officer in both wars. The general gist was that the man enjoyed his comforts in the safety of his command post while keeping well out of harm's way, if you get my drift. He was deemed to be reckless with the lives of the men in the ranks. In addition, he was deemed to be an extremely harsh disciplinarian, even an unfair one by many officers and enlisted alike.

"Our questioning of Major Donelly revealed an area of interest, one that we are actively pursuing at present. He and the general both served in the postwar occupation internment camps for German POWs. It was the major's opinion that the general had little sympathy for the German prisoners. They had returned from Soviet prison camps, and the general was of the opinion that the 'huns'—as he always insisted on calling them—deserved every ill treatment they received. On more than one occasion–according to the major–Gen. Hill-Brownwell's stated purpose in dealing with the POWs was to ensure that they would never to be allowed to occupy significant positions in the new Germany being created by the Allies."

"I presume you have followed up on that lead," Eugène commented.

"Indeed. We learned—to our chagrin and shame as a matter-of-fact—that the British-run camps like those of the Americans and the French were no better than the Nazi camps or the Soviet gulags. We have delved into that sordid subject sufficiently to be convinced that any survivors would prime persons of interest to our investigation. All of the camps kept good records, which is surprising given the nature of the conditions existing there. We are quite certain of the names of those men who entered the camps; but the death rate was high; and it is not quite so clear which of those men were alive when the camps were finally closed in the late fifties.

"We do have a list, but it is undoubtedly incomplete. The most difficult part of the investigation is locating the whereabouts of the released men today. We have succeeded in locating approximately thirty-two hundred of them, and are going through the tedium of contacting every one of them. We are less than a quarter of the way through the task."

"Any names catch your attention?"

"A few we have not been able to trace after the final release. It is as if they vanished into thin air. Our attention was drawn to several SS officers with French names, which seemed odd to us. They had all been interned in a couple of those especially wretched gulags in far north Siberia and were among the very few who survived what our Soviet 'allies' termed 'special treatment.' I have a list of those men whom we intend to track down if it is possible. It should be interesting to learn what they are about. I will telex the list as soon as I can find it in the pile of clutter on my desk. Neatness is DI Snowden's forte, not mine. I will probably have to enlist her help as I usually do. She is indispensable."

Eugène laughed. "I know what you mean. I would be lost without my senior INTERPOL technician, Forensic Specialist Marianne de la Reynie. She maintains my sanity at the office the same way my wife keeps me from complete chaos at home. We are of the opinion from several of our investigators that you may well be on a productive track. Keep me posted through Marianne; she is the central data coordinator for now. At the rate information is coming in, we will have to hire a significantly larger staff pretty soon. Thank you for your cooperation, Linc. We will talk again soon."

After the conversation, Linc sat lost in thought and pondered the ramifications of his conversation with the INTERPOL superintendent. It was his way to think a problem through thoroughly, weighing and analyzing every scrap of information. His critics believed that he was prone to overthinking and were annoyed by his periodic lapses of attention to them and to their brilliant discoveries. Detective Chief Inspector Lincoln Crandall-White was professorial in appearance and in his thought processes. He was the quintessential Oxford tweedy, tieless, brown- or gray-shirted, wool pants, and brogans, thinker and lecturer. He seldom spoke unless he had something to say, and that something was usually directly on target to open an avenue of investigation in a fruitful direction. When asked for his opinion, he almost always came back with the nut of the issue and the investigation.

He was forty-seven years old, had bushy gray-brown hair, eyebrows, mustache and sideburns, and intense riveting eyes partly because one of them was hazel and the other blue. He used his unusual eyes skillfully to keep his listener looking at his face and then hearing what he had to say. The first thing his thinking produced at this point in time was that this investigation could either be the making of his career or a colossal international failure which would force his retirement. Linc was not inclined overmuch towards caution, and he vowed to pursue his case and its relationship to the other murders until the truth—the whole truth—was known. For the moment, it was time for lunch.

British Pub Recipes

Welsh Rarebit

Ingredients
-2 tbsps unsalted butter, 2 tbsps all-purpose flour, 1 tsp Dijon mustard, 1 tsp Worcestershire sauce, ½ tsp kosher salt, ½ tsp freshly ground black pepper, ½ cp porter beer, ¾ cp heavy cream, 6 oz (~1½ cps) shredded Cheddar cheese, 2 drps hot sauce, 4 slices toasted rye bread.

Preparation
-In a medium saucepan over low heat, melt the butter and whisk in the flour. Cook, whisking constantly for 2–3 mins., being careful not to brown the flour.
-Whisk in mustard, Worcestershire sauce, salt, and pepper until smooth. Add beer and whisk to combine. Pour in cream and whisk until well-combined and smooth.
-Gradually add cheese, stirring constantly until cheese melts and sauce is smooth; this will take 4–5 mins. Add hot sauce. Pour over toast; garnish with bacon, diced tomatoes, and chives before serving.

Ploughman's Lunch

Ingredients
-1 tbsp kosher dill relish, assorted English cheeses: Cotswold, Huntsman, Stilton, Shropshire Blue, English Cheddar, substantial chunk of crusty bread, pickled onions, bull pickled onions, assorted cold cuts like Black Forest Ham and pâtés, a variety of sliced apples, several hard-boiled and pickled eggs, and a pint of good dark English ale.

Preparation: Eat and drink.

Shepherd's Pie

Ingredients
3 lg peeled and quartered potatoes, 1 stick salted butter, 1½ cps onion, 1–2 cps diced carrots, corn, peas mixture, 1½ lbs lean ground sirloin, ½ cp beef broth, 1 tsp Worcestershire, salt, pepper, garlic, hot sauce to taste.

Preparation

-Place the peeled and quartered potatoes in medium-sized pot and cover with 1+ in. cold water. Add tsp salt and bring to a boil, reduce to a simmer, and cook until tender.

-While the potatoes are cooking, melt 4 tbsps butter in a large sauté pan on med. heat. Add chopped onions and cook until tender. Add vegetables separately (best to cook them individually according to their cooking times to achieve al dente firmness).

-Add ground beef to the pan with the onions and vegetables. Cook until no longer pink. Season with salt and pepper. Add the Worcestershire and beef broth. Bring the broth to a simmer and reduce heat to low. Cook uncovered for 10 mins. Add more beef broth at intervals to prevent meat from drying out.

-When the potatoes are done cooking (soft), remove them from the pot and place them in a bowl with the remaining 4 tbsps butter. Mash and season with salt and pepper to taste.

-Preheat oven to 400° F. Spread the beef, onions, and vegetables in an even layer in a large baking dish and spread mashed potatoes over the top of the ground beef. Rough up the surface of mashed potatoes with a fork so there are peaks that will get well-browned.

-Sprinkle grated cheddar cheese over the top of the mashed potatoes before baking. Cook in oven at 400° F until potatoes are brown and bubbling~30 min. May have to broil for the last few mins. to help the surface of the mashed potatoes brown. Serve hot with stout British ale (wine is for sissies).

CHAPTER FIFTY-ONE

Corporate Offices of European International Conglomerate, No. 13 Upper Belgrave Street, London, August 22, 1962

Antoine was growing increasingly concerned about the health of his friend, Michaele. Michaele walked about like an old man—older than he was chronologically. He seemed to have lost energy and drive, which was quite unlike him since they had finally gotten away from the gulag and the Allied POW camps. When they first came to London, Michaele was a dynamo who attacked their business with a dizzyingly frenetic enthusiasm, and they had prospered beyond their wildest expections as a result. As of the present date, their legitimate income was almost the equal to their income from their organized crime pursuits.

Michaele was pale and had lost a significant amount of weight, and now coughed constantly. When they first left the gulag, Michaele had been extremely thin, but now he looked more like the keeper of the crypt. Antoine decided that today was the day to confront him and to find out what was the matter. He elected to have the talk with his old friend and Herr Caussidière—their Swiss partner—before their meeting with the architects and construction people from Argentina, where they were about to start three new building complexes. The two men had decided to relocate to the highly accommodating South American country sometime during the upcoming year as soon as the projects were completed.

Michaele was sitting at the conference table coughing—having a particularly bad spell. Antoine saw that Michaele's handkerchief was soaked with blood even though his old friend quickly put it into his pocket and gave Antoine a wan smile.

"Good morning, Michaele. Sounds like your cough is getting worse."

"No, my friend—about the same. Probably a bronchitis. It'll pass."

Antoine shook his head. "Don't think so, Michaele. You still have some blood on your cheek."

Michaele did not want to bring out the blood-soaked handkerchief; so, he struggled to get up and find a box of tissues. Antoine produced a box of fancy French *"Le Troubadour"* tissues from a cabinet and handed it to Michaele. The effort to stand caused another spasm of coughing, and now he was embarrassed to be filling multiple tissues with thick blood.

"I'd better get to the bathroom," he said.

"Don't be embarrassed, Michaele. It's only you and me here. You can't keep things from me—certainly not things like this. This is serious; it's certainly more than just a little cold or bronchitis. You know that, my friend. You've been sick for a while, and we need to get you to a doctor today as soon as the meeting is over. For that matter, I can handle the Argentines myself. Why don't you go have a lie down for a while? Leave business to me, all right?"

To his considerable surprise, Michaele nodded his head. Another surprise came when he offered his arm to Antoine for help getting up.

The meeting was efficient and productive. The Argentine businessmen and builders presented complete construction and business plans which met Antoine's specifications in all aspects. There was no explicit statement about the obvious overages in the labor and materials estimates. Everyone in the room knew that this was the Argentine way. There were palms to be greased all along the way, not the least being the paranoid kleptocratic administration of José María Guido, who was serving as the interim president while the country's two military factions created political chaos.

The general upheaval was—remarkably enough—not particularly bad for business. The prospect of any foreign investment in the country was greeted favorably by all participants in the current Argentinian drama, and they all left the businessmen and builders to their own devices. In fact, there was a decidedly positive aspect to the conflict and the administration's both-hands-in-the-public-trough approach. Regulations were ignored, and bribes were kept to a reasonable level to avoid discouraging investment. All in all, things were moving smoothly for the European International Conglomerate. Antoine signed for the president and CEO—as Laird Eagen and Randolph Bellwether, the respective pseudonyms for himself and Michaele. He and the Argentinians drank a champagne toast, and they wished Randolph a speedy recovery.

Antoine called the consumption service at the Royal Brompton Hospital because he was more than just suspicious that Michaele had the disease. Since Michaele did not smoke, Antoine figured that it was not cancer. He decided that the Royal Brompton was as good a place to start as any.

The physicians of the sanatorium were extremely busy, since the Royal Brompton was one of only a few hospitals equipped to treat consumption. Triple the usual fee for Doctor Evan Goodefellow's surgery and a promise of a handsome grant to the hospital magically cleared the way for Michaele to be seen the following day.

Michaele was too tired and sick to speak for himself; so, he readily agreed to let Antoine do the talking with the doctors. Antoine provided such history as he could, and the doctor examined Michaele.

"We will need a chest x-ray," the doctor said.

"Let's get it done as quickly as possible, if you please," Antoine requested.

The doctor brought the radiographic plates and showed the two men.

"You can see here that almost the entire right lung is opaque—white—and has pushed the heart and left lung to the left. This is a big mass. While it could be cancer, my examination of the sputum revealed acid fast bacilli; so, consumption is the better diagnosis."

"Could you explain that in lay terms, Doctor?" Antoine asked.

"Of course—pardon me for getting too technical. The dye or stain used to identify the tuberculosis germ is called acid fast and when it is positive, the patient—you, Mr. Bellwether, has active growing tuberculosis. Because the stain colors the bacteria red, we medical people irreverently refer to them as 'red snappers.' The old name for TB was 'consumption.'"

Michael spoke up; his voice soft and his speech punctuated with productive bloody cough, "I understand that TB is untreatable, is that right?"

"Definitely not—not anymore. In fact, I want you to start on two medications this very day and to get plenty of rest. If you have the means, you might want to go to a sanatorium in the desert area of the United States. They are working wonders there. But this is getting ahead of the game. Take the medications for six months along with the rest, then we will see if you are a candidate for pneumonectomy."

Antoine raised his eyebrows.

"Sorry again," the physician said. "Surgery. The left lung will have to be removed in order to allow the healthy tissues to be successfully treated by the medications."

Michaele went pale, "Can a man survive with only one lung, Doctor Goodefellow?"

"Indeed, he can. In fact, my prognosis is that you will live for many more years; but, of course, with a lessened ability to exercise due to reduced lung capacity. You should be able to get out and about on walks, play golf if you are so inclined, and swim. That is one of the recommended treatments in those desert sanatoria."

"We'll do it all. We put ourselves into your hands, Doctor."

"That's the spirit. I will write you a prescription for one year of isoniazid and p-aminosalicylic acid. That is now the standard of care. Let's see you back in say a month to see how things are going."

CHAPTER FIFTY-TWO

Corporate Offices of European International Conglomerate, No. 13 Upper Belgrave Street, London, August 22, 1962, later that day

Michaele was too tired to argue with Antoine when they got back to the office. He agreed to take to his bed for the rest of the day, but he insisted on having a serious talk with his partner later that evening. Antoine agreed.

While Michaele slept, Antoine and the office staff swung into motion. One of the conference rooms was rapidly converted into a hospital room with all of the modern comforts available to an English gentleman. The room was ready for its first occupant by the time Michaele awakened and downed a pot of good English chicken noodle soup and buttered toast. Tuberculosis was one of the major public health problems that doctors and nurses dealt with for fifty years prior to Michaele's visit to the sanatorium. Early on, treatment consisted of the use of special diets, bed rest in sanatoria, and lung collapse therapy. The medical world was loath to change to different treatment, and in England and rural America it was not uncommon for people to have their lungs collapsed or removed. The case fatality rate five years after diagnosis was fifty percent and treatment in a sanatorium was expensive and available only to the privileged few like Michaele. Combination treatment introduced in the 1950s reduced the fatality rate to five percent for the lucky minority who were able to obtain the medications and the sanatoria treatment in time.

Starting in the 1960s, ambulatory treatment of tuberculosis outside sanatoria along with one year of isoniazid and p-aminosalicylic acid drug therapy came to be recognized as being as effective for patients and their families as treatment in a sanatorium, but that was after Michaele's time in Europe. The result was a drastic reduction in surgeries, domiciliary care, the death rate, and the huge burdensome costs which could only be afforded by the rich.

Fortified by the rest and the chicken soup, Michaele insisted on getting his say in before Antoine could interrupt him.

"I have given considerable thought to the doctor's orders. I intend to comply with them because I want to live. However, Antoine, you know our life's work is not done, and I don't mean constructing buildings in Argentina."

Antoine nodded his understanding.

"The rest did me good. I have confidence that the medication will help. I do think that the surgery doesn't need to be done right away, and I want us to take a trip to America and to Russia. Of the more than a hundred names still on our list, there are two that I want to be sure are eliminated before I die and while I can still be a part of the missions."

"I don't know, Michaele. Wouldn't it be enough for me to do the heavy work and you just work with me on the planning?"

"Not for those two. The memories are too vivid for me to be left out of any part of the action for those monsters."

"I understand. Let's work on the plans, and I'll do the legwork to get ready. Then I'll take you to the place we choose; and you can be the avenger for all of our brothers in the Charlemagne Division, at least for those two special cases."

He did not have to say the names. Their names and faces were inextricably entrenched into the psyches of both Antoine and Michaele. Both of them considered the removal of those two to be the most important missions in their remaining lives' work.

Michaele improved after a month with the strict regimen of rest, good food, exposure to sunshine, and Dr. Goodefellow's pills. He was able to get up and walk short distances. Antoine took him on seemingly innocuous and therapeutic excursions to the countryside. There, the two old friends practiced long distance shooting for hours at a time. English gentlemen had taken to the sport and were now entering and faring decently in international matches; so, no one paid Antoine and Michaele any heed. The process and activity were very tiring for Michaele, but he kept at it with determination until he could place three rounds out of four within two inches of dead center at five hundred yards and one out of four near the center at eight hundred yards, and three more into what would be the head or heart and probably would count as kill shots. He grew fond of the fine English Parker Hale C3A1 sniper rifle and facile with the process of loading the 7.62×51mm NATO cartridges while lying prone.

"You're ready," Antoine pronounced. "We'll leave tomorrow for the US state of Texas. I made arrangements for you to be admitted as a Swiss citizen into one of the fine sanatoria in the desert state. Our people have been shadowing our quarry for the past three weeks. He has weaknesses for routine, sweet young Mexican girls, and tequila. Next Friday he will leave Presidio, Texas, and cross the Texas-Mexico border on Federal highway 67 over the Presidio–Ojinaga International Bridge and into Ojinaga, Chihuahua State, Mexico at eleven-forty-five, in time to have his usual lunch at the Cantina Rojas in the center of town. After that, he will walk three blocks to the Chihuahua Caballero's Club—a whorehouse. That is his usual pattern. However–on this particular Friday–he will not even make it to his lunch. You will be lying on top of a two-story building less than a hundred yards from the sidewalk. You will have a perfectly clear view as he approaches the cantina because there is a vacant lot between your building and the sidewalk.

"*Sturmbannführer* Hugues Beauchamp will follow him into Mexico in an old pickup truck and will walk ahead of him. You will recognize Hugues easily because he will be wearing a very large touristic straw sombrero. As soon as you see Hugues, get ready. You will only get one shot. *Hauptsturmführer* Jérôme Christophe Mailhot and I will be parked behind your building. As soon as the mission is accomplished, all you need to do is to walk down the stairs, out the back door, and into our car. We will be back in the United States in less than hour."

The four old comrades arranged to sit in different seats on different rows of the TransWorld Airlines flight from Heathrow to Dallas Love Field. The Boeing 720 touched down on time, and Michaele Dupont—aka Randolph Bellwether—aka Dennis Cunningham Lord Downfort—checked into the Tarrant County Elmwood Sanatorium—orginally the Poor Farm, but recently spruced up for more discerning clientele. The reception staff was a bit awed to have an expatriate

English lord who now called Switzerland home as a paying patient in the sanatorium. It was a brilliantly sunny and dessicatingly hot day, typical for Fort Worth.

The Elmwood Sanatorium was ideally situated—in the perfect middle of nowhere—between Dallas and Fort Worth with miles and miles of miles and miles between the TB hospital and either city. The locals in Dallas described the distance between Dallas and Fort Worth as thirty-two miles and a century apart.

On Friday morning very early, friends in a partially rusted 1955 Ford Fairlane Crown Victoria with a souped-up V8 took Lord Downfort on a desert excursion and picnic, expecting to be gone the entire day—so they told the Elmwood managers. Overnight, Hugues had staked out the modest tract home of Major Rick Avery Saunders, USA ret—former aide-de-camp of the late WW2 General Glen Gabler—in the eastern Dallas suburb of Mesquite, a plodding hot town with a slowly growing population of about 30,000. True to his rigid and presumably fatal routine, Saunders headed like a homing pigeon for Chihuahua. An hour before Major Saunders left Mesquite, Antoine, Michaele, and Jérôme took the more direct route towards Mexico. All three vehicles traveled the same final, almost dirt, track route into Mexico; but Saunders was the last of the three to reach the little border town of Presidio on the Farm to Market Road 170 and US Route 67, 145 miles northeast of Chihuahua. The assassins were in Ojinaga, Chihuahua state, nearly an hour ahead of the selected victim waiting for him.

CHAPTER FIFTY-THREE

Empty lot next to Cantina Rojas, Ojinaga, Chihuahua State, Mexico, September 29, 1962

Antoine got Michaele comfortably settled on a backpacker foam mattress on the rooftop of the autobody repair shop which looked out onto the empty lot and the sidewalk. Cantina Rojas was on his left, and an open-front discount women's clothing store was on the right. Across the street the view was stale view of the slab side of a cinder brick building—a *maquiladora* [small factory that assembles prefabricated goods—in this case, chimney, venting, and air distribution products]. Ojinaga serves as a support center and market community for the surrounding area. The *maquiladora* was humble enough to lack even a sign to identify it. Antoine set down two small plastic bottles of Evian water and a cellophane-wrapped egg salad sandwich.

Michaele coughed a small amount of blood into a pile of paper napkins he brought with him to the scene.

"You all right, Michaele?" Antoine asked solicitously with genuine concern on his face. "Think you can pull this off?"

"*Jawohl, Bruder,*" Michaele said with determination equal to Antoine's concern.

"You have to suppress that cough until it's over. That'll be tough, but you can't draw attention to yourself."

"I know, I know. If I have to cough, I'll bury my face in the pile of napkins. Nobody will hear a thing."

Antoine looked over the edge of the flat top roof at the scene two stories below and approximately fifty yards away. It was approaching noon. The situation was ideal for a sniper: sun at Michaele's back, noisy cantina next to the planned kill site, fairly busy rural Mexican road traffic on the pothole ridden street. The ambient noise would muffle almost all the sound Michaele was likely to make, even the actual firing of the rifle to some degree.

One of the more famous famous *norteño* musical groups from Ojinaga, and one of the loudest—Los Diamantes de Ojinaga—was already heating up the sound waves on the block; and the crowd inside the cantina and out on the sidewalk was getting drunker and more boisterous as the morning drew closer to noon. Unlike many other regional bands that used only accordions as the lead band instrument, Los Diamantes used saxophones and accordions together to get a richer and louder sound production, and one that reached a hundred yards away from the rowdy beer and tequila joint.

Sidewalk traffic was intermittent and not heavy. Ojinaga retained its rural culture, environment, and poverty. Most of the people walking along the hot sidewalk were peons—hardscrabble farmers-who never saw a surplus enough to turn an actual profit. The dusty border town was a way station for narcotic smuggling and illegal immigration; so, it was not hard to pick out the occasional small band of illegals led by their unfeeling and often thieving coyotes as they made their weary way towards the border and the riches of Los Estados Unidos [USA]. The pedestrians were either too tired, too thirsty and hungry, or too frightened to look up at the building where Michaele lay in wait. Antoine took one last reconnoitering look over the eight-inch high rain gutter border of the autobody shop to be sure there were no federales in view, bade Michaele good hunting, and crawled back to the rooftop enterway into the stairwell which led to the street on the opposite side of the cantina and the *maquiladora*. He could just make out muffled coughing by his old friend lying outstretched in the sweltering noonday sun as he descended the trash strewn stairs.

Rick Saunders had intentionally skipped breakfast and made the long trip from Dallas on an empty and increasingly noisy stomach. He was looking forward to satiating his appetites—both of them, but food first. He wore a light blue denim shirt, faded blue jeans, and scuffed desert boots, the better to make him fit in with the nondescript flow of people along the sidewalks and streets. He kept a hand on his wallet all the time, fearing pickpockets or brazen bandits. His broad brimmed

Stetson shielded his head and eyes from the brilliant sun and from any view of the world above his eyebrows as he sauntered along the uneven pavement of the sidewalk without a care in the world.

Jérôme was waiting a block ahead of Rick. As the Texan rounded the corner and approached the former German POW who had suffered at his hands in an Allied POW camp not so long ago, Jérôme started walking towards Cantina Rojas, making sure to gauge his pace to equal that of Rick. He was wearing a large brimmed straw sombrero which he had intentionally dusted with road and coal dust and a sarape *gabán* [poncho] typical of the Mexican state of Coahuila in northeastern Mexico. It was old, worn, and dirty, but the bright bands of color were still evident—dark brown base with haphazard bands of yellow, orange, red, blue, green, purple, and chartreuse. Its purpose was to cover the machine pistol he concealed beneath it.

He allowed Rick to get closer—about ten yards now. He passed the discount store and walked purposefully along the sidewalk that faced the empty lot. He stopped for a second, lifted his sombrero, and wiped the sweat off his forehead—the signal to Michaele that the target was close behind him. He then turned and walked across to the other side of the street and back the way he had come. Jérôme never looked back. He met Antoine waiting at the next street in his Ford Fairlane Crown Victoria—now so covered with dust that its colors could not be distinguished with certainty—the engine idling. They moved the large four-seat sedan as swiftly through the gathering crowds on their way to market as they could without drawing attention to themselves and parked in front of the stairway of the autobody shop.

Michaele coughed up a large thick quarter cupful of bloody sputum and wiped his mouth with a napkin which was now nearly soaked with blood. The signal had been given; so, he chambered a 7.62×51mm NATO cartridge into the barrel of the English Parker Hale C3A1 sniper rifle and drew a bead on the head of a passing farmer to approximate the correct angle of his shot. In less than ten seconds, Rick Saunders walked into view. It was eleven-forty; he was five minutes early.

Michaele suppressed a nagging cough and felt the wad of bloody sputum trying to cough its way out. He suppressed the droplets of sweat running down his forehead and into his eyes. He suppressed the almost impossible craving to pull the trigger until Rick walked into a portion of the sidewalk where he was separated by three feet from the nearest other pedestrian on the sidewalk.

Rick never varied his pace or his direction of gaze. He wore an anticipatory smile.

Michaele centered the reticle on a point just above Rick's cheek-bone and directly in front of the upper third of his ear. He took in a breath, fought the need to cough and to blink, and slowly squeezed the fine-tuned trigger.

Rick Saunders, Major, USA, retired, felt nothing as his head exploded. He was dead before his body crumpled to the ground.

At first, the few people on the street and the sidewalk scattered in terror, then slowly they began to gather to get a view of the macabre scene, looking around and finally up to see where the shot came from. It would be foolish for Michaele to look over at his handiwork or to allow anyone on the ground to see him. He thought about gathering up the blood-soaked napkins scattered by his backpacking cushion, but thought better of the idea and crawled on his belly towards the opening to the stairs. He released a mighty exhalation and cough, and sprayed the roof and the upper stairs with a copius blood spatter. He hurried down the stairs heedlessly, stepping in the blood and marking his path with the prints of his desert boots all the way down the stairs, across the sidewalk, and into Antoine and Jérôme's Ford.

As the crowd gathered on the opposite side of the building where the Ford was parked, the three assassins threaded their way north on back-streets until they left Ojinaga proper. They traveled at a speed between sixty and seventy miles per hour across the nearly 15,000 acres of open farmland with nothing but cattle pasture and plots of soy, cotton, corn, wheat, onions, peanuts, canteloupes, and assorted vegetables, to reach the border station at the Presidio–Ojinaga International Bridge. It was a modestly busy day; so, there was an uneasy wait of half an hour before the US Border and Customs agents finally got to them.

"Identification papers, please," the Hispanic agent requested politely.

Antoine reached his driver's license and all of the car's occupants' US passports to the woman.

"Thank you, gentlemen," she said. "I appreciate seeing your pass-ports. Technically your driver licences are sufficient, but the US is soon going to require passports of everyone. Mexico is a foreign country, which seems to be news to lots of American tourists. What was the nature of your visit, gentlemen?"

"Tourism, Officer," Antoine responded.

"Bringing anything back?" she asked.

"Oh, we certainly hope not," he answered with a big bad-boy smile.

She laughed, even though it was joke that was getting time and repetition worn. She raised a quizzical eyebrow.

"No, Ma'am," Antoine answered, serious this time.

"Drive safely, gentlemen. Remember the speed limit is fifty."

"Thank you, Officer. We'll be careful."

As he started to roll down the window, Michaele developed a severe coughing spell. The customs agent looked at him sitting in the backseat and took note of the blood he was coughing up.

"That's a really nasty cough," she said. "You okay?"

Michaele could only nod.

"Cancer," Antoine said with a sad look. "The trip was probably too much for him. We're headed back to Tucson to get him into the hospital there. Appreciate your concern."

"I won't keep you then. My best wishes," she said, leaning into the open window to say it to Michaele.

They exceeded the speed limit only by a little all the way back to Fort Worth and the Tarrant County Elmwood Sanatorium outside of the city, arriving before dark. Antoine and Jérôme got Michaele settled into bed after receiving a scolding by the evening shift nurse. When she had vented her spleen, she strutted out of the room still angry.

"She's right, you know, Michaele. You have to get rest. Stay here for a month, then get back to London. If that's a problem, I have left instructions for the staff to call me at the corporation offices. Jérôme and I will come back and get you if we have to."

"You have more important things to do than to nursemaid me," Michaele said. "I'll be fine."

That bit of unlikely optimism was given the lie by another coughing spell.

"You will, *Bruder*. You will," Jérôme lied as they parted.

The word of Rick Saunder's assassination reached the Texas Rangers office in Presidio the following day. The Mexican federales had been called that morning and hurried into Ojinaga to discover the body of a murdered man whose wallet contained a Texas state driver's license and a retired Army officer ID card along with a wad of cash. They did not want anything to do with an international incident which would bring a spotlight into the activities into their lucrative region of northern Mexico where the Río Conchos River drains into the Rio Bravo [known as the Rio Grande in the US]—an area called La Junta de los Rios. Their meager Mexican salaries did not support the Federales or their families, and scrutiny on their extracurricular activities would be counterproductive.

Mexican authorities had a grudging respect for the Texas Rangers and regularly worked with them on selected cases. Two rangers—Tom Packer and Eldred Drake—were allowed in and conducted a cursory crime scene evaluation. Intuition led them to the rooftop of the auto-body repair shop, where they found a single brass casing and a bushel basket full of very bloody tissues. With the help of the Federales, they measured and photographed the bloody footprints on the roof and the stairs, noting that the prints were not from cowboy boots or any familiar American or Mexican-made boots. They took note of the fact that their Mexican counterparts seemed anxious to get the body back to the States and that the wallet was empty of cash.

Back in the Presidio office, Tom said, "This here was a professional hit. One shot from a sniper rifle, and no one seen a thing."

Tom was twenty-five years older than Eldred and looked like he had stepped out of an 1870 Texas Ranger recruiting lithograph. Although the current approved attire included a white shirt and tie, tan trousers, a light-colored western cowboy hat, a ranger belt, and cowboy boots which Eldred had worn ever since he graduated from ranger school, Tom was old style. He wore whatever clothes he could afford or muster, which were usually—like today—worn out from heavy use. Unlike his junior associate, Tom dressed more like a compromise between Mexican *vaqueros* and some kind of gringo police officer. Unlike most modern rangers, he preferred to wear broad-brimmed *sombrero* as opposed to a neat new Stetson and wore throwback square-cut, knee-high boots with a high heel and pointed toes—the Spanish style. He still wore silver spurs because he liked the jangling sound—and he insisted that the ladies were unable to resist a ranger in real boots and spurs. Both rangers groups—new and old—carried their guns the same way, with the holsters positioned high around their hips instead of low on the thigh. This placement made it easier to draw and shoot while riding a horse, although now they more often used motorized travel.

Ranger Eldred Drake had ambitions. He intended to move up the ranks in the ranger organization; so, he was a stickler for details in the manual and in his dress. He wore clean crisp, freshly laundered and pressed Levis, a wide belt with his rodeo championship buckle, and a snap button long-sleeve white cotton shirt and a string tie. His boots were polished every morning and dusted off from his day's work every noon and just at quitting time. He was scrupulous about shaving twice a day because of his fast-growing and heavy black beard. He had wavy black hair and an Indian nose. His teeth were big, and there was a conspicuous gap between his front two incisors—all harking back to the distant point in his genealogy when a great-great grandfather had married a Native American woman. Together they produced twelve Mestizos. The subsequent generations did little to dilute the strong genetic contribution of the Natchitoches Indians whose genealogical contribution was now lost to the mists of time.

Eldred made the decisive point: "But even big-time pros make mistakes. The guy or guys who did this hit made three big ones: we have the slug, and it is intact enough to find out the make and model of the gun, at least. We have bloody footprints that don't match anything we see on men's feet around here. And, there is all that bloody toilet paper up there on the roof. I don't think that's from an injury. I think somebody is mighty sick. I'm gonna take some of the globs of blood over to Doc Pinter's. I have a hunch about what this is. He used to work up at the Elmwood Sanatorium by Fort Worth, and he can confirm my hunch."

Pinter's office was only three blocks away.

Ranger Drake walked in and asked to see the doctor right away on ranger business.

"I'll get him," Ruby Dempsey, the office girl, said.

"What's up?" asked the doc when he came out from seeing a pregnant patient.

"Need to have you look at a blood sample under the microscope, Doc."

He handed the doctor the mass of paper tissue with the large blood clot.

"See that gray snotty-lookin's stuff mixed in with the blood, Eldred?"

"I noticed it. That's why I brought it to you for confirmation."

"First thing I do will be to make a Ziehl–Neelsen stain prep. It's also called the acid-fast stain."

"For TB, right?"

"Good boy. Who says the Texas Rangers are just dumb thugs?"

"We do, Doc. Keeps the yokels scared of us."

They both laughed.

With a few manipulations, Dr. Pinter looked under the microscope and said without a bit of reservation, "Acid-fast bacilli—Mycobacterium tuberculosis. Good call, Eldred. Take a look at all of those red streaks. Your sniper has TB, and a well advanced case. Given the amount of blood he's coughin' up and all that bacterial sludge, he's in a world of hurt. He's actually coughin' up chunks of lung."

"I need an opinion, Doc. Is he too sick to travel any big distance?"

"I would bet the barn on it. He's about to slough his mortal coil. I wouldn't be surprised to learn that he's already dead."

"Where do ya'll think him and his friends would likely head?"

"Exactly one place, Eldred. That's Elmwood up by Fort Worth. Ya'll skiddadle up there right away, and I'd bet plenty that he's layin' up there coughin' out his lungs and maybe his brains."

"So don't think I'm impolite, Doc; but that's exactly what I'm gonna do right now."

Eldred reported the doc's findings and suggestion to Tom and started out the office door to get in the car.

"Hold up a sec. You hearda that new invention—the telephone?" Tom asked.

"Oh, yeah, good idea. We can put a hold on the guy before he can git outta there. That's why you're the captain with the fancy gold badge and I'm the guy with the lowly silver one."

The 1960s badge of a Texas Ranger was the same size as compared to a 1948 *cinco pesos* coin from which both Tom and Eldred had theirs made. Shortly after the Texas Rangers were merged with the Department of Public Safety, a new badge design was issued by the state. Roughly oval-shaped, it contained the legend "Dept. of Public Safety," the letters T-E-X-A-S, and a star with the rank in the center. The two mavericks kept their old style badges like many of the old-timers, and no one made a complaint.

"Get on with it and make the call, lowly ranger. Probably oughta call Austin first."

"Politics," grumbled Eldred.

"It's how to keep yer job, young fella. I been at this for nearly thirty-five years. I hadda make a lotta compromises in that time."

"I'm still learnin'.'"

He made the call to headquarters in Austin and gave the duty officer the shorthand version.

"Ya'll need to git on over there to Fort Worth [pronounced Fot Wuth] asap, ya heah!" the duty officer said unnecessarily.

"Thank ya'll very much, Ranger. Idda never have thought of that.

"Anyhow, me and Tom will head out from Presidio. See ya'll at the sanatorium. Be careful out there. We think these're bad dudes. Might wanna bring along the cavalry."

The ranger captain, Reggie Cutler, in Austin, acted immediately after learning about the military status of the victim and called the DOD and the DOJ. The DOD call took half an hour to wend its way to Tucker Nicholsen SAC, 83rd MP Det CID, in Fort Richardson, Alaska.

"Nicholsen," Tucker answered.

"This is Captain Reggie Cutler, chief of the Texas Rangers office in Austin, Special Agent. We are investigating a murder that the DOD told us may be related to one you have going—the killing of a US general named Glen Gabler."

"Yes, sir. You've come to the right place. What's new?"

"I'm going to keep this real simple because it's kind of urgent right now. The Mexican federales called us about a sniper murder—obvious professional hit—in a little border town called Ojinaga, Chihuahua State. Our rangers confirmed that the deceased is one Major Rick Avery Saunders, USA retired. That ring a bell?"

"A loud one. What have you learned?"

"I'll fax up the info, but right now things are in the hurry-up phase. We have a lead that suggests that the perp may be currently in Fort Worth. Specifically in the Tarrant County Elmwood Sanatorium outside of the city. Rangers, Fort Worth police, and fibbies, are all gearing up to descend on the place. It's a TB sanatorium. If he's still there, this may be a breakthrough for you and us."

"And maybe a half dozen or dozen other cases around the world, Ranger. We'll get our people there as fast as humanly possible. I know you have to protect your people, but try if at all possible not to kill the guy. We need to sweat him."

"Understood. I'll let you go. See you or one of your agents in Fort Worth."

"Thanks for the call."

Tucker called Major Darrin Higgins, Chief Officer MCU, Alaska State Police, in Juneau to give him a heads up and then made arrangements for the Army criminal investigation service in Dallas to send special agents with lights ablaze and sirens blaring. His only other requests—and the strongest ones—were not to kill the arrestee and to try and play nice with all the other jurisdictions involved.

Capt. Cutler's next call was to AAG Spencer Reynolds, assistant attorney general for the criminal division of the DOJ, who in turn called DFBI Warren Brent Gaines and Superintendent Axel Baird INTERPOL agent in charge in New York City, and Eugène Léon Dentremont, Senior Detective Chief Superintendent of INTERPOL, who had his deputy, Marianne de la Reynie senior INTERPOL technician, forensic specialist, contact the French, Russian, British, and Argentinian law enforcement officers in the cohort of investigators of the murders of senior military officers. Then all eyes and ears focused on Fort Worth—a dusty backwater city in north central Texas—a place most had never heard about before that day.

The rangers stopped at a burger joint and picked up some Tex-Mex to eat on the way to Fort Worth.

Tex-Mex Recipes

Tex-Mex BLT—Serves 2

Ingredients
$\frac{1}{4}$ cp mayo, 1 pinch chili powder, 1 pinch fresh chopped jalapeno, 1 pinch pepper, 4 thick slices whole wheat bread, 8 slices crisply fried bacon, 6 thinly sliced tomatoes, 1 slice thinly sliced avocado, 1 sprig roughly chopped cilantro, 1 washed lettuce leaf.

Preparation
Mix mayo with pinch of chili powder and jalapeno and set aside. Toast the bread lightly and spread both sides with mayo. Pile on bacon, tomato, avocado, cilantro sprigs, and lettuce, and top with other slice of toast.

Tex-Mex Stuffed Chilies—Serves 10

Ingredients
-1 med. diced red onion, 1 lb ground turkey or good beef, 1 (1½ oz) envelope taco seasoning, 1 11 oz drained can corn, 1 4 ounce can green Ortega chilies, 1 15 oz can rinsed and drained black beans, ½ 15 oz can refried beans, $\frac{1}{2}$ cup salsa, 4 cps shredded cheddar cheese, 5 med. bell peppers of all colors. Include Ortegas or jalapenos as desired.

Preparation
-Brown ground meat with onion in skillet until done, drain grease. Add taco seasoning and water as per envelope simmer 5 mins., remove from heat and let cool.
-Cut peppers in half from top to bottom, remove all seeds and membrane.
-Place in 2 greased 13 x 9 in. pans.
-Mix salsa and refried beans. To the meat mixture add corn, black beans, green chilies, refried mix, and 2 cps cheddar cheese.
-Stuff raw peppers with mix. Cover and bake ~1 hour at 350º F, uncover and top with remaining cheese, then place back in oven ~5 min. until cheese is melted.

Tex-Mex Barbecued Salmon—4 Servings

Ingredients
$\frac{1}{4}$ cup fresh orange juice, 2 tbsps fresh lemon juice, 4 6 oz salmon fillets, 2 tbsps brown sugar, 1 tbsp chili powder, 2 tsps lemon zest, $\frac{3}{4}$ tsp ground cumin, $\frac{1}{4}$ tsp salt, $\frac{1}{4}$ tsp cinnamon, 1 lemon slice.

Preparation
-In a ziplock plastic bag, combine first orange juice, lemon juice, and salmon; seal and marinate in refrigerator 1 hour, turning occasionally. Remove fish from bag, discard marinade.
-In a small bowl, combine next sugar, chili powder, lemon zest, cumin, salt, and cinnamon. Place fillets in the mixture and soak in same (but fresh) marinade longer.
-Place fillets on grill on medium-high heat and cover with grill lid. Baste fish with the sauce occasionally. Cook for 10–12 min. or until fish flakes easily when tested with fork. Serve with lemon slice.

CHAPTER FIFTY-FOUR

Tarrant County Elmwood Sanatorium, outside Fort Worth, Texas, September 31, 1962, evening

After enduring the irate nurse's scolding and seeing to it that their old and sick friend was as comfortable as possible, Antoine and Jérôme bade Michaele a reluctant farewell, then drove quickly across the desolate highway thirty-three miles to Love Field in Dallas. No transatlantic flights were available at that time of night;so, Antoine had to make emergency and incredibly expensive arrangements to take the two of them alone on a TWA flight to London. The cost was not Antoine's main concern; the attention they would stir up with their extravagance was. At least Michaele was out of it for now.

When they arrived back at the corporate offices of European International Conglomerate in London, the two men were greeted with an urgent telegram message from Nicolai Andreavich Putansky *russkaya mafiya* under boss to Leonid Zaslavskevich Breslava. Breslava was the *Pakhan* of the *vory v zakone* [thieves-in-law] and Putansky was Breslava's brigadier.

The telegram message was simple: "We have information regarding the whereabouts of Lt. Gen. Dimitri Sobrieski, as per your request. Stop. Contact us soonest possible. Stop."

It was six-thirty in London and nine-thirty in Moscow. Antoine assumed the chieftains of the *russkaya mafiya* would be just starting an evening of rough drinking and gluttony. His call would not be a disturbance. He called Nicolai first and got no answer; so, he called the *Pakhan* and was surprised to get an answer on the first ring.

"Who is this?" came the gravelly voice.

"Leonid Zaslavskevich, this is Laird Eagen in London. I received an urgent telegram from Nicolai Andreavich. What do I need to know?"

Every message or service between the two men was a matter of goods, money, or services transfer: goods for goods, money for money, services—including transmittal of information—for services. It was a good, clean, and efficient business arrangement that left nothing to the imagination or to mistakes.

"I am glad you called before the evening is over. We have a hurry-up situation here, one you have told me is of primary importance to you."

Braslava was speaking English in case anyone was listening in. He had little confidence in the English ability of the KGB watchers who hounded him.

"I just got back from the US. It would be best to make this as direct as possible, Leonid Zaslavskevich, because my brain may be rather foggy from jet lag."

"I understand perfectly, Laird. I hate to fly. The message is that we have a time and a location for the man who interests you. He will be in a meeting at the Moscow Military District headquarters, A-252, Chapayevskiy Per., Dom 14, at 1800 hours Moscow time tomorrow, and tomorrow only. We have determined a location across the street in an apartment building which should prove to be very useful. Everyone who enters or leave the district headquarters must use the main entry facing onto Chapayevskiy for the building."

Antoine took hurried notes.

"Any problem providing us the necessary equipment?"

"Not really, my friend; but you realize that all of this will be very costly."

"How costly?"

"Thirty million rubles for expenses and an additional ten million for our … efforts."

Antoine did a quick bit of math. He had just been in the US; so, he was thinking in terms of the US dollar. Thirty rubles to one dollar—$1.3 million dollars. It was steep, but not really a problem. It would be something of a problem to raise that much overnight.

"Will that include a safe exit from the USSR, Leonid Zaslavskevich?"

"Of course. Any place you want to go."

"I had not prepared for such a quick response to our request. I will have difficulty raising the money tonight, but our Swiss bankers can wire the funds tomorrow morning. Will that be acceptable?"

"Of course, my friend. We operate on a basis of trust. I will alert my bankers to anticipate the funds in the morning. I presume you will leave on what the Americans call the 'red-eye' tonight?"

"Yes. I have some familiarity with the Aeroflot schedule. We should be able to arrive at the secret Sheremetyevo Airport early tomorrow with a little influence from you."

"Until then," Leonid said and hung up.

Antoine put in a call to Geneva, Switzerland, to the private line of the CEO of Caussidière Enterprises International, François Gaspard Caussidière.

"I hope your venture in the Western Hemisphere went satisfactorily, *Mein Freund*," François said as soon as his secretary told him who was calling.

"It did. The second half of the mission has presented itself much sooner than expected. I will need you to wire $1.3 million to our associate in Moscow tomorrow morning at the opening of business. I believe you already have the account number."

"Are we still dealing with Moscow Narodny Bank Ltd?"

"Yes."

"A wire for that amount will be forwarded from UBS to Narodny as soon as the Geneva branch opens."

"Good. Take your usual fee from the account but not from the $1.3 million. Understood?"

"Of course. Will that be all?"

"For today, but we have big plans developing in our South American areas of interest."

"As always, I will remain at your service."

§§§§§

Fort Worth PD and Tarrant County sheriff's deputies arrived in the parking lot of the Tarrant County Elmwood Sanatorium less than twenty minutes after the first calls were received. There were four cars in all, and the law enforcement officers got out and stood in the oppressive heat for a short pre-raid conference. Sgt. Billie Wayne McAfee was the acknowledged lead until the rangers or fibbies got there.

Billie Wayne had been a Fort Worth PD cop since he was eighteen years old. He was now fifty-six going on seventy after a hard working, hard playing, and hard drinking life. His sun-bronzed face showed a deeply etched line for every near miss and long night of his career. He wore an old sweat-stained straw cowboy hat and a pair of badly scuffed boots with old-fashion high heels and pointy toes capped with steel protectors. He was still wearing the same snap button bright red cowboy shirt he had on yesterday. He had the dunlop syndrome— his belly dunlop over his belt. His facial stubble was three days old, and his eyes showed a considerable amount of red from a night or two of carousing.

"We don't know for real what we ah gonna encounta in this heah situation. No use us gettin' all shot up because we don' know what's what. How 'bout you two fine depities go on round the back, and Dayne and me'll check out the front. Give a sqwak on ya'll's horns if ya'll see somethin' ya don' lak," Billie Wayne suggested.

To get along, Fort Worth PD and Tarrant County sheriffs did not give each other orders, just suggestions.

The two teams split up. The deputies gave a short call indicating that everything was clear.

"Me and Dayne're fixin' ta go in the front. Ya'll go in the back. Say in thirty seconds."

"Copy."

Both front and rear entries into the sanatorium were locked. Billie Wayne knocked several times, but could not get anyone to come and open the doors.

He called the department to let them know they were going in and to warn the FBI and all other reinforcements that their entrance into the old sanatorium to arrest the possible killer of the Army officer was in progress. Dayne was larger than Billy Wayne, and he kicked in the door. He and Billy Wayne entered the facility, guns drawn. The commotion of knocking in the door brought the attention of a busy nurses' aide who was passing out the day's doses of isoniazid. He rushed out of the ward towards the front door where the noise was coming from and nearly got himself shot for his efforts.

"Hands in the air! Keep 'em where we can see 'em,!" yelled Dayne, pointing his revolver at the aide's heart.

"Who're you, guys?" the aide asked, less excited than the two law officers once he realized they were cops.

"Fot Wuth po-lice and sheriff's depahtment. Who's in charge heah?"

"That'd be Nurse Digby. Ruth Digby. She's in a patient's room workin' to clean him up."

"Put ya'lls hands down and take us to him. Let's all keep rat quite, y'heah. We gotta surprise for a killah comin' up."

They made their way down the poorly lit hallway. Paint was peeling of the walls and ceiling, and patches of plywood showed through worn linoleum.

"This here's where Mizz Digby is, Officers. Want me to announce ya'll?"

"No, thanks. We'll take it from heah. Ya'll get yuhsef back to the wahd like nuthin's goin' on. Don't let on we're heah. Awrat?"

"Yes, suh."

Billy Wayne knocked softly on the door to avoid startling the head evening nurse.

"Weah in the middle a thengs in heah. Can ya'll wait a bit?"

"Afraid not, Mizz Digby. Weah frum the po-lice. We need ta talk with ya. We got a urgent mattah goin' on."

As soon as Billy Wayne gave his order to the nurse, he regretted it and wished that he and Dayne had had the good grace to step out of the room. The stench was overwhelming—worse than a rural privy.

"Pe-u!" said Dayne. "That'd gag a maggot."

"So, what's so impotant, Officers?" Nurse Digby asked, more than a little perturbed at the interruption.

"We have information that a professional killah might just be hidin' in ona the Elmwood buildin's. Ah ya'll aweah of any patient comin' inta the establishment coughin' a lotta blood this evenin', Ma'am?"

"This place is full of patients coughin' up blood, most frum the white plague, Officah. Could be in any ona these waitin' rooms for death. Anythin' bettah ta go on?"

"Man wuz probly outta the hospital mosta the day, oh mebbe he come in fresh today oah yestiddy. Cain't be shua about that. What we'a shua 'bout, though, is that he was bleedin' purty bad—coughin' up big clarks a blood, usin' lottsa hankies oah toilet papah."

"We did get a kinda strange one yestiddy oah the day befoah. Name wuz somethin' lak a fancy English gentaman, wouldn' ya know. C'mon ovah ta the desk, an' ah'll do ma best ta find the one ah mean."

She paused then opened the door to the room with the fragrant patient and called into the nurses' aide, "Sally Rose, honey, sorry;but ah haveta go with the po-lice men foah a bit. Finish up, please, then we'll havta do oah rounds. Be a bit late tonaght, ah'm afraid."

The law enforcement officers followed the tired-looking nurse to her desk. She opened a metal medical record holder and ran her finger down a list of names.

"This heah's the one ya'll maght be a lookin' foah. Take a gander at this heah name."

They read "Dennis Cunningham Lord Downfort."

"Sound's lak a pimp name," Dayne said. "How old's this fella?"

"Look's oldah than he probly is, Deputy. My guess is that he's pushin' sixty, but he looks more like eighty with one foot in the grave and t'other on a banana peel. We hadda give him morphine to calm down that god-awful cougha his. He don' look lak much uv a killah—moah lak a victim."

"Let's go and see this famous English Lo-ad Downfort. Ya'll stand back frum the doah when we git theah, Mizz Digby," said Billy Wayne.

"Whatevah ya'll say, Sergeant."

She took the police officers to the next-to-the-last door in the hallway. It was fairly dark there owing to the absence of the overhead light.

"Sorry, ya'll. County don' keep the place up all that well nowah days," Nurse Digby said by way of a halfhearted apology.

Wasn't her fault.

The officers drew their revolvers. Billy Wayne motioned to the nurse to stay back. Dayne softly turned the doorknob and then flung the door open wide. The two armed men rushed in to the room with Billy Wayne moving to the right, and Dayne to the left. It was evident when they got into the fully lit room that they could have ridden horses and given banshee yells without waking up the patient. He was almost comatose but breathing easily, with only occasional soft coughing productive of bubbles of bright red blood. He was thin—emaciated—and had the sallow complexion of a man about to meet his maker and glad of it.

"Don' look all that dangerous ta me," Dayne observed, and Billy Wayne nodded.

"Exceptin' fa gettin' the red snappers on ya frum ona the poah souls lak this here one. His bedroom mate is likely ta heah him coughin' hissef ta exhaustion and then seein' an empty bed with clean sheets in the mahnin'."

"Any uthahs coughin' up lottsa blood lak this'un, Ma'am?" Billy Wayne asked Nurse Digby.

"We gotta lotta fairly sick old lungers in heah, gentlemen; this'un is bah fah the wusta the lot. And he's the only one that come in heah last coupla days. Record says his friends took him out foah little excursion yestiddy—kinda constitutional outing. Gone the whole day."

"Must be our guy. Don' look all that dangerous."

"Not now that he's been sedated, Dayne; but ya'll nevah know. Mebbe he was bettah earleah."

"Oah mebbe he made one last effort today."

"Could be. Ah thenk we bettah leave him be 'til the rangers and the FBI agents git heah. Ah don' want him to croak on oah watch. Let's ya'll and me set a spell in heah and watch him. Ah'll go out and use the desk phone, call this in. We don' need the cavalry gallopin' in heah scarin' these poah foaks haf outta theah minds."

"Ah agree. Let's hope the rest of 'em gits heah PDQ, or else this one ain't gonna be much of a witness."

Recipes for Sanatorium Food, ca 1950s

The ideal diet for tuberculosis patients consists of good nutrition with leafy, dark-colored greens like kale and spinach, for their high iron and B-vitamin content, plenty of whole grains including whole wheat pastas, breads, and cereals, antioxidant-rich, brightly-colored vegetables, such as carrots, peppers, and squash, and fruits like tomatoes, blueberries, and cherries, unsaturated fats like vegetable or olive oil instead of butter, a daily multivitamin with minerals, and high calorie energy foods. The patient is encouraged to eat hearty portions of lean protein sources like poultry, beans, tofu, and fish. No coffee or other caffeinated drinks and a bare minimum of refined products like sugar, white breads, or white rice, alcohol, or drugs of abuse.

In the 1940s and 50s, the reality in sanatoria was different owing not to ignorance or stinginess, but to lack of funding in some counties. In those days, and in those places, staffing was limited, and the aides had to hurry. The patient experienced a brief encounter with a harried nurse or aide delivering a plate with two or three stale slices of bread and a pat of butter, and a large thick mug holding a knife and fork. A later meal was likely to feature a plate of cold meat and potatoes with a large enamel mug of tea or cocoa. Patients like jail inmates referred to the fare as "Indian rubber beefsteak, disconnected cheese, and coffee that tastes like tobacco juice." The best food the patients received, but the least appreciated, was a daily tablespoonful of cod liver oil. Teaspoons were in short supply; the patient had the choice of stirring with the meaty end or the handle end of his or her fork and licking it clean before proceeding with the meat, if it was meat day. Besides the tedium of the same food schedule week in and week out, it was a bit dispiriting and jail-like since plates, mugs, and utensils were all marked with the patient's admission number and engraved with the phrase, "Stolen from Elmwood," to discourage thievery.

CHAPTER FIFTY-FIVE

Tarrant County Elmwood Sanatorium, outside Fort Worth, Texas, September 31, 1962, late evening

Fort Worth PD Sgt. Billie Wayne McAfee and Tarrant County Deputy Sheriff Dayne Brown had a conundrum: follow procedure and wait until their superiors and the other agencies' people arrived on the scene and risk having the old man die in his sleep without giving up any vital information, or they take the initiative and wake him up and risk getting him so excited that he croaks resulting in IA, bringing them up on charges for violating protocol or worse, for police harassment and involuntary manslaughter, or some such b———t like that.

"Whadda ya'll think we oughta do, Dayne?" Billie Wayne asked after they had talked the problem to death.

"Punt."

"How? Take the option of just waitin' and lettin' the brass handle it?"

"No. What ah mean is see what Nurse Digby thinks about the Lo-ad Downfart's condition. Is the man lak as not goin' ta have a heart attack or a stroke or somethin' if we try and wake him up?"

"Ah lak that idee. Let's fetch the woman and git her expertise."

The question was posed to the nurse.

"Not relevant, ya'll. The lord in there is out fa the naght. He had a big sulga morphine. Mess with 'im an' about all ya'll'l git is a few mumbles. No amounta coffee, yellin', or manhandlin' is gonna change that."

"We got oah answer, Billie Wayne. Let's jist set and jaw fah a bit 'till the higha-ups, the fibbies, an' the rangers show up. If it's okay with ya'll, I'll call in the info this time; and you get yoah dispatch ta put ya'll

418

in touch with the rangers and whoevah else is fixin' ta descend on us poah hick cops heah on the scene."

"Good. Give us somethin' ta do," Billie Wayne said.

He asked one deputy and one PD cop to guard the door—nobody in or out without permission by McAfee or Brown until the brass arrived. Nurse Digby was the exception, of course. He asked the other pair to start a canvass throughout the hospital—including patients, nurses, and staff.

After calling dispatch at police headquarters and the sheriff's department and giving a brief, typical beat cop, Dick-and-Jane-and-Spot rendition of the status of the activity at the scene, Dayne took the initiative to get dispatch to put him through to the rangers. They talked his language. Billie Wayne was busy on the horn with the brass back in Fort Worth PD headquarters.

"This heah's Depity Sheriff Dayne Brown at the Elmwood TB hospital. Me an' Foat Wuth Sergeant Billie Wayne McAfee have the subject under control and in ouah surveillance. He's a real sick dude. What's yoah ETA?"

"Hey, Dayne. This heah's Ranger Eldred Drake. We ah comin'— laghts an' sirens. Be theah mebbe ten-fifteen minutes."

"Ya got the raght idee. Man's fixin' to meet his makah PDQ. Hope we kin get somethin' outta him befoah he does."

"Copy that."

Billie Wayne got through to the FBI special agents on their way from Dallas and the INTERPOL chief from New York. The former told him that they would be on scene in less than half an hour, and the latter said it would be maybe two or three hours owing to problems with air traffic. Then, Billie Wayne redialed Fort Worth PD and asked the night duty officer to start a search for anything they could learn about Dennis Cunningham Lord Downfort.

Nurse Ruth Digby ventured a suggestion, "Ah looked up the insurance info on the great lord. He don' have none. The bill's goin' to a corporation—name's European International Conglomerate."

"Any chance of a address an' telephone numbah, ma'am?"

"Ah knew ya'll'd axe me that, Sergeant. Answer's yes. No. 13 Upper Belgrave Street, London. An' ah don' mean the London ovah theah in Kimble county. Got a pencil? The numbah's different than our'n. Heah ya go: 01-WHItehall 1321. Instructions ah to dial up the 01 foah the city, then the WHI, then wait. An operatah will come on and axe ya'll foah the rest of the numbahs—the 1321. She could axe ya'll for the numbahs that correspond to the 't-e-h-a-l-l.' That's just what's above the telephone metal ring foah dialin';, so, it's 8 foah the t, 3 foah the e, 4 foah the h, 2 foah the a, and then finally 55 foah the two l's. Got that?"

"Ah wrote it down. I thank ah kin handle it. Seems purty complicated if ya'll axe me."

While Billie Wayne was working out the complex foreign system, Dayne had a sudden inspiration. He put in a call to the sheriff's department and asked his deputy on call to see what he could learn about the European International Conglomerate.

"Get the FBI involved if ya'll need to."

Billie Wayne decided against making the call to London without authorization. Instead, he called the FBI special agents again and got them involved. They called back to their main headquarters in the J. Edgar Hoover FBI building and arranged for them to deal with INTERPOL and the London office of the FBI.

INTERPOL dispatch informed Senior Detective Chief Superintendent of INTERPOL Eugène Dentremont, Detective Chief Inspector Lincoln Crandall-White—the New Scotland Yard senior homicide detective on the British murder case—and SAC Douglas Wilson of the London FBI bureau office who arranged for a joint task force to obtain a warrant for a no-knock raid on the Upper Belgrave Street offices.

§§§§§

Soviet Naval Aviation Office, A-253, Chapayevskiy Per., Dom 19, across from the Moscow Military District Headquarters, 1600 hours Moscow time, the same late evening

Antoine—known to his *russkaya mafiya* confederates as Laird Eagen—sat and fidgeted on the uncomfortable couch ten feet from the windows that looked down at the Moscow Military District Headquarters entrance on Chapayevskiy Per below the room in which he was sitting. The office staff of the naval aviation office got a special treat that afternoon; they were all given the rest of the day off. The officers of the aviation office got the credit and a nice bonus; the *russkaya mafiya* were paid what amounted to a year's salary for one of the clerks in the office; and Antoine had his front row seat. He just had to be patient and to wait until the Moscow Military District meeting came to an end. He knew that one of the attendees was Lt. Gen. Dimitri Sobrieski who was to receive a commendation for his service in Novosibirsk. It was rumored that the commendation was a smooth way to move him out of his post and into retirement.

Antoine had conducted the business of setting all of this up with the *pakhan* and his brigadier, Krespin Brundinovich, who was in charge of all of the on-site activities except for the actual sniper shot—Antoine had reserved that strictly for himself. Krespin was the leader of a crew made up of six *boyeviks* and *shestyorkas* [warriors]. The warriors were almost robotic in their slavish deference and obedience to Krespin. They served as lookouts to alert Antoine and Krespin as soon as Antoine's quarry showed himself on the street.

Antoine and two of the *boyeviks* set up the gun—a Finnish RK 62 modified into a sniper rifle. A fifteen-round magazine of 7.62×39mm Soviet rounds was locked in place; a round was chambered; and the safety was off. The rifle was guaranteed to be in perfect working order and to be sighted in at two hundred yards. One useful addition appreciated by Antoine was the 4x Zeiss ZF42 telescopic sight the *pakhan* himself had mounted and verified for its accuracy.

Antoine knew that he had only one shot, and he had to make it a good one.

The hands of the utilitarian Soviet wall clock moved with glacial slowness towards the 1800 hour when the warriors and Antoine had been promised that the lieutenant general would make his brief appearance on the sidewalk and even more briefly on the street as he would be helped into a waiting limo.

Four-thirty ... five-fifteen ... five-forty ... five-fifty. Antoine was sitting in place leaning across a table and sighting the rifle scope at a point where men's heads on the sidewalk had been unwittingly giving the assassin an opportunity for precise positioning of his weapon. Five-fifty-three. Five-fifty-five. Antoine was sweating, and it annoyed him. Couldn't be helped. He was not getting any younger, and he was out of practice. He was pleased that his hands were as steady as they were during his days as a leader of sniper units in the Charlemagne Division of the SS.

Five-fifty-six. A noncom stepped out of the entrance and looked up and down Chapayevskiy Per. Apparently seeing nothing amiss, he returned back inside. Antoine and his two *boyeviks* gently slid the office window open and moved the rifle forward enough that it was about three inches beyond the level of the glass. He resighted through the 4x Zeiss ZF42 telescopic sight at full magnification and was pleased with the enlargement and the famous Zeiss clarity. Five-fifty-eight.

Several senior officers moved out of the building surrounded by their security personnel at six on the dot. Sobrieski was not one of them. Antoine became more nervous than he should have been.

"*Patience, patience,*" he said to himself and worked on controlling his respirations.

Two huge security men dressed in Siberian heavy fur caps stepped out and surveyed the area. Then one of them gestured at the door. Lt. Gen. Dimitri Sobrieski—in the flesh—stepped out and took his own surveillance of the street before starting towards his limo.

Antoine's heart skipped a beat when he saw his tormentor. He wanted to start a hail of bullets—use up his entire magazine, blow the man's head and chest into oblivion.

Again, he cautioned himself, "*Patience, patience.*"

With the hubris of Soviet command, Sobrieski strode across the sidewalk, gave a couple of friendly casual salutes and waves to other senior officers, then stood ramrod stiff by the rear passenger door waiting for his security officer to open the door for him.

The limousine door opened wide, and the security detail stepped back to give the general room to enter. He was standing in the clear, head and shoulders visible for three seconds. Antoine Duvalier—former SS general, former Soviet, American, and French POW, and survivor—drew in a long slow breath. His hand and eye were steady. He exhaled—and, as he did, he carefully and deliberately squeezed the trigger. The rifle jumped in his hands, and for a moment he lost sight of his target. He knew he would not get another chance. As he pulled the barrel of the rifle back into the fourth floor room, he had time to see a cloud of blood, bone, and brains come from the extinguished life of Lt. Gen. Dimitri Sobrieski, butcher of the Butugychag Tin Mine Soviet Gulag for "Special Treatment Prisoners." It was a moment of pure ecstasy.

§§§§§

The two Texas rangers—Tom Packer and Eldred Drake—arrived at the Elmwood Sanatorium shortly before midnight and were informed that the suspected assassin "Lord Downfort" was still in a drug-induced stupor.

"Nurse tells us that the man is basically ahraht, but we gotta be patient and wait until he wakes up befoah we can hope to get anythin' outta him," Sgt. Billie Wayne McAfee told the two rangers.

"Ah'm itchin' ta get at 'im," Tom said. "Time's awastin', an' who knows how many othahs were in on that killin' of onna our vets."

"Or if we ah bakhen up the wrong tree altagethah," Eldred mentioned parenthetically.

All four men nodded their heads.

Twenty minutes later, four special agents of the FBI showed up and took their place in the hallway to wait for "Lord Downfort" to come around.

"He's sleepin' an' gainin' strength while he does, gentlemen," Ruth Digby told them. "Ah thenk he'll be able talk with ya'll by mornin'. My bet's that ya'll will be able to get at him befoah eight."

"Let us pray on that," Eldred said.

At seven-thirty in the morning, Superintendent Axel Baird, INTERPOL agent in charge in New York City, arrived close on the heels of an even score of local reporters from the *Fort Worth Telegram*, the *Fort Worth Press*, the weekly *Fort Worth Chief*, the *Dallas Morning News*, the *Dallas World*, and even the *Texas Catholic*. There were radio station reporters from the local NBC affiliate and KLIF radio. KERA-TV and channel 8 WFAA-TV who parked their broadcast trucks in the parking lot which was rapidly becoming overcrowded.

Deputy Sheriff Dayne Brown was delegated to control traffic because the numbers of vehicles were becoming unmanageable.

"We ah goin' ta haf ta install a stoplight heah befoah the day's ovah," he quipped.

Ranger Capt. Packer received a call from Austin headquarters. Texas Ranger Captain Reggie Cutler asked how things were going and what—if anything—they had learned from the person of interest there in Fort Worth.

"Nuthin' wuthwhile, I gotta say. Man's still out cold. Has TB and is low sick. Weah not raht certain he's gonna make through the nat. The man looks lak he's fixin' tah slough his mortal coil any moment.

"Ah don' know how the news got out, but we gotta news circus goin' on in the pahkin' lot ahready, and ain't nuthin' happened yet. Cain't imagine what's gonna be lahk heah if we make some sorta announcement."

"Last thing we need is a buncha hysteria, Tom. Rumors are worse than the real thing. Get somebody out there to get control. Try to get the news people to hold it down until we make a formal and vague announcement."

"Okay, Boss, I copy."

"Keep me posted."

Tom gathered the officers waiting in the hallway outside "Lord Duck's" room as it had come to be known.

"The head of the rangers made a suggestion that we get the rumor mill quietened down befoah this theng gits outta hand. Somebody's gotta go out and tell those buzzards that we don' have nuthin' heah yet."

"And maybe we could get some of that famous Texas breakfast while we're waiting," Tom Packer suggested.

Recipes

Texas Breakfast—Serves 12 (Effete Easterners) or 8 (Real Texans)
Grandma's Old-fashioned Pancakes

Ingredients
-1 cp each finely ground whole wheat flour, white flour complete pancake mix, buckwheat, instant oat meal, 2 heaping tsps baking powder, 3 tbsps soy protein powder, 4 tbsps nondairy creamer, 4 heaping tbsps brown sugar, ¼ tsp natural vanilla, ¼ tsp maple flavoring, spices to taste (nutmeg, cinnamon).
-Buttermilk, whole milk in equal portions, and 4 large or extra large separated eggs to establish the perfect Goldilocks consistency.

Preparation
-Break eggs and separate into yolks and whites. Add yolks to buttermilk/milk, vanilla, and maple flavoring mixture and mix thoroughly. Beat egg whites until they are fluffy and firm and fold carefully into liquid mixture.
-Preheat griddle to the point that water skittles on its surface. Cover with cooking spray.
-Gradually add liquid mixture to the thoroughly mixed solids for the Goldilocks consistency—not too thick, not too thin, just right for pancakes.

-Immediately pour pancake mixture onto griddle~½ cp each. Carefully check to see if first side is golden brown, then turn and poke a hole in the top of the pancake. Cooking will not take long, so check early in the process. It is a good idea to test the first pancake to be sure it is done—it will be fluffy. Do not let the pancakes burn. Serve immediately as each set of pancakes comes off the griddle.

Central Texas Breakfast Tacos

Ingredients
-4 medium russet potatoes, 5 strips extra thick peppered bacon, 1½ lb meat (chopped tongue, chopped steak, or lean angus burger), ½ cp chorizo (requires ½ lb ground pork, 1 can chipotle peppers), white vinegar, 1 cp shredded sharp cheddar cheese and ½ cp shredded Swiss, 1 cp mixed chopped peppers (equal parts green, red, yellow, orange, and jalapeño), ½ cp chopped onions, 5 crushed garlic cloves, 4 pureed raw jalapeños, grapeseed oil, 1 bunch cilantro, 6–8 large flour tortillas.

Preparation
1. Green Salsa (never red in Texas)
-The goal is a slightly bitter, thin, creamy salsa to complement the chorizo. Salsa verde is best created by emulsification of pureed jalapeños and grapeseed oil. Leave in the seeds and add garlic to taste to make the salsa picante. Mix ingredients well and to taste and pour over tacos to serve.
2. Chorizo
-Combine ground pork with canned chipotle peppers (use the type packed in spicy acidic adobo sauce), crushed garlic paste, and a splash of white vinegar. Saute and save. Should be made in advance of your breakfast.
3. Potatoes
-Par-cook potatoes in vinegar first, let them cool, and then fry to crispness in extra virgin olive oil and a little butter on the stovetop
4. Final preparation—scramble eggs, allowing for areas to begin to solidify, then add chorizo, ½ cp shredded cheese, ¼ cp chopped onions, potatoes, and fry until fairly crisp. Immediately, pile onto tortilla and fold. After the taco itself is closed, garnish generously with all the toppings: shredded cheese, sliced avocado, cilantro leaves, mixed chopped peppers (equal parts green, red, yellow, orange, and jalapeño), ¼ cp chopped onions. Cover with green salsa. Add hot sauce to taste.

Mexico Border Texas Breakfast Burritos

Ingredients
-4 small links of spicy sausage or chorizo (see recipe above), 8 baby yellow potatoes, 8 eggs, 2/3 cup of grated Cheddar cheese, plus another 1/3-2/3 cp for topping, 1 cp milk, 8–10 tbsps olive oil, 4 flour tortillas, salt, pepper, Cajun seasoning, and spicy salsa to taste.

Preparation

-Remove the sausages from their casing and add to a small pan over medium heat. Break up the sausage with a spatula as it cooks to crumble it. Once cooked~8–10 mins., set aside and reserve.

-While the sausage is cooking, put a small pot of salted water on to boil. Add the potatoes and cook until just slightly undercooked~10–15 mins. Run under cold water, then drain. When slightly cooled, dice into small cubes.

-In a small bowl, mix eggs together with 2/3 cup of grated Cheddar cheese, splash of milk, salt and pepper and other seasonings and small amount of salsa. Add the mixture to a small pan over medium-low heat and slowly scramble the eggs~5–7 mins.

-While the eggs are cooking, add oil to another pan over medium heat; when hot, add the potatoes and sprinkle with a little Cajun seasoning, and fry until very crisp.

-Final preparation—Divide the cooked egg mixture in generous amounts among the tortillas. Cover each filled tortilla with the crumbled sausage and potatoes. Sprinkle remaining cheese on top and drizzle salsa. Eat with your hands. If it isn't messy, you haven't done it right.

CHAPTER FIFTY-SIX

Soviet Naval Aviation Office, A-253, Chapayevskiy Per., Dom 19, across from the Moscow Military District Headquarters, 1622 hours Moscow time, the same late evening

The killing room was swept clean of any trace of the assassination team that had been there, including wiping down every surface, removing the brass from the spent cartridge, and replacing the furniture back in its original position. The process took less than ten minutes. Antoine, Krespin Brundinovich, and his six *boyeviks* moved down the back stairway and out into the trash-strewn alley, sending rats scurrying for cover. Three AZLK Moskvitch 401s owned by the thieves-in-law were waiting. The assassination team crammed themselves into the three small Russian-built vehicles; and, a minute later, the hit squad was lost to view of the frantic military police and soldiers who were searching the area in a fury. They checked out the aviation office where the shot had been fired and never knew that it was the site.

Antoine spent the night at the safest of safe houses—House No. 6, Maly Patriarshy Pereulok, southwest Side of Patriarshiye Ponds, Moscow. It was safe because it was untouchable: it was the home of Leonid Zaslavskevich Breslava, the *vory v zakone* [syndicate boss and chief of the thieves-in-law] of the *Solntsevskaya Bratva, russkaya mafiya* [Russian mafia].

In the morning, Krespin brought disturbing news from America to the *pakhan* in the form of an article published in *Pravda* that morning. The story warranted only a few paragraphs, but it appeared on the front page under the fold. Leonid handed the paper to Antoine without comment as soon as he read it.

The headline read: *Assassins Kill American Officer in Mexico*. The first paragraph was: "Snipers murdered retired American Army Major Richard Saunders in the Mexican border town of Ojinaga. It is believed that he was assassinated by the American CIA because he was about to divulge information to Mexican authorities that could be embarrassing to the American intelligence service. It is a common response by that terrorist organization.

"One of the assassins is currently under siege in a hospital in the American state of Texas where it is reported that he has been severely wounded. Our informants consider it unlikely that the man—whose real identity is not known for certain—will leave the hospital alive. He may possess knowledge that the CIA cannot allow to become public. The only clue to the man's identity is that he was registered into the hospital under a presumably false name, Dennis Cunningham Lord Downfort. He was described as having a German accent. It is widely known that the United States regularly uses former German SS personnel to carry out their dirty work."

Antoine digested the information quickly and made a life-changing decision just as quickly.

"Leonid Zaslavskevich, this is serious news. I will be unable to return to London in the foreseeable future. I will need your assistance to travel incognito to Argentina where I have contacts. I will need to make some overseas telephone calls, and then I will need to have the *Solntsevskaya Bratva* move me out of Russia."

Leonid sat quietly, thinking, for a couple of minutes.

"That is a most difficult request, my friend. I am sure you know that."

Antoine nodded.

"We have little direct contact with backdoor operatives either here or in Argentina who would be willing to provide such a service. As you might imagine, the ODESSA and Spider organizations are not altogether friendly with Russians in general; and any kind of relationship between ODESSA and official Soviet agencies is strictly prohibited."

"But the *Solntsevskaya Bratva* has what the Americans call a 'behind-the-scenes' arrangement with ODESSA," Antoine stated, knowing for certain that it was true; and he was not asking a question.

"Perhaps there is some truth to that, Laird."

Not even Breslava knew Antoine's real name.

"I presume it would be somewhat expensive."

"That makes you the master of understatement, my friend," Leonid said. "First of all, the assassin or assassins of an American Army officer would make you what the American FBI would call 'Public Enemy Number One'; and there will be a worldwide manhunt. ODESSA will be most reluctant to come under scrutiny."

Antoine was growing weary at having to endure Breslava's usual haggling game; so, he decided to cut to the chase, even if it might appear to be somewhat discourteous. He was too tired and too anxious to prolong the negotiation like Arabs in a souk sipping tea.

"How much do you think it will cost, Leonid Zaslavskevich?"

Leonid thought for a moment, then scribbled a figure on a piece of note paper.

Antoine's only outward expression change was a slight tightening of his facial muscles, an almost imperceptible response.

"Let us do it today, Leonid Zaslavskevich."

Leonid had to work to suppress a smile of satisfaction. He left the room and put in a call to *Schloss* Krupp in the southeast corner of Lietzenburger and Pfalzburger Strassen, Charlottenburg Section of City West Berlin. He made immediate connection via the private line to his old sometimes nemesis and sometimes friend, Anton Friedrich Krupp von Bohlen und Halbach.

"To what do I owe the pleasure of this call, Leonid Zaslavskevich?" the head of the ODESSA asked.

"I have a mutually beneficial business proposition to offer you. Your organization is uniquely suited to perform a service."

§§§§§

Tarrant County Elmwood Sanatorium, outside Fort Worth, Texas, October 1, 1962, 0830

Michaele Dupont started to dream and shortly thereafter realized that he was waking up. He was mildly confused and disoriented, and he felt sick. His mouth was dry and coated with a residue of bloody phlegm, but he was pleased to find that he was in possession of his faculties. Nurse Digby discovered that her patient was awake and offered him tea.

"Thank you, that would be helpful," Michaele said.

"Ya'll drink yoah tea, Lord Downfort; and I will get you some breakfast."

Michaele did not like the heavy breakfasts that Germans and Americans preferred when he was healthy, and he was not sure he would even be able to get the tea down, let alone bacon, eggs, heavy pancakes, toast, corn meal mush, fruit, Texas tacos and burritos, and coffee, now that he was sick. He did feel well enough to recognize that he was actually having some hunger pangs.

Ruth left the room and went straight to ranger Capt. Tom Packer, whom she considered to be the ranking officer among the law enforcement officers gathered in the hallway, the FBI notwithstanding.

"He's awake, and he's not coughin'; that's the good news. He's weak and hungry, which might be bad for ya'll. Mah advice to ya'll is to wait just a bit whilst ah fetch him up some breakfast. He'll be able to concentrate better then."

"Awraht, Ruth. But we ain't got all day. We might be dealin' with a bigger plot heah; so, the more we learn and the sooner we learn it, the better we'll be at protectin' and servin' the people of the great state of Texas."

"Ah understand, and ah will do mah best ta hurrah thengs along, Captain."

The large coterie of brother law enforcement officers fidgeted impatiently for two hours finishing their huge breakfasts while "Lord Downford" slept fitfully, coughing frequently, and mumbling confusedly. Finally, Ruth let the two rangers in.

"Hey theah, Lord Downfort. How ya'll feelin'?" Tom Packer asked with just the right solicitous tone.

"Some better."

"That's real good," Tom observed and was instantly aware of the man's decidedly German accented English, hardly the Etonian accent he was expecting from this man who was supposedly a peer of the realm. "Ya'll up to answerin' a few questions, suh?"

"Depends."

"Whatta ya'll mean ... 'depends' Lord Downfort?"

"If the questions are not too stressful. As you can see, *respecté agent de police*," he said, not mindful that in his weariness he had slipped into his native French. "A stressful question or two might cause me harm."

It did not escape Ranger Packer that the man's French slip of the tongue was uttered with a perfect French accent. More than a little was not kosher here, but Tom was not at all sure what it meant.

"Tell me, please, what is your full name, suh?"

Michaele paused briefly, trying to remember. His brain was foggy, but he knew he needed to be careful.

"Dennis Cunningham Lord Downfort," he responded.

"Ya'll ah an Englishman, Ah presume?"

"I am."

"Please give me ya'll's address and telephone numbah; so, we can contact ya'll's relations ovah theah."

Michaele had prepared for that question and replied with the street number of one of European International Conglomerate's warehouses, certain that these Texas hicks would not have the resources to verify his statement. He was very careful not to slip and tell the hick cop about No. 13 Upper Belgrave Street, London—the address of the corporate offices.

Tom made a note then proceeded, "Whatta ya'll doin' heah in Texas, suh?"

"Business. However, my aggravating cough worsened; and I must have lapsed into unconsciousness because I woke up here in this hospital."

"What kinda business, Lord Downfort?"

"Import-export."

"Does yoah business require you to go into Mexico?"

Michaele's antennae went up—way up.

"We have a worldwide type of business as you might imagine … respected officer."

The stilted English came out with a decided Germanic accent, and it was basically the same words the suspect had used when he slipped momentarily into French. One thing Tom decided at that point was that the man was doing an acting job pretending to be an English lord and was not doing a very good job at it. What he could not decide was whether the man was a Jerry or a Frenchie. He would have some questions to ask INTERPOL as soon as he was done with the questions.

"Ah need a definite answah to mah next question, Yoah Lordship. Exactly what were ya'll doin' in Ojinaga, Chihuahua State, Mexico yesterday mornin'?"

Michaele paled visibly and closed his eyes.

"I'm afraid you will have to come back in an hour or two when I have had time to rest. I am rather ill–as you can see–and I am not up to any further questions."

He began to cough vigorously, which seemed even more theatrical than his fake lordship accent to Tom; but he decided to let it go for the moment. "Lord Downfort" lapsed quickly—remarkably quickly—into a deep sleep.

Tom left the sick room with all of its bacteria floating around in the fetid air. He sought out INTERPOL agent Superintendent Axel Baird——who had been smart and polite enough not to interfere up to this point.

"Axel," Tom said, "okay if Ah call ya'll bah ya'll's fust name?"

"Sure,"Axel replied, "that's how we do business for the most part in INTERPOL. How can I be of help?"

"Ah need a coupla thengs, Axel. Ah got this heah address for ouah 'Lord Downfort' in theah. Can ya'll check it out, raht quick like?"

"Sure."

"And, while ya'll ah at it, see if this heah name is legit. Ah thenk he's as phony as a three dollah bill, but mebbe Ah'm just ona those untrustin' old rinchers [Mexican slang for Texas cop]."

"I'll get right on it."

Axel called Eugène Léon Dentremont to expedite the gathering of that specific piece of information.

After Axel's call, Eugène dialed the number for Detective Chief Inspector Lincoln Crandall-White at New Scotland Yard.

The secretary took a few minutes to locate the chief inspector.

"Hello, Eugène, how can I be of service?"

"We may have a small break in our case involving murders of important officials in several countries. You no doubt remember the assassination of Lieutenant-General Sir Cyril Goeffrey Robert Hill-Brownwell, RA, Retired?"

"Most certainly; and how could I forget, Eugène? Ten Downing pesters me daily about why we have not cracked the case. It will be refreshing to have something to report."

Eugène gave him the pertinent information.

"I'll get right on it. I'll ring you up as soon as I have anything."

Linc thumbed through his rolodex and located the name of the London detectives in charge of the investigation—DI [Detective Inspector of New Scotland Yard] Angela Snowden and DI Anthony Bourden-Clift.

When he had them both on the line, he did not waste a syllable, "I telexed the information you need. Drop everything and get on this. Call me directly, and I will let INTERPOL and the Texas Rangers know. Be prepared to follow up on what ever comes of this."

"Yes, sir," both detective inspectors chimed at the same time.

The search was ridiculously easy: Anthony found a current copy of *Burke's Peerage*, and Angela opened the *British Phone Book*. No such person as Dennis Cunningham Lord Downfort was ever listed in the genealogies of English peerage, and the address—although a real one—was for a warehouse of a large company called the European International Conglomerate. Angela found the names of the two main executives—CEO Laird Eagen and President Randolph Bellwether—and a number for the headquarters office at No. 13 Upper Belgrave Street, London. The two detective inspectors presumed it was too easy, and that the names would either be phonies like the address, or the officers would be legitimate and would have nothing to do with the case. It seemed like picking their names out of a hat.

Anthony called DCI Crandall-White and gave him a status report. The time between their two calls that morning was less than ten minutes. Linc called INTERPOL headquarters in Lyon and informed the senior detective chief superintendent. Eugène called his New York City superintendent, Axel Baird. The call came to nurse Ruth Digby, who trotted promptly to the waiting room where all of the law enforcement agents were sitting in suspended animation.

"Superintendent Baird, Ah got a call from the head of INTERPOL. He says to tell y'all and everybody else that there's no sucha person as Lord whatshisname. The address was a good one, but not for him. British murder detectives ah on theah way raht now to talk to the heads of the company. News at elem."

She said all without taking a breath. Less than twenty minutes had elapsed since Axel Baird had made his call. Axel got it all except for "news at elem," but he decided to forego asking in the interest of time.

Almost simultaneously three more things happened which were pertinent to the case: Lieutenant of *militsiya* Trushin Vasilyovich Stepanovich from the USSR called Eugène Dentremont in Lyon.

"Hello, Lieutenant Stepanovich … Trushin. Nice to hear from you," answered Eugène. "Something new in the murder of Lieutenant General Lagounov, I hope?"

"Nothing new there, Eugène. Instead, I am calling to report a new murder that I am pretty sure relates to Gen. Lagounov's killing."

He told Eugène the pertinent details—in standard cop-talk—about the assassination of Lt. Gen. Dimitri Sobrieski by a professional sniper.

"I could go into great detail about this man—the victim—but for the time being I will telex the voluminous details of his life and career and the evidence from the crime scene. The link I see between Gen. Sobrieski and Gen. Lagounov is that both had serious roles in the Soviet gulag system. They were called the butchers of the Butugychag Tin Mine Soviet Gulag for 'Special Treatment Prisoners.'"

"Who warranted 'special treatment'?"

"Political prisoners, university professors who refused to follow the party line, and German SS officers. They got the worst of it."

"I didn't think those people survived."

"Probably only a few, Chief Superintendent; but anyone who did and could still breathe and walk would be bearing a huge grudge even at this late date."

"I'm sure your people can get something of a list of the prisoners who survived or of family members and friends of prisoners. Those people could be carrying around an equally bitter grudge. Let me know as soon as you can. Check your telex reports from this morning. Maybe the people we are looking for are part of this. We all need a break."

"Yes, sir. We will put all of our resources into that search for now."

The second piece of information to surface came from Friedrich Schneider Graf von der Lippe, the police chief of Wiesbaden regarding a call he received from Anton Friedrich Krupp von Bohlen und Halbach, the head of the ODESSA. He called INTERPOL.

"Greetings, Chief, to what do I owe the pleasure of this call?" Eugène Dentremont asked in response the German police chief's "*Guten morgen.*"

"Apparently ODESSA has developed a concern which could make the organization's activities more difficult."

"Pardon me, Chief, but that can't be all bad news."

"Not for us in Germany either, Eugène. Von Bohlen und Halbach wanted to let me know that his organization had been contacted very recently by individuals who are seeking to move their fortunes from Europe to South America."

"That can't be all that unusual, *mein freund*."

"Usually no; and usually, we would not hear about it from the head of ODESSA. The difference is that the individual seeking help provided information to further his bona fides to von Bohlen und Halbach, and it is that information that raised flags in the Nazi organization and probably should for us in our murder investigations."

"I'm all ears."

"Although he was sworn to secrecy, von Bohlen und Halbach is known to defend ODESSA above any other consideration. In this instance, he perceived a threat of sorts. It seems that the man called from Moscow—from a number our German police have traced to the home of Leonid Zaslavskevich Breslava, one of the chieftains of the *Solntsevskaya Bratva* which—in case you may not be aware—is the strongest group in the *vory v zakone* or, as we all know them, the "thieves-in-law"—in effect, the Russian *mafiya*. They emerged as leaders of prison groups in gulags and are now among the most dangerous and effective organized crime groups in the world."

"Sorry, Friedrich, but I don't quite see how this is germane to our murder cases."

"Patience, Eugène. This is all necessary background. The call came in three hours after the assassination of a Russian general named Sobrieski. He was related to the Gen. Lagounov. I'm sure you are aware of that murder. There is a relationship between the two generals, and maybe to our recent caller. He would not give me his current—and presumably fake—name, but it is ODESSA's policy to require a true SS officer name that can be verified. The name von Bohlen und Halbach got was *Gruppenführer und Generalleutnant der Waffen-SS* Antoine Duvalier. His unit was the 33rd Waffen-Grenadier Division of the SS, the so-called Charlemagne Division. I contacted a counterpart of mine in Moscow—Rudolph Vladimirovich Fedorchuck II, head of the KGB's Fifth Directorate, responsible for ideology and countersubversion, and the Agitprop Department. He knows everyone and everything, including the classified KGB records. Duvalier was a prisoner in one of the worst POW gulags—one whose commandant was Gen. Lagounov. His deputy was Gen. Sobrieski. The last the KGB knows of Duvalier is that he was one of the few survivors and one of only a handful of such prisoners released around 1956 when the camp was closed down. My team thinks the evidence for motive is there, and this Duvalier likely has help from Nazi sympathizers. We are looking for anything more we can learn about him and suggest that you put him high on your list of suspects."

"I very much appreciate this timely message, Friedrich. Maybe you could get your detectives *Kriminalkommissar* Horst Schäfer and *Oberwachtmeister* Eberhard Zimmermann to investigate the records on German POWs released back into Germany after the war. I have been in contact with them on the Gunther Emil Sondregger murder case. Sondregger's real name was Heinrich Rudolf Gajewski, an SS officer who worked for IG Farben in chemical war crimes. I will get my people in INTERPOL to find anything about possible internment in Allied POW camps after release from Russia or if he might have been listed in the DP [Displaced Persons] records. Maybe together we can trace this man or people he knows and find out if he is involved. Great work and thanks, Friedrich. Keep in touch."

The third piece of information on that busy day came from Nurse Digby.

"Listen up, y'all. I been tunin' in to Little Lord Downfort's nightmare talk. Funniest thing about that is that he speaks gibberish—maybe French, maybe German, or maybe just his fever talkin'; but Ah thenk y'all oughta take a listen. Might learn somethin' while he's not guardin' himself."

The two rangers pointed at Axel Baird, whose INTERPOL background required that he be conversant in French and German. He donned a face mask and took up a chair beside the elderly tuberculosis patient and began to take notes.

Michaele mumbled and groaned as he slept fitfully, obviously uncomfortable from his frequent coughing and nightmares. It was apparent that his nightmares reflected the life of a man with bad memories in four languages: French, German, English, and Russian.

CHAPTER FIFTY-SEVEN

Tarrant County Elmwood Sanatorium, outside Fort Worth, Texas, October 3, 1962, early morning

Abel sat patiently through the night listening to the rantings of the feverish old man as he thrashed about in his sickbed. He made notes of everything he could understand. The rest of the law enforcement team finally found places to sleep and agreed to wait until morning to find out what Abel would glean from his vigil.

Abel's notes were as rambling and nonsensical as the speaker's delirious mumblings: "*Mon ami, de revenir ici...*" [Fr. "My friend, get back here..."]; "*Ya ne neudachnik...*" [Rus. "I am not a loser..."]; "*Je vais vivre ... Antoine, mon frère, un de mes oignons...*" [Fr. "I'll live ... Antoine, my brother, have one of my onions..."]; "*Ja, mein General, werde ich die Lösung der Untermenschen machen passieren heute...*" [Ger. "Yes, my general, I will make the solution of the subhumans happen today..."]; "Don't let them take us alive..."; "*Rester éveillé, ne meurent pas die, Ne meurs pas...*" [Fr. "Stay awake, don't die.... Don't die..."]; "*My vernemsya k nim...*" [Rus. "We'll get to them..."]; "*Accrochez-vous, mon frère...*" [Fr. "Hang on, my brother..."].

The fake English lord began to awaken about seven-thirty. Abel felt like he was too fatigued to do the questioning; so, he prepared a report as best he could of what he had translated and delivered it to the rest of the law enforcement team to use in subsequent interrogations.

The general gist of Abel's conclusions indicated that: "Our man did not give up his identity. He was apparently placed in what must have been a prison or POW camp and was badly maltreated. He spoke in French, German, English, and Russian. The French seemed to be directed mainly at a friend or his brother, called Antoine; and the German sounded like military orders, battle commands, references to murdering Jews, and expressed fears. The Russian was largely about his suffering and humiliation and about his determination to live on despite all of the odds against him. Look, I'm no doctor, but I would hazard the guess that this guy's about to shuffle off his mortal coil—as Shakespeare put it—and we'd better get what we can out of him before he croaks."

The other officers decided to have a tag-team approach to the questioning; so, they could remain mentally sharp while the mystery prisoner wore down. They drew straws to decide the order of the questioning. Major Darrin Higgins, Chief Officer MCU, Alaska State Police, and Tucker Nicholsen, SAC, 83rd MP Det CID, Fort Richardson, Alaska—new head of the investigation of Gen. Gabler's murder—drew the short straws and became the team to do the first round of questioning.

Major Higgins's first question was delivered with calculated abruptness, "Look, whateveryour name is, we know it isn't any Dennis Cunningham Lord Downfort. So cut the nonsense and tell us who you really are. It will shorten your ordeal … and ordeal it will be if we don't start getting some truthful answers immediately. We have officers in London headed to the Corporate Offices of European International Conglomerate, No. 13 Upper Belgrave Street, London, even as we speak. We know that's where your office is; so, cooperate and save yourself grief."

Michaele stared at Major Higgins with a disinterested expression and then at Tucker and was mute.

"You give us the names of your helpers in the murder of Major Rick Avery Saunders, a retired US Army major right now; and we'll put in a good word to the judge. You could spend the rest of your days in a rest home rather than a prison. Most assuredly you won't like our prisons. A bread and water diet gets real old real fast. You'll get three hots and a cot in our prison hospital, maybe a TV, get to play a lot of dandy games with the other geezers in the place. Nurses'll treat you real nice, unlike the American prisoners who don't take to foreigners," Tucker said.

Michaele bristled at the mention of a prison. He spoke for the first time, his tongue loosened by the sedatives he had been given and in response to the pent-up anger that had been simmering just below his dogged appearance.

"I've been in prisons—worse ones than you can imagine. You don't scare me."

"Maybe this will: you won't get treatment for that bloody cough, and we'll see you hang and be buried in an unmarked grave out here in some dusty hillside. Like that idea, my Lord?"

A crack appeared in Michaele's armor.

"Will I get drugs for my TB? How about plenty of pain medications? How about a little nip of some something from your Jack Daniels Company and some of that Coors beer we read about in England if I cooperate?"

"Anything within reason. So what'll you give us?"

"I have to think on it for a bit. I'll give you an answer tomorrow."

The Alaska trooper and the ACIS special officer could not pry anything more out of their stubborn detainee; so, they left the room and met with their brother officers. Half an hour later, Tom Packer and Eldred Drake–the Texas rangers–went into Michaele's room to take up the rapid-fire question format of the first two officers. They pushed the man hard about his known associates, his friends, his neighbors, and the helpers in the sniper death of Rick Saunders in Mexico.

The annoyed rangers gave it up temporarily but returned to go at him again after he had a short nap, hoping they could find his weak spot and capitalize on it. Michaele gave stubborn nonsense answers. Without even so much as a nod of one of their heads or any promise of food improvements, the two seasoned officers left the room and ignored his whining and pleas for relief of his cough, a change of venue, and a better diet.

Michaele did not get breakfast and could hear his stomach growling. He had known severe hunger during his POW days which should have toughened him against a privation technique. However, he had grown weaker instead of stronger over the years when it came to need for good food and warmth. He was coughing copious amounts of blood now and had a strong premonition that he was dying. He did not want to die alone in a strange country, and he did not think he could endure starvation or freezing again. His mind began to wander. His memories of Antoine began to narrow down to the times his fellow prisoner had stolen his food, took his blanket when he was sick and freezing, and when he berated him for being weak. He owed his superior officer nothing.

Two new officers entered the room—Dayne Brown, Tarrant County Deputy Sheriff and Sgt. Billie Wayne McAfee, Fort Worth PD Sergeant, took the shift for the late afternoon.

"Ya'll look purty hungry," Dayne said. "Wanna have somethin' tah eat?"

"Yes, sir, I do."

"This here's a game of give a little and then git a little," Billie Wayne said. "Like, you tell me where this Antoine fella is and ya'll git a plate a gri-ets smuthed in buttah, little salt and peppah, and mebbe a little brown sugah. Sound good?"

Michaele nodded his head almost against his better judgment. He had no idea what gri-ets were, but they sounded good.

"Ya'll unnerstan' how this here game is suppos' tah be played, raht, Dennis?"

"I don't really know. That's the truth."

His stomach growled and began to ache. He was afraid to lie. It would not be very hard to trace Antoine's movements, and it was only a matter of time. He shrugged his shoulders.

"I do have sort of an idea where he was going."

"You mean after he dumped you here in this little hick hospital where you could catch some sorta deadly virus or somethin' instead of getting medicine to help you'all beat this heah disease yuh already got? Seems like he wants to get as far away from you as possible. We think he was the mastermind for the Mexican hit, and ya'll ah the fall guy in this heah muhdah. That about the sum and substance of it, Dennis?"

"I want to have some guarantees if I tell you about what you want to know."

Dayne mentally clicked his fingers and shouted silently, still keeping a soda cracker expression on his face. "*Gotcha*!!"

Michaele paused for almost a minute.

Then, he asked the golden question: "What immunity and medical care and housing—that sort of thing—will you guarantee me if I give you everything I know?"

"Depends on what ya'll know, how soon ya'll get it out, and how valuable it proves to be. Ah can't altogethah promise things; but since it looks like ya'll ah about to go off to hell in a handbasket befoah the week's out, Ah think immunity is on the table."

"You might understand if I don't feel completely trusting. I'll tell you what I'll do: I'll tell all for some guarantees; but every one of the police persons out there has to be present; and a secretary has to take down everything that is said. It has to be written down and signed by me, by the police persons in charge, and by the prosecutors—even the attorney general of the United States."

"Ya'll don' want that much, huh, Dennis? Ah'll get alla that goin' in the next few minutes. Ya'll get a little rest while Ah gathah up the troops and git on the horn tah the state capitol and to Washington DC. Written stuff takes a bita time. How 'bout ya'll make a compromise with me and agree to start talkin' while all of the back and forths are goin' on?"

Michaele looked a little confused.

"Sorry, but what does 'back-and-forths' mean?"

"Ah, shucks, pahtnah, that's just Texas talk comin' out. Ah mean the calls, the answers, the telegrams and all that;so, everythin' is legal and in agreement with what ya'll and me say tah one anothah."

"Understood."

Dayne made a beeline for the door to the hospital room and started all of the "back-and-forths" into motion. Abel Baird called INTERPOL, where Eugène Dentremont set up a phone tree to get agreement from the Germans, the French, the Russians, and the Argentines; Major Higgins contacted the attorney general of Alaska; Special Agent Xavier Gonzales-Soto immediately got through to DFBI Warren Brent Gaines, who passed on the message to AAG Spencer Reynolds, assistant attorney general for the criminal division of the DOJ of the US. Tom Packer ran to the hospital gedunk to call Texas Ranger Captain Reggie Cutler. Cutler contacted the governor of Texas, who called Tomás Delacruz, the governor of the State of Chihuahua in Mexico. Dayne himself had to call the Tarrant County sheriff on field phone while his partner in all of this—Fort Worth PD Sgt. Billie Wayne McAfee—dealt with the nearest locals which included getting a court recorder to the hospital in a police cruises with lights flashing and siren blaring.

It was a measure of the importance the law enforcement and prosecutorial members of the world's governments placed on this mass murder case that the grants of immunity began flooding the Tarrant County Western Union telegraph office. Rural Texans living between Dallas and Fort Worth wondered if the cops were launching some sort of drug raid on the Elmwood Sanatorium what with all of the sirens and flashing lights converging on the sleepy little hospital.

Every officer in the hospital was waiting for the most important of all of the telegrams—that coming from the Department of Justice. It arrived in half an hour and was signed by Attorney General Robert F. Kennedy himself. It was a grant of immunity for everything the "Lord" wanted, but contained a proviso that any or all of the grant could be cancelled if the subject failed to fulfill his end of the bargain.

The law enforcement officers had a quick in-family argument about who should present the writ of immunity to the suspect and conduct the formal interrogation. Because the man might be most impressed by an agent of the United States Federal Bureau of Investigation, the rest of the officers grudgingly agreed that Special Agent Xavier Gonzales-Soto would do the honors; and, as Dayne Brown and Billie Wayne McAfee said, have the fibbies take all the credit. Xavier signaled to Lydia Heppleweight, the court stenographer who rushed to the hospital from Fort Worth; and they strode into Dennis Cunningham Lord Downfort's sick room.

Xavier introduced himself and told Michaele, "This is Lydia Heppleweight, court stenographer for Tarrant County, Texas. She will take down everything that you and I say to each other. Here is the grant of full immunity and guarantees of good hospital care in a pleasant location and provision of reasonable amenities for the rest of your life. Those things will occur only under certain conditions. First, you answer every question put to you honestly. Second, you leave nothing out. Third, you provide us with information that leads to the arrest and conviction of all of your confederates in the murders and other crimes we know about and any others we may not yet know about. Do you understand?"

"I understand," Michaele answered in a clear strong voice, having just cleared his throat with a prolonged bout of coughing.

"Do you agree to the terms?"

"I do."

"Then, let us begin. What is your real name?"

"*Oberführer der Waffen-SS* Michaele Dupont."

That got the FBI agent's full attention.

CHAPTER FIFTY-EIGHT

Arbat Street, No. 83, Moscow, October 3, 1962, late morning

Antoine Duvalier was in trouble. His coconspirators—the "thieves-in-law"—showed him new daily *Pravda* articles on the recent assassination of Lt. Gen. Dimitri Sobrieski which left nothing to doubt regarding the determination of the police, the KGB, the *nomenklatura* [the power elite of the country, corrupt officials all], and the military forces of the Soviet Union to apprehend and to interrogate anyone who was complicit in the murder. Antoine could imagine his own fate if any of the members of the *russkaya mafiya* who were presently hiding him capitulated under "questioning." His death would not come quickly or easily. He shuddered at his thoughts.

From the killing site at the Soviet Naval Aviation Office, A-253, Chapayevskiy Per., Dom 19, across from the Moscow Military District Headquarters, the *mafiya* killers, led by *Avtoritet* Krespin Brundinovich, had efficiently whisked Antoine in the trunk of an AZLK Moskvitch 401 to the safest of safe houses—the home of *mafiya* boss Leonid Zaslavskevich Breslava. Breslava decided the heat was too intense; so, he allowed Antoine only one night at his house then had him taken to one of the *Solntsevskaya Bratva*'s safe houses—Arbat Street, No. 83—near the trolleybus station and the city's first metro station, an extremely busy section of Moscow where almost anyone could be lost in the crowd. No. 83 was an apartment building where an earlier comfortable single apartment had been made into a *kommunalka*, where more than one family lived together, glad to have a roof over their heads in the era of Soviet "transition." One of the *Bratva* families served as caretakers of the apartment, and all family members knew how to keep their mouths shut.

Antoine knew his days in Russia were numbered, and the number was small and growing smaller by the hour. *Pravda* reported mass arrests and questioning at the KGB's Lubyanka Prison—said to be the tallest building in Moscow, since Siberia could be seen from its basement. *Pravda*—the official newspaper of the Soviet Union—suggested that apprehension and arrest of the assassin was imminent. Antoine knew that *Pravda* echoed the party line without having an opinion of its own.

He approached Krespin with his interpretation of what needed to be done.

"Krespin, my *drug* [Rus. friend], I cannot impose on you and *Pakhan* Breslava much longer; and I cannot go back to Europe. I have contacts in Argentina where I can assume a new identity and be safe. From there, I can continue our profitable business arrangements with the *Solntsevskaya Bratva*; and our lives can get back to normal. Of course I will need your help, and I realize it require considerable expense."

The stolid thick-bodied Krespin was a man of very few words. "Eight million rubles [$27,000]," he said tersely.

Antoine nodded. "I will contact my banker and have the transfer made today, if you can arrange communication."

"Not a problem."

It took a day to be able to make contact with Liert Beili Amstutz from UBS in Geneva. The money—plus $10,000 extra for incidentals—was wired to MNB [Moscow Narodny Bank Ltd] and recorded in the account of the Worker's Cooperative of Arbat Section, a wholly owned subsidiary of the *Solntsevskaya Bratva*. Travel plans were necessarily complex and elaborate with cost overruns—the principal of which was the necessity to involve the cooperation of the ODESSA, officials of the Argentine government, and two agents of the KGB border patrol. The overruns came to a grand total of twenty-two million rubles [$74,000]—a price Antoine considered relatively cheap in comparison to his life and to his earning potential in Argentina.

Disguised as a workman with papers indicating he was Vasislav Andropovich, a mechanic for the Worker's Cooperative of Arbat Section Heavy Machinery Company, Antoine was driven to the Odessa—the third largest city in Ukraine—the major Soviet seaport and transportation hub located on the northwestern shore of the Black Sea. He boarded a Soviet oil tanker, *The Red Star Petrochemical Vessel* number 8503, leaving the port of Illichivsk southwest of Odessa bound for Helsinki. Aboard ship, he was identified with official documents as Ivan Nureyev, fourth engineer's assistant. In Helsinki, he was met by one of Breslava's men and given new papers including a Finnish passport bearing his photograph and the name Mikke Herppa Tuomala. Five days later, having exited Europe from Madrid, he landed at the International Airport *Ingeniero Talavella*, Córdoba, Argentina. He was on his own from then on.

Antoine was exhausted, but before he dared to sleep, he had to find a room where he would be anonymous. He knew exactly where to go because the ODESSA had instructed him carefully. From the Córdoba airport, he boarded an overcrowded normal bus to the city center, then caught a taxi to the red light district near Rio Suquía, known as the *Ex Abasto* because of the presence of the huge *Mercado de Abasto* market area. He took the most expensive room available for a week in the Abasto Transient Hotel because it at least offered a none-too-clean private bathroom and access to a telephone for a price, and because it was located about midway between the main metro station and the trolleybus station. He was also close to the river and its boats, which gave him three choices of escape routes if that became necessary.

He slept for the better part of two days, then did a thorough standing spit bath and changed clothes. He found a busy restaurant on Calle Lillo west of the market and near his hotel and feasted on the skimpy fare Argentines consider breakfast: a cup of *café con leche*, a few *medialunas* [croissants], and two shot glasses of *agua con gas* [carbonated water]. It was hugely unsatisfying; so, he purchased half a dozen containers of unflavored yogurt and some overripe fruit to tide him over until he could find real food. With his hunger pangs settled down for the moment, he telephoned Erich Boehme, former SS *Hauptsturmführer*, restauranteer, and current ODESSA officer in Bariloche.

§§§§§

Tarrant County Elmwood Sanatorium, outside Fort Worth, Texas, October 3, 1962, early afternoon

Xavier asked Michaele, "I don't suppose you go around telling everyone your birth name or your SS rank or history. So, what name do you use in your private and business life?"

"I am known as Randolph Bellwether."

"What is your occupation—the legitimate one?"

"President of European International Conglomerate."

"I'll need to know the address of your company."

"No. 13 Upper Belgrave Street, London."

"What exactly do you do for the European International Conglomerate, Michaele?"

There was a considerable pause. Michaele figeted for a few moments, obviously uncomfortable with the question and how to answer it. Xavier's antennae went up, but he kept his facial expression completely bland.

Finally, Michaele answered, "I am the executive responsible for all imports and exports of the products we deal with. I manage the personnel, review the invoices, hire and fire people, attend in-house meetings and any meetings with senior executives from other companies."

"What kinds of products, Michaele?"

"Armaments, heavy machinery, refrigerators, stoves, communications equipment, office furniture—that sort of thing."

"All legal?"

Another pause.

This time Xavier interrupted, "You have immunity for everything you tell me and nothing you hide from me. Michaele, frankly you have nothing to lose and everything to gain by giving me everything."

"It is difficult to say. We do some ... quite a lot, actually ... of business with the Italian and American mafia and organized crime people from France, Germany, and especially Russia."

"Such as?"

"Prostitution, drugs, kidnapping, extortion...."

"And murder?"

"That, too. We have a unique position in the organized crime world. We never compete with the others; so, they use our influence to settle disputes. The way that works is that both sides have to agree to abide by our final decision. If they agree and then ... how do you say ... fail...."

"Renege?"

"That's the word. Then, we have enforcers. All of the crime families fear us because we operate with total secrecy and with no mercy for offenders. We never give up, and we have never failed to find and punish a man or woman who … reneges. In reality, we seldom have to resort to violence … or killing, because of our reputation. No one wants to be on our bad side. They know they sign their death warrant if they make trouble for the other families after we have been involved."

"I seem to recall something from Greek history like that."

"Yes. The Italian mafia and later in America, the members saw themselves as Roman warriors, and they made reference to the Greeks who preceded them. They teach every new man about Omerta—the code of silence and also about how the Greeks would call in a particular Spartan to broker a peace settlement. If one party failed to live up to the agreement, that city-state could find itself at war with Sparta—and nobody ever wanted that. If the Spartan were to be injured or killed by one or the other of the disputing parties, Sparta would seek a terrible vengeance. The word comes from the Latin *invicta* or 'to vindicate,' which in practical terms means 'to avenge.' Whole cities were reduced to rubble, all men were slaughtered, and all women and children who were part of the offending city were sold into slavery, and they did not live long. That is the understanding about our role—or main role—in the organized crime world."

"You murdered for this purpose yourself?"

"Yes."

"Did you have partners?"

"Really, just one partner, but we had trusted and well-paid members of our organization who lived in multiple countries simply waiting for our call. They are very good at what they do."

"You must have a great many enemies."

"Hard as it is to believe, we don't. We provide a critical service. Because of our role, gang wars and other hostile actions are relatively uncommon. The families can do productive work and make a great deal of money without having to look over their shoulders for the most part."

"Why did you kill Rick Saunders in Mexico?"

"That was personal business for Antoine and me, not part of our crime syndicate work. He was a devil who did unspeakable things to us. We waited a long time to avenge those wrongs."

"We suspect you of several other murders of former military officers. Did you do that?"

"Twenty-one of them. We were quite successful, but our work has not been completely finished."

"I need you to write down all of the people you have killed for your personal reasons. You can do that after we finish our questions. You mentioned someone called Antoine … did I get that right?"

"Yes, we were in the war together; then we were POWs. We had to get revenge for what was done to his and to our division."

"What division?"

"The 33ʳᵈ Waffen-Grenadier Division of the SS."

"Your name is French, not German. How did that come about?"

"It was an all-French division. We were called 'Hitler's Gauls.' We were the last division defending the Führer's bunker until the very last."

"You and Antoine."

"I am proud to say that we were loyal to the end."

Xavier shook his head. It was the first time he had ever heard of an all-French Nazi division. He would have to check this part of Michaele's story out very thoroughly before giving it credence.

"I'm guessing that you have a long story about how the men you murdered figured into your story. For now, let's just get some information on this Antoine and any other people who aided and abetted the murders we are investigating."

"As you wish."

"Tell me about Antoine. Full name, address, where he is at the present, and how we can find him."

He was taking notes as fast as he could write along with the court reporter. The detainee did not even seem to notice either of them.

"He is *Gruppenführer und Generalleutnant der Waffen-SS* Antoine Duvalier. He is now living under the name of Laird Eagen, a citizen of Great Britain. We share the same business address: No. 13 Upper Belgrave Street, London. We share the penthouse nearby in the Halkin Hotel, in Belgravia—5 and 6 Halkin Street, London. It is less than five minutes from Hyde Park Corner and about ten minutes or so walk from the Buckingham Palace."

"Do you think he is in London now?"

"Probably. He is either at the corporate offices or at home. He and I tend to keep to ourselves."

That was his first lie, and Michaele uttered it out without any change in his facial expression, not even so much as a blink.

"Write down the name of everyone who had to do with the murders you described. I have to get my people going on the information you have given me. I don't know if you are a praying man, Michaele; but if you are lying to me, you should start getting in touch with the man upstairs because it will go very badly for you. Understand?"

"I understand perfectly. As you Americans like to say, 'I am being straight with you.' I think you are an honest man and are straight with me. I will have a good kind of immunity."

"Anything else I need to know? I am not a believer in second chances."

"Nothing, other than the things I will write down."

Xavier and the court reporter left the room and quickly brought all of the other law enforcement officers up to date. A flurry of activity directed at No. 13 Upper Belgrave Street, London, commenced immediately.

§§§§§

Abasto Transient Hotel, Ex Abasto District, Córdoba, Argentina, the same afternoon

Antoine called four times over a five-hour period before he was able to connect with Erich Boehme, the ODESSA officer he had been told would help him get started in Argentina.

"*Guten tag*," Erich answered with his usual Prussian brusqueness.

"I am the man from Russia you were told to expect."

"Name?"

"Not over the telephone. I need to have transport to Bariloche where we can meet in private and talk. Can you arrange that?"

"Have you money?"

"Only a little with me, but I am sure that you have been informed of my holdings and ability to pay any necessary expenses. Exchange of funds will have to wait until I can communicate with Europe over a secure telephone system."

Erich pondered that for a quiet moment.

"All right. But, my friend, you need to know that we do not tolerate Jewish tricks to get us to expose ourselves."

"Of course I do, Herr *Hauptsturmführer*. I am a *Gruppenführer und Generalleutnant der Waffen-SS*. That is all you need to know to understand that my word is my sacred bond. We can work together for our mutual profit; but I, like you, have no tolerance for those who would betray those of us who are the architects of the Fourth Reich. You will meet me by the Rio Suquia in the Ex Abasto area of Córdoba. Are you familiar with that part of the city?"

"Not intimately. I know it as the red light district. But I have contacts who will know the area like the back of their hands. Be more specific, General."

"There is a small gelato kiosk under a stand of three tall trees about midway between the trolleybus station and the main metro station. I will be wearing a red cap. If I see police, you can consider yourself to be a dead man."

"And I say the same thing to you. We are both careful man, General."

"As all of us must be in these troubled times. I expect to see you tomorrow evening at dusk."

"That will be a good time. Welcome to Argentina."

CHAPTER FIFTY-NINE

Corporate Offices of European International Conglomerate, No. 13 Upper Belgrave Street, London, October 3, 1962, late morning

"Nice digs," commented Angela Snowden to her partner Anthony Bourden-Clift—both DIs [Detective Inspectors] of the New Scotland Yard homicide bureau, as they exited the elevator and faced the impressive glass doors of the European International Conglomerate.

"Maybe too nice," Anthony responded. "Wonder what they actually do."

"Let's go in and shake them up a bit."

"Shouldn't get too high up on our moral horse, partner. After all, this may be nothing but a red herring."

"Never discount a woman's intuition, Anthony. I have a hunch."

"Uh-oh," Anthony said half under his breath as they marched into the posh surroundings of the company's corporate headquarters.

Angela announced herself and her partner to the receptionist, and they showed their badges and credentials.

The receptionist looked to be the counterpart of the gunhildas who staffed every German office the two detectives had ever been in—formidable, uncommunicative, precise, and proper to a fault. She looked to be in her mid-fifties and Aryan to the core. She had gray hair with an attractive interlacing of golden strands which indicated that she once was probably quite a striking blond. She was tall, willowy, and severe—in her person, her hair, and her hauteur. Her hair was held back in a tight small bun held in place with six bobby pins located precisely equidistant from each other. Her starched white blouse closed with three buttons mid-neck and was held firmly in place with a broach designed with an eagle on a pale pink background. She wore a gray business suit, light-gray nylons, and sturdy gray office shoes ornamented with a gold buckle. She wore an amythest signet ring on her right fifth finger. Her fingers were long and graceful, and her hands were strong. Her face was authoritative and unsmiling—evidently an expression that graced her face most of the time because she had no smile wrinkles around her mouth or eyes. She wore no makeup.

"We have been expecting you, detectives. I have a message for you to call Detective Chief Inspector Lincoln Crandall-White at New Scotland Yard as soon as you arrive. You may use the telephone in Mr. Harringer's office. He is out for the day on company business. You will have complete privacy there."

"Thank you," Angela said, and the two DIs walked into a glass bubble of a room.

Angela made the call.

"DCI Crandall-White, here."

"What's up, Chief?"

"News and a heads up. The suspect in Texas appears to be spilling his guts. He gave us his name ... names actually: *Oberführer der Waffen-SS* Michaele Dupont, aka Randolph Bellwether, aka Dennis Cunningham Lord Downfort, which was the name he used when he was checked in to the TB sanatorium there in Texas. His partner, and the man you are after, is *Gruppenführer und Generalleutnant der Waffen-SS* Antoine Duvalier, aka Laird Eagen. You should use the Bellwether and Eagen names to start with. You should also know that the Bellwether individual has given a full confession to all of the murders after he got a writ of immunity from every country where the murders were committed. It is quite a story. A write-up will be on your desks when you get back to the Yard."

"We'll ring you up when we get out of here. Judging by the battleax receptionist, it is likely to be a trying day for us."

"You two are up to it. Stiff upper lip and all that," Crandall-White said with a brief chuckle.

The two detectives returned to the receptionist and asked to see Mssrs. Bellwether and Eagen.

"I'm afraid they are not here. They are out of the country on foreign business at the time being," the receptionist said, her expressionless face betraying nothing.

"We are here on official police business under direction of the Crown Prosecution Service [CPS)] with direct orders from the DPP [Director of Public Prosecutions] through our New Scotland Yard senior homicide detective. We are not here to be trifled with. Obstruction of a police investigation is a crime. Consider that as you hear our orders."

"Do you have a warrant, Detective Inspectors?"

"Do we need one, Madam?" asked DI Bourden-Clift. "Because if we do, this will be a formal affair all the way—everyone in this office or who works for this company will spend whatever time is necessary at the Yard waiting his or her turn to be questioned. We will bring in crime scene investigators, dogs, forensic accountants, and a great deal of hostility. Now what is it going to be?"

"What do you need, Detective Inspector?" the receptionist directed her question to Anthony with a completely emotion-free expression, not bored nor insolent, just stonily proper.

"For starters," Angela said, "we need the names, addresses, and telephone numbers of every employee of the office. Right this minute we need useful information on how to get in contact with the president and CEO of the company."

"I'm not at liberty to supply you with that information. It is private."

As Angela was about to offer her angry rejoinder, the reception desk telephone rang.

"Yes, sir, they are still here," the receptionist answered.

"DI Snowden—Detective Chief Inspector Crandall-White is asking for you."

"Just a moment, Chief, I'll have to get a pen and paper."

The receptionist handed Angela the necessary items so quickly it was as if she could hear Chief Crandall-White on the other end of the line or was clairvoyant.

"Go ahead, Chief."

Angela wrote, "Penthouse, Halkin Hotel, in Belgravia; 5 and 6 Halkin Street. Telephone number 020 7730 6942." As an aside, she wrote, "WRWMIN."

She said, "Thank you, Chief. And Chief, would you be so kind as to put a rush on a warrant for the Corporate Offices of European International Conglomerate?"

She listened for a moment then responded, "Yes, Chief, I'm afraid we are definitely meeting with that kind of obstruction… Yes, sir, we will also need the warrant to cover all employees, their homes, vehicles, bank records, and everything else you can think of. I agree that this seems to be the focal point and that we are getting closer. Thank you for your help."

"Surely all of that or even none of that is necessary, Detective Inspector," said a now subdued receptionist.

"You are quite wrong there. In the first place, we do in fact have need of all of that information because we have information indicating that this is an ongoing criminal enterprise. In the second place, you chose the wrong pair of detectives to antagonize while in the course of their lawful investigation. Now, Madam, let us start with your name."

The receptionist responded with her name, her address, her telephone number, her husband's name, and that of her solicitor. She was now pale and much chastened. It was unfair; she was only doing what her two employers required of her. However, she was not about to be caught up in a dragnet for "an ongoing criminal enterprise."

"Addresses and telephone numbers for the president and CEO."

Quinella Montgomery quickly supplied the information from the black address book in her desk. Angela checked the information against that given to her by the chief inspector and was happy to note that it was a perfect match.

"DI Bourden-Clift will use the telephone. We will wait for the bobbies to arrive, and then we will be leaving. No one in this office is to leave until the uniform officers give permission, no matter how long this takes. You requested a warrant—you have one. It will arrive in about twenty minutes. You might wish to call your solicitor now and get him or her over here, because the warrant is going to be lengthy, complicated, and not to your liking. That is the only telephone call that can be made from here for the rest of the day."

"My goodness," said Mrs. Montgomery, "oh, my goodness!"

"Goodness has nothing to do with it, Mrs. Montgomery. This is the law and your government in action, and your cooperation is now required; whereas when we were being nice; and you were being nasty, it was a polite request. We can get it here or at the Yard. Which will it be?"

"I will render every assistance at my disposal. Here will be fine."

"Good. We have an understanding. We know where Mr. Bellwether is. You will supply me with any information you possibly can about the whereabouts of Mr. Eagan."

"I was accurate about him being out of the country. The last place I have him listed is in the Metropol Hotel in Moscow. However, he has not contacted the office in the past four days; and when I tried to contact him at the hotel, I was informed that he was traveling and would not return to Moscow for two weeks."

"Now, that wasn't so hard was it, Mrs. Montgomery? Let's push this a little harder. Does Eagan have a wife, children, a mistress, friends, or business associates we can contact?"

"Neither the president nor the CEO have any family. I am not aware of any … special friends. Neither of them seemed to be the social type. They dealt with hundreds of business acquaintances; but if they had any kind of personal relationship with any of them, it is not known to me."

"Please be diligent in gathering all information available on anyone those two men know or knew. I will ring you up later today to check on your progress and will send by a uniform to collect what you have prepared at the close of the business day. Right now, DI Bourden-Clift and I will be heading to the Halkin to have a look-see at your superiors' residence. You may call us there if something comes to mind."

Mrs. Montgomery nodded her assent and held her angry grimace until the detectives entered the elevator. She was good at angry grimaces, which usually intimidated even the most persistent inquirers. She was sixty-two years old and underneath the harsh and tentlike cover of her exterior, Mrs. Montgomery had an excellent female form. It was apparent that she—or her employers—decided against allowing such attributes to be exhibited. She was once beautiful—-statuesque and willowy—with a Danish youthful face. Now she was still attractive if she relaxed her severe features, which was a rarity. Her long service in the SS had lined her face with worry and cruelty.

CHAPTER SIXTY

Abasto Transient Hotel, Ex Abasto District, Córdoba, Argentina, October 4, 1962, late morning

Erich Boehme was not in a good mood. He disliked flying, and he had just gotten off a bumpy ride which the stewardesses had euphemistically called "turbulence." He did not like to hurry; he much preferred a careful Prussian plan; but he had rushed out of Bariloche so quickly that he had forgotten his toothbrush and camel hairbrush. Even after seventeen years, he remained very leery about leaving his very protective little Germanic enclave in Bariloche. He had vivid memories of the manhunts for his fellow SS officers during the past few years—especially Adolf Eichmann who was kidnapped in front of his house on Garibaldi Street in Buenos Aires in May 1960, and his personal friends, Ustasha Dinko Šakić, the former commandant of the Jasenovac concentration camp—Auschwitz of the Balkans—and Richard Walther Darré, who served as part of the Führer's cabinet. Erich had nightmares of being arrested even after all of these years. And here he was in Córdoba among strangers, most of whom seemed to be in queues outside whorehouses. Who knew how many Mossad spies, Jewish Avengers, or other Nazi hunters might be all around him?

He muttered to himself that this French Nazi *SS Gruppenführer und Generalleutnant der Waffen-SS* Antoine Duvalier was nothing to him, certainly not important enough to put himself at risk. But the ODESSA had its stern code. He had benefited and accepted a significant position in the organization—a lucrative one, he had to admit—so he was obligated. He had set the operation in motion to get this

Duvalier person to Bariloche and to let him go on about his business. He sighed quietly as he knocked on the flimsy door to the horrible little hotel room.

He was unpleasantly surprised to find not one, but nine, men standing in the room. He frowned his Prussian officer frown and tried to determine which of the men was the general. It was easy, as it turned out, because all of rest of the men deferred to the tall patrician gray-haired man with the Frankish nose and hard hazel eyes.

Antoine said, "*Hauptsturmführer* Boehme, I presume?"

Erich stood more erect when he heard his rank given correctly, "*Jawohl, mein Gruppenführer und Generalleutnant!*"

He reflexively clicked his heels.

"May I present my comrades-in-arms: *Waffen SS-Obersturmbannführer* [Lieutenant Colonel] Serge Alain Rounsavall, *Waffen SS-Hauptsturmführer* [Head Company Unit Storm Leader] Jérôme Christophe Mailhot, *Waffen SS-Sturmbannführer* [Senior Battalion Leader], Hugues Beauchamp, Berthold Küppers, Rolf Kohns, Clause Fischer, Willibald Movius, *und* Gerhard Jungermann. These fine Third Reich soldiers are all that is left of what we like to call ourselves—the *Gebirsjägers.*"

That broke the ice. Even stolid and wary Erich managed a semblance of a laugh at the almost forgotten reference to the light infantry mountain troops formed in Norway and especially pertinent to the present group of Frenchmen for the unit's heroics in the battles in the Vosges region of France. All of the men gave each other a well-executed *Hitlergrüss.*

"What am I to do with nine of you when I was only warned to expect one?"

It was rhetorical, but Antoine answered anyway, "Help us get to Bariloche; so, we can make you rich. We are presently in need, and will always be in your debt, *Hauptsturmführer.* However, we do not come as beggars to the feast. We have excellent resources. In fact, once we are settled, I will ask that you bring major investors of our same persuasion; and we will all begin to build a financial empire. You will benefit without making a financial contribution; your expertise will suffice. Others will profit beyond their wildest dreams. We have already done what we need to do in Bariloche to get started and have full confidence that our financial infusion will sweep away any lingering doubts on anyone's part."

"But, of course, Herr General. I hope to help you all to a rapid and successful assimilation into Argentinian life. I have found the country to be most accommodating and cordial."

§§§§§

Headquarters, Metropolitan Police Service/New Scotland Yard, Criminal Investigation Department [CID], Victoria Embankment, London, the same day

DIs Angela Snowden and Anthony Bourden-Clift reported to DCI Lincoln Crandall-White and Superintendent Guy Mutz, chief of the INTERPOL, in the western suburb of St. Cloud in Paris on their day's investigation into the little known affairs of two men presumed to be the mass murderers of World War II senior Allied officers.

Angela was—as usual—terse: "We learned two things. The first is that the most important of the killers—presumably the ring leaders— were the man in the Texas hospital, Randolph Bellwether, and Antoine Duvalier aka Laird Eagen. Duvalier was traced to Moscow on information from his office and with the good work of our tech department. However, he has disappeared off the face of the earth it would appear. The second thing we learned is that there are several potential confederates. We found a list of names, all presumably aliases, but still perhaps in use."

She passed out a printed Xerox copy of the list they found. It included the names of eleven men: Laird Eagen, Randolph Bellwether, Pedro T. Rodriguez, Gonzalez Martin Sanchez, Dominico Lobos, Antonio de Castro, Guglielmo Pardini, Humberto Garrido, Ismael García-Iglesias, Augustín Ruiz-Rubalcaba, and José María Zapatero.

"Of these, we only know the original identity of the first two. Laird Eagen is the putative leader of the group—correctly, Antoine Duvalier—and Randolph Bellwether is the former Michaele Dupont who is now lying in a Texas hospital under the remarkably improbable alias of Dennis Cunningham Lord Downfort. He has given a full confession and has been granted immunity. The officers at the hospital are under the impression that he is suffering from an advanced case of tuberculosis and is not long for this world. Our office is attempting to get more old French and German army records about the Nazi SS unit they all served in during the war—the 33rd Waffen-Grenadier

Division, better known as the Charlemagne Division—and the Russian and Allied POW records. It is slow going. INTERPOL, under Superintendent Mutz and DCS Dentremont,wehave a liason with Soviet law enforcement, and are working directly with a Moscow police detective, Lieutenant of *Militsiya* Trushin Vasilyovich Stepanovich. He has connections to the KGB which—miracle of miracles—is willing to open its files on the Siberian POW camps to help trace the activities of the German SS officer corps internees after their release in 1956. It is a significant understatement to observe that the KGB has a very efficient record system and ability to find people it wants to find.

"The second part of the answer to your question is something Chief Superintendent Dentremont suggested. Maybe the perpetrators are all old Nazi SS officers who now recognize that they can no longer live in Europe. Like most good Nazis, they may have been secreted out of Europe by the ODESSA and are now living comfortably in Argentina, the US, or even Asia. SS fugitives have the help of the Vatican, the Swiss, and the CIA. INTERPOL sources are investigating all of those helpers. Because the move must have been quite recent, we are concentrating on Argentina first. The Mossad has a very thorough and intense interest in the South American Nazi havens, and they have agreed to help. We have begun to work with Argentine police who are willing to help to a degree because an influential citizen of theirs was one of the murder victims.

Our liason agent in Argentina is *Teniente Policía de la Provincia de Policía de Córdoba, PPC* José Emanuel de Corsos. INTERPOL has an agent in Córdoba as we speak. We have spread a wide net and are beginning to close it down bit by bit as we obtain more information. We have a set of Spanish names; so, Argentina is where the net will tighten the quickest and the tightest."

"Angela, tell us about the ongoing efforts with organized crime. We are getting hints that Eagan and Bellwether have a role in that world," said Superintendent Mutz.

"We have only known about that connection for a little while; so, everything is preliminary. I don't have to tell you that the mafia or its counterparts is a very close-mouthed bunch. They tend to respond only to serious threats to their ongoing enterprises or to promises of illicit profiteering. We are employing both tactics at the same time. Our INTERPOL and regular law enforcement agencies all over the free world are putting the screws on organized criminals, starting with the mid-level gangsters who usually know the most and do the most. As with the other efforts, we are concentrating on Argentina to begin with. One of the murders occurred in France, and there is a Corsican connection to that murder and to Argentine organized crime. Benedettu Paganucci and his two underlings, Dominic Rizzuto and Tony Lagomarsino, have a lucrative confidential informant relationship with *Enquêteur*] Grégoire Laurent De Vincent and Research Unit Officer-Assistant to Inspector De Vincent Gendarmerie Lieutenant Sylvain Piétri.

"Our preliminary information from those sources indicates that the organized crime families are beginning to doubt the effectiveness of the so-called *Gebirgsjägers* and are losing their fear of them. The profit motive is beginning to take over. Paganucci has given some good intel into the underbelly of Argentine society—who can be bought, who does the buying, and where the skeletons are buried. Most importantly, he seems to know where the criminal money is being spent to branch into legitimate businesses. All of that information comes at a cost;and INTERPOL is working with the French, the Americans, and the Israelis to pay the cost. We are in hopes that the information coming in is good, because Paganucci, Rizzuto, and Lagomarsino are going to be rich men from the payments for the dribs and drabs of information they are supplying. We'll see whether or not the cost is worth it.

"We know that there are Catholic, organized crime, and ODESSA, tentacles intertwined into certain Swiss financial organizations. There is a 'fixer' by the name of François Caussidière, an enthusiastic Swiss Nazi collaborator before and after the war. He has connections with Paganucci, the Vatican, and the UBS [Union Bank of Switzerland] in Geneva. He is a pure mercenary and can be bought for the right price; but we have to tread lightly since his sympathies lie with the Nazis. Our tack is to convince him that the *Gebirgsjägers'* day is done. We are trying to squeeze him to find out any financial information about, or the whereabouts of, the still-surviving *Gebirgsjägers.* Not much in the way of results yet, but the wily fox seems to be negotiating rather than outright refusing. It is an early work in progress, I'm afraid."

CHAPTER SIXTY-ONE

Boehme New Alemana Delicatessen 420 Avenida Pepito Moreno, San Carlos de Bariloche, Argentina, October 8, 1962

For more than two centuries, the northern portion of the Andean Patagonia country rested at the feet of the majestic Andes largely unspoiled by development or intrusion by Europeans. However, those foreigners who did see the place agreed with the Patagonian pioneer, Francisco P. Moreno, that it was "a beautiful piece of Argentine Switzerland." No one agreed more fervently and longingly than the former German SS officer *Hauptsturmführer* Erich Walther Boehme, now a minor businessman in the hub city of the area—San Carlos de Bariloche. Bariloche was founded only as recently as 1902 and—with the advent of the railroad in the 1930s—had grown to a population of 22,000 year-round residents and hosted several hundred thousand tourist visitors to Iguazú Falls and Nahuel Huapi National Park which surrounded the city. In the mind of Erich Boehme—and a fairly large number of other similarly entrepreneurially-minded men—Bariloche was ripe for development and to make millionaires of the developers.

The arrival of the "*Gebirgsjägers*" would have been the answer to his prayers had Erich been a praying man. They brought with them a financial portfolio that rivaled that of the duly elected politicians of the Argentine government and sufficient worldwide influence to be able to gather a meeting of men who could—with the swipe of a pen—make a hotel, a resort, or even a new city happen. Seated in the backroom office of his delicatessen were twenty-three well-dressed affluent men who were unknown to him a month previously but were now about to make him rich and powerful.

The close quarters of the office afforded the opportunity for all of the men to speak quietly and still be heard.

As they waited for everyone to gather and take a seat, Antoine turned to Benedettu Paganucci and said, "My friend, there are some things you and I should decide upon before we talk business with the others."

"I agree, Laird. First, a question: what name do you use here in Argentina?"

"I am Don Pedro Altenhofen. It says so on my well-worn Argentine passport. If you care to check, you will find that I have lived in Argentina for over twenty years, having moved here from Essen. My parents were in the import-export business, and I grew up there. However, back twenty years ago, I developed a strong desire to live in the land of my ancestors—Argentina. You could check all of that out if you wished to do so. It is good to be at home."

The thuggish Mafioso looked at Antoine's eyes and then began to laugh.

"I was getting used to you being a three-generation Englander named Laird Eagen."

Laughing or even smiling did not come quite naturally to the taciturn Sicilian. He was a block of a man—all muscle. He was five feet three inches tall and weighed 212 pounds. He had a knife-cut scar on his left cheek, and pockmarked skin from a bad case of untreated adolescent acne. To deflect attention from himself, he chose a conservative soft white cotton bosom fronted fitted shirt. Benedettu's heavily muscled arms strained the shirt's fabric.

Benedettu had tight curled black hair, an olive complexion, a strong chin and nose, large white teeth, and he rarely smiled, let alone let himself have a laugh. Even in his modified gaucho pants, he came across as the Italian thug he was.

Antoine laughed with him, then abruptly said, "Benedettu, I want you to know that all of us in the *Gebirgsjägers* intend to get out of our mutual business and to live ordinary, but rich, lives here in Argentina. We have no further interest in the business where you do so well, and we wish you well. However, should anyone feel that we have become weak or afraid or that we hide from them who truly know us, you can tell them that they are quite mistaken in that belief. If anyone of us should encounter violence, remember that we still have a network of very loyal people who would happily cut a few throats. I say to you, my friend, it is in your best interest and that of the Mafia or *Unione Corse* [Corsican crime syndicate] to let us go our separate ways in peace. Our meeting today is to offer you an opportunity to make a great deal of money in a legitimate investment—one the authorities will not question."

Benedettu grunted his understanding as the others entered the room and were introduced to each other. Antoine's nine *Gebirgsjägers* were familiar with Benedettu Paganucci, Dominic Rizzuto, and Tony Lagomarsino from the *Unione Corse*; and it was almost laughably awkward to be rentroduced with their new Argentine names. The nine men had not had adequate time to become used to being Pedro T. Rodriguez, Gonzalez Martin Sanchez, Dominico Lobos, Antonio de Castro, Guglielmo Pardini, Humberto Garrido, Ismael García-Iglesias, Augustín Ruiz-Rubalcaba, and José María Zapatero. Most of the names were hard for the *Gebirgsjägers* to pronounce, but the Corsicans knew better than to allow anything but a slight smile of acknowledgement to crease their faces. They were also familiar with the two Swiss men—the fixer, François Gaspard Caussidière, and the banker from UBS, Liert Beili Amstutz. Liert was the only man in the room wearing a suit, and the only one whose naturally stiff demeanor did not match the faux bonhomie written on the faces of all of the other men.

The Argentines and other attendees were—until that day—strangers to the others. Besides Erich Boehme, there was a Buenos Aires banker named Gunther Horn—an unapologetic Prussian. He was as Catholic as the pope for all of his Germanic background. He had six daughters: Maria Innocenta, Maria Guadalupe, Maria Veronica, Maria Immaculata, Maria Angela, and Maria Crosifissa. Gunther was huge, massively obese—so much so that he wore what looked like an oversized priest's cassock made of the finest silk and cotton blend. He was intolerably bigoted towards Mestizos, Negroes, Protestants, and assorted non-Germans.

The most unusual of the men in the room was an American investment banker with the Negro Industrial Bank of Washington—the oldest and largest Negro-owned commercial bank in the metropolitan Washington, DC, region. Evert Williams had been intentionally selected because of the relative obscurity of the Industrial Bank in banking circles around the world, and because he and his bank were hungry for a good new investment outside the United States to start the board's program of diversification. He was a tall, thin, sophisticated Southern gentleman with no pretensions of fighting for equality of races. He was about money and about accumulating a good deal of it for his bank, with the source not being contested by the White establishment in the eastern United States.

He was what Negroes called a "Cordon"—a derivative of the name of a popular champagne, Cordon Negro—and a "Bear," because he was very light-skinned and because he was (b)lack, (e)ducated, (a)nd (r)ich. He had been called worse. When he lived in Jones Beach, New York City, he had been dubbed an "African Rock Fish," a term for Negroes indicating that all of them were very poor swimmers; and throughout his rising career, he had been called behind his back by his fellow Negroes, a "chocolate-covered marshmallow"—a black man who acts white. He ignored them all.

Evert made himself an expert on the legislative efforts to repeal the Glass-Steagall separation of commercial and investment banking act of 1933. In the first two years of the 1960s, he had been influential in persuading the Office of the Comptroller of the Currency to issue aggressive interpretations of Glass-Steagall to permit national banks to engage in certain securities activities. His main credential so far as the developers were concerned was that he brought very large amounts of investment capital to the table.

The final three men in the room were there to bring the dream to physical reality. Heinrich Stracher was the artist/architect/civil engineer who conceived the actual plan. He was a pale, small, intense, nervous, man who wore pince-nez spectacles, a French beret, and a flouncy blouse and gaucho pants. He had a wispy mustache and beard that set off his face to match his intended appearance of a French impressionist painter. Despite his *sui generis*—almost cartoon character—appearance, he received full attention from the rest of the men due to his obvious genius, his intense passion for the project, and the captivating plans and drawings he produced.

Daniel Urquiza was the experienced developer having built similar grand projects in Buenos Aires, San Clemente del Tuyú on the Atlantic coast, and Ushuaia—El Fin del Mundo—in Tierra del Fuego, Argentina. He was famous for his accomplishments in Santiago de Chile, Viña del Mar, and Concepción Chile. Daniel was a bluff man with sandy hair, a stubble beard, and the coarse features, topographical bronzed skin, and hard hands of a construction worker. He had intense silvery blue eyes, high cheek bones, and muscular arms revealed by a clean white tee shirt. He was the only man in the room wearing American three-button Levi 501 denims as a proud Germanic signature—in his mind—because the inventor of the first blue jeans was Levi Strauss, who was born in Buttenheim, Bavaria. He wore scuffed knee-high gaucho boots with spurs. As soon as he could, Daniel dominated the conversation with his intentions for bringing Heinrich's artistry into reality.

Of course, every major project requires a necessary evil—an attorney. In the case of the newly named Pueblo Parque National Nahuel Huapi, a team of attorneys was required. The firm of Xavier Manriquez-Huelsmann and Mitarbeiter Abogados la Ley [Attorneys-atLaw], Buenos Aires, had handled almost every major building project in Argentina for the past thirty years. The firm held distinct advantages for its clients which made it indispensable. In order of importance, those advantages were: 1. Connections with the Casa Rosada. Xavier was related personally to Interim President José María Guido through his mother and to Argentine Chief of the Cabinet of Ministers, Guillermo Fernández, by marriage which gave him ready access to the Argentine seat of government at will. His large extended family had done mutually lucrative business with the government of Argentina for three decades. 2. The Huelsmann family had deep roots—five generations in Argentina—with the behind-the-scenes ruling elite and kingmakers of the German community. 3. Xavier's perfect record of contributing an honest kickback of fifteen percent of every project profit for which his firm served as the *abogados*. Therefore, having the firm involved as attorneys guaranteed unexcelled three way profits—for the clients, for the firm, and for the government. 4. And, Xavier knew everyone and everything in Argentina that mattered. He was extraordinarily—almost miraculously so—effective and efficient. His presence in the back room of Erich Boehme's delicatessen that day guaranteed the project's success.

Xavier Manriquez-Huelsmann looked every bit the role as the major player in any room. He was fifty years old, tall, patrician, and slender. His full head of dark blond hair was beginning to gray at the temples, which gave him the appearance of mature wisdom. His slender handsome face and imperial sneer gave him the air of invincible power. He had a perfect Germanic dueling scar on his left cheek, and an athletic physique which removed any doubt about his virility and energy. He dressed the part—a freshly pressed beige linen suit, silk shirt tie made from Thailand, highly polished $2,400 Gucci horsebit loafers imported from Italy, and a diamond-encircled Rolex.

Even his car shouted his affluence. He had a chauffeur-driven Citroën DS estate wagon—a front-engine, front-wheel-drive executive car manufactured and marketed by the French company Citroën. The automobile had a most definite artistic flair and was de rigor among the very rich of Argentina. The vehicle was designed by sculptor and industrial designer Flaminio Bertoni. French aeronautical engineer André Lefèbvre styled and engineered the car. The Citroën DS was one of the few cars in the world to have the modern hydropneumatic self-levelling suspension which provided a pillow-smooth ride. The work of the designers guaranteed that Manriquez-Huelsmann's car would be appreciated and envied for its aerodynamic, futuristic body design and innovative technology. It served Manriquez-Huelsmann's need for subtle austentation, and in addition to its baby cheek soft ride; his car was the first mass production car to have disc brakes.

It was a measure of his importance and his wide circle of fawning associates that Daniel Urquiza, Heinrich Stracher, and Gunther Horn—the three important Argentinians—greeted Attorney Manriquez-Huelsmann—with the most respectful French etiquette. Social class distinctions imported into Argentina from the haughty French determined the importance of certain time-honored forms of correct social behavior. The classes below the rich and powerful in general greet each other by shaking hands. An embrace with a kiss on both cheeks—called the *faire la bise*—is reserved for two people who are close friends or relatives and of the same social class. Manriquez-Huelsmann was particularly sensitive to such nuances; so, he ignored the other lesser mortals in the room. The embrace shared among the four men took place only the first time they entered the room together and again when they parted. The men maintained their formality in their verbal greetings, so that Manriquez-Huelsmann was always Monsieur and never referred to by his given name. The men were in a public space; so, it was neither unusual nor rude that none of the four smiled or made eye contact with them. Antoine was all too aware of this set of affectations of the French, and it had chaffed him all the years he spent in France.

"Thank you for traveling all the way to my humble delicatessen in Bariloche," Erich said when everyone was seated and enjoying some of his regionally famous delicacies—onion, cheese, and corn empanadas, Spanish sausage, Italian bruschetta, hot sweet Chilean crab cakes, torta de merengue con calafate berry frutilla, and pisco sours. "Your time is very valuable; so, I will ask Heinrich Stracher to make the formal presentation of the project."

Stracher did so with a flair. He had fine water color renditions of the Pueblo Parque National Nahuel Huapi drawn to scale and showing— with almost breathtaking flair—the artistic conception of an attractive wedding of Bavarian and Andean mountain lodge leitmotifs—sturdy tuff stone, slate, and fitzroya structures. He showed large color photographs of the Civic Center, the Edificio Movilidad, Plaza Perito Moreno, the Neo-Gothic San Carlos de Bariloche Cathedral, the Llao Llao Hotel, the Domingo Sarmiento Library, the Francisco Moreno Museum of Patagonia, the City Hall, the handsome and quaint Post Office, the Police Station, and the Customs Buildings. He spread the elaborate plans around tables in the office showing skiing, trekking, mountaineering, golfing, and swimming facilities, hotels and restaurants, and of course, chocolate shops for which Bariloche was famous— all yet to be developed. The proposed streets were wide and left space for outdoor cafes and boutique shops. He included plans for a large casino, a shopping mal, a business center, and a diversity of churches, synagogues, and even a small mosque.

Stracher's concepts and the flair with which he presented them received approbation from the serious men in the room which was unprecedented. They applauded. Daniel Urquiza provided a concise but detailed discussion of the practical elements of construction of the development and was greeted with similar enthusiasm.

Erich stood again and introduced Xavier Manriquez-Huelsmann, Evert Williams, Gunther Horn, Liert Beili Amstutz, Benedettu Paganucci, and Don Pedro Altenhofen—the financial might of the project. In the interests of brevity, the assembled financiers had elected Don Pedro to be their spokesman since he and his *Gebirgsjägers* were slated to be the major shareholders by virtue of their dominant financial contribution.

Antoine [aka Don Pedro] was brief. He gave a listing of the agreed-upon financial makeup of the project. Each financial institution's contribution and percentage profit share was listed in order of amount. The list contained the signatures of the men in the room. The project's estimated cost was to be eight billion US dollars over a ten-year period. The estimated profits were forty-five billion dollars over twenty to twenty-five years. The number of full-time employees of the corporation was expected to be between three and four thousand.

Xavier then stood and explained tersely how the government would be involved and how it would be rewarded. He omitted names and his personal trade secrets. The measure of his status was such that such details were not expected, and his guarantee of success was accepted by all of the powerful men without demurrer. The Pueblo Parque National Nahuel Huapi development was officially underway, and Antoine and his *Gebirgsjägers* breathed mutual sighs of relief and pleasure at the prospect that—at last—they would be truly free: free of the gulags, the crime syndicates, the world's law enforcement authorities, the Nazi hunters, and of the fear of financial want.

They were unaware of the forces marshalled against them, headed by INTERPOL.

Recipes for Lunch in "The Little Switzerland or Little Bavaria of South America"

Steamed Chilean Crab—Serves 1 per Crab

Ingredients
-4 Chilean crabs, one loaf fresh warm bread, 4 garlic cloves, assorted fresh herbs (especially fresh dill), 1 cube salted butter, 1 red chili pepper.
Preparation
-Steaming crabs—add about 2 in. salted water in the bottom of a large steam pot. Place crabs into boiling water in a steamer basket to ensure even cooking—otherwise the bottom crabs will be boiled and not steamed. Allow~15–20 min. to cook through.
-Cleaning cooked crabs—As soon as the crabs are cooled, clean by removing the triangular panel on the back of the crab (easy to lift, remove, and discard). Hold crab body firmly and remove or crack open the top shell and use the open cavity as a bowl. Chilean crabs have copious meat in that space. Discard the so-called "crab butter" which is bitter. Remove the gray gills and discard. Clean interior with copious amounts of cools water. An alternative is to break the crab in half and set halves on a platter for serving.

-Preparation of Red Chile butter:
Ingredients
-1 cube melted, salted butter, 4 minced garlic cloves (1–4 as preferred), 8 tbsps fresh chopped dill, 1 finely diced red chili pepper
-Mix ingredients, warm, and pour over crab.
-Serving crab—forget about potatoes or rice, etc. Include a simple fresh garden salad with lots of herbs and garlicky Red Chile butter with fresh dill.

Schweinshaxe
Zutaten
-Salz, Pfeffer, Paprika, 1–2 Zwiebeln, 1 Karotte, 1 Lauch, 1 Stange Sellerie, 1 Stück Brotrinde, 3/8 to 1/2 Liter kochende Flüssigkeit.

Zubereitung
Schweinshaxe mit Salz, Pfeffer und etwas Paprika einreiben, zunächst mit wenig kochendem Wasser in geschlossenem Bräter dämpfen. Gemüse grob schneiden. Nach etwa 15–20 Minuten Schwarte karoartig einschneiden. Dann Bratzutaten zugeben und bei guter Mittelhitze (220-200° C) unter öfterem Begießen etwas 1 1/2 Stunden braten, bei Bedarf etwas kochende Flüssigkeit seitlich nachgießen. Kurz vor beendeter Garzeit mehrmals mit Bier bestreichen und kurz überbraten, wodurch Schwarte schön knusprig wird.

Ham hocks
Ingredients
-salt, pepper, paprika, 1-2 onions, 1 carrot, 1 leek, 1 celery stalk, bread crust, 3/8 to 1/2 liter boiling liquid.

Preparation
-Rub the ham hocks with salt, pepper, and some paprika. Steam them with a little boiling water in a covered pan. Chop the vegetables in large chunks. After 15–20 minutes, make diagonal cuts in the ham hock rind. Add the vegetables and roast uncovered at 220–200° Celsius for about 1 1/2 hours while basting frequently. Add boiling liquid as needed. Before it is done, brush well with beer and turn the heat up briefly until the rind is nice and crisp.

Hasenpfeffer
Zutaten
-1 Kaninchen ca 500 g, 1 Karotte, 2 Stangen Sellerie, 3 Zehen Knoblauch, 1 Zweig Rosmarin, 3 Lorblattblätter, 500 ml Rotwein, 250 ml Fleischbrühe, 6 Esslöffel Olivenöl

Rabbit Stew
Ingredients
-1 young-½ lb. rabbit, 1 carrot, 2 stalks celery, 3 cloves garlic, 1 sprig rosemary, 3 bay leaves, 500 ml red wine, 250 ml meat stock, 6 tbsps olive oil.

Zubereitung

-*Zerteiles Kaninchen waschen und abtrocknen. Sehnen entfernen. Karotte und Selleriestangen grob zerkleinern. Knoblauchzehen halbieren. Rosmarinzweig mit den Lorbeerblättern zusammenbinden. Alles mit dem Fleisch zusammen in eine Schüssel geben und mit dem Rotwein angießen. Diese Marinade abgedeckt an einem kühlen Ort 24 Stunden stehen lassen.*

-*Das Fleisch dann herausnehmen, abtrocknen und mit Mehl bestäuben. Die Marinade durchsieben, Wein und Gemüse bereitstellen. In einem Bräter das Olivenöl erhitzen, das Fleisch rundum kräftig anbraten, salzen und pfeffern. Temperatur verringern. Gemüse, Knoblauch und Kräuter mit andünsten, Rotwein und 250 ml Brühe angießen. Den Bräter zudecken und das Fleisch bei geringer Hitze etwas 2,5 Stunden weichschmoren. Das Fleisch und den Kräuterbund herausnehmen, die Sauce pürieren, abschmecken und mit dem Fleisch servieren.*

Preparation

-Cut up, trim, wash and dry meat. Chop carrot and celery. Halve garlic cloves. Tie rosemary and bay leaves together. Put all in a bowl with meat and add wine. Cover marinade and set in a cool place for 24 hours.

-Take meat out and strain marinade. Put liquid and vegetables aside. Heat olive oil in roasting pan. Sear meat and add salt and pepper. Lower temp. Braise vegetables and herbs. Add wine and meat stock. Cover pan and stew meat on low heat for about 2½ hrs. Remove meat and bundled herbs, puree remaining sauce, season to taste, and serve with meat.

CHAPTER SIXTY-TWO

Le Bureau Central National (BCN) d'*INTERPOL** ***pour la France **[The International Criminal Police Organization, or INTERPOL], Office of Senior Detective Chief Superintendent Eugène Léon Dentremont, 200 Quai Charles de Gaulle, 69006 Lyon, France, June 12, 1963**

In the Lyon office of INTERPOL, mountains of evidence were accumulating, set aside for the task force investigating the serial killings of senior military officers in the few months since the formal investigation was instigated. The names and whereabouts of many of the mid-level gangsters who were associated with the *Gebirgsjägers*, some ODESSA agents, a few Nazis shipped by the underground railroad to South America, and two close lieutenants of the presumed head of the criminal enforcer outfit. The general consensus at this point was that the criminals had escaped to Paraguay, Argentina, or perhaps, even somewhere in Italy. Most of the money in the bet was on Argentina, but no real direct evidence was available. But it looked like the stalemate was about to shift in favor of INTERPOL and the rest of the international force working on the case.

Three days previously, DCS Dentremont met with Levi Appleman ben Cohen, *Hoypt* [Yiddish for chief] Director of the Mossad—known in the intelligence world only as "C"—in an undisclosed location.

"Dark in here, Levi—or 'C,' if you prefer," Eugène said. "Certainly adds to the cloak and dagger character of our meeting."

Levi laughed, "And the abandoned warehouse décor fits the scene perfectly."

Eugène shrugged, knowing that it was always like this with the Mossad.

"With all of this secrecy, I'm sure that you have something earth-shattering to offer up, my friend."

"Maybe not earth-shattering, but I am hoping it will be helpful in your investigation into the ODESSA fugitives. As you know, we have a mutual interest. We have learned something that has piqued our interest from one of our Sayanim in Argentina."

"Our people have considerable interest in that Nazi country, but we have not been able to make much progress through official channels as you might imagine. What have you got?" Eugène asked.

"Eugène, you realize that this might turn out to be nothing; so, don't get your hopes up too high."

Eugène nodded his understanding.

"Our woman—as it turns out—works in a small exclusive chocolate shop on General San Martin Avenue in a very German city located within Nahuel Huapi National Park. She is one of our people, but has kept her religion a strict secret, even though Jews suffer very little prejudice or harassment there. She is blond and blue-eyed—as Aryan as they get in looks; so, the locals talk freely around her assuming that she is one of them. She informed our resident agent in Córdoba that until the last few months, Bariloche has been a rather sleepy Bavarian or Swiss Alpine town—whichever you prefer. About nine months ago, a group of obviously rich men—bankers, developers, and planners—came into town. They all bought some of the region's fine chocolate from our girl and ignored her presence as they talked business in hushed tones. She learned that they were there for a meeting with the local ODESSA leader—a man known as Erich Walther Boehme, whom we know to be a former SS *Hauptsturmführer*—in his delicatessen. A number of the men were hard-looking and militaristic, with Aryan features and Argentine names."

"Phony?"

"Presumably. Since that time, those militaristic men have settled in and are doing business. That business is to begin the construction of a multibillion-dollar development which will be known as Pueblo Parque National Nahuel Huapi and will likely make all of those already rich men a good deal richer and more securely entrenched in the community. The militarists she described are already fitting in very nicely, apparently. Their obvious leader—a man called Don Pedro Altenhofen—is being touted to take over the position as the vice president of the town's German Argentinian Cultural Association as soon as the current officer's term expires. That man is Erich Walther Boehme.

"Perhaps this would all be nothing more than mundane local goings-on were it not for our investigation into the past of the newcomers. In brief, they have no past. There is no credible record of their having ever existed before October of last year. More damning potentially is that my agents from the Institute were able to find obviously forged documents used to allow them to pass through customs, to be known as previous home and business owners in the capital, Buenos Aires, etc."

"Sounds like transplants facilitated by ODESSA."

"That's our take. The head of our Nazi hunter teams, Moises Silverman, is bringing a team into Argentina to try and find out who they really are and the extent—if any—of crimes they have committed against the children of Israel. You have informed us that you are searching for a man or a few men who may be fugitives after having committed several murders of prominent military officers. Since a man fitting that description recently admitted to the killings and has since died of a lung disease in the American state of Texas, there has been this spate of hyperactivity there in Argentina. We think that is more than mere coincidence."

On the strength of that information, Dentremont informed the closed circle of investigators working on the murder cases that it was time for them to meet in Lyon for an important strategy session. As indication of the high value they all placed on the importance of their ongoing cooperative investigation, all of them dropped what they were doing and booked flights to Lyon.

The investigators included: *Kriminalkommissar* Schäfer and *Oberwachtmeister* Zimmermann from Ludwigshafen; police chief von der Lippe, *Kriminalpolitzei* forensics sciences senior secretary Weiss-Krüger, *Kriminalkommissar* Boehme, head of the FIU [Financial Intelligence Unit] of the *Bundespolitzei*, and INTERPOL special secretary Hertzog—the individual assigned to gather and collate every piece of information available from both official and unofficial sources about the German/Nazi/ODESSA connection, from Wiesbaden; Major Higgins, Chief Officer MCU, Alaska State Police, in Juneau and SAC, 83rd MP Det CID, Nicholsen, Fort Richardson, Alaska; Superintendent Baird, INTERPOL agent-in-charge, New York City; FBI Special Agent Gonzales-Soto from Washington DC; Texas Ranger Captain Cutler from Austin, Texas; *Enquêteur* De Vincent, Senior INTERPOL technician, Forensic Specialist and Research Unit Officer de la Reynie, and Gendarmerie Lieutenant Piétri from Paris; Lieutenant of *militsiya* Stepanovich and *Uchastkovyi* Lebedinsky from Moscow; *Teniente Policía de la Provincia de Policía de Córdoba, PPC* de Corsos and *Sargentopolicíaprovbsas Policía de la Provincia de Córdoba, PPC* de Jesus, from Córdoba; and DCI Crandall-White and DI Snowden, New Scotland Yard, London.

They were all tired but keyed up enough to pay full attention to Eugène, whose first communication, by way of greeting was, "Thank you for coming on such short notice. Let us have two rules today: first, let one of us speak at a time. Second, let us all use first names only. The titles and some of the last names are different enough to cause a little confusion and distraction."

Everyone nodded approval.

"Now, let me tell you what 'C' communicated to me three days ago. To be very brief, his Mossad agents have been tracking Nazis all around the world since the end of the war, and especially in Argentina, as you all know. That concentration may have paid off for us. There are newly hatched Argentinians—heretofore unknown to history—who arrived four months ago in a little mountain town in Argentina called Bariloche. They brought with them hundreds of millions of dollars which will eventually be billions of dollars and are creating a tourist housing and facilities development in the area. Work is already underway. Why we should be interested is that several men came bearing fully Argentinian names but fully Aryan faces? The Mossad hazarded the none-too-wild a guess that their appearance was that of ex-military men. The name of the development is Pueblo Parque National Nahuel Huapi. Our contact person in Bariloche is named Davido Parades. He is in fact Jewish, and a top-notch Mossad agent.

"As soon as you can, José and Manuel, get your team in contact with Davido and set up a round-the-clock surveillance schedule of the newcomer Argentinians. We want photos on all of them, wiretaps, and information about known associates. We are particularly interested in photographs of the man called Don Pedro Altenhofen.

"Grégoire, Sylvain, and Marianne: concentrate on the Vatican, Nazi, and German interconnections having to do with Nazis escaping into Switzerland and depositing their money in that nice neutral country. Follow the money; find out the accounts where physical treasures are being stored as well as the cash. Use the French government—as many branches as necessary—and call in favors or twist arms but get that money trail. Where was the money sent initially and where is it being funneled to now? INTERPOL knows for a certainty that the USB holds a great deal of ill-gotten Nazi money. Furthermore, we have certain knowledge about a slippery French-Swiss collaborator with the Nazis and facilitator for sham bank accounts as well as émigré assistance by the name of François Gaspard Caussidière who will be easy to find, but a tough nut to crack. He is an inveterate liar and a double agent. He can be bought if the price offered is high enough. He often works with a Swiss banker employed by the Union Swiss Bank of Geneva by the name of Liert Beili Amstutz. He is brilliant, cunning, and ruthless. However, our Mossad friends have certain information about his personal life that should prove useful. Don't hesitate to use that information.

"Also, put a task force on Indochina because we know that many ex-SS made it to Viet Nam and Laos as planters and with the foreign legion.

"Lincoln and Angela: get your team working on the Middle East; those nice Muslims have extended both arms and a big hug to the escaping Nazis, especially those with weapons expertise. It is possible that some survivors of both the gulags and the Allied slave labor POW camps finally made it to the warm and sunny climes of those deserts. Find them and squeeze them for information on our quarries. We will let sleeping dogs lie about their past crimes and their current benefactors and employers for all who cooperate. Get MI-5 and MI-6 to work on their records of any Germans who were taken into service in the British defense programs. You will need to interrogate them. Try and overlook the fact that both the British and the Germans committed uncounted and unconscionable atrocities and concentrate on what you can learn about the Germans or any possible members of the French unit that served in the SS. Do they know their current whereabouts?

"Trushin, Ivan, and Katrinka—please do two difficult things: get Colonel-General Boris Vadimovich Ilyushin, your old war commander, on board to get every record available on our suspects. And it will be a considerable stretch; but get Alexander Shelepin, the current head of the KGB, to clear the way to let you see all of the records about the released SS officer corps POWs especially–of course–those who served in the Charlemagne Division. There can't be many of them left; and, if anyone knows who or where they are, it will be the KGB. The other difficult thing I ask is that you get along with your German counterparts. And Friedrich, Horst, and Eberhard: please give the same cooperation to the Soviets. Your principal tasks will be to squeeze the ODESSA; call in any old markers, bribe, lie to, extort, cajole, or anything else you can think of to get what we need. They are key. Your defense, security, diplomatic, and intelligence services know where the money is. Bring to bear everything all of our organizations have to get that information. We must become able to freeze their assets. That is an imperative."

Eugène paused for a good draught of cold water and then finished with the query to open up the discussion of his panel of dedicated experts, "Any questions?"

There were a great many, and it was late evening before they finished and adjourned for a well-earned dinner at the La Cave d'à Côté. It was a frequent haunt of Eugène's not well known to any but the elite locals and rare gourmand tourists who learned of it by word of mouth. It was located down a dark, narrow alleyway which would give the faint of heart a moment of pause. The eighteenth century restaurant and soaring vaulted wine cellar—now a trendy wine bar—made it one of Lyon's most popular evening meeting places. The visiting law enforcement officers lounged on a leather sofas to drink before dinner cocktails that sat around a large communal tables and shared plates of charcuterie and cheese, *rosette de Lyon* sausage, Saint-Marcellin cheese, and saucisse à la pistache accompanied by specialty wines. The officers shared bottles of Côtes-du-Rhônes and Beaujolais—the favorite being a crisp aged Beaujolais Blanc that the owner produced in his own vineyard. La Cave d'à Côté served to solidify Lyon's reputation as France's gastronomic capital. They were all nicely drunk by the time Eugène deposited them in their rooms in the Hotel Foch. Lieutenant of Soviet *militsiya* Trushin Vasilyovich Stepanovich thought he had died and gone to the heaven he so vigorously did not believe in.

CHAPTER SIXTY-THREE

Construction Headquarters, Pueblo Parque National Nahuel Huapi Project, Bariloche, Argentina, September 23, 1963, 0900

Antoine had a mixed day. The bad news was learning that his oldest friend, Michaele Dupont, had died. That information came from Switzerland by way of a terse note from François Gaspard Caussidière, his go-between for his business dealings in Switzerland, both legal and illegal. The news was frustratingly slow in coming. Michaele died of his tuberculosis March 6, 1963; but it was not news in the US State of Texas, and went almost entirely unnoticed except for an automatic notification to the UBS in Geneva that one of their major customers had died. Caussidière learned about the death from the banker—Liert Beili Amstutz—nearly two weeks previously, but the Argentine postal service was notoriously slow and inefficient. Antoine had had very few friends during his life as a Nazi sympathizer in France, then as an SS general, then as a POW, and now as a fugitive.

There was good news, however, and he was receiving it now from the ever optimistic and enthusiastic developer, Daniel Urquiza.

"I am pleased to report, Don Pedro, that we are well underway and should be done with construction in eighteen months. That puts us well ahead of schedule and also under budget, which is almost unheard of in one of my projects. I must not be doing something right."

He laughed; and Antoine laughed with him, glad to have something to lighten his barely suppressed gloom.

"Are you suggesting that I might not be a bankrupt by the time this project is completed, Daniel?"

"Far from it, Don Pedro. I predict for you a long and happy life as a very rich billionaire."

He smiled broadly.

"Thank you. Even if you are lying, Daniel. Thank you for giving me a bright spot in my day."

§§§§§§

Chocolatería Más Rico de Bariloche, No. 669 Avenida General José de San Martin, San Carlos de Bariloche, September 23, 1963, 0910

Moises Silverman and Davido Parades spread out an array of fifty-seven surveillance photographs on the marble chocolate cutting table in the factory section of the chocolatería alongside the letter from "C" at the Institute. The photos were front, side, and oblique views of twelve men whom the Mossad operatives had targeted as possible suspects in the serial murders of military officers as well as being Nazi war criminals.

Moises said, "'C' had Elie Wiesel and his cohorts on the International Commission for the Study of the Holocaust go over the pictures, his own files, and those of the *Algemeiner Journal* and the *Yedioth Ahronoth*. They felt fairly sure about six of the fourteen men whose pictures were submitted. They know them only by their German names."

Davido Scotch taped a name on the corresponding photograph for the six: Pedro T. Rodriguez, Gonzalez Martin Sanchez, Dominico Lobos, Antonio de Castro, Guglielmo Pardini, and Humberto Garrido. Moises put a tag on each of the photos with at least a preliminary agreement that he was an SS criminal. Those tagged were: *Gruppenführer und Generalleutnant der Waffen-SS* Antoine Duvalier, *Waffen SS-Obersturmbannführer* Serge Alain Rounsavall, *Waffen SS-Sturmbannführer* Hugues Beauchamp, *Waffen SS-Hauptsturmführer* Jérôme Christophe Mailhot, SS officers of uncertain rank Berthold Küppers, Rolf Kohns, and Clause Fischer. Davido attached a second tag to each of the photos using the information forwarded by Senior INTERPOL technician, Forensic Specialist Marianne de la Reynie.

They now could match the SS officer with his current alias: Antoine Duvalier was Don Pedro T. Rodriguez; Hugues Beauchamp was

Gonzalez Martin Sanchez; Jérôme Christophe Mailhot was Dominico Lobos; Berthold Küppers was Antonio de Castro; Rolf Kohns was Guglielmo Pardini; and Clause Fischer was Humberto Garrido. There were three additional men whose photographs were taken in various conversations or activities in association with the six identified by Marianne: Ismael García-Iglesias, Augustín Ruiz-Rubalcaba, and José María Zapatero according to their passport photos, which Marianne had been given access to by the Argentine customs service through the intercession of the Argentine police partners, Manuel de Jesus, José Emanuel de Corsos, Gerhardt Möller, and Adolf Henckel. It had taken all four of them working around the clock to obtain the passport photos, and they all had to give up a number of their personal markers to get that access.

An enlarged copy of each passport photo was attached to the corresponding surveillance photo, and from Marianne, a copy of each man's official SS photo obtained from ODESSA with promises of immunity that exceeded anything INTERPOL wanted to grant to the Nazi rescue and export organization. While they worked, Emilia Glücksmann—the Sayanim who had alerted the Mossad and started the entire process—entered a side door quietly and escorted José Emanuel de Corsos and Manuel de Jesus—the Córdoba police officers—into the small room. The Mossad operatives were informed that the two police officers had spearheaded the passport search and had participated in the around-the-clock surveillance of the new Bariloche businessmen which had produced the photos spread out on the marble chocolate cutting table. The owner of the chocolataria was aware of and sympathetic to the Israelis and their Argentine counterparts' cause, but was too afraid to be in close contact with the conspirators. He strongly preferred to maintain plausible deniability and to be the lookout for unwanted visitors from the safety of his comfortable shop front location. That suited Moises and Davido's purposes well also.

"Anything new?" Moises asked Manuel.

"Nothing."

Emilie observed, "Our covers seem to be intact. I overheard two of our suspects talking about coming by to get chocolates for their girl friends this afternoon. All seemed to be routine."

"Good," Davido said. "We should get to work and to commit these names to the photos and into our memories; so, we can be long gone when our nice Nazi friends come by for chocolates from '*la* chocolat-ería *más rica de Argentina*' as the advertisement says."

Emilia served as instructor and quizzed each man by showing him a photo and having him give the name, or showing him a name and having him pick out the correct passport photo or current surveillance photo. This took two hours.

Moises asked, "Emilia, how about you go down to Boehme's delicatessen and get us some sandwiches and beer for lunch while the rest of us strategize about our next moves?"

She was about to protest, but she knew well enough not to question orders from the Mossad leader. She had been drilled on the necessity of the 'need-to-know' principle of tradecraft. She was content with the knowledge that she was becoming something of a good amateur agent and let it go at that.

Moises was so stereotypical Jewish in appearance—dark hair, dark olive skin, bushy eyebrows, narrow face with a large hooked nose occupying its center—that it hampered his undercover work. He had the body of a power lifter and the agile movements of a gymnast. He smiled often, revealing crooked teeth, the result of poor dental care in the Kibbutz during his formative years. From those years, he became a dedicated Israeli soldier and then a Mossad agent.

Davido was anybody's and everybody's stereotypical western European. In fact, his family was among the first Zionists to pour into Palestine in the early 1900s. He was tall, slim, and had blond curly hair. His features were fine and symmetrical. He—unlike Moises—had benefited from European dentistry when he attended Cambridge during his college years. He habitually wore desert khakis and boots. He played the role of a bon vivant when he needed to while under-cover; but by nature, he was rather shy and retiring. He had taken a liking to Emilia and had been warned by Moises not to let that cloud his thinking or his dedication.

Emilia was young, slim, and had red hair and freckles like a rather sizable minority of Israeli Jews. She was flat-chested which caused her dismay, but it seemed that a skimpy figure was become more the style of late; so, she stopped complaining about her physique to her girl friends. She dressed in casual denim shirts, Levi five-button jeans, and desert boots for her size-four feet. She was small and seemed delicate or fragile. She was neither. And she had taken a shine to Davido, which is how she came to be involved in the current Mossad mission.

Moises took the lead, and he and Davido outlined the plan they had honed down to the finest detail during wireless communications with "C." It was a conservative operation designed to create as little stir in the growing town as possible and with as little overt violence as possible. They took great pains to stress how crucial it was to avoid tipping off the group of suspects by doing anything premature or public.

§§§§§

*Le Bureau Central National (BCN) d'*INTERPOL *pour la France,* Office of Senior Detective Chief Superintendent Eugène Léon Dentremont, 200 Quai Charles de Gaulle, 69006 Lyon, France, 1300, the same day.

Because of the sensitivity of what they were about to do—or attempt to do—DCS Dentremont enlisted the official aid of his superior, INTERPOL Secretary General Ronald Swing, to smooth the way and to be present when the questioning of two prominent Swiss citizens took place in Lyon. Swing had gone promptly to Melchior Martin Dubs, Head of the *Département fédéral de justice et police,* and to Jakob Furrer, president of the Swiss Confederation, to obtain their written approval. They were reluctant and took their time—three weeks—to grant INTERPOL the right to pursue its investigation into Swiss banking as it pertained to the murders of important military officers.

The interrogators in the office that day were Dentremont, General Secretary Swing, Superintendent Guy Mutz, chief of the INTERPOL office in the western suburb of St. Cloud in Paris, Antoine Louis Comtessa, superintendent of the Geneva INTERPOL office, Friedrich Schneider Graf von der Lippe, *Der Polizeipräsident* in Wiesbaden representing the Bundeskriminalamt [BKA-Federal Criminal Police Office], and *Enquêteur* Grégoire Laurent De Vincent, Paris police detective. Also present were two attorneys: Arnold Blocher, representing INTERPOL, and Camille von Steiger, representing the two men being questioned: François Gaspard Caussidière and Liert Beili Amstutz.

After introductions, DCS Dentremont asked if anyone would like to take a drink of water from the crystal pitcher set in the middle of the conference table. Everyone shook their heads to indicate "no."

"Herr Amstutz, no doubt you are wondering why you have been asked here for questioning. And, you may also question the need for such strict formality. The reason is that at least six very prominent former military generals have been assassinated in the past several years, all by the same gang of criminals, and all funded by illegal accounts held in the Union Bank of Switzerland in Geneva. There may have been as many as a couple of dozen."

Before Attorney von Steiger or bank officer Amstutz could launch into an objection or a protest, Dentremont held up his hand and said, "In due time, in due time. You will be able to voice your denials and defenses. Right now, we are going to lay out our case; so, you will be fully aware of your precarious predicament. That goes double for you, Monsieur Caussidière. You are a Swiss collaborator with the Nazis and facilitator for sham bank accounts and émigré assistance. Be patient and learn."

Camille started to raise her hand to demand proof, but thought better of it and held her peace. Eugène gestured to Antoine Comtessa, and the INTERPOL superintendent for Geneva stood and passed out a set of bound documents.

"You may peruse these handouts at your leisure, including as I speak. You will find that everything I have said is borne out by evidence, facts, and provable assertions. The purpose of this meeting is to give you advance notice that charges will be filed. As we speak, INTERPOL, FBI, BKA, magistrates of the *Sûreté Nationale*, and investigators from the United Nations International Court of Justice are waiting in the lobby of the Union Bank of Switzerland in Geneva with warrants. A similar set of officials are waiting in the Vatican. They will move in force once I give the signal.

"This is what will happen to you Herr Amstutz, Monsieur Caussidière, and to your bank: the records of the bank will be made fully public, especially those with regards to collaborating with the Nazis to rob Jewish victims of the Holocaust. It will be necessary to examine and make public all bank records to be certain that nothing is overlooked. The relationship of the Vatican and the Nazis and your bank will be part of that public record. We have arrest warrants already prepared for high-ranking bank officials, members of the ODESSA whom we can identify and about whom we have stacks of evidence. In the end, your careers will be ruined, your property confiscated, and you will go to prison. It will be a long and complicated process–undoubtedly–but a thorough one with an inevitable conclusion."

Camille von Steiger hurriedly conferred with her clients, François Caussidière and Liert Amstutz. The three nodded their heads in agreement as the DCS of INTERPOL waited patiently, his face a mask of placid indifference.

"There must be something we can do to stave off this worldwide financial and social disaster, Chief Superintendent," Camille said with an expectant look.

"Perhaps not all of what I have outlined needs to take place. As the three of you were having your short talk, I considered how things might be hastened and made less onerous. This is what I decided, and it is a take-it-or-leave-it choice for you. The decision must be made now. If you fail to comply with my offer and elect to leave this meeting without an agreement, I will make three calls and set all I have threatened into motion. Do you understand, *Mandataire* von Steiger?"

"I do. Please continue, Chief Superintendent."

"Good. This is the only offer you will ever receive. I can state that because all present are in agreement. We wish the names of all SS officers who have benefitted from your financial and émigré assistance since 1943. We wish every bit of information you possess regarding several specific officers."

He handed them a list of the known *Gebirgsjägers*.

"We know that you have a rather large account for General Antoine Duvalier aka Laird Eagen, aka Don Pedro Altenhofen and for Brigadier Michaele Dupont, aka Randolph Bellwether, aka Dennis Cunningham Lord Downfort, who is deceased. Effective immediately, you will close the account, freeze the assets, and agree to management of the account by a team of law enforcement officers headed by my office here in Lyon. Secondly, you will refrain from any communication of any kind at any time with Duvalier/Eagen/Altenhofen in perpetuity. Thirdly, all assets will be placed at the disposal of the aforementioned team to be used in the fugitive manhunt for Altenhofen and his confederates. Anything left over after the arrest and conviction of Altenhofen will be tendered to the State of Israel to use to help the victims of the Holocaust. Fourthly, the bank will cease and desist forever to do business with the ODESSA or like-minded organizations or with any individual with a past history of Nazi activity or sympathy. We will supply a list for you to use as a preliminary set of information. The bank will actively surrender all artifacts, *objets d'art*, and the like, and ship them posthaste to the State of Israel.

"Finally, each of you will resign from your bank and all other business interests and submit to regular parole-type visits. You will each be fined $100 million. That is not negotiable. You will never again do business in the financial sector. That will be monitored by the parole officer assigned to you.

"In return, you will not go to prison. Your heinous activities will not be made public. The bank will resume business as usual, absent the presence of Nazis or their money. You will make yourself obscure, and you will engage in useful work—the kind of work where you pack a lunch pail, wear blue collar clothes, and work at least eight hours a day at manual labor. Do you understand and agree to these terms?"

A pall had settled over Attorney von Steiger and her clients. They once again held a hurried and this time anguished consultation.

With gloom on her face and in her voice, Camille said, "We do."

"INTERPOL officers will accompany you back to the bank where you will obtain and produce the records we demand, and you will present them to the officers before the close of business today."

Eugène picked up his telephone and had a brief conversation with his agents waiting in the UBS lobby in Geneva. He put down the receiver and with a backhand wave, he dismissed the three miscreants with prejudice. In Geneva, the INTERPOL and other officers served their warrants—the ones with the limited objectives. Eugène had never really expected that he would be able to pull off the grand attack that he truly wished he could. This would have to do.

CHAPTER SIXTY-FOUR

Department of Justice, Office of the Assistant Attorney General, Criminal Division, 950 Pennsylvania Avenue Washington, DC, September 23, 1963, afternoon

AAG Spencer Reynolds was tired, and it was still early in the day. Perhaps it was because he, his staff, and several FBI agents had stayed up all night preparing for the encounter scheduled to take place in fifteen minutes. All of the people for his side of the encounter were present, accounted for, and prepared. They, too, all looked tired. DFBI Warren Brent Gaines, Special Agent Xavier Gonzales-Soto, INTERPOL superintendent for New York, Axel Baird, FBI Assistant Director Malcolm Albright, the head of the CID [Criminal Investigative Division], and three agents specializing in financial crimes were seated on the law enforcement side of the conference table. Cecil Prathers from the Transnational Criminal Enterprise Section was there because of links in the murders of the generals to organized crime had recently turned up in the investigation. SA Don Peterson and SA Cynthia Broderick-Carter from the Financial Crimes Section were there because they were the two best brains regarding banking, banking fraud, and linking to out of CONUS financial affairs, including money laundering.

The security detail showed in a very unlikely set of bedfellows including highly successful bankers, even more successful Mafia dons, and two quite unsuccessful CIA agents. Bank of America vice president Creighton Wilberforce and Evert Williams, an American investment banker with the Negro Industrial Bank of Washington—the oldest and largest Negro-owned commercial bank in the metropolitan

Washington, DC, region took seats near the head of the table. The two Mafiosos—Giuseppe "The Boss" D'Aquila and Gaetano "Numbers" Terranova—swaggered in demonstrating an almost theatrical blasé indifference—been-there-done-that, and "You ain't gotten nuthin' on us; so, whyah we heah?" attitude. They sat squarely in the middle of the conference table facing the government agents. Two of the special agents of the CIA were middle-aged and seasoned Financial Threat and Asymmetric Warfare Advisors who had agreed to come only because they knew they were impervious to any investigation the DOJ might want to open into their handling of financial affairs of the Farm. Two other special agents—Kenneth Lawson and Donald Martin Allenton—were older men. They had grim faces and were stolidly silent. Those two men had been ranking officials of Operation Paper Clip—and still supervised the Nazi war criminal scientists they had spirited out of Germany at the end of the war. The CIA agents all sat on the same side of the long table as the other government agents but as far away from the FBI and DOF officials as they could and still be in the same room.

AAG Spencer Reynolds took a quick look around the table to ascertain if everyone was there.

"Thank you for coming on such short notice. We all have busy schedules and our times are valuable to us; so, I will get right to it. The reason you are here is to help the US government, the UN, and INTERPOL in an investigation of Nazi war criminals who are now operating brazenly in Argentina. You all have other activities that you would prefer not to be made public, and we have no wish to venture into those areas...," he paused for effect, "unless we absolutely have to do so. We are here to talk about money.

"All of you are engaged in financing a real estate venture in Bariloche, Argentina. We have every intention to have you volunteer to stop doing so. The reason is that the prime movers of the project are murderous Nazi war criminals and fugitives who are living and working in Argentina illegally. We ask your help. Because our operation is so sensitive, we are going to ask you to volunteer to be sequestrated for a few days while our operation is carried out."

Everyone on the other side of the table began to argue that their rights would be violated, that there was no due process in what the government was requiring; and the government had no jurisdiction ... etc., etc.

Spencer waited until the furor subsided then said, "As simply as I can put it, gentlemen, we have both the legal right and the authority to do so. It is in the interest of national security, and we have a presidential order. Relax. This will pass quickly. We also require that you say nothing about this mission for the next thirty years. That is a requirement of the National Secrets Act."

"So, what exactly do you want from us?" Evert Williams, the only black man in the room, asked with authority in his voice.

"I'll answer that in a moment. First, I want you to know why in some detail. That's why Special Agents of the FBI Cecil Prathers from the Transnational Criminal Enterprise Section and SAs Don Peterson and Cynthia Broderick-Carter from the Financial Crimes Section are here. They will present a legal history of the case in question."

Prathers explained the links between the murders of the generals and organized crime, and Broderick-Carter presented a prosecutorial legal brief explaining why the financial involvement of anyone was considered part of a criminal conspiracy and was in violation of the treating-with-the-enemy clauses of the National Security Act. She pointedly directed her eyes towards CIA agents Kenneth Lawson and Donald Martin Allenton for her next explanation.

"The CIA has a plan called Operation Paperclip which secretly—even to the Congress—brought Nazi war criminals to the United States and gave money to Italy, Germany, the UK, and Argentina to either extricate the Nazi SS scientists and bring them to the US or keep them in safe situations in England, Germany, and Argentina where they could continue their work with the United States being the recipient of the scientific knowledge harvest."

"So," interrupted Spencer, "what we want and are prepared to enforce and to monitor is for each and all of you to cease and desist immediately from funding this one particular enterprise. That should bring down the elaborate and expensive assistance program which keeps the criminals we are after from being protected. We can tighten the noose around their necks and bring them to justice."

"This is racist!" exclaimed Evert. "I hate to play the race card, but we will never allow ourselves to be bullied."

"Our business is perfectly legit!" blurted out the two Mafiosos almost simultaneously.

"Operation Paperclip is classified!" the two older CIA agents snarled.

"These are the requests and the conditions for your release back into society: as soon as you leave this meeting, both banks will call their Argentine receiving banks and cancel all further payments. You Italian gentlemen will sever your financial connections with the Corsican Union Corse and all of their offshoot Gitans having to do with this Bariloche project. The same thing applies for you two bankers. It is time to recognize that you have gotten into business with dogs. You may be aware of the old Spanish saw that says, '*Si usted se acuesta con perros te levantas con pulgas,*' which roughly translates to 'If you lie down with dogs, you get up with fleas.' It is in your best interests to cut these war criminals off immediately. The same goes for the CIA. You have been funding this project in order to reap profits which will allow you to maintain your Operation Paperclip well into the future. I am here to tell you that I—for one—do not in the least approve of what you are doing. In this instance I can do something about it. Cease and desist with your Argentine adventure."

There was a self-confident but reserved chorus from the attendees, "And if we don't?"

DFBI Gaines chose to answer. "Glad you asked. If you decide to persist, the first thing I will do is turn over all the information the bureau has to the IRS CI [Internal Revenue Service, Criminal Investigation division]. They—along with the FBI and incidentally, the CIA offices on the right side of the law—will make everything you are doing public and with the full force of our investigative bodies. Heads will roll, and I think several of yours will be part of the rolling. Our agencies will see to it that you are bankrupt in the end. If I have anything to do with it, some or all of you will go to prison. Now, I ask you, are those Nazi war criminals worth it?"

The accused men realized that the government's options and power would destroy them in the end, but they hated being bullied and cornered. Evert Williams was the only one to raise a challenge, and it was halfhearted.

"We will not be bullied, sir."

"Yes, Mr. Evert, you will."

"Is that a threat?"

"Yes. Think for a moment what the tenacious and patient bulldogs of the IRS CI did to Al Capone. Do you think–even for a moment–that you can withstand their scrutiny and ill will?"

"I suppose not, but you are overstepping your authority."

"Perhaps so, but should you resist, in the end, we will outlast you; and you will be nothing but a negative footnote in the history of finance and a hiss and a byword for the cause of Negro equality."

At the end of the meeting, there was general unhappiness on the part of the targeted financiers, but they all reluctantly agreed to accompany the DOJ security personnel to their new vacation homes in Fort Meade, Maryland. Most of them were aware that it was the ultimately secure and most comfortable prison or safe house in the world—whichever one warranted. They were allowed one call each, and that was to set the processes of cessation of funding into accelerated motion.

§§§§§

Palais de Justice Boulevard du Palais in the Île de la Cité in central Paris, *SDM* [*Service de Contrôle Budgétaire et Comptable Ministériel*—Office of Accounting and Budget], Office of Philippe Jean Joseph de Douai, assistant minister, that same afternoon

Assistant Minister de Douai and his accountants, *Directeur Général de la Police Nationale*—the Sûreté—and his two senior subordinates, and chief of police for Ajaccio, Corsica, Ange-Pierre Persie, faced Don Agapito, the ruthless chieftain of the Guérini clan—the ruling dynasty of the *Unione Corse* on Corsica and one of the driving forces which earned the French protectorate the title of "Murder Island"—and his three principal underchieftains— Benedettu Paganucci, Dominic Rizzuto, and Tony Lagomarsino. The men looked across a table laden with Corsican Brocciu, Pulenda, and Figatellu, and *niulincu, balaninu, bastilicacciu,* and *sartinesu* goat's milk cheeses. The Corsican meats included generous slices of Corsican pork produced from pigs bred with wild boars and then castrated at an early age. The Corsican beverage was *biera accumudata cu a castagna* [chestnut beer], and for both the Corsicans and the Parisians, there was fresh sangria. For the tastes of the Frenchmen, de Douai set out a fine young red wine— Beaujolais Nouveau.

The etiquette of France demanded that no business be conducted until after lunch, even high-level police communications with known criminals; this was Paris, after all. The men enjoyed Cuban cigars and an after-dinner digestif of Cointreau, a brand of triple sec—an orange-flavoured *liqueur*—produced in Saint-Barthélemy-d'Anjou. As a sign that the business for which Don Agapito and his men had been summoned to Paris could begin, the Corsican oligarch pushed back his chair and rested on its back two legs in an exaggeratedly relaxed position.

Agapito was fat with a face so porcine and fleshy he could hardly keep his eyes open. He had ruddy streaks lined with spidery veins indicative of his advancing liver cirrhosis. Like many of his paisanos, the don had bad teeth—full of caries and gaps where teeth had been removed. His gums were swollen and enflamed from poor dental hygiene; they oozed a small amount of odoriferous purulent material which he constantly spat into a fine monogramed silk handkerchief. The lifelong failure to practice even a minimum of mouth care produced a neglect that gave his teeth a green color. He had halitosis powerful enough to keep all but the most obsequious at an arm's length distance. He wore a dirty white shirt with sweat-stained armpits and a short tie that had once been red and black but was now a splotchy maroon and gray. His pants were held up by a pair of overwide leather braces. His clothing had not been cleaned in days, and the body odor he emitted increased the distance created between him and anyone with whom he talked.

He scratched his proturant abdomen then asked, "Now, Minister de Douai, to what do we humble Corsicans owe the honor of sharing lunch and fine things to drink with the head of the SDM and our esteemed Ange-Pierre Persie? Your presence suggests matters related only to money, and Chief Persie's presence makes one wonder about criminal matters."

"Some of both, Don Agapito. We report to you that we have a criminal and monetary interest in several former SS officers and fugitives currently living in Argentina. They are guilty of truly heinous crimes which have no statute of limitations under the United Nations Rule 160—the non-applicability of statutory limitations to war crimes and crimes against humanity including retroactive reach to noncurrent wars. As part of an international fugitive manhunt, the interest of the *Service de Contrôle Budgétaire et Comptable Ministériel* is to interdict the flow of money to and from the fugitives in order to impede their defenses. We French shall do our part—which is to halt the commerce and bribery—while others attend to the more regular police actions.

"What does that have to do with the *Unione Corse*, Minister?" asked Don Agapito.

"You have invested in a development project in Bariloche, Argentina, which is known to be active in the establishment of the status of the war criminals into Argentine society and protection by the Argentine government. They have murdered senior military officers from around the world, and we cannot allow that to go uncorrected."

"I see. And what exactly can we do for you? I presume that we are not being accused of a financial crime?"

"Not yet. If you were to cut off all funding and all business transactions of any kind with the men involved—and we know that you are fully aware of their names and crimes—all interest by the French and Corsican governments in your financial affairs would cease until or unless there should be new such crimes. We require that that divorcement from those people come from you today."

"Would that be a matter put into writing, Minister de Douai?"

"I have a document already prepared, Don Agapito. All it lacks is your signature and that of Mssrs. Paganucci, Rizzuto, and Lagomarsino who are all signatories to the legal documents in Argentina which got the project there underway and which keep it afloat. We do not want that project to succeed. We are serious enough about that to make life … shall we say … *greviously difficile* … for individuals or organizations that thwart our intentions. We would be aggrieved to have to do that given our long-standing history of cordial cooperation."

The Corsican crime lord reached for the paper, signed it with a flourish, and handed it to his three subordinates.

"What real interest do we Frenchmen and Corsicans have in some nothing business transaction a backward place such as Argentina?"

"Indeed," agreed Asst. Minister de Douai, "and it goes without saying that there will be no further involvement by your Sicilian, American, and Campanian … associates?"

Don Agapito gave only the slightest nod of his head to convey his assent. Nothing more was necessary. The *Unione Corse* and the governments of Corsica and France had a long and productive gentlemens' agreement which neither party wished to jeopardize. The *Unione* provided invaluable assistance to France when it was in its extremity by supplying highly capable resistance fighters against the invading Nazis during World War II and served very effectively as strike breakers and to keep Marseille out of communist hands after the war.

The French government, law enforcement officials, the SDECE [*Service de Documentation Extérieure et de Contre-Espionnage*—France's external intelligence agency], and the American Central Intelligence Agency, for their part, "deemphasized" law enforcement of such celebrated criminal enterprizes as the French Connection—a highly lucrative heroin industry—after World War II in exchange for Corsicans working vigorously to prevent French communists from bringing the old port of Marseille under their control.

The French Connection was an elaborate and complicated scheme by which smugglers moved morphine from Indochina to Turkey and Beirut and then to *Unione Corse* laboratories in Marseille for processing into high quality heroin. The final product was then sent to the United States after first passing through Canada. It was a winning arrangement for everyone involved.

BOOK FOUR

ENDGAME

CHAPTER SIXTY-FIVE

Israeli Institute for Intelligence and Special Operations [Mossad *LeAliyah Bet*], Headquarters of Director Levi Appleman ben Cohen, Glilot Junction on Highway 2, Ramat Aviv Neighborhood of Tel Aviv, September 28, 1963, afternoon

The Mossad director of *katsas* [field agents] and the director of the most secret department—the *kidons* [legal assassins]—met with "C," as the director was known. Most directors of the world's smallest—and arguably, the most effective—intelligence service were secretive individuals by personal preference and by operational necessity; so, they usually went by only the first initial of their surnames. The issue at hand was the eradication of a business, its finances, and its senior officers in faraway San Carlos de Bariloche, Argentina. Mossad's interest was tangential to that of the intelligence services of the US, the UK, Germany, France, the Soviet Union, INTERPOL, and—oddly enough—Argentina itself. For Mossad, it was a payment of debts owed the CIA for assistance in the Arab-Israeli conflict of 1956 and the establishment of defense measures thereafter and the opportunity to erase another set of protected SS war criminals. For the other countries, the purpose was the apprehension, if possible—or the death, if necessary—of the international murderers of their senior military officers.

Abraham ben Levy, the senior *katsa*, gave "C" a succinct and to-the-point current status of what Israel and its partners were calling Project Save the Generals. His information came from twice daily updates from Moises Silverman and Davido Parades, the Mossad agents on site in Bariloche.

"All of the main group of killers are known to be in Bariloche as of noon today, Director. They will attend a meeting of financial supporters and their attorney for the Pueblo Parque National Nahuel Huapi project after siesta—about four in the afternoon. Moises has twelve men in place and set to go once you give the signal, "C." Davido says that it is unlikely that financial supporters and the killers will meet anytime soon after today. One of our Sayanim working in the project office told Moises and Davido that there appears to be some sort of tension or greater concern than usual among the principals. The meeting was a surprise to all of the Bariloche residents involved in the project other than the president and CEO apparently."

"Are we ready?"

"Moises and Davido tell us they are," Abraham said.

"Separately, our two *kidons* reported to me that they have an additional ten men hidden in the town ready to strike inside the delicatessen where the meeting is to be held. The *kidons* will lead the on-site approach; and the other ten are seasoned IDF combat veterans who will handle defenses from outsiders, police, and bystanders. They have four well-trained snipers. It is a Nazi-supporting town; so they are prepared for the worst," Lev Mizrahi, the leader of the *kidon* squad, added.

"Any CIA or other security services presence?"

"Conspicuous by their absence."

"Have all of our people gotten rid of their Israeli papers and identities and have appropriate papers on them to convince the local authorities that the troublemakers are—or better, *were*—Argentines if things don't go as planned?"

"Yes, sir. If you don't mind me saying so, they didn't just fall off the turnip truck, as the Texans like to say."

"Of course, Lev. I am understandably nervous about this adventure. We seem to be out on a limb, as usual. The CIA and the rest of our 'comrades' are out there busily establishing plausible denial."

"Not unexpected, sad to say."

"So, let me be paranoid. Do our people have the right kind of clothes to fit in with the citizens of Argentina? Are their weapons traceable to somebody else besides the Children of Israel? Does every man and woman have an L-pill? Are their legends good enough to pass muster and to keep the wolves away from Israel's doorsteps? Are their communications secure?"

"Yes to all of that. The Institute's documents officers have been very thorough. I defy anyone to prove that these men and women are anything but what they appear in public to be. As to communications, we have been strict about using only a one-time pad for all our communiqués [Irregular-sized strings of random numbers for one-time use as a key in enciphering messages; the proper use of a one-time pad renders a message all but mathematically unbreakable.]," Lev stated definitively, with Abraham adding his agreement with a positive head nod.

"Anything I forgot to ask or otherwise need to know?" "C" asked earnestly.

"We can't think of anything. My thinker's sore from trying," Abraham said.

"Then, I'll call the old sabra. He's waiting for my call. We'll have a signed directive in the next fifteen minutes.

"Sabra" was an apt descriptor for the prime minister. He was one of the Israelis who were born in Palestine, and he—as the word signifies—was indeed a thorny character.

§§§§§

Boehme New Alemana Delicatessen 420 Avenida Pepito Moreno, San Carlos de Bariloche, Argentina, that same afternoon, four o'clock

At three-thirty—before the appointed hour for the meeting on the strange events swirling around financing of the Pueblo Parque National Nahuel Huapi Project—only Antoine, his *Gebirgsjägers*, the project's attorney, Xavier Manriquez-Huelsmann, and the project manager, Daniel Urquiza, showed up. They sat stiffly in near silence for almost thirty minutes waiting for the expected financiers to enter the back room of the delicatessen, but not a single one came in by five to four.

Antoine stepped out of the back room office and called to Erich Boehme, "Erich, *mein freund*, please have your staff contact the airports and the bus lines to see if there is some problem in travel. If I may, I would like to use your other telephone to contact New York, Corsica, and Switzerland myself. You may record it as a business expense."

"Of course, call as much as you need, *Generalleutnant*."

For the first time, Antoine began to get angry and to have a nagging fear when he could not reach anyone at the six numbers he called. They were out; or they were occupied; or the one answering was unfamiliar with the name of Don Pedro Altenhofen. Alarm klaxons began to go off in Antoine's head. His biggest struggle was to maintain a calm demeanor.

He strode purposefully back into the small room in the back of the delicatessen.

"Meeting is over. Our financiers are not coming and are not available for my calls."

Erich Boehme walked back in and interrupted, "No luck on my efforts to learn any reason why your money people would have been unable to get here: —weather is good, no flights cancelled, no problems with roads or buses. The conclusion is that they did not come. Charitably, all of them failed to get the message to come, or they collectively forgot."

The implications were simple and clear. A trace of urgency had entered Erich's voice.

"Are you a gambling man, Erich?" Antoine asked.

"I am, Don Pedro."

"How are you going to place your bets on this issue?"

"Ninety-nine to one against this being some convoluted mistake. One hundred to none says that this means Nazi hunters."

Antoine and the *Gebirgsjägers* did not have the tiniest inkling to bet against the former Nazi's salient observation.

Antoine had had a long life of moving into action when it was necessary, and he did not hesitate now.

"Xavier and Daniel, leave by the back door right now and don't stop until you board the nearest bus going north. The Nazi hunters and INTERPOL won't really be after you right now, and they won't expect you to stoop so low as to take a bus. Giving up your limos is a small price to pay for the peace of mind you will gain from having your freedom. Once back in the cities, make your records disappear, and deny any involvement."

The lawyer and the project manager did not hesitate. They walked as fast as they could out of the room and away from Boehme's delicatessen, avoiding main streets and drawing any attention to themselves. They found a bus terminal three kilometers east of central Bariloche next to the train station on RN237 [Ave. 12 de Octubre]. There were plenty seats available on El Crucero del Norte bus lines super cama class which had wide and large seats, steward onboard, working lavatories, and edible safe food. They paid cash at ticket station number 122 and booked a nonstop trip all the way to Lima, Peru. Twenty minutes later they were moving swiftly and comfortably on Ruta Nacional No. 237—the *main* Neuquén-*Bariloche highway*—bound for Lima and safety 2032 miles north.

Despite the tedium of the three-day trip, the grand vistas they witnessed from the large bus windows were rewarding and eye-opening to these city men. South America has some of the most startling scenery on earth, and they saw a great expanse and variety of it. They passed snowcapped mountains—many of them volcanoes—apparently endless barren deserts and salt flats, bizarre rose-colored rock formations shaped by the elements, lush tropical jungles, ancient ruins, and deep canyons before they finally stepped out into the bus terminal in La Ciudad de los Reyes—the Metropolitan Municipality of Lima. Had they gone by air like civilized men instead of potential fugitives, Xavier and Daniel would have only taken four hours and thirteen minutes, but then they would have missed what was the real Argentina and points north.

Antoine gave Xavier and Daniel ten minutes, then he and the other *Gebirgsjägers* left the delicatessen through a side window and kept close to the building walls as they made their way along a circuitous route through the labyrinthine alleyways behind the myriad new stores and restaurants surrounding the delicatessen. Antoine ran the escape like an army maneuver. He sent Serge to the escape cache of fresh passports—two for each man—and cash enough to last a frugal fugitive two weeks. He dispatched Hugues and Jérôme out as scouts to make sure that there were no Jew or INTERPOL patrols ahead. Each man reported back every five minutes. Antoine ordered a somewhat reluctant Berthold to cover their backs to be sure they were not being followed. The three made their reports twice, but Berthold failed to return after another fifteen minutes.

"They got him," Clause said unemotionally.

It was the fortunes of war.

"I'm sure you're right. So we take a vote on the route."

Hugues took a moment to tell the rest where he had come from and had encountered no Nazi hunters.

"Good. Hugues, you lead the way for Jérôme and you. Clause and I will go our own separate way to the bus station. Be very careful when you get there. Watch for the hunters. If it's the Israelis, you can bet that their attack has been planned for some time; and they may be hard to spot. Buy a one-way nonstop ticket for Ushuaia aboard a super cama. Then go to the next ticket station and buy another ticket for Santiago. I think we'll be safer in Chile than spending a long time here in Argentina. We have friends in Puerto Varas, and we'll all make our separate ways there and meet up and plan our next moves. *Verstehen sie?*"

All the men responded that they understood, and they set off looking grim and feeling as if they were bare naked at the Führer's birthday celebration. There were sightings of suspicious-looking strangers, but each man stepped into a tourist kiosk and bought wide-brimmed strawhats and bright-colored ponchos. By some small miracle, all of them made it safely to the main bus terminal. They followed Antoine's directions and bought tickets for both destinations, with each bus leaving at different times from those chosen by the other *Gebirgsjägers*.

Antoine did not do quite the same thing that he asked his partners to do. He purchased one ticket for Brazil and the second for Puerto Varas, Chile. He booked a Via Bariloche bus company trip on común class—the lowest category which provided only the minimal and basic technical standards for bus transportation. Locals came rushing to the bus passengers with offers of accommodation, money exchange, and food and drinks. A local police officer told Antoine to beware of his luggage and belongings at the Bariloche Bus Terminal. He would have a six– to eight-hour ride, so he spent his hour buying very cheap and rough workman's clothes. Part of the time he spent scuffing his heavy uncomfortable shoes. He could remember the years in the POW camps when his footwear hardly met the definition of shoes; so, he did not complain to himself.

§§§§§

Chocolatería Más Rico de Bariloche, No. 669 Avenida General José de San Martin, San Carlos de Bariloche, that same afternoon, four o'clock

Moises and Davido had a hasty last-minute consultation before giving final orders to proceed to the irrevocable last move of their operation. The small back room was heavily overcrowded and rank with the smell of sweaty nervous bodies.

Moises ticked off the intended assignments: "I'll go in the front with the two INTERPOL guys. Lev will make a final check on the snipers. You take Manny and Aaron and go in through the back door in the alley. Eban, Micah, and Eliot: circle the streets and alleys surrounding the delicatessen in the two tour buses and watch for us to give the thumbs-up signal to pick us up. We hope against all hope that the pickup will be able to take place in the alley and not on the Avenida. Enos, Gavriel, Ezra, Haggai, and Yachin: you mingle around outside. If cops or Nazis come in force, it will be your responsibility to buy us enough time to get the war criminals into the buses and get out of Bariloche. I don't need to tell you that we will all be in mortal danger if shooting starts, and you guys will have to be the front lines. So, have I missed anything?"

Davido said, "Equipment check."

"Sure. Everybody empty then reload your weapons and set them to auto fire."

Thirteen well-oiled Uzis were checked and again made ready for the third time that day.

"Hoods? Handcuffs? Ropes? Blankets? Food and water? Extra ammunition? Extra fuel tanks on the buses?"

A small quiet chorus of voices answered "Yes," each man answering for his specific assignment.

"Any last-minute issues with the escape route?"

"No," Lev said.

"Everybody okay and ready to go?"

Another quiet chorus of yeses.

"Synchronize watches."

Gavriel said, "Let's do it. I am getting nervous as a kitten in a room full of rocking chairs."

"All right, let's move out. May YHWH protect this mission and all who serve Him this day," Moises said, and the thirteen specially chosen protectors of Israel quietly left the chocolateria in separate small groups to ensure no undue attention would be generated.

Entry time had been set for 1610, and everything depended on precise timing. At 1609, everyone was in place. At exactly 1610, Moises and two Argentine INTERPOL agents strode casually through the front door of the Boehme New Alemana Delicatessen at 420 Avenida Pepito Moreno.

"Will you be staying for lunch or having take-away, gentlemen?" asked the sweet-voiced young Aryan girl.

One of the INTERPOL agents stood by the front door, and Moises and the other agent ignored the girl and walked directly around the display counter and opened the door to the back room.

She just managed to get out, "That's private, you are not allowed...!" before the two men rushed into the room.

Davido, Manny, and Aaron quietly opened the rear door and entered the room simultaneously with Moises and his INTERPOL officers. The six men looked at each other in consternation. They were alone in the room. It was obvious that the war criminals had made a very hasty exit as evidenced by spilled coffee that was still warm, half-eaten sandwiches, and papers strewn over the table and the floor.

"They knew we were coming!" Davido growled. "How? Spies? A traitor?"

"Spies or intelligent criminals who learned that their funding had been cancelled," Moises said. "It happened only a few minutes ago. Some of them went out through that open window. They probably headed for their cars or the bus station. Let's round up the troops and get down to the main train station and the metro bus stop on Ave. 12 de Octubre. Eban, Micah, and Eliot: get in the buses and start to patrol the backstreets. Don't attract a lot of attention when you do."

In five minutes all of the thirteen Project Save the Generals agents were aware of the highly disappointing and now more dangerous development, and every man knew his assignment for this next phase of their operation. Ten minutes later, the agents were mingling with the sparse crowds around the train and bus station and were circling the town, eyes flicking into every alley and street. Several were walking about looking for suspicious activity taking place in any and every building they passed.

Enos caught the first break.

CHAPTER SIXTY-SIX

Vicinity of the Bariloche Train and Bus Terminals, 1622 the same day

Antoine found a group of *Porteños* squatting among their belongings waiting for their train to the outskirts of Bariloche—Rio Negro Province. He insidiously insinuated himself into the group, avoiding physical or verbal contact as much as possible. He kept the brim of his cap down to hide his eyes and pretended to be asleep. In common with other Third World countries, the periphery of San Carlos de Bariloche included poorly integrated areas which encroached upon the rural settlements with their antiquarian ways. The poverty and constantly increasing ramshackle buildings inadequate to provide the shelter and privacy needed of the rural and the urban groups sometimes fomented violent interactions. Only four months of the year could be considered to have pleasant climatic conditions which aggravated the interrelations among the more or less permanent residents. It was four-thirty when he became aware of a series of incidents taking place in and around the two stations. The small commotions—which were commonplace among the *Porteños*—produced almost negligible interest–let alone disruption–among the men and women sitting or squatting, smoking, and snacking; so, there was no general excitement.

But to Antoine's trained and anxiety-enhanced eye and mind—now at a considerably heightened level of focus—there was dismay. In two separate scuffles, he saw small groups of very fit men wrestle down Rolf Kohns and Clause Fischer and drag them into alleys close at hand. His first impulse was to race to their aid, but his rational mind forbade him to do so. As he watched the minor dramas, he saw Serge Rounsavall, Hugues Beauchamp, Jérôme Christophe Mailhot, and Willibald Movius enter Pullman buses and saw the buses pull out of the station. He presumed that Berthold Küppers should now be considered a casualty—if not a KIA—and had to be written off along with Rolf and Clause.

"Worse," he muttered to himself, "the three men possess vital secrets which could bring all of the rest of us five *Gebirgsjägers* down."

He and his remaining men were not out of danger yet—not by a long shot. Serge, Hugues, Jérôme, and Willibald watched the same scene and felt equally helpless. It was rapidly becoming an every-man-for-himself situation.

After an excruciating delay to get a new steward on the Via Bariloche bus, Antoine's escape vehicle pulled out and made its way onto Highway 213 headed west towards the border. He knew that a man who had not been through all of the trials that he had might have gone out to save his men, but he could not afford to take the chance. He bid a mental farewell and set his face towards Puerto Varas.

It was almost twenty past four when the Mossad members of the Project Save the Generals arrived in the station area. They had to become less careful of risks and more assertive if this was not to become an almost complete loss with all the consequences. Moises mentally begged someone, somewhere, to supply a solution and quickly.

While he mused, he became more convinced that all of the criminals had successfully fled the area, if not even the jurisdiction. Enos walked past an alley and happened to see two men changing their clothes. That was altogether suspicious; so, he decided to walk up to the two and demand to see identification as if he were a policeman. It was a bluff, and he knew it. But he needed to have time to have his team catch up. He believed it would not be long before the two found a ride and disappeared.

"Hey, you, what are you doing? Come out where I can see you."

His voice carried all the sound of authority despite that he was nothing but a spy and an assassin. It would go very badly for him if he were to be caught. He fingered the L-pill in his front pocket.

Rolf spotted him and casually stepped up to the intruder and asked, "What's the problem, Officer?"

"The department is searching for several criminal fugitives. You were changing your clothes in the back of that alley which makes you seem suspicious. Show me your papers quickly; so, I can be on my way."

Rolf debated for a moment, but his options were very limited. He thought about bulldozing over the smaller man facing him and running away or alternatively of wrestling him to the ground and killing him. His other option was to bluff his way out. He trusted the ODESSA's papers; they looked completely authentic to him. He showed the officer his passport. Enos did not care whether the papers were genuine or not. He had hit the jackpot. There in his hands was proof positive that he had the right man. The name—Guglielmo Pardini—on the passport matched up with the name of the Nazi war criminal, Rolf Kohns. The passport photo was also a dead giveaway.

"I need you and your friends to come with me. We will have some questions for you at the station. Do I need to put cuffs on you, Sr. Pardini?"

"What cause have you to arrest me?" Rolf demanded.

"No arrest, sir. We simply need to have you answer some questions at headquarters. Your cooperation in this matter will be in your favor if anything improper should ever be brought forward about you."

The other man—Clause Fischer—was attentive to the interaction between Rolf and the police officer. He knew they could not spend any more time chatting; if the cop committed to putting cuffs on Rolf, their chances for escape would evaporate. He moved closer, as unobtrusively as possible.

Rolf caught a glimpse of Clause in the corner of his peripheral vision. He gave Clause a quick glance and a nod then returned his attention back to the officer. He calculated his chances of overpowering the smaller man—with the help of Clause, if necessary—and they were good. He outweighed the officer by probably eighty pounds and was eight inches taller. He had had combat experience, and he doubted that the small man had never been in a real fight. Besides, he had big, slow, but powerfully-built Clause on his side. The odds were completely in his favor.

Rolf was wrong on all points of his calculations. He plunged ahead to grab the small cop in a powerful bear hug. Enos was ready. His other job—when he was not out stalking Nazi war criminals—was being the main instructor in Krav Maga for the IDF [Israel Defense Forces], in the Institute in Tel Aviv. Rolf found himself flat on his back and unable to catch his breath on the filthy pavement of the alley.

Clause flung himself at Enos, but instead of landing a powerful round-house punch to the face of the smaller man, he caught a stone-hard pointed elbow to his delicate nose before he was upended by a quick and accurate leg sweep. He landed on his back, and Enos chopped his Adam's Apple with a flat fist blow that caused the much larger man to believe he was going to suffocate.

Manny, Aaron, and Lev quickly joined Enos, swarming over the two barely conscious *Gebirgsjägers,* trussing them up and gagging them with well-practiced efficiency. In less than a minute, the two were sitting on the floor of a large tourist bus trying to regain their wits. Lev left Aaron to guard the two fugitives, and he and Manny exited the bus to continue the search for the rest of the elusive war criminals. One of the ODESSA men drove the escape bus quickly out of the area. The search—which lasted less than an hour—proved to be futile. Rather than risk being identified as Mossad, Moises decided to call it off in Bariloche. He made a guess that the Nazis would not stay in the city, even with the large number of fairly fanatical sympathizers.

"The question is," he said, "did they go north, or did they go south?"

The distances going north were longer, and the number of Nazi sympathizers ready to offer assistance fewer, which made the risks of getting apprehended worse. He had limited manpower but an adult lifetime of experience to make his hunches better than most men's objective reasoning.

"South," he said.

"Shorter distance, more stops, narrow country. They may be in a lorry or a car, but they were not likely to be able to get taxis willing to cross the border or to find a fast traveling bus. We don't have to worry about the niceties of bus travel. We can drive at twice the speed of the tourist bus to the border and then set up ambushes in towns along the way," said Davido.

"Puerto Varas or Porto Montt are the best choices for the Nazis," said Gavriel. "I've been studying the maps of Patagonia for the last ten days. They have to get to an airport in Chile, hoping that they are not expected there or that they have good enough papers to get them on a plane and back to Europe or even the US"

"I agree," said Moises. "Let's go ahead on that presumption and try and get to Puerto Varas first. From there we can call back and see if the police or INTERPOL have heard of any older military-looking men getting off anywhere down the line. We'll leave a couple of men in Puerto Varas; and the rest of us can go to Port Montt and see if our fugitives were able to get on a ferry, ship, or a boat. I think that will tighten the net the most."

Lev told the rest that he was not so sure, but at least the plan included immediate action, and that was the kind of solution he like best. All of the agents of Project Save the Generals agreed that it was the most logical direction and plan. Since Argentina is huge—almost 2,500 miles long and more than 620 miles wide—they would have the advantage of a narrower search area in Chile, but their work would still be considerable. Chile occupies a land mass more than triple the length of the state of California and almost four times the length of Italy. The saving grace for the project officers was that Chile is a long but very narrow country; it has an average width of only about 110 miles, with a maximum of 217 miles at Antofagasta and a minimum of 9.6 miles near Puerto Natales.

At the Argentina/Chile border station located at Paso Cardenal Antonio Samoré, the buses carrying the fugitives and the ones carrying the pursuing agents had to wait in a long tedious line while uncaring customs agents scrutinized the identification papers of every passenger in every vehicle and questioned vigorously whether anyone was carrying any forbidden food products such as peanuts, almonds, trail mix, cheese, raw meat, yogurt, clove garlic, or fresh vegetables or fruit. All of the men involved were Europeans and were finding that crossing this isolated border was a considerably more lengthy process than they were used to in Europe. The fugitives were sweating from the stress and fear of being surprised by the agents coming after them, and the agents were worried that their quarries would be long gone by the time they were able to cross into Chile. Moises and his agents had stopped for a quick check in Villa La Angostura, just eighteen and a half miles from the crossing. No one had seen anyone matching the descriptions and photo arrays the agents showed them.

The border crossing is located at an altitude of almost 4,300 feet— low by comparison to many of the other crossings—making it one of the easiest of the Argentina/Chile passes and even had a paved road part of the way. The agents' bus was jammed between two Tas Choapa buses, and the fugitives had to wait impatiently with a view of the front end of one Via Bariloche bus and the back end of a Tas Choapa bus. Beyond the border crossing, the fugitives crossed the Cordillera de Los Andes from Argentiina to Chile and passed through a fairly barren region with leafless tall trees in a partially inhabited part of Chile with more than an hour's head start on their pursuers. They traveled gradually west down the lower elevations, further along passing into a country of mountains, lush forests, and lakes.

CHAPTER SIXTY-SEVEN

Entre Lagos, Chile, Ruta 215-CH, late evening the same day.

Six hours after finally clearing Chilean customs and leaving the Paso Cardenal Antonio Samoré, the *Gebirgsjägers*—Serge Rounsavall, Hugues Beauchamp, Jérôme Christophe Mailhot, and Jérôme Movius—on the Pullman bus pulled into the small bus station in Entre Lagos. They were famished, tired from the strain, and sleepy from the tedium of the long bus ride. All passengers and the driver alighted from the bus. The women ran for the toilets, and the men had a leisurely look around before going into the separate bathroom building for men. Considerably relieved, they all converged on the small café which served the many travelers passing through the main town of Puyehue commune in Osorno Province. It was a beautiful, tranquil evening in the Los Lagos Region of southern Chile, and a good chance to relax and stretch one's cramped legs. There was just time enough to grab a bowl of the café's signature *arroz con leche*.

Shortly after the arrival of the Pullman bus, a Via Bariloche bus pulled up to the station. Soon, the café was crowded with passengers clamoring for food and drink. Serge and Hugues made a visual inventory of the passengers from the second bus. There were the usual backpackers, trekkers, and sightseers, and about a dozen rural Chileans in family groups. Without being obvious about it, their eyes and minds concentrated on another dozen—more accurately, eleven—men who seemed somewhat out of place among the usual passengers. They were young to middle-aged, appeared to be European or Slavic or perhaps Semitic; and they seemed to be making an effort not to look at the *Gebirgsjägers*.

Nothing about the newcomers shouted 'law enforcement' or 'military,' but nothing about them whispered 'regular tourists' either.

"It's too crowded in here," Serge whispered.

"I know what you mean," Hugues responded. "Time to finish up and get back to the bus."

"Um hmmh, before the rest of the passengers. I'll start out and give a nod to the rest, and you hang back a little and see if anybody takes notice or gets up."

Serge nodded, and the two men got up slowly and sauntered towards the door, being scrupulously careful not to make eye contact with anyone in the room. The rest of the *Gebirgsjägers* followed suit, paid their bills from their small cache of Chilean pesos, and made their way out of the building and into the growing darkness. Serge was the last to leave, and noted that nobody seemed to be paying attention to them.

As soon as the last of the five men left, Moises and Lev signaled the other Project Save the Generals agents by twisting their mouths in the direction of the door leading to the kitchen, and they all got up one by one and made their way to the kitchen. The mouth movement was a little Argentinian custom Davido had taught Moises to indicate a direction of interest. It was usefully discreet. Lev had already reconnoitered the entrance to the kitchen and found that the work area also had a door to the outside where the workers could deposit garbage and have a smoke. The kitchen workers were not too happy to be bumped aside as the agents pushed their way through the crowded and smoky kitchen, but they were too busy to make a point of it.

Outside, the eleven men became a disciplined commando force. Lev took half of the men and circled around through the trees and back to their Via Bariloche bus where they extracted an Uzi from each bag— one for each of the agents. Along with the handguns each of them carried in the waistband of their pants or in an ankle holster, the team was quickly well armed for whatever eventuality presented itself. The lights of the café provided the only illumination on the buses, and the agents worked their way along the shadows until they came to the Pullman bus. There were no men by the bus; so, the agents fanned out separately to try and locate the men who had left the café ahead of them. They moved silently and without speaking. This was the type of operation and the kind of conditions for which they had trained. The tension and level of alertness among the agents was electric.

Serge became aware of the agents when they got out of their Via Bariloche bus.

He whispered, "Keep down, and stay away from the bus until I give a signal. They have to be Mossad or some other set of hostiles. Be quiet. If you have to fight, do it with your knife and kill, don't wound anyone. We can't have a wounded man calling out to his friends."

They were about fifteen yards from their Pullman bus. It was standard practice for bus drivers to leave the keys in the ignition, and there was a free road in front of the bus which would allow a fast escape. The *Gebirgsjägers* moved in nearly absolute silence and with glacial celerity towards their bus, keeping their eyes and ears fully trained on the surrounding grounds to locate any enemies.

The agents had lain flat on their bellies in wait for movement from the Nazis. Their patience was rewarded by the sound of shuffling feet moving through the gloom of the moonless night. The occasional dark figure moved from one shadow to another, and it was soon evident that all movement was in the direction of the Pullman bus.

First contact came when Willibald Movius crawled on his hands and knees over a patch of grass located in a pitch-black corner of the parking area, almost crawling right on top of Yachin Gottesman and Manny Levin who were lying motionless in the darkness. As Willibald made his slow way past, Yachin sprang onto his back and applied a *mata leao* sleeper choke hold around his neck and rendered him unconscious in five seconds. There was a little stir as Willibald made his futile attempt to struggle which alerted Jérôme, who spun around to see what was happening. His motion carried the point of his chin into the hard fist of Manny. There was a sharp crack, then silence. Yachin and Manny trussed up their victims and began crawling on their bellies in the direction of the bus for which their opponents had been heading.

Serge made it to the bus and slid up the steps through the open door before anyone saw him. He waited until he heard a soft hiss come from Hugues before making any kind of move. He reached out and took Hugues' hand and helped him aboard. The two men crawled along the aisle until they came to their seats. They opened their escape bags and found a handgun and made ready for an attack.

"I heard some rustling a couple of minutes ago," Serge whispered. "I think we lost at least one man, maybe two. Those guys out there—whoever they are—are very good. We're in for a fight."

Hugues whispered back, "I'm sure of it. How long should we wait before revving up the bus and taking off without Willibald and Jérôme do you think?"

"If they're not on board by the time, I get to the driver's seat, they're on their own. If we wait any longer, those guys after us will realize we're here and trapped in the bus with no place to run. It's now or never."

The two men made their way back to the area of the driver's seat as quickly and quietly as circumstances allowed. Serge twisted his way into the driver's seat and maintained a low profile. Hugues held a gun in each hand, tapped Serge on the shoulder to let him know that he was ready, then quickly reached out and pulled the door of the bus closed.

The noise was like a rocket went off there in the silent night. Hell broke loose as soon as the sound made it to the ears of the agents. The ignition on the powerful bus engine roared into action; the Israeli agents advanced on the bus with guns blazing at the area of the front of the coach compartment; and Hugues returned fire out the windows without any thought of having an actual target. Eban and Micah pounded on the front entry door, and Eliot and Enos attacked the rear door—without success. Haggai and Aaron ran to the opposite side of the bus and fired a heavy fusillade from that side with equally disappointing lack of success. Lev, Moises, Gavriel, and Ezra all gathered near the front of the bus and opened fire from protective positions behind nearby trees and vehicles, all to no avail. The ponderous bus roared straight ahead, scattering all of the agents. Ezra was too slow, and the bus ran over his left leg, crushing it. He was the only casualty in the opening gun battle.

Before they could do anything to halt the Pullman bus's progress, it careered out of the parking lot and back onto Ruta 215.

"Pick up Ezra and the two prisoners and everybody get to our bus!" Lev ordered.

It took time to do that. They were also briefly hampered by curious Chileans and tourists coming out of the café to see what the commotion was about. Moises and Gavriel covered the rear as the agents hauled their human cargo onto their bus. The two rear guards were obliged to fire a few rounds into the roof of the café to discourge the onlookers, who scrambled back into the relative safety of the well-lit room.

Lev took the driver's seat of the Via Bariloche bus and started the engine. It was sluggish and took two turns of the ignition before getting going, which wasted precious seconds.

"Which way?" asked Eliot who sat in the front row behind the driver.

"Fifty-fifty chance, but I'll bet on south," Lev answered and pulled out onto Ruta 215 and floored the accelerator.

Lev calculated that they would have just enough fuel to make it to Puerto Varas before they had to stop. Every agent on the bus strained his eyes looking at the darkness along the gravel road to see if there was any sign of the other bus or of any men walking. They actually stopped twice and frightened an ebriated husband headed home from one of the several small drinking establishments along the way. Nothing more than that was accomplished; the Pullman bus had too great of a head start on them to be seen, let alone be caught. The Via Bariloche bus had a much smaller and slower engine than its Pullman counterpart.

Manny, Aaron, and Micah worked to stabilize Ezra's obviously fractured leg. The knee was bent at an obscene lateral angle from his thigh. Haggai and Enos assumed the role of interrogators of the two captured Nazi criminals; but even with not-so-gentle persuasion, they were unable to learn anything about the plans or present location of the leader of the group, the man known as Antoine. In fact, neither man knew the answers to either question. After a few good kicks just to vent anger, the agents left the criminals alone.

Chilean Dessert Recipes

Arroz con Leche de Chile—Rice Pudding with Milk and Raisins

Ingredients
-1 cp white rice, 2 cps water, 1 cup whole milk, 2 large eggs, ½ cp gran. sugar, 1 tsp vanilla extract, 1 tsp grated lemon peel, 1 tsp butter, 1 cp heavy cream, 1–2 cps raisins (dark, golden, or mixed), cinnamon for dusting.

Preparation
-Put rice and water in a med. saucepan and bring to a boil. Reduce heat to low and cook rice until soft~15–20 mins. Stir milk, eggs, sugar, vanilla, raisins, and lemon peel in a medium bowl until blended. Add the rice and stir until all ingredients are well mixed.
-Butter a 9 in. pan and spoon the rice mixture into it.

-Bake in a preheated 350º F oven for 25 mins. Remove rice pudding from oven, stir well, and allow to cool~15 mins. Whip cream to soft peaks with an electric mixer. Fold the rice pudding into the whipped cream. Transfer to a serving dish, dust with cinnamon (and maybe a little nutmeg).
-Serve warm or chilled.

Dulce de Leche

Ingredients
-1 qt whole milk, 12 oz sugar (~1 ½ cps), 1 vanilla bean, split and seeds scraped ½ tsp baking soda.

Preparation
-Combine milk, sugar, vanilla bean, and seeds in a large, 4-qt saucepan and place over med. heat. Bring to a simmer, stirring occasionally, until sugar has dissolved. Once the sugar has dissolved, add the baking soda and stir to combine. Reduce the heat to low and cook uncovered at a bare simmer. Stir occasionally, but do not reincorporate the foam that appears on the top of the mixture. Continue to cook for 1 hr. Remove the vanilla bean after 1 hr. and continue to cook until the mixture is a dark caramel color and has reduced to~1 cp~1½—2 hrs. Strain mixture through a fine mesh strainer. Store in the refrigerator in a sealed container (for up to a month).

CHAPTER SIXTY-EIGHT

Municipal Bus Terminal, Puerto Montt, Chile, six a.m. the following day

Antoine's Via Bariloche bus company trip on común class was a test of endurance. The passengers had had only one bathroom stop in seven hours and no stop for food. It was expected that passengers in común class would bring their own. He had not spoken a word to anyone. He was not inclined to have himself be remembered, and the peasants on the bus were a taciturn bunch who never warmed to strangers. He was parched and famished, but his fear overrode the temptation to rush into one of the restaurents near the bus terminal in Puerto Varas.

He relieved himself in a clump of bushes but was too nervous to find a place to eat. He expected to be accosted by his pursuers any minute and felt unsafe being in the attractive little tourist community. As quickly as he could, Antoine walked to Del Salvador to a waiting small blue-gray local bus and stepped aboard. He paid the driver and settled into an uncomfortable seat and listened to his empty stomach growl. The buses left the town every ten minutes; so, less than thirty minutes after having arrived in Puerto Varas, he was in Puerto Montt where—for some reason he could not explain—he felt safer. He was in the middle of town near the harbor. He stood for a moment or two on Diego Portales and Lillo streets and oriented himself. In English, he asked a tourist where he could find the best food.

"Just go down Avenida Diego Portales to Angelmó. The fish market is fun, and the restaurants are all pretty good. Lots of raw stuff and some fruits of the sea that I wouldn't eat, but that's just me."

Antoine thanked the man and began walking briskly away from the bus station, taking care to look around and behind himself as he went. He saw no one who seemed to be interested in him or to be following him. The farther he went, the hungrier he got, and the less ill at ease. At intervals he could see the deep blue ocean to the west, and at others he could see the towering jagged peaks of the southern Andes to the east. Puerto Montt is the southernmost city on the mainland of Chile before the land breaks up into the islands of Tierra Del Fuego. The street on the way to Angelmó was crowded with little stalls selling traditional Chilean handicrafts, tourist souvenirs made of the alerce tree which grows in the Lake Region nearby, and leather products.

He meandered a little further down Ave. Diego Portales until he came to the fish markets and the restaurants. For a man as hungry as Antoine, Angelmó was a seafood extravaganza. He salivated at the large variety of fresh fish and *frutes del mar* which were guaranteed fresh because he could see his dinner being taken out of small boats a few yards from where he could eat them.

He exchanged his Argentine pesos for the Chilean variety and realized that Argentina's money was not worth much on the international market. He checked out several restaurants in the artisan area—Pueblito Melipulli—and harbor open air places that served delicacies which had been on a boat ten minutes before. His final choices included: *ceviche* [minced raw sea bass in lemon juice] and *almejas con limón* [raw clams with lemon juice] as starters, then had a small bowl of *Caldillo de Congrio* [conger-eel soup with onions, potatoes, and carrots]. He ate slowly to avoid upsetting his very empty stomach or getting too full to enjoy a good variety. Next, he ordered *ostiones a la parmesana* [sea scallops on their shells in melted butter and covered with grilled Parmesan cheese] and *Pastel de Jaiba* [Chilean crab pie—the sweetest in the world—served in its own hard rough shell]. He left just enough room to have a small bowl of cinnamony *Arroz con Leche* [rice pudding—lit. rice with milk and raisins].

He drank bottled water, presuming that the water from taps was not fit to drink, just as it was in Argentina. He avoided taking any alcohol because he wanted to be as mentally sharp as he could be. He satisfied himself that no one had been observing or tailing him, then he made his way in an unnecessarily circuitous walk to the Club Aleman just off Ave. Diego Portales. During his stay in Bariloche and his preparation of an escape plan, he learned that the club not only catered to Germans, but was overtly accommodating when possible SS officers came by.

Antoine was confident that his German could pass for a native; so, he walked with confidence up the steep entry steps and knocked with the large brightly polished brass door knocker. The building was in the old colonial style, one of the few such buildings left in Chile.

He was greeted by a liveried butler who worked to hide his contempt for the blue-collar worker standing before him.

"*Wie kann ich Ihnen behilflich zu sein, sir?*" ["How may I be of service to you, sir?"]

"*Ich bin hier mit bezeichnet Anton Friedrich Krupp von Bohlen und Halbach, und ich bin in der Notwendigkeit von speziellen Unterkunft für die ich gut bezahlen.*" ["I am referred here by Anton Friedrich Krupp von Bohlen und Halbach, and I am in need of special accommodation for which I can pay well."]

His delivery was that of an autocratic-ranking SS officer, and that and the mention of the head of the ODESSA in Germany had the instantaneous effect of leveling their social status despite his rough clothes. The butler showed him in and politely offered Antoine a chair.

A gentleman in a beautifully tailored three-button, three-piece gray suit, Armani power tie, and freshly pressed white shirt came to see Antoine in a few minutes and welcomed him.

"How can I be of help?"

"I will need a proper suit of clothing, shirts, ties, dress shoes, and some casual wear as well. First, however, I must make a telephone call to your brother club in Puerto Varas."

"But of course," the executive said smartly. "Follow me."

Antoine made the call to the Puerto Varas club and left instructions for anyone with an authentic SS tattoo who asked for him to be directed to the Puerto Montt club.

"Now for clothing," he said.

"I will take you personally. I presume that you would not care to be the object of interest from anyone on the street; so, it would be best for you to ride in the club limo and to keep your head down at all times."

"That would be fine, Herr Butler."

After the shopping trip—which was twice as expensive as it would have been for a local without the baggage of being a Nazi who was illegal in the country, Antoine realized how tired he was.

Antoine slept in his old clothes because he was too tired to remove them. The sleep lasted fourteen hours and concluded only because the butler nudged his shoulder to awaken him. It took a few moments for Antoine to return to a semi-sentient mental status.

"You have a telephone call, *Mein Generalleutenant*. Would you care to accompany me to the club's office where you may speak with privacy?"

Antoine followed the butler down the two flights of stairs, shaking his head to get rid of the cobwebs.

"Altenhofen here," he said, still not sure enough to use his Germanic credentials over the phone.

"Antoine, it's Serge. Hugues and I are in Puerto Varas hiding out in the Club Aleman. You know the place?"

"I know about it. What about the others?"

"All dead or captured. We can only presume that we have been badly compromised."

"Yes," Antoine said thoughtfully and with regret. "Arrange a wire transfer of the Chilean funds to the club; they are more than willing to help. Be generous in sharing with the club to further its activities. Have them get you some seamen's outfits, then have them get you here to Puerto Montt to the Club Aleman. Do it this morning. Trust no one but the butler there. He—like the one here—is a major ODESSA contact. I will arrange for us to get on a cargo ship bound for Lima and then another means of transportation to Indochina. I have some contacts in Saigon who will be glad to have us join their unit."

"French Foreign Legion?"

"Perhaps, but don't get ahead of yourselves."

"We will do everything we can to get to you before sundown."

"Be here before noon. We need to get away as soon as possible. The Nazi hunting Jews from the Levant are efficient and effective; never underestimate them."

Recipes for Frutes del Mar in Southern Chile

Chilean Sea Bass Ceviche—Serves 8

Ingredients
-2 lbs Chilean sea bass (may substitute pompano, red snapper, or sole), all bones removed, juice of 2 large lemons and 4–6 limes, ½ red onion thinly sliced and separated into rings, 1 clove minced garlic, 1 hot red chili, and 1 sweet orange pepper seeded and cut into thin strips, 2 tbsps chopped fresh flat-leaf parsley, 3 tbsps minced fresh cilantro, coarse sea salt, freshly ground black pepper, and extra virgin olive oil to taste, 6 halved, peeled, and pitted ripe avocadoes.

Preparation
-Rinse fish; pat dry and slice thinly into bite-size pieces.
-In a 2-quart stainless steel bowl, combine the citrus juices, onion, garlic, peppers, parsley, and cilantro. Add the fish, making sure the citrus juices generously cover the fish. Season with salt and pepper. Allow the fish to marinate in the fridge for at least 4 hrs—until the fish no longer looks raw. Season as desired and drizzle with a bit of olive oil. Serve in avocado halves. As variety, may add shrimp, scallops, or different firm fish, octopus, and calamari.

Almejas con limón

Ingredientes
-½ kg. de almejas, 2 ajos, 1 par de ramitas de perejil fresco, 2 limones, aceite de olive, pimiento y sal.

Cómo preparer
-Antes de comenzar la elaboración de las almejas con limón, lo mejor será tener las almejas en agua
con sal durante un buen rato, para que expulsen la arena que pudieran tener dentro. Finalmente
las escurrimos y las reservamos.
-Ponemos una cazuela al fuego con un chorrito de agua y un poco de zumo de limón y añadimos las almejas. Las tapamos y dejamos que se abran. Las que permanezcan cerradas deberán desecharse, ya que estarán malas y podríamos intoxicarnos.
-Quitamos las almejas con limón del fuego y las escurrimos. Reservamos el caldo aparte. -Ponemos una sartén al fuego con un chorreón de aceite de oliva, agregamos los ajos picados y dejamos que se doren un poquito. A continuación rociamos el zumo de los dos limones, un poco de perejil fresco picadito, una pizca de sal y pimienta molida y, por fin, el caldo de la cocción de las almejas con limón bien colado.
-Dejamos que reduzca y, cuando esté listo, lo echamos por encima de las almejas y a chuparse los dedos.

Clams with lemon

Ingredients
-½ kg clams, 2 garlic cloves, 2 sprigs of fresh parsley, 2 lemons, extra virgin olive oil, pepper and salt.

Preparation
-Before commencing preparation, soak clams in salted water for a while, to expel any sand. Drain and reserve.
-Heat a pan with a little water lemon juice and add the clams [Open clamshells and leave open. If closed, clams must be discarded because they are poor and could be infectious.]
-Remove clams and drain. Reserve broth. Place in frying pan with a dash of olive oil, add garlic and let brown a little. Sprinkle juice of 2 lemons, some fresh chopped parsley, a pinch of salt and ground pepper, and finally the cooking juices from the clams with lemon. When ready, drizzle reduction over the clams and serve.

Caldillo de Congrio [Conger Eel Soup]

Ingredients
-2–3 tbsps extra virgin olive oil, 1 thinly sliced white onion, 3–4 minced garlic cloves, 1 tbsp paprika, 2 cps seeded and chopped tomatoes, 1 cp good white wine, 4 cps rich fish stock, 2 tbsps finely chopped parsley, 1 bay leaf, salt and pepper to taste, 1 lb conger eel fillets (may substitute white fish or a mixture of both) cut into chunks, ½ cp heavy cream, ½ bunch chopped cilantro.

Preparation
-Heat oil in a large pot over medium-high heat. Add onion and saute until translucent~3 to 4 min. Stir in the garlic and paprika and saute for another 1–2 mins.
-Stir in the tomatoes and simmer for another 4–5 minutes to cook the tomatoes down. Add wine and cook down for another~1 min.
-Pour in the fish stock and add the parsley, bay leaf, salt, and pepper. Bring to a boil, then reduce heat to medium-low and simmer for 15–20 min.
-Add the fish or eel and simmer until the fish is cooked through~5–8 mins.
-Stir in cream and adjust seasoning with salt and pepper. Serve in bowls, garnished with some of the chopped cilantro and a few dashes of *salsa de ají* or other hot pepper sauce.

Ostiones a la parmesana—Sea Scallops on Their Shells in Melted Butter and Covered with Grilled Parmesan Cheese

Ingredients
-1½ lbs bay scallops, 1 cp extra virgin olive oil, 2–3 large finely minced garlic cloves, 1 *ají cacho de cabra* or serrano chile, minced or dried to taste, salt.

Preparation
-Heat oil in a sauté pan until almost smoking, then add chile and garlic.
-When garlic is almost golden~30 secs, turn the heat to high and add scallops.
-When the scallops are done~1–2 mins. and before the garlic turns brown, remove from heat and divide the entire contents among the preheated pailas*. Serve immediately with crusty bread and chilled white wine.
*Pailas are small pans with two handles which do double-duty as plates, going directly from the stove to the table.

CHAPTER SIXTY-NINE

Casa Fischer Guesthouse, Calle Mirador 20, Puerto Varas, Chile, the same morning

The eleven members of the Project Save the Generals had spent the day walking the streets of Puerto Varas one by one and, in some instances, two by two, looking for any Nazi fugitive that was still alive and in action. They got a few promising leads—promising enough to spur them on to the opinion that the SS officers were more likely than not still in the town. The Mossad agents knew they were living on borrowed time; either they had to find one or more of their quarries; or they would have to leave the area as the Argentine secret police— who were notoriously pro-Nazi—would learn about them and close in, even in Chile.

The meeting they were about to have would determine whether they would be able to push their luck a little further or if they would give up and try the southern towns of Puerto Montt or one of the smaller towns like Valdivia, or Cochamó to the east and southeast, Calbuco to the southwest, and Maullín and Los Muermos to the west.

They were sitting in the outdoor café of the bright, fairly new Casa Fischer Guesthouse. The views were beautiful and soporific; they were only 160 or so feet from the tranquil blue Lake Llanquihue, and three city blocks from the town's Plaza de Armas. The place was small; so, only five of the Israelis had taken lodging in the container studios with their terraces. None of them wanted to draw attention to themselves; so, they had cheaper rooms without private bathrooms. Pretending to be tourists, they pumped the owners for tourist information and learned all about local markets, restaurants, Calbuco and Osorno volcanoes, and about the nearby towns.

The casino was 650 feet away and several of the agents spent time in it losing money but gaining some useful information. Moises had been able to bring up the topic of Germans living in Puerto Varas and learned—without seeming to be overly nosy—that the center of German life in the city was the Club Aleman and its outstanding restaurant a few blocks away just off Av. San Francisco, near Gramado Street.

"Either they are hiding out in the club, or the Nazi sympathizing members have helped them to escape," Moises said quietly. "I propose that we leave two men to surveil the club night and day for say … three days … while the rest of us head down south. If we fail to locate them there, we will just have to admit that we lost yet another battle against the fugitive Nazis; and we will have to go back home and wait until something new shows up."

There was reluctant agreement with the alteration in plans. With a certain level of resignation, they all ate their succulent portions of red Chilean King Crab and a course of Congrio Frito [deep-fried conger eel] washed down with Almaviva, a Chilean blend of Cabernet Sauvignon, Merlot, Camenere, and Cabernet Franc produced in Chile's Maipo valley.

"I know in my gut that ODESSA is hiding them either here or in Puerto Montt," said Lev. "It will give me an ulcer to leave here without them, knowing full well that they will laugh at our backs."

All of the team except for two of the INTERPOL agents—who drew the black bean and had to sit through a mind-numbing stakeout of the Pte Varas Club Aleman—caught train or bus rides to Puerto Montt and began the tedious and tiring secret canvassing of the city and its neighboring communes. Egan and Micah had watched the arrivals and departures at El Tepual Airport; Eliot, Enos, and Gavriel came to know every street and alley in Valdivia; the rest of the INTERPOL contingent exhausted the potential of Cochamó and learned nothing in Calbuco, Maullín, and Los Muermos. After a fruitless three-day search—which included around-the-clock surveillance of the Pte Montt Club Aleman by Ezra, Haggai, Yachin, and Enos and a useless tour of the rural countryside by Moises, Manny, and Aaron—Moises decided it was time for the team to fold its figurative tents and get back to their desert before they were caught up in a futile international incident.

Lev muttered that the place lived up to what the locals called it, "*Muerto Montt*"['Dead Montt'] and expressed his frustrated description of the deadly boring Puerto Montt unpolished working-class and the complete lack of worldly charm of this pocket of the Chilean atmosphere.

§§§§§

Club Aleman, 264 Ave. Antonio Varas, Puerto Montt, September 29, 1963, midnight

"There are always two of them. I'm not sure if it is always the same two; and I can't be certain that there are not any others hidden around the area; but I have not seen any sign of anyone else," said Christof Weishuhn, who had been chosen to provide security for the fugitive *Gebirgsjägers*.

"How do we get past them?" Antoine asked.

"We send out four delivery trucks in fairly close succession, *Mein General*," said Christof. "One to the airport, one to the metro bus station, one to the railroad station, and then, a last one to the port."

"The theory being that two men cannot possibly keep track of four trucks, any one or none of which could be carrying anyone of us," Antoine said.

"That's the idea. The escapees will go out in the third truck, and the fourth will wait longer than the rest then drive very rapidly and directly for the airport. We will have a gurney waiting at the airport and will lift a man out and cover him with blankets after he lies on the gurney."

"And, the boat is waiting?"

"All preparations are ready and onboard. The captain and crew have been paid enough to render them deaf, blind, and mute until long after you men are well out of Chilean waters and to keep them amnesiac afterwards."

It was a night devoid of stars or the light of the moon. Ezra and Haggai had the night watch while Yachin and Enos went to bed in the guesthouse. All four were certain they might as well be pounding sand down a rat hole for all the good they were doing. The case was dead, at least this phase of it. It was time to head back to Tel Aviv and to wait until another bit of evidence presented a new location and a new direction.

Ezra yawned again, and Haggai said, "Go ahead and sleep. I'll watch for the next four hours, then, I'll wake you up; and you can let me get a little rest. I think Moises will send us out of Chile tomorrow. It won't be a moment too soon."

"Moises and Lev would kill us or at least get us thrown out of the Institute if either of them got wind that we had a nap on the job, you know that, *AHKH* [Heb.—Brother]."

Boredom and weariness got the best of them. In a little over an hour, both of them were sound asleep. It was midnight. Christof Weishuhn changed into a Puerto Montt police constable's uniform and made one more walk-around outside to be sure that there was nothing stirring and that there was no one watching. At the end of the block, near the intersection with Ave. Diego Portales, he walked past a florist's lorry. Ordinarily, he would not have paid any attention to a parked business truck; but this one had a feature that drew his attention: two men were sitting in the front seat sound asleep. He checked to see if there were any other potential watchers along the front and the back of the club, then hurried back to where his men and the three *Gebirgsjägers* were anxiously waiting.

"Gerhardt, go up towards Diego Portales. There's a florist's truck parked almost on the corner with two men sitting asleep in the front seat. Plant yourself in front of the truck and watch to see if they do anything that makes them seem to be awake. If they are awake, kill them."

Gerhardt slipped out the front door and took up his position. The four clubcatering lorries drove out of the rear garage and into the alley behind the club in the planned order and turned in opposite directions and with different destinations. Antoine, Hugues, and Serge lay on the floor in the back of the third lorry clutching lugers which Christof had provided them. They each had a small canvas seaman's bag containing all of their belongings to last them for the next two or three weeks. Antoine soothed himself with the memory that he was carrying more than he owned during the prison and fugitive years. The three men shared a still warm batch of *kuchen*—a German fruit flan—and three bottles of the local Kuntsmann beer during the short ride to the harbor.

Puerto Montt was a small city set into a deep, almost V-shaped cut in a mountain at the northern end of Reloncaví Sound. It was a town seemingly plucked out of Bavaria and set down in the picturesque Patagonian Andes. Prior to World War II, Puerto Montt was a small, ramshackle seaport perched on a ledge between an inland Patagonian fjord and the dramatic volcanoes of the southern Andes. Because of its deep waters and strategic commercial location, the harbor became the main seaport at the lower end of Chile's western continental land mass. The harbor made Puerto Montt the principal commercial, services, and financial hub of Chilean Northern Patagonia—the Zona Austral—and the de facto capital of Chilean Patagonia. The city was becoming the hub of one of the largest salmon aquaculture industries in the world. Hatcheries, fisheries, and packing plants were mostly located south of Puerto Montt. From the port, fresh salmon was being flown daily to world markets; and frozen salmon was shipped by ocean to all five continents. The region was beginning to see tremendous growth due to the salmon industry, the rapid expansion of forestry, cattle, and burgeoning tourism. The main advantage of that commercial activity for the *Gebirgsjägers* was that the hum of activity—even at night—made one more lorry on the dock and one more boat in the water nothing to attract attention. As it was, there were no watchers; the Israelis and INTERPOL searchers had already called it quits and were getting a good night's sleep before returning to their headquarters empty-handed.

The night was dark and misty with visibility down to less than a hundred yards when the ship's tender delivered Antoine, Serge, and Hugues alongside the seventy-yard-long German super seiner, the *Port of Emden* 220, a factory freezer trawler. The *Gebirgsjägers* reported aboard as seagoing factory workers with contracts to work all the way to Hong Kong. With an initial period of trawling for salmon, the entire trip was expected to take between six and eight weeks. The ship, its crew, and the rapid, strenuous, and tedious work requirements made for nearly perfect anonymity. The men were taken below decks and showed to their assigned bunks. Then the factory crew chief led them to the purser's office where they presented their papers.

The ODESSA and Club Aleman forgers had done an expert job preparing passports, seaman's contracts, work histories, and medical documentations for the three new men about to begin their first time on the *Port of Emden* 220, although—according to their papers—not their first time on a factory ship. They were hired through a ship worker contracting company called JobMonkey with a base pay of $3,000 USD per month plus a small percentage of the vessel's earnings. Although it was well past midnight when they finished being processed aboard, the three new men were expected to be on the factory line at first bell of the morning watch—0430—and to work until four bells of the first dog watch [1800 hours] seven days a week. The three men knew they were too old for this kind of backbreaking labor, but they also knew they had no choice but to keep their eyes down and never to complain and draw attention to themselves.

Antoine, Serge, and Hugues stood side-by-side in the production line most days since they were unskilled and novices to the ship. They were usually employed as "slimers" [low-level factory workers]. The monotony was occasionally broken by being reassigned as cooks helpers or even quality control jobs. They were all smart enough and good enough workers to have days when they worked as "combies" [combination factory worker and deckhand], which meant they could have a little time on deck occasionally to work at hand-hauling nets, making repairs, or clearing fish off the vast stretches of hook-laden nets. Deckhand work took place in fresh air performing less monotonous work than when they were entombed below decks in the factory. On good days there were remarkably beautiful and fascinating sights that lifted their spirits.

For the first three weeks, the catching process dominated everything. The *Gebirgsjägers* joined the frenetic action on deck as the fish poured onto the decks from the massive nets. They worked as sorters pulling nontargeted fish—by-catch—from the salmon being processed. The pace was grueling because at all times everyone had to work very quickly to ensure the rest of the factory never ran out of fish to process. Because he was big and strong, Serge worked in the early days as a fillet machine operator. As the fish were sorted, they moved on a conveyor belt to a table in front of the driver. The operators had to grab the fish off the belt and pass them into the filleting machine which was able to fillet 135 to 145 fish per minute—two fish per second—and the operator had to fill the trays uniformly without missing any one of them.

Another job for the former senior SS officers was to be flippers or candlers. The fillets moved from the filleting machine to a table belt that is lit from underneath. The job of the processor, or the "flipper," was to straighten all the fillets very quickly. "Candlers" inspected the fillets for bones or worms then–after passing inspection–the fillets that passed were placed in trays to be frozen. These positions were only on those boats that freeze whole fillets as a final product, called a "block" or "shatter-pack." Among the worst jobs was to move the guts, heads, and offal into vats to be processed into fish meal and fertilizer.

Hugues seemed to draw the black bean more often than chance would have it and have to join the freezer crew. The freezer crew was divided into different positions. The "loader" took the pans of finished product and placed them in plate freezers. After freezing, the "freezer breaker" took the pans back out of the freezer and sent them to the "pan breaker," who broke the product out of the pans. The product—still wrapped in plastic—then went to "case-up," where it was put into boxes stamped with the product grade and date. These boxes were glued or taped shut, and sent to the "stacker," who stacked the product in the freezer hold—day after monotonous and freezing day. The only thing standing between the three men and insanity was the knowledge that they were safe and obscure and that at the end of the exhausting voyage, they would start new lives in the Orient—lives as rich men who were not being hunted.

Having picked up a little Japanese during his POW time in Siberia, Antoine was able to communicate on a crude level with the very exacting Japanese surimi expert—the surimi master. Because of that, he spent time assisting the factory boss in charge of making the important Japanese delicacy. It was hardly a lofty job. Surimi was made by filleting the fish, mincing the fillets, washing the mince many times, then squeezing out the water, which produced a doughy paste that could be shaped and flavored to make artificial crab, scallops, and other artificial seafood products. Most of the time he worked as an extruder—a processor at the end of the surimi line—who mixed sugar with the finished surimi paste, then placed the mixed surimi in bags and pans to be frozen. His intelligence and capable bearing gave Antoine some respite from the drudgery when he was called upon to work under the surimi master as inspector, a job he found surprisingly easy to learn for all of its complexity and finicky exactness.

The *Port of Emden* 220 was two days out from Hong Kong's Victoria Harbor when the *Gebirgsjägers* first ran into trouble. Hugues Beauchamp had been keeping his head down and his hands busy at the grueling factory workload for the six-and-a-half weeks of the voyage from Puerto Montt to the British Crown Colony. His strict obedience, reliability, and careful work ethics were almost his undoing. He came to the notice of the surimi master, Junji Hirokatsu Shimazaki.

Mr. Shimazaki regularly went headhunting in the factory to find men with the skill, intelligence, and quickness to be able to comply with his exacting requirements. Hugues stood out. Mr. Shimazaki had begun to think his previous favorite, a German Chilean named Adolf Ramirez-Böhler, was showing his age and was not quite up to the rigors of the Japanese way. He walked up behind Hugues and tapped him on the shoulder.

Shimizaki was diminutive, even by Japanese standards. As a result he was an arrogant martinet who paid slavish attention to his coiffure, his trim pencil mustache, and his olive drab clothing that harked back to the era of Japanese power in their East Asian Co-Prosperity Sphere. His hands were as clean as a surgeon's from frequent washings and application of lotions to get rid of the smell of fish. His nails were manicured twice a month by one of his subservient assistants. He had coal-black squinting eyes with unusually prominent medial epicanthial folds. In strong light his lids covered all but a thin slit through which he saw everything. He carried a clipboard and pen in one hand and a long, thin skinning knife in the other.

"Mr. Resseguie," he said, "come with me to my surimi production area. I am in need of a new man, one with fresh energy."

He turned imperiously away and walked up the three flights of ships ladders, through the hatch on the second deck and down the passageway to the pristine laboratory/factory—which he operated like an antiquarian *Bushi* [Samurai] daimyo of the Tokugawa shogunate—without so much as glancing behind him to see of Hugues was trotting along behind him at a respectful distance. Antoine watched the two men leave the hot, smelly factory deck with mixed feelings. Mostly he was concerned about Hugues' hair-trigger temper and how he would react to being treated like a *Burakumin* [outcast group at the bottom of the Japanese social order that was historically victimized by the higher-ranking members of the feudal society]. Master Shimazaki certainly treated Antoine like a subhuman, and the former SS general was not likely ever to forget or forgive those slights. However, he continuously reminded himself what the real goal was for himself and his men—to be affluent, safe, and anonymous, beyond the reach of Western law enforcement. He was not so sure how well Hugues would control himself.

Hugues remembered back to the late nineteen thirties when he and the French Charlemagne division volunteered to help the increasingly powerful anticommunist Nazi party in Germany. Early on, he had been treated like something of an *untermenschen* [subhuman] by the imperious Nazis until the division's heroics and unflinching devotion to the Führer earned them the respect of even the most arrogant of the SS officers. He could still remember the slights and what he had had to endure to achieve status in the German ranks.

Now, this physically frail and effeminate dwarf of an Oriental lorded it over him like an SS general over a buck private—a nothing. It grated his soul.

He had been a student in the surimi manufactory for three days when things came to a head.

"You, *Burakumin*, come while I show you how to use a knife, assuming you are even capable of using the simplest of tools like a chimpanzee."

Hugues bit his lip and watched with feigned interest as the master took a prerigor fresh salmon and extracted the thirty-six pinbones by hand, yielding a perfect piece of fresh meat.

"Do that, *Gaijin* [a Japanese word for foreigners and non-Japanese, connoting an "outside person," a negative and pejorative term], and you stay. Fail me again and you go back to the lowest deck and work with the other swine."

He said it with a denigrating sneer. Hugues was not exactly sure what the word "*Gaijin*" meant, but the connotation of the word was clearly written on the master's implacable face. That night, Hugues told Antoine about his latest encounter and how much he hated the arrogance of the "yellow dwarf."

"Tell me what '*Gaijin*' means, Antoine."

"Put up with it for a few more days, *Mon Frère*," Antoine advised.

"What does it mean?"

The look on Hugues' face brooked no denial; so, Antoine responded directly, "Bastard, *untermenschen*," he said.

"I will kill him," Hugues said, and the look on his face was deadly serious.

CHAPTER SEVENTY

Super Seiner Factory Ship *Port of Embden* 220, in the South China Sea near the Spratley Islands, Six bells on the middle watch, October 18, 1963

Antoine said sharply, "If you do, they will arrest you; and all our efforts to escape to a new life will be lost."

"Help me like you always have, Antoine, and we can get our revenge with no one being the wiser. I have asked but very little during the long years we have suffered together. This I ask."

Antoine hated the dimunitive Japanese martinet as much as Hugues did. He paused in thought for a moment.

"All right. But we will plan this carefully. No one can even guess about you and me being involved. He must disappear. Be patient."

"I will try my best, *Mon Frère*; but I cannot endure forever."

Antoine nodded. He knew where the surimi master's stateroom was located. After dark that same night, he, Hugues, and Serge reconnoitered the passageway containing the stateroom and the possible places where the man's body could be hidden or dumped overboard without them being detected.

Serge located a cold storage room where the off-line fish were held frozen for transportation to an onshore fertilizer plant. There were huge vats of frozen fish of all kinds except salmon which were waiting to be ground up unceremoniously as soon as the ship docked.

Each of the men carried a fish-killing club. Serge tapped on Master Shimazaki's stateroom door while the other two stood well off to the side. It was very late, nearing three bells of the middle watch [one-thirty]. The master opened the door and peered groggily out into the companion way trying to make sense of what he was seeing.

He managed to start a sentence with, "What's the…," but those were his last words.

Serge brought his fish club up from where it was hanging at his side and struck the small Japanese in the middle of his skull. Shimazaki dropped like a sack of fish salt, and his eyes turned blank. The three attackers pushed him into his room and were about to take out all of their frustrations when Antoine had a moment of clarity.

"Stop!" he hissed. "No blood. Break his neck."

"My turn," Hugues said.

He knelt down and applied the thumbs of his powerful hands and crushed the man's neck's hyoid bones and thyroid cartilages. It was unnecessary. The surimi master was already dead.

Hugues fought to control his bloodlust, knowing that Antoine was right, as always.

"You are the *Burakumin* and *Gaijin*, you little *sonderbar* [queer]."

He spat on him, then moved back to get better control of himself.

"Serge, check the companionway. Hugues and I will wrap him up in his extra bedsheets and blankets; so, no one will be able to be sure what we're carrying if they should happen out into the companionway while we're carting him to the off-line fish storage."

No one was out and about. It was an uncomfortable night, and the ship was experiencing some of every motion the ocean could dish out: pitching, yawing, swaying, sinking, surging, and heaving. The three *Gebirgsjägers* were hampered in their movements to avoid banging into the bulkheads or falling. They shuffled along with very wide-based stances until they made their way into the ice-cold fish storage area. Antoine closed and locked the hatch while Serge and Hugues removed a center portion of frozen fish from one large container to make room for the sirimi master's corpse. Their hands were nearly frozen by the time they muckled the body—which now seemed very heavy—into the pit in the center of the great mound of frozen fish. Then they all pitched in to shovel the fish over Shimazaki until his body was covered about two feet deep. They forced the lid down as tightly as they possibly could; and Serge found the metal seal placer and clamped it on the hinge, signifying that this batch was ready for transport off the ship and into Hong Kong lorries bound for the interior of the People's Republic of China.

Master Shimazaki was not missed for three days, and then his absence became a mystery. No one held out much hope that the man or his body would be found in the vastness of the South China Sea—which extends over an area from the Singapore and Malacca Straits to the Strait of Taiwan, a water territory over a million and a quarter square miles. The ship's security force combed the ship from top to bottom and interrogated every man aboard who had had anything to do with the man. It was all to no avail. No one saw anything. No one knew anything. No one could even imagine anyone having ill feelings towards him such that they would commit murder and throw the man's body overboard. Mostly no one talked; they just kept their eyes down and mumbled monosyllabic non-answers when questioned and went about their routines as if nothing had happened. To the vast majority of the men, nothing had happened. Nobody cared.

CHAPTER SEVENTY-ONE

Victoria Harbor Port Facilities, Hong Kong Island, Hong Kong British Crown Colony, November 2, 1963

When the *Port of Embden* 220 pulled into the busy and sheltering waters of Hong Kong's Victoria Harbor, the entire ship's company took a very unusual break and stood on deck to see the beauty of the natural land-form harbor as they sailed between Hong Kong Island and Kowloon. They glided carefully past the entrance of the Zhu Jiang [Pearl River] and cautiously approached the Kwai Chung Container Terminals in the western part of the harbor, threading the ship through the traffic of one of the world's busiest harbors—hosting more than 200,000 ships a year. The waters of the harbor were overloaded by oceangoing and river vessels and local junks, all carrying passengers or a wide variety of goods because of its deep ocean advantages, the shelter afforded it by the surrounding hills, and its strategic location. The captain of the pilot boat had his work cut out for him as he led the huge fishing trawler into its berth in the container terminal.

Hugues looked furtively over his shoulder and spoke quietly to Antoine and Serge. "Think security knows the miserable little nip is dead and is just waiting to spring it on us? Do you think they know it was us?"

"I don't know the answer to either question for sure, but I do know this: once we walk off this rust bucket and into the great masses of anonymous humanity in the terminal area, no one could possibly locate us even if they had us cold. Our plan is to keep our heads down and eyes straight forward. No issues with anyone over anything until we are out of Hong Kong altogether, *Est-ce que tu comprends* [do you understand]?"

The three men were grim-faced but kept their wits about them. They took their turns in the customs and paymaster lines without entering into the usual complaints and arguments among the men trying to get off the ship more quickly than their shipmates. They were patient while the paymaster crew totaled the base pay and share income for each man, checking and rechecking. Every man was paid in cash, in the currency of his choice. The *Gebirgsjägers* took just enough pay in Hong Kong dollars and British pounds sterling to tide them over until they could get established in a more anonymous and secure location.

As soon as they cleared all procedures, they headed straight for the centrally located Shun Tak Centre in Sheung Wan, immediately west of the main business district. They bought business suits and tropical linens, white shirts, and appropriate shoes in the night market for the next stop on their odyssey to secure freedom. They had a choice of taking the cheaper *Tak Sing, Dai Loy,* or *Fat Shan* ferries, but they were feeling flush; so, they opted for the more luxurious and more expensive *Macao*. The trip took four hours, during which the three lowered their anxiety levels with good eighteen-year-old British Glenturret Scotch which was a far cry from the swill they had to drink aboard the *Port of Emden* 220 for the past nearly eight months. They slept most of the way, feeling the waves of anxiety melting away because they were now free of potential accusations from law enforcement for the murder of Junji Hirokatsu Shimazaki. Antoine was not quite so sure they had heard or seen the last of INTERPOL, the FBI, the Sûreté, or the Mossad, however.

§§§§§

Le *Bureau Central National (BCN) d'*INTERPOL *pour la France* [The International Criminal Police Organization, or INTERPOL], Office of Senior Detective Chief Superintendent Eugène Léon Dentremont, 200 Quai Charles de Gaulle, 69006 Lyon, France, November 28, 1963

The law enforcement officers gathered in the office of Senior Detective Chief Superintendent Dentremont's office were glum. They all realized the inevitability of what Eugène's decision was going to be.

He skipped preliminary chit-chat, the usual small French treats, and the introductions as he began to speak to the senior officers of his own INTERPOL service, the FBI, French national police, and a representative from the *Mishteret Yisra'el* [National Police of Israel]. No one raised an eyebrow at the absence of Levi Appleman ben Cohen ["C"] or anyone else from the Institute in Tel Aviv.

"Our Detective Vinciguerra will sum up what we know about the manhunt for the fugitives—the alleged killers of the senior military officers."

He turned to Vinciguerra.

"Thank you, Chief Superintendent. There is not a great deal to tell; so, I will keep it simple. For the past several weeks, it has been my task—along with Forensic Specialist Marianne de la Reynie—to monitor every detail from every agency and department around the world involved in the manhunt for the SS fugitives. This has included American CIA, FBI, Alaska and Texas state police, and US Army military police; Israeli National Police and the Mossad; French Paris police and the Sûreté; British New Scotland Yard; Argentine provincial police of Córdoba, Buenos Aires, and Ushuaia, the national police, and more than a few Argentine government officials known to be flagrant Nazi sympathizers; Chilean police in Santiago, Valparaiso, and Puerto Montt and their national police, the coast guards of Argentina, Chile, and Peru, and civilian Nazi sympathizers like the Club Aleman; Soviet KGB's Fifth Directorate and Moscow *militisya* detectives; German state *Kriminalpolitzei* detectives, forensic sciences officers, and detectives in several west and east German cities.

There is not an airport, railway station, or seaport that we have not investigated and monitored. We have been a thorn in the side of organized crime throughout the world—the Sicilian mafia, the *russ-kaya mafiya*, the *Unione Corse*, the yakusa, Chinese triads, and all of their known associates. We have pressured everyone we know of in the ODESSA and Spider organizations and their Swiss and Vatican sympathizers. So far as we can determine—and to the limit of our resources—we have turned over every possible stone."

"And found nothing," DCS Dentremont said morosely.

"That's about it, sir. We have followed leads that suggested that they escaped by securing a private airplane to take them to Peru, or that they boarded some sort of fishing boat or other cargo ship out of a Chilean port, or that they joined one of the legions of tourist trekkers headed north overland through Chile or Argentina. None of the leads panned out. All I can say for certain is that the last time any of the fugitives was seen for certain was on September the twenty-eighth of this year in the vicinity of the Bariloche, Argentina, train and bus terminals. Even that information came from a classified source. There are no official law enforcement records even of that small piece of information."

"So, where are we now, Chief Superintendent?" asked FBI Special Agent Xavier Gonzales-Soto.

"At an impasse. We will—of necessity—scale back our hunt until we have credible evidence of a location for these criminals. We know they are part of the worldwide criminal organizations and that they have huge resources at their disposal. We will have to be patient—we have no other choice. We will get them—mark my words—but it will take time. And, at the risk of repeating myself, we will have to be patient."

Recipe for Marinated Macaw

<u>**Tropical Marinated Macaw**</u>

Ingredients
-2 young adult macaws (fresh), pineapple, lemon, pomegranate, and chicozapote juice from fully ripened fruit, 1 cp each of Bacardi rum, *Mezcal* liquor, *acachú* liquor, aguardiente brandy, *caxtila* Veracruz rum, *taberna* palm liquor—about 1 pt. each.
-2 thin cedar planks, lengths of stout twine.

Preparation
Note: Because macaw is very tough, it is essential to follow the preparation instructions to the letter.
-Very carefully pluck the bird, leaving no roots of feathers in the skin.

-Cut bird open and attach to plank with twine, breast up (in crucifix posture). Immerse in ice-cold mix of all juices and refrigerate for 1 day. Remove, then heat bird in its marinade to low boil and leave at boil for 1 hr. Bring heat down to simmer and maintain at that temperature for 6 hrs.

-Remove bird from hot juice, discard juice, allow to cool in refrigerator for 6 hrs. Be sure bird is completely cold.

-Place bird on its plank into a mix of the rums and palm liquor, heat to low boil, then turn down to simmer for 4–6 hrs. Test tenderness with a fork.

-When fairly tender, remove from hot liquid and discard liquid.

-Refrigerate until cool~2–3 hrs, then place bird on its plank into a mixture of the *Mezcal*, brandy, and *acachú* so that it is completely immersed and repeat cooling process for another~2–3 hrs.

-Then place bird on its plank and cold liquid into a 360º F oven for 4 hrs. Lower heat to 225º for ~2 hrs. so that it is nice and warm for serving.

-Note that the dish is considered to taste somewhere between spotted owl and bald eagle.

To Serve
-Discard liquid.
-Discard bird.
-Eat the board.

CHAPTER SEVENTY-TWO

Continental Hotel, 132 Đnen Khởi, Bến Nghé, Quận 1, Saigon, December 12, 1963

The three remaining *Gebirgsjägers* arrived in war-torn Vietnam on December the eighth and were met at Tan Son Nhat International Airport by a holdover French planter called Jean-Yves Sarrazin—which was not his birth name. Sarrazin was a former French Foreign Legion colonel who had escaped capture after the debacle and chaos of the defeat of the French army at Dien Bien Phu in May 1954, which ended the first Indochina War. He changed his name, disavowed his military past, and became a harmless employee of a French plantation outside Saigon. He gradually accumulated enough capital to buy his own large rubber plantation and to become assimilated into the new society of the country. He was chronically short of money because of his proclivity for beautiful women, fast horses, gambling, and poor business decisions. When former comrades in the Legion told him that three old and very rich army men were in need of a safe haven, he enthusiastically volunteered.

Sarrazin was in his mid-sixties, tall with short cropped white hair, a Frankish nose which led him and the other Frenchmen to be known as the "big-noses" by the Vietnamese in their private conversations. His once lean, fit physique was softer now with a noticeable ponch which was beginning to lap over his belt. He wore the uniform of the French colonial planters—white linen suit, light pink silk shirt and tie decorated with a dragon figure imported from China, a wide belt from which an evil dagger hung in an embroidered leather scabbard, and heavy leather sandals with no stockings—a protection against fungal foot infections in the cloying wet tropical climate.

"General Duvalier, I presume," Jean-Yves said and extended his hand to Antoine.

"I prefer Pierre Deneuve, Monsieur Sarrazin," Antoine answered warily.

"Please, we should be on first name basis. I am Jean-Yves."

Antoine nodded in agreement.

He and the other *Gebirgsjägers* were more than uncomfortable in the crowded airport where Vietnamese and American military personnel teemed among the civilians and *Canh Sat* [government of South Vietnam's national police, the "white mice" as they were known, because of their uniform white helmets and gloves] were in abundance.

"I understand your discomfort … Pierre. Let us adjourn to more inviting surroundings."

He snapped his fingers, and two peasant porters rushed to his side and gathered up the few suitcases belonging to the *Gebirgsjägers*. They pushed their way onto Quang Trung Street and joined the cacophony and chaos of morning traffic in one of the most densely populated cities in the world. They made the mandatory stops at the three checkpoints—American and South Vietnamese—and finally arrived at their first destination, the venerable old Grand Hôtel Continental in the heart of the city. The driver opened the doors for Jean-Yves and the *Gebirgsjägers,* then sat patiently in the shade of a café umbrella to await the pleasure of his employer and the guests.

"Let us get something to drink in the Continental Shelf where we can speak in private, my friends," Jean-Yves said, and led them into the designated first floor—but technically located on the second floor of the hotel—bar which was given its nickname by war correspondents who joked that they were safe from grenades up the stairs and in the bar.

Jean-Yves settled into his place in the booth he had reserved the prevous day and invited his guests to do the same. They all ordered drinks and–after the obsequious waiter thanked Jean Yves effusively and left– they got down to business.

"All of that bowing and scraping could get on one's nerves," said Antoine. "And I understand that the Vietnamese people don't believe in tipping."

"Maybe someplace," said Jean Yves and laughed, "but not in the Continental."

"Tell me, please, Jean-Yves, what our agenda will be."

They were all speaking French because their booth was situated next to one occupied by a loud and obviously intoxicated group of American Marine officers.

"We will whisk you out to my plantation where you will stay in one of my guesthouses for as long as you desire or need to. I have trusted friends from the Legion who will arrive at my home day after tomorrow, and we will be able to have a useful conversation with them that evening. You realize that they will be most careful around the Vietnamese because they are … shall we say … persona non grata in the country for the time being. They will be posing as German businessmen. It will be best for you to speak German with them."

"Thank you, Jean-Yves. We are in your debt and will compensate you accordingly."

Jean-Yves nodded dismissively, a hypocritical gesture, Antoine knew, because he had already paid the man several thousand American dollars through his bank in Algiers.

Late the following evening, a light tap on the *Gebirgsjägers'* cottage door signaled the arrival of the Legionnaires. Serge went out the back door and circled surreptitiously around to where he had a good line of sight on the visitors. Antoine and Hugues held their Lugers at their right sides with the hand and gun held out of sight while Antoine opened the door.

A smiling Jean-Yves greeted him, "*Mon ami*, Pierre," he said, taking care to use Antoine's current pseudonym for the time being, "these are my friends from Algiers. I am hoping they will be yours as well. May we come in?"

Antoine took two quick looks outside, then invited the three men into the cosy Indochinese decorated room. All of the visitors entered with bare hands extended, and did 360 degree turns to demonstrate that they were not armed. Antoine nodded at Hugues; and the two of them did the same thing, except that they placed their handguns on the entryway table. The five men nodded at each other in acceptance, and Pierre made introductions.

"This is Col. Didier Amirault and Lt. Col. Édouard Melerine of the Legion in Algeria. May I present Pierre Deneuve, Frédéric Charron, and…."

On cue, Serge entered the room through the front door and said, "Georges Thibault."

The two Legionnaires nodded crisply, and the three *Gebirgsjägers* returned the gesture. Antoine waved the three newcomers into the room and pointed out chairs for them.

When they were all seated, Col. Amirault took command of the conversation, "We cannot be in Vietnam for long for obvious reasons. We came at the request of Col. Danvier, whom you know as Jean-Yves Sarrazin. My fellow Legionnaire officer and I will not be coy. We have complete dossiers on all of you courtesy of a mutual friend, Anton Friedrich Krupp von Bohlen und Halbach."

Upon hearing the name of the secretive head of the ODESSA, the eyebrows and the antennae of all three *Gebirgsjägers* sprang to attention.

"You need not be alarmed, *mes amis*. Our war is over. We share a common enemy in the communists, and Anton has all of our best interests in mind. He remains secretive about himself and about you three and about our visit here. You are in need of anonymity and a purpose in life, and we are in need of seasoned officers for our struggles in Algeria and elsewhere. Anton assured us that you would fit in well with the Legion."

"It would be good to serve France again. What would our positions be, *mon Colonel?*"

"We are aware that you were a *gruppenführer und generalleutnant der Waffen-SS*," he said, nodding at Antoine. "And you were, I believe, a *sturmbannführer*," he said to Hugues, "and you were an *obersturmbannführer*," he nodded to Serge.

Serge acknowleged Col. Amirault's accuracy.

"At present, we have no positions on the general staff; and frankly, none of us will ever achieve that rank. There is too much favoritism towards the old guard for that to happen. We do need officers, and I want each of you to have a colonelcy. I recognize that we are asking a distinguished *Général de Division* to step down to the same rank as me. Would that be acceptable?"

The rank of colonel would indeed be a significant drop-down for Antoine; but to be a senior French officer, anonymous to the rest of the world and safe from it, and able to return to his first love—a military career—trumped all other considerations. He did not hesitate and answered for all three *Gebirgsjägers*.

"When do we start and where, *mon Colonel?*"

"First, let me make one thing entirely clear, gentlemen," Col. Amirault said in all seriousness. "The Legion as it stands today is 100 percent loyal to Gen. de Gaulle. No French officer who sided with the Algerian insurgency or separatist movement may have rank above major in the Legion. You have been vetted, and your complete separation from such groups is a given because of your SS background. And—I might add— your presumed involvement in the assassination of *Général de division* Étienne Malboeuf—a former bitter enemy of de Gaulle—was quietly received with good marks. Never forget that you enter the service on de Gaulle and his loyalists' side. We, of course, pray that no Legionnaire will ever have to bear arms against another Frenchman during his entire career. You will be required to sign the oath."

"We will be happy to do it now," Antoine said definitively.

"We have the papers."

Lt. Col. Melerine opened a thin brief case and produced three parchment sheets which the three *Gebirgsjägers* signed with alacrity.

"This second set of documents are your official enlistment papers. Congratulations on your becoming French Foreign Legionnaires."

The *Gebirgsjägers* signed the five-year service contracts as well. They signed with the pseudonyms they were using in Viet Nam which was perfectly acceptable to the Legion. The Legion gives or allows all recruits a new name and strictly guards their anonymity.

"Now, in answer to when and where, let me tell you that you can travel to Algiers beginning tomorrow. It will take a couple of days given the continuing poor relations between the governments of Vietnam and Algeria. The final *where* is Sidi-bel-Abbès, Algeria, another day's flight."

Vietnamese Recipes

Banh mi

There are many different varieties of *banh mi*, only limited by the cook's imagination. The following is the basic sandwich.

Ingredients
-crusty baguette, sliced pork and other lunch meats, shredded cured pork skin, various kinds of pâté, Miracle Whip, Jack Daniels mustard, or mayo., Vietnamese radish, carrot pickles, lettuce, sliced cucumbers, sprigs of cilantro, fresh pounded chilies, sliced cheeses, preferably strong tasting ones. *Banh mi*

calls out for variation: sausage, shredded meats, bok choy, meat loaf, white and dark meat of chicken, sliced beef pot roast, or steak.

Preparation
-Buy the baguette freshly made from the vendor so it is crusty on the outside and soft and white inside. Slice it lengthwise with a sharp serrated knife or even good kitchen shears, taking care to avoid crushing the bread at the point of cutting. Layer the slabs of bread with the choices of the moment, lean over the sink or the ground or a plate because it's messy. It is also filling. Vietnamese often eat only two meals a day, with *Banh mi* being one of those.

Bún mắm (bun mam)

Ingredients
-sufficient homemade rice noodles [vermicelli preferred], *nouc mam* [fermented fish sauce], tamarind juice, sugar, variety of meats [such as squid, prawns, pork, beef (*bo*), and chicken (*ga*)], sliced eggplant, bok choy, boiling water.

Preparation
-Bring a soup pot ¾ full of water to a rolling boil. Add *nouc mam*, tamarind juice, sugar to taste.
-Pile noodles on the bottom, then the entire assortment of meats on top of them, then the sliced egg plant (which soaks up the broth. Serve very hot. May have hot sauce, salt, and pepper to taste.

Phở (pho)

Ingredients
-noodles, choices of meat (as with *Bún mắm*), chopped green onions, sweet onions, ±bok choy, assorted herbs (such as mint, sawtooth, cilantro) to taste, homemade chili sauce.

Preparation
-flash-boil noodles until soft, top with meat choices, sprinkle chopped green and sweet onions.
-serve hot with buttered baguette and 333 beer (which can be added to the broth for a little extra flavor kick if desired).

Nước chẩm (nouc mam)

Ingredients
-½ cp fish sauce, ⅓ cp fresh lime juice, ¼ cp sugar, 1 minced clove garlic, 1 tsp sambal olek, ½ cp water. Chili, salt, pepper, sugar, ±333, to taste.

Preparation
-fish sauce:
The process of making the favored fish sauce of Viet Nam is one that Americans are better off not knowing about if they are to enjoy the pungent final product. First, a layer of ungutted raw fish is spread over an open area. Salt is then liberally applied to the layer of fish. Additional layers of fish and salt, about ten to fifteen in all, are heaped on and allowed to putrefy for three or four weeks in the broiling sun until an oily black liquid runs off the sides. That piquant effluent is collected in bowls and served over rice, often with pieces of fish or vegetables added. It was irreverently called "armpit sauce" by American GIs with uneducated palates.
-add fish sauce, lime juice, sugar, garlic, sambal olek, water, chili, salt, pepper, and sugar. Mix thoroughly and allow to chill in fridge for 1–2 days. *Nước chấm* is found on virtually every table at every meal, and every day in both North and South Viet Nam. This ubiquitous amalgam sauce is at once salty, tangy, spicy, fishy, and sweet. It is perfect for dunking, dipping, adding to, or pouring over foods. Some people like to drink it straight.

Elephant Ear Fish

Ingredients
-2 kg *Osphronemus Exodon* or Elephant ear fish—preferred—(may substitute tilapia or other flaky white fish), 2 tbsps olive oil, 1 lime, juiced, ¾ tsp sea salt and 1 tbsp sea salt, ¼ tsp black pepper. 1 pkg of rice vermicelli noodles~250 g., 1 cp mint, 1 cp Thai basil, 1 cp cilantro, 16+ rice paper wrappers.

Preparation
-Gut fish, but leave whole. Combine fish, olive oil, lime juice, salt, and pepper. Marinate 10 min.
Preheat oven to 350° F. Heat grill pan over high heat and sear fish for 30 secs. on each side. Place in oven and bake 10 mins. until cooked through. Cool.
-In a soup pot, boil 1 l. water with 1 tbsp sea salt. Add rice noodles, stirring to separate. Cook 3–5 mins. until soft. Drain. Rinse with cold water and drain again. Set aside.
-Carefully place whole fish into boiling oil and cook until it is rigid and can be manipulated without breaking. When dry and cool enough to handle, pick up with chopsticks and stand vertically in a narrow pot and support it with bamboo sticks on both sides at intervals to keep it erect.
-Slice herbs into thin strips and mix together. Place 2 rice paper sheets in soup pot and cover with 6 in. lukewarm water to soften~20 secs. When soft and pliable, remove one carefully and place on a paper towel in front of you. Place 1 tbsp of the herbs in the center of the circle ⅓ of the way from the bottom in a rectangular shape 6 in. x 2 in. high. Break off pieces of whole fish (consistency of thick potato chips) and place on top of rice paper sheet. Place 2 tbsps vermicelli noodles on top of that. Roll the bottom of the rice paper up and over the filling,

tucking the ends in to close (like rolling a cigar). Fold both right and left flaps into the center, creating blunt ends of a roll. Be careful not to roll too tightly or the rice paper will rip. Roll the filling gently towards the top of the circle, taking care to tuck the filling in to make a snug package.

-Repeat with next sheet of rice paper and add 2 more to the soup pot to soften. Serve with a bowl of *nuoc mam* for dipping.

Vietnamese sea urchin

Ingredients
-1 sea urchin for each guest. Mustard, lemon juice, soy sauce, chilis, hard roasted peanuts, boiled broccoli, sea salt and pepper, herbs of choice.

Preparation
-Crack open and clean sea urchins so that the opening allows urchin to serve as the bowl. Add lemon juice, mustard, soy sauce, and mix thoroughly, gathering up urchin meat into mix. Add chilies, peanuts, and broccoli.

-Eat fresh (no cooking required): this gives the spiciness of the mustard, the texture of the broccoli, the sweet fat of the sea urchins, the aromatic flavor of the peanuts, and the added flavor of the salt, pepper, and herbs. It is useful to wash down with plenty of 333.

Bạch Tuộc Hấp Hành—Steamed Baby Octopus with Ginger and Onion

Ingredients
-300 g octopus, 1 small branch of ginger, 2 cloves of spring onion, sea salt, *nouc mam*, garlic, chili, sugar

Preparation
-Pull out octopus organs. Put head and tentacles on basket, add 1 tsp salt. Scrape firmly to reduce grease, wash then wash again.

-Peel off cover of the ginger, slice into long and thin pieces. Use the white part of spring onion, slice into long pieces.

-Add sliced ginger and spring onion on top of octopus bowl, bring to steam until they are cooked~5–10 mins.

-Pour *nouc mam* over mixture in salad bowl and enjoy. 333 is a good beverage with this salad.

CHAPTER SEVENTY-THREE

EMT [*État-major tactique*, Tactical Command Post], La Légion Étrangère, Sidi-bel-Abbès, Algeria, December 29, 1964

The day was one more oppressively hot test of human endurance in a long string of such days. The *Gebirgsjägers* celebrated their first year as Legionnaires this month and wondered privately among themselves if they could tolerate even one more year, let alone the entire five-year tour for which they had contracted. They all knew they were safe out in the middle of the drabness of the Algerian desert. No one in his right mind would ever bother to look for them in this godforsaken hot hell. There was nothing to do but play cards, intervene in fights among the eighty-six nationals represented in the Legion just in this small outpost, or seek out a Bedouin woman—almost unthinkable for the arrogant Aryan *Gebirgsjägers*. The place was once the headquarters city of the French Foreign Legion, but that all changed two years previously when the Algerian War of Independence officially ended, and Algeria's sovereignty was certified. The French and their sympathizers were evacuated, and the Legion moved its headquarters and museum to Aubagne in southern France. Only two sites were maintained: the naval base at Mers El Kébir and the small desert EMT post in Sidi-bel-Abbès. All that was left in Sidi Bel Abbès were the training center of the Algerian National Gendarmerie and the EMT—Tactical Command Post—of *La Légion Étrangère*. Most of the Legionnaires proper were part of the 1st Foreign Regiment—the so-called "*Perle de oust.*"

The *tenue de jour* [uniform of the day] was the usual because of the almost perpetual heat—blue tunic, white linen trousers tucked into short leather leggings substituting for regular day red serge because of the hot weather, white kepi, and epaulettes. Even though it was a parade day, the red sash could not be worn to offset the monotony of the uniform. The *Gebirgsjägers* and the other Legionnaire officers were wearing the same dark blue-black tunics as their fellow officers in the French line regiments, except that black replaced red as a facing color on collar and cuffs. This was a full-dress day; so, all the officers were wearing gold-fringed epaulettes; and rank was shown by the five gold ring stripes on both kepi and cuffs.

The occasion for this full-dress parade was to impress the Israeli *Mahal* [acronym for *Mitnadvei Ḥutz LaAretz, Volunteers from outside the Land*]. The *Mahal* was a unit the IDF [Israeli Defense Forces] patterned after the French Foreign Legion. It maintained close ties with the Legion and the armed forces of France. The *Mahal*—like the Legion—was originally a unit of non-Israelis [the *Mahalniks*] serving in the Israeli military. The term originated with approximately 4,000 Jewish and non-Jewish volunteers who went to Israel to fight in the 1948 Arab–Israeli War, including the *Aliyah Bet* [illegal Jewish immigrants during the British Mandate]. Most of the original *Mahalniks* were World War II veterans from American and British armed forces. To the present day, the Israeli Defense Ministry allows the enlistment of non-Israeli citizens to join Israel's armed forces if they have at least one grandparent of Jewish descent.

No unit in the world can hold a better or more disciplined parade than the Legion. All ranks were represented, and the colors shown brilliantly in the Algerian sun on the nearly white sand of the parade ground. The tricolor waved from each of the four corners; and the marching men were a symphony of black, white, red, gold, khaki, and for some, green (berets). The starch-white kepis reflected the noonday sun, and the marchers' heads held a disciplined nearly perfect unision. The Legion's flag with its *Honneur et Fidélité* [Honour and Fidelity] lettering led the ranks. To its right, the First Regiment's regimental flag fluttered showing its motto—*Ad unum* [To the end]. A distinct difference maintained between the Legion and all other French military unit is its motto. The other units fly a banner reading: *Honneur et Patrie* [Honour and Fatherland]. Behind the flags two men—one huge and black, the other small and fair—carried the banner bearing the motto of the Legion: *Legio Patria Nostra* [The Legion is our Fatherland].

The Israelis and *Mahalniks* stood at rigid attention as the Legionnaires slow-marched past the reviewing stand. Unlike the 116-step-per-minute pace of other French units, the Foreign Legion has an 88-step-per-minute marching speed which the Legionnaires fondly refer to as the "crawl." The reason for the slow march and its origins are argued. There may be some truth to the popular belief that the slow pace might have been due to a need to preserve energy and fluids during long marches under the hot dry Algerian sun. Officially, the slow pace began in 1945, but it also reflected the slow marching pace of the *Ancien Régime*, and was reintroduced as a return to traditional roots.

The men marching to the Legion's *Le Boudin* that day were reduced in number and diversity in comparison to the makeup of the Legion prior to 1962. After the independence of Algeria and the shame the Legion felt for those Legionnaires and many other units who sided against France—the *Armée d'Afrique*: Zouaves, Tirailleurs, Méharistes, Harkis, Goums, Chasseurs d'Afrique, and most of the Spahi regiments—which were disbanded; the Foreign Legion was severely reduced in numbers and diversity but not completely disbanded. The recruitment requirements were intensified, and many postings were eliminated. The changed Legion rightfully maintained its reputation as an elite unit ready to engage in serious fighting, but the recruitment practices tended to remove the concept that the Legion was a place for disgraced or wronged men looking to leave behind their old lives and start new ones. There were holdovers from the old ways like the *Gebirgsjägers* who still occupied something of a romanticized place in the hearts of the Legionnaires and their admirers.

The new Legion intensified the general concept that the units were ready for rapid deployment to the hot spots of the world. This was particularly true for the *état-major tactique* stationed in the lonely outpost of Sidi-bel-Abbès. The Legion also intensified the basic adherence to the motto of *Legio Patria Nostra* by codifying the core activities and loyalties designed to preserve French interests everywhere in the world. In addition, the concept of adoption of the Foreign Legion as a new fatherland and military career was based on careful vetting and training to amplify the professionalism of the unit which—for all of its diversity—was unified in purpose and performance. The Legion did not require repudiation by the Legionnaire of his original nationality, but rather, respected the original fatherland loyalties of the Legionnaires and worked to steer the men to a pride of self, their origins, and their comrades in the Legion. They were free to preserve their nationalities. All of the changes enhanced the value and performance of the Legion and made the Legionnaires proud of their service. For the *Gebirgsjägers*, it was home, country, fatherland, and family all rolled into one package of *esprit de corps*.

After the parade, the entire garrison and its Israeli guests gathered for a sumptuous lunch in the post pavilion. The usual fare for Legionnaires was actually quite good: things like rabbit, *haricots verts*, green salad, fresh baked bread and strawberry crepes, often canned pate, potted mushrooms, preserved pears, and a flavor-locked package of Gruyere cheese. Each French ration box contained small bottles of red and white wine and a fortifying shot-bottle of cognac.

However, on this occasion, the EMT base caporal chefs and servers outdid themselves. Algerian servers dressed in crisp white shirts and trousers, black boots, and red, white, and blue sashes swept through the crowd serving champagne, an assortment of beer for those of less French taste, and large platters of the multiple regions of Algerian food. The rich and exotic foods included: *Kabylie*—the Algiers couscous— a large range of Mediterranean fruits—including tropical ones—and vegetables, lamb, and Mediterranean seafood. Special dishes included: *kesra*, a traditional Amazigh flatbread, *merguez*, a spicy lamb sausage from the Atlas Mountains, *shakshouka*, *karantita*, *marqa bel a'assel*— a speciality from Tlemcen—and the *chakhchoukha* from Chaoui. The food was spicy and required ample supplies of bottled water and libations. The spices featured multiple different dried red chilies, caraway, *ras el hanout*, black pepper, cumin, nutmeg, coriander, fennel, ginger, mace, and star anise. The chefs cooked with tagines and clay vessels, handmade in Algeria. There were a wide variety of Algerian salads with clear influence by the French and the Turks such as beetroot and anchovies, and a Algerian recipes for dishes of Spanish origin such as *Gaspacho Oranais*, an Algerian version of a *Manchego* [Spanish Castillian] cheese dishes, *pisto* [vegetable stew with tomato sauce], washed down with the sweet white wine of La Mancha and the strong red wine from Valdepeñas. The Algerians made no complaint about the consumption of alcohol and were inclined to take a nip or two themselves despite their Muslim religion. However, liberalism did not extend to the consumption of pork which was expressly prohibited in the Sharia law. The Israeli and other Jews among the *Mahalniks* appreciated not having even to see pork being consumed.

The rest of the afternoon was spent in siesta and dips in the regimental pools. Part of that period was occupied for Lev and Moises Silverman to meet with a local indigenous Jewish tailor, a member of the sayanim. Jacob ben Amsallem was a throwback to the Jews of sixty years previously in his Jewish culture and dress and his fierce loyalty to France. He wore a scarlet *tarbush* [oblong turban with silken tassel], a bright copper-colored *ṣadriyyah* [vest with large sleeves], and *sarwal* trousers [pantaloons] fastened by an orange *ḥizam* [girdle], all covered by a multicolored *burnoose* [mantle], and a large red, white, and blue silk handkerchief, the tassels of which hung down to his feet. He wore new soft black leather shoes which were shaped to fit either foot. Jacob confirmed that three older Legionnaire officers were fairly new to the first regiment and did not associate much with the other officers. Although they usually spoke French, the three men sometimes spoke German to the Legionnaires from German-speaking countries, including southern Chile.

Thus nourished and refreshed, the men of the Legion and the Israeli guests gathered on huge mats for the Krav Maga tournament for which they had all gathered. This contest was inspired by a highly successful previous gathering held on April 30—Camarone Day—one of the Legion's most important anniversary celebrations. At that time, the Legionnaires were new to the extremely effective Israeli martial art form and were chagrined and impressed at how easily the smaller Israelis defeated the larger Foreign Legion fighters who took a great deal of pride in their ability to fight mano-a-mano. The French were far better prepared for today's contest, having trained every day since that time in order to make a better showing. Antoine Duvalier—now known as Col. Antoine Toussaint—was the oldest man and most senior officer to be listed as a contestant.

The tournament had a few rules designed to avoid maiming injury and allowed for "tapping-out" as a submission before real damage would occur. Unlike advanced IDF training, protective gear was used in all matches; so, the opponents could make real attacks without resulting in the real injury that Krav Maga was developed to inflict. Serge and

Hugues lasted three matches before finally submitting, which was three matches better than their previous showing in April. Antoine met Lev Mizrahi in the quarterfinals. Antoine only knew Lev by his reputation as a Master of Krav Maga and his success as a competition fighter. Lev, however, was the leader of the Mossad *kidon* [assassination] squad and was privy to all information pertaining to the Project Save the Generals. His recognition of Antoine for who he really was came as a complicated series of serendipitous events.

After the Mossad failed to make a capture or prevent an escape from Puerto Montt, Chile, no new information had turned up, and—for all intents and purposes—the murderers of the senior generals in multiple countries had vanished without even a hint as to how or where. By April 1964, the active search was placed on hold. None of the law enforcement agencies around the world who had an interest in the Project Save the Generals had the slightest inkling that the murderers might be hiding relatively in plain sight by resuming a military career. Israel had been in regular contact with the Foreign Legion for several years, and the two entities had traded valuable and mutually beneficial information. For the Israelis, they were able to copy everything useful they could glean from the Legion's recruiting, training, and how to maintain a multinational, highly diverse military force separate from regular French army units. With a worldwide Jewish support for Israel, there were many men and women who wished to aid the IDF but to retain their own national identity and citizenship. What worked well for the French worked well for Israel. The Mossad recognized from the beginning the intelligence-gathering potential of the multiethnic, multinational force loyal to Israel and did all it could to foster good relations.

For its part, especially after 1962, having the plucky and militarily successful little country flatter the Legion by emulation was a morale booster and gave the Legionnaires an opportunity to train with and to learn from the IDF and Mossad. They learned in April 1964 of an area where they were deficient, and they bonded with the Israelis to correct that deficiency. As a result of their humiliation in the first Krav Maga competition, they enlisted the help of Israeli instructors and began to drill Legionnaires in the IDF model—an intensive three-month, six-days-a-week, twelve-hours-a-day regimen of training. In order to enter an Israeli governmental security unit, a candidate spends six hours a day honing shooting skills and six hours of full contact Krav Maga sparring. The IDF Krav Maga instructor course is five weeks in duration above and beyond the "basic" course, and an increasing number of Legionnaires were becoming proficient enough to reach the formal rank of Expert. No one yet had achieved a full level-five expert rank, and no one was even being considered for the rank of Master.

Lev Mizrahi was a Master and one of the elite instructors. He practiced what he preached and competed regularly in full contact, no-pads, sparring with the best of the best in Israel and around the world. He had never been beaten by anyone outside the corps of top instructors in the Mossad. Antoine Toussaint was presumed to be no exception.

Antoine was fifteen years older than Lev, forty years less experienced in Krav Maga; and his body was tired after the abuse he had suffered during his military career and beyond. The match lasted twenty-five minutes, which was a good showing against Lev Mizrahi. Lev was the epitome of a self-defender—able to perform within the Krav Maga principle of *retzev* [Hebrew for "continuous motion"] with the aim of neutralizing his enemies by any means necessary and without suffering injury himself. Despite having been fully active in training, Antoine's experience was no match for Lev's. The stepping side kicks, horizontal elbow strikes, uppercut elbow strikes and fist punches, hammer fists, hook punches, outside and inside chops, and several hip and leg throws and trips came too fast and furiously and with too much sustained intensity for the old soldier to cope with. He was finally finished with a trick. Lev was one move ahead of Antoine. He tried an armbar which led Antoine to make a mistake by turning onto his abdomen to protect his arm. This gave Lev the opening to put the older and tireder man into a rear naked Brazilian jiu-jitsu choke—the *mata leão* [Portuguese—lion killer]. The choke, also known as the *hadaka jime* in judo, is designed to cut off blood supply to the head resulting in rapid onset of unconsciousness. Antoine was aware that his consciousness was rapidly deteriorating, and he would soon be helpless; so, he admitted defeat and tapped out. When Antoine fully regained his senses, Lev helped him to his feet and shook his hand.

"You did well, my friend. You outlasted any of my other opponents. Don't be discouraged. I have been at this for forty years. Keep working and we will meet again next year."

Antoine gave the Israeli Master a grudging smile and a casual salute.

"I saw the other two men who seem to be older than the rest of the officers. I would like to meet them. Maybe we could all get a drink after the matches finish tonight—in the spirit of good sportsmanship and among comrades-in-arms."

Antoine should have been suspicious at the request, but he was only flattered that this world's champion wanted to meet him and the rest of the *Gebirgsjägers*. He thought nothing more of it, and Serge and Hugues were equally ready to find camaraderie with the Israeli experts.

The entire Israeli contingent, including the *Mahalniks*, were already in the EMT bar when the *Gebirgsjägers* entered. Lev introduced all of the Israeli team—which included his Project Save the Generals undercover officers: Moises, Eban, Micah, Eliot, Enos, Gavriel, Ezra, Haggai, Yachin, Enos, Manny, and Aaron. Antoine formally introduced Serge and Hugues—at least their aliases—and the newly acquired friends enjoyed an evening of drinking—the Israelis, a little too much local Carignan wine and strong domestic Groupe Castel whiskey—and the Legionnaires, considerably too much absinthe—*la fée verte* [the green fairy]—a worldwide illegal, anise-flavored high alcohol spirit derived from botanicals, including grand wormwood, green anise, sweet fennel, and other differing medicinal and culinary herbs depending on the producer. Absinthe usually has a natural green color, hence the popular name.

Recipes for Algerian Food

Kabylie—[Couscous Algérien]—Serves 8

Ingredients
-2 lg. chopped onions, 1 tsp turmeric, ½ tsp cayenne pepper, 1 cp vegetable stock, 1 tbsp cinnamon, 3 tsps black pepper, 1 tsp salt, 10 tbsps tomato puree, 7 whole cloves, 6 med. cloves, 6 med. zucchini, 8 small yellow squash, 1½ large carrots, 8 med. unpeeled yellow potatoes, 2 lg red bell peppers, 1 15 oz. can garbanzo beans. 2 cps dried currents, 2 pkgs couscous.

Preparation
-Saute onion in vegetable stock over med. low heat until translucent. Add all spices and cook for a few more mins., stirring as needed. Add tomato paste, stir and simmer 2 mins.
-Cut vegetables in large chunks and add all—except beans—and a dash of cinnamon; add water to cover. Bring to a low boil, reduce heat and simmer, covered~1 hour. Alternatively, may cook slowly for 2–3 hours.

-Add drained garbanzo beans~ about 5 mins. before taking vegetables off heat.
-Put couscous and currents in a bowl. Pour boiling water over couscous and wait~5 mins.[~1½-1 ratio water or vegetable stew water to couscous], then fluff lightly with fork. Alternatively, add cooked whole shrimp and/or sea scallops sautéed in Fresca soda pop, and/or grilled white fish and/or salmon to the stew. Serve the stew over the couscous. Another alternative is to add cold diced fresh tomatoes to the entire mix just before serving.

Merguez [Spicy Lamb Sausage from the Atlas Mountains]—Serves 8

Ingredients
-Red spicey Merguez link lamb sausages—4 per person, 2–4 tbsps EVOO [preferably crushed fresh young olives to extract oil, uncooked], but extra virgin olive oil will suffice. It loses some nutritional value when cooked.

Preparation
-Prick holes in sausages with a sharp instrument. Lightly rub EVOO onto each or pour extra virgin olive oil into grill pan.
-In a cast iron grill pan, cook the *Merguez* sausages until they begin to take on color. Do not overcook [dries sausages out]. Remove from the heat and keep warm in a 200° F oven. Do not use gas grill because it imparts an odor and taste to the sausages. Alternatively, cut sausages into 1 in. sections, or mash with a spoon. Serve over couscous.

Chakhchoukha—Serves 8

General note: The *marqa* or stew is made with diced lamb cooked with spices [dried red chilies, caraway, *ras el hanout*, black pepper, cumin], tomatoes, chopped onions, chick peas, potatoes, zucchini, carrots.
The *rougag* or *khobz* [flat bread] is made with fine semolina and, after baking, is torn by hand into small pieces. When eating in individual plates, about two handfuls are put in the plate and then the sauce or stew is poured on top.

Ingredients for khobz
-500 g fine semolina, 500 g white or half and half white and whole grain flour, 1 tsp salt, water

Ingredients for the Marga (sauce)
-8 lamb chops or 8 skinless chicken pcs, on bone but skin and fat free, 1 lg onion, 3 garlic cloves, 2 med. carrots, 2 med. zucchini, 2 lg potatoes, ¼ swede (another of the turnip family) or ¼ turnip, 1 peeled chopped parsnip, 1 cp drained chickpeas, 2 tsps *ras el hanout* spice mix, salt, pepper, 1 pinch dried mint, 1 tbsp sunflower or vegetable oil, 1 cp tomato puree with added liquid, 1½ l. water, 1 lg chopped green chili.

Preparation
khobz
Roll out dough on a floured smooth surface, grease cookie sheet, transfer flat bread dough to sheet, and bake at 350° F for ~30 mins. until crisp and browning.

Marga
Cut meat into 1–2 in. cubes or cook whole. Saute in spiced extra virgin olive oil until done through.
Mix all other ingredients of the sauce into a pot and boil until soft but not mushy. May be better to cook different vegetables separately since they differ in cook times. Cook couscous (or brown rice may be used as a second-rate substitute). Place hot couscous on a plate. Mix meat in or pour sauce over meat on the couscous.

To Serve
Serve with mint tea and assorted fresh fruits. Break pieces of bread and scoop up the *Marga* with the bread. Algerians and people who know eat this dish with their fingers. It is considered gauche to use utensils.

CHAPTER SEVENTY-FOUR

EMT [*État-major tactique*, Tactical Command Post], La Légion Étrangère, Sidi-bel-Abbès, Algeria, December 29, 1964, late evening

Prior to going to the EMT bar to socialize with the Legionnaires—the suspected murderers of the generals—Lev and Moises cautioned their men to avoid consuming more than just a little social alcohol; so, they would have their wits about them at all times. Moises told them to let the Nazis get drunk and talkative. They would be good listeners. Lev paid their waiter a double tip to water down the Israeli contingent's drinks and to make the Legionnaire's drinks extra concentrated. Nonetheless, they did not learn much from the mildly inebriated Legionnaires. After the social meeting, Lev and Moises retired to their rooms and made a call to the Institute.

A measure of the importance attached to the transmission was that "C" himself answered the encrypted call.

"Lev, Moises, I presume this call relates to our discussion about events in your current location last April."

"Yes, sir. We have confirmed the presence of three subjects whom we last saw in South America. It is not feasible to meet with them in Tel Aviv anytime soon without creating difficulties. We will have to return at a future date and with a solid plan."

"Will you be back to the Institute tomorrow?"

"Jehovah willing and good luck with the weather and the rather unreliable transportation facilities we will face."

"Overcome, brothers. I am sure this is an issue that won't wait."

§§§§§

Le *Bureau Central National (BCN) d'*INTERPOL *pour la France* [The International Criminal Police Organization, or INTERPOL], Office of Senior Detective Chief Superintendent Eugène Léon Dentremont, 200 Quai Charles de Gaulle, 69006 Lyon, France, December 29, 1964, late evening

DCS Dentremont was called into headquarters from a black tie soiree honoring President Deutraine's appointment of a new chief of staff of the French air force. Now ensconced in his office with a fully secure line, he returned the direct line call from "C" at Israel's Institute.

"C" answered the telephone himself. "Thank you for getting back to me so promptly, Eugéne. I would not have troubled you unless it was about a matter of some gravity."

"I'm glad to be 'bothered,' 'C'; I hate black tie affairs. What's up?"

"Some of our agents have located the fugitives being sought in the Project Save the Generals case."

"Confirmed?"

"As nearly absolutely as possible. My most senior *katsa* [field agent] and *kidon* [assassin] have identified all three. In fact, they participated in an athletic contest and spent the evening having drinks with them. As important as that, we have one of our sayanim in the area to keep a close watch on them while we plan our move."

"Can you give me the area, 'C'?"

"Of course, but we all must understand that this must be handled with the utmost delicacy for any number of reasons: the political fallout with the French, the Muslims, Israel, and the Algerian government; the risk of causing an international incident that leads to armed conflict among countries; and certainly the possibility that a premature, gauche, or mishandled operation could result in the permanent loss of our access to these SS monsters. The place is Sidi-bel-Abbès, Algeria."

"The French Foreign Legion!!?" Léon exclaimed, quite unlike his usual unflappable self. "Do you wish to handle this alone, 'C'? Cutting out the FBI, the CIA, the Sûreté, the SDECE [*Service de Documentation Extérieure et de Contre-Espionnage*—external security], and the DGSI [*Direction générale de la sécurité intérieure*—internal security]—to name but a few—will not help you win friends; and it won't get you any help you might find that you need."

"Nor INTERPOL, I presume?"

"We will not be happy. However, we are good at keeping secrets; and we will not betray you."

"Thank you for that. I, of course, would not expect anything less. Frankly, our experience with the FBI and the CIA has not filled us with confidence; and the French would have a conflict of interest of the first order. They would be highly averse to allowing French Foreign Legion soldiers to be taken, and they would be loath to admit ever that they were employing former Nazis in senior military positions."

"I understand, and I pledge INTERPOL assistance in any way we can should you make a request."

"Thank you, Léon. The Institute will consider this to be a marker we owe you, payable at some future date."

§§§§§

Oval Office, the White House, Washington, DC, December 31, 1964, 0600

President Johnson listened intently and without interrupting as the DCIA presented the PDB [Presidential Daily Briefing] for the previous day. The PDB was a top secret document produced each morning for the president of the United States under the direction of the DCIA, DDIA, the NSA, and other members of the United States Intelligence Community as became necessary. There was only one topic covered in today's PDB.

Director McCone summarized.

"Mr. President, 'C' communicated to us—as a courtesy—that they have intelligence that they consider comes from absolutely reliable sources relating to the whereabouts of the murderers of the senior generals around the world, including one of our own, Gen. Glen Gabler, USA/Ret. You will recall that they almost captured them in September 1963 in Bariloche, Argentina, and Puerto Montt, Chile. The fugitives have been in the wind ever since, seemingly having vanished from the earth. Then, in April 1964, a group of Israelis took part in a Krav Maga martial arts competition with French Foreign Legionnaires in Sidi-bel-Abbès, Algeria."

"That's the world headquarters for the Foreign Legion, isn't it?"

"Used to be up until two years ago when they got booted out of country after Algeria got its independence."

"Let me guess," the president said, "those old Nazis are now in the Foreign Legion and fighting for France."

"Seems so."

"Lot of strange bedfellows since the war seems to me."

"And this is about as strange as it gets, Mr. President. Apparently, the Legion and the Mossad have close ties; and the old Nazis are thick as thieves with the Israeli Jews."

The president shook his head.

"As I said in the beginning of this PDB, the Mossad has officially informed us that they are planning to capture or to terminate the three fugitives they know about and any others they run into in Algeria. They invite our help, but I have to say that 'C' didn't seem all that enthusiastic or hopeful that we would want to get involved."

"Involved how?"

"They are going to run a black-op to kidnap or kill the Nazis."

"Where … exactly?"

"On the base. It's a Foreign Legion outpost EMT or Tactical Command Post for rapid deployment missions."

"With French Foreign Legionnaires protecting their comrades, Director?"

"Probably with some stealth, Mr. President; but in a nutshell, that's about it."

"And what do they want from us in return for destroying every diplomatic endeavor from now until kingdom come, or even risking war with the French?!"

"At the minimum they'd like some equipment … like two Beechcraft King Air Multirole Transports and flight crews to get the people in and out, two C-97 Stratofreighters to haul in all the stuff, and a few third-generation jet fighters—including, but not limited to Airforce F-111 Tactical Strike Aircraft and F4 Phantom IIs with our air-to-air missiles, more sophisticated radars and medium-range RF AAMs for stand-off ranges, our improved electronic countermeasures (ECM) for spoofing radar seekers, and chain-guns for starters, sir."

"C-97s are the pregnant guppies that we now have for civilian use?"

"Basically."

"Anything else suit their fancy, Director?"

"Boots on the ground would not be rejected. 'C' specifically hinted at SEALs and Army Rangers."

"Large force?"

"No, they want a small force, but the crème de la crème."

"Any idea what this would cost in American money, Director?"

"Depends on the length of time involved and the exact equipment we contribute, but I'd think nothing less than $100 million."

"I know that a lot of you think I take too long of a time to make up my mind about things, especially when it comes to military action. However true that may be in general, in this specific instance I will give you my decision right now: it's no. Plain unvarnished no. Risk a war with the touchy French; so, the world will be safe from a couple or three old Nazis? I don't think so. Tell 'C' that for me, and wish them luck. They're gonna need it."

§§§§§

Israeli Institute for Intelligence and Special Operations [Mossad LeAliyah Bet], Headquarters of Director Levi Appleman ben Cohen, Glilot Junction on Highway 2, Ramat Aviv Neighborhood of Tel Aviv, January 1, afternoon

"C" sat at his simple old desk in the Institute and surveyed his most trusted *katsa*, Abraham Levy, and the designated head of the *kidon* squad, Lev Mizrahi, who would direct the mission and turn it into an assassination if necessary. That was Lev's specialty. There were a total of nineteen men in the room including Moises Silverman, the senior Mossad field agent who had been part of the Project Save the Generals since its inception, and an unprecedented fourteen *katsas*. There were only thirty-five *katsas* [foreign field agents] in the entire world; so, the significant percentage of them involved in this project underscored the gravity with which it was regarded. "C" was well aware that if the mission became a disaster, his coterie of agents would be severely depleted; and he would almost certainly lose his job. Each man was special and known personally by "C"; and he cared about them, knew their families, and was cognizant of what they had already sacrificed for *Éres Yisra'el*. He was on a first name basis with them: Eban, Micah, Eliot,

Enos, Gavriel, Ezra, Haggai, Yachin, Enos, Manny, and Aaron. The force was rounded out by five IDF commandoes who came with the personal recommendation of the IDF chief of staff.

"C" did not waste time on formalities or warm up chit-chat.

"Thank you for your willingness to be involved in this mission. You are volunteers, and a great deal rides on what you do, not the least of which is the reputation of Israel … and … my job. And, oh, yes … your lives. We are in this alone. President Johnson and DCIA McCone flatly turned us down when I requested operational assistance. They want nothing to do with what could well turn out to be an international incident.

"You men will fly to Sidi-bel-Abbès, Algeria, tomorrow night and do a HALO parachute drop in the mountains just north of the city. You will travel in three separate companies to a location outside the west gates of the city on the side opposite the Legion headquarters. There you will meet our sayanim who lives in the city. He will be your guide. Others of our sayanim who live in Algiers have arranged trucks to haul in heavy weapons and troop trucks to aid in your escape. When you leave this room, each of you will be issued an L-pill—just in case—and false ID papers including Moroccan passports. In part, you have been selected because of your fluency in Arabic; that is important should this venture come unglued; and you have to make it back to Israel on your own. You know the drill: should you be captured or killed, we will disavow you. You know better than to carry anything that identifies your real person, anything that originated in Israel, or any personal photos or memorabilia. No *Magen Davids* [Star of David] on you anywhere or in any form."

There were no demurrers, even from the minority of the men who were religious.

CHAPTER SEVENTY-FIVE

Tell Atlas Mountains, Northwestern Algeria, January 3, 0 dark-30

The INS [Israeli Navy Ship] S class submarine, *Tanin* [Tz-71], surfaced in international waters offshore from the bustling North African city of Sidi-bel-Abbès, Algeria, in radio silence and all-lights-out precautions. The ship had earned the affectionate name "Sugar Boat" among the crew and the commandoes from the smooth voyage and easy and silent surfacing maneuver. Nineteen men dressed all in black and with black-painted faces stepped swiftly onto the deck and took a moment to gain their sea legs. As they assembled, two zodiacs were put into the ocean on the starboard side; and crew men lined the bridge, coming to aid the commandoes as they entered the boats.

The zodiacs sped in the direction of the shoreline, and the *Tanin* submersed. The entire time on the surface of the Mediterranean had been less than seven minutes. Five minutes into Algerian waters, two Sikorsky S-58 helicopters—a longer and more powerful version of the earlier Sikorsky model S-55—appeared out of the blackness and hovered over the zodiacs. A trail line was dropped from the helicopters to each of the zodiacs and secured only by two men holding the line. A rescue basket was lowered and two men gingerly entered it and stretched out to avoid imbalance. The basket was retracted into the helicopter, and the two men were quickly helped out and into the cargo bay of the aircraft. The process was repeated three times, then the rescue basket apparatus was retracted into the helicopter for the last time. The final action was to pull the trail line back into the aircraft with six backpacks full of weaponry and emergency supplies. The boat drivers headed back to sea for the predetermined GPS site where they rejoined the sub. The Sikorskys moved swiftly at low altitude towards the Tell Atlas Mountains north of Sidi-bel-Abbès. It was largely an instrument flight since they could not risk lights.

The Sikorsky rose well above the mountains, and at the predetermined location, began to release the parachutists and their gear in a HALO [high altitude, low opening] drop. There was real danger in the process: it was pitch-black dark, they were landing in unfamiliar territory, and—unlike most of the rest of the archetypal barren North African habitat—their landing site was in the steep well-watered and forested mountains north of that vast desert. Had the landing been in the light, the men would have been treated to a striking green background with a surprisingly densely populated area of North African towns.

The mountains–with their inhospitable environment–have provided a refuge for the original inhabitants, who fled successive invasions. Here the Berber people survived, preserving their own languages, traditions, and beliefs, while at the same time accepting Islam to some extent. Village communities still live according to a code of customary law–known as *kanun*–which deals with all questions of property and persons. The family unit traces its descent from a single ancestor, preserving its cohesion by the sense of solidarity that unites its members; an injury to the honor of one affects the group as a whole and demands vengeance.

The Kabyle Berber society in the Tell Atlas Mountains had struggled for centuries to preserve its individuality apart from the majority Arabs. Nowhere is that more evident than in their choice of habitat. Their fortified villages are largely perched high up on mountain crests. Most of the villages are small, consisting of a few dwellings, a mosque, a threshing floor, and a place for the assembly of the elders—the *djemaa* which governs the affairs of each community altogether separate from adjacent villages. The fortified villages guard against predation by any outsiders, including the government. Families live in separate rooms in the form of a square around a closed interior courtyard. Parachutists would be greeted with a hail of gunfire if sighted.

Women grow vegetables in small gardens adjoining their houses. Fig and olive trees cover the mountain slopes below and around the villages, and those carefully tended trees are the principal resources of the clans and are husbanded communally. The Kabyle are also skilled craftsmen working with wood, silver, and wool. They supplement their families' incomes by working as peddlers and selling carpets and jewelry to the people of the plains below.

The landing went relatively well; for seventeen of the nineteen commandoes, it was safe, efficient, and successful. For one thing, none of the men parachuted into a town by mistake. For two of the IDF noncommissioned officers, it did not go so well. *Rav samal mitkadem* [*Rasam*-advanced chief sergeant) Levi McGuire hit a rocky outcrop, fell fifteen feet, and fractured his right femur, and *Rav samal rishon* [*Rasar*-chief sergeant first class] Shaul Shraga ben Peretz landed on a spike of a dried up cork oak tree which penetrated his left foot through-and-through. Unfortunately for the unit, and especially for the two soldiers, they were out of commission; and they had to be dealt with appropriately. Fortunately—and as the result of good planning—Jacob ben Amsallem, the sayanim from Sidi-bel-Abbès, was waiting for the commando unit in the drop site with his pack mules. The little tailor knew a village situated near the mountaintops which was populated by a small clan of strict Orthodox Jewish families who were as private, protected, and prickly as their Berber neighbors—the nearest of whom lived forty-five miles away. He loaded the two injured men onto mules and led them up the rough trails to the village where the rabbi was happy to serve as an auxiliary sayanim and to provide nursing and protective care for his coreligionists, who were a rarity in his mountains.

The seventeen still fit commandoes donned night vision goggles and began to pick their laborious way down the mountainside through moist forests of cork oaks, an undergrowth of cane apple and heather shrub, and treacherously irregular carpets of rockroses and lavender. The footing was especially difficult in areas of crumbling limestone where they encountered heavy roots of green oak, arborvitae, stands of cedar, and thin bushy undergrowth covering the rocky soil. There were decent trails and even two gravel roads which would have been navigable for a family automobile. Lev insisted on avoiding both of those options for the sake of security. It was slowgoing due to the need for silence. Occasionally a small herd of wild boars or an infrequent jackal startled the advance guard, but they were well enough trained not to utter a sound. Besides the uneven terrain they had to descend, the march was difficult because of the weight of their packs.

Every man carried a backpack holding weapons that could not be traced back to Israel: a Russian Stechkin APS—A 9x18mm Makarov 1951 modified to the AO-44/APB variant with attaching silencer and steel wire stock, a select-fire machine pistol; a Walther or Pistole P38, a 9 mm semiautomatic handgun which was the service pistol of the Wehrmacht during World War II. The Israelis had the late 1963 postwar military model P1 with an aluminum frame rather than the steel frame of the original design. The pistol held eight rounds in a single row, detachable box magazine, and was fitted with a silencer; twelve Soviet F1 RPG-6 [*Ruchnaya Protivotankovaya Granata*] hand grenades and plastic explosives; and a Soviet *spetsnaz* force NRS-2 survival knife worn in an ankle holster with a built-in single-shot firing mechanism able to fire a 7.62x42mm SP-4 cartridge. The packs also contained three days of emergency rations and water, injectable morphine, tetanus antitoxin, and antibiotics—penicillin and streptomycin—a tourniquet, tape, plastic splints, and powder antibiotic wound packs.

For all of that encumbrage, the unit made good time and with no mishaps. The outskirts of the city were barren and burned—a landscape somewhere in composition between Galilee and the face of the moon. The city itself—located forty-six-and-a-half miles inland from the Mediterranean Sea—was now the populous commercial center of an important agribusiness area of vineyards, market gardens, orchards, and grain fields. It was formerly surrounded by a wall with four gates, but all that was left for the commandoes to see and to stumble over were some small piles of rock rubble. They silently passed the university which served as a landmark. Wide boulevards and squares replaced the traditional quarters, causing the town to lose much of its former character beginning in 1962. It was still completely dark when they arrived at the northwestern gates of Sidi-bel-Abbès—the side opposite the location of the Foreign Legion headquarters–giving the city something of a desert ghost town quality. Once again, Jacob ben Amsallem was waiting in the shadows.

"Following me, please, sirs," he said, looking down to minimize the possibility that it could appear that he was giving orders.

The commando unit fell in behind the sayanim, and they moved like shadows. The sky was overhung, making it a moonless and starless night—perfect for the task at hand. They walked quickly and cautiously to avoid brushing debris on the streets but in what were obviously semicircles; the commandoes presumed it was for the purpose of security. They circled the Sidi Bel Abbès Domestic Airport and the Metropolitan Police station—which was a decaying remnant of the colonial era—before splitting into two groups and focusing on the EMT station. Jacob led one arm of the commando unit and Lev led the other. Their objective was the BOQ [Bachelor Officers' Quarters].

§§§§§

BOQ [Bachelor Officers Quarters], EMT [*État-major tactique*, Tactical Command Post], La Légion Étrangère, Sidi-bel-Abbès, Algeria, early morning

"It's the dark romance of the French Foreign Legion: haunted men from everywhere, fighting anywhere, dying for causes not their own. Legionnaires need war, certainly ... [and] there's always the hopeless battle.... The real lesson here was not about combat tactics. It was about do not ask questions, do not make suggestions, do not even think of that. Forget your civilian reflexes. War has its own logic."

-William Langewiesche

Antoine cursed the time of day—not yet 0500—his insistent bladder, his arthritic joints, his insomnia, and his old age for not allowing him more than four to six hours of sleep a night. He was too old to be a soldier, he thought. He was too old to be still sleeping in a narrow utilitarian bed in a Spartan room, in a godforsaken desert, among dark-faced strangers he detested. Otherwise, he loved the Legion and the safety and the anonymity it provided. He pushed his creaky bones up out of bed and began to curse the heat—the omnipresent heat. He was already sweating by the time he made it to the narrow veranda overlooking the now rarely used parade grounds. His bladder forced him to hurry. He unzipped and leaned out as far as possible and let flow a narrow and frustrating stream of urine down onto the walkway in front of his building.

He cursed his fellow *Gebirgsjägers*—now Legionnaires—his real friends, Hugues Beauchamp and Serge Rounsavall, and all the rest of the sleeping Legionnaires. He cursed all of the men in the unit, indeed all men everywhere who were not rapidly going bald like him. He was just in a foul mood. He needed to stretch his limbs and to get his blood flowing; so, he threw on a blouse and shoes and walked down to the walkway he had just besmirched to go for a walk. The command post was empty of people. If there were sentries, they were likely asleep—the lazy good-for-nothings. Such conduct would never have been tolerated in his old unit, the 33rd Waffen Grenadier Division of the SS *Charlemagne* (1st French) Regiment. During the war, such a miscreant would have stood before a summary court martial and been shot the same day. He missed the glory days in the SS, the absolute power, the adventure. He missed being important. His regiment had been personally assigned to be the last defenders of the Führer in the final Battle of Berlin.

He had to admit that now he was somewhat awake he enjoyed the early morning quiet. It was peaceful. He tallied the positive aspects of his life as he slowly walked around the streets of Sidi-bel-Abbès and tried to imagine—there in the dark—what the place had been like during its glory days as the international headquarters of the French Foreign Legion. Nothing like Berlin with the SS regiments marching down the *Ku'damm* in perfect order; but still, the Legion had its own pomp and tradition that could still make an old Frenchman's heart swell.

He heard a shuffling sound. Rats. The place was crawling with them. It was more than a decent human being's life to venture into an alley at night. The thought made his skin crawl. He listened again but heard nothing else; so, he moved on, a little more wary now. He stepped into shadows and listened intently. There was a distinct sound—as if a man had brushed against a building or alley wall. Now, Antoine's antennae went up. He went into reflexive combat vigilance mode. The night became quiet again, but Antoine refused to believe that he was hearing things that were not there. There were bandits—marauding Berbers who would love to kidnap a senior Legion officer—or maybe just a drunk sliding along a wall for balance trying to get home. That thought gave him an immediate goal. He crept silently into a dark alley and made his way quickly back to the barracks.

He tapped first on Serge's door, then on Hugues's.

"Quiet," he said. "Maybe this is nothing, but I am sure I was being watched. At least there's somebody out there that shouldn't be. Get dressed. My old defensive prickle is back. I think we need to get ready for something."

Both men were groggy and a little confused. But they both had been with Antoine long enough to trust his sixth sense about danger.

"What do you want to do, *Mein General?*" Serge asked, but thought, *What are we doing up in the middle of the night?*

"This will sound stupid, but I want to overreact. If there's nothing to this, we can just slip back to our rooms; and nobody will be the wiser."

In the street below, Lev gave Haggai a withering look. He had stumbled over a bag of trash and bumped into a wall. To Lev in his heightened state of awareness, it sounded as if he had fired his pistol. Lev did not need to say anything; Haggai and everyone else got the message. Moises took five men and made their way through the narrow alleys around to the back of the BOQ. Every man in the unit could remember when a fugitive had escaped out the back when they went in the front. They were determined that this not be another one of those times. A long foot chase would be noisy and would attract a lot of highly unwanted attention.

Antoine, Serge, and Hugues made their way down the connecting hallways of the three barracks buildings until they came to the west facing exit. Serge took point and popped his head out of the door to take a quick look. Nothing there. He was beginning to feel rather sheepish. He signaled, and the other two *Gebirgsjägers* followed point just as they had done for all their years of combat.

Serge stepped up to Antoine, cupped his hands over Antoine's right ear, and whispered very softly with careful enunciation, "Where to?"

Antoine did the same thing to Serge. His whisper was terse: "Armory."

They were less than twenty-five yards away if they had chosen the most direct route, but their instincts pushed them to walk through the darkest alleys and past the broken streetlights they were familiar with. They made their way to the back of the armory, being careful not to fall over the trash strewn back there. Antoine felt a twinge of disgust that he was part of an outfit that permitted such lack of military order. He determined to report this to the CO later that morning ... if nothing came of his foray in the night.

Lev and Moises whispered orders into their Bulgarian *Radioelektronika* handheld radio transceivers.

"Two sentries in the street in front and in back of the BOQ. The rest of the teams get up to the second floor. Jacob says they are in rooms 210, 211, and 212. Be on the lookout for sentries. Radio silence from here on out."

There were no guards, and the Israelis met no resistance. They lined up two men to each door while the rest stood guard in the halls and stairwells. Lev gave a twisting finger signal, and a man tried the doorknob of each of the three rooms. To no one's surprise, they were all locked. The locks were ridiculously simple—skeleton keyholes with no bolt locks. The doors were unlocked in less than five seconds and very nearly silently.

"Look for booby traps," Lev whispered as he pushed his door slowly open.

Ten seconds later, the commandoes returned to the hall and shook their heads.

"At least we didn't wake the garrison," Lev whispered.

He was wrong, as it turns out. Before he could ask the obvious question—*Where are they?*—two men peeked out of their partly opened doors, one in the first third of the hallway, the other nearer the other end. An IDF master sergeant took down the man at his end, and did it in lethal silence. At the other end, the Legionnaire recognized instantly that he was facing a much superior force and rushed back into his room, threw on pants, and went out through the window facing the front of the building. He jumped to the veranda—which made a serious crashing noise—and got a severely strained ankle for his reward. He leaped off the veranda onto the top of a small Fiat and crumpled the bonnet in with a resounding crash. Micah was one of the guards on the street. He saw the man's two landings, and was at the Fiat to dispatch him before the Legionnaire could get off the car. Micah cut his throat and did it quietly, but the damage was already done.

Half-dressed Legionnaires began pouring into the street, opening the barracks room doors and rattling sabers and locking and loading rifles and pistols. Micah Freiburg and *Rasar* Evon Meir were shot dead by men who saw Micah cut the throat of one of their brothers-in-arms. The Legion drilled the *Code d'honneur du Legionnaire* into every recruit, including officers from their first day in the Legion, and required frequent rote recitation of the men to ensure that it was never out of their minds when Legionnaires came under fire.

"Légionnaire, tu es un volontaire, servant la France avec honneur et fidélité.

["Legionnaire, you are a volunteer serving France with honour and fidelity.]

Chaque légionnaire est ton frère d'armes, quelle que soit sa nationalité, sa race ou sa religion. Tu lui manifestes toujours la solidarité étroite qui doit unir les membres d'une même famille." [Each Legionnaire is your brother-in-arms whatever his nationality, his race, or his religion might be. You show him the same close solidarity that links the members of the same family."]

Then hell broke loose.

CHAPTER SEVENTY-SIX

Armurerie, EMT [État-major tactique, Tactical Command Post], La Légion Étrangère, Sidi-bel-Abbès, Algeria, January 3, 1964, 0715

The battle outside the armory was sporadic, with small arms fire crackling around the barracks buildings for a few minutes followed by men shouting in three or four different languages. After nearly three hours of fighting, no one seemed to have discovered the whereabouts of the *Gebirgsjägers*. It appeared the commandoes who had invaded the EMT were conducting a guerrilla-type fight with the Legionnaires with alternating running, hiding, and stopping to fire at pursuers. In the darkness and smoke and chaos, men were being wounded and some were dead on both sides; but the chaos made it impossible to determine an accurate and up-to-the-minute casualty count.

"Maybe they've forgotten about us," Hugues said, "and maybe they've gotten themselves into too much trouble to be able to concentrate on their mission."

"Maybe ... but I don't think that will last very long," said Antoine.

The three men were taking a breather from their work of fortifying the inside of the building for when—not if—the interests of the outsiders shifted to them. They had opened three bottles of rather good Cote du Rhone red wine from the storage racks reserved for officers and were quenching their thirst. There was no water in the armory and no food.

Serge sat looking out of the first floor front windows—the only windows in the building.

"White flag," he said.

"Whose?" Antoine asked.

"The commandoes. The Jews. One of them is walking out to parlay with Capitaine Duris."

"Let me have a look," Antoine said. "It's the Krav Maga master, Lev Mizrahi. That can't be any good for us. He has real juice with the Legion, and he's a smooth talker. My bet is that they are going to try to make the best of out a terrible situation for both of them. Once they do, our time here is over despite all that 'Each Legionnaire is your brother-in-arms whatever his nationality.' I can almost hear the reasoning about how Nazis—and especially SS—are the natural enemies of the Legion, and certainly for mother France. The best we can hope for is to get the chance to escape with a head start, and the worst is that we have a small last Battle of Berlin here today."

"I won't surrender. No POW camp for me. I'll never go back to one. So, if we're going to have a battle, it will be my last one," said Serge.

"I have no intention of giving up. But I will go down fighting. Hopefully we can take down a few Jews as we go," Antoine added.

Hugues said, "I hate to be fighting Frenchmen again, but so be it. We are effectively persons with no country. My only allegiance is to you two. Don't let them take me. Kill me if it looks like I can no longer fight, or if I get surrounded."

Antoine put his right hand in the air, and all three touched palms in a pact to the death.

"*Sichern und laden* [lock and load]," he said, "*zum vernichtungskrieg* [to a war of annilation, an ultimate offensive]."

§§§§§

"Watching him watch ... I asked how [it] was going. He answered that the boat was sinking normally. It was a figure of speech. He knew from experience that the [men] were doing well enough."

-William Langewiesche

Lev stepped out of the morning shadows cast by the rising sun. He was keenly aware of the dozens of Legionnaire guns pointed at him and knew he was as close to death as he had ever been, white flag or not.

Captaine Duris glared at him with a mixed look of hatred for an enemy, profound disappointment for having been betrayed by a man and a country he had counted upon as friends, and a face full of quizzical bewilderment. Lev stopped halfway between the barracks and the Legion captain, slowly turned around a full 360 degrees, and opened his hands to show empty palms.

Duris gave a curt jerk of his head to signal Lev to approach. All around him came the sound of locking rifles. Duris turned slowly and gestured with his hands in a downward fashion to signal his men to point their rifles at the ground. All guns lowered and aimed at a forty-five degree angle towards the hard pack of the parade ground.

Lev walked directly to Captaine Duris and stopped two feet from him. His eyes held the captaine's in a look of courage that he scarcely felt, and a deep conviction that he would not signal anything suggesting aggression, anger, or that he was an enemy.

"Thank you for agreeing to speak with me, Capitaine. I offer no excuses. My commandoes and I came here uninvited and with a military mission. I wish to assure you that we never intended to harm even a single Legionnaire. Our mission is to arrest, detain, and remove back to Israel three mass murderers. We believe them to be common enemies of both of our countries. We are sorrowful that there has been blood shed on both of our sides. We ask that you allow us to deal with the three Nazi *Totenkopfverbände* [Deaths Head units who specialized in extermination camp duty] who not long ago were murdering our defenseless countrymen, women, and children, and who betrayed France by collaborating—even worse—by forming the infamous 33rd Waffen SS division—the *Charlemagne* regiment—to kill Frenchmen. They should have been nothing more than *scheiss kommandoes* [men assigned to latrine detail by the *Konzentrationslager*]."

"What is it you expect me to do, Lev?"

The question was posed in a manner of resignation fully expecting that his Legionnaires would shortly be fighting to the death against the elite IDF and Mossad commandoes—a lose-lose situation with unthinkable international ramifications. At the very least, he knew his career would be over; and he would be cashiered out in disgrace.

"Let us reason together, *mon ami*. We have already lost men we can ill-afford to lose. No matter what happens from this point on, we will lose more. Both you and I and our respective countries will suffer great loss of face if a battle occurs between us. I would like to avoid that if it is humanly possible. I think there can still be a solution, one which may yet allow us to prove our true friendship towards the Legion and to France. Have your Legionnaires back away a safe distance and remain ready to annihilate our men should it even appear that we will do anything other than what I promise."

"And what is it that you promise, Lev? What possible good can come of what you have already done?"

"Allow us to arrest and take the three homicidal monsters back to stand trial in Israel … or to die trying. Perhaps they will elect to fight to their own deaths. That would be no great loss to you, to the Legion, to France, or to the world if that is their choice. When we finish our mission, we will leave with the same secrecy that governed our arrival. No one outside of this location need ever know what took place here. I pledge you my personal honor that the Mossad, the IDF, and the government of Israel will never breathe a word of it beyond our top secret councils."

Duris pondered the offer for a few moments.

"We will place a *cordon sanitaire* around the EMT and all entrances and exits of Sidi-bel-Abbès. We will neither hinder nor help you. You will be on your own to find your way out. You know I cannot speak for the ungovernable Kabyle Berbers. They live by their own law— the *kanum*—and like nothing better than to kidnap and torture or sell a senior Legion officer. They are wild men but know that they are Muslims to their cores. They would not hesitate for a fraction to kill or torture you or your men or any other Jew they might encounter. I hope you have a plan for your escape; but if you don't, we will not remember nor mourn you. Are we clear on our agreement?"

"Entirely. Please allow me to return to the barracks before you move your men back and out of harm's way. We will approach the armory with great caution. We will control our fire as much as is humanly possible to prevent collateral damage to civilians or to Legionnaires. We will even try as much as we can to avoid serious damage to buildings."

The two men saluted, and Lev did a smart about-face and walked purposefully back to the barracks and his men without so much as a backward glance.

Duris stood with his men in the square until Lev was out of sight, then he ordered them to follow him away from the parade grounds.

They set up a perimeter and placed snipers on every building that had a view of the armory.

§§§§§

The three surviving *Gebirgsjägers* watched through the armory window as the Jew and the capitaine parlayed under the white flag. The next thing that happened was a surprise and perplexing. The Jew—which Antoine now recognized as Lev Mizrahi, the Krav Maga master—turned away from Capitaine Duris and disappeared into the barracks. Duris led his Legionnaire detachment away from the parade ground, out of sight, and presumably out of the action.

"We're going to be attacked by the Jews," Hugues said. "Better get ready."

"I don't think that's what will happen first," Antoine observed. "They'll want to parlay, have us surrender peacefully and without any more bloodshed. My bet is that a couple or more of them got wounded or killed by the Legionnaires, and that won't sit well with the Jew bosses in the Hebrew Entity."

The sun was up and blazing at ten a.m. when Lev Mizrahi and Moises Silverman walked out into the ovenlike heat and dazzling whiteness of the sandy parade ground under a white flag. The two Israelis walk slowly and cautiously. Moises carried the white flag, waving it constantly. They were unarmed and exposed and would be for the 120 yards from the first barracks to the armory building.

Serge glued his eyes on the two Mossad agents. His finger twitched on the trigger of his F1 sniper rifle—not out of fear or out of concern that lives would surely be lost in the coming minutes, but out of his hatred for Jews and everything Jewish. He started to hum the marching song of the Waffen SS—the *SS Marshiert in Feindesland*.

In a few moments, Antoine and Hugues joined in the music that was indelibly etched into their memories. Antoine had a fine baritone voice and began to sing the lyrics. His voice was quiet and calming, and the words evoked the glories of their time of power and pride. Serge and Hugues joined him lustily. As the Israelis grew close enough to hear them, the three SS officers began to sing louder, finally reaching the loudest they could manage to be sure the Jews heard their defiance and would be afraid as they always had been when the Waffen SS marched into a village or city with Jews.

Antoine opened the front door a crack; so, the sound of the song which was once familiar to every German—but was now prohibited in both East and West Germany—could carry fully:

"Wo wir sind da geht's immer vorwärts,
Und der Teufel der lacht nur dazu!
Ha, ha, ha, ha, ha!
Wir kämpfen für Deutschland,
Wir kämpfen für Hitler,
Der Rote kommt nie mehr zur Ruh.'
Der Rote kommt nie mehr zur Ruh.'"

[Where we are it always goes forward!
And the devil merely laughs,
Ha, ha, ha, ha, ha!
We fight for Germany,
We fight for Hitler,
The red one (communism) never gets a rest.
The red one never gets a rest.]

Hugues pushed a standard-issue MAS 49/56 service rifle obtained from the armory racks through a small crack opening of the door. He liked the gun—a semiautomatic rifle holding only ten 7.5 x 54mm cartridges—with a good range of effectiveness, but was not happy with its lack of power. Any shot he made would have to be fatal, or he and his fellow *Gebirgsjägers* would not last long. The presence of the menacing rifle was not lost on Lev or Moises. Behind him, Antoine held a MAT-49 submachine gun. What that weapon lacked in range—only about one hundred yards—it made up for in power and magazine capacity. The gun was a confidence builder: it held thirty-two rounds of 9mm ammunition and could fire 600 rounds per minute on full automatic. The limited range mattered little since the fight between the *Gebirgsjägers* and the Jews or maybe even with their fellow Legionnaires would be at relatively close quarters like the SS men were used to from their days in the war when they spread fear from door to door. The benefits of their MAT-49s outweighed the minor disadvantage, and they felt ready for whatever was to come. Serge's sniper rifle could handle anything requiring accuracy at a distance, and he was a deadly accurate shooter. The armory had enough readily available ammunition to allow them to hold out for weeks.

When the Israelis were within twenty feet of the door, Hugues yelled at them, "Far enough! You have five minutes; so speak your piece. After that, your white flag won't mean a thing, Jew."

He punctuated his harsh rhetoric with two shots fired near their feet. He was impressed that neither man flinched.

Lev spoke calmly but loud enough for the men in the armory to hear every word. "You know this is the end for you here. The Legion won't have you anymore after the dossier we gave them about you. As I told you when we had our little Krav Maga contest, Antoine, we have a strong and enduring relationship with the French and the Legion."

"Is that why we heard them shooting at you early this morning—that kind of 'strong and enduring relationship'?"

"We violated their trust in order to get into the EMT barracks to arrest you without a fight or without the Legion even knowing what had happened. As you correctly recognized, that didn't work out well. Two of our people were killed for sure, maybe more. However, once we identified ourselves, Capitaine Duris allowed me to apologize and accepted our assurances that we truly do value our relationship with the Legion. He also ordered his Legionnaires to back away and to let us deal with you separately," Lev said calmly.

"Time's almost up, Jew. What do you want?"

"You are charged in the *Cour Internationale de Justice* with the postwar murder of retired military officers, with crimes against the Jewish people, war crimes, crimes against humanity, and illegal flight to avoid prosecution. We are here to give you a chance to defend yourself in court against these accusations."

"In a Jew court? How stupid do you think we are?"

"Israel is a country of laws and legal procedures, unlike your Nazi Germany. I promise you safe passage and a fair hearing and trial."

"Or what?"

"We settle things finally here today in this godforsaken desert."

"Time's up. Go back to Jew country now. As cowards or as corpses ... makes no difference to us. We fought to the end in the Battle of Berlin, and we are ready to do so again to day. You have a minute to run and hide, Jew. Go to hell!"

"You first, *Scheiss Kommando*!" Moises said.

Antoine flashed the sign of the fig in total disrespect.

Lev and Moises began to back away.

Moises got in the last word, "Justice will be done today, Nazi!"

The two men separated and began to move swiftly in opposite directions. When they were almost 100 yards away from the armory, Hugues fired one shot close to the shoulder of each man, and the two Mossad agents ducked into building entrances for safety.

CHAPTER SEVENTY-SEVEN

Armurerie, EMT [État-major tactique, Tactical Command Post], La Légion Étrangère, Sidi-bel-Abbès, Algeria, January 3, 1964, noon

The heat in the armory was rising by the hour and would become unbearable by mid-afternoon. The *Gebirgsjägers* were beginning to realize the extent of their predicament. In their crucial haste to get away from the Mossad commandoes pouring into the barracks building during the night, all they had been able to think about was getting to a defensible location and obtaining necessary arms. Now, with dry mouths, parched throats, and empty stomachs, they had to deal with other necessities.

"Why don't they come after us?" Hugues asked.

He was sweating profusely and had soaked his Legionnaire shirt. He felt feverish.

Antoine said, "Because they don't have to. They can just sweat us out, or starve us out, or let our thirst force us to give in and to go with them without a fight."

"Did you find anything to eat or drink in the building when you reconnoitered?"

"No. There is no faucet for running water, not even a toilet. There is no food storage here."

Serge asked, "So, *Gruppenführer*, what are our options?"

"Between slim and none," Antoine replied with his usual candor and alacrity.

Hugues said, "What if I find a way to sneak out and see if I can find food and water or an escape route?"

"I think we should all stay together through this whole thing," Serge said.

"Hugues has the germ of an idea, Serge. Why don't you take first watch for any attack or suspicious activity? Hugues and I will go over every inch of the building to determine if there is a hidden tunnel, a sewer passage, or a way to sneak out to a different building. I don't think we're likely to find anything, but we can't just give up."

"Yes, sir," Serge said, standing at attention.

Antoine and Hugues made a cursory tour of the building and determined immediately that the option of sneaking out by entering the outdoors was not feasible. The armory sat alone at the end of the parade ground with no less than fifty feet between it and any other building. By Legion regulation, the surroundings should be pristine clean and free of any debris, trash containers, garages, or vegetation. The policy had not been adhered to with anything near perfection, but they would be like sitting ducks in a shooting gallery if they tried that route. They proceeded to tear up floors and ceilings to see if there was a crawl space out of the building. There was not enough room for a man even to crawl in any under floor or above ceiling space, and none of the small spaces led anywhere except around the space itself. Their efforts on the basement floor were more work, but also somewhat more successful.

They found the fairly large utility pipes and were able to follow them to the left side of the concrete foundation walls under the floor. There was enough space around the piping that a man could slither on his belly. It would be very difficult going, but it was not impossible. The work was backbreaking and time-consuming. Both men were approaching heat exhaustion, and dehydration was beginning to take its toll.

Antoine said, "Our shifts can only be about half an hour long, or we will get exhausted and too weak to be useful. It will take a lot of time; and we have precious little of that; but let's try. I'll go relieve Serge, and he can do a half-hour turn."

He removed a 100 Santeem [Fr. Centime] Dinar coin and said to Hugues, "Let's flip for which one of us takes the next turn. After that, we will rotate digging and guard shifts among all three of us. All right?"

"No problem."

They flipped, and Hugues won. Antoine would take over digging in half an hour, and Serge would go next, then Hugues again. Hugues lay down on the concrete floor and was asleep in minutes. Serge—the strongest of all of them—came down the steps and began the arduous task of making a tunnel to the foundation wall. He moved much more quickly than the other two had. By 1400, there was a passageway to the wall. Now the problem was to break through the thick wall and see what conditions were like under the parade ground above.

The only tools available to them in the armory were entrenching tools. Each small shovel lasted only about an hour before breaking up or becoming so bent that it was useless. The walls were very thick and had rebar reinforcements every eight inches. Antoine worried about the amount of noise they were creating and about the glacial slowness of their progress. They were all worried about their physical condition. The longer they worked the hotter it got, and the more exhausted, famished, and dehydrated they became.

On Antoine's watch at 1530, he saw an Israeli commando dash across the parade ground and situate himself behind a stone pillar and a stone flower bed.

"We have action," he called to his comrades-in-arms.

"We better stop digging and all of us come up and watch for a while. Maybe this is the time we get to fight instead of trying to be sappers or combat engineers," Serge said. "The attempts to get through that four-foot thick concrete foundation are futile."

"Even if the Jew-dogs don't attack, we can't just sit here until we are too weak to fight. That's what they want us to do, Antoine," Hugues said.

"I agree. It's a good day to die," Antoine said. "We need to let them commit themselves a little more; so, we at least know where some of them are before we take them on. We have to make it a good day for as many of them to die as possible; so, the day is not wasted, *meine Brüder*."

Serge and Hugues nodded their agreement.

CHAPTER SEVENTY-EIGHT

Armurerie, EMT [État-major tactique, Tactical Command Post], La Légion Étrangère, Sidi-bel-Abbès, Algeria, January 3, 1964, 1900 hours

"The loneliest moment in someone's life is when they are watching their whole world fall apart, and all they can do is stare blankly."

-F. Scott Fitzgerald, *The Great Gatsby*

Hugues asked Serge and Antoine, "What do you remember best about our early days in the SS?"

"Marching through Polish villages rounding up the *untermenschen*. Our lines were perfect; our black uniforms and polished high black boots shined like mirrors. I loved those days," Serge said.

Then Serge asked, "What was your worst day in the war?"

"Easy," Hugues answered, "the day the Führer died at the end of the Battle of Berlin."

Antoine smiled and asked facetiously, "What was your best meal during our stay in the Butugychag Tin Mine—the Soviet gulag camp for us 'special treatment' POWs?"

The very question brought a pall over the men, but Antoine still smiled. Serge got his drift.

"Rat stew."

They all laughed.

Antoine asked again, "What was your best meal in the American POW Camp 63 Brienne le Cheteâu in France?"

"That's easy," said Serge, "dirt cakes."

They all gave macabre laughs remembering the Hobbesian nightmare of their stays in the Soviet and then the American and French murder camps. They were somehow amused, knowing they were whistling in their walk past the graveyard.

As the insufferable day wore on, Antoine pulled from his shirt pocket a worn pack of Italian playing cards he obtained from one of the Croatian Legionnaires. It was 1600 hours, and the merciless sun was still providing the source of furnace level heat in the armory.

"Let's play a little game of *Briskula* to pass the time until the sun goes down. I hate to fight in the heat."

Briskula is the Croatian name for the Italian card game better known as Brisk. The Spanish version is *Brisca*. Antoine proposed that they play the Spanish variant, *Mano o Sola Negra* [the Black Hand]. The game was appropriate to the day since it is played by each participant attempting to play tricks on all other players. It was commonly played by bored Legionnaires while waiting for assignments and at rest stops.

Hugues hummed *Frère Jacques*—his favorite song from his childhood in Marseilles—a sign of his resignation to the fates that awaited him. He allowed himself a moment of longing for those days of safety and peace. Antoine and Hugues began to sing the familiar words; and for a few moments they forgot their cards, the oppressive heat, and their untenable predicament.

> "*Frère Jacques,*
> *Frère Jacques,*
> *Dormez vous?*
> *Dormez vous?*
> *Sonnez les matines,*
> *Sonnez les matines,*
> *Din, din, don!*
> *Din, din, don!*"

> [Are you sleeping,
> Are you sleeping?
> Brother John?
> Brother John?
> Morning bells are ringing,

Morning bells are ringing,
Ding ding dong,
Ding ding dong.]

Serge then started *Au clair de la lune* [By the light of the moon], and finally they all sang *Alouette,* an angry and sadistic little children's song about the wrath of a man awakened by the cheery sound of a lark's song in which he threatens to pluck off the bird's feathers, then its beak, then its head. It aroused anger and a longing for revenge in the three *Gebirgsjägers.*

"Alouette, gentile alouette,
Alouette, je te plumerai,
Je te plumerai la tête
Je te plumerai la tête
Et la tête! Et la tête!
Alouette! Alouette!
A-a-a-aha tête.
Alouette! Alouette!
A-a-a-ah"

[Lark, nice lark,
Lark, I will pluck you.

I will pluck your head,
I will pluck your head,
And your head! And your head!
Lark! Lark!
O-o-o-oh!]

Hugues stopped singing and reported seeing two more Mossad agents take up positions along the columns of the barracks building. Others began to run out with pieces of furniture to create barricades.

Antoine ordered, "Serge, check the back."

Serge returned to report, "Jew-boys in position at the back and snipers on the rooftops on both sides."

The prospects were dismal at the very best. They waited until dusk, parched, hungry, and weakened by heat; then Antoine gave orders

585

to each of his comrades-in-arms and himself to fix bayonets to their MAT-49 submachine guns and to attach scabbarded combat knives to their belts.

"Take as many of the Jew-dogs as possible. We go out in glory in our last fight."

He opened the front door of the armory building as wide as it could go. The three men began to sing at the top of their lungs as they emerged from their last place of refuge:

"Au revoir, au revoir, au revoir tout le monde.
Au revoir tout le monde, au revoir.
Au revoir, au revoir, au revoir tout la monde.
Au revoir, au revoir, au revoir tout le monde."

[Goodbye everyone.]

Then they burst out of the armory, guns blazing. The Mossad agents were caught by surprise, and three of them paid with their lives for their lack of vigilance. The three *Gebirgsjägers* were cut to ribbons by a withering fire from five directions. The SS 33rd Waffen Grenadier Division-*Charlemagne* 1st French – ceased to exist.

EPILOGUE

Israeli Institute for Intelligence and Special Operations [*Mossad Le Aliyah Bet*], Headquarters of Director Levi Appleman ben Cohen, Glilot Junction on Highway 2, Ramat Aviv Neighborhood of Tel Aviv, February 28, 1964

Lev had dreaded this encounter since the debacle unfolded in Sidi-bel-Abbès, Algeria, almost two months previously. There was nothing new to report; "C" had already received the written after-action report. Now, Lev had to face "C" and his fellow *katsas*, including Abraham Levy, senior *katsa* [Mossad field officer] tasked with the leadership of Project Save the Generals; senior officers of the Israeli Defense Forces including *Rav aluf* [Lt. Gen. and Chief of the General Staff] Mordechai ben Frazier and Prime Minister Yaron Naguisa and to repeat the details of what he considered the greatest failing of his life. He knew that—in all likelihood—he would be cashiered out of the Mossad this very day.

Director Cohen's office was somber. No chit-chat, inquiries about the health of families, or jovial banter. There was a funereal pall in the air of the small room.

"Take a seat, Lev. There is no need to stand on formality. We wish to hear about the Algerian mission and then to decide about what to do about it," "C" said.

"Yes, sir. I will begin with a flat and simple statement: I take full responsibility for any and all mistakes that led to a failed mission."

"What was the goal of the mission, Lev?"

"To capture the infamous SS mass murderers and recent serial killers of senior military officers around the world. The fallback plan was to kill them all if there was no way to avoid doing so. We failed in the primary goal. We did kill the SS criminals—the last remaining members of Hitler's French division. My failure—and I accept full responsibility—was twofold. Nine elite Israeli fighters, including Mossad *katsas*, were killed and had to be left in the desert. The other failure is that this mission has become a potential international incident. The result is that we have lost serious ground in our efforts at detente with the French, and it will be decades before we can regain the very important trust of the French Foreign Legion.

"In all candor, we were lucky to get as many of our men out as we did. The Legionnaires reluctantly stood aside while we marched to the small Sidi Bel Abbès Airport. We helicoptered our wounded by IAF Sikorsky S-58s to Es-Sénia—Ahmed Ben Bella Airport—seventy kilometers to the north, the closest international airport. The presence of helicopters that might be traced back to the IAF was bad enough, but the airport was where we had real public exposure. We brazened it out and were able to land a big old 1933 de Havilland DH.89 Dragon Rapide transport originally captured from the Brits and to fly out before it could become apparent who we were."

"What could you have done differently with this mission, Lev?"

"I'm not sure. I decided against a diplomatic overture to the Legion as taking too long. We might have taken in a larger contingent of men, but I feared that the logistics would have been too complicated and cumbersome so, I decided on going in with a small group of elite soldiers and agents. Even in retrospect, I do not think I would have considered either of the other options. We could have attempted a surgical airforce strike; but, in my opinion, the risks of such an attack would have been more likely to provoke a serious incident with the nation of France. I did not then and do not now believe we could have flown IDF fighters in without casting strong suspicion on Israel."

The PM asked, "So, Lev, give me your take on the international incident. Do you believe news of this event will come out in the future to the embarrassment of the governments of France and Israel?"

"No, Prime Minister. I believe it is contained. The French and the Legion do not want knowledge of what happened in the remote desert of Algeria to become known in the world at large any more than we do. I had a serious discussion with the Legion commander in Sidi-bel-Abbès about secrecy. I gave him my solemn promise that we would never divulge even the existence of the raid, let alone the killing of Legionnaires and Israeli commandoes. He agreed fully with me that saving face was crucial, laying blame was not."

"You were correct, as it turns out, Lev," the PM said. "We had a secret meeting with the President of France and with the commander of the Legion, Brigade General François Jacques de Négrier. The president and the general want nothing greater than to be able to deny that the incident ever happened. I pledged our sacred honor to the agreement that nothing would ever be reported of the incident to anyone outside this room, and they took a solemn oath that nothing would ever be learned about the Algerian incident outside the highest ranks of the French government and the Legion. It is in our mutual interest to forget that it ever happened, at least in any public forum. Privately we will mourn our dead, care for their widows and children, and lie to them. There was an unfortunate training accident in Laos. A plane crash killed everyone aboard. The news media will never be otherwise informed. Any leak about the incident will be considered a violation of both the French and Israeli National Secrets Acts."

Lev nodded humbly.

"C" said, "Still, Lev, we need to know what happened; so, we can avoid such an incident in the future. We also need to begin the healing process. First, we mourn. Then we begin to find and to train elite armed forces personnel to be able to fill the huge gaps in our services. That will take time—ten years or more."

"Do you wish to have my resignation, Director?"

"Certainly not. You have a fine record. Perhaps you made mistakes, but it is not for us to make judgments against you from the comfort of our armchairs. No, my friend, you must suck up your personal hurt and bring our secret forces back up to strength. We need you."

"I cannot tell you how important that is to me, sir. I have always been fully loyal and fully dedicated to Israel's defense. My mistakes will be studied; so, we all can benefit."

Lev proceeded to tell the assembled officers everything he knew about the Nazi officers his men had killed. He spared himself nothing as he told of the logistics and decisions of the Project Save the Generals mission. He listed the names of the Legionnaires who were killed and the Israelis who gave their last full measure of devotion and now are becoming bleached bones in the arid desert: Moises Silverman, Eban Alpert, Micah Freiburg, Eliot Frank, Enos Lovitz, Gavriel Neuberger, Joshua Rantzen, Michael Sachs, Maurice Howard, and Danny Chomsky.

Lev bowed his head, and for a moment it did not appear that he would be able to go on.

"I don't need to remind that you are never to divulge what took place to the military establishments whose officers were murdered and who participated in the manhunt. They will have to adjust to the reality that the criminals have vanished."

Lev took a deep breath and said, "That will require a great deal of lying, Mr. Prime Minister. However, I find that I have been honing that skill to a high degree over these past two months."

§§§§§

J. Edgar Hoover Building, FBI [Federal Bureau of Investigation] Headquarters, Office of the DFBI [Director FBI] Warren Brent Gaines, 935 Pennsylvania Avenue, NW Washington, DC, later that same afternoon

Director Gaines, his personal secretary, Harriet Margolis, and the communications director, Max Brendamann, struggled with the logistics and the equipment to make the first conference call from his office. The world's first telephone call occurred March 10, 1876, between Alexander Graham Bell—the inventor of the telephone—and his assistant, Thomas Watson. The first commercial transcontinental phone line was inaugurated Janury 25, 1915 and involved a tedious series of stops along the way in every city on the direct line. Just to get to San Francisco to hook up to the transcontinental cable took ten minutes and required massive amplifiers to get the sound from New York to San Francisco. It also required a courtesy hookup with President Woodrow Wilson. The first device useful for telephone conferencing was the Jordanphone invented by a Bulgarian in 1945. The work to accomplish successful commercial telephone conferencing began in 1956.

The DFBI groused that "you'd think they could have gotten it working better after eighty-eight years of working on the problem!"

Gaines was exceedingly impatient after a forty-five minute delay before all of the participants were hooked up.

"Gentleman," he said, "I got a telegram from our Israeli counterpart which indicated that they have run into a dead-end in the Project Save the Generals. He believes the three Nazi perpetrators have either met deservedly bad ends or have gone into a hole somewhere and may never be heard from again. "C" made a salient observation. It may be for the best for all of us to file this case in the cold case file—the very deep cold case file. It seems that INTERPOL and the Mossad have turned over some stones which ought to be put quietly down again regarding the treatment of POWs by the Allies during and after World War II. These are things any good lawyer would use against all of our countries, and would be better kept in the past. We will no longer be able to blame it all on the Germans, and our citizens are not going to like that.

"President Johnson has ordered US investigations and fugitive searches to cease, and General Secretary Brezhnev has issued the same orders. I presume that will meet with approval by Chancellor Erhard, don't you, Chief Schneider Graf von der Lippe?"

"Most assuredly, Director. I will inform him as soon as we get off the line," the police chief of Wiesbaden replied.

"Is there any jurisdiction opposed to this decision?"

A chorus of 'nos' came from all of the chiefs on the line.

"Good. Then we can consider the Project Save the Generals to be officially closed until such time as convincing evidence leads us to reopen the investigation."

In the background—unheard by any of the chiefs—was an undertone in nearly a dozen languages which—translated and paraphrased—was, "And politics trumps police work again," uttered with a collective sigh of resignation and murmured invectives against politics and politicians all over the world.

-END-

APPENDICES

CAST OF CHARACTERS

GERMANS	
Gruppenführer und Generalleutnant der Waffen-SS Antoine Duvalier, aka Laird Eagen, aka Don Pedro Altenhofen, aka Pierre Deneuve, aka Antoine Toussaint	Charlemagne Division officer who survived the gulag
Oberführer der Waffen-SS Michaele Dupont, aka Randolph Bellwether, aka Dennis Cunningham Lord Downfort	Charlemagne Division officer who survived the gulag
Waffen SS-Obersturmbannführer [*Lieutenant Colonel*] Serge Alain Rounsavall, aka Pedro T. Rodriguez, aka Georges Thibault	Charlemagne Division officer who survived the gulag
Waffen SS-Sturmbannführer [Senior Battalion Leader], Hugues Beauchamp, aka Gonzalez Martin Sanchez, aka Frédéric Charron	Charlemagne Division officer who survived the gulag
Waffen SS-Hauptsturmführer [Head Company Unit Storm Leader] Jérôme Christophe Mailhot, aka Dominico Lobos	Charlemagne Division officer who survived the gulag
Waffen SS-Sturmbannführer [Major] Jean Luc Latendresse	Charlemagne Division officer who survived the gulag

Berthold Küppers, aka Antonio de Castro	Former SS officer who joined Antoine and Michaele when they were sent to France
Rolf Kohns, aka Guglielmo Pardini	Former SS officer who joined Antoine and Michaele when they were sent to France
Clause Fischer, aka Humberto Garrido	Former SS officer who joined Antoine and Michaele when they escaped from the French POW camp
Willibald Movius, aka Ismael García-Iglesias	Former SS officer who joined Antoine and Michaele when they escaped from the French POW camp
Gebirgsjägers	Men associated with the Russian POWs: Duvalier, Dupont, Rounsavall, Beauchamp, Mailhot, Latendresse, Küppers, Kohns, Fischer, Movius
Gerhard Jungermann, aka Augustín Ruiz-Rubalcaba	Former SS officer who joined Antoine and Michaele when they escaped from the French POW camp
Obersturmführer [SS-Senior Storm Leader] Jacob Friedrich Bunnemann, aka José María Zapatero	Charlemagne Division officer who was saved by Antoine and Michaele and helped with their escape to France after the war and internment
François Gaspard Caussidière	Swiss collaborator with the Nazis and facilitator for sham bank accounts and émigré assistance
Liert Beili Amstutz	Swiss banker in UBS, Geneva
Gunther Emil Sondregger aka Heinrich Rudolf Gajewski (his original name)	German IG Farben war criminal and subsequent murder victim
Joachim Becker	IG Farben Administration security officer
Kriminalkommissar [Detective Lieutenant] Horst Schäfer	Lead detective for the state police criminal division investigating the Sondregger murder
Senior Constable [*Oberwachtmeister*] Eberhard Zimmermann	Lower ranked criminal detective (A5) under Schäfer
Friedrich Schneider Graf von der Lippe	The Police Chief of Wiesbaden

Hilda Weiss-Krüger	Senior secretary and analyst in the *Kriminalpolitzei* forensic sciences division
Kriminalkommissar Leopold Boehm	Head of the FIU [Financial Intelligence Unit] of the *Bundespolitzei*
Aline Hertzog	INTERPOL agent, Weisbaden
Heinrich Kohler	WestBerlinImportExport Corporation. *Stellvertretender Direktor* [Deputy Director] and 2nd in command of organized crime syndicate
Anton Friedrich *Krupp von* Bohlen und Halbach	Head of the ODESSA
Hauptsturmführer Erich Walther Boehme	Former SS officer, present Bariloche Argentine businessman and local head of ODESSA
Jean-Yves Sarrazin (a pseudonym)	Former French foreign legionnaire, now planter after the defeat at Dien Bien Phu.

RUSSIANS	
Lieutenant of militsiya Trushin Vasilyovich Stepanovich	Moscow police detective
Katrinka Stepanovich	Vasily's wife
Ivan Viktorovich Lebedinsky	Police (militsiya) underofficer (Underofficer *uchastkovyi* militsioner)
Lada Kornikova	Police (militsiya) private
Georgy Artyomovich Yesipov	Police (militsiya) private, illiterate, huge, and strong. Intensely loyal to Stepanovich. Driver
Lieutenant Zakhar Rostislavovich Rumyantsev	Backup militsiya officer for Stepanovich
Lieutenant General of Cavalry Grigory Yegorivich Lagounov, Cavalier of the Order of the Red Banner	Murder victim in the Arkhangelskoye Military Convalescent Home, USSR, Oct. 1961
Lieutenant Dimitri Sobrieski	Aide-de-camp of Gen. Lagounov
Militsioner Private Yuri Alexandreovich Inozemtsev	Lebedinsky's next-in-command
Sister Ludmila Mikhailovna Kovalevsky	Gen. Lagounov's floor nurse

Sister Maria Nikolayovna Ilyushkin	Gen. Lagounov's head nurse
Colonel-General Boris Vadimovich Ilyushin	Lt. Stepanovich's old Great War commanding officer, now Colonel General—Komandarm Commander First Rank—of the Red Army.
Alexander Shelepin	Current head of the KGB
Rudolph Vladimirovich Fedorchuck II	Head of the KGB's Fifth Directorate, responsible for ideology and countersubversion, and the Agitprop Department
Col. Gavril Davidovich Nabatov.	KGB colonel who provides information for the investigation of Gen. Lagounov's murder
Abram Kirillovich Yerkulayev, Konstintin Leonidovich Zubkov, and Matvei Nikitavich Akhremenko	KGB officers humiliated by Gen. Lagounov and bore a grudge against him.
Vitali Mikhailovich Bakatinshov, second in command to Ivan Aleksandrovich Serov when he was the chairman from 1954 until 1958	KGB senior officer whipped and humiliated by Gen. Lagounov and bore a grudge against him
Gen. Vladimir Yefimovich Semichastny who was once second in command to Gen. Lagounov in Siberia	Current Director of the KGB, once second-in-command to Gen. Lagounov, and bore a grudge against him
Oleg Petrovich Latsis was the son of an especially prominent and educated Kulak family	Red Army noncom, son of a Kulak family. He was falsely charged as a deserter by Gen. Lagounov but escaped execution. He and his family sent to Siberia. They all bore a grudge against him.
Presbyter Athanasius Mogila	Russian Orthodox priest persecuted by Gen. Lagounov and bore a grudge against him
Karl Rudolf Kirschstein, Jakob Josef Potthoff, and Rolf Herman Schwindt	Pseudonyms for Red Army deserters persecuted by Gen. Lagounov and fled to Germany
Karp and Marita Petrenko	Old couple murdered by Antoine Duvalier and Michaele Dupont in Magadan, Siberia

Leonid Zaslavskevich Breslava	*russkaya mafiya* boss or the *Pakhan*—the Boss or *Krestnii Otets* [Godfather] of the *vory v zakone* thieves-in-law] *Solntsevskaya Bratva* [brothers or brotherhood]
Nicolai Andreavich Putansky	russkaya mafiya under boss
Ivan Dragonovich Brudzinski	*russkaya mafiya* Sovietnik [support person, advisor and close trusted friend of the Boss, Breslava—comparable to the Consigliere of Cosa Nostra]

AMERICANS	
General Glen Gabler, USA ret	Murder victim at the Alaskan Bear Lodge
Glen's three sons—Glen, Jr., Trace, and Jackson	Part of the fishing party at the Alaskan Bear Lodge
Major Rick Avery Saunders, USA ret.	Long suffering aide-de-camp of Gen. Gabler
Neille Bastrup	Owner, operator of the Alaskan Bear Lodge
Neille's four sons—Kevin, Able, Michael, and Donovan	Part of the Alaskan Bear Lodge crew
Corporal Daniel Olsen	Mountie with the RCMP at the Atlin, BC station
Nasnana	Athabaskan girl, Alaskan Bear Lodge worker
Asaaluk	Tlingit girl from Hoonah, Alaskan Bear Lodge worker
Major Darrin Higgins	Chief officer MCU, Alaska State Police, in Juneau
Lt. Oscar Perez	MCU (Juneau) first responding officer
Tucker Nicholsen	SAC, 83rd MP Det CID, Fort Richardson, Alaska, new head of the investigation of Gen. Gabler's murder
Henry and Anotklosh Peratrovich	Hoonah Tlingit headmen
Sergeant Major Owen Briggs, USA	Senior NCO in charge of Bad Kreuznach Allied slave camp

Superintendent Axel Baird	INTERPOL agent in charge in New York City, investigating the death of Gen. Glen Gabler
AAG Spencer Reynolds	Assistant attorney general for the criminal division of the DOJ of the US
DFBI Warren Brent Gaines	Director of the FBI
Special Agent Xavier Gonzales-Soto	FBI agent in charge of interrogating Michaele
Lydia Heppleweight	Fort Worth court stenographer
Tom Packer and Eldred Drake	Texas Rangers from Presidio, Texas
Texas Ranger captain, Reggie Cutler	Chief Texas Ranger headquarters, Austin, Texas
Dayne Brown	Tarrant County Deputy Sheriff
Sgt. Billie Wayne McAfee	Fort Worth PD Sergeant
Ruth Digby	Tarrant County (Fort Worth) Elmwood Sanatorium evening nurse
Evert Williams	American investment banker with the Negro Industrial Bank of Washington
Creighton Wilberforce	American investment banker, vice-president of Bank of America
Giuseppe "The Boss" D'Aquila	American Mafioso involved in financial crimes
Gaetano "Numbers" Terranova	American Mafioso involved in financial crimes
Kenneth Lawson Donald Martin Allenton	CIA agent involved in Operation Paper Clip
Donald Martin Allenton	CIA agent involved in Operation Paper Clip
Evert Williams	Investment banker from the Negro Industrial Bank of Washington— the oldest and largest Negro-owned commercial bank in the metropolitan Washington, DC, region. The bank partially funded the Pueblo Parque National Nahuel Huapi Project

ARGENTINES	
Carlos Aguillara-Dominguez, aka Hörst Dietsel	Argentine murder victim
Anna Maria Lobos	Carlos's mistress
Manuel de Jesus	Sargentopolicíaprovbsas Policía de la Provincia de Córdoba, PPC [Corporal, Police of the Province of Córdoba]
José Emanuel de Corsos	Teniente Policía de la Provincia de Policía de Córdoba, PPC [Detective, Police of the Province of Córdoba]
Gerhardt Möller	Oficial de Policía [Police Officer] Policía de la Provincia de Córdoba, PPC
Adolf Henckel	*Inspector de Policia* [Inspector of Police—third ranking field officer in the department] *de la Provincia de Policía de Córdoba, PPC*
Dr. Konrad Schmidt von Dresden	Córdoba Provincial Police Medical Examiner
Erich Walther Boehme	Former SS *Hauptsturmführer*, and current ODESSA officer in Bariloche, Argentina.
Xavier Manriquez-Huelsmann	Head of the law firm of Xavier Manriquez-Huelsmann and Mitarbeiter Abogados la Ley representing the Pueblo Parque National Nahuel Huapi Project
Daniel Urquiza	Project manager of the Pueblo Parque National Nahuel Huapi Project
Heinrich Stracher	Artist/architect/civil engineer. Designer of the Pueblo Parque National Nahuel Huapi Project
Gunther Horn	Banker who partially funded the Pueblo Parque National Nahuel Huapi Project
Christof Weishuhn	Chilean—Puerto Montt—Club Aleman Nazi sympathizer

FRENCH	
Général de division (Ret.) Étienne Malboeuf	French murder victim
Monica Roussin-Malboeuf	General Malboeuf's wife
Damien Malboeuf	Estranged son of Gen. Malboeuf
René Malboeuf	Estranged son of Gen. Malboeuf
Antoinette de Baudry	Malboeuf's mistress
Grégoire Laurent De Vincent	*Enquêteur* [plain clothes detective of the Paris police]
Gendarmerie Lieutenant Sylvain Piétri	Research Unit Officer-Assistant to Inspector De Vincent
Benedettu Paganucci	Corsican syndicate criminal and former lover of Antoinette de Baudry
Dominic Rizzuto	Associate of Paganucci
Tony Lagomarsino	Associate of Paganucci
Eugène Léon Dentremont	Senior Detective Chief Superintendent of INTERPOL
Superintendent Guy Mutz	Chief of the INTERPOL office in the western suburb of St. Cloud in Paris
Marianne de la Reynie	Senior INTERPOL technician, Forensic Specialist
Ronald Swing	INTERPOL Secretary General
Jean-Yves Sarrazin	Current French planter in Vietnam, former foreign Legion colonel Danvier
Col. Col. Didier Amirault	French foreign Legionnaire in Algeria
Lt. Col. Édouard Melerine	French foreign Legionnaire in Algeria
Captaine Émile Duris	Commandant of the EMT [*État-major tactique*, Tactical Command Post], *La Légion Étrangère* [French Foreign Legion], Sidi-bel-Abbès, Algeria

BRITISH	
Lieutenant-General Sir Cyril Goeffrey Robert Hill-Brownwell, RA, Ret	British murder victim
Major Algernon Donelly, RA	Witness of British murder

Clifford Brewster	Major Domo at the Army and Navy Club where the British murder took place
Detective Chief Inspector Lincoln Crandall-White.	New Scotland Yard senior homicide detective
DI [Detective Inspector] Angela Snowden	New Scotland Yard homicide detective
DI [Detective Inspector] Anthony Bourden-Clift	New Scotland Yard homicide detective
Doctor Evan Goodefellow	Physician at Royal Brompton Sanatorium

ISRAELIS	
Levi Appleman ben Cohen ["C"]	Director of Mossad, involved in Project Save the Generals
Moises Silverman	Senior covert Mossad agent involved in Project Save the Generals
Davido Parades	Mossad agent-in-place in Bariloche, Argentina, involved in Project Save the Generals
Lev Mizrahi	Leader of the Mossad *kidon* [assassination] squad involved in Project Save the Generals
Abraham Levy	Senior *katsa* [Mossad field officer] tasked with the leadership of Project Save the Generals

III. A BRIEF NONFICTION HISTORY OF THE CHARLEMAGNE DIVISION

"It was the best of times, it was the worst of times, it was the age of wisdom, it was the age of foolishness, it was the epoch of belief, it was the epoch of incredulity, it was the season of Light, it was the season of Darkness, it was the spring of hope, it was the winter of despair, we had everything before us, we had nothing before us, we were all going direct to Heaven, we were all going direct the other way—in short, the period was so far like the present period, that some of its noisiest authorities insisted on its being received, for good or for evil, in the superlative degree of comparison only."

-Charles Dickens, *Tale of Two Cities*,
opening paragraph, London: Chapman & Hall, April-

November, 1859

"Someone praising a man for his foolhardy bravery, Cato the elder said, 'There is a wide difference between true courage and a mere contempt for life.'"

-Plutarch

The book—*The Charlemagne Murders*—is a novel, a fiction, a story, and most certainly is not a factual history of the 33rd Waffen-Grenadier

Division [*Der SS (Französische NR 1 Division Charlemagne)*]. The division, however, certainly existed—as incredible as it may seem—because literally thousands of Frenchmen fought—with full knowledge of what they were doing—for Germany's Nazis, and in the most feared and hated division in the armed forces—*Der Schutzstaffel* or SS—or as the Germans euphemistically called them: the protection squadron or defense corps. The SS was an elite, jingoistic, military, paramilitary, and police unit sworn to fanatical personal fealty to Adolf Hitler and all he advocated and practiced. That is in the face of the fact—for the Frenchmen involved—that Nazi armies invaded and occupied France and subjected the French to terrible treatment and humiliation such as the atrocities of Tulle and Oradour-sur-Glane. Why would any patriotic Frenchman do such a thing, for apparently the volunteers regarded themselves as patriots?

To understand the underlying motivation, it is necessary to see the historical perspective of the subset of Frenchmen who saw socialism and communism as the greatest threat against civilization and French values that was ever conceived. From 1934 onward, French communism—the PCF or Popular Front—openly supported Stalin and the Russian Communist Party socially, politically, and financially and regarded the worst threat to France to be Hitler's Nazism. The early communist party began to resist all overtures towards Hitler and to demonstrate against war. The demonstrations became progressively violent, and the party became increasingly active in illegal and clandestine activities.

Hardcore nationalist anticommunist families fought back politically, financially, and as an insurgency. Their sons became imbued and seduced by the anticommunist rhetoric. Hitler's burning of the Reichstag signaled to the French that invasion was imminent, and the communists launched a fight to protect the nation against the Nazi threat. In 1934, the far right wing staged riots to protest the actions of the communists. The growing strength of the PCF/communist party in France alarmed thousands of right wing-leaning French patriots by their rhetoric and actions. It was widely presumed that atheistic communism was set to take over the world and destroy civilization as the conservative French knew it. They sent their sons to Germany in the thousands to join in the only effective organization acting against the apparently overwhelming influence and power of Stalin's Soviet Union.

Those sons stayed in their French units, and a considerable number of them proved their loyalty to Hitler by becoming worthy to be in the SS.

The history of the Charlemagne Division began decades earlier in the trench carnage of World War I. Postwar France was a place of chaos, political and social unrest, and economic distress; and the Frenchmen who returned home found a much changed and inhospitable homeland. The French had won the war technically; but it was a hollow victory: one and a half million men were killed and four million were wounded, which overwhelmed France's depleted resources in the aftermath of the most horrific war in the world's history. Much of that devastating war took place in France itself, and a significant portion of northern France was in ruins.

Between the end of the war and 1940 when the next war began in earnest, France had forty-two governments—averaging about six months each in duration. This chaotic and ruined France was the seedbed of French communism among the young people in the desperate working class. They—much like the poor Muslims of the current era—were easily radicalized. They stormed the Bastille and started the Paris Commune.

The old guard right wing families were aghast at the growing power, radicalism, and threat posed by the ever-increasing menace of the far Left. That majority segment of the French populace balanced the extremes of the Left by joining the politics of the far Right. Traditional monarchists, working-class nationalists, big business, and the firmly entrenched French bourgeoisie came together in an unlikely union whose core purpose was to defeat communism and to restore law and order, whatever the cost. *L'Action Française* became the focus group to stand up to the evils of communism, as the Right deemed them.

The extremists of the Right matched rhetoric for rhetoric, riot for riot, and armed conflict for armed conflict with the Left. On the Right, Great War veterans flocked to such groups as the *Croix de Feu* with its penchant for armed response and secret paramilitary activity. The youth of Right wing families joined organizations such as the *Jeunesses Patriotes* which became the forerunner of the Hitler Youth in neighboring Germany. In 1934, the Right staged bloody riots with protracted fighting between French police and the Right-wingers. The more moderate French reacted by electing left-leaning governments, especially that led by Prime Minister Léon Blum. It was not inconsequential for the anti-Semite Right that Blum was Jewish. That inflamed the Right's core bigotry and led to an approval of the Nazi policies being unleashed in Germany. The Right seethed under what it felt to be unfair treatment by the socialist/communist regimes of the country and longed for revenge.

Many on the Right so despised the Jewish, communist, rabble-led governments that they espoused a united states of Europe with a bent towards approval of Germany's policies; and, after the invasion, collaboration with the Nazis. Although today's perspective is much different, at the time, the prism through which the Right saw the world of France, such ideology, political stances, and intellectual writing favored a world of cooperation between Nazi Germany and Right wing France. A generation of thousands of Frenchmen was reared in that milieu.

Imperial Germany was created by unifiying disparate German states by the staunch nationalist Otto von Bismarck in the late nineteenth century after German victories in European conflicts. World War I was a challenge by the power and economic strength of Germany against the governments and economies of Europe and later the United States. The humiliating defeat of Germany cost them precious land: Schleswig-Holstein was ceded to Denmark, Eupen-Malmédy to Belgium, and Danzig to Poland, and Alsase-Lorraine was returned to France. War reparations required by the Treaty of Versailles were crippling. The Spanish flu ravaged the European world, including Germany, all still reeling from the Great War. A British blockade resulted in food shortages and near-starvation. Then, the coup de grâce came to any thought of a return to democracy by the Germans in the shape of the Great Depression.

Enter the National Socialist Party—the Nazis—and its charismatic leader, Adolf Hitler. Very soon, the new chancellor—the putative Fúhrer—abandoned any pretense of paying reparations, of having an emasculated German military, or allowing the hated Jewish race any longer to be the ruling class, as Hitler saw them. He rearmed Germany, rounded up the Jews and other undesirables, and created an intensely well-ordered and efficient government with only Nazis allowed to govern.

In part to balance his own power against that of the German military—the Wehrmacht—Hitler established his own military organization, the SS, which was dedicated to his principles of anti-Semitism,

Aryan supremacy, and the establishment of a United States of Europe with Hitler's Germany at the helm. This fit the aspirations and ideologies of the French Right wing to a T, and French youth flocked to join the dynamic movement in Europe—which was deemed to be the answer to France's quagmire problems as well as those in Germany. The SS started as a protection unit for the Fúhrer, evolved into a national police force, and morphed into his personal political army.

It was deemed to be a singular honor that a unit of Frenchmen should be accepted as a fully recognized Waffen SS division. Other units were formed by Danes, Belgians, Norwegians, Dutch, Estonia, Latvia, the Ukraine, Belarus, Georgia, Armenia, and even Poles. Altogether, there were 200,000 volunteers in the SS from other countries including Great Britain: there were 40,000 Spanish volunteers, 40,000 volunteers from Belgium, 50,000 Dutch volunteers, and three divisions from Finland. Late in the war, Soviet opponents of Stalin, personnel from the Soviet Union, including the Caucasian Muslims, Turkestanis, Crimean Tatars, ethnic Ukrainians and Russians, and Cossacks were absorbed into the Wehrmacht, but the Charlemagne Division's all-French makeup was unusual, if not unique.

Although the story of the division has largely been lost to any but inquisitive historians, it should be remembered that the transition of Frenchmen into sociopathic German SS paramilitarists was not just a social and political movement. It is in fact a story of French individuals who made a conscious choice to turn their back on their country and to fight for a murderous enemy. The 33rd Waffen Grenadier Division of the SS *Charlemagne* (1st French) and *Charlemagne* Regiment are collective names used for units of French volunteers in the *Wehrmacht* and later *Waffen-SS* during World War II. From estimates of 7,400 to 11,000 at its peak in 1944, the strength of the Division fell to just sixty men in May 1945. Even late in the war, after it was clear that Germany's cause was lost—and the Waffen SS was known worldwide as a hiss and a byword—Frenchmen still joined up and participated in the barbarities being committed on the Eastern Front. They recognized and later admitted that they understood the horrors of the actions of the SS, but they pitied the German elitists because they faced the world alone as a crumbling bulwark against the inevitable encroachment of godless communism.

The Frenchmen were volunteers, not men unwillingly pressed into service. They came from common bourgoise families and had no prior strong political involvement, from militarists produced by the long tradition of French men of war, and many had served France in the Great War and in Indochina and North Africa. The ranks of the Charlemagne Division included such diversity as former teachers and school boys, farmers, and clerks, along with the warriors. At intervals, there were as many as 20,000 Frenchmen in the Charlemagne Division from France, and there was a Flemish Division from Flanders. At first, the volunteers for the LVF [*Légion des Voluntaires Français*] had to be Aryan and in good health. At that point, there was an unspoken policy that the volunteers come from good Catholic families and have the appropriate political convictions.

The majority of these men and their families were fearful anticommunists who were galvanized into action by the Russian invasion of Finland in 1939. By the following year, Germany itself had ten million young men of its own of which six and a half million were part of the German military machine. They hardly lacked for manpower at the time. Some 50,000 were in the SS, quite a sufficient number to commit the atrocities they were already perpetrating. Nevertheless, young Frenchmen flocked to Germany to join up. In large part, this enthusiasm for Germany was a result of a sort of ennui of defeatism and political despair that gripped France.

In actual fact, France was a vastly superior military force than Germany, and Germany was occupied with its invasion of Poland and would have been very hard-pressed to have protected its western border and to have withstood a second war front with France. France missed its opportunity—as did the rest of the civilized world—to stop the onslaught of Nazism that was beginning to sweep Europe.

When Germany swept into France almost effortlessly trampling over the much-vaunted Maginot Line, the French were gripped with disbelief and utter inability to mount an adequate defense. This crisis of self-confidence within the French society led a significant percentage of the young men to evacuate decaying and conquered France to join the triumphant Germans. The tall, blond, very fit, black uniformed, disciplined SS troopers with their double lightning flashes (runes) on their uniforms became an irresistible draw. Rather than joining De Gaulle and the Free French, those malcontents elected to leave Vichy France with all its weakness and failure altogether and to join the winning side: the new world of the Third Reich.

The French world was ambiguous during this time of confusion. Contrary to revisionist history which cast the French as determined insurgents or at least subtle saboteurs against the Nazi puppet administration of General Pétaine, the popular *Service d'Ordre Legionnaire* (SOL) enthusiastically supported the official stance and actions of the Vichy government in the belief that the occupying German army was the last bulwark of protection against the evils of Bolshevism. Many young SOL members chose to join German forces outright. As early as October 1940, Marshall Pétain spoke to the nation of "collaboration," a practical necessity since nearly two million French soldiers were residing in German POW camps by that time.

As revenge for the egregious Versailles Treaty which ended WWI, the Germans made everything French subordinate to Germany. But even among the conquered French, there was a surprisingly large amount of sympathy for Germany post-Versailles; many people felt they had been harshly treated. Viewed through the prism of the times, as difficult as it is to comprehend in the second decade of the twenty-first century, there was popular and vigorous support for Nazi ideas. Anti-Semitism was common in France, and Hitler was admired there for fixing Germany's Jewish problem.

Not unlike the view of big business currently, the power elites in most Western countries, viewed communism or any brand of socialism or push for improvement in the lives and status of the working class as threatening to their ownership of the means of production. Then as now, the capitalist elites believed that if this populous ideology took over, they would lose their businesses and financial empires. So, in France—and, indeed, most Western nations—National Socialism with its vicious racism and Aryan Supremacy may have been unsavory to many and not fit conversation for the dinner table; but a considerable number of those moguls did not perceive this ideology as something that threatened their bottom lines; so, they really did not care. The prospect of war looming in Europe, in fact, was perceived by many business leaders in France and elsewhere as being potentially highly positive for their profit making. They were considerably more afraid of the Communists than the Nazis as a result.

In France and many other Western countries, socialists—with their social justice agendas—were already threatening the business class of the 1930s and 1940s. They were gaining influence by attracting working class voters, and in some instances—as occurred in Germany—there had been attempts at Soviet-style revolutions which met with more approval than was comfortable to the moguls and the workers they controlled. From the 1920s on, Socialism was supported by millions of people—probably the majority of working-class Germans—and this Soviet-style incursion into the culture of Germany and its neighbors was most unsettling. The defining line for the moguls was that these socialist revolutions, whether through the ballot box or on the streets, had almost succeeded in Europe and one did succeed in Russia. The moguls and bankers—the one percent—were alarmed by the potential for spread of this—to them—poisonous doctrine, which was obviously so appealing to an expanding number of oppressed workers. The excesses and the massive crimes of Stalin had not yet been fully recognized to begin to discredit the ideology of communism. At the less oppressive end of the socialist continuum—the end favored by the moguls and their polictical supporters—lay the fact that the largest political party in Germany in the years before the Nazis took power was the Social Democratic Party which aimed to install a socialist economic system, albeit by democratic means. It—the Weimar Republic—was an epic economic failure.

The juggernaut of Nazism, even in its naked physical form, moved in an incremental fashion which was not particularly alarming to the moguls, the bankers, and their politicians. The Anschluss in Austria took place with wild cheering in the streets and a smooth transition to the Greater Germany under the Nazi policies. Alsace-Lorraine—a set of provinces bordering France and Germany had a strong intermingling of the two languages, family relationships, commerces, and political preferences—historically was once French, then German, then French again. When Germany consolidated its victory over France, it absorbed Alsace and Lorraine into Greater Germany and applied all German laws to the region, including conscription of soldiers. When France became part of the Allies victorious over the Germans, Frenchmen in German uniforms were imprisoned and tried for atrocities while serving Germany—often having been drafted into the armed services of the country then controlling the region. The ambiguity led to a movement to quash the convictions and sentences passed upon the soldiers and to avoid the embarrassment of having to explain away how it is that Frenchmen fought on the side of the Nazis. This was an important face-saving measure by De Gaulle's new France, and it resulted in hiding the past of the war which included collaboration—a fact the new France would rather have relegated to the misty past. History was rewritten to eliminate mention of the uncomfortable facts, and the mythology became simplified to an untruth—all, or most, Frenchmen fought the Germans as underground partisans.

The true French partisans conducted a war of attrition by murdering supporters of groups favoring the concept that the Nazis were protectors of true French values, and that drove still more young Frenchmen to defect to the German side. Many Frenchmen were torn in their loyalties and rationalized that active collaboration with the Germans did not mean full adherence to the Nazi ideology and cause, but collaboration was an acceptable alternative to the decadent downhill slide into Bolshevism. The Right-wing families shared the fear expressed by Pierre-Joseph Proudhon that "Communism is exploitation of the strong by the weak," and that was antithetical to the traditions of those families.

The more zealous of those who had even that lukewarm tilt towards the Nazis found it only logical to pursue their deeply held convictions to the logical conclusion of joining with the putative enemy of official France. Defection was a process: French veterans aligned with the official French forces, became disillusioned at the growing strength of communism as it was pitted against the nationalistic forces, and moved forward to the next logical step of actually joining the Nazi heroic fight against the seemingly unstoppable and corrupting ideology and strength of Bolshevism. In many instances, the individual and group choice to align with the forces of anticommunism was greeted with fairly widespread and strongly supported enthusiasm by the populace. The anticommunism attitude was visceral as put by Ernest Renan: "Communism is in conflict with human nature." Adlai E. Stevenson said, "Communism is the death of the soul. It is the organization of total conformity—in short, of tyranny—and it is committed to making tyranny universal." And that sentiment was almost worldwide except for the frankly communist countries. Even Karl Marx himself said,

[The *Communist Manifesto, Chapter One*] "There is a specter haunting Europe, the specter of communism."

Germany's attitude appealed to a significant minority of the French at the time. The sentiments of Heinrich Heine resonated with them: "Communism possesses a language which every people can understand—its elements are hunger, envy, and death." Farsighted politicians and businessmen were pragmatic about the situation, however much they might have disliked the excesses of the occupying regime. They were Francophiles to the core, but worked to have France be a part of what they viewed as an inevitable German-dominated future in Europe, and perhaps the rest of the world. They might have disapproved of Hitler's tactics, but at least they could communicate with the man and his minions with a shared background of experience. He was—as they said—"A man we can do business with." They provided material and psychological support to the youth who were abandoning France to fight for the winning side and for the common good of France in the new world that was coming.

Germany—for its part—viewed conquered France as an inferior nation with inferior people, which should be plundered of its farm produce, manufactury, and its labor force. The Germans kept two million French soldiers in Germany as prisoners doing forced labor as hostages to ensure that Vichy France would reduce its military forces and pay a heavy tribute in gold, food, and supplies to Germany. While they did not for a moment consider the French as equals in the struggle against communism, they willingly exploited the French people to accept their best young people into their military machinery.

That provided enticing incentives which further increased the exodus into German collaboration and service. Even the very young, chaffing at the indecision and ineffectiveness of French efforts to curb the advance of communism, flocked to German recruiting offices to volunteer to serve in the Wehrmacht and even more enthusiastically to become part of the respected elite Waffen SS. At first the regular German army and naval forces became aware of the value of the French conscriptees, but later—as German successes increased—the SS targeted the young French devotees. Early on, the idea was to volunteer for the glory of France. Soon, however, the French volunteers became frank German soldiers fighting for the Reich, for Europe, for France's inclusion in the greater German sphere of power and control, and for a national-socialist *German* victory.

In September 1941, a unit of volunteers was mustered into the Wehrmacht's *Infantrie-Regiment 638* under the command of a former colonel of the French colonial forces. They were strongly influenced to do so by their Roman Catholic padre, Monsignor de Mayol de Lupé, an ardent national socialist enthusiast, like many of his coreligionists. Outside France, the unit wore German uniforms with a French tricolor patch on their sleeves, and inside France, they were allowed to wear their French uniforms. Military awards were presented after parades in Les Invalides in Paris and a march to Notre Dame and a celebration of mass.

The Waffen SS became symbolic of the right wing values of courage, fearlessness, endurance, fitness, toughness, and ruthlessness in battle that harked back to a mythical time of the Teutonic Knights for the Germans and to the time when France was one of the greatest military forces in the world for the Frenchmen. They sent home glowing reports of the rigors and successes of the SS training program and the seemingly unstoppable advances of the SS which was seen to be the savior of French values. That enthusiasm contributed to even more fervor among rightests to join the SS ranks. The old values of battle success at any cost, complete devotion to leaders, and great personal conviction that they were fighters—not just soldiers—engaged in a righteous cause stirred a deep emotional center in the minds of the youth. The recruitment by Germany—capitalizing on that propaganda—was eminently successful. In training, the ideal of becoming an officer candidate became the paramount goal for many aspirants, such as this author's fictional characters, and spurred even more zeal.

The young French farmers and working class boys came to see from reports filtering back into France—from their fellow Frenchmen now actively engaged with the SS—a meritocracy unlike the decadent French society where family status and wealth gave preference even to inferior men. The SS was their chance to excel, and the Nazis used that conviction to their significant advantage. Unlike the aristocracy top-heavy French forces, popular opinion in the right wing of France saw in the SS an organization where officers were respected by noncoms and privates because of their fairness, merit, and identification with their men. Rank was earned, and a good man could advance despite his family's lowly status. It was a way up and out of the stagnant world of the France which still clung to antiquarian notions of aristocratic superiority. Early on, a powerful incentive to join the SS lay in the knowledge of the fact that the Waffen SS had the best discipline among the fittest men who were supplied with the best military equipment of any armed force in the history of the world.

SS recruits had to meet rigid standards: to be of excellent character, to be free of any criminal record, to be of strict Aryan descent, to be between seventeen and twenty-two years of age, to be of greater than average intelligence, to have good dental health, and excellent physical fitness. They were carefully screened for "Nordic" features, and that—like the other attributes of the men chosen to be in the SS—appealed to the latent or even overt anti-Semitism among the French who sought admission. However, it was not until later when the war was well underway that French were allowed into the officer candidate schools because early on they were not considered Aryan enough. Of the initial 13,400 who signed up at the recruitment office in Paris, only about 6,000 were accepted—largely due to dental issues.

The inclusion of foreigners into the Waffen SS came about because the Wehrmacht became unable to provide men meeting the exacting requirements of the SS schools, and they agreed to the inclusion of foreigners of superior qualifications. Himmler's dream was to unite Aryans from all over the world into the Third Reich's unstoppable forces—to separate them from the *untermenschen* in those countries. The kindred Aryans were welcomed as part of the "family" as what were termed the "*Freewilligen*." After the Nazis fought their way to control in Western Europe in 1940, they found highly willing legions ready and waiting for recruitment, such as the Norwegian *Nasjonal Samling*, the Swedish *Svensk Socialistik Samling*, the Flemish *Volunteer Legion Flandern*, the Dutch *Volunteer Legion Niederlande*, and the Danish *Freikorps Danmark*. The French army sponsored what they called the *French Legion des Volontaires Française contre le bolchevisme*, or LVF which—wittingly or unwittingly—vetted Frenchmen for duty and led to those men being diverted to Nazi service. These legions were promptly sent to war on the Eastern front after training. The inclusion of the foreign legions allowed for rapid expansion of the Waffen SS and decidedly increased its importance in the German military machine.

Despite that almost exponential growth, the SS could not keep up with the unprecedented level of slaughter on the Russian front. Between 1941 and 1944 with Operation Barbarossa, almost 1.5 million Germans were killed, another million were MIA, and 3.5 million were wounded. That Russian enterprise resulted in more KIA and MIA than Great Britain and the United States suffered in the entire war put together. Despite the terrible carnage, the French were both fully accepted into the German ranks and were fully dedicated to service because of the close-up fight against their mutual enemy, the Red Menace.

The French served the Nazi cause in the SS as the Charlemagne Division, but also in the Heer [the German army or Wehrmacht], the Kriegsmarine [Navy], and the Luftwaffe [Air Force]. They were drivers, mechanics, logistics personnel, sailors, ground support staff for the air force, and some were in the secretive German special forces.

Those Frenchmen and other officer candidates received a remarkable education—two sets of Charlemagne men were sent to the officer candidate school at Neweklau, some directly from the POW camps where they had been held since the invasion of France—which included such mind and body-improving classes as golf and tennis, and attended operatic, musical, and theatrical performances. Strangely enough, the French were allowed to keep their French identity throughout training and service with a French flag on their sleeves, and were not required to adopt the stringent German attention to discipline and uniforms. Because there were so many former French soldiers among the recruits with actual combat experience, the French LVF units were ready for service after only two months of the hard German and self-imposed rigorous French training. The LVF's first blooding took place outside Moscow in the winter of 1941. Two French battalions took part in the drive to capture Moscow. Twelve men were killed and fifty-five were wounded, a small but clear harbinger of things to come. They—like their German comrades—were very ill-equiped to endure the terrible cold, and they suffered serious hardships.

In 1942 the LVF was assigned to antipartisan duties in the Byelorussian SSR (Belarus). By the end of December 1942, the unit had lost half of its men. In February, the second battalion was almost completely wiped out. By that summer, the Vichy government recognized the battlefield decoration of the LVF—the *Croix de Guerre Léé gionnaire*—despite a widespread push inside France among the moderates and the left wing to charge the French who joined the Germans with treason and a dreadful violation of the patriotism of France.

In June 1944, after the significant victories by the LVF in the battle over the Bohr, the unit was disbanded and sent back to France. They achieved a conspicuous number of medals for bravery, and had withstood their withering standoff against the better manned and equipped Russians. They carried that *esprit de corps* with them into the newly-formed SS Charlemagne Division. The total number of men accepted into the LVF during its existence had been just under 6,500. More than ten percent of them were buried in Russia. Most—but not all—volunteered to serve in the SS, some were pressed into service, and a few refused and were sent to labor camps to suffer out the war.

In 1943, Hitler ordered the establishment of an SS recruiting station in France with an eye towards keeping a steady flow of men coming into his rapidly depleting armed forces. He was not nearly as dainty about recruitment as Himmler or the Wehrmacht: he needed the men. Initially, they decided on a regiment-sized unit with the name of Charlemagne, the Holy Roman Frankish emperor. They wanted to call it the Karl der Grosse, the Germanic rendering of the Frenchman's name and title, but the French prevailed in the naming at least. On January 30, 1943, Pierre Leval—the most senior minister of the Vichy government—made public for the first time a law which sanctioned direct enlistment of French citizens into the Waffen SS.

With both official German and French sanction, entrance requirements for the Waffen SS were reduced to make it possible for a wider population to have the privilege to enter the elite corps. Recruitment became very active and invited in hundreds of people already working for the Germans—former French veterans and members of the French Right-wing political groups: the PPF, RNP, PSF, the MSR, and the large reservoir of French STO workers already in the employ of the Nazi government in Germany. This change in policy brought in an astonishing number and variety of new recruits from all over the world—as far-flung as French Indochina, North African blacks, and Sri Lanka. Not all recruits were accepted into the Waffen SS owing to their still stringent requirements. Only thirty percent of applicants were ever actually sent to Waffen SS training camp in Sennheim, Alsace Lorraine.

Along the way to becoming the Charlemagne Division, there were several iterations of names of the outfit: Karl der Gross, Fanzösisches SS Regiment, SS Freiwilligen Regiment, Freiwilligen-Sturmbrigade Nr 8, SS Sturmbridge Frankreich. Originally, what came to be the fully accepted Waffen 33rd Division der SS Charlemagne was looked upon as a unit of inferiority composed of non-Aryans, Eastern Europeans, and even Russians. All of that began to change rapidly after D-Day— June 6, 1944. First of all, the French who collaborated with or fought with the Germans had to abandon France and take up their lot with what was beginning to look like the losing side—they had no other viable choice. As the Germans and collaborationists fled the now liberated soil of France, they encountered a bloody and hypocritical orgy of vengeance. Those who stayed professed involvement with De Gaulle's Free French or at least the partisan resistance underground. They committed atrocities against remaining and fleeing collaborationists and the girls who shared their sexual favors with the occupiers. Many of those fleeing to safety were ambushed and killed before they could reach the safety of Germany.

In the spring of 1944, an OKW [German High Command] general order laid out plans to unite all foreign soldiers into the Waffen SS. During that summer of 1944, the French Legionnaires fighting for Germany began to coalesce and to build their legend. Their fighting reputation was enhanced by their defense at the Bohr in Russia and in Galicia at the junction between Poland and the Ukraine. Germany now was in the throes of a three-front war: Russia, Western Europe, and Italy, and the situation was changing from "negative" to "dire." Acting out of necessity, Germany approved a French unit—the *Milice*—for recruitment services in unoccupied countries and assigned them to the task of rounding up Jews for deportation to death camps and to fight against Resistance units, including those in France. They were also active in carrying out political assassinations. This all included intimidation, overt brutality and torture, and resulted in a minor civil war in France. In 1944, when France was liberated by the Allies, the *Milice* unit members and their families fled to Germany. Most of the *Milice* members joined the Charlemagne Division shortly thereafter. They formed the bulk of the Division when it was ordered to the Eastern Front.

Although the French brigade was not yet considered combat-ready, it became necessary for the German high command to form them up into a 1st Battalion under *Waffen-Hauptstürmführer* Pierre Cance, a French volunteer. That put a thousand minimally-trained French volunteers with twenty officers and nine-hundred-eighty noncoms to face the Red hordes. They had only light weapons—no tanks, planes, or heavy artillery, and all around them seasoned German companies and regiments were being obliterated by the onslaught of seemingly unstoppable Red Army units advancing west. The French unit seemed doomed, but despite all the odds against them, the survivors lived to form the hardcore center of the final iteration of the French volunteer units—the Charlemagne Division—in 1945. In early 1945, the division commander at the time, SS-*Oberführer* Puaud, received assurance from *Reichsführer-SS* Heinrich Himmler that his men would not be sent to the western front, where they might have to fight fellow Frenchmen. He was also told that they would fight under the French flag and continue to have Catholic military chaplains. Himmler also promised that France would regain its sovereignty after Germany's victory.

The task of effecting the formal organization of the Charlemagne Division fell to SS Major General Dr. Gustav Krukenberg. In a sense the legendary story of the division started then, and lasted only one year.

At the critical point in 1944, the French Battalion was pressed into action to seal off the gap in the Wehrmacht's eastern front. On August 8, section commander Sturmmann Delatte became technically the first French Waffen SS soldier to be killed in action. He was certainly not to be the last. The second company of the Charlemagne Division was next put into action under Léon Gaultier, a former history teacher who left his profession to fight in the anticommunism movement. August 10, 1944 was a bad day for the Charlemagne Division: twenty men were killed, including the commanders—a company commander, six platoon commanders, and twenty section commanders. The worst thing for the division was that there were no replacements for those commanders. However, they succeeded in sealing the gap, and the fighting at Sanok died down. It was the usual practice to send the SS troops to the hottest combat areas, so after minimal rest, the division was moved two hundred kilometers west—a harbinger of things to come. By then, six officers and 130 other ranks were killed; eight officers and 661 other ranks were wounded and forty men were MIA—846 out of the original 1000 men were out of commission.

The French Division had proved itself in combat. Fifty-eight Iron Crosses were awarded later that month—twenty-nine posthumously. They moved west under constant combat pressure from the Russians until they finally established a base camp in northern Germany. Himmler decided on August 10, 1944 to unite all forces made up of Frenchmen into the final entity—The *Waffen-Grenadier-Brigade der SS Charlemagne (franz. Nr.1)* with Oberst Edgar Punaud of the LVF placed in command. The unit's initial battles were fought in Pomerania, and its final battle—indeed, the end of its existence—was fought in Berlin in 1945. Honorific titles were seldom awarded to any SS organization, but Himmler believed that the French had earned the right to be known by the name Charlemagne—a Frankish-Carolingian king of the near-modern era—and by then a pan-Germanic iconic hero. Other honorific units often proved to be a disappointment or even an embarrassment to the SS by achieving notoriety not for combat heroism, but for the slaughter of helpless civilians—e.g. the Bosnian Muslim Division. The division was assigned the number 33 after a Hungarian unit of *volksdeustchemen*. An elite subunit within the division was created as the *kampfschule* Close Combat School for the final battle in Berlin.

The division had only five infantry battalions, limited heavy firepower, and almost no chance for reinforcement, even from its inception. That would have required considerable time to improve, and, as it turned out, time was a commodity sorely lacking for the Charlemagne Division and Hitler. To compensate for the lack of volunteers and the severe attrition from combat, the SS ceased from all its elitist requirements and let any volunteer in from January 1945 until the end. For the first time, men were conscripted for SS service; it was no longer a privilege, and it no longer represented a military force with mythic Germanic honor attached to it. The final pre-Battle of Berlin count for the division was a scanty 7,340 men. Many of the original anticommunist fighters objected to the integral union of German and French soldiers, but all of them knew that any such elitism was absurd. They were—like it or not—united in the final defense of Nazi Germany.

The Charlemagne Division began to receive hastily trained outsiders to beef up its ranks—men who had had to attend crash courses in how the division functioned. The French, like their German SS counterparts, had all sworn to be *fidèle et brave jusqûà la mort* [to be brave and loyal to Adolf Hitler until death], and that would have to be enough to sustain them in the coming battles which they all knew were doomed to defeat and the end of the Third Reich. They were in a short period of *wildflecken* [the calm before the inevitable storm gathering and advancing from the east].

The division moved west by railway, defending itself in a rearguard action all the way against overwhelming superiority in Red Army numbers, reinforcements, heavy armaments, and mobility. The Charlemagne mounted a nearly suicidal series of battles to protect the railway corridor. Russian casualties were horrendous, with whole companies and brigades of tanks reduced to naught by well-placed German/French fire. Finally, however, the massive power of the Soviets overwhelmed the French positions and broke the Charlemagne lines. Tanks and corpses littered the ground everywhere as the still fighting Frenchmen made an orderly retreat further west through a hell in the snow.

The Charlemagne Division was becoming splintered, and its ability to continue fighting came under question. At Elsenau, the *Compagnie d'Honneur* school reinforcements and the nearly exhausted Charlemagne soldiers hunkered down under sheets commandeered from German farmers to camouflage them under the snow. Having been prewarned of the advancing Soviet tanks, the division staged an ambush and destroyed the armored vehicles in an unprecedented victory. The hapless and unexpecting Soviet infantry was massacred by French machinegun fire coming from hiding holes all along the road. Supporting Russian infantry arrived too late and slaughtered as well. Again and again the Soviets charged and were mowed down by the withering fire of revenge-seeking Frenchmen. It was sheer butchery. The Soviet dead lay in piles all along the road. At five-thirty in the afternoon, the division made an orderly retreat further west to avoid contact with the oncoming Soviet armor divisions. The cost for the Charlemagne was very great. More than a thousand men were lost—a number that could not be fully replaced.

The division retreated west on the fifth of March and found itself in an open field, exhausted, almost out of ammunition, and most of them wounded, freezing, and starving. Russian infantry and heavy armor flanked them and began a systematic and pulpifying fire on the French SS lines. The Soviet infantrymen ran amok, slaughtering any Frenchman who moved. The battle—if it could be dignified as such—

was over in minutes, and the field was littered with almost exclusively French dead. Only a handful escaped. The defenders of the town they had been defending scattered into the hills, and many of them froze to death after simply sitting down in the snow too exhausted to walk any further. Objectively, the Charlemagne Division had ceased to exist as a formal unit.

The last action of the Charlemagne Division, such as still existed— and indeed the once invincible German military machine—occurred in the *Gotterdämmerung* [End of Days] in Berlin. When the division was deployed for the first time in February 1945, there were eight thousand men. In April, they regrouped south of Berlin with only a little over a thousand men. The German empire was decimated, shrinking from all sides by the day. The German military machine was being ground to pieces, and the Red Army was at the gates of Berlin. The only question remaining was who would arrive first in the bleeding heart of the runt Germany; that group or nation would hold all the cards in the postwar era.

The last stand defense of Hitler and Berlin rested on hastily reassembled units of the LVII Corps of the Wehrmacht, a few Kriegsmarine companies, some Luftwaffe stragglers, and three Waffen SS divisions— none of which was made up of Germans. Those foreign divisions were the Nordland Division (Sweden, Norway, Denmark, and Switzerland), 15th Waffen SS Latvian, and lastly, the battered and bedraggled 33rd Waffen SS Charlemagne Division. Though few in number and most of them wounded at least once, the division was still proud of its ongoing contribution to the destruction of communism.

Stalin's Russia amassed a two-and-a-half million men, nearly forty-two thousand big guns and mortars, six-and-a-quarter thousand tanks and self-propelled guns, and seventy-five hundred airplanes. As it happened, the greater part of the Waffen SS was absent: they were defending Austria. The total number of Germans defending Berlin was no more than one hundred thousand, and they collectively had only one hundred tanks. No one expected a prolonged siege—a Stalingrad. What happened in this *Gotterdämmerung*, this much-vaunted final cataclysm according to Goebbels, was—for the Germans, at least—a hopeless and forlorn anticlimax. The heroes of the German side were not even Germans: they were French.

To prepare for the struggle, Hitler's remaining generals reorganized the Waffen SS divisions and released from service those whose hearts were no longer in the fight. Some stragglers filtered in from the massacre in Pomerania. The entire Compagnie d'Honneur elected to fight to the end. About four hundred hardcore Frenchmen joined the defectors. The extremely uneven fight to the finish commenced on the morning of April 16, 1945.

The masses of Russian men and machines rushed towards Berlin, taking out the meager tank and infantry units scattered along the way to impede the Russian juggernaut. Zukhov's army was hardly unscathed. When the last resistance outside the city was quashed, 30,000 Russians were dead. The dire straits of the men defending Berlin was highlighted by a change of command of the majority of the defenders because of a severe illness. The new commander was the Nordlander, Joachim Ziegler, who rallied the remaining Charlemagne grenadiers into a cohesive unit. The almagamated unit which now formed the Charlemagne Division consisted of about 400–500 men who formed a *kampfgruppe*. A few trucks and even private automobiles were found to move the fighting unit into the heart of Berlin. They pounded their way through the mounting chaos on the roads which were, by then, glutted with terrified civilian refugees and deserting military men. The Charlemagne Division drove to the Reichsportsfeld in Charlottenburg—the site of the 1936 Olympics—and regrouped. They stocked up on the abundant supplies abandoned by the fleeing Luftwaffe.

The reequipped, well-fed, and reformed battalion drove out towards the east and the waiting Russians in the morning. The scene in the innermost part of Berlin was surreal. It was unnaturally quiet for a weekday, and many people were still going to work. What was missing was a defense buildup proportional to the threat. Further out in Hasenbeide, the scene was war and chaos. The Charlemagne headquarters was bombed. Ziegler was relieved of command, and the division moved into the central city and made their headquarters in the Berlin Opera House. During the night, Charlemagne commandoes destroyed two Russian tanks, and the division planned a major counterattack in the morning. The French grenadiers proved to be very effective in the street-by-street and house-to-house highly mobile combat. Antitank guns were employed to great effect by destroying the front and the rear tanks of a Russion battalion, thus rendering the entire one hundred tanks either destroyed or helpless. The advance was successful in driving the Russians back a significant distance, but at a cost of one quarter of their strength.

Russian artillery caught a company of grenadiers in the open and killed fifteen of them. Elsewhere, the great Russian onslaught was rushing towards Berlin's center, cracking the Nazi defenses as they went. At this point, the division was reinforced by a unit of Hitler youth—mere boys. Each boy carried a *panzerfäust* [a simple metal tube with an attached hollow charge which had an effective range of less than one hundred yards], a World War I Mauser rifle, and a handful of ammunition. The very ignorance and youthful enthusiasm of the reinforcements made them absurdly unafraid, and they were able to destroy tanks and kill infantrymen with the weapons they carried which were often bigger than they were. They were able to hold off attack after attack of the heavy armor of the Russian tank corps. Despite such consummate bravery and success, a great many of the boys and old men were hanged by mobile SS units for failure to defend their sectors.

As the pincers of the Russian tanks and infantry closed inexorably in, yet another reorganization occurred, this one placing the Charlemagne Division in command of the final defenses around the Chancellery and Hitler himself. At that point, two of the remaining five company commanders had been killed, and half of the men. Finally, on April 28, the defense was reduced to a ring around the Belle-Alliance-Platz; and the Russians stormed in. Attack after attack was defeated by the Frenchmen, and Soviet casualties mounted to a horrific level. Corpses of dead Russians lay in piles that impeded their progress. Whole buildings fell in on the defenders, finally leaving alive only the exceptional among them. Krukenberg described the night as "darkness, chased away by this enormous brazier the city has become, has vanished...." The rumbling upheaveal of the battle submerged the city, as Krukenberg described it. The French Charlemagne Division established their reputation that day. The remaining grenadiers now knew they were not going to win, but they remained determined to resist.

The noise was deafening, and conversation, even shouting, was impossible. The men of the division became essentially solitary and independent, effectively taking out huge numbers of the enemy as the Russians closed in by the sheer mass of their numbers and the superiority of their equipment. As that dreadful Saturday drew to a close, the Charlemagne grenadiers were still in control. Russian tanks still fell prey to the courageous employment of the crude *panzerfäusts*, but the incredible number of the tanks advancing down the rubble-strewn streets was becoming overwhelming. Now they began to blow any building to pieces from which German fire came, and grenadiers were being crushed in the falling buildings. Any SS soldier who surrendered was murdered. All contact with other fighting units was lost. The divison fought, died, pulled back and regrouped, and fought again. Any relief achieved was temporary. Incredibly they were still cohesive and effective throughout the twenty-ninth, despite the apparently inexhaustible supply of Soviet fighting units and equipment. The Charlemagne guns began to run out of ammunition.

On April 30, SS headquarters was moved to a library cellar where the ever-dwindling coterie of French soldiers gathered to plot and plan their desperate resistance. Men received paper bandages and two hours rest before returning to battle. Evacuation of wounded was no longer possible. By some nearly superhuman demonstration of grit, the library was surrounded by twenty-one hulks of burned-out tanks by nightfall of that long day. The Soviet tankers and infantry recognized that the battle was nearly at an end, and they were reluctant to launch another suicidal attack, preferring to let the wider nature of the conflict take its course.

That same day, Hitler and Eva Braun were married then retired to a private room and killed themselves. It was all over, but no one told the Charlemagne Division in their shrunken world. There were now fifty men capable of fighting in the division. The library location became indefensible, so they moved once again, this time to the *Sicherheitshauptamt*, the Ministry of Security next to the old Gestapo headquarters and torture cellars on Prinz-Albrecht Strasse. There was little ammunition left and no guns that were effective at any real distance. They waited for the inevitable Soviet advance. They knew full well that there would be no quarter asked and none given. In sporadic fighting, another handful of Charlemagne grenadiers were killed that day.

In the Führer bunker, things were going from bad to worse. General Krukenberg described the situation: "SS General Mohnke asked me if I—being the most senior officer in my rank—would continue to assure the defense of the city, in which case all troops still available would be placed under my command. I rejected that stupid idea" [since all was lost]. The Goebbels murdered their six children then killed themselves. At least some common sense was allowed at that point, and the few remaining members of the Charlemagne Division were given the option of breaking out if they could. Krukenberg assembled what was left of his defenders and began to plan their own breakout.

Those who chose to get away left an hour before midnight on that May Day. It was an unmitigated disaster from the moment it started. The escapees met with what could only be called sheer butchery. They died by the hundreds. They had few weapons, only a handful of ammunition, and the fighting separated them into small disparate groups with no real leadership. Only a very small number of the division got out, and many of them met with murder by the waiting French army. One small group elected to stay in the *Sicherheitshauptamt* to fight to the bitter end.

An eerie and unnerving silence fell over the city as the Charlemagne grenadiers awaited their fate. Sporadic patrols searched the nearby city streets, and all returned with the thoroughly disheartening news that no one else was there. One patrol went to the Air Ministry and learned that complete capitulation had taken place and that German and Russian soldiers were resting, eating, and trading cigarettes with each other. The last holdouts took up all of their remaining arms and ammunition and walked towards the U-Bahn station where they saw an armada of Soviet tanks, red banners everywhere, and armies of drunken Soviet soldiers engaged in an orgy of looting. The last few dozen Charlemagne troops decided to sneak into the subways to find a way to reach other units of the German military machine still fighting—or so they were informed.

It was a doomed decision. In the night, Soviet soldiers captured the remaining few Charlemagne soldiers who had fought with such distinction in the Battle of Berlin and hauled the survivors away to uncertain futures in the gulag system. There were approximately 1,200 men stationed at Wildflecken and 700 remnants left behind at Carpin; 400 of them were deemed noncombatants. Their hopeless resistance was overwhelmed by Soviet tanks and masses of Soviet infantry on April 27. The remaining Charlemagne members became fleeing refugees and scattered. The last 600 organized members were ordered to go to Bavaria to the Mountain Redoubt to stage a last-ditch stand. They

and the escapees that headed south all finally disintegrated as any semblance of fighting units and it became every man for himself.

In the aftermath of the great battle and the horrific war, there was an
orgy of revenge, rape, murder, and destruction. Adolf Hitler's parting
legacy to Europe was based on his orders that nothing was to be left
for the victorious Allies. Where there had been cities, they would find
rubble. Where there had been cultivated fields, they would find wilder-
ness. The *Führer* and his henchmen came close to achieving this goal.
Agricultural production had ground to a halt, while in urban centers
millions had been bombed out of their homes and were living on the
edge of starvation. Distribution of the limited stockpiles of food was
severely constrained by the smashed state of Central Europe's rail and
transport infrastructure. There was an ominous uptick of premature
postwar deaths in many of these countries—between a million and
1.5 million deaths in Germany alone. Added to those killed by civil
war in Yugoslavia, Greece, Poland, Ukraine and the Baltic states, and
then those who died because of poor nutrition throughout Europe and
Asia, the numbers of premature deaths almost certainly were in excess
of two million.

"Borders were redrawn and homecomings, expulsions, and burials
were under way. But the massive efforts to rebuild had just begun. When
the war began in the late 1930s, the world's population was approximately two billion. In less than a decade, the war between the Axis
and the Allied powers had resulted in eighty million deaths—killing
off about four percent of the whole world. Allied forces now became
occupiers, taking control of Germany, Japan, and much of the territory
they had formerly ruled. Efforts were made to permanently dismantle
the war-making abilities of those nations, as factories were destroyed
and former leadership was removed or prosecuted. War crimes trials
took place in Europe and Asia, leading to many executions and prison
sentences," Alan Taylor, *World War II, After the War*. Whole popula-
tions had lost almost everything and everyone—witness the Holocaust.

There was an orgy of postwar anti-Semitism, mostly due to fights
over property. When the Jews had been deported from Poland or
Hungary or Romania, all their possessions had been confiscated by
Nazis, Nazi sympathizers, and opportunistic anti-Semites and shared
out. When the survivors returned to their homelands, they wanted this

property back, which made many of the new owners feel threatened and resentful. Most of the time it was easy to frighten returning Jews away, but all too often when Jews insisted on having their possessions returned to them, local communities got violent. It did not take much. There was very little evidence of soul-searching involved. In some areas the people had become so used to violence against Jews during the war that it did not feel at all abnormal.

With due acknowledgment of Mr. Taylor, more than a hundred million people were dead if the fifty million Chinese are included. "Millions of POWs—including two million Axis detainees—languished in appalling pestilential inhuman internment camps. Entire cities lay in complete ruin. Economies were inoperative. There was widespread anarchy, famine, crime, pestilence, and violent conflict, with millions of uprooted people wandering the ruined lands.... The continent was filled with people who regarded violence as a normal way of life," Keith Lowe, *Savage Continent*.

Hence, mercy was in very short supply, especially for the defeated German veterans and the civilian population. Things were even worse for the foreign soldiers who had fought for the Third Reich and who had committed unspeakable atrocities—witness the *Totenkopfverbände* concentration camp officials and guards—including the 33rd Waffen-SS Division Charlemagne—who tormented, humiliated, tortured, and murdered several million hapless Jews, homosexuals, political dissidents, captured Russian civilians, gypsies, and mentally retarded people. Records are replete that the SS committed atrocities, but no records directly incriminate the Charlemagne Division other than their service in the concentration camps. The members of the division who lived long enough to write articles or memoirs back in France denied such service.

Records are limited as to what became of the few survivors of the Charlemagne Division beyond those who lie in unmarked graves or as carrion food throughout the countries they invaded or nearby the dreadful Russian, French, American, and British POW camps. On VE Day, May 8, 1945, French soldiers of the 2nd Armored Division—acting on the orders of French General Leclerk—murdered a dozen defenseless grenadiers near Karlstein, southeastern Bavaria. Many others found it their lot to pay the price for defeat. Some—including those who opted out of the final Battle of Berlin and were captured—went to Russian gulags in 1945, like the infamous Butugychag Tin Mine in Siberia; those designated as war criminals and assigned to "special treatment" camps—including most SS officers and men—were not released until 1956. A million of them died in that period. The period of misery was not over for them, even after their release from Siberia. Most of them were repatriated to Europe and began internment in Allied POW camps which were the equal of those in Soviet Siberia. Hundreds of thousands starved, froze, were worked to death, or died while being forced to march as human shields across unrehabilitated minefields. Soviet prisoners suffered similar terrible mistreatment; only a fraction returned home alive after more than a decade in captivity—a grim parity in atrocities.

The cost was very great for the SS paramilitary soldiers: by 1942, almost every member of the 1934–1935 SS training school at Bad Tölz Junkerschulen—the international school for officer candidates—was dead, and that statistic applied almost across the board at the other training centers. The Death's Head SS soldiers could be sent to the battle front at any time, and Waffen-SS soldiers could be sent to the camps for guard duty when they were wounded in battle and could no longer fight. By D-Day, 35 percent of all German soldiers had been wounded at least once, and by late 1944, the Waffen SS accounted for 10 percent of the German military and had an even higher WIA, KIA, and MIA rate. By the end of World War II, the Waffen-SS had grown to thirty-nine divisions, which served as elite combat troops alongside the Wehrmacht which finally had to accord them grudging respect.

The twelve-day-long Battle of Berlin was the final major offensive of the European theatre of World War II; the Soviets lost over 78,000 men killed and 274,000 men wounded in that one final battle. The Waffen SS and the few remaining disorganized Wehrmacht units suffered—according to initial Soviet estimates based on kill claims— 458,080 killed and 479,298 captured, but later German research puts the number of dead at approximately 92,000–100,000. Both figures were likely inflated or deflated for political purposes, but by any reckoning were enormous.

Among those extremely hardy survivors of the Charlemagne Division were a few who turned themselves in to the headquarters of the French sector and were promptly placed in handcuffs and taken to Tegel Prison. A very few actually made it back to France. Many of those repatriates—often against their will—were tried and sent to prison at hard labor. Many were stripped of their citizenship. Some were executed by hanging; others served prison sentences and then were hanged or shot by firing squad. They were all regarded as pariahs, traitors, and murderers of innocent French people; they were the losers in the war, after all; and justice was defined by the victors. If a French soldier was killed by a repatriated Waffen-SS traitor, fifty repatriated prisoners were rounded up to be executed. Women who bore children by Germans or division men suffered greatly during the postwar period, and their two hundred thousand children—the "Bosche bastards"—also paid the price of their parents' sins.

Around 761 division members living in France after the war received pensions from the German government and were officially deemed to be traitors by the French government. After pressure from the postwar government of France, they were struck from the pensioner roles of Germany. Some division members made their way into the Foreign Legion and served in Indochina or Algeria, including surviving SS members recruited directly from prisoner of war camps. Others were men from lost German lands who had nowhere to go home to. Highly regarded by the French for their discipline and bravery, an estimated 35,000 Germans and Frenchmen who served the Germans took part in France's war in Vietnam. Those men made up over half the Foreign Legion units in Vietnam that bore much of the heaviest fighting against the communist Viet Minh forces of Ho Chi Minh. In this brutal conflict, more than 10,000 Legionnaires were killed out of about 70,000 who fought.

Some Charlemagne men made it to South America and joined other Nazis living there. A few of those were hunted down and murdered by French security agents of the *Deuxième Bureau* [later, the *Service de documentation extérieure et de contre-espionnage*—the SDECE, Foreign Documentation and Counter-Espionage Service]. Most imprisoned members were given early release by the government after it passed the *loi d'armistie* act in 1947. Most of those faded into intentional obscurity, but a few extremely dedicated anticommunists among them became politically active and publically voiced their views—an act of bravery or foolhardiness of the highest order. Later, some of them attended gatherings of former SS men and were received with great warmth. Some were even allowed to wear a regular French army uniform and to continue being warriors for France.

While he was yet speaking, there came also another, and said, the fire of God is fallen from heaven, and hath burned up the sheep, and the servants, and consumed them; and I only am escaped alone to tell thee.

-The Book of Job,
KJV 1:13–19

"It occurred to Susan that men were always waiting for something cataclysmic—love or war or a giant asteroid.... Men just wanted to focus on one big thing, leaving the thousands of smaller messes for the women around them to clean up."
-Bonnie Jo Campbell, *American Salvage*

"So we beat on, boats against the current, borne back ceaselessly into the past."
-F. Scott Fitzgerald, *The Great Gatsby*

Based on:

- Jonathan Trigg, *HITLER'S GAUL'S, The History of the 33rd Waffen SS Division Charlemagne*, Spellmount, History Press.
- Philippe Garrard, *THE FRENCH WHO FOUGHT FOR HITLER: Memories from the Outcasts*, Cambridge University Press.
- Tony Le Tissier, *CHARLEMAGNE: The 33rd Waffen-Grenadier Division of the SS*, Pen and Sword, Military.
- Robert Forbes, *POUR L'EUROPE—French Volunteers of the Waffen-SS*, Trowbridge: Redwood Books, 2000.
- David Schoenbrun, *SOLDIERS OF THE NIGHT*, London, Robert Hale, 1981.

www.ingramcontent.com/pod-product-compliance
Lightning Source LLC
Chambersburg PA
CBHW071330020726
47502CB00001B/36